Ray Bradbury, one of �578�578 horror fiction in the wo�578�578 Illinois, USA in 1920. �578�578 monsters, circuses, dino�578�578 started writing short stor�578�578 carnival 'Mr Elictrico', �578�578 story-writing in the 1940's. In 1944 he sold about forty stories for a total of $800.

His tales set on Mars were collected into _The Martian Chronicles_. His famous _Fahrenheit 451_ was filmed by Truffaut in 1966, and many of his stories have been adapted successfully for TV and the cinema. The film based on his book _Something Wicked This Way Comes_ is being released shortly.

By the same author

The Stories of

Ray Bradbury

VOLUME 1

with an introduction by the author

GRANADA
London Toronto Sydney New York

Published in paperback by Granada Publishing Limited in 1983

ISBN 0 586 05485 5

First published in Great Britain by
Granada Publishing Limited 1981

Published by arrangement with Alfred A. Knopf, Inc.

Most of the stories in this book were previously published in the
following books:

The Illustrated Man, The Martian Chronicles, R is for Rocket, The
Machineries of Joy, S is for Space, The Golden Apples of the Sun, A
Medicine for Melancholy, Fahrenheit 451, I Sing the Body
Electric!, Dandelion Wine, Long After Midnight, Dark Carnival
and The October Country

and the following magazines:

American Mercury, Arkham Sampler, Charm, Collier's, Ellery
Queen's Mystery Magazine, Eros, Esquire, Famous Fantastic
Mysteries, Galaxy, Harper's, Maclean's, Mademoiselle, Magazine
of Fantasy and Science Fiction, Marvel Science Fiction, McCall's,
Penthouse, Planet Stories, Playboy, Saint Detective, Saturday
Evening Post, Seventeen, Shenandoah, Star Science Fiction Stories
3, Startling Stories, Super Science Fiction Stories, Thrilling
Wonder Stories, Today and Weird Tales.

Granada Publishing Limited
Frogmore, St Albans, Herts AL2 2NF
and
36 Golden Square, London W1R 4AH
515 Madison Avenue, New York, NY 10022, USA
117 York Street, Sydney, NSW 2000, Australia
100 Skyway Avenue, Rexdale, Ontario, M9W 3A6, Canada
61 Beach Road, Auckland, New Zealand

Printed and bound in Great Britain by
Cox & Wyman Ltd, Reading
Set in Plantin

Granada ®
Granada Publishing ®

And this one, with love,
for Nancy Nicolas and Robert Gottlieb,
whose arguments about favourites
put this book together

Contents

Drunk, and in Charge of a Bicycle

an introduction by Ray Bradbury

In 1953 I wrote an article for *The Nation* defending my work as a science-fiction writer, even though that label only applied to perhaps one third of my output each year.

A few weeks later, in late May, a letter arrived from Italy. On the back of the envelope, in a spidery hand, I read these words:

> B. Berenson
> I Tatti, Settignano
> Firenze, Italia

I turned to my wife and said, 'My God, this can't be from *the* Berenson, can it, the great art historian?!'

'Open it,' said my wife.

I did, and read:

Dear Mr Bradbury:

In 89 years of life, this is the first fan letter I have written. It is to tell you that I have just read your article in *The Nation* — 'Day After Tomorrow'. It is the first time I have encountered the statement by an artist in any field, that to work creatively he must put flesh into it, and enjoy it as a lark, or as a fascinating adventure.

How different from the workers in the heavy industry that professional writing has become!

If you ever touch Florence, come to see me.

Sincerely yours, B. BERENSON.

Thus, at the age of thirty-three, I had my way of seeing, writing and living approved of by a man who became a second father to me.

I needed that approval. We all need someone higher, wiser, older to tell us we're not crazy after all, that what we're doing is all right. All right, hell, *fine*!

But it is easy to doubt yourself, because you look around at a community of notions held by other writers, other intellectuals, and they make you blush with guilt. Writing is supposed to be difficult, agonizing, a dreadful exercise, a terrible occupation.

But, you see, my stories have led me through my life. They shout, I follow. They run up and bite me on the leg — I respond by writing down everything that goes on during the bite. When I finish, the idea lets go, and runs off.

That is the kind of life I've had. Drunk, and in charge of a bicycle, as an Irish police report once put it. Drunk with life, that is, and not knowing where off to next. But you're on your way before dawn. And the trip? Exactly one half terror, exactly one half exhilaration.

When I was three my mother snuck me in and out of movies two or three times a week. My first film was Lon Chaney in *The Hunchback of Notre Dame*. I suffered permanent curvature of the spine *and* of my imagination that day a long time ago in 1923. From that hour on, I knew a kindred and wonderfully grotesque compatriot of the dark when I saw one. I ran off to see all the Chaney films again and again to be deliciously frightened. The Phantom of the Opera stood astride my life with his scarlet cape. And when it wasn't the Phantom it was the terrible hand that gestured from behind the bookcase in *The Cat and the Canary,* bidding me to come find more darkness hid in books.

I was in love, then, with monsters and skeletons and

circuses and carnivals and dinosaurs and, at last, the red planet, Mars.

From these primitive bricks I have built a life and a career. By my staying in love with all of these amazing things, all of the good things in my existence have come about.

In other words, I was *not* embarrassed at circuses. Some people are. Circuses are loud, vulgar, and smell in the sun. By the time many people are fourteen or fifteen, they have been divested of their loves, their ancient and intuitive tastes, one by one, until when they reach maturity there is no fun left, no zest, no gusto, no flavour. Others have criticized, and they have criticized themselves, into embarrassment. When the circus pulls in at five of a dark cold summer morn, and the calliope sounds, they do not rise and run, they turn in their sleep, and life passes by.

I did rise and run. I learned that I was right and everyone else wrong when I was nine. Buck Rogers arrived on scene that year, and it was instant love. I collected the daily strips, and was madness maddened by them. Friends criticized. Friends made fun. I tore up the Buck Rogers strips. For a month I walked through my fourth-grade classes, stunned and empty. One day I burst into tears, wondering what devastation had happened to me. The answer was: Buck Rogers. He was gone, and life simply wasn't worth living. The next thought was: Those are not my friends, the ones who got me to tear the strips apart and so tear my own life down the middle; those are my enemies.

I went back to collecting Buck Rogers. My life has been happy ever since. For that was the beginning of my writing science fiction. Since then, I have never listened to anyone who criticized my taste in space-travel, sideshows or gorillas. When such occurs, I pack up my dinosaurs and leave the room.

For, you see, it is all mulch. If I hadn't stuffed my eyes and stuffed my head with all of the above for a lifetime, when it came round to word-associating myself into story ideas, I would have brought up a ton of ciphers and a half-ton of zeros.

'The Veldt', collected herein, is a prime example of what goes on in a headful of images, myths, toys. Back some thirty years ago I sat down to my typewriter one day and wrote these words: 'The Playroom'. Playroom where? The Past? No. The Present? Hardly. The Future? Yes! Well, then, what would a Playroom in some future year be like? I began typing, word-associating around the Room. Such a Playroom must have wall-to-wall television in each wall, and in the ceiling. Walking into such an environment, a child could shout: River Nile! Sphinx! Pyramids! and they would appear, surrounding him, in full colour, full sound, and, why not? glorious warm scents and smells and odours, pick one, for the nose!

All this came to me in a few seconds of fast typing. I knew the Room, now I must put characters in the Room. I typed out a character named George, brought him into a future-time kitchen, where his wife turned and said:

'George, I wish you'd look at the Playroom. I think it's broken – '

George and his wife go down the hall. I follow them, typing madly, not knowing what will happen next. They open the door of the Playroom and step in.

Africa. Hot sun. Vultures. Dead meats. Lions.

Two hours later the lions leaped out of the walls of the Playroom and devoured George and his wife, while their TV-dominated children sat by and sipped tea.

End of word-association. End of story. The whole thing complete and almost ready to send out, an explosion of idea, in something like 120 minutes.

The lions in that room, where did they come from?

From the lions I found in the books in the town library when I was ten. From the lions I saw in the real circuses when I was five. From the lion that prowled in Lon Chaney's film *He Who Gets Slapped* in 1924!

1924! you say, with immense doubt. Yes, 1924. I didn't see the Chaney film again until a year ago. As soon as it flashed on the screen I knew that that was where my lions in 'The Veldt' came from. They had been hiding out, waiting, given shelter by my intuitive self, all these years.

For I am that special freak, the man with the child inside who remembers all. I remember the day and the hour I was born. I remember being circumcised on the second day after my birth. I remember suckling at my mother's breast. Years later I asked my mother about the circumcision. I had information that couldn't have been told me, there would be no reason to tell a child, especially in those still-Victorian times. Was I circumcised somewhere away from the lying-in hospital? I was. My father took me to the doctor's office. I remember the doctor. I remember the scalpel.

I wrote the story 'The Small Assassin' twenty-six years later. It tells of a baby born with all its senses operative, filled with terror at being thrust out into a cold world, and taking revenge on its parents by crawling secretly about at night and at last destroying them.

When did it all really begin? The writing, that is. Everything came together in the summer and fall and early winter of 1932. By that time I was stuffed full of Buck Rogers, the novels of Edgar Rice Burroughs, and the night-time radio serial *Chandu the Magician*. Chandu said magic and the psychic summons and the Far East and strange places which made me sit down every night and from memory write out the scripts of each show.

But the whole conglomeration of magic and myths and falling downstairs with brontosaurs only to arise with La of Opar, was shaken into a pattern by one man, Mr Electrico.

He arrived with a seedy two-bit carnival, The Dill

Brothers Combined Shows, during Labor Day weekend of 1932, when I was twelve. Every night for three nights, Mr Electrico sat in his electric chair, being fired with ten billion volts of pure blue sizzling power. Reaching out into the audience, his eyes flaming, his white hair standing on end, sparks leaping between his smiling teeth, he brushed an Excalibur sword over the heads of the children, knighting them with fire. When he came to me, he tapped me on both shoulders and then the tip of my nose. The lightning jumped into me. Mr Electrico cried: *'Live forever!'*

I decided that was the greatest idea I had ever heard. I went to see Mr Electrico the next day, with the excuse that a nickel magic trick I had purchased from him wasn't in working order. He fixed it, and toured me around the tents, shouting at each, 'Clean up your language,' before we entered to meet the dwarfs, acrobats, fat women, and Illustrated Men waiting there.

We walked down to sit by Lake Michigan where Mr Electrico spoke his small philosophies and I talked my big ones. Why he put up with me, I'll never know. But he listened, or it seemed he listened, maybe because he was far from home, maybe because he had a son somewhere in the world, or had no son at all and wanted one. Anyway he was a defrocked Presbyterian minister, he said, and lived down in Cairo, Illinois, and I could write him there, any time I wished.

Finally he gave me some special news.

'We've met before,' he said. 'You were my best friend in France in 1918, and you died in my arms in the battle of the Ardennes forest that year. And here you are, born again, in a new body, with a new name. Welcome back!'

I staggered away from that encounter with Mr Electrico wonderfully uplifted by two gifts: the gift of having lived once before (and of being told about it) . . . and the gift of trying somehow to live forever.

A few weeks later I started writing my first short stories about the planet Mars. From that time to this, I have never stopped. God bless Mr Electrico, the catalyst, wherever he is.

If I consider every aspect of all the above, my beginnings almost inevitably had to be in the attic. From the time I was twelve until I was twenty-two or -three, I wrote stories long after midnight — unconventional stories of ghosts and haunts and things in jars that I had seen in sour armpit carnivals, of friends lost to the tides in lakes, and of consorts of three in the morning, those souls who had to fly in the dark in order not to be shot in the sun.

It took me many years to write myself down out of the attic, where I had to make do with my own eventual mortality (a teenager's preoccupation), make it to the living room, then out to the lawn and sunlight where the dandelions had come up, ready for wine.

Getting out on the front lawn with my Fourth of July relatives gave me not only my Green Town, Illinois, stories, it also shoved me off towards Mars, following Edgar Rice Burroughs' and John Carter's advice, taking my childhood luggage, my uncles, aunts, my mom, dad, and brother with me. When I arrived on Mars I found them, in fact, waiting for me, or Martians who looked like them, pretending me into a grave. The Green Town stories that found their way into an accidental novel titled *Dandelion Wine* and the Red Planet stories that blundered into another accidental novel called *The Martian Chronicles* were written, alternately, during the same years that I ran to the rainbarrel outside my grandparents' house to dip out all the memories, the myths, the word-associations of other years.

Along the way, I also re-created my relatives as vampires who inhabited a town similar to the one in *Dandelion Wine*, dark first cousin to the town on Mars where the Third Expedition expired. So, I had my life three ways, as town explorer, space-traveller, and wanderer with Count Dracula's American cousins.

I realize I haven't talked half enough, as yet, about one variety of creature you will find stalking this collection, rising here in nightmares to founder there in loneliness and despair: dinosaurs. From the time I was seventeen until I was thirty-two, I wrote some half-dozen dinosaur stories.

One night when my wife and I were walking along the beach in Venice, California, where we lived in a thirty-dollar-a-month newlyweds' apartment, we came upon the bones of the Venice Pier and the struts, tracks, and ties of the ancient roller-coaster collapsed on the sand and being eaten by the sea.

'What's that dinosaur doing lying here on the beach?' I said.

My wife, very wisely, had no answer.

The answer came the next night when, summoned from sleep by a voice calling, I rose up, listened, and heard the lonely voice of the Santa Monica bay fog horn blowing over and over and over again.

Of course! I thought. The dinosaur heard that lighthouse fog horn blowing, thought it was another dinosaur arisen from the deep past, came swimming in for a loving confrontation, discovered it was only a fog horn, and died of a broken heart there on the shore.

I leaped from bed, wrote the story, and sent it to the *Saturday Evening Post* that week, where it appeared soon after under the title 'The Beast from 20,000 Fathoms.' That story, titled 'The Fog Horn' in this collection, became a film two years later.

The story was read by John Huston in 1953, who promptly called to ask if I would like to write the screenplay for his film *Moby Dick*. I accepted, and moved from one beast to the next.

Because of *Moby Dick*, I re-examined the life of Melville

and Jules Verne, compared their mad captains in an essay written to re-introduce a new translation of *20,000 Leagues Beneath the Sea,* which, read by the 1964 New York World's Fair people, put me in charge of conceptualizing the entire upper floor of the United States Pavilion.

Because of the Pavilion, the Disney organization hired me to help plan the dreams that went into Spaceship Earth, part of Epcot, a permanent world's fair, now building to open in 1982. In that one building, I have crammed a history of mankind, coming and going back and forth in time, then plunging into our wild future in space.

Including dinosaurs.

All of my activities, all of my growing, all of my new jobs and new loves, caused and created by that original primitive love of the beasts I saw when I was five and dearly cherished when I was twenty and twenty-nine and thirty.

Look around among these stories and you will probably find only one or two that actually happened to me. I have resisted, most of my life, being given assignments to go somewhere and 'sponge up' the local colour, the natives, the look and feel of the land. I learned long ago that I am not seeing directly, that my subconscious is doing most of the 'sponging' and it will be years before any usable impressions surface.

As a young man I lived in a tenement in the Chicano section of Los Angeles. Most of my Latino stories were written years after I had moved from the tenement, with one terrifying, on-the-spot, exception. In late 1945, with World War II freshly over, a friend of mine asked me to accompany him to Mexico City in an old beat-up Ford V-8. I reminded him of the vow of poverty that circumstances had forced on me. He rebutted by calling me a coward, wondering why I didn't rev up my courage and send out three or four stories which I had hidden away. Reason for the hiding: the stories had been rejected once or twice by various magazines.

Pummelled by my friend, I dusted the stories off and mailed them out, under the pseudonym William Elliott. Why the pseudonym? Because I feared that some Manhattan editors might have seen the name Bradbury on the covers of *Weird Tales* and would be prejudiced against this 'pulp' writer.

I mailed off three short stories to three different magazines, in the second week of August 1945. On August 20, I sold one story to *Charm*, on August 21, I sold a story to *Mademoiselle*, and on August 22, my twenty-fifth birthday, I sold a story to *Collier's*. The total monies amounted to $1,000, which would be like having $10,000 arrive in the mail today.

I was rich. Or so close to it I was dumbfounded. It was a turning point in my life, of course, and I hastened to write to the editors of those three magazines confessing my true name.

All three stories were listed in *The Best American Short Stories of 1946* by Martha Foley, and one of them was published in Herschel Brickell's O. Henry Memorial Award *Prize Stories* the following year.

That money took me to Mexico, to Guanajuato, and the mummies in the catacombs. The experience so wounded and terrified me, I could hardly wait to flee Mexico. I had nightmares about dying and having to remain in the halls of the dead with those propped and wired bodies. In order to purge my terror, instantly, I wrote 'The Next in Line'. One of the few times that an experience yielded results almost on the spot.

Enough of Mexico. What about Ireland?

There is every kind of Irish story here because after living in Dublin for six months I saw that most of the Irish I met had a variety of ways of making do with that dreadful beast Reality. You can run into it head-on, which is a dire business, or you can skirt around it, give it a poke, dance for it, make up a song, write you a tale, prolong the gab, fill up the flask.

Each partakes of Irish cliché, but each, in the foul weather and the foundered politics, is true.

I got to know every beggar in the streets of Dublin, the ones near O'Connell's Bridge with maniac pianolas grinding more coffee than tunes and the ones who loaned out a single baby among a whole tribe of rainsoaked mendicants, so you saw the babe one hour at the top of Grafton Street and the next by the Royal Hibernian Hotel, and at midnight down by the river, but I never thought I would write of them. Then the need to howl and give an angry weep made me rear up one night and write 'McGillahee's Brat' out of terrible suspicions and the begging of a rainwalking ghost that had to be laid. I visited some of the old burnt-out estates of the great Irish landowners, and heard tales of one 'burning' that had not quite come off, and so wrote 'The Terrible Conflagration up at the Place'.

'The Anthem Sprinters', another Irish encounter, wrote itself down years later when, one rainy night, I recalled the countless times my wife and I had sprinted out of Dublin cinemas, dashing for the exit, knocking children and old folks to left and right, in order to make it to the exit before the National Anthem was played.

But how did I begin? Starting in Mr Electrico's year, I wrote a thousand words a day. For ten years I wrote at least one short story a week, somehow guessing that a day would finally come when I truly got out of the way and let it happen.

The day came in 1942 when I wrote 'The Lake'. Ten years of doing everything wrong suddenly became the right idea, the right scene, the right characters, the right day, the right creative time. I wrote the story sitting outside, with my typewriter, on the lawn. At the end of an hour the story was finished, the hair on the back of my neck was standing up, and I was in tears. I knew I had written the first really good story of my life.

All during my early twenties I had the following schedule.

On Monday morning I wrote the first draft of a new story. On Tuesday I did a second draft. On Wednesday a third. On Thursday a fourth. On Friday a fifth. And on Saturday at noon I mailed out the sixth and final draft to New York. Sunday? I thought about all the wild ideas scrambling for my attention, waiting under the attic lid, confident at last that, because of 'The Lake', I would soon let them out.

If this all sounds mechanical, it wasn't. My ideas drove me to it, you see. The more I did, the more I wanted to do. You grow ravenous. You run fevers. You know exhilarations. You can't sleep at night, because your beast-creature ideas want out and turn you in your bed. It is a grand way to live.

There was another reason to write so much: I was being paid twenty to forty dollars a story, by the pulp magazines. High on the hog was hardly my way of life. I had to sell at least one story, or better two, each month in order to survive my hot-dog, hamburger, trolley-car-fare life.

In 1944 I sold some forty stories, but my total income for the year was only $800.

It suddenly strikes me that there is much in this collection I haven't commented on yet. 'The Black Ferris' Volume 2 is of interest here because early one autumn twenty-three years ago it changed itself from a short short story into a screenplay and then into a novel, *Something Wicked This Way Comes*.

'The Day It Rained Forever' was another word-association I handed myself one afternoon, thinking about hot suns, deserts, and harps that could change the weather.

'The Leave-Taking' is the true story of my great-grandmother who nailed shingles on rooftops well into her seventies, then took herself up to bed when I was three and said farewell to everyone and went to sleep.

'Calling Mexico' sprang into being because I visited a friend of mine one afternoon in the summer of 1946 and, as I entered the room, he handed me the telephone and said, 'Listen.' I listened and heard the sounds of Mexico City coming from two thousand miles away. I went home and wrote about my telephone experience to a friend in Paris. Halfway through my letter, the letter turned into the story, which went off in the mail that day.

'Skeleton' happened because I went to my doctor when I was twenty-two, complaining that my neck, my throat, felt strange. I touched all around the tendons and muscles of my neck. The doctor did likewise and said, 'You know what you're suffering from?'

'What?'

'A bad case,' he said, 'of discovery of the larynx. We all discover, at one time or another, various tendons, various bones, in our bodies we never noticed before. That's you. Take an aspirin and go home.'

I went home, feeling my elbows, my ankles, my ribs, my throat, and my medulla oblongata.

'Skeleton', a contest between a man and his hidden bones, wrote itself that night.

'The Picasso Summer' was the result of my walking on the shoreline with friends and my wife one late afternoon. I picked up a Popsicle stick, drew pictures in the sand and said: 'Wouldn't it be awful, if you'd wanted to own a Picasso all your life, and suddenly bumped into him here, drawing mythological beasts in the sand . . . your very own Picasso "etching" right in front of you . . . '

I finished the story, about Picasso on the beach, at two in the morning.

Hemingway. 'The Parrot Who Met Papa'. One night in 1952 I drove across Los Angeles with friends to invade the printing plant where *Life* was publishing their issue with Hemingway's *Old Man and the Sea* in it. We grabbed copies, hot off the press, sat in the nearest bar, and talked about Papa, Finca Vigía, Cuba, and, somehow, a parrot who had lived in that bar and talked to Hemingway every night. I went home, made a notation about the parrot, and put it away for sixteen years. Prowling my file folders in 1968 I came upon just the note for a title: 'The Parrot Who Met Papa'.

My God, I thought, Papa's been dead eight years. If that parrot is still around, remembers Hemingway, can speak with his voice, he's worth millions. And what if someone kidnapped the parrot, held it for ransom?

'The Haunting of the New' happened because John Godley, Lord Kilbracken, wrote me from Ireland describing his visit to a house that had burned and been replaced, stone by stone, brick by brick, in imitation of the original. Within half a day of reading Kilbracken's postcard, I had first-drafted the tale.

Enough now. There you have it. Here are one hundred stories from almost forty years of my life, containing half the damning truths I suspected at midnight, and half of the saving truths I re-found next noon. If anything is taught here, it is simply the charting of the life of someone who started out to somewhere – and went. I have not so much thought my way through life as done things and found what it was and who I was after the doing. Each tale was a way of finding selves. Each self found each day slightly different from the one found twenty-four hours earlier.

It all started that autumn day in 1932 when Mr Electrico gave me the two gifts. I don't know if I believe in previous lives, I'm not sure I can live forever. But that young boy believed in both and I have let him have his head. He has written my stories and books for me. He runs the Ouija Board and says Aye or Nay to submerged truths or half-truths. He is the skin through which, by osmosis, all the stuffs pass and put themselves on paper. I have trusted his passions, his fears, and his joys. He has, as a result, rarely failed me. When it is a long damp November in my soul, and I think too much and perceive too little, I know it is high time to get back to that boy with the tennis shoes, the high fevers, the multitudinous joys, and the terrible nightmares. I'm not sure where he leaves off and I start. But I'm proud of the tandem team. What else can I do but wish him well, and at the same time acknowledge and wish two other people well? In the same month that I married my wife Marguerite, I became affiliated with my literary representative and closest friend, Don Congdon. Maggie typed and criticized my stories, Don criticized and sold the results. With the two of them as teammates these past thirty-three years, how could I have failed? We are the Connemara Lightfoots, the Queen's Own Evaders. And we're still sprinting for that exit.

Here are the stories. Turn the page.

The Stories of

RAY BRADBURY

The Night

You are a child in a small town. You are, to be exact, eight years old, and it is growing late at night. Late for you, accustomed to bedding in at nine or nine-thirty; once in a while perhaps begging Mom or Dad to let you stay up later to hear Sam and Henry on that strange radio that is popular in this year of 1927. But most of the time you are in bed and snug at this time of night.

It is a warm summer evening. You live in a small house on a small street in the outer part of town where there are few street lights. There is only one store open, about a block away: Mrs Singer's. In the hot evening Mother has been ironing the Monday wash and you have been intermittently begging for ice cream and staring into the dark.

You and your mother are all alone at home in the warm darkness of summer. Finally, just before it is time for Mrs Singer to close her store, Mother relents and tells you:

'Run and get a pint of ice cream and be sure she packs it tight.'

You ask if you can get a scoop of chocolate ice cream on top, because you don't like vanilla, and Mother agrees. You clutch the money and run barefooted over the warm evening cement sidewalk, under the apple trees and oak trees, towards the store. The town is so quiet and far off, you can only hear the crickets sounding in the spaces beyond the hot indigo trees that hold back the stars.

Your bare feet slap the pavement, you cross the street and find Mrs Singer moving ponderously about her store, singing Yiddish melodies.

'Pint ice cream?' she says. 'Chocolate on top? Yes!'

You watch her fumble the metal top off the ice-cream freezer and manipulate the scoop, packing the cardboard pint chock full with 'chocolate on top, yes!' You give the money, receive the chill, icy pack, and rubbing it across your brow and cheek, laughing, you thump barefootedly homeward. Behind you, the lights of the lonely little store blink out and there is only a street light shimmering on the corner, and the whole city seems to be going to sleep . . .

Opening the screen door you find Mom still ironing. She looks hot and irritated, but she smiles just the same.

'When will Dad be home from lodge-meeting?' you ask.

'About eleven-thirty or twelve,' Mother replies. She takes the ice cream to the kitchen, divides it. Giving you your special portion of chocolate, she dishes out some for herself and the rest is put away. 'For Skipper and your father when they come.'

Skipper is your brother. He is your older brother. He's twelve and healthy, red-faced, hawk-nosed, tawny-haired, broad-shouldered for his years, and always running. He is allowed to stay up later than you. Not much later, but enough to make him feel it is worthwhile having been born first. He is over on the other side of town this evening to a game of kick-the-can and will be home soon. He and the kids have been yelling, kicking, running for hours, having fun. Soon he will come clomping in, smelling of sweat and green grass on his knees where he fell, and smelling very much in all ways like Skipper; which is natural.

You sit enjoying the ice cream. You are at the core of the deep quiet summer night. Your mother and yourself and the night all around this small house on this small street. You lick each spoon of ice cream thoroughly before digging for another, and Mom puts her ironing board away and the hot iron in its case, and she sits in the armchair by the phonograph, eating her dessert and saying, 'My lands, it was a hot day today. It's still hot. Earth soaks up all the heat and lets it out at night. It'll be soggy sleeping.'

You both sit there listening to the summer silence. The dark is pressed down by every window and door, there is no sound because the radio needs a new battery, and you have played all the Knickerbocker Quartet records and Al Jolson and Two Black Crows records to exhaustion; so you just sit on the hardwood floor by the door and look out into the dark dark dark, pressing your nose against the screen until the flesh of its tip is moulded into small dark squares.

'I wonder where your brother is?' Mother says after a while. Her spoon scrapes on the dish. 'He should be home by now. It's almost nine-thirty.'

'He'll be here,' you say, knowing very well that he will be.

You follow Mom out to wash the dishes. Each sound, each rattle of spoon or dish is amplified in the baked evening. Silently, you go to the living room, remove the couch cushions and, together, yank it open and extend it down into the double bed that it secretly is. Mother makes the bed, punching pillows neatly to flump them up for your head. Then, as you are unbuttoning your shirt, she says:

'Wait awhile, Doug.'

'Why?'

'Because I say so.'

'You look funny, Mom.'

Mom sits down a moment, then stands up, goes to the door, and calls. You listen to her calling and calling Skipper, Skipper, Skiiiiiiiiiperrrrrrrr over and over. Her calling goes out into the summer warm dark and never comes back. The echoes pay no attention.

Skipper. Skipper. Skipper.

Skipper!

And as you sit on the floor a coldness that is not ice cream and not winter, and not part of summer's heat, goes through you. You notice Mom's eyes sliding, blinking; the way she stands undecided and is nervous. All of these things.

She opens the screen door. Stepping out into the night she walks down the steps and down the front sidewalk under the lilac bush. You listen to her moving feet.

She calls again. Silence.

She calls twice more. You sit in the room. Any moment now Skipper will reply, from down the long long narrow street.

'All right, Mom! All right, Mother! Hey!'

But he doesn't answer. And for two minutes you sit looking at the made-up bed, the silent radio, the silent phonograph, at the chandelier with its crystal bobbins gleaming quietly, at the rug with the scarlet and purple curlicues on it. You stub your toe on the bed purposely to see if it hurts. It does.

Whining, the screen door opens, and Mother says:

'Come on, Shorts. We'll take a walk.'

'Where to?'

'Just down the block. Come on. Better put your shoes on, though. You'll catch cold.'

'No, I won't. I'll be all right.'

You take her hand. Together you walk down St James Street. You smell roses in blossom, fallen apples lying crushed and odorous in the deep grass. Underfoot, the concrete is still warm, and the crickets are sounding louder against the darkening dark. You reach a corner, turn, and walk towards the ravine.

Off somewhere, a car goes by, flashing its lights in the distance. There is such a complete lack of life, light, and activity. Here and there, back off from where you're walking towards the ravine, you see faint squares of light where people are still up. But most of the houses, darkened, are sleeping already, and there are a few lightless places where the occupants of a dwelling sit talking low dark talk on their front porches. You hear a porch swing squeaking as you walk near.

'I wish your father was home;' says Mother. Her large hand tightens around your small one. 'Just wait'll I get that boy. I'll spank him within an inch of his life.'

A razor strop hangs in the kitchen for this. You think of it, remember when Dad has doubled and flourished it with muscled control over your frantic limbs. You doubt Mother will carry out her promise.

Now you have walked another block and are standing by the holy black silhouette of the German Baptist Church at the corner of Chapel Street and Glen Rock. In the back of the church a hundred yards away, the ravine begins. You can smell it. It has a dark sewer, rotten foliage, thick green odour. It is a wide ravine that cuts and twists across the town, a jungle by day, a place to let alone at night, Mother has often declared.

You should feel encouraged by the nearness of the German Baptist Church, but you are not — because the building is not illumined, is cold and useless as a pile of ruins on the ravine edge.

You are only eight years old, you know little of death, fear, or dread. Death is the waxen effigy in the coffin when you were six and Grandfather passed away — looking like a great fallen vulture in his casket, silent, withdrawn, no more to tell you how to be a good boy, no more to comment succinctly on politics. Death is your little sister one morning when you awaken at the age of seven, look into her crib and see her staring up at you with a blind blue, fixed and frozen stare until the men come with a small wicker basket to take her away. Death is when you stand by her high chair four weeks later and suddenly realize she'll never be in it again, laughing and crying, and make you jealous of her because she was born. That is death.

But this is more than death. This summer night wading deep in time and stars and warm eternity. It is an essence of all the things you will ever feel or see or hear in your life again, being brought steadily home to you all at once.

Leaving the sidewalk, you walk along a trodden, pebbled, weed-fringed path to the ravine's edge. Crickets, in loud full drumming chorus now, are shouting to quiver the dead. You follow obediently behind brave, fine, tall Mother who is defender of all the universe. You feel braveness because she goes before, and you hang back a trifle for a moment, and then hurry on, too. Together, then, you approach, reach, and pause at the very edge of civilization.

The ravine.

Here and now, down there in that pit of jungled blackness is suddenly all the evil you will ever know. Evil you will never understand. All of the nameless things are there. Later, when you have grown you'll be given names to label them with. Meaningless syllables to describe the waiting nothingness. Down there in the huddled shadow, among thick trees and trailed vines, lives the odour of decay. Here, at this spot, civilization ceases, reason ends, and a universal evil takes over.

You realize you are alone. You and your mother. Her hand trembles.

Her hand *trembles*.

Your belief in your private world is shattered. You feel Mother tremble. Why? Is she, too, doubtful? But she is bigger, stronger, more intelligent than yourself, isn't she? Does she, too, feel that intangible menace, that groping out of darkness, that crouching malignancy down below? Is there, then, no strength in growing up? no solace in being an adult? no sanctuary in life? no flesh citadel strong enough to withstand the scrabbling assault of midnights? Doubts flush you. Ice cream lives again in your throat, stomach, spine and limbs; you are instantly cold as a wind out of December-gone.

You realize that all men are like this. That each person is to himself one alone. One oneness, a unit in a society, but always afraid. Like here, standing. If you should scream now, if you should holler for help, would it matter?

You are so close to the ravine now that in the instant of your scream, in the interval between someone hearing it and running to find you, much could happen.

Blackness could come swiftly, swallowing; and in one titanically freezing moment all would be concluded. Long before dawn, long before police with flashlights might probe the disturbed pathway, long before men with trembling brains could rustle down the pebbles to your help. Even if they were within five hundred yards of you now, and help *certainly* is, in three seconds a dark tide could rise to take all eight years of life away from you and —

The essential impact of life's loneliness crushes your beginning-to-tremble body. Mother is alone, too. She cannot look to the sanctity of marriage, the protection of her family's love, she cannot look to the United States Constitution or the City Police, she cannot look anywhere, in this very instant, save into her heart, and there she'll find nothing but uncontrollable repugnance and a will to fear. In this instant it is an individual problem seeking an individual solution. You must accept being alone and work on from there.

You swallow hard, cling to her. Oh Lord, don't let her die, please, you think. Don't do anything to us. Father will be coming home from lodge-meeting in an hour and if the house is empty . . . ?

Mother advances down the path into the primeval jungle. Your voice trembles. 'Mom. Skip's all right. Skip's all right. He's all right. Skip's all right.'

Mother's voice is strained, high. 'He always comes through here. I tell him not to, but those darned kids, they come through here anyway. Some night he'll come through and never come out again — '

Never come out again. That could mean anything. Tramps. Criminals. Darkness. Accident. Most of all — death.

Alone in the universe.

There are a million small towns like this all over the world. Each as dark, as lonely, each as removed, as full of shuddering and wonder. The reedy playing of minor-key violins is the small towns' music, with no lights but many shadows. Oh the vast swelling loneliness of them. The secret damp ravines of them. Life is a horror lived in them at night, when at all sides sanity, marriage, children, happiness, are threatened by an ogre called Death.

Mother raises her voice into the dark.

'Skip! Skipper!' she calls. 'Skip! Skipper!'

Suddenly, both of you realize there is something wrong. Something very wrong. You listen intently and realize what it is.

The crickets have stopped chirping.

Silence is complete.

Never in your life a silence like this one. One so utterly complete. Why should the crickets cease? Why? What reason? They have never stopped ever before. Not ever.

Unless. Unless —

Something is going to happen.

It is as if the whole ravine is tensing, bunching together its black fibres, drawing in power from all about sleeping countrysides, for miles and miles. From dew-sodden forests and dells and rolling hills where dogs tilt heads to moons, from all around the great silence is sucked into one centre, and you at the core of it. In ten seconds now, something will happen, something will happen. The crickets keep their truce, the stars are so low you can almost brush the tinsel. There are swarms of them, hot and sharp.

Growing, growing, the silence. Growing, growing, the tenseness. Oh it's so dark, so far away from everything. Oh God!

And then, way way off across the ravine:

'Okay, Mom! Coming, Mother!'

And again:

'Hi, Mom! Coming, Mom!'

And then the quick scuttering of tennis shoes padding down through the pit of the ravine as three kids come dashing, giggling. Your brother Skipper, Chuck Redman, and Augie Bartz. Running, giggling.

The stars suck up like the stung antennae of ten million snails.

The crickets sing!

The darkness pulls back, startled, shocked, angry. Pulls back, losing its appetite at being so rudely interrupted as it prepared to feed. As the dark retreats like a wave on a shore, three kids pile out of it, laughing.

'Hi, Mom! Hi, Shorts! Hey!'

It smells like Skipper all right. Sweat and grass and his oiled leather baseball glove.

'Young man, you're going to get a licking,' declares Mother. She puts away her fear instantly. You know she will never tell anybody of it, ever. It will be in her heart though, for all time, as it is in your heart, for all time.

You walk home to bed in the late summer night. You are glad Skipper is alive. Very glad. For a moment there you thought —

Far off in the dim moonlit country, over a viaduct and down a valley, a train goes rushing along and it whistles like a lost metal thing, nameless and running. You go to bed, shivering, beside your brother, listening to that train whistle, and thinking of a cousin who lived way out in the country where that train is now; a cousin who died of pneumonia late at night years and years ago . . . You smell the sweat of Skip beside you. It is magic. You stop trembling. You hear footsteps outside the house on the sidewalk, as Mother is turning out the lights. A man clears his throat in a way you recognize.

Mom says, 'That's your father.'

It is.

Homecoming

'Here they come,' said Cecy, lying there flat in her bed.

'Where are they?' cried Timothy from the doorway.

'Some of them are over Europe, some over Asia, some of them over the Islands, some over South America!' said Cecy, her eyes closed, the lashes long, brown, and quivering.

Timothy came forward upon the bare plankings of the upstairs room. 'Who are they?'

'Uncle Einar and Uncle Fry, and there's Cousin William, and I see Frulda and Helgar and Aunt Morgiana and Cousin Vivian, and I see Uncle Johann! They're all coming fast!'

'Are they up in the sky?' cried Timothy, his little grey eyes flashing. Standing by the bed, he looked no more than his fourteen years. The wind blew outside, the house was dark and lit only by starlight.

'They're coming through the air and travelling along the ground, in many forms,' said Cecy, in her sleeping. She did not move on the bed; she thought inward on herself and told what she saw. 'I see a wolflike thing coming over a dark river — at the shallows — just above a waterfall, the starlight shining up his pelt. I see a brown oak leaf blowing far up in the sky. I see a small bat flying. I see many other things, running through the forest trees and slipping through the highest branches; and they're *all* coming this way!'

'Will they be here by tomorrow night?' Timothy clutched the bedclothes. The spider on his lapel swung like a black pendulum, excitedly dancing. He leaned over his sister. 'Will they all be here in time for the Homecoming?'

'Yes, yes, Timothy, yes,' sighed Cecy. She stiffened. 'Ask

no more of me. Go away now. Let me travel in the places I like best.'

'Thanks, Cecy,' he said. Out in the hall, he ran to his room. He hurriedly made his bed. He had just awakened a few minutes ago, at sunset, and as the first stars had risen, he had gone to let his excitement about the party run with Cecy. Now she slept so quietly there was not a sound. The spider hung on a silvery lasso about Timothy's slender neck as he washed his face. 'Just think, Spid, tomorrow night is Allhallows Eve!'

He lifted his face and looked into the mirror. His was the only mirror allowed in the house. It was his mother's concession to his illness. Oh, if only he were not so afflicted! He opened his mouth, surveyed the poor, inadequate teeth nature had given him. No more than so many corn kernels — round, soft and pale in his jaws. Some of the high spirit died in him.

It was now totally dark and he lit a candle to see by. He felt exhausted. This past week the whole family had lived in the fashion of the old country. Sleeping by day, rousing at sunset to move about. There were blue hollows under his eyes. 'Spid, I'm no good,' he said, quietly, to the little creature. 'I can't even get used to sleeping days like the others.'

He took up the candleholder. Oh, to have strong teeth, with incisors like steel spikes. Or strong hands, even, or a strong mind. Even to have the power to send one's mind out, free, as Cecy did. But, no, he was the imperfect one, the sick one. He was even — he shivered and drew the candle flame closer — afraid of the dark. His brothers snorted at him. Bion and Leonard and Sam. They laughed at him because he slept in a bed. With Cecy it was different; her bed was part of her comfort for the composure necessary to send her mind abroad to hunt. But Timothy, did he sleep in the wonderful polished boxes like the others? He did not! Mother let him

have his own bed, his own room, his own mirror. No wonder
the family skirted him like a holy man's crucifix. If only the
wings would sprout from his shoulder blades. He bared his
back, stared at it. And sighed again. No chance. Never.

Downstairs were exciting and mysterious sounds, the slither-
ing black crape going up in all the halls and on the ceilings
and doors. The sputter of burning black tapers in the banis-
tered stairwell. Mother's voice, high and firm. Father's
voice, echoing from the damp cellar. Bion walking from
outside the old country house lugging vast two-gallon jugs.

'I've just got to go to the party, Spid,' said Timothy. The
spider whirled at the end of its silk, and Timothy felt alone.
He would polish cases, fetch toadstools and spiders, hang
crape, but when the party started he'd be ignored. The less
seen or said of the imperfect son the better.

All through the house below, Laura ran.

'The Homecoming!' she shouted gaily. 'The Homecoming!' Her footsteps everywhere at once.

Timothy passed Cecy's room again, and she was sleeping
quietly. Once a month she went belowstairs. Always she
stayed in bed. Lovely Cecy. He felt like asking her, 'Where
are you now, Cecy? And *in* who? And what's happening? Are
you beyond the hills? And what goes on there?' But he went
on to Ellen's room instead.

Ellen sat at her desk, sorting out many kinds of blond, red
and black hair and little scimitars of fingernails gathered
from her manicurist job at the Mellin Village beauty parlour
fifteen miles over. A sturdy mahogany case lay in one corner
with her name on it.

'Go away,' she said, not even looking at him. 'I can't work
with you gawking.'

'Allhallows Eve, Ellen; just think!' he said, trying to be
friendly.

'Hunh!' She put some fingernail clippings in a small white

sack, labelled them. 'What can it mean to you? What do you know of it? It'll scare hell out of you. Go back to bed.'

His cheeks burned. 'I'm needed to polish and work and help serve.'

'If you don't go, you'll find a dozen raw oysters in your bed tomorrow,' said Ellen, matter-of-factly. 'Good-bye, Timothy.'

In his anger, rushing downstairs, he bumped into Laura.

'Watch where you're going!' she shrieked from clenched teeth.

She swept away. He ran to the open cellar door, smelled the channel of moist earthy air rising from below. 'Father?'

'It's about time,' Father shouted up the steps. 'Hurry down, or they'll be here before we're ready!'

Timothy hesitated only long enough to hear the million other sounds in the house. Brothers came and went like trains in a station, talking and arguing. If you stood in one spot long enough the entire household passed with their pale hands full of things. Leonard with his little black medical case, Samuel with his large, dusty ebon-bound book under his arm, bearing more black crape, and Bion excursioning to the car outside and bringing in many more gallons of liquid.

Father stopped polishing to give Timothy a rag and a scowl. He thumped the huge mahogany box. 'Come on, shine this up, so we can start on another. Sleep your life away.'

While waxing the surface, Timothy looked inside.

'Uncle Einar's a big man, isn't he, Papa?'

'Unh.'

'How big is he?'

'The size of the box'll tell you.'

'I was only asking. Seven feet tall?'

'You talk a lot.'

About nine o'clock Timothy went out into the October

weather. For two hours in the now-warm, now-cold wind he walked the meadows collecting toadstools and spiders. His heart began to beat with anticipation again. How many relatives had Mother said would come? Seventy? One hundred? He passed a farmhouse. If only you knew what was happening at our house, he said to the glowing windows. He climbed a hill and looked at the town, miles away, settling into sleep, the town-hall clock, high and round, white in the distance. The town did not know, either. He brought home many jars of toadstools and spiders.

In the little chapel belowstairs a brief ceremony was celebrated. It was like all the other rituals over the years, with Father chanting the dark lines, Mother's beautiful white ivory hands moving in the reverse blessings, and all the children gathered except Cecy, who lay upstairs in bed. But Cecy was present. You saw her peering, now from Bion's eyes, now Samuel's, now Mother's, and you felt a movement and now she was in you, fleetingly, and gone.

Timothy prayed to the Dark One with a tightened stomach. 'Please, please, help me grow up, help me be like my sisters and brothers. Don't let me be different. If only I could put the hair in the plastic images as Ellen does, or make people fall in love with me as Laura does with people, or read strange books as Sam does, or work in a respected job like Leonard and Bion do. Or even raise a family one day, as Mother and Father have done . . . '

At midnight a storm hammered the house. Lightning struck outside in amazing, snow-white bolts. There was a sound of an approaching, probing, sucking tornado, funnelling and nuzzling the moist night earth. Then the front door, blasted half off its hinges, hung stiff and discarded, and in trooped Grandmama and Grandpapa, all the way from the old country!

From then on people arrived each hour. There was a flutter at the side window, a rap on the front porch, a knock at the back. There were fey noises from the cellar; autumn wind piped down the chimney throat, chanting. Mother filled the large crystal punch bowl with a scarlet fluid poured from the jugs Bion had carried home. Father swept from room to room lighting more tapers. Laura and Ellen hammered up more wolfsbane. And Timothy stood amidst this wild excitement, no expression to his face, his hands trembling at his sides, gazing now here, now there. Banging of doors, laughter, the sound of liquid pouring, darkness, sound of wind, the webbed thunder of wings, the padding of feet, the welcoming bursts of talk at the entrances, the transparent rattlings of casements, the shadows passing, coming, going, wavering.

'Well, well, and *this* must be Timothy!'

'What?'

A chilly hand took his hand. A long hairy face leaned down over him. 'A good lad, a fine lad,' said the stranger.

'Timothy,' said his mother. 'This is Uncle Jason.'

'Hello, Uncle Jason.'

'And over here — ' Mother drifted Uncle Jason away. Uncle Jason peered back at Timothy over his caped shoulder, and winked.

Timothy stood alone.

From off a thousand miles in the candled darkness, he heard a high fluting voice; that was Ellen. 'And my brothers, they *are* clever. Can you guess their occupations, Aunt Morgiana?'

'I have no idea.'

'They operate the undertaking establishment in town.'

'What!' A gasp.

'Yes!' Shrill laughter. 'Isn't that priceless!'

Timothy stood very still.

A pause in the laughter. 'They bring home sustenance for Mama, Papa and all of us,' said Laura. 'Except, of course, Timothy . . . '

An uneasy silence. Uncle Jason's voice demanded, 'Well? Come now. What about Timothy?'

'Oh, Laura, your tongue,' said Mother.

Laura went on with it. Timothy shut his eyes. 'Timothy doesn't — well — doesn't *like* blood. He's delicate.'

'He'll learn,' said Mother. 'He'll learn,' she said very firmly. 'He's my son, and he'll learn. He's only fourteen.'

'But I was raised on the stuff,' said Uncle Jason, his voice passing from one room on into another. The wind played the trees outside like harps. A little rain spatted on the windows — 'raised on the stuff,' passing away into faintness.

Timothy bit his lips and opened his eyes.

'Well, it was all my fault.' Mother was showing them into the kitchen now. 'I tried forcing him. You can't force children, you only make them sick, and then they never get a taste for things. Look at Bion, now, he was thirteen before he . . .'

'I understand,' murmured Uncle Jason. 'Timothy will come around.'

'I'm sure he will,' said Mother, defiantly.

Candle flames quivered as shadows crossed and recrossed the dozen musty rooms. Timothy was cold. He smelled the hot tallow in his nostrils and instinctively he grabbed at a candle and walked with it around and about the house, pretending to straighten the crape.

'*Timothy*,' someone whispered behind a patterned wall, hissing and sizzling and sighing the words, '*Timothy is afraid of the dark*.'

Leonard's voice. Hateful Leonard!

'I like the candle, that's all,' said Timothy in a reproachful whisper.

More lightning, more thunder. Cascades of roaring laughter. Bangings and clickings and shouts and rustles of clothing. Clammy fog swept through the front door. Out of the fog, settling his wings, stalked a tall man.

'Uncle Einar!'

Timothy propelled himself on his thin legs, straight through the fog, under the green webbing shadows. He threw himself across Einar's arms. Einar lifted him.

'You've wings, Timothy!' He tossed the boy light as thistles. 'Wings, Timothy: fly!' Faces wheeled under. Darkness rotated. The house blew away. Timothy felt breezelike. He flapped his arms. Einar's fingers caught and threw him once more to the ceiling. The ceiling rushed down like a charred wall. 'Fly, Timothy!' shouted Einar, loud and deep. 'Fly with wings! Wings!'

He felt an exquisite ecstasy in his shoulder blades, as if roots grew, burst to explode and blossom into new, moist membrane. He babbled wild stuff; again Einar hurled him high.

The autumn wind broke in a tide on the house, rain crashed down, shaking the beams, causing chandeliers to tilt their enraged candle lights. And the one hundred relatives peered out from every black, enchanted room, circling inward, all shapes and sizes, to where Einar balanced the child like a baton in the roaring spaces.

'Enough!' shouted Einar, at last.

Timothy, deposited on the floor timbers, exaltedly, exhaustedly fell against Uncle Einar, sobbing happily. 'Uncle, uncle, uncle!'

'Was it good flying? Eh, Timothy?' said Uncle Einar, bending down, patting Timothy's head. 'Good, good.'

It was coming towards dawn. Most had arrived and were ready to bed down for the daylight, sleep motionlessly with no sound until the following sunset, when they would shout out of their mahogany boxes for the revelry.

Uncle Einar, followed by dozens of others, moved towards the cellar. Mother directed them downwards to the crowded row on row of highly polished boxes. Einar, his wings like sea-green tarpaulins tented behind him, moved with a curious whistling down the passageway; where his wings touched they made a sound of drumheads gently beaten.

Upstairs, Timothy lay wearily thinking, trying to like the darkness. There was so much you could do in darkness that people couldn't criticize you for, because they never saw you. He *did* like the night, but it was a qualified liking: sometimes there was so much night he cried out in rebellion.

In the cellar, mahogany doors sealed downwards, drawn in by pale hands. In corners, certain relatives circled three times to lie, heads on paws, eyelids shut. The sun rose. There was a sleeping.

Sunset. The revel exploded like a bat nest struck full, shrieking out, fluttering, spreading. Box doors banged wide. Steps rushed up from cellar damp. More late guests, kicking on front and back portals, were admitted.

It rained, and sodden visitors laid their capes, their water-pelleted hats, their sprinkled veils upon Timothy who bore them to a closet. The rooms were crowd-packed. The laughter of one cousin, shot from one room, angled off the wall of another, ricocheted, banked, and returned to Timothy's ears from a fourth room, accurate and cynical.

A mouse ran across the floor.

'I know you, Niece Leibersrouter!' exclaimed Father, around him but not to him. The dozens of towering people pressed in against him, elbowed him, ignored him.

Finally, he turned and slipped away up the stairs.

He called softly. 'Cecy. Where are you now, Cecy?'

She waited a long while before answering. 'In the Imperial Valley,' she murmured faintly. 'Beside the Salton Sea, near the mud pots and the steam and the quiet. I'm inside a farmer's wife. I'm sitting on a front porch. I can make her move if I want, or do anything or think anything. The sun's going down.'

'What's it like, Cecy?'

'You can hear the mud pots hissing,' she said, slowly, as if speaking in a church. 'Little grey heads of steam push up the mud like bald men rising in the thick syrup, head first, out in the boiling channels. The grey heads rip like rubber fabric, collapse with noises like wet lips moving. And feathery plumes of steam escape from the ripped tissue. And there is a smell of deep sulphurous burning and old times. The dinosaur has been abroiling here ten million years.'

'Is he done yet, Cecy?'

The mouse spiralled three women's feet and vanished into a corner. Moments later a beautiful woman rose up out of nothing and stood in the corner, smiling her white smile at them all.

Something huddled against the flooded pane of the kitchen window. It sighed and wept and tapped continually, pressed against the glass, but Timothy could make nothing of it, he saw nothing. In imagination he was outside staring in. The rain was on him, the wind at him, and the taper-dotted darkness inside was inviting. Waltzes were being danced; tall thin figures pirouetted to outlandish music. Stars of light flickered off lifted bottles; small clods of earth crumbled from casques, and a spider fell and went silently legging over the floor.

Timothy shivered. He was inside the house again. Mother was calling him to run here, run there, help, serve, out to the kitchen now, fetch this, fetch that, bring the plates, heap the food – on and on – the party happened.

'Yes, he's done. Quite done.' Cecy's calm sleeper's lips turned up. The languid words fell slowly from her shaping mouth. 'Inside this woman's skull I am, looking out, watching the sea that does not move, and is so quiet it makes you afraid. I sit on the porch and wait for my husband to come home. Occasionally, a fish leaps, falls back, starlight edging it. The valley, the sea, the few cars, the wooden porch, my rocking chair, myself, the silence.'

'What now, Cecy?'

'I'm getting up from my rocking chair,' she said.

'Yes?'

'I'm walking off the porch, towards the mud pots. Planes fly over, like primordial birds. Then it's quiet, so quiet.'

'How long will you stay inside her, Cecy?'

'Until I've listened and looked and felt enough: until I've changed her life some way. I'm walking off the porch and along the wooden boards. My feet knock on the planks, tiredly, slowly.'

'And now?'

'Now the sulphur fumes are all around me. I stared at the bubbles as they break and smooth. A bird darts by my temple, shrieking. Suddenly I am in the bird and fly away! And as I fly, inside my new small glass-bead eyes I see a woman below me, on a boardwalk, take one two three steps forward into the mud pots. I hear a sound as of a boulder plunged into molten depths. I keep flying, circle back. I see a white hand, like a spider, wriggle and disappear into the grey lava pool. The lava seals over. Now I'm flying home, swift, swift, swift!'

Something clapped hard against the window. Timothy started.

Cecy flicked her eyes wide, bright, full, happy, exhilarated.

'Now I'm *home*!' she said.

After a pause, Timothy ventured, 'The Homecoming's on. And everybody's here.'

'Then why are you upstairs?' She took his hand. 'Well, ask me.' She smiled slyly. 'Ask me what you came to ask.'

'I didn't come to ask anything,' he said. 'Well, almost nothing. Well — oh, Cecy!' It came from him in one long rapid flow. 'I want to do something at the party to make them look at me, something to make me good as them, something to make me belong, but there's nothing I can do and I feel funny and, well, I thought you might . . . '

'I might,' she said, closing her eyes, smiling inwardly. 'Stand up straight. Stand very still.' He obeyed. 'Now, shut your eyes and blank out your thought.'

He stood very straight and thought of nothing, or at least thought of thinking nothing.

She sighed. 'Shall we go downstairs now, Timothy?' Like a hand into a glove, Cecy was within him.

'Look everybody!' Timothy held the glass of warm red liquid. He held up the glass so that the whole house turned to watch him. Aunts, uncles, cousins, brothers, sisters!

He drank it straight down.

He jerked a hand at his sister Laura. He held her gaze, whispering to her in a subtle voice that kept her silent, frozen. He felt tall as the trees as he walked to her. The party now slowed. It waited on all sides of him, watching. From all the room doors the faces peered. They were not laughing. Mother's face was astonished. Dad looked bewildered, but pleased and getting prouder every instant.

He nipped Laura, gently, over the neck vein. The candle flames swayed drunkenly. The wind climbed around on the roof outside. The relatives stared from all the doors. He popped toadstools into his mouth, swallowed, then beat his arms against his flanks and circled. 'Look, Uncle Einar! I can fly, at last!' Beat went his hands. Up and down pumped his feet. The faces flashed past him.

At the top of the stairs, flapping, he heard his mother cry, 'Stop, Timothy!' far below. 'Hey!' shouted Timothy, and leaped off the top of the well, thrashing.

Halfway down, the wings he thought he owned dissolved. He screamed. Uncle Einar caught him.

Timothy flailed whitely in the receiving arms. A voice burst out of his lips, unbidden. 'This is Cecy! This is Cecy! Come see me, all of you, upstairs, first room on the left!' Followed by a long trill of high laughter. Timothy tried to cut it off with his tongue.

Everybody was laughing. Einar set him down. Running through the crowding blackness as the relatives flowed upstairs towards Cecy's room to congratulate her, Timothy banged the front door open.

'Cecy, I hate you, I hate you!'

By the sycamore tree, in deep shadow, Timothy spewed out his dinner, sobbed bitterly and thrashed in a pile of autumn leaves. Then he lay still. From his blouse pocket, from the protection of the matchbox he used for his retreat, the spider crawled forth. Spid walked along Timothy's arm. Spid explored up his neck to his ear and climbed in the ear to tickle it. Timothy shook his head. 'Don't, Spid. Don't.'

The feathery touch of a tentative feeler probing his eardrum set Timothy shivering. 'Don't, Spid!' He sobbed somewhat less.

The spider travelled down his cheek, took a station under the boy's nose, looked up into the nostrils as if to seek the brain, and then clambered softly up over the rim of the nose to sit, to squat there peering at Timothy with green-gem eyes until Timothy filled with ridiculous laughter. 'Go away, Spid!'

Timothy sat up, rustling the leaves. The land was very bright with the moon. In the house he could hear the faint ribaldry as Mirror, Mirror was played. Celebrants shouted, dimly muffled, as they tried to identify those of themselves whose reflections did not, had not ever, appeared in a glass.

'Timothy.' Uncle Einar's wings spread and twitched and came in with a sound like kettledrums. Timothy felt himself plucked up like a thimble and set upon Einar's shoulder. 'Don't feel badly, Nephew Timothy. Each to his own, each in his own way. How much better things are for you. How rich. The world's dead for us. We've seen so much of it, believe me. Life's best to those who live the least of it. It's worth more per ounce, Timothy, remember that.'

The rest of the black morning, from midnight on, Uncle Einar led him about the house, from room to room, weaving and singing. A horde of late arrivals set the entire hilarity off afresh. Great-great-great-great and a thousand more great-greats Grandmother was there, wrapped in Egyptian cerements. She said not a word, but lay straight as a burnt ironing board against the wall, her eye hollows cupping a distant, wise, silent glimmering. At the breakfast, at four in the morning, one-thousand-odd-greats Grandmama was stiffly seated at the head of the longest table.

The numerous young cousins caroused at the crystal punch bowl. Their shiny olive-pit eyes, their conical, devilish faces and curly bronze hair hovered over the drinking table, their hard-soft, half-girl half-boy bodies wrestling against each other as they got unpleasantly, sullenly drunk. The wind got higher, the stars burned with fiery intensity, the noises redoubled, the dances quickened, the drinking became more positive. To Timothy there were thousands of things to hear and watch. The many darknesses roiled, bubbled, the many faces passed and repassed . . .

'Listen!'

The party held its breath. Far away the town clock struck its chimes, saying six o'clock. The party was ending. In time to the rhythm of the striking clock, their one hundred voices began to sing songs that were four hundred years old, songs Timothy could not know. Arms twined, circling slowly, they sang, and somewhere in the cold distance of morning the town clock finished out its chimes and quieted.

Timothy sang. He knew no words, no tune, yet the words and tune came round and high and good. And he gazed at the closed door at the top of the stairs.

'Thanks, Cecy,' he whispered. 'You're forgiven. Thanks.'

Then he just relaxed and let the words move, with Cecy's voice, free from his lips.

Good-byes were said, there was a great rustling. Mother and Father stood at the door to shake hands and kiss each departing relative in turn. The sky beyond the open door coloured in the east. A cold wind entered. And Timothy felt himself seized and settled in one body after another, felt Cecy press him into Uncle Fry's head so he stared from the wrinkled leather face, then leaped in a flurry of leaves up over the house and awakening hills . . .

Then, loping down a dirt path, he felt his red eyes burning, his fur pelt rimed with morning, as inside Cousin William he panted through a hollow and dissolved away . . .

Like a pebble in Uncle Einar's mouth, Timothy flew in a webbed thunder, filling the sky. And then he was back, for all time, in his own body.

In the growing dawn, the last few were embracing and crying and thinking how the world was becoming less a place for them. There had been a time when they had met every year, but now decades passed with no reconciliation. 'Don't forget,' someone cried, 'we meet in Salem in 1970!'

Salem. Timothy's numbed mind turned the words over. Salem, 1970. And there would be Uncle Fry and a thousand-times-great Grandmother in her withered cerements, and Mother and Father and Ellen and Laura and Cecy and all the rest. But would he be there? Could he be certain of staying alive until then?

With one last withering blast, away they all went, so many scarves, so many fluttery mammals, so many sere leaves, so many whining and clustering noises, so many midnights and insanities and dreams.

Mother shut the door. Laura picked up a broom. 'No,' said Mother. 'We'll clean tonight. Now we need sleep.' And the family vanished down cellar and upstairs. And Timothy moved in the crape-littered hall, his head down. Passing a party mirror, he saw the pale mortality of his face all cold and trembling.

'Timothy,' said Mother.

She came to touch her hand on his face. 'Son,' she said, 'we love you. Remember that. We all love you. No matter how different you are, no matter if you leave us one day.' She kissed his cheek. 'And if and when you die, your bones will lie undisturbed, we'll see to that. You'll lie at ease forever, and I'll come visit every Allhallows Eve and tuck you in the more secure.'

The house was silent. Far away the wind went over a hill with its last cargo of dark bats, echoing, chittering.

Timothy walked up the steps, one by one, crying to himself all the way.

Uncle Einar

'It will take only a minute,' said Uncle Einar's sweet wife.

'I refuse,' he said. 'And that takes but a *second*.'

'I've worked all morning,' she said, holding to her slender back, 'and you won't help? It's drumming for a rain.'

'Let it rain,' he cried, morosely. 'I'll not be pierced by lightning just to air your clothes.'

'But you're so quick at it.'

'Again, I refuse.' His vast tarpaulin wings hummed nervously behind his indignant back.

She gave him a slender rope on which were tied four dozen fresh-washed clothes. He turned it in his fingers with distaste. 'So it's come to this,' he muttered, bitterly. 'To this, to this, to this.' He almost wept angry and acid tears.

'Don't cry; you'll wet them down again,' she said. 'Jump up, now, run them about.'

'Run them about.' His voice was hollow, deep, and terribly wounded. 'I say: let it thunder, let it pour!'

'If it was a nice, sunny day I wouldn't ask,' she said, reasonably. 'All my washing gone for nothing if you don't. They'll hang about the house – '

That *did* it. Above all, he hated clothes flagged and festooned so a man had to creep under on the way across a room. He jumped up. His vast green wings boomed. 'Only so far as the pasture fence!'

Whirl: up he jumped, his wings chewed and loved the cool air. Before you'd say Uncle Einar Has Green Wings he sailed low across his farmland, trailing the clothes in a vast fluttering loop through the pounding concussion and backwash of his wings!

'Catch!'

Back from the trip, he sailed the clothes, dry as popcorn, down on a series of clean blankets she'd spread for their landing.

'Thank you,' she cried.

'Gahh!' he shouted, and flew off under the apple tree to brood.

Uncle Einar's beautiful silk-like wings hung like sea-green sails behind him, and whirred and whispered from his shoulders when he sneezed or turned swiftly. He was one of the few in the Family whose talent was visible. All his dark cousins and nephews and brothers hid in small towns across the world, did unseen mental things or things with witch-fingers and white teeth, or blew down the sky like fire-leaves, or loped in forests like moon-silvered wolves. They lived comparatively safe from normal humans. Not so a man with great green wings.

Not that he hated his wings. Far from it! In his youth he'd always flown nights, because nights were rare times for winged men! Daylight held dangers, always had, always would; but nights, ah, nights, he had sailed over islands of cloud and seas of summer sky. With no danger to himself. It had been a rich, full soaring, an exhilaration.

But now he could not fly at night.

On his way home to some high mountain pass in Europe after a Homecoming among Family members in Mellin Town, Illinois (some years ago) he had drunk too much rich crimson wine. 'I'll be all right,' he had told himself, vaguely, as he beat his long way under the morning stars, over the moon-dreaming country hills beyond Mellin Town. And then — crack out of the sky —

A high tension tower.

Like a netted duck! A great sizzle! His face blown black by a blue sparkler of wire, he fended off the electricity with a terrific back-jumping percussion of his wings, and fell.

His hitting the moonlit meadow under the tower made a noise like a large telephone book dropped from the sky.

Early the next morning, his dew-sodden wings shaking violently, he stood up. It was still dark. There was a faint bandage of dawn stretched across the east. Soon the bandage would stain and all flight would be restricted. There was nothing to do but take refuge in the forest and wait out the day in the deepest thicket until another night gave his wings a hidden motion in the sky.

In this fashion he met his wife.

During the day, which was warm for November first in Illinois country, pretty young Brunilla Wexley was out to udder a lost cow, for she carried a silver pail in one hand as she sidled through thickets and pleaded cleverly to the unseen cow to please return home or burst her gut with unplucked milk. The fact that the cow would have most certainly come home when her teats needed pulling did not concern Brunilla Wexley. It was a sweet excuse for forest-journeying, thistle-blowing, and flower-chewing; all of which Brunilla was doing as she stumbled upon Uncle Einar.

Asleep near a bush, he seemed a man under a green shelter.

'Oh,' said Brunilla, with a fever. 'A man. In a camp-tent.'

Uncle Einar awoke. The camp-tent spread like a large green fan behind him.

'Oh,' said Brunilla, the cow-searcher. 'A man with wings.'

That was how she took it. She was startled, yes, but she had never been hurt in her life, so she wasn't afraid of anyone, and it was a fancy thing to see a winged man and she was proud to meet him. She began to talk. In an hour they were old friends, and in two hours she'd quite forgotten his wings were there. And he somehow confessed how he happened to be in this wood.

'Yes, I noticed you looked banged around,' she said. 'That right wing looks very bad. You'd best let me take you home and fix it. You won't be able to fly all the way to Europe on it, anyway. And who wants to live in Europe these days?'

He thanked her, but he didn't quite see how he could accept.

'But I live alone,' she said. 'For, as you see, I'm quite ugly.'

He insisted she was not.

'How kind of you,' she said. 'But I am, there's no fooling myself. My folks are dead, I've a farm, a big one, all to myself, quite far from Mellin Town, and I'm in need of talking company.'

But wasn't she afraid of him? he asked.

'Proud and jealous would be more near it,' she said. '*May I?*' And she stroked his large green membraned veils with careful envy. He shuddered at the touch and put his tongue between his teeth.

So there was nothing for it but that he come to her house for medicaments and ointments, and my! what a burn across his face, beneath his eyes! 'Lucky you weren't blinded,' she said. 'How'd it happen?'

'Well . . . ' he said, and they were at her farm, hardly noticing they'd walked a mile, looking at each other.

A day passed, and another, and he thanked her at her door and said he must be going, he much appreciated the ointment, the care, the lodging. It was twilight and between now, six o'clock, and five the next morning, he must cross an ocean and a continent. 'Thank you; good-bye,' he said, and started to fly off in the dusk and crashed right into a maple tree.

'Oh!' she screamed, and ran to his unconscious body.

When he waked the next hour he knew he'd fly no more in the dark again ever; his delicate night-perception was gone. The winged telepathy that had warned him where towers, trees, houses and hills stood across his path, the fine clear vision and sensibility that had guided him through mazes of forest, cliff, and cloud, all were burnt forever by that strike across his face, that blue electric fry and sizzle.

'How?' he moaned softly. 'How can I go to Europe? If I flew by day, I'd be seen and — miserable joke — maybe shot down! Or kept for a zoo perhaps, what a life *that'd* be! Brunilla, tell me, what shall I do?'

'Oh,' she whispered, looking at her hands. 'We'll think of something . . . '

They were married.

The Family came for the wedding. In a great autumnal avalanche of maple, sycamore, oak, elm leaf, they hissed and rustled, fell in a shower of horse-chestnut, thumped like winter apples on the earth, with an over-all scent of farewell-summer on the wind they made in their rushing. The ceremony? The ceremony was brief as a black candle lit, blown out, and smoke left still on the air. Its briefness, darkness, upside-down and backward quality escaped Brunilla, who only listened to the great tide of Uncle Einar's wings faintly murmuring above them as they finished out the rite. And as for Uncle Einar, the wound across his nose was almost healed and, holding Brunilla's arm, he felt Europe grow faint and melt away in the distance.

He didn't have to see very well to fly straight up, or come straight down. It was only natural that on this night of their wedding he take Brunilla in his arms and fly right up into the sky.

A farmer, five miles over, glanced at a low cloud at midnight, saw faint glows and crackles.

'Heat lightning,' he observed, and went to bed.

They didn't come down till morning, with the dew.

The marriage took. She had only to look at him, and it lifted her to think she was the only woman in the world married to a winged man. 'Who else could say it?' she asked her mirror. And the answer was: 'No one!'

He, on the other hand, found great beauty behind her face,

great kindness and understanding. He made some changes in his diet to fit her thinking, and was careful with his wings about the house; knocked porcelains and broken lamps were nerve-scrapers, he stayed away from them. He changed his sleeping habits, since he couldn't fly nights now anyhow. And she in turn fixed chairs so they were comfortable for his wings, put extra padding here or took it out there, and the things she said were the things he loved her for. 'We're in our cocoons, all of us. See how ugly I am?' she said. 'But one day I'll break out, spread wings as fine and handsome as you.'

'You broke out long ago,' he said.

She thought it over. 'Yes,' she had to admit. 'I know just which day it was, too. In the woods when I looked for a cow and found a tent!' They laughed, and with him holding her she felt so beautiful she knew their marriage had slipped her from her ugliness, like a bright sword from its case.

They had children. At first there was fear, all on his part, that they'd be winged.

'Nonsense, I'd love it!' she said. 'Keep them out from under foot.'

'Then,' he exclaimed, 'they'd be in your *hair*!'

'Ow!' she cried.

Four children were born, three boys and a girl, who, for their energy, seemed to have wings. They popped up like toadstools in a few years, and on hot summer days asked their father to sit under the apple tree and fan them with his cooling wings and tell them wild starlit tales of island clouds and ocean skies and textures of mist and wind and how a star tastes melting in your mouth, and how to drink cold mountain air, and how it feels to be a pebble dropped from Mt Everest, turning to a green bloom, flowering your wings just before you strike bottom!

This was his marriage.

And today, six years later, here sat Uncle Einar, here he was, festering under the apple tree, grown impatient and unkind; not because this was his desire, but because after the long wait, he was still unable to fly the wild night sky; his extra sense had never returned. Here he sat despondently, nothing more than a summer sun-parasol, green and discarded, abandoned for the season by the reckless vacationers who once sought the refuge of its translucent shadow. Was he to sit here forever, afraid to fly by day because someone might see him? Was his only flight to be as a drier of clothes for his wife, or a fanner of children on hot August noons? His one occupation had *always* been flying Family errands, quicker than storms. A boomerang, he'd whickled over hills and valleys and like a thistle, landed. He had always had money; the Family had good use for their winged man! But now? Bitterness! His wings jittered and whisked the air and made a captive thunder.

'Papa,' said little Meg.

The children stood looking at his thought-dark face.

'Papa,' said Ronald. 'Make more thunder!'

'It's a cold March day, there'll soon be rain and plenty of thunder,' said Uncle Einar.

'Will you come watch us?' asked Michael.

'Run on, run on! Let Papa brood!'

He was shut of love, the children of love, and the love of children. He thought only of heavens, skies, horizons, infinities, by night or day, lit by star, moon, or sun, cloudy or clear, but always it was skies and heavens and horizons that ran ahead of you forever when you soared. Yet here he was, sculling the pasture, kept low for fear of being seen.

Misery in a deep well!

'Papa, come watch us; it's March!' cried Meg. 'And we're going to the Hill with all the kids from town!'

Uncle Einar grunted. 'What hill is that?'

'The Kite Hill, of course!' they all sang together.

Now he looked at them.

Each held a large paper kite, their faces sweating with

anticipation and an animal glowing. In their small fingers
were balls of white twine. From the kites, coloured red and
blue and yellow and green, hung caudal appendages of cotton
and silk strips.

'We'll fly our kites!' said Ronald. 'Won't you come?'

'No,' he said, sadly. 'I mustn't be seen by anyone or
there'd be trouble.'

'You could hide and watch from the woods,' said Meg.
'We made the kites ourselves. Just because we know how.'

'How do you know?'

'You're our father!' was the instant cry. 'That's why!'

He looked at his children for a long while. He sighed. 'A
kite festival, is it?'

'Yes, sir!'

'I'm going to win,' said Meg.

'No, *I'm*!' Michael contradicted.

'Me, *me*!' piped Stephen.

'God up the chimney!' roared Uncle Einar, leaping high
with a deafening kettledrum of wings. 'Children! Children! I
love you dearly!'

'Father, what's wrong?' said Michael, backing off.

'Nothing, nothing, nothing!' chanted Einar. He flexed his
wings to their greatest propulsion and plundering. Whoom!
They slammed like cymbals. The children fell flat in the
backwash! 'I have it, I *have* it! I'm free again! Fire in the flue!
Feather on the wind! Brunilla!' Einar called to the house. His
wife appeared. 'I'm free!' he called, flushed and tall, on his
toes. 'Listen, Brunilla, I don't need the night any more! I can
fly by day! I don't need the night! I'll fly *every* day and *any*
day of the year from now on! – but, God, I waste time,
talking. Look!'

And as the worried members of his family watched, he
seized the cotton tail from one of the little kites, tied it to his
belt behind, grabbed the twine ball, held one end in his teeth,
gave the other end to his children, and up, up into the air he

flew, away into the March wind!

And across the meadows and over the farms his children ran, letting out string to the daylit sky, bubbling and stumbling, and Brunilla stood back in the farmyard and waved and laughed to see what was happening; and her children marched to the far Kite Hill and stood, the four of them, holding the twine in their eager, proud fingers, each tugging and directing and pulling. And the children from Mellin Town came running with *their* small kites to let up on the wind, and they saw the great green kite leap and hover in the sky and exclaimed:

'Oh, oh, what a kite! What a kite! Oh, I wish I'd a kite like that! Where, where did you *get* it!'

'Our father made it!' cried Meg and Michael and Stephen and Ronald, and gave an exultant pull on the twine and the humming, thundering kite in the sky dipped and soared and made a great and magical exclamation mark across a cloud!

The Traveller

Father looked into Cecy's room just before dawn. She lay upon her bed. He shook his head uncomprehendingly and waved at her.

'Now, if you can tell me what good she does, lying there,' he said, 'I'll eat the crape on my mahogany box. Sleeping all night, eating breakfast, and then lying on top her bed all day.'

'Oh, but she's so helpful,' explained Mother, leading him down the hall away from Cecy's slumbering pale figure. 'Why, she's one of the most adjustable members of the Family. What good are her brothers? Most of them sleep all day and do nothing. At least Cecy is *active*.'

They went downstairs through the scent of black candles; the black crape on the banister, left over from the Homecoming some months ago and untouched, whispering as they passed. Father unloosened his tie, exhaustedly. 'Well, we work nights,' he said. 'Can we help it if we're — as you put it — old-fashioned?'

'Of course not. Everyone in the Family can't be modern.' She opened the cellar door; they moved down into darkness arm in arm. She looked over at his round white face, smiling. 'It's really very lucky I don't have to sleep *at all*. If you were married to a night-sleeper, think what a marriage it would be! Each of us to our own. None of us the same. All wild. That's how the Family goes. Sometimes we get one like Cecy, all mind; and then there are those like Uncle Einar, all wing; and then again we have one like Timothy, all even and calm and normal. Then there's you, sleeping days. And me, awake all and all of my life. So Cecy shouldn't be too much for you to understand. She helps me a million ways each day. She sends her mind down to the green-grocer's for me, to see what he sells. She puts her mind inside the butcher. That saves me a long trip if he's fresh out of good cuts. She warns me when gossips are coming to visit and talk away the afternoon. And, well, there are six hundred other things — !'

They paused in the cellar near a large empty mahogany box. He settled himself into it, still not convinced. 'But if she'd only contribute more,' he said. 'I'm afraid I'll have to ask her to find some sort of work.'

'Sleep on it,' she said to him. 'Think it over. You may change your mind by sunset.'

She was closing the lid down on him. 'Well,' he said, thoughtfully. The lid closed.

'Good morning, dear,' she said.

'Good morning,' he said, muffled, enclosed, within the box.

The sun rose. She hurried upstairs to make breakfast.

Cecy Elliott was the one who Travelled. She seemed an ordinary eighteen-year-old. But then none of the Family looked like what they were. There was naught of the fang, the foul, the worm or wind-witch to them. They lived in small towns and on farms across the world, simply, closely re-aligning and adapting their talents to the demands and laws of a changing world.

Cecy Elliott awoke. She glided down through the house, humming. 'Good morning, Mother!' She walked down to the cellar to recheck each of the large mahogany boxes, to dust them, to be certain each was tightly sealed. 'Father,' she said, polishing one box. 'Cousin Esther,' she said, examining another, 'here on a visit. And — ' she rapped at a third, 'Grandfather Elliott.' There was a rustle inside like a piece of papyrus. 'It's a strange, cross-bred family,' she mused, climbing to the kitchen again. 'Night-siphoners and flume-fearers, some awake, like Mother, twenty-five hours out of twenty-four; some asleep, like me, fifty-nine minutes out of sixty. Different species of sleep.'

She ate breakfast. In the middle of her apricot dish she saw her mother's stare. She laid the spoon down. Cecy said, 'Father'll change his mind. I'll show him how fine I can be to have around. I'm family insurance; he doesn't understand. You wait.'

Mother said, 'You were inside me a while ago when I argued with Father?'

'Yes.'

'I thought I felt you looking out my eyes,' the mother nodded.

Cecy finished and went up to bed. She folded down the blankets and clean cool sheets, then laid herself out atop the covers, shut her eyes, rested her thin white fingers on her small bosom, nodded her slight, exquisitely sculptured head back against her thick gathering of chestnut hair.

She started to Travel.

Her mind slipped from the room, over the flowered yard, the fields, the green hills, over the ancient drowsy streets of Mellin Town, into the wind and past the moist depression of the ravine. All day she would fly and meander. Her mind would pop into dogs, sit there, and she would feel the bristly feels of dogs, taste ripe bones, sniff tangy-urined trees. She'd hear as a dog heard. She forgot human construction completely. She'd have a dog frame. It was more than telepathy, up one flue and down another. This was complete separation from one body environment into another. It was entrance into tree-nozzling dogs, men, old maids, birds, children at hopscotch, lovers on their morning beds, into workers a sweat with shovelling, into unborn babies' pink, dream-small brains.

Where would she go today? She made her decision, and went!

When her mother tiptoed a moment later to peek into the room, she saw Cecy's body on the bed, the chest not moving, the face quiet. Cecy was gone already. Mother nodded and smiled.

The morning passed. Leonard, Bion and Sam went off to their work, as did Laura and the manicuring sister; and Timothy was despatched to school. The house quieted. At noontime the only sound was made by Cecy Elliott's three young girl-cousins playing Tisket Tasket Coffin Casket in the back yard. There were always extra cousins or uncles or grand-nephews and night-nieces about the place; they came and went; water out of a faucet, down a drain.

The cousins stopped their play when the tall loud man banged on the front door and marched straight in when Mother answered.

'That was Uncle Jonn!' said the littlest girl, breathless.

'The one we hate?' asked the second.

'What's he want?' cried the third. 'He looked mad!'

'*We're* mad at *him*, that's what,' explained the second, proudly. 'For what he did to the Family sixty years ago, and seventy years ago and twenty years ago.'

'Listen!' They listened. 'He's run upstairs!'

'Sounds like he's cryin'.'

'Do grown-ups cry?'

'Sure, silly!'

'He's in Cecy's room! Shoutin'. Laughin'. Prayin'. Cryin'. He sounds mad, and sad, and fraidy-cat, all together!'

The littlest one made tears, herself. She ran to the cellar door. 'Wake up! Oh, down there, wake up! You in the boxes! Uncle Jonn's here and he might have a cedar stake with him! I don't want a cedar stake in my chest! Wake up!'

'Shh,' hissed the biggest girl. 'He hasn't a stake! You can't wake the Boxed People, anyhow. Listen!'

Their heads tilted, their eyes glistened upwards, waiting.

'Get off the bed!' commanded Mother, in the doorway.

Uncle Jonn bent over Cecy's slumbering body. His lips were misshaped. There was a wild, fey and maddened focus to his green eyes.

'Am I too late?' he demanded, hoarsely, sobbing. 'Is she gone?'

'Hours ago!' snapped Mother. 'Are you blind? She might not be back for days. Sometimes she lies there a week. I don't have to feed the body, she finds sustenance from whatever or whoever she's in. Get away from her!'

Uncle Jonn stiffened, one knee pressed on the springs.

'Why couldn't she wait?' he wanted to know, frantically, looking at her, his hands feeling her silent pulse again and again.

'You heard me!' Mother moved forward curtly. 'She's not to be touched. She's got to be left as she is. So if she comes home she can get back in her body exactly right.'

Uncle Jonn turned his head. His long hard red face was pocked and senseless, deep black grooves crowded the tired eyes.

'Where'd she go? I've *got* to find her.'

Mother talked like a slap in the face. 'I don't know. She has favourite places. You might find her in a child running along a trail in the ravine. Or swinging on a grape vine. Or you might find her in a crayfish under a rock in the creek, looking up at you. Or she might be playing chess inside an old man in the court-house square. You know as well as I she can be anywhere.' A wry look came to Mother's mouth. 'She might be vertical inside me now, looking out at you, laughing, and not telling you. This might be her talking and having fun. And you wouldn't know it.'

'Why — ' He swung heavily around, like a huge pivoted boulder. His big hands came up, wanting to grab something. 'If I *thought* — '

Mother talked on, casual quiet. 'Of course she's *not* in me, here. And if she was there'd be no way to tell.' Her eyes gleamed with a delicate malice. She stood tall and graceful, looking upon him with no fear. 'Now, suppose you explain what you want with her?'

He seemed to be listening to a distant bell, tolling. He shook his head, angrily, to clear it. Then he growled. 'Something . . . inside me . . . ' He broke off. He leaned over the cold, sleeping body. 'Cecy! Come back, you hear! You can come back if you want!'

The wind blew softly through the high willows outside the sundrifted windows. The bed creaked under his shifted weight. The distant bell tolled again and he was listening to it, but Mother could not hear it. Only he heard the drowsy summer-day sounds of it, far far away. His mouth opened obscurely:

'I've a thing for her to do to me. For the past month I've been kind of going — insane. I get funny thoughts. I was going to take a train to the big city and talk to a psychiatrist but he wouldn't help. I know that Cecy can enter my head and exorcise those fears I have. She can suck them out like a vacuum cleaner, if she wants to help me. She's the only one can scrape away the filth and cobwebs and make me new again. That's why I need her, you understand?' he said, in a tight, expectant voice. He licked his lips. 'She's *got* to help

'After all you've done to the Family?' said Mother.

'I did nothing to the Family!'

'The story goes,' said Mother, 'that in bad times, when you needed money, you were paid a hundred dollars for each of the Family you pointed out to the law to be staked through the heart.'

'That's unfair!' he said, wavering like a man hit in the stomach. 'You can't prove that. You lie!'

'Nevertheless, I don't think Cecy'd want to help you. The Family wouldn't want it.'

'Family, Family!' He stomped the floor like a huge, brutal

child. 'Damn the Family! I won't go insane on their account! I need help, God damn it, and I'll get it!'

Mother faced him, her face reserved, her hands crossed over her bosom.

He lowered his voice, looking at her with a kind of evil shyness, not meeting her eyes. 'Listen to me, Mrs Elliott,' he said. 'And you, too, Cecy,' he said to the sleeper. 'If you're there,' he added. 'Listen to this.' He looked at the wall clock ticking on the far, sun-drenched wall. 'If Cecy isn't back here by six o'clock tonight, ready to help clean out my mind and make me sane, I'll – I'll go to the police.' He drew himself up. 'I've got a list of Elliotts who live on farms all around and inside Mellin Town. The police can cut enough new cedar stakes in an hour to drive through a dozen Elliott hearts.' He stopped, wiped the sweat off his face. He stood, listening.

The distant bell began to toll again.

He had heard it for weeks. There was no bell, but he could hear it ringing. It rang now, near, far, close, away. Nobody else could hear it save himself.

He shook his head. He shouted to cover the sound of those bells, shouted at Mrs Elliott. 'You heard me?'

He hitched up his trousers, tightened the buckle clasp with a jerk, walked past Mother to the door.

'Yes,' she said. 'I heard. But even I can't call Cecy back if she doesn't want to come. She'll arrive eventually. Be patient. Don't go running off to the police –'

He cut her. 'I can't wait. This thing of mine, this noise in my head's gone on eight weeks now! I can't stand it much longer!' He scowled at the clock. 'I'm going. I'll try to find Cecy in town. If I don't get her by six – well, you know what a cedar stake's like . . . '

His heavy shoes pounded away down the hall, fading down the stairs, out of the house. When the noises were all gone, the mother turned and looked, earnestly, painfully, down upon the sleeper.

'Cecy,' she called, softly, insistently. 'Cecy, come home!'

There was no word from the body. Cecy lay there, not moving, for as long as her mother waited.

Uncle Jonn walked through the fresh open country and into the streets of Mellin Town, looking for Cecy in every child that licked an ice-pop and in every little white dog that padded by on its way to some eagerly anticipated nowhere.

The town spread out like a fancy graveyard. Nothing more than a few monuments, really – edifices to lost arts and pastimes. It was a great meadow of elms and deodars and hackmatack trees, laid out with wooden walks you could haul into your barn at night if the hollow sound of walking people irked you. There were tall old maiden houses, lean and narrow and wisely wan, in which were spectacles of coloured glass, upon which the thinned golden hair of age-old bird nests sprouted. There was a drug shop full of quaint wire-rung soda-fountain stools with plywood bottoms, and the memorious clear sharp odour that used to be in drug stores but never is any more. And there was a barber emporium with a red-ribboned pillar twisting around inside a chrysalis of glass in front of it. And there was a grocery that was all fruity shadow and dusty boxes and the smell of an old Armenian woman, which was like the odour of a rusty penny. The town lay under the deodar and mellow-leaf trees, in no hurry, and somewhere in the town was Cecy, the one who Travelled.

Uncle Jonn stopped, bought himself a bottle of Orange Crush, drank it, wiped his face with his handkerchief, his eyes jumping up and down, like little kids skipping rope. I'm afraid, he thought. I'm afraid.

He saw a code of birds strung dot-dash on the high telephone wires. Was Cecy up there laughing at him out of sharp bird eyes, shuffling her feathers, singing at him? He suspicioned the cigar-store Indian. But there was no animation in that cold, carved, tobacco-brown image.

Distantly, like on a sleepy Sunday morning, he heard the

bells ringing in a valley of his head. He was stone blind. He stood in blackness. White, tortured faces drifted through his inturned vision.

'Cecy!' he cried, to everything, everywhere. 'I know you can help me! Shake me like a tree! Cecy!'

The blindness passed. He was bathed in a cold sweating that didn't stop, but ran like a syrup.

'I know you can help,' he said. 'I saw you help Cousin Marianne years ago. Ten years ago, wasn't it?' He stood, concentrating.

Marianne had been a girl shy as a mole, her hair twisted like roots on her round ball of head. Marianne had hung in her skirt like a clapper in a bell, never ringing when she walked; just swithering along, one heel after another. She gazed at weeds and the sidewalk under her toes, she looked at your chin if she saw you at all — and never got as far as your eyes. Her mother despaired of Marianne's ever marrying or succeeding.

It was up to Cecy, then. Cecy went into Marianne like fist into glove.

Marianne jumped, ran, yelled, glinted her yellow eyes. Marianne flickered her skirts, unbraided her hair and let it hang in a shimmery veil on her half-nude shoulders. Marianne giggled and rang like a gay clapper in the tolling bell of her dress. Marianne squeezed her face into many attitudes of coyness, merriment, intelligence, maternal bliss, and love.

The boys raced after Marianne. Marianne got married.

Cecy withdrew.

Marianne had hysterics; her *spine* was gone!

She lay like a limp corset all one day. But the habit was in her now. Some of Cecy had stayed on like a fossil imprint on soft shale rock; and Marianne began tracing the habits and thinking them over and remembering what it was like to have Cecy inside her, and pretty soon she was running and shouting and giggling all by herself; a corset animated, as it were, by a memory!

Marianne had lived joyously thereafter.

Standing with the cigar-store Indian for conversation, Uncle Jonn now shook his head violently. Dozens of bright bubbles floated in his eyeballs, each with tiny, slanted, microscopic eyes staring in, in at his brain.

What if he never found Cecy? What if the plain winds had borne her all the way to Elgin? Wasn't that where she dearly loved to bide her time, in the asylum for the insane, touching their minds, holding and turning their confetti thoughts?

Far-flung in the afternoon distance a great metal whistle sighed and echoed, steam shuffled as a train cut across valley trestles, over cool rivers, through ripe cornfields, into tunnels like finger into thimble, under arches of shimmering walnut trees. Jonn stood, afraid. What if Cecy was in the cabin of the engineer's head, now? She loved riding the monster engines across country far as she could stretch the contact. Yank the whistle rope until it screamed across sleeping night land or drowsy day country.

He walked along a shady street. Out of the corners of his eyes he thought he saw an old woman, wrinkled as a dried fig, naked as a thistle-seed, floating among the branches of a hawthorn tree, a cedar stake driven into her breast.

Somebody screamed!

Something thumped his head. A blackbird, soaring skywards, took a lock of his hair with it!

He shook his fist at the bird, heaved a rock. 'Scare me, will you!' he yelled. Breathing rawly, he saw the bird circle behind him to sit on a limb waiting another chance to dive for hair.

He turned slyly from the bird.

He heard the whirring sound.

He jumped about, grabbed up. 'Cecy!'

He had the bird! It fluttered, squalled in his hands.

'Cecy!' he called, looking into his caged fingers at the wild black creature. The bird drew blood with its bill.

'Cecy, I'll crush you if you don't help me!'

The bird shrieked and cut him.

He closed his fingers tight, tight, tight.

He walked away from where he finally dropped the dead bird and did not look back at it, even once.

He walked down into the ravine that ran through the very centre of Mellin Town. What's happening now? he wondered. Has Cecy's mother phoned people? Are the Elliotts afraid? He swayed drunkenly, great lakes of sweat bursting out under his armpits. Well, let *them* be afraid awhile. He was tired of being afraid. He'd look just a little longer for Cecy and then go to the police!

On the creek bank, he laughed to think of the Elliotts scurrying madly, trying to find some way round him. There was no way. They'd have to make Cecy help him. They couldn't afford to let good old Uncle Jonn die insane, no, sir.

B-B-shot eyes lay deep in the water, staring roundly up at him.

On blazing hot summer noons, Cecy had often entered into the soft-shelled greyness of the mandibled heads of crayfish. She had often peeked out from the black egg eyes upon their sensitive filamentary stalks and felt the creek sluice by her, steadily, and in fluid veils of coolness and captured light. Breathing out and in the particles of stuff that floated in water, holding her horny, lichened claws before her like some elegant salad utensils, swollen and scissor-sharp. She watched the giant strides of boy feet progressing towards her through the creek bottom, heard the faint, water-thickened shout of boys searching for crayfish, jabbing their pale fingers down, tumbling rocks aside, clutching and tossing frantic flippery animals into open metal cans where scores of other crayfish scuttled like a basket of waste-paper come to life.

She watched pale stalks of boy legs poise over her rock, saw the nude loin-shadows of boy thrown on the sandy muck of the creek floor, saw the suspenseful hand hovered, heard the suggestive whisper of a boy who's spied a prize beneath a stone. Then, as the hand plunged, the stone rolled, Cecy flirted the borrowed fan of her inhabited body, kicked back in a little sand explosion and vanished downstream.

On to another rock she went to sit fanning the sand, holding her claws before her, proud of them, her tiny glass-bulb eyes glowing black as creek-water filled her bubbling mouth, cool, cool, cool . . .

The realization that Cecy might be this close at hand, in any live thing, drove Uncle Jonn to a mad fury. In any squirrel or chipmunk, in a disease germ, even, on his aching body, Cecy might be existing. She could even enter amoebas . . .

On some sweltering summer noons, Cecy would live in an amoeba, darting, vacillating, deep in the old tired philosophical dark waters of a kitchen well. On days when the world high over her, above the unstirred water, was a dreaming nightmare of heat printed on each object of the land, she'd lie somnolent, quivering and cool and distant, settling in the well-throat. Up above, trees were like images burned in green fire. Birds were like bronze stamps you inked and punched on your brain. Houses steamed like manure sheds. When a door slammed it was like a rifle shot. The only good sound on a simmering day was the asthmatic suction of well water drawn up into a porcelain cup, there to be inhaled through an old skelatinous woman's porcelain teeth. Over-head, Cecy could hear the brittle clap of the old woman's shoes, the sighing voice of the old woman baked in the August sun. And, lying lowermost and cool, sighting up up through the dim echoing tunnel of well, Cecy heard the iron suction of the pump handle pressed energetically by the sweating old lady; and water, amoeba, Cecy and all rose up the throat of the well in sudden cool disgorgement out into the cup, over which waited sun-withered lips. Then, and only then, did Cecy withdraw, just as the lips came down to sip, the cup tilted, and porcelain met porcelain . . .

Jonn stumbled, fell flat into the creek water!

He didn't rise, but sat dripping stupidly.

Then he began crashing rocks over, shouting, seizing upon and losing crayfish, cursing. The bells rang louder in his ears. And now, one by one, a procession of bodies that couldn't exist, but seemed to be real, floated by on the water. Worm-white bodies, turned on their backs, drifting like loose marionettes. As they passed, the tide bobbed their heads so their faces rolled over, revealing the features of the typical Elliott family member.

He began to weep, sitting there in the water. He had wanted Cecy's help, but now how could he expect to deserve it, acting a fool, cursing her, hating her, threatening her and the Family?

He stood up, shaking himself. He walked out of the creek and up the hill. There was only one thing to do now. Plead with individual members of the Family. Ask them to inter-cede for him. Have them ask Cecy to come home, quickly.

In the undertaking parlour on Court Street, the door opened. The undertaker, a short, well-tonsored man with a mous-tache and sensitively thin hands, looked up. His face fell.

'Oh, it's *you*, Uncle Jonn,' he said.

'Nephew Bion,' said Jonn, still wet from the creek, 'I need your help. Have you seen Cecy?'

'Seen her?' said Bion Elliott. He leaned against the marble table where he was working on a body. He laughed. 'God, don't ask me *that*!' he snorted. 'Look at me, close. Do you know me?'

Jonn bristled. 'You're Bion Elliott, Cecy's brother, of course!'

'Wrong.' The undertaker shook his head. 'I'm Cousin Ralph, the butcher! Yes, the *butcher*.' He tapped his head. 'Here, inside, where it counts, I'm Ralph. I was working in my refrigerator a moment ago over at the butcher's shop when suddenly Cecy was inside me. She borrowed my mind, like a cup of sugar. And brought me over here just now and sifted me down into Bion's body. Poor Bion! What a joke!'

'You're — you're *not* Bion!'

'No, ah, no, dear Uncle Jonn. Cecy probably put Bion in *my* body! You see the joke? A meat-cutter exchanged for a meat-cutter! A dealer in cold-cuts traded for another of the same!' He quaked with laughter. 'Ah, that Cecy, what a child!' He wiped happy tears from his face. 'I've stood here for five minutes wondering what to do. You know something? Undertaking isn't hard. Not much harder than fixing pot roasts. Oh, Bion'll be mad. His professional integrity. Cecy'll probably trade us back, later. Bion never was one to take a joke on himself!'

Jonn looked confused. 'Even *you* can't control Cecy?'

'God, no. She does what she does. We're helpless.'

Jonn wandered towards the door. 'Got to find her somehow,' he mumbled. 'If she can do this to you, think how she'd help me if she wanted . . . ' The bells rang louder in his ears. From the side of his eyes he saw a movement. He whirled and gasped.

The body on the table had a cedar stake driven through it.

'So long,' said the undertaker to the slammed door. He listened to the sound of Jonn's running feet, fading.

The man who staggered into the police station at five that afternoon was barely able to stand up. His voice was a whisper and he retched as if he'd taken poison. He didn't look like Uncle Jonn any more. The bells rang all the time, all the time, and he saw people walking behind him with staked chests, who vanished whenever he turned to look.

The sheriff looked up from reading a magazine, wiped his brown moustache with the back of one clawlike hand, took his feet down off a battered desk and waited for Uncle Jonn to speak.

'I want to report a family that lives here,' whispered Uncle Jonn, his eyes half-shut. 'A wicked family, living under false pretences.'

The sheriff cleared his throat. 'What's the family's name?'

Uncle Jonn stopped. 'What?'

The sheriff repeated it. 'What's the family's name?'

'Your voice,' said Jonn.

'What about my voice?' said the sheriff.

'Sounds familiar,' said Jonn. 'Like — '

'Who?' asked the sheriff.

'Like Cecy's mother! That's who you sound like!'

'Do I?' asked the sheriff.

'That's who you are inside! Cecy changed you, too, like she changed Ralph and Bion! I can't report the Family to you, now, then! It wouldn't do any good!'

'Guess it wouldn't,' remarked the sheriff, implacably.

'The Family's gotten around me!' wailed Uncle Jonn.

'Seems that way,' said the sheriff, wetting a pencil on his tongue, starting a fresh crossword puzzle. 'Well, good day to you, Jonn Elliott.'

'Unh?'

'I said "Good day".'

'Good day.' Jonn stood by the desk, listening. 'Do you — do you *hear* anything?'

The sheriff listened. 'Crickets?'

'No.'

'Frogs?'

'No,' said Uncle Jonn. 'Bells. Just bells. Holy church bells. The kind of bell a man like me can't stand to hear. Holy church bells.'

The sheriff listened. 'No. Can't say as I hear 'em. Say, be

careful of that door there; it slams.'

The door to Cecy's room was knocked open. A moment later, Uncle Jonn was inside, moving across the floor. The silent body of Cecy lay on the bed, not moving. Behind him, as Jonn seized Cecy's hand, her mother appeared.

She ran to him, struck him on head and shoulders till he fell back from Cecy. The world swelled with bell sounds. His vision blacked out. He groped at the mother, biting his lips, releasing them in gasps, eyes streaming.

'Please, please tell her to come back,' he said. 'I'm sorry. I don't want to hurt anyone any more.'

The mother shouted through the clamour of bells. 'Go downstairs and wait for her there!'

'I can't hear you,' he cried, louder. 'My head.' He held his hands to his ears. 'So loud. So loud I can't stand it.' He rocked on his heels. 'If only I knew where Cecy was — '

Quite simply, he drew out a folded pocket knife, unfolded it. 'I can't go on — ' he said. And before the mother moved he fell to the floor, the knife in his heart, blood running from his lips, his shoes looking senseless one atop the other, one eye shut, the other wide and white.

The mother bent down to him. 'Dead,' she whispered, finally. 'So,' she murmured, unbelievingly, rising up, stepping away from the blood. 'So he's dead at last.' She glanced around, fearfully, cried aloud.

'Cecy, Cecy, come home, child, I need you!'

A silence, while sunlight faded from the room.

'Cecy, come home, child!'

The dead man's lips moved. A high clear voice sprang from them.

'Here! I've been here for days! I'm the fear he had in him; and he never guessed. Tell Father what I've done. Maybe he'll think me worthy now . . . '

The dead man's lips stopped. A moment later, Cecy's body

on the bed stiffened like a stocking with a leg thrust suddenly into it, inhabited again.

'Supper, Mother,' said Cecy, rising from bed.

The Lake

They cut the sky down to my size and threw it over the Michigan lake, put some kids yelling on yellow sand with bouncing balls, a gull or two, a criticizing parent, and me breaking out of a wet wave, finding this world very bleary and moist.

I ran up on the beach.

Mama swabbed me with a furry towel. 'Stand there and dry,' she said.

I stood there, watching the sun take away the water beads on my arms. I replaced them with goose-pimples.

'My, there's a wind,' said Mama. 'Put on your sweater.'

'Wait'll I watch my goose-bumps,' I said.

'Harold,' said Mama.

I put the sweater on and watched the waves come up and fall down on the beach. But not clumsily. On purpose, with a green sort of elegance. Even a drunken man could not collapse with such elegance as those waves.

It was September. In the last days when things are getting sad for no reason. The beach was so long and lonely with only about six people on it. The kids quit bouncing the ball because somehow the wind made them sad, too, whistling the way it did, and the kids sat down and felt autumn come along the endless shore.

All of the hot-dog stands were boarded up with strips of golden planking, sealing in all the mustard, onion, meat odours of the long, joyful summer. It was like nailing summer into a series of coffins. One by one the places slammed their covers down, padlocked their doors, and the wind came and touched the sand, blowing away all of the million footprints of July and August. It got so that now, in September, there was nothing but the mark of my rubber tennis shoes and Donald and Delaus Schabold's feet, down by the water curve.

Sand blew up in curtains on the sidewalks, and the merry-go-round was hidden with canvas, all of the horses frozen in mid-air on their brass poles, showing teeth, galloping on. With only the wind for music, slipping through canvas.

I stood there. Everyone else was in school. I was not. Tomorrow I would be on my way west across the United States on a train. Mom and I had come to the beach for one last brief moment.

There was something about the loneliness that made me want to get away by myself. 'Mama, I want to run up the beach a ways,' I said.

'All right, but hurry back, and don't go near the water.'

I ran. Sand spun under me and the wind lifted me. You know how it is, running, arms out so you feel veils from your fingers, caused by wind. Like wings.

Mama withdrew into the distance, sitting. Soon she was only a brown speck and I was all alone.

Being alone is a newness to a twelve-year-old child. He is so used to people about. The only way he can be alone is in his mind. There are so many real people around, telling children what and how to do, that a boy has to run off down a beach, even if it's only in his head, to get by himself in his own world, with his own miniature values.

So now I was really alone.

I went down to the water and let it cool up to my stomach. Always before, with the crowd, I hadn't dared to look, to come to this spot and search around in the water and call a certain name. But now —

Water is like a magician. Sawing you in half. It feels as if you were cut half in two, part of you, the lower part, sugar, melting, dissolving away. Cool water, and once in a while a very elegantly stumbling wave that falls with a flourish of lace.

I called her name. A dozen times I called it.

'Tally! Tally! Oh, Tally!'

Funny, but you really expect answers to your calling when you are young. You feel that whatever you may think can be real. And sometimes maybe that is not so wrong.

I thought of Tally, swimming out into the water last May, with her pigtails trailing, blonde. She went laughing, and the sun was on her small twelve-year-old shoulders. I thought of the water settling quiet, of the life-guard leaping into it, of Tally's mother screaming, and of how Tally never came out . . .

The life-guard tried to persuade her to come out, but she did not. He came back with only bits of water-weed in his big-knuckled fingers, and Tally was gone. She would not sit across from me at school any longer, or chase indoor balls on the brick streets on summer nights. She had gone too far out, and the lake would not let her return.

And now in the lonely autumn when the sky was huge and the water was huge and the beach was so very long, I had come down for the last time, alone.

I called her name over and over. Tally, oh, Tally!

The wind blew so very softly over my ears, the way wind blows over the mouths of sea-shells to set them whispering. The water rose, embraced my chest, then my knees, up and down, one way and another, sucking under my heels.

'Tally! Come back, Tally!'

I was only twelve. But I know how much I loved her. It was that love that comes before all significance of body and morals. It was that love that is no more bad than wind and sea and sand lying side by side forever. It was made of all the warm long days together at the beach, and the humming quiet days of droning education at the school. All the long autumn days of the years past when I had carried her books home from school.

Tally!

I called her name for the last time. I shivered. I felt water on my face and did not know how it got there. The waves had not splashed that high.

Turning, I retreated to the sand and stood there for half an hour, hoping for one glimpse, one sign, one little bit of Tally to remember. Then, I knelt and built a sand-castle, shaping it fine, building it as Tally and I had often built so many of them. But this time, I only built half of it. Then I got up.

'Tally, if you hear me, come in and build the rest.'

I walked off towards that faraway speck that was Mama. The water came in, blended the sand-castle circle by circle, mashing it down little by little into the original smoothness.

Silently, I walked along the shore.

Far away, a merry-go-round jangled faintly, but it was only the wind.

The next day, I went away on the train.

A train has a poor memory; it soon puts all behind it. It forgets the cornlands of Illinois, the rivers of childhood, the bridges, the lakes, the valleys, the cottages, the hurts and the joys. It spreads them out behind and they drop back of a horizon.

I lengthened my bones, put flesh on them, changed my young mind for an older one, threw away clothes as they no longer fitted, shifted from grammar to high school, to college books, to law books. And then there was a young woman in Sacramento. I knew her for a time, and we were married.

I continued my law study. By the time I was twenty-two, I had almost forgotten what the East was like.

Margaret suggested that our delayed honeymoon be taken back in that direction.

Like a memory, a train works both ways. A train can bring rushing back all those things you left behind so many years before.

Lake Bluff, population ten thousand, came up over the sky. Margaret looked so handsome in her fine new clothes. She watched me as I felt my old world gather me back into its living. She held my arm as the train slid into Bluff Station and our baggage was escorted out.

So many years, and the things they do to people's faces and bodies. When we walked through the town together I saw no one I recognized. There were faces with echoes in them. Echoes of hikes on ravine trails. Faces with small laughter in them from closed grammar schools and swinging on metal-linked swings and going up and down on teeter-totters. But I didn't speak. I walked and looked and filled up inside with all those memories, like leaves stacked for autumn burning.

We stayed on two weeks in all, revisiting all the places together. The days were happy. I thought I loved Margaret well. At least I thought I did.

It was on one of the last days that we walked down by the shore. It was not quite as late in the year as that day so many years before, but the first evidences of desertion were coming upon the beach. People were thinning out, several of the hot dog stands had been shuttered and nailed, and the wind, as always, waited there to sing for us.

I almost saw Mama sitting on the sand as she used to sit. I had that feeling again of wanting to be alone. But I could not force myself to speak of this to Margaret. I only held on to her and waited.

It got late in the day. Most of the children had gone home and only a few men and women remained basking in the windy sun.

The life-guard boat pulled up on the shore. The life-guard stepped out of it, slowly, with something in his arms.

I froze there. I held my breath and I felt small, only twelve years old, very little, very infinitesimal and afraid. The wind howled. I could not see Margaret. I could see only the beach, the life-guard slowly emerging from the boat with a grey sack in his hands, not very heavy, and his face almost as grey and lined.

'Stay here, Margaret,' I said. I don't know why I said it.

'But, why?'

'Just stay here, that's all − '

I walked slowly down the sand to where the life-guard stood. He looked at me.

'What is it?' I asked.

The life-guard kept looking at me for a long time and he couldn't speak. He put the grey sack down on the sand, and water whispered wet up around it and went back.

'What is it?' I insisted.

'She's dead,' said the life-guard quietly.

I waited.

'Funny,' he said, softly. 'Funniest thing I ever saw. She's been dead. A long time.'

I repeated his words.

He nodded. 'Ten years, I'd say. There haven't been any children drowned here *this* year. There were twelve children drowned here since 1933, but we recovered all of them before a few hours had passed. All except one, I remember. This body here, why it must be ten years in the water. It's not − pleasant.'

I stared at the grey sack in his arms. 'Open it,' I said. I don't know why I said it. The wind was louder.

He fumbled with the sack. 'The way I know it's a little girl, is because she's still wearing a locket. There's nothing much else to tell by −'

'Hurry, man, *open it*!' I cried.

'I better not do that,' he said. Then perhaps he saw the way my face must have looked. 'She was such a *little* girl − '

He opened it only part way. That was enough.

The beach was deserted. There was only the sky and the wind and the water and the autumn coming on lonely. I looked down at her there.

I said something over and over. A name. The life-guard looked at me. 'Where did you find her?' I asked.

'Down the beach, that way, in the shallow water. It's a long time for her, ain't it?'

I shook my head.

'Yes, it is. Oh God, yes it is.'

I thought: People grow. I have grown. But she has not changed. She is still small. She is still young. Death does not permit growth or change. She still has golden hair. She will be forever young and I will love her forever, oh God, I will love her forever.

The life-guard tied up the sack again.

Down the beach, a few moments later, I walked by myself. I stopped, and looked down at something. This is where the life-guard found her, I said to myself.

There, at the water's edge, lay a sand-castle, only half-built. Just like Tally and I used to build them. She half and I half.

I looked at it. I knelt beside the sand-castle and saw the little prints of feet coming in from the lake and going back out to the lake again and not ever returning.

Then – I knew.

'I'll help you to finish it,' I said.

I did. I built the rest of it up very slowly, then I arose and turned away and walked off, so as not to watch it crumble in the waves, as all things crumble.

I walked back up the beach to where a strange woman named Margaret was waiting for me, smiling . . .

The Coffin

There was any amount of banging and hammering for a number of days; deliveries of metal parts and oddments which Mr Charles Braling took into his little workshop with a feverish anxiety. He was a dying man, a badly dying man, and he seemed to be in a great hurry, between racking coughs and spittlings, to piece together one last invention.

'What are you doing?' inquired his younger brother, Richard Braling. He had listened with increasing difficulty and much curiosity for a number of days to that banging and rattling about, and now he stuck his head through the work-room door.

'Go far far away and let me alone,' said Charles Braling, who was seventy, trembly and wet-lipped most of the time. He trembled nails into place and trembled a hammer down with a weak blow upon a large timber and then struck a small metal ribbon down into an intricate machine, and, all in all, was having a carnival of labour.

Richard looked on, bitter-eyed, for a long moment. There was a hatred between them. It had gone on for some years and now was neither any better nor any worse for the fact that Charlie was dying. Richard was delighted to know of the impending death, if he thought of it at all. But all this busy fervour of his old brother's stimulated him.

'Pray tell,' he said, not moving from the door.

'If you must know,' snarled old Charles, fitting in an odd thingumabob on the box before him, 'I'll be dead in another week and I'm — I'm building my own coffin!'

'A coffin, my dear Charlie. That doesn't *look* like a coffin. A coffin isn't that complex. Come on now, what are you up to?'

'I tell you it's a coffin! An odd coffin, yes, but nevertheless,' the old man shivered his fingers around in the large box, ' – nevertheless a coffin!'

'But it would be easier to buy one.'

'Not one like this! You couldn't buy one like this anyplace, ever. Oh, it'll be a real fine coffin, all right.'

'You're obviously lying.' Richard moved forward. 'Why, that coffin is a good twelve feet long. Six feet longer than normal size!'

'Oh, yes?' The old man laughed quietly.

'And that transparent top; who ever heard of a coffin lid you can see through? What good is a transparent lid to a corpse?'

'Oh, just never you mind at all,' sang the old man heartily. 'La!' And he went humming and hammering about the shop.

'This coffin is terribly thick,' shouted the young brother over the din. 'Why, it must be five feet thick; how utterly unnecessary!'

'I only wish I might live to patent this amazing coffin,' said old Charlie. 'It would be a god-send to all the poor peoples of the world. Think how it would eliminate the expenses of most funerals. Oh, but, of course, you don't know how it would do that, do you? How silly of me. Well, I shan't tell you. If this coffin could be mass-produced – expensive at first, naturally – but then when you finally got them made in vast quantities, gah, but the money people would save.'

'To hell with you!' And the younger brother stormed out of the shop.

It had been an unpleasant life. Young Richard had always been such a bounder he never had two coins to clink together at one time; all of his money had come from old brother Charlie, who had the indecency to remind him of it at all times. Richard spent many hours with his hobbies; he dearly loved piling up bottles with French wine labels, in the garden. 'I like the way they glint,' he often said, sitting and sipping, sipping and sitting. He was the only man in the county who could hold the longest grey ash on a fifty-cent cigar for the longest recorded time. And he knew how to hold his hands so his diamonds jangled in the light. But he had not bought the wine, the diamonds, the cigars — no! They were all gifts. He was never allowed to buy anything himself. It was always brought to him and given to him. He had to ask for everything, even writing paper. He considered himself quite a martyr to have put up with taking things from that rickety old brother for so long a time. Everything Charlie ever laid his hand to turned to money; everything Richard had ever tried in the way of a leisurely career had failed.

And now, here was this old mole of a Charlie whacking out a new invention which would probably bring Charlie additional specie long after his bones were slotted in the earth!

Well, two weeks passed.

One morning, the old brother toddled upstairs and stole the insides out of the electric phonograph. Another morning he raided the gardener's greenhouse. Still another time he received a delivery from a medical company. It was all young Richard could do to sit and hold his long grey cigar ash steady while these murmuring excursions took place.

'I'm finished!' cried old Charlie on the fourteenth morning, and dropped dead.

Richard finished out his cigar, and, without showing his inner excitement, he laid down his cigar with its fine long whitish ash, two inches long, a real record, and arose.

He walked to the window and watched the sunlight playfully glittering among the fat beetlelike champagne bottles in the garden.

He looked towards the top of the stairs where old dear brother Charlie lay peacefully sprawled against the banister. Then he walked to the phone and perfunctorily dialled a number.

'Hello, Green Lawn Mortuary? This is the Braling residence. Will you send around a wicker, please? Yes. For brother Charlie. Yes. Thank you. Thank you.'

As the mortuary people were taking brother Charlie out in their wicker they received instructions. 'Ordinary casket,' said young Richard. 'No funeral service. Put him in a pine coffin. He would have preferred it that way – simple. Good-bye.'

'Now!' said Richard, rubbing his hands together. 'We shall see about this "coffin" built by dear Charlie. I do not suppose he will realize he is not being buried in his "special" box. Ah.'

He entered the downstairs shop.

The coffin sat before some wide-flung French windows, the lid shut, complete and neat, all put together like the fine innards of a Swiss watch. It was vast, and it rested upon a long table with rollers beneath for easy manoeuvring.

The coffin interior, as he peered through the glass lid, was six feet long. There must be a good three feet of false body at both head and foot of the coffin, then. Three feet at each end which, covered by secret panels that he must find some way of opening, might very well reveal – exactly what?

Money, of course. It would be just like Charlie to suck his riches into his grave with himself, leaving Richard with not a cent to buy a bottle with. The old bastard!

He raised the glass lid and felt about, but found no hidden buttons. There was a small sign studiously inked on white paper, thumbtacked to the side of the satin-lined box. It said:

THE BRALING ECONOMY CASKET. Copyright, April, 1946. Simple to operate. Can be used again and again by morti-cians and families with an eye to the future.

Richard snorted thinly. Who did Charlie think he was fooling?

There was more writing:

DIRECTIONS: SIMPLY PLACE BODY IN COFFIN –

What a fool thing to say. Put body in coffin! Naturally! How else would one go about it? He peered intently and finished out the directions:

SIMPLY PLACE BODY IN COFFIN – AND MUSIC WILL START.

'It can't be – ' Richard gaped at the sign. 'Don't tell me all this work has been for a – ' He went to the open door of the shop, walked out upon the tiled terrace and called to the gardener in his greenhouse. 'Rogers!' The gardener stuck his head out. 'What time is it?' asked Richard.

'Twelve o'clock, sir,' replied Rogers.

'Well, at twelve-fifteen, you come up here and check to see if everything is all right, Rogers,' said Richard.

'Yes, sir,' said the gardener.

Richard turned and went back into the shop. 'We'll find out – ' he said, quietly.

There would be no harm in lying in the box, testing it. He noticed small ventilating holes in the sides. Even if the lid were closed down there'd be air. And Rogers would be up in a moment or two. SIMPLY PLACE BODY IN COFFIN – AND MUSIC WILL START. Really, how naive of old Charlie! Richard hoisted himself up.

He was like a man getting into a bathtub. He felt naked and watched over. He put one shiny shoe into the coffin and crooked his knee and eased himself up and made some little remark to nobody in particular, then he put in his other knee and foot and crouched there, as if undecided about the temperature of the bath-water. Edging himself about, chuckling softly, he lay down, pretending to himself (for it was fun pretending) that he was dead, that people were dropping tears on him, that candles were fuming and illuminating and that the world was stopped in mid-stride because of his passing. He put on a long pale expression, shut his eyes, holding back the laughter in himself behind pressed, quivering lips. He folded his hands and decided they felt waxen and cold.

Whirr. Spung! Something whispered inside the box-wall. *Spung!*

The lid slammed down on him!

From outside, if one had just come into the room, one would have imagined a wild man was kicking, pounding, blathering, and shrieking inside a closet! There was a sound of a body dancing and cavorting. There was a thudding of flesh and fists. There was a squeaking and a kind of wind from a frightened man's lungs. There was a rustling like paper and a shrilling as of many pipes simultaneously played. Then there was a real fine scream. Then — silence.

Richard Braling lay in the coffin and relaxed. He let loose all his muscles. He began to chuckle. The smell of the box was not unpleasant. Through the little perforations he drew more than enough air to live on, comfortably. He need only push gently up with his hands, with none of this kicking and screaming, and the lid would open. One must be calm. He flexed his arms.

The lid was locked.

Well, still there was no danger. Rogers would be up in a minute or two. There was nothing to fear.

The music began to play.

It seemed to come from somewhere inside the head of the coffin. It was green music. Organ music, very slow and melancholy, typical of Gothic arches and long black tapers. It smelled of earth and whispers. It echoed high between stone walls. It was so sad that one almost cried listening to it. It was music of potted plants and crimson and blue stained-glass windows. It was late sun at twilight and a cold wind blowing. It was a dawn with only fog and a faraway fog horn moaning.

'Charlie, Charlie, Charlie, you old fool you! So this is your odd coffin!' Tears of laughter welled into Richard's eyes.

'Nothing more than a coffin which plays its own dirge. Oh, my sainted grandma!'

He lay and listened critically, for it was beautiful music and there was nothing he could do until Rogers came up and let him out. His eyes roved aimlessly, his fingers tapped soft little rhythms on the satin cushions. He crossed his legs idly. Through the glass lid he saw sunlight shooting through the French windows, dust particles dancing on it. It was a lovely blue day.

The sermon began.

The organ music quieted and a gentle voice said:

'We are gathered here together, those who loved and those who knew the deceased, to give him our homage and our due – '

'Charlie, bless you, that's *your* voice!' Richard was delighted. 'A mechanical funeral, by God. Organ music and lecture. And Charlie giving his own oration for himself!'

The soft voice said, 'We who knew and loved him are grieved at the passing of – '

'What was *that*?' Richard raised himself, startled. He didn't quite believe what he had heard. He repeated it to himself just the way he had heard it:

'We who knew and loved him are grieved at the passing of Richard Braling.'

That's what the voice had said.

'Richard Braling,' said the man in the coffin. 'Why, *I'm* Richard Braling.'

A slip of the tongue, naturally. Merely a slip. Charlie had meant to say 'Charles' Braling. Certainly. Yes. Of course. Yes. Certainly. Yes. Naturally. Yes.

'Richard was a fine man,' said the voice, talking on. 'We shall see no finer in our time.'

'My name again!'

Richard began to move about uneasily in the coffin.

Why didn't Rogers come?

It was hardly a mistake, using that name twice. Richard Braling. Richard Braling. We are gathered here. We shall miss — We are grieved. No finer man. No finer in our time. We are gathered here. The deceased. Richard Braling. *Richard* Braling.

Whirrrr, Spung!

Flowers! Six dozen bright blue, red, yellow, sun-brilliant flowers leaped up from behind the coffin on concealed springs!

The sweet odour of fresh-cut flowers filled the coffin. The flowers swayed gently before his amazed vision, tapping silently on the glass lid. Others sprang up until the coffin was banked with petals and colour and sweet odours. Gardenias and dahlias and daffodils, trembling and shining.

'Rogers!'

The sermon continued.

' — Richard Braling, in his life, was a connoisseur of great and good things — '

The music sighed, rose and fell, distantly.

'Richard Braling savoured of life, as one savours of a rare wine, holding it upon the lips — '

A small panel in the side of the box flipped open. A swift bright metal arm snatched out. A needle stabbed Richard in the thorax, not very deeply. He screamed. The needle shot him full of a coloured liquor before he could seize it. Then it popped back into a receptacle and the panel snapped shut.

'Rogers!'

A growing numbness. Suddenly he could not move his fingers or his arms or turn his head. His legs were cold and limp.

'Richard Braling loved beautiful things. Music. Flowers,' said the voice.

'Rogers!'

This time he did not scream it. He could only think it. His

tongue was motionless in his anaesthetized mouth.

Another panel opened. Metal forceps issued forth on steel arms. His left wrist was pierced by a huge sucking needle.

His blood was being drained from his body.

He heard a little pump working somewhere.

' – Richard Braling will be missed among us – '

The organ sobbed and murmured.

The flowers looked down upon him, nodding their bright-petalled heads.

Six candles, black and slender, rose up out of hidden receptacles, and stood behind the flowers, flickering and glowing.

Another pump started to work. While his blood drained out one side of his body, his right wrist was punctured, held, a needle shoved into it, and the second pump began to force formaldehyde into him.

Pump, pause, *pump*, pause, *pump*, pause, *pump*, pause.

The coffin moved.

A small motor popped and chugged. The room drifted by on either side of him. Little wheels revolved. No pallbearers were necessary. The flowers swayed as the casket moved gently out upon the terrace under a blue clear sky.

Pump, pause. *Pump*, pause.

'Richard Braling will be missed –'

Sweet soft music.

Pump, pause.

'Ah, sweet mystery of life, at last –' Singing.

'Braling, the gourmet –'

'Ah, at last I have the secret of it all –'

Staring, staring, his eyes egg-blind, at the little card out of the corners of his eyes:

THE BRALING ECONOMY CASKET . . .

DIRECTIONS: SIMPLY PLACE BODY IN COFFIN – AND MUSIC WILL START.

A tree swung by overhead. The coffin rolled gently through the garden, behind some bushes, carrying the voice and the music with it.

'Now it is the time when we must consign this part of this man to the earth —'

Little shining spades leaped out of the sides of the casket.

They began to dig.

He saw the spades toss up dirt. The coffin settled. Bumped, settled, dug, bumped and settled, dug, bumped and settled again.

Pulse, pause, *pulse*, pause. *Pump*, pause, *pulse*, *pump*, pause.

'Ashes to ashes, dust to dust —'

The flowers shook and jolted. The box was deep. The music played.

The last thing Richard Braling saw was the spading arms of the Braling Economy Casket reaching up and pulling the hole in after it.

'Richard Braling, Richard Braling, Richard Braling, Richard Braling, Richard Braling . . . '

The record was stuck.

Nobody minded. Nobody was listening.

The Crowd

Mr Spallner put his hands over his face.

There was the feeling of movement in space, the beautifully tortured scream, the impact and tumbling of the car with wall, through wall, over and down like a toy, and him hurled out of it. Then – silence.

The crowd came running. Faintly, where he lay, he heard them running. He could tell their ages and their sizes by the sound of their numerous feet over the summer grass and on the lined pavement, and over the asphalt street; and picking through the cluttered bricks to where his car hung half into the night sky, still spinning its wheels with a senseless centrifuge.

Where the crowd came from he didn't know. He struggled to remain aware and then the crowd faces hemmed in upon him, hung over like the large glowing leaves of down-bent trees. They were a ring of shifting, compressing, changing faces over him, looking down, looking down, reading the time of his life or death by his face, making his face into a moon-dial, where the moon cast a shadow from his nose out upon his cheek to tell the time of breathing or not breathing any more ever.

How swiftly a crowd comes, he thought, like the iris of an eye compressing in out of nowhere.

A siren. A police voice. Movement. Blood trickled from his lips and he was being moved into an ambulance. Someone said, 'Is he dead?' And someone else said, 'No, he's not dead.' And a third person said, 'He won't die, he's not going to die.' And he saw the faces of the crowd beyond him in the night, and he knew by their expressions that he wouldn't die.

And that was strange. He saw a man's face, thin, bright, pale; the man swallowed and bit his lips, very sick. There was a small woman, too, with red hair and too much red on her cheeks and lips. And a little boy with a freckled face. Others' faces. An old man with a wrinkled upper lip, an old woman, with a mole upon her chin. They had all come from — where? Houses, cars, alleys, from the immediate and the accident-shocked world. Out of alleys and out of hotels and out of streetcars and seemingly out of nothing they came.

The crowd looked at him and he looked back at them and did not like them at all. There was a vast wrongness to them. He couldn't put his finger on it. They were far worse than this machine-made thing that happened to him now.

The ambulance doors slammed. Through the windows he saw the crowd looking in, looking in. That crowd that always came so fast, so strangely fast, to form a circle, to peer down, to probe, to gawk, to question, to point, to disturb, to spoil the privacy of a man's agony by their frank curiosity.

The ambulance drove off. He sank back and their faces still stared into his face, even with his eyes shut.

The car wheels spun in his mind for days. One wheel, four wheels, spinning, spinning, and whirring, around and around.

He knew it was wrong. Something wrong with the wheels and the whole accident and the running of feet and the curiosity. The crowd faces mixed and spun into the wild rotation of the wheels.

He awoke.

Sunlight, a hospital room, a hand taking his pulse.

'How do you feel?' asked the doctor.

The wheels faded away. Mr Spallner looked around.

'Fine — I guess.'

He tried to find words. About the accident. 'Doctor?'

'Yes?'

'That crowd — was it last night?'

'Two days ago. You've been here since Thursday. You're all right, though. You're doing fine. Don't try to get up.'

'That crowd. Something about wheels, too. Do accidents make people, well, a — little off?'

'Temporarily, sometimes.'

He lay staring up at the doctor. 'Does it hurt your time sense?'

'Panic sometimes does.'

'Makes a minute seem like an hour, or maybe an hour seem like a minute?'

'Yes.'

'Let me tell you then.' He felt the bed under him, the sunlight on his face. 'You'll think I'm crazy. I was driving too fast, I know. I'm sorry now. I jumped the kerb and hit that wall. I was hurt and numb, I know, but I still remember things. Mostly — the crowd.' He waited a moment and then decided to go on, for he suddenly knew what it was that bothered him. 'The crowd got there too quickly. Thirty seconds after the smash they were all standing over me and staring at me . . . it's not right they should run that fast, so late at night . . .'

'You think it was thirty seconds,' said the doctor. 'It was probably three or four minutes. Your senses —'

'Yeah, I know — my senses, the accident. But I was conscious! I remember one thing that puts it all together and makes it funny, God, so damned funny. The wheels of my car, upside down. The wheels were still spinning when the crowd got there!'

The doctor smiled.

The man in bed went on. 'I'm positive! The wheels were spinning and spinning fast — the front wheels! Wheels don't spin very long, friction cuts them down. And these were really spinning!'

'You're confused,' said the doctor.

'I'm not confused. That street was empty. Not a soul in sight. And then the accident and the wheels still spinning and all those faces over me, quick, in no time. And the way they looked down at me, I *knew* I wouldn't die . . . '

'Simple shock,' said the doctor, walking away into the sunlight.

They released him from the hospital two weeks later. He rode home in a taxi. People had come to visit him during his two weeks on his back, and to all of them he had told his story, the accident, the spinning wheels, the crowd. They had all laughed with him concerning it, and passed it off.

He leaned forward and tapped on the taxi window.

'What's wrong?'

The cabbie looked back. 'Sorry, boss. This is one helluva town to drive in. Got an accident up ahead. Want me to detour?'

'Yes. No. No! Wait. Go ahead. Let's – let's take a look.'

The cab moved forward, honking.

'Funny damn thing,' said the cabbie. 'Hey, *you*! Get that fleatrap out the way!' Quieter, 'Funny thing – more damn people. Nosy people.'

Mr Spallner looked down and watched his fingers tremble on his knee. 'You noticed that, too?'

'Sure,' said the cabbie. 'All the time. There's always a crowd. You'd think it was their own mother got killed.'

'They come running awfully fast,' said the man in the back of the cab.

'Same way with a fire or an explosion. Nobody around. Boom. Lotsa people around. I dunno.'

'Ever seen an accident – at night?'

The cabbie nodded. 'Sure. Don't make no difference. There's always a crowd.'

The wreck came in view. A body lay on the pavement. You knew there was a body even if you couldn't see it. Because of the crowd. The crowd with its back towards him as he sat in the rear of the cab. With its back towards him. He opened the window and almost started to yell. But he didn't have the nerve. If he yelled they might turn around.

And he was afraid to see their faces.

'I seem to have a penchant for accidents,' he said, in his office. It was late afternoon. His friend sat across the desk from him, listening. 'I got out of the hospital this morning and first thing on the way home, we detoured around a wreck.'

'Things run in cycles,' said Morgan.

'Let me tell you about my accident.'

'I've heard it. Heard it all.'

'But it was funny, you must admit.'

'I must admit. Now how about a drink?'

They talked on for half an hour or more. All the while they talked, at the back of Spallner's brain a small watch ticked, a watch that never needed winding. It was the memory of a few little things. Wheels and faces.

At about five-thirty there was a hard metal noise in the street. Morgan nodded and looked out and down. 'What'd I tell you? Cycles. A truck and a cream-coloured Cadillac. Yes, yes.'

Spallner walked to the window. He was very cold and as he stood there, he looked at his watch, at the small minute hand. One two three four five seconds — people running — eight nine ten eleven twelve — from all over, people came running — fifteen sixteen seventeen eighteen seconds — more people, more cars, more horns blowing. Curiously distant, Spallner looked upon the scene as an explosion in reverse, the fragments of the detonation sucked back to the point of impulsion. Nineteen, twenty, twenty-one seconds and the crowd was there. Spallner made a gesture down at them, wordless.

The crowd had gathered so fast.

He saw a woman's body for a moment before the crowd swallowed it up.

Morgan said, 'You look lousy. Here. Finish your drink.'

'I'm all right, I'm all right. Let me alone. I'm all right. Can you see those people? Can you see any of them? I wish we could see them closer.'

Morgan cried out, 'Where in hell are you going?'

Spallner was out the door, Morgan after him, and down the stairs, as rapidly as possible. 'Come along, and hurry.'

'Take it easy, you're not a well man!'

They walked out on to the street. Spallner pushed his way forward. He thought he saw a red-haired woman with too much red colour on her cheeks and lips.

'There!' He turned wildly to Morgan. 'Did you see her?'

'See *who*?'

'Damn it; she's gone. The crowd closed in!'

The crowd was all around, breathing and looking and shuffling and mixing and mumbling and getting in the way when he tried to shove through. Evidently the red-haired woman had seen him coming and run off.

He saw another familiar face! A little freckled boy. But there are many freckled boys in the world. And, anyway, it was no use; before Spallner reached him, this little boy ran away and vanished among the people.

'Is she dead?' a voice asked. 'Is she dead?'

'She's dying,' someone else replied. 'She'll be dead before the ambulance arrives. They shouldn't have moved her. They shouldn't have moved her.'

All the crowd faces – familiar, yet unfamiliar, bending over, looking down, looking down.

'Hey, mister, stop pushing.'

'Who you shovin', buddy?'

Spallner came back out, and Morgan caught hold of him before he fell. 'You damned fool. You're still sick. Why in hell'd you have to come down here?' Morgan demanded.

'I don't know, I really don't. They moved her, Morgan, someone moved her. You should never move a traffic victim. It kills them. It kills them.'

'Yeah. That's the way with people. The idiots.'

Spallner arranged the newspaper clippings carefully.

Morgan looked at them. 'What's the idea? Ever since your accident you think every traffic scramble is part of you. What are these?'

'Clippings of motor-car crackups, and photos. Look at them. Not at the cars,' said Spallner, 'but at the crowds around the cars.' He pointed. 'Here. Compare this photo of a wreck in the Wilshire District with one in Westwood. No resemblance. But now take this Westwood picture and align it with one taken in the Westwood District ten years ago.' Again he motioned. 'This woman is in both pictures.'

'Coincidence. The woman happened to be there once in 1936, again in 1946.'

'A coincidence once, maybe. But twelve times over a period of ten years, when the accidents occurred as much as three miles from one another, no. Here.' He dealt out a dozen photographs. 'She's in *all* of these!'

'Maybe she's perverted.'

'She's more than that. How does she *happen* to be there so quickly after each accident? And why does she wear the same clothes in pictures taken over a period of a decade?'

'I'll be damned, so she does.'

'And, last of all, why was she standing over *me* the night of my accident, two weeks ago?'

They had a drink. Morgan went over the files. 'What'd you do, hire a clipping service while you were in hospital to go back through the newspapers for you?' Spallner nodded. Morgan sipped his drink. It was getting late. The street lights were coming on in the streets below the office. 'What does all this add up to?'

'I don't know,' said Spallner, 'except that there's a universal law about accidents. *Crowds gather.* They always gather. And like you and me, people have wondered year after year, why they gathered so quickly, and how? I know the answer. Here it is!'

He flung the clippings down. 'It frightens me.'

'These people — mightn't they be thrill-hunters, perverted sensationalists with a carnal lust for blood and morbidity?'

Spallner shrugged. 'Does that explain their being at all the accidents? Notice, they stick to certain territories. A Brentwood accident will bring out one group. A Huntington Park another. But there's a norm for faces, a certain percentage appear at each wreck.'

Morgan said, 'They're not *all* the same faces, are they?'

'Naturally not. Accidents draw normal people, too, in the course of time. But these, I find, are always the *first* ones there.'

'Who are they? What do they want? You keep hinting and never telling. Good Lord, you must have some idea. You've scared yourself and now you've got me jumping.'

'I've tried getting to them, but someone always trips me up, I'm always too late. They slip into the crowd and vanish. The crowd seems to offer protection to some of its members. They see me coming.'

'Sounds like some sort of clique.'

'They have one thing in common, they always show up together. At a fire or an explosion or on the sidelines of a war, at any public demonstration of this thing called death. Vultures, hyenas, or saints, I don't know which they are, I just don't know. But I'm going to the police with it, this evening. It's gone on long enough. One of them shifted that woman's body today. They shouldn't have touched her. It killed her.'

He placed the clippings in a briefcase. Morgan got up and

slipped into his coat. Spallner clicked the briefcase shut. 'Or, I just happened to think . . . '

'What?'

'Maybe they *wanted* her dead.'

'Why?'

'Who knows. Come along?'

'Sorry. It's late. See you tomorrow. Luck.' They went out together. 'Give my regards to the cops. Think they'll believe you?'

'Oh, they'll believe me all right. Good night.'

Spallner took it slow driving downtown.

'I want to get there,' he told himself, 'alive.'

He was rather shocked, but not surprised, somehow, when the truck came rolling out of an alley straight at him. He was just congratulating himself on his keen sense of observation and talking out what he would say to the police in his mind, when the truck smashed into his car. It wasn't really his car, that was the disheartening thing about it. In a preoccupied mood he was tossed first this way and then that way, while he thought, What a shame, Morgan has gone and lent me his extra car for a few days until my other car is fixed, and now here I go again. The windshield hammered back into his face. He was forced back and forth in several lightning jerks. Then all motion stopped and all noise stopped and only pain filled him up.

He heard their feet running and running and running. He fumbled with the car door. It clicked. He fell out upon the pavement drunkenly and lay, ear to the asphalt, listening to them coming. It was like a great rainstorm, with many drops, heavy and light and medium, touching the earth. He waited a few seconds and listened to their coming and their arrival. Then, weakly, expectantly, he rolled his head up and looked.

The crowd was there.

He could smell their breaths, the mingled odours of many

people sucking and sucking on the air a man needs to live by. They crowded and jostled and sucked and sucked all the air up from around his gasping face until he tried to tell them to move back, they were making him live in a vacuum. His head was bleeding very badly. He tried to move and he realized something was wrong with his spine. He hadn't felt much at the impact, but his spine was hurt. He didn't dare move.

He couldn't speak. Opening his mouth, nothing came out but a gagging.

Someone said, 'Give me a hand. We'll roll him over and lift him into a more comfortable position.'

Spallner's brain burst apart.

No! Don't move me!

'We'll move him,' said the voice, casually.

You idiots, you'll kill me, don't!

But he could not say any of this out loud. He could only think it.

Hands took hold of him. They started to lift him. He cried out and nausea choked him up. They straightened him out into a ramrod of agony. Two men did it. One of them was thin, bright, pale, alert, a young man. The other man was very old and had a wrinkled upper lip.

He had seen their faces before.

A familiar voice said, 'Is — is he dead?'

Another voice, a memorable voice, responded, 'No. Not yet. But he will be dead before the ambulance arrives.'

It was all a very silly, mad plot. Like every accident. He squealed hysterically at the solid wall of faces. They were all around him, these judges and jurors with the faces he had seen before. Through his pain he counted their faces.

The freckled boy. The old man with the wrinkled upper lip.

The red-haired, red-cheeked woman. An old woman with a mole on her chin.

I know what you're here for, he thought. You're here just as you're at all accidents. To make certain the right ones live and the right ones die. That's why you lifted me. You knew it would kill. You knew I'd live if you left me alone.

And that's the way it's been since time began, when crowds gather. You murder much easier, this way. Your alibi is very simple; you didn't know it was dangerous to move a hurt man. You didn't mean to hurt him.

He looked at them, above him, and he was curious as a man under deep water looking up at people on a bridge. Who are you? Where do you come from and how do you get here so soon? You're the crowd that's always in the way, using up good air that a dying man's lungs are in need of, using up space he should be using to lie in, alone. Tramping on people to make sure they die, that's you. I know *all* of you.

It was like a polite monologue. They said nothing. Faces. The old man. The red-haired woman.

Someone picked up his briefcase. 'Whose is this?'

It's mine! It's evidence against all of you!

Eyes, inverted over him. Shiny eyes under tousled hair or under hats.

Faces.

Somewhere — a siren. The ambulance was coming.

But, looking at the faces, the construction, the cast, the form of the faces, Spallner saw it was too late. He read it in their faces. They *knew*.

He tried to speak. A little bit got out:

'It — looks like I'll — be joining up with you. I — guess I'll be a member of your — group — now.'

He closed his eyes then, and waited for the coroner.

The Scythe

Quite suddenly there was no more road. It ran down the valley like any other road, between slopes of barren, stony ground and live oak trees, and then past a broad field of wheat standing alone in the wilderness. It came up beside the small white house that belonged to the wheat field and then just faded out, as though there was no more use for it.

It didn't matter much, because just there the last of the gas was gone. Drew Erickson braked the ancient car to a stop and sat there, not speaking, staring at his big, rough farmer's hands.

Molly spoke, without moving where she lay in the corner beside him. 'We must of took the wrong fork back yonder.'

Drew nodded.

Molly's lips were almost as white as her face. Only they were dry, where her skin was damp with sweat. Her voice was flat with no expression in it.

'Drew,' she said. 'Drew, what are we a-goin' to do now?'

Drew stared at his hands. A farmer's hands, with the farm blown out from under them by the dry, hungry wind that never got enough good loam to eat.

The kids in the back seat woke up and pried themselves out of the dusty litter of bundles and bedding. They poked their heads over the back of the seat and said:

'What are we stoppin' for, Pa? Are we gonna eat now, Pa? Pa, we're awful hungry. Can we eat now, Pa?'

Drew closed his eyes. He hated the sight of his hands.

Molly's fingers touched his wrist. Very light, very soft. 'Drew, maybe in the house there they'd spare us somethin' to eat?'

A white line showed around his mouth. 'Beggin',' he said harshly. 'Ain't none of us ever begged before. Ain't none of us ever goin' to.'

Molly's hand tightened on his wrist. He turned and saw her eyes. He saw the eyes of Susie and little Drew, looking at him. Slowly all the stiffness went out of his neck and his back. His face got loose and blank, shapeless like a thing that has been beaten too hard and too long. He got out of the car and went up the path to the house. He walked uncertainly, like a man who is sick, or nearly blind.

The door of the house was open. Drew knocked three times. There was nothing inside but silence, and a white window curtain moving in the slow, hot air.

He knew it before he went in. He knew there was death in the house. It was that kind of silence.

He went through a small, clean living room and down a little hall. He wasn't thinking anything. He was past thinking. He was going towards the kitchen, unquestioning, like an animal.

Then he looked through an open door and saw the dead man.

He was an old man, lying out on a clean white bed. He hadn't been dead long; not long enough to lose the last quiet look of peace. He must have known he was going to die, because he wore his grave clothes – an old black suit, brushed and neat, and a clean white shirt and black tie.

A scythe leaned against the wall beside the bed. Between the old man's hands there was a blade of wheat, still fresh. A ripe blade, golden and heavy in the tassel.

Drew went into the bedroom, walking soft. There was a coldness on him. He took off his broken, dusty hat and stood by the bed, looking down.

The paper lay open on the pillow beside the old man's head. It was meant to be read. Maybe a request for burial, or to call a relative. Drew scowled over the words, moving his pale, dry lips.

To him who stands beside me at my death bed:

Being of sound mind, and alone in the world as it has been decreed, I, John Buhr, do give and bequeath this farm, with all pertaining to it, to the man who is to come. Whatever his name or origin shall be, it will not matter. The farm is his, and the wheat; the scythe, and the task ordained thereto. Let him take them freely, and without question — and remember that I, John Buhr, am only the giver, not the ordainer. To which I set my hand and seal this third day of April, 1938.

[Signed] *John Buhr.* Kyrie eleison!

Drew walked back through the house and opened the screen door. He said, 'Molly, you come in. Kids, you stay in the car.'

Molly came inside. He took her to the bedroom. She looked at the will, the scythe, the wheat field moving in a hot wind outside the window. Her white face tightened up and she bit her lips and held on to him. 'It's too good to be true. There must be some trick to it.'

Drew said, 'Our luck's changin', that's all. We'll have work to do, stuff to eat, somethin' over our heads to keep rain off.' He touched the scythe. It gleamed like a half-moon. Words were scratched on its blade: WHO WIELDS ME — WIELDS THE WORLD! It didn't mean much to him, right at that moment.

'Drew,' Molly asked, staring at the old man's clasped hands, 'why — why's he holdin' that wheat stalk so hard in his fingers?'

Just then the heavy silence was broken by the sound of the kids scrambling up the front porch. Molly gasped.

They lived in the house. They buried the old man on a hill and said some words over him, and came back down and swept the house and unloaded the car and had something to eat, because there was food, lots of it, in the kitchen; and they did nothing for three days but fix the house and look at the land and lie in the good beds, and then look at one another in surprise that all this was happening this way, and their stomachs were full and there was even a cigar for him to smoke in the evenings.

There was a small barn behind the house and in the barn a bull and three cows; and there was a well-house, a spring-house, under some big trees that kept it cool. And inside the well-house were big sides of beef and bacon and pork and mutton, enough to feed a family five times their size for a year, two years, maybe three. There was a churn and a box of cheese there, and big metal cans for the milk.

On the fourth morning Drew Erickson lay in bed looking at the scythe, and he knew it was time for him to work because there was ripe grain in the long field; he had seen it with his eyes, and he did not want to get soft. Three days' sitting were enough for any man. He roused himself in the first fresh smell of dawn and took the scythe and held it before him as he walked out into the field. He held it up in his hands and swung it down.

It was a big field of grain. Too big for one man to tend, and yet one man had tended it.

At the end of the first day of work, he walked in with the scythe riding his shoulder quietly, and there was a look on his face of a puzzled man. It was a wheat field the like of which he had never seen. It ripened only in separate clusters, each set off from the others. Wheat shouldn't do that. He didn't tell Molly. Nor did he tell her the other things about the field. About how, for instance, the wheat rotted within a few hours after he cut it down. Wheat shouldn't do that, either. He was not greatly worried. After all, there was food at hand.

The next morning the wheat he had left rotting, cut down, had taken hold and come up again in little green sprouts, with tiny roots, all born again.

Drew Erickson rubbed his chin, wondered what and why

and how it acted that way, and what good it would be to him – he couldn't sell it. A couple of times during the day he walked far up in the hills to where the old man's grave was, just to be sure the old man was there, maybe with some notion he might get an idea there about the field. He looked down and saw how much land he owned. The wheat stretched three miles in one direction towards the mountains, and was about two acres wide, patches of it in seedlings, patches of it golden, patches of it green, patches of it fresh-cut by his hand. But the old man said nothing concerning this; there were a lot of stones and dirt in his face now. The grave was in the sun and the wind and silence. So Drew Erickson walked back down to use the scythe, curious, enjoying it because it seemed important. He didn't know just why, but it was. Very, very important.

He couldn't just let the wheat stand. There were always new patches of it ripened, and in his figuring out loud to no one in particular he said, 'If I cut the wheat for the next ten years, just as it ripens up, I don't think I'll pass the same spot twice. Such a damn big field.' He shook his head. 'That wheat ripens just *so*. Never too much of it so I can't cut all the ripe stuff each day. That leaves nothin' but green grain. And the next mornin', sure enough, another patch of ripe stuff . . . '

It was damned foolish to cut the grain when it rotted as quick as it fell. At the end of the week he decided to let it go a few days.

He lay in bed late, just listening to the silence in the house that wasn't anything like death silence, but a silence of things living well and happily.

He got up, dressed, and ate his breakfast slowly. He wasn't going to work. He went out to milk the cows, stood on the porch smoking a cigarette, walked about the back yard a little and then came back in and asked Molly what he had gone out to do.

'Milk the cows,' she said.

'Oh, yes,' he said, and went out again. He found the cows waiting and full, and milked them and put the milk cans in the spring-house, but thought of other things. The wheat. The scythe.

All through the morning he sat on the back porch rolling cigarettes. He made a toy boat for little Drew and one for Susie, and then he churned some of the milk into butter and drew off the buttermilk, but the sun was in his head, aching. It burned there. He wasn't hungry for lunch. He kept looking at the wheat and the wind bending and tipping and ruffling it. His arms flexed, his fingers, resting on his knee as he sat again on the porch, make a kind of grip in the empty air, itching. The pads of his palms itched and burned. He stood up and wiped his hands on his pants and sat down and tried to roll another cigarette and got mad at the mixings and threw it all away with a muttering. He had a feeling as if a third arm had been cut off of him, or he had lost something of himself. It had to do with his hands and his arms.

He heard the wind whisper in the field.

By one o'clock he was going in and out of the house, getting underfoot, thinking about digging an irrigation ditch, but all the time really thinking about the wheat and how ripe and beautiful it was, aching to be cut.

'Damn it to hell!'

He strode into the bedroom, took the scythe down off its wall-pegs. He stood holding it. He felt cool. His hands stopped itching. His head didn't ache. The third arm was returned to him. He was intact again.

It was instinct. Illogical as lightning striking and not hurting. Each day the grain must be cut. It had to be cut. Why? Well, it just did, that was all. He laughed at the scythe in his big hands. Then, whistling, he took it out to the ripe and waiting field and did the work. He thought himself a little mad. Hell, it was an ordinary-enough wheat field, really, wasn't it? Almost.

The days loped away like gentle horses.

Drew Erickson began to understand his work as a sort of dry ache and hunger and need. Things built in his head.

One noon, Susie and little Drew giggled and played with the scythe while their father lunched in the kitchen. He heard them. He came out and took it away from them. He didn't yell at them. He just looked very concerned and locked the scythe up after that, when it wasn't being used.

He never missed a day, scything.

Up. Down. Up, down, and across. Back and up and down and across. Cutting. Up. Down.

Up.

Think about the old man and the wheat in his hands when he died.

Down.

Think about this dead land, with wheat living on it.

Up.

Think about the crazy patterns of ripe and green wheat, the way it grows!

Down.

Think about . . .

The wheat whirled in a full yellow tide at his ankles. The sky blackened. Drew Erickson dropped the scythe and bent over to hold his stomach, his eyes running blindly. The world reeled.

'I've killed somebody!' he gasped, choking, holding to his chest, falling to his knees beside the blade. 'I've killed a lot —'

The sky revolved like a blue merry-go-round at the county fair in Kansas. But no music. Only a ringing in his ears.

Molly was sitting at the blue kitchen table peeling potatoes when he blundered into the kitchen, dragging the scythe behind him.

'Molly!'

She swam around in the wet of his eyes.

She sat there, her hands fallen open, waiting for him to finally get it out.

'Get the things packed!' he said, looking at the floor.

'Why?'

'We're leavin',' he said, dully.

'We're leavin'?' she said.

'That old man. You know what he did here? It's the wheat, Molly, and this scythe. Every time you use the scythe on the wheat a thousand people die. You cut across them and – '

Molly got up and put the knife down and the potatoes to one side and said, understandingly, 'We travelled a lot and haven't eaten good until the last month here, and you been workin' every day and you're tired – '

'I hear voices, sad voices, out there. In the wheat,' he said. 'Tellin' me to stop. Tellin' me not to kill them!'

'Drew!'

He didn't hear her. 'The field grows crooked, wild, like a crazy thing. I didn't tell you. But it's wrong.'

She stared at him. His eyes were blue glass, nothing else.

'You think I'm crazy,' he said, 'but wait 'til I tell you. Oh, God, Molly, help me; I just killed my mother!'

'Stop it!' she said firmly.

'I cut down one stalk of wheat and I killed her. I felt her dyin', that's how I found out just now – '

'Drew!' Her voice was like a crack across the face, angry and afraid now. 'Shut up!'

He mumbled. 'Oh – Molly – '

The scythe dropped from his hands, clamoured on the floor. She picked it up with a snap of anger and set it in one corner. 'Ten years I been with you,' she said. 'Sometimes we had nothin' but dust and prayers in our mouths. Now, all this good luck sudden, and you can't bear up under it!'

She brought the Bible from the living room.

She rustled its pages over. They sounded like the wheat

rustling in a small, slow wind. 'You sit down and listen,' she said.

A sound came in from the sunshine. The kids, laughing in the shade of the large live oak beside the house.

She read from the Bible, looking up now and again to see what was happening to Drew's face.

She read from the Bible each day after that. The following Wednesday, a week later, when Drew walked down to the distant town to see if there was any General Delivery mail, there was a letter.

He came home looking two hundred years old.

He held the letter out to Molly and told her what it said in a cold, uneven voice.

'Mother passed away — one o'clock Tuesday afternoon — her heart — '

All that Drew Erickson had to say was, 'Get the kids in the car, load it up with food. We're goin' on to California.'

'Drew — ' said his wife, holding the letter.

'You know yourself,' he said, 'this is poor grain land. Yet look how ripe it grows. I ain't told you all the things. It ripens in patches, a little each day. It ain't right. And when I cut it, it rots! And next mornin' it comes up without any help, growin' again! Last Tuesday, a week ago, when I cut the grain it was like rippin' my own flesh. I heard somebody scream. It sounded just like — And now, today, this letter.'

She said, 'We're stayin' here.'

'Molly.'

'We're stayin' here, where we're sure of eatin' and sleepin' and livin' decent and livin' long. I'm not starvin' my children down again, ever!'

The sky was blue through the windows. The sun slanted in, touching half of Molly's calm face, shining one eye bright blue. Four or five water drops hung and fell from the kitchen faucet slowly, shining, before Drew sighed. The sigh was husky and resigned and tired. He nodded, looking away. 'All right,' he said. 'We'll stay.'

He picked up the scythe weakly. The words on the metal leaped up with a sharp glitter.

WHO WIELDS ME – WIELDS THE WORLD!

'We'll stay . . . '

Next morning he walked to the old man's grave. There was a single fresh sprout of wheat growing in the centre of it. The same sprout, reborn, that the old man had held in his hands weeks before.

He talked to the old man, getting no answers.

'You worked the field all your life because you *had* to, and one day you came across your own life growin' there. You knew it was yours. You cut it. And you went home, put on your grave clothes, and your heart gave out and you died. That's how it was, wasn't it? And you passed the land on to me, and when I die, I'm supposed to hand it over to someone else.'

Drew's voice had awe in it. 'How long a time has this been goin' on? With nobody knowin' about this field and its use except the man with the scythe . . . ?'

Quite suddenly he felt very old. The valley seemed ancient, mummified, secretive, dried and bent and powerful. When the Indians danced on the prairie it had been here, this field. The same sky, the same wind, the same wheat. And, before the Indians? Some Cro-Magnon, gnarled and shag-haired, wielding a crude wooden scythe, perhaps, prowling down through the living wheat . . .

Drew returned to work. Up, down. Up, down. Obsessed with the idea of being the wielder of *the* scythe. He, himself! It burst upon him in a mad, wild surge of strength and horror.

Up! WHO WIELDS ME! Down! WIELDS THE WORLD!

He had to accept the job with some sort of philosophy. It

was simply his way of getting food and housing for his family. They deserved eating and living decent, he thought, after all these years.

Up and down. Each grain a life he neatly cut into two pieces. If he planned it carefully — he looked at the wheat — why, he and Molly and the kids could live forever!

Once he found the place where the grain grew that was Molly and Susie and little Drew he would never cut it.

And then, like a signal, it came, quietly.

Right there, before him.

Another sweep of the scythe and he'd cut them away.

Molly, Drew, Susie. It was certain. Trembling, he knelt and looked at the few grains of wheat. They glowed at his touch.

He groaned with relief. What if he had cut them down, never guessing? He blew out his breath and got up and took the scythe and stood back away from the wheat and stood for a long while looking down.

Molly thought it awfully strange when he came home early and kissed her on the cheek, for no reason at all.

At dinner, Molly said, 'You quit early today? Does — does the wheat still spoil when it falls?'

He nodded and took more meat.

She said, 'You ought to write to the Agriculture people and have them come look at it.'

'No,' he said.

'I was just suggestin',' she said.

His eyes dilated. 'I got to stay here all my life. Can't nobody else mess with that wheat; they wouldn't know where to cut and not to cut. They might cut the wrong parts.'

'What wrong parts?'

'Nothin',' he said, chewing slowly. 'Nothin' at all.'

He slapped his fork down, hard. 'Who knows *what* they might want to do! Those gover'ment men! They might even

— might even want to plough the whole field under!'

Molly nodded. 'That's just what it needs,' she said. 'And start all over again, with new seed.'

He didn't finish eating. 'I'm not writin' any gover'ment,

and I'm not handin' this field over to no stranger to cut, and that's that!' he said, and the screen door banged behind him.

He detoured around that place where the lives of his children and his wife grew up in the sun, and used his scythe on the far end of the field where he knew he would make no mistakes.

But he no longer liked the work. At the end of an hour he knew he had brought death to three of his old, loved friends in Missouri. He read their names on the cut grain and couldn't go on.

He locked the scythe in the cellar and put the key away. He was done with the reaping, done for good and all.

He smoked his pipe in the evening on the front porch, and told the kids stories to hear them laugh. But they didn't laugh much. They seemed withdrawn, tired and funny, like they weren't his children any more.

Molly complained of a headache, dragged around the house a little, went to bed early, and fell into a deep sleep. That was funny, too. Molly always stayed up late and was full of vinegar.

The wheat field rippled with moonlight on it, making it into a sea.

It wanted cutting. Certain parts needed cutting *now*. Drew Erickson sat, swallowing quietly, trying not to look at it.

What'd happen to the world if he never went in the field again? What'd happen to people ripe for death, who waited the coming of the scythe?

He'd wait and see.

Molly was breathing softly when he blew out the oil lamp

and got to bed. He couldn't sleep. He heard the wind in the wheat, felt the hunger to do the work in his arms and fingers.

In the middle of the night he found himself walking in the field, the scythe in his hands. Walking like a crazy man, walking and afraid, half-awake. He didn't remember unlocking the cellar door, getting the scythe, but here he was in the moonlight, walking in the grain.

Among these grains there were many who were old, weary, wanting so very much to sleep. The long, quiet, moonless sleep.

The scythe held him, grew into his palms, forced him to walk.

Somehow, struggling, he got free of it. He threw it down, ran off into the wheat, where he stopped and went down on his knees.

'I don't want to kill any more,' he said. 'If I work with the scythe I'll have to kill Molly and the kids. Don't ask me to do that!'

The stars only sat in the sky, shining.

Behind him, he heard a dull, thumping sound.

Something shot up over the hill into the sky. It was like a living thing, with arms of red colour, licking at the stars. Sparks fell into his face. The thick, hot odour of fire came with it.

The house!

Crying out, he got sluggishly, hopelessly, to his feet, looking at the big fire.

The little white house with the live oaks was roaring up in one savage bloom of fire. Heat rolled over the hill and he swam in it and went down in it, stumbling, drowning over his head.

By the time he got down the hill there was not a shingle, bolt or threshold of it that wasn't alive with flame. It made blistering, crackling, fumbling noises.

No one screamed inside. No one ran around or shouted.

He yelled in the yard. 'Molly! Susie! Drew!'

He got no answer. He ran close in until his eyebrows withered and his skin crawled hot like paper burning, crisping, curling up in tight little curls.

'Molly! Susie!'

The fire settled contentedly down to feed. Drew ran around the house a dozen times, all alone, trying to find a way in. Then he sat where the fire roasted his body and waited until all the walls had sunken down with fluttering crashes, until the last ceiling bent, blanketing the floors with molten plaster and scorched lathing. Until the flames died and smoke coughed up, and the new day came slowly; and there was nothing but embering ashes and an acid smouldering.

Disregarding the heat fanning from the levelled frames, Drew walked into the ruin. It was still too dark to see much. Red light glowed on his sweating throat. He stood like a stranger in a new and different land. Here – the kitchen. Charred tables, chairs, the iron stove, the cupboards. Here – the hall. Here the parlour and then over there was the bedroom where –

Where Molly was still alive.

She slept among fallen timbers and angry-coloured pieces of wire spring and metal.

She slept as if nothing had happened. Her small white hands lay at her sides, flaked with sparks. Her calm face slept with a flaming lath across one cheek.

Drew stopped and didn't believe it. In the ruin of her smoking bedroom she lay on a glittering bed of sparks, her skin intact, her breast rising, falling, taking air.

'Molly!'

Alive and sleeping after the fire, after the walls had roared down, after ceilings had collapsed upon her and flame had lived all about her.

His shoes smoked as he pushed through piles of fuming litter. It could have seared his feet off at the ankles, he wouldn't have known.

'Molly . . . '

He bent over her. She didn't move or hear him, and she didn't speak. She wasn't dead. She wasn't alive. She just lay there with the fire surrounding her and not touching her, not harming her in any way. Her cotton nightgown was streaked with ashes, but not burnt. Her brown hair was pillowed on a tumble of red-hot coals.

He touched her cheek, and it was cold, cold in the middle of hell. Tiny breaths trembled her half-smiling lips.

The children were there, too. Behind a veil of smoke he made out two smaller figures huddled in the ashes sleeping.

He carried all three of them out to the edge of the wheat field.

'Molly. Molly, wake up! Kids! Kids, wake up!'

They breathed and didn't move and went on sleeping.

'Kids, wake up! Your mother is – '

Dead? No, not dead. But –

He shook the kids as if they were to blame. They paid no attention; they were busy with their dreams. He put them back down and stood over them, his face cut with lines.

He knew why they'd slept through the fire and continued to sleep now. He knew why Molly just lay there, never wanting to laugh again.

The power of the wheat and the scythe.

Their lives, supposed to end yesterday, May 30, 1938, had been prolonged simply because he refused to cut the grain. They should have died in the fire. That's the way it was meant to *be*. But since he had not used the scythe, nothing could hurt them. A house had flamed and fallen and still they lived, caught halfway, not dead, not alive. Simply – waiting. And all over the world thousands more just like them, victims of accidents, fires, disease, suicide, waited, slept just like Molly and her children slept. Not able to die, not able to live. All because a man was afraid of harvesting the ripe grain. All because one man thought he could stop working with a scythe and never work with that scythe again.

He looked down upon the children. The job had to be done every day and every day with never a stopping but going on, with never a pause, but always the harvesting, forever and forever and forever.

All right, he thought. All right. I'll use the scythe.

He didn't say good-bye to his family. He turned with a slow-feeding anger and found the scythe and walked rapidly, then he began to trot, then he ran with long jolting strides into the field, raving, feeling the hunger in his arms, as the wheat whipped and flailed his legs. He pounded through it, shouting. He stopped.

'Molly!' he cried, and raised the blade and swung it down.

'Susie!' he cried. 'Drew!' And swung the blade down again.

Somebody screamed. He didn't turn to look at the fire-ruined house.

And then, sobbing wildly, he rose above the grain again and again and hewed to left and right and to left and to right and to left and to right. Over and over and over! Slicing out huge scars in green wheat and ripe wheat, with no selection and no care, cursing, over and over, swearing, laughing, the blade swinging up in the sun and falling in the sun with a singing whistle! Down!

Bombs shattered London, Moscow, Tokyo.

The blade swung insanely.

And the kilns of Belsen and Buchenwald took fire.

The blade sang, crimson wet.

And mushrooms vomited out blind suns at White Sands, Hiroshima, Bikini, and up, through, and in continental Siberian skies.

The grain wept in a green rain, falling.

Korea, Indo-China, Egypt, India trembled; Asia stirred, Africa woke in the night . . .

And the blade went on rising, crashing, severing, with the fury and the rage of a man who has lost and lost so much that he no longer cares what he does to the world.

Just a few short miles off the main highway, down a rough dirt road that leads to nowhere, just a few short miles from a highway jammed with traffic bound for California.

Once in a while during the long years a jalopy gets off the main highway, pulls up steaming in front of the charred ruin of a little white house at the end of the dirt road, to ask instructions from the farmer they see just beyond, the one who works insanely, wildly, without ever stopping, night and day, in the endless fields of wheat.

But they get no help and no answer. The farmer in the field is too busy, even after all these years; too busy slashing and chopping the green wheat instead of the ripe.

And Drew Erickson moves on with his scythe, with the light of blind suns and a look of white fear in his never-sleeping eyes, on and on and on . . .

There Was an
Old Woman

'No, there's no lief arguin'. I got my mind fixed. Run along with your silly wicker basket. Land, where you ever get notions like that? You just skit out of here; don't bother me, I got my tattin' and knittin' to do, and no never minds about tall, dark gentlemen with fangled ideas.'

The tall, dark young man stood quietly, not moving. Aunt Tildy hurried on with her talk.

'You *heard* what I said! If you got a mind to talk to me, well, you can talk, but meantime I hope you don't mind if I pour myself coffee. There. If you'd been more polite, I'd offer you some, but you jump in here high and mighty and you never rapped on the door or nothin'. You think you *own* the place.'

Aunt Tildy fussed with her lap. 'Now, you made me lose count! I'm makin' myself a comforter. These winters get on mighty chill, and it ain't fittin' for a lady with bones like rice-paper to be settin' in a draughty old house without warmin' herself.'

The tall, dark man sat down.

'That's an antique chair, so be gentle,' warned Aunt Tildy. 'Start again, tell me things you got to tell, I'll listen respectful. But keep your voice in your shoes and stop starin' at me with funny lights in your eyes. Land, it gives me the collywobbles.'

The bone-porcelain, flowered clock on the mantel finished chiming three. Out in the hall, grouped around the wicker basket, four men waited, quietly, as if they were frozen.

'Now, about that wicker basket,' said Aunt Tildy. 'It's past six feet long, and by the look, it ain't laundry. And those four men you walked in with, you don't need them to carry that basket — why, it's light as thistles. Eh?'

The dark young man was leaning forward on the antique chair. Something in his face suggested the basket wouldn't be so light after a while.

'Pshaw,' Aunt Tildy mused. 'Where've I seen a wicker like that before? Seems it was only a couple of years ago. Seems to me — oh! Now I remember. It was when Mrs Dwyer passed away next door.'

Aunt Tildy set her coffee cup down, sternly. 'So *that's* what you're up to? I thought you were workin' to sell me somethin'. You just set there until my little Emily trounces home from college this afternoon! I wrote her a note last week. Not admittin', of course, that I wasn't feelin' quite ripe and pert, but sort of hintin' I want to see her again, it's been a good many weeks. Her livin' in New York and all. Almost like my own daughter, Emily is.

'Now, she'll take care of you, young man. She'll shoo you out'n this parlour so quick it'll — '

The dark young man looked at Aunt Tildy as if she were tired.

'No, I'm *not!*' she snapped.

He weaved back and forth on the chair, half shutting his eyes, resting himself. O, wouldn't she like to rest, too? he seemed to murmur. Rest, rest, nice rest . . .

'Great sons of Goshen on the Gilberry Dike! I got a hundred comforters, two hundred sweaters and six hundred potholders in these fingers, no matter they're skinny! You run off, come back when I'm done, maybe I'll talk to you.' Aunt Tildy shifted subjects. 'Let me tell you about Emily, my sweet, fair child.'

Aunt Tildy nodded thoughtfully. Emily, with hair like yellow corn tassels, just as soft and fine.

'I well remember the day her mother died, twenty years ago, leavin' Emily to my house. That's why I'm mad at you and your wickers and such goin's-on. Who ever heard of people dyin' for any good cause? Young man, I don't *like* it. Why, I remember —'

Aunt Tildy paused; a brief pain of memory touched her heart. Twenty-five years back, her father's voice trembled in the late afternoon.

'Tildy,' he whispered, 'what you goin' to *do* in life? The way you act, men don't walk much with you. You kiss and skedaddle. Why don't you settle down, marry, raise children?'

'Papa,' Tildy shouted back at him, 'I like laughin' and playin' and singin'. I'm not the marryin' kind. I can't find a man with my philosophy, Papa.'

'What "philosophy's" that?'

'That death is ridiculous! It run off with Mama when we needed her most. You call *that* intelligent?'

Papa's eyes got wet and grey and bleak. 'You're always right, Tildy. But what can we do? Death comes to everybody.'

'Fight!' she cried. 'Strike it below the belt! Don't *believe* in it!'

'Can't be done,' said Papa sadly. 'We all stand alone in the world.'

'There's got to be a change sometime, Papa. I'm startin' my own philosophy here and now! Why, it's silly people live a couple of years and are shoved like wet seeds in a hole; but nothin' sprouts. What good do they do? Lay there a million years, helpin' no one. Most of them fine, nice, neat people, or at least tryin'.'

But Papa wasn't listening. He bleached out, faded away, like a photo left lying in the sun. She tried to talk him out of it, but he passed on, anyway. She spun about and ran. She couldn't stay on once he was cold, for his coldness denied her philosophy. She didn't attend his burial. She didn't do anything but set up this antique shop on the front of an old house and live alone for years, that is, until Emily came. Tildy didn't want to take the girl in. Why? Because Emily believed in dying. But her mother was an old friend and Tildy had promised help.

'Emily,' continued Aunt Tildy, to the man in black, 'was the first to live in this house with me in all the years. I never got married. I feared the idea of livin' with a man twenty-thirty years and then have him up and die on me. It'd shake my convictions like a house of cards. I shied off from the world. I screamed at people if they so much as mentioned death.'

The young man listened patiently, politely. Then he lifted his hand. He seemed to know everything, with the dark, cold shining of his eyes, before she opened her mouth. He knew about her and World War II, when she shut off her radio forever and stopped the newspapers and beat a man's head with an umbrella, driving him from her shop when he insisted on describing the invasion beaches and the long, slow tides of the dead drifting under the silent urgings of the moon.

Yes, the dark young man smiled from the antique rocker, he knew how Aunt Tildy had stuck to her nice old phonograph records. Harry Lauder singing 'Roamin' in the Gloamin' ', Madame Schumann-Heink and lullabies. With no interruptions, no foreign calamities, murders, poisonings, auto accidents, suicides. Music stayed the same each day, every day. So the years ran, while Aunt Tildy tried to teach Emily her philosophy. But Emily's mind was fixed on mortality. She respected Aunt Tildy's way of thinking, however, and never mentioned – eternity.

All this the young man knew.

Aunt Tildy sniffed. 'How do you know all those things? Well, if you think you can talk me into that silly wicker basket, you're way off the trestle. You lay hands on me, I'll spit right *in* your face!'

The young man smiled. Aunt Tildy sniffed again.

'Don't simper like a sick dog. I'm too old to be made love at. That's all twisted dry, like an old tube of paint, and left behind in the years.'

There was a noise. The mantel clock chimed three. Aunt Tildy flashed her eyes to it. Strange. Hadn't it chimed three o'clock just five minutes ago? She liked the bone-white clock with gold angels dangling naked about its numeralled face and its tone like cathedral bells, soft and far away.

'Are you just goin' to *sit* there, young man?'

He was.

'Then, you won't mind if I take a little cat nap. Now, don't you stir off that chair. Don't come creepin' around me. Just goin' to close my eyes for a spell. That's right. That's right . . .'

Nice and quiet and restful time of day. Silence. Just the clock ticking away, busy as termites in wood. Just the old room smelling of polished mahogany and oiled leather in the Morris chair, and books sitting stiff on the shelves. So nice. Nice . . .

'You aren't gettin' up from the chair, are you, mister? Better not. I got one eye open for you. Yes, indeed I have. Yes, I have. Oh. Ah, hmmmm.'

So feathery. So drowsy. So deep. Under water, almost. Oh, so nice.

Who's that movin' around in the dark with my eyes closed?

Who's that kissin' my cheek? You, Emily? No. No. Guess it was my thoughts. Only – dreamin'. Land, yes, that's it. Driftin' off, off, off . . .

Ah? What say? Oh!

'Wait while I put on my glasses. There!'

The clock chimed three again. Shame, old clock, now, shame. Have to have you fixed.

The young man in the dark suit stood near the door. Aunt Tildy nodded.

'You leavin' so soon, young man? Had to give up, didn't you? Couldn't convince me; no, I'm mule-stubborn. Never get me free of this house, so don't bother comin' back to try!'

The young man bowed with slow dignity.

He had no intention of coming again, ever.

'Fine,' declared Aunt Tildy. 'I always told Papa I'd win! Why, I'll knit in this window the next thousand years. They'll have to chew the boards down around me to get me out.'

The dark young man twinkled his eyes.

'Quit lookin' like the cat that ate the bird,' cried Aunt Tildy. 'Get that old fool wicker away!'

The four men trod heavily out the front door. Tildy studied the way they handled the empty basket, yet staggered with its weight.

'Here, now!' She rose in tremulous indignation. 'Did you steal my antiques? My books? The clocks? What you got in that wicker?'

The dark young man whistled jauntily, turning his back to her, walking along behind the four staggering men. At the door he pointed to the wicker, offered its lid to Aunt Tildy. In pantomime he wondered if she would like to open it and gaze inside.

'Curious? Me? Pshaw, no. Get out!' cried Aunt Tildy.

The dark young man tapped a hat on to his head, saluted her crisply.

'Good-bye!' Aunt Tildy slammed the door.

There, there. That was better. Gone. Darned fool men with their maggoty ideas. No never minds about the wicker. If they stole something, she didn't care, long as they let her alone.

'Look.' Aunt Tildy smiled. 'Here comes Emily, home from college. About time. Lovely girl. See how she walks. But, land, she looks pale and funny today, walkin' so slow. I wonder why. Looks worried, she does. Poor girl. I'll just fix some coffee and a tray of cakes.'

Emily tapped up the front steps. Aunt Tildy, rustling around, could hear the slow, deliberate steps. What *ailed* the girl? Didn't sound like she had no more spunk than a flue-lizard. The front door swung wide. Emily stood in the hall, holding to the brass doorknob.

'Emily?' called Aunt Tildy.

Emily shuffled into the parlour, head down.

'Emily! I been waitin' for you! There was the darndest fool men here with a wicker. Tryin' to sell me somethin' I didn't want. Glad you're home. Makes it right cosy – '

Aunt Tildy realized that for a full minute Emily had been staring.

'Emily, what's wrong? Stop starin'. Here, I'll bring you a cup of coffee. There!

'Emily, why you backin' away from me?

'Emily, stop screamin', child. Don't scream, Emily! Don't! You keep screamin' that way, you go crazy. Emily, get up off the floor, get away from that wall! Emily! Stop cringin', child, I won't hurt you!

'Land, if it ain't one thing it's another.

'Emily, what's *wrong*, child . . . ?'

Emily groaned through her hands over her face.

'Child, child,' whispered Aunt Tildy. 'Here, sip this water. Sip it, Emily, that's it.'

Emily widened her eyes, saw something, then shut them, quivering, pulling into herself. 'Aunt Tildy, Aunt Tildy, Aunt – '

'Stop that!' Tildy slapped her. 'What *ails* you?'

Emily forced herself to look up again.

She thrust her fingers out. They vanished inside Aunt Tildy.

'What fool notion!' cried Tildy. 'Take your hand away! Take it, I say!'

Emily dropped aside, jerked her head, the golden hair

shaking into shiny temblors. 'You're not here, Aunt Tildy. I'm dreaming. You're dead!'

'Hush, baby.'

'You *can't* be here.'

'Land of Goshen, Emily – '

She took Emily's hand. It passed clean through her. Instantly, Aunt Tildy raised straight up, stamping her foot.

'Why, why!' she cried angrily. 'That – fibber! That sneak-thief!' Her thin hands knotted to wiry, hard, pale fists. 'That dark, dark fiend; he stole it! He toted it away, he did, oh he did, he did! Why, I – ' Wrath steamed in her. Her pale blue eyes were fire. She sputtered into an indignant silence. Then she turned to Emily. 'Child, get up! I need you!'

Emily lay, quivering.

'Part of me's here!' declared Aunt Tildy. 'By the Lord Harry, what's left will have to do, for a bit. Fetch my bonnet!'

Emily confessed. 'I'm scared.'

'Certainly, oh, certainly not of *me*?'

'Yes.'

'Why, I'm no spook! You known me most of your life! Now's no time to snivel-sop. Fetch up on your heels or I'll slap you crack across your nose!'

Emily rose, in sobs, stood like something cornered, trying to decide which direction to bolt in.

'Where's your car, Emily?'

'Down at the garage – ma'am.'

'Good!' Aunt Tildy hustled her through the front door. 'Now – ' Her sharp eyes poked up and down the street. 'Which way's the mortuary?'

Emily held to the step rail, fumbling down. 'What're you going to do, Aunt Tildy?'

'Do?' cried Aunt Tildy, tottering after her, jowls shaking in a thin, pale fury. 'Why, get my body back, of course! Get my body back! Go on!'

The car roared, Emily clenched to the steering wheel, staring straight ahead at the curved, rain-wet streets. Aunt Tildy shook her parasol.

'Hurry, child, hurry, before they squirt juices in my body and dice and cube it the way them persnickety morticians have a habit of doin'. They cut and sew it so it ain't no good to no one!'

'Oh, Auntie, Auntie, let me go, don't make me drive! It won't do any good, no good at all,' sighed the girl.

'Here we are.' Emily pulled to the kerb, and collapsed over the wheel, but Aunt Tildy had already popped from the car and trotted with mincing skirt up the mortuary drive, around behind to where the shiny black hearse was unloading a wicker basket.

'You!' She directed her attack at one of the four men with the wicker. 'Put that down!'

The four men looked up.

One said, 'Step aside, lady. We're doing our job.'

'That's my body tucked in there!' She brandished the parasol.

'That I wouldn't know anything about,' said a second man. 'Please don't block traffic, madam. This thing is heavy.'

'Sir!' she cried, wounded. 'I'll have you know I weigh only one hundred and ten pounds.'

He looked at her casually. 'I'm not interested in your heft, lady. I'm due home for supper. My wife'll kill me if I'm late.'

The four of them moved on, Aunt Tildy in pursuit, down a hall, into a preparations room.

A white-smocked man awaited the wicker's arrival with a rather pleased smile on his long, eager-looking face. Aunt Tildy didn't care for the avidity of that face, or the entire personality of the man. The basket was deposited, the four men wandered off.

The man in the white smock glanced at Auntie and said:

'Madam, this is no fit place for a gentlewoman.'

'Well,' she said, gratified, 'glad you feel that way. It's exactly what I tried to tell that dark-clothed young man!'

The mortician puzzled. 'What dark-clothed young man is that?'

'The one that came puddlin' around my house, that's who.'

'No one of that description works for us.'

'No matter. As you just so intelligently stated, this is no place for a lady. I don't want me here. I want me home cookin' ham for Sunday visitors, it's near Easter. I got Emily to feed, sweaters to knit, clocks to wind —'

'You are quite philosophical, and philanthropical, no doubt of it, madam, but I have work. A body has arrived.' This last, he said with apparent relish, and a winnowing of his knives, tubes, jars, and instruments.

Tildy bristled. 'You put so much as a fingerprint on that body, and I'll —'

He laid her aside like a little old moth. 'George,' he called with a suave gentleness, 'escort this lady out, please.'

Aunt Tildy glared at the approaching George.

'Show me your backside, goin' the other way!'

George took her wrists. 'This way, please.'

Tildy extricated herself. Easily. Her flesh sort of — slipped. It even amazed Tildy. Such an unexpected talent to develop at this late day.

'See?' she said, pleased with her ability. 'You can't budge me. I want my body back!'

The mortician opened the wicker lid casually. Then, in a recurrent series of scrutinies he realized the body inside was . . . it   seemed . . . could   it   be? . . . maybe . . . yes . . . no . . . no . . . it just *couldn't* be, but . . . 'Ah,' he exhaled, abruptly. He turned. His eyes were wide, then they narrowed.

'Madam,' he said, cautiously. 'This lady here is — a —

relative — of yours?'

'A very dear relation. Be careful of her.'

'A sister, perhaps?' He grasped at a straw of dwindling logic, hopefully.

'No, you fool. Me, do you hear? *Me!*'

The mortician considered the idea. 'No,' he said. 'Things like this don't happen.' He fumbled with his tools. 'George, get help from the others. I can't work with a crank present.'

The four men returned. Aunt Tildy crossed her arms in defiance. 'Won't budge!' she cried, as she was moved like a pawn on a chessboard, from preparations room to slumber room, to hall, to waiting chamber, to funeral parlour, where she threw herself down on a chair in the very centre of the vestibule. There were pews going back into grey silence, and a smell of flowers.

'Please, ma'am,' said one of the men. 'That's where the body rests for the service tomorrow.'

'I'm sittin' right plumb here until I get what I want.'

She sat, pale fingers fussing with the lace at her throat, jaw set, one high-buttoned shoe tapping with irritation. If a man got in whopping distance, she gave him a parasol whop. And when they touched her, now, she remembered to — slip away.

Mr Carrington, Mortuary President, heard the disturbance in his office and came toddling down the aisle to investigate. 'Here, here,' he whispered to everyone, finger to mouth. 'More respect, more respect. What is this? Oh, madam, may I help you?'

She looked him up and down. 'You may.'

'How may I be of service, please?'

'Go in that room back there,' directed Aunt Tildy.

'Yee-ess.'

'And tell that eager young investigator to quit fiddlin' with my body. I'm a maiden lady. My moles, birthmarks, scars, and other bric-a-brac, includin' the turn of my ankle, are my own secret. I don't want him pryin' and probin', cuttin', or hurtin' it any way.'

This was vague to Mr Carrington, who hadn't correlated bodies yet. He looked at her in blank helplessness.

'He's got me in there on his table, like a pigeon ready to be drawn and stuffed!' she told him.

Mr Carrington hustled off to check. After fifteen minutes of waiting silence and horrified arguing, comparing notes with the mortician behind closed doors, Carrington returned, three shades whiter.

Carrington dropped his glasses, picked them up. 'You're making it difficult for us.'

'*I* am?' raged Aunt Tildy. 'Saint Vitus in the mornin'! Looky here, Mister Blood and Bones or whatever, you tell that — '

'We're already draining the blood from the — '

'What!'

'Yes, yes, I assure you, yes. So, you just go away, now; there's nothing to be done.' He laughed nervously. 'Our mortician is also performing a brief autopsy to determine cause of death.'

Auntie jumped to her feet, burning.

'He can't do that! Only coroners are allowed to do that!'

'Well, we sometimes allow a little —'

'March straight in and tell that Cut-'em-up to pump all that fine New England blue blood right back into that fine-skinned body, and if he's taken anything out, for him to attach it back in so it'll function proper, and then turn that body, fresh as paint, into my keepin'. You hear!'

'There's nothing I can do. Nothing.'

'Tell you *what*. I'm settin' here for the next two hundred years. You listenin'? And every time any of your customers come by, I'll spit ectoplasm right squirt up their nostrils!'

Carrington groped that thought around his weakening mind and emitted a groan. 'You'd ruin our business. You wouldn't do that.'

Auntie smiled. *'Wouldn't* I?'

Carrington ran up the dark aisle. In the distance you could hear him dialling a phone over and over again. Half an hour later cars roared up in front of the mortuary. Three vice-presidents of the mortuary came down the aisle with their hysterical president.

'What seems to be the trouble?'

Auntie told them with a few well-chosen infernalities.

They held a conference, meanwhile notifying the mortician to discontinue his homework, at least until such time as an agreement was reached . . . The mortician walked from his chamber and stood smiling amiably, smoking a big black cigar.

Auntie stared at the cigar.

'Where'd you put the *ashes*?' she cried, in horror.

The mortician only grinned imperturbably and puffed.

The conference broke up.

'Madam, in all fairness, you wouldn't force us out on the street to continue our services, would you?'

Auntie scanned the vultures. 'Oh, I wouldn't mind at all.'

Carrington wiped sweat from his jowls. 'You can have your body back.'

'Ha!' shouted Auntie. Then, with caution: 'Intact?'

'Intact.'

'No formaldehyde?'

'No formaldehyde.'

'Blood in it?'

'Blood, my God, yes, blood, if only you'll take it and go!'

A prim nod. 'Fair enough. Fix 'er up. It's a deal.'

Carrington snapped his fingers at the mortician. 'Don't *stand* there, you mental incompetent. Fix it up!'

'And be careful with that cigar!' said the old woman.

'Easy, easy,' said Aunt Tildy. 'Put the wicker on the floor where I can step in it.'

She didn't look at the body much. Her only comment was, 'Natural-lookin'.' She let herself fall back into the wicker.

A biting sensation of arctic coldness gripped her, followed by an unlikely nausea and a giddy whorling. She was two drops of matter fusing, water trying to seep into concrete. Slow to do. Hard. Like a butterfly trying to squirm back into a discarded husk of flinty chrysalis!

The vice-presidents watched Aunt Tildy with apprehension. Mr Carrington wrung his fingers and tried to assist with boosting and pushing moves of his hands and arms. The mortician, frankly sceptical, watched with idle, amused eyes.

Seeping into cold, long granite. Seeping into a frozen and ancient statue. Squeezing all the way.

'Come alive, damn ye!' shouted Aunt Tildy to herself. 'Raise up a bit.'

The body half-rose, rustling in the dry wicker.

'Fold your legs, woman!'

The body grabbled up, blindly groping.

'See!' shouted Aunt Tildy.

Light entered the webbed blind eyes.

'Feel!' urged Aunt Tildy.

The body felt the warmth of the room, the sudden reality of the preparations table on which to lean, panting.

'Move!'

The body took a creaking, slow step.

'Hear!' she snapped.

The noises of the place came into the dull ears. The harsh, expectant breath of the mortician, shaken; the whimpering Mr Carrington; her own crackling voice.

'Walk!' she said.

The body walked.

'Think!' she said.

The old brain thought.

'Speak!' she said.

The body spoke, bowing to the morticians.

'Much obliged. Thank you.'

'Now,' she said, finally, 'cry!'

And she began to cry tears of utter happiness.

And now, any afternoon about four, if you want to visit Aunt Tildy, you just walk around to her antique shop and rap. There's a big, black funeral wreath on the door. Don't mind that! Aunt Tildy left it there; that's how her humour runs. You rap on the door. It's double-barred and triple-locked, and when you rap her voice shrills out at you.

'Is that the man in black?'

And you laugh and say, 'No, no, it's only me, Aunt Tildy.'

And she laughs and says, 'Come on in, quick!' and she whips the door open and slams it shut behind, so no man in black can ever slip in with you. Then she sets you down and pours your coffee and shows you her latest knitted sweater. She's not as fast as she used to be, and can't see as good, but she gets on.

'And if you're 'specially good,' Aunt Tildy declares, setting her coffee cup to one side, 'I'll give you a little treat.'

'What's that?' visitors will ask.

'This,' says Auntie, pleased with her little uniqueness, her little joke.

Then with modest moves of her fingers she will unfasten the white lace at her neck and chest and for a brief moment show what lies beneath.

The long blue scar where the autopsy was neatly sewn together.

'Not bad sewin' for a man,' she allows. 'Oh, some more coffee? *There!*'

There Will Come
Soft Rains

In the living room the voice-clock sang, *Tick-tock, seven o'clock, time to get up, time to get up, seven o'clock!* as if it were afraid that nobody would. The morning house lay empty. The clock ticked on, repeating and repeating its sounds into the emptiness. *Seven-nine, breakfast time, seven-nine!*

In the kitchen the breakfast stove gave a hissing sigh and ejected from its warm interior eight pieces of perfectly browned toast, eight eggs sunnyside up, sixteen slices of bacon, two coffees, and two cool glasses of milk.

'Today is August 4, 2026,' said a second voice from the kitchen ceiling, 'in the city of Allendale, California.' It repeated the date three times for memory's sake. 'Today is Mr Featherstone's birthday. Today is the anniversary of Tilita's marriage. Insurance is payable, as are the water, gas, and light bills.'

Somewhere in the walls, relays clicked, memory tapes glided under electric eyes.

Eight-one, tick-tock, eight-one o'clock, off to school, off to work, run, run, eight-one! But no doors slammed, no carpets took the soft tread of rubber heels. It was raining outside. The weather box on the front door sang quietly: 'Rain, rain, go away; rubbers, raincoats for today . . . ' And the rain tapped on the empty house, echoing.

Outside, the garage chimed and lifted its door to reveal the waiting car. After a long wait the door swung down again.

At eight-thirty the eggs were shrivelled and the toast was like stone. An aluminium wedge scraped them into the sink, where hot water whirled them down a metal throat which digested and flushed them away to the distant sea. The dirty dishes were dropped into a hot washer and emerged twinkling dry.

Nine-fifteen, sang the clock, *time to clean*.

Out of warrens in the wall, tiny robot mice darted. The rooms were acrawl with the small cleaning animals, all rubber and metal. They thudded against chairs, whirling their moustached runners, kneading the rug nap, sucking gently at hidden dust. Then, like mysterious invaders, they popped into their burrows. Their pink electric eyes faded. The house was clean.

Ten o'clock. The sun came out from behind the rain. The house stood alone in a city of rubble and ashes. This was the one house left standing. At night the ruined city gave off a radioactive glow which could be seen for miles.

Ten-fifteen. The garden sprinklers whirled up in golden founts, filling the soft morning air with scatterings of brightness. The water pelted windowpanes, running down the charred west side where the house had been burned evenly free of its white paint. The entire west face of the house was black, save for five places. Here the silhouette in paint of a man mowing a lawn. Here, as in a photograph, a woman bent to pick flowers. Still farther over, their images burned on wood in one titanic instant, a small boy, hands flung into the air; higher up, the image of a thrown ball, and opposite him a girl, hands raised to catch a ball which never came down.

The five spots of paint — the man, the woman, the children, the ball — remained. The rest was a thin charcoaled layer.

The gentle sprinkler rain filled the garden with falling light.

Until this day, how well the house had kept its peace. How carefully it had inquired, 'Who goes there? What's the password?' and, getting no answer from lonely foxes and whining cats, it had shut up its windows and drawn shades in an old-maidenly preoccupation with self-protection which bordered on a mechanical paranoia.

It quivered at each sound, the house did. If a sparrow brushed a window, the shade snapped up. The bird, startled, flew off! No, not even a bird must touch the house!

The house was an altar with ten thousand attendants, big, small, servicing, attending, in choirs. But the gods had gone away, and the ritual of the religion continued senselessly, uselessly.

Twelve noon.

A dog whined, shivering, on the front porch.

The front door recognized the dog voice and opened. The dog, once huge and fleshy, but now gone to bone and covered with sores, moved in and through the house, tracking mud. Behind it whirred angry mice, angry at having to pick up mud, angry at inconvenience.

For not a leaf fragment blew under the door but what the wall panels flipped open and the copper scrap rats flashed swiftly out. The offending dust, hair, or paper, seized in miniature steel jaws, was raced back to the burrows. There, down tubes which fed into the cellar, it was dropped into the sighing vent of an incinerator which sat like evil Baal in a dark corner.

The dog ran upstairs, hysterically yelping to each door, at last realizing, as the house realized, that only silence was here.

It sniffed the air and scratched the kitchen door. Behind the door, the stove was making pancakes which filled the house with a rich baked odour and the scent of maple syrup.

The dog frothed at the mouth, lying at the door, sniffing, its eyes turned to fire. It ran wildly in circles, biting at its tail, spun in a frenzy, and died. It lay in the parlour for an hour.

Two o'clock, sang a voice.

Delicately sensing decay at last, the regiments of mice hummed out as softly as blown grey leaves in an electrical wind.

Two-fifteen.

The dog was gone.

In the cellar, the incinerator glowed suddenly and a whirl of sparks leaped up the chimney.

Two thirty-five.

Bridge tables sprouted from patio walls. Playing cards fluttered onto pads in a shower of pips. Martinis manifested on an oaken bench with egg-salad sandwiches. Music played.

But the tables were silent and the cards untouched.

At four o'clock the tables folded like great butterflies back through the panelled walls.

Four-thirty.

The nursery walls glowed.

Animals took shape: yellow giraffes, blue lions, pink antelopes, lilac panthers cavorting in crystal substance. The walls were glass. They looked out upon colour and fantasy. Hidden films clocked through well-oiled sprockets, and the walls lived. The nursery floor was woven to resemble a crisp, cereal meadow. Over this ran aluminium roaches and iron crickets, and in the hot still air butterflies of delicate red tissue wavered among the sharp aromas of animal spoors! There was the sound like a great matted yellow hive of bees within a dark bellows, the lazy bumble of a purring lion. And there was the patter of okapi feet and the murmur of a fresh jungle rain, like other hoofs, falling upon the summer-starched grass. Now the walls dissolved into distances of parched weed, mile on mile, and warm endless sky. The animals drew away into thorn brakes and water holes.

It was the children's hour.

Five o'clock. The bath filled with clear hot water.

Six, seven, eight o'clock. The dinner dishes manipulated like magic tricks, and in the study a *click*. In the metal stand opposite the hearth where a fire now blazed up warmly, a cigar popped out, half an inch of soft grey ash on it, smoking, waiting.

Nine o'clock. The beds warmed their hidden circuits, for nights were cool here.

Nine-five. A voice spoke from the study ceiling:

'Mrs McClellan, which poem would you like this evening?'

The house was silent.

The voice said at last, 'Since you express no preference, I shall select a poem at random.' Quiet music rose to back the voice. 'Sara Teasdale. As I recall, your favourite . . .

> *There will come soft rains and the smell of the ground,*
> *And swallows circling with their shimmering sound;*
>
> *And frogs in the pools singing at night,*
> *And wild plum trees in tremulous white;*
>
> *Robins will wear their feathery fire,*
> *Whistling their whims on a low fence-wire;*
>
> *And not one will know of the war, not one*
> *Will care at last when it is done.*
>
> *Not one would mind, neither bird nor tree,*
> *If mankind perished utterly;*
>
> *And Spring herself, when she woke at dawn*
> *Would scarcely know that we were gone.'*

The fire burned on the stone hearth and the cigar fell away into a mound of quiet ash on its tray. The empty chairs faced each other between the silent walls, and the music played.

At ten o'clock the house began to die.

The wind blew. A falling tree bough crashed through the

kitchen window. Cleaning solvent, bottled, shattered over the stove. The room was ablaze in an instant!

'Fire!' screamed a voice. The house lights flashed, water pumps shot water from the ceilings. But the solvent spread on the linoleum, licking, eating, under the kitchen door, while the voices took it up in chorus: 'Fire, fire, fire!'

The house tried to save itself. Doors sprang tightly shut, but the windows were broken by the heat and the wind blew and sucked upon the fire.

The house gave ground as the fire in ten billion angry sparks moved with flaming ease from room to room and then up the stairs. While scurrying water rats squeaked from the walls, pistolled their water, and ran for more. And the wall sprays let down showers of mechanical rain.

But too late. Somewhere, sighing, a pump shrugged to a stop. The quenching rain ceased. The reserve water supply which had filled baths and washed dishes for many quiet days was gone.

The fire crackled up the stairs. It fed upon Picassos and Matisses in the upper halls, like delicacies, baking off the oily flesh, tenderly crisping the canvases into black shavings.

Now the fire lay in beds, stood in windows, changed the colours of drapes!

And then, reinforcements.

From attic trapdoors, blind robot faces peered down with faucet mouths gushing green chemical.

The fire backed off, as even an elephant must at the sight of a dead snake. Now there were twenty snakes whipping over the floor, killing the fire with a clear cold venom of green froth.

But the fire was clever. It had sent flame outside the house, up through the attic to the pumps there. An explosion! The attic brain which directed the pumps was shattered into bronze shrapnel on the beams.

The fire rushed back into every closet and felt of the

clothes hung there.

The house shuddered, oak bone on bone, its bared skeleton cringing from the heat, its wire, its nerves revealed as if a surgeon had torn the skin off to let the red veins and capillaries quiver in the scalded air. Help, help! Fire! Run, run! Heat snapped mirrors like the first brittle winter ice. And the voices wailed, Fire, fire, run, run, like a tragic nursery rhyme, a dozen voices, high, low, like children dying in a forest, alone, alone. And the voices fading as the wires popped their sheathings like hot chestnuts. One, two, three, four, five voices died.

In the nursery the jungle burned. Blue lions roared, purple giraffes bounded off. The panthers ran in circles, changing colour, and ten million animals, running before the fire, vanished off towards a distant steaming river . . .

Ten more voices died. In the last instant under the fire avalanche, other choruses, oblivious, could be heard announcing the time, playing music, cutting the lawn by remote-control mower, or setting an umbrella frantically out and in, the slamming and opening front door, a thousand things happening, like a clock shop when each clock strikes the hour insanely before or after the other, a scene of maniac confusion, yet unity; singing, screaming, a few last cleaning mice darting bravely out to carry the horrid ashes away! And one voice, with sublime disregard for the situation, read poetry aloud in the fiery study, until all the film spools burned, until all the wires withered and the circuits cracked.

The fire burst the house and let it slam flat down, puffing out skirts of spark and smoke.

In the kitchen, an instant before the rain of fire and timber, the stove could be seen making breakfasts at a psychopathic rate, ten dozen eggs, six loaves of toast, twenty dozen bacon strips, which, eaten by fire, started the stove working again, hysterically hissing!

The crash. The attic smashing into kitchen and parlour.

The parlour into cellar, cellar into sub-cellar. Deep freeze, armchair, film tapes, circuits, beds, and all like skeletons thrown in a cluttered mound deep under.

Smoke and silence. A great quantity of smoke.

Dawn showed faintly in the east. Among the ruins, one wall stood alone. Within the wall, a last voice said, over and over again and again, even as the sun rose to shine upon the heaped rubble and steam:

'Today is August 5, 2026, today is August 5, 2026, today is . . .'

Mars Is Heaven

The ship came down from space. It came from the stars and the black velocities, and the shining movements, and the silent gulfs of space. It was a new ship; it had fire in its body and men in its metal cells, and it moved with a clean silence, fiery and warm. In it were seventeen men, including a captain. The crowd at the Ohio field had shouted and waved their hands up into the sunlight, and the rocket had bloomed out great flowers of heat and colour and run away into space on the *third* voyage to Mars!

Now it was decelerating with metal efficiency in the upper Martian atmospheres. It was still a thing of beauty and strength. It had moved in the midnight waters of space like a pale sea leviathan; it had passed the ancient Moon and thrown itself onward into one nothingness following another. The men within it had been battered, thrown about, sickened, made well again, each in his turn. One man had died, but now the remaining sixteen, with their eyes clear in their heads and their faces pressed to the thick glass ports, watched Mars swing up under them.

'Mars!' cried Navigator Lustig.

'Good old Mars!' said Samuel Hinkston, archaeologist.

'Well,' said Captain John Black.

The rocket landed on a lawn of green grass. Outside, upon this lawn, stood an iron deer. Further up on the green stood a tall brown Victorian house, quiet in the sunlight, all covered with scrolls and rococo, its windows made of blue and pink and yellow and green coloured glass. Upon the porch were hairy geraniums and an old swing which was hooked into the porch ceiling and which now swung back and forth, back and forth, in a little breeze. At the summit of the house was a cupola with diamond leaded-glass windows and a dunce-cap roof! Through the front window you could see a piece of music titled 'Beautiful Ohio' sitting on the music rest.

Around the rocket in four directions spread the little town, green and motionless in the Martian spring. There were white houses and red brick ones, and tall elm trees blowing in the wind, and tall maples and horse chestnuts. And church steeples with golden bells silent in them.

The rocket men looked out and saw this. Then they looked at one another and then they looked out again. They held to each other's elbows, suddenly unable to breathe, it seemed. Their faces grew pale.

'I'll be damned,' whispered Lustig, rubbing his face with his numb fingers. 'I'll be damned.'

'It just can't be,' said Samuel Hinkston.

'Lord,' said Captain John Black.

There was a call from the chemist. 'Sir, the atmosphere is thin for breathing. But there's enough oxygen. It's safe.'

'Then we'll go out,' said Lustig.

'Hold on,' said Captain John Black. 'How do we know what this is?'

'It's a small town with thin but breathable air in it, sir.'

'And it's a small town the like of Earth towns,' said Hinkston, the archaeologist. 'Incredible. It can't be, but it *is*.'

Captain John Black looked at him idly. 'Do you think that the civilizations of two planets can progress at the same rate and evolve in the same way, Hinkston?'

'I wouldn't have thought so, sir.'

Captain Black stood by the port. 'Look out there. The geraniums. A specialized plant. That specific variety has only been known on Earth for fifty years. Think of the thousands of years it takes to evolve plants. Then tell me if it is logical that the Martians should have: one, leaded-glass windows;

two, cupolas; three, porch swings; four, an instrument that looks like a piano and probably *is* a piano; and five, if you look closely through this telescopic lens here, is it logical that a Martian composer would have published a piece of music titled, strangely enough, "Beautiful Ohio"? All of which means that we have an Ohio River on Mars!'

'Captain Williams, of course!' cried Hinkston.

'What?'

'Captain Williams and his crew of three men! Or Nathaniel York and his partner. That would explain it!'

'That would explain absolutely nothing. As far as we've been able to figure, the York expedition exploded the day it reached Mars, killing York and his partner. As for Williams and his three men, their ship exploded the second day after their arrival. At least the pulsations from their radios ceased at that time, so we figure that if the men were alive after that they'd have contacted us. And anyway, the York expedition was only a year ago, while Captain Williams and his men landed here some time during last August. Theorizing that they are still alive, could they, even with the help of a brilliant Martian race, have built such a town as this and *aged* it in so short a time? Look at that town out there; why, it's been standing here for the last seventy years. Look at the wood on the porch newel; look at the trees, a century old, all of them! No, this isn't York's work or Williams'. It's something else. I don't like it. And I'm not leaving the ship until I know what it is.'

'For that matter,' said Lustig, nodding. 'Williams and his men, as well as York, landed on the *opposite* side of Mars. We were very careful to land on *this* side.'

'An excellent point. Just in case a hostile local tribe of Martians killed off York and Williams, we have instructions to land in a further region, to forestall a recurrence of such a disaster. So here we are, as far as we know, in a land that Williams and York never saw.'

'Damn it,' said Hinkston, 'I want to get out into this town, sir, with your permission. It may be there *are* similar thought patterns, civilization graphs on every planet in our sun system. We may be on the threshold of the greatest psychological and metaphysical discovery of our age!'

'I'm willing to wait a moment,' said Captain John Black.

'It may be, sir, that we're looking upon a phenomenon that, for the first time, would absolutely prove the existence of God, sir.'

'There are many people who are of good faith without such proof, Mr Hinkston.'

'I'm one myself, sir. But certainly a town like this could not occur without divine intervention. The *detail*. It fills me with such feelings that I don't know whether to laugh or cry.'

'Do neither, then, until we know what we're up against.'

'Up against?' Lustig broke in. 'Against nothing, Captain. It's a good, quiet green town, a lot like the old-fashioned one I was born in. I like the looks of it.'

'When were you born, Lustig?'

'Nineteen fifty, sir.'

'And you, Hinkston?'

'Nineteen fifty-five, sir. Grinnell, Iowa. And this looks like home to me.'

'Hinkston, Lustig, I could be either of your fathers. I'm just eighty years old. Born in 1920 in Illinois, and through the grace of God and a science that, in the last fifty years, knows how to make *some* old men young again, here I am on Mars, not any more tired than the rest of you, but infinitely more suspicious. This town out here looks very peaceful and cool, and so much like Green Bluff, Illinois, that it frightens me. It's too *much* like Green Bluff.' He turned to the radioman. 'Radio Earth. Tell them we've landed. That's all. Tell them we'll radio a full report tomorrow.'

'Yes, sir.'

Captain Black looked out the rocket port with his face that

should have been the face of a man eighty but seemed like the face of a man in his fortieth year. 'Tell you what we'll do, Lustig; you and I and Hinkston'll look the town over. The other men'll stay aboard. If anything happens they can get the hell out. A loss of three men's better than a whole ship. If something bad happens, our crew can warn the next rocket. That's Captain Wilder's rocket, I think, due to be ready to take off next Christmas. If there's something hostile about Mars we certainly want the next rocket to be well armed.'

'So are we. We've got a regular arsenal with us.'

'Tell the men to stand by the guns then. Come on, Lustig, Hinkston.'

The three men walked together down through the levels of the ship.

It was a beautiful spring day. A robin sat on a blossoming apple tree and sang continuously. Showers of petal snow sifted down when the wind touched the green branches, and the blossom scent drifted upon the air. Somewhere in the town someone was playing the piano and the music came and went, came and went, softly, drowsily. The song was 'Beautiful Dreamer'. Somewhere else a phonograph, scratchy and faded, was hissing out a record of 'Roamin' in the Gloamin' ', sung by Harry Lauder.

The three men stood outside the ship. They sucked and gasped at the thin, thin air and moved slowly so as not to tire themselves.

Now the phonograph record being played was:

> *Oh, give me a June night*
> *The moonlight and you . . .*

Lustig began to tremble. Samuel Hinkston did likewise.

The sky was serene and quiet, and somewhere a stream of water ran through the cool caverns and tree shadings of a ravine. Somewhere a horse and wagon trotted and rolled by, bumping.

'Sir,' said Samuel Hinkston, 'it must be, it *has* to be, that rocket travel to Mars began in the years before the First World War!'

'No.'

'How else can you explain these houses, the iron deer, the pianos, the music?' Hinkston took the captain's elbow persuasively and looked into the captain's face. 'Say that there were people in the year 1905 who hated war and got together with some scientists in secret and built a rocket and came out here to Mars —'

'No, no, Hinkston.'

'Why not? The world was a different world in 1905; they could have kept it a secret much more easily.'

'But a complex thing like a rocket, no, you couldn't keep it secret.'

'And they came up here to live, and naturally the houses they built were similar to Earth houses because they brought the culture with them.'

'And they've lived here all these years?' said the captain.

'In peace and quiet, yes. Maybe they made a few trips, enough to bring enough people here for one small town, and then stopped for fear of being discovered. That's why this town seems so old-fashioned. I don't see a thing, myself, older than the year 1927, do you? Or maybe, sir, rocket travel is older than we think. Perhaps it started in some part of the world centuries ago and was kept secret by the small number of men who came to Mars with only occasional visits to Earth over the centuries.'

'You make it sound almost reasonable.'

'It has to be. We've the proof here before us; all we have to do is find some people and verify it.'

Their boots were deadened of all sound in the thick green grass. It smelled from a fresh mowing. In spite of himself,

Captain John Black felt a great peace come over him. It had been thirty years since he had been in a small town, and the buzzing of spring bees on the air lulled and quieted him, and the fresh look of things was a balm to the soul.

They set foot upon the porch. Hollow echoes sounded from under the boards as they walked to the screen door. Inside they could see a bead curtain hung across the hall entry, and a crystal chandelier and a Maxfield Parrish painting framed on one wall over a comfortable Morris chair. The house smelled old, and of the attic, and infinitely comfortable. You could hear the tinkle of ice in a lemonade pitcher. In a distant kitchen, because of the heat of the day, someone was preparing a cold lunch. Someone was humming under her breath, high and sweet.

Captain John Black rang the bell.

Footsteps, dainty and thin, came along the hall, and a kind-faced lady of some forty years, dressed in the sort of dress you might expect in the year 1909, peered out at them.

'Can I help you?' she asked.

'Beg your pardon,' said Captain Black uncertainly. 'But we're looking for — that is, could you help us — ' He stopped. She looked out at him with dark, wondering eyes.

'If you're selling something — ' she began.

'No, wait!' he cried. 'What town is this?'

She looked him up and down. 'What do you mean, what town is it? How could you be in a town and not know the name?'

The captain looked as if he wanted to go sit under a shady apple tree. 'We're strangers here. We want to know how this town got here and how you got here.'

'Are you census takers?'

'No.'

'Everyone knows,' she said, 'this town was built in 1868. Is this a game?'

'No, not a game!' cried the captain. 'We're from Earth.'

'Out of the *ground*, do you mean?' she wondered.

'No, we came from the third planet, Earth, in a ship. And we've landed here on the fourth planet, Mars — '

'This,' explained the woman, as if she were addressing a child, 'is Green Bluff, Illinois, on the continent of America, surrounded by the Atlantic and Pacific Oceans, on a place called the world, or, sometimes, the Earth. Go away now. Good-bye.'

She trotted down the hall, running her fingers through the beaded curtains.

The three men looked at one another.

'Let's knock the screen door in,' said Lustig.

'We can't do that. This is private property. Good God!'

They went to sit down on the porch step.

'Did it ever strike you, Hinkston, that perhaps we got ourselves somehow, in some way, off track, and by accident came back and landed on Earth?'

'How could we have done that?'

'I don't know, I don't know. Oh God, let me think.'

Hinkston said, 'But we checked every mile of the way. Our chronometers said so many miles. We went past the Moon and out into space, and here we are. I'm *positive* we're on Mars.'

Lustig said, 'But suppose, by accident, in space, in time, we got lost in the dimensions and landed on an Earth that is thirty or forty years ago.'

'Oh, go away, Lustig!'

Lustig went to the door, rang the bell, and called into the cool dim rooms: 'What year is this?'

'Nineteen twenty-six, of course,' said the lady, sitting in a rocking chair, taking a sip of her lemonade.

'Did you hear that?' Lustig turned wildly to the others. 'Nineteen twenty-six! We *have* gone back in time! This *is* Earth!'

Lustig sat down, and the three men let the wonder and terror of the thought afflict them. Their hands stirred fitfully on their knees. The captain said, 'I didn't ask for a thing like this. It scares the hell out of me. How can a thing like this happen? I wish we'd brought Einstein with us.'

'Will anyone in this town believe us?' said Hinkston. 'Are we playing with something dangerous? Time, I mean. Shouldn't we just take off and go home?'

'No. Not until we try another house.'

They walked three houses down to a little white cottage under an oak tree. 'I like to be as logical as I can be,' said the captain. 'And I don't believe we've put our finger on it yet. Suppose, Hinkston, as you originally suggested, that rocket travel occurred years ago? And when the Earth people lived here a number of years they began to get homesick for Earth. First, a mild neurosis about it, then a full-fledged psychosis. Then threatened insanity. What would you do as a psychiatrist if faced with such a problem?'

Hinkston thought. 'Well, I think I'd rearrange the civilization on Mars so it resembled Earth more and more each day. If there was any way of reproducing every plant, every road, and every lake, and even an ocean, I'd do so. Then by some vast crowd hypnosis I'd convince everyone in a town this size that this really *was* Earth, not Mars at all.'

'Good enough, Hinkston. I think we're on the right track now. That woman in that house back there just *thinks* she's living on Earth. It protects her sanity. She and all the others in this town are the patients of the greatest experiment in migration and hypnosis you will ever lay eyes on in your life.'

'That's *it*, sir!' cried Lustig.

'Right!' said Hinkston.

'Well.' The captain sighed. 'Now we've got somewhere. I feel better. It's all a bit more logical. That talk about time and going back and forth and travelling through time turns my stomach upside down. But *this* way − ' The captain smiled.

'Well, well, it looks as if we'll be fairly popular here.'

'Or will we?' said Lustig. 'After all, like the Pilgrims, these people came here to escape Earth. Maybe they won't be too happy to see us. Maybe they'll try to drive us out or kill us.'

'We have superior weapons. This next house now. Up we go.'

But they had hardly crossed the lawn when Lustig stopped and looked off across the town, down the quiet, dreaming afternoon street. 'Sir,' he said.

'What is it, Lustig?'

'Oh, sir, *sir*, what I *see* – ' said Lustig, and he began to cry. His fingers came up, twisting and shaking, and his face was all wonder and joy and incredulity. He sounded as if at any moment he might go quite insane with happiness. He looked down the street and began to run, stumbling awkwardly, falling, picking himself up, and running on. 'Look, look!'

'Don't let him get away!' The captain broke into a run.

Now Lustig was running swiftly, shouting. He turned into a yard halfway down the shady street and leaped up upon the porch of a large green house with an iron rooster on the roof.

He was beating on the door, hollering and crying, when Hinkston and the captain ran up behind him. They were all gasping and wheezing, exhausted from their run in the thin air. 'Grandma! Grandpa!' cried Lustig.

Two old people stood in the doorway.

'David!' their voices piped, and they rushed out to embrace and pat him on the back and move around him. 'David, oh, David, it's been so many years! How you've grown, boy; how big you are, boy. Oh, David boy, how are you?'

'Grandma, Grandpa!' sobbed David Lustig. 'You look fine, fine!' He held them, turned them, kissed them, hugged them, cried on them, held them out again, blinking at the little old people. The sun was in the sky, the wind blew, the grass was green, the screen door stood wide.

'Come in, boy, come in. There's iced tea for you, fresh, lots of it!'

'I've got friends here.' Lustig turned and waved at the captain and Hinkston frantically, laughing. 'Captain, come on up.'

'Howdy,' said the old people. 'Come in. Any friends of David's are our friends, too. Don't stand there!'

In the living room of the old house it was cool, and a grandfather clock ticked high and long and bronzed in one corner. There were soft pillows on large couches and walls filled with books and a rug cut in a thick rose pattern, and iced tea in the hand, sweating, and cool on the thirsty tongue.

'Here's to our health.' Grandma tipped her glass to her porcelain teeth.

'How long you been here, Grandma?' said Lustig.

'Ever since we died,' she said tartly.

'Ever since you what?' Captain John Black set down his glass.

'Oh yes.' Lustig nodded. 'They've been dead thirty years.'

'And you sit there calmly!' shouted the captain.

'Tush.' The old woman winked glitteringly. 'Who are you to question what happens? Here we are. What's life, anyway? Who does what for why and where? All we know is here we are, alive again, and no questions asked. A second chance.' She toddled over and held out her thin wrist. 'Feel.' The captain felt. 'Solid, ain't it?' she asked. He nodded. 'Well, then,' she said triumphantly, 'why go around questioning?'

'Well,' said the captain, 'it's simply that we never thought we'd find a thing like this on Mars.'

'And now you've found it. I dare say there's lots on every planet that'll show you God's infinite ways.'

'Is this Heaven?' asked Hinkston.

'Nonsense, no. It's a world and we get a second chance. Nobody told us why. But then nobody told us why we were on Earth, either. That other Earth, I mean. The one you came from. How do we know there wasn't *another* before *that* one?'

'A good question,' said the captain.

Lustig kept smiling at his grandparents. 'Gosh, it's good to see you. Gosh, it's good.'

The captain stood up and slapped his hand on his leg in a casual fashion. 'We've got to be going. Thank you for the drinks.'

'You'll be back, of course,' said the old people. 'For supper tonight?'

'We'll try to make it, thanks. There's so much to be done. My men are waiting for me back at the rocket and − '

He stopped. He looked towards the door, startled.

Far away in the sunlight there was a sound of voices, a shouting and a great hello.

'What's that?' asked Hinkston.

'We'll soon find out.' And Captain John Black was out the front door abruptly, running across the green lawn into the street of the Martian town.

He stood looking at the rocket. The ports were open and his crew was streaming out, waving their hands. A crowd of people had gathered, and in and through and among these people the members of the crew were hurrying, talking, laughing, shaking hands. People did little dances. People swarmed. The rocket lay empty and abandoned.

A brass band exploded in the sunlight, flinging off a gay tune from upraised tubas and trumpets. There was a bang of drums and a shrill of fifes. Little girls with golden hair jumped up and down. Little boys shouted, 'Hooray!' Fat men passed around ten-cent cigars. The town mayor made a speech. Then each member of the crew, with a mother on one arm, a father or sister on the other, was spirited off down the street into little cottages or big mansions.

'Stop!' cried Captain Black.

The doors slammed shut.

The heat rose in the clear spring sky, and all was silent. The brass band banged off around a corner, leaving the rocket to shine and dazzle alone in the sunlight.

'Abandoned!' said the captain. 'They abandoned the ship, they did! I'll have their skins, by God! They had orders!'

'Sir,' said Lustig, 'don't be too hard on them. Those were all old relatives and friends.'

'That's no excuse!'

'Think how they felt, Captain, seeing familiar faces outside the ship!'

'They had their orders, damn it!'

'But how would you have felt, Captain?'

'I would have obeyed orders — ' The captain's mouth remained open.

Striding along the sidewalk under the Martian sun, tall, smiling, eyes amazingly clear and blue, came a young man of some twenty-six years. 'John!' the man called out, and broke into a trot.

'What?' Captain John Black swayed.

'John, you old son of a bitch!'

The man ran up and gripped his hand and slapped him on the back.

'It's you,' said Captain Black.

'Of course, who'd you *think* it was?'

'Edward!' The captain appealed now to Lustig and Hinkston, holding the stranger's hand. 'This is my brother Edward. Ed, meet my men, Lustig, Hinkston! My brother!'

They tugged at each other's hands and arms and then finally embraced. 'Ed!' 'John, you bum, you!' 'You're looking fine, Ed, but, Ed, what *is* this? You haven't changed over the years. You died, I remember, when you were twenty-six and I was nineteen. Good God, so many years ago, and here you are and, Lord, what goes on?'

'Mom's waiting,' said Edward Black, grinning.

'Mom?'

'And Dad too.'

'Dad?' The captain almost fell as if he had been hit by a mighty weapon. He walked stiffly and without co-ordination. 'Mom and Dad alive? Where?'

'At the old house on Oak Knoll Avenue.'

'The old house.' The captain stared in delighted amaze. 'Did you hear that, Lustig, Hinkston?'

Hinkston was gone. He had seen his own house down the street and was running for it. Lustig was laughing. 'You see, Captain, what happened to everyone on the rocket? They couldn't help themselves.'

'Yes. Yes.' The captain shut his eyes. 'When I open my eyes you'll be gone.' He blinked. 'You're still there. God, Ed, but you look *fine*!'

'Come on, lunch's waiting. I told Mom.'

Lustig said, 'Sir, I'll be with my grandfolks if you need me.'

'What? Oh, fine, Lustig. Later, then.'

Edward seized his arm and marched him. 'There's the house. Remember it?'

'Hell! Bet I can beat you to the front porch!'

They ran. The trees roared over Captain Black's head; the earth roared under his feet. He saw the golden figure of Edward Black pull ahead of him in the amazing dream of reality. He saw the house rush forward, the screen door swing wide. 'Beat you!' cried Edward. 'I'm an old man,' panted the captain, 'and you're still young. But then, you *always* beat me, I remember!'

In the doorway, Mom, pink, plump, and bright. Behind her, pepper-grey, Dad, his pipe in his hand.

'Mom, Dad!'

He ran up the steps like a child to meet them.

It was a fine long afternoon. They finished a late lunch and they sat in the parlour and he told them all about his rocket and they nodded and smiled upon him and Mother was just the same and Dad bit the end off a cigar and lighted it thoughtfully in his old fashion. There was a big turkey dinner at night and time flowing on. When the drumsticks were sucked clean and lay brittle upon the plates, the captain leaned back and exhaled his deep satisfaction. Night was in all the trees and colouring the sky, and the lamps were halos of pink light in the gentle house. From all the other houses down the street came sounds of music, pianos playing, doors slamming.

Mom put a record on the Victrola, and she and Captain John Black had a dance. She was wearing the same perfume he remembered from the summer when she and Dad had been killed in the train accident. She was very real in his arms as they danced lightly to the music. 'It's not every day,' she said, 'you get a second chance to live.'

'I'll wake in the morning,' said the captain. 'And I'll be in my rocket, in space, and all this will be gone.'

'No, don't think that,' she cried softly. 'Don't question. God's good to us. Let's be happy.'

'Sorry, Mom.'

The record ended in a circular hissing.

'You're tired, Son.' Dad pointed with his pipe. 'Your old bedroom's waiting for you, brass bed and all.'

'But I should report my men in.'

'Why?'

'Why? Well, I don't know. No reason, I guess. No, none at all. They're all eating or in bed. A good night's sleep won't hurt them.'

'Good night, Son.' Mom kissed his cheek. 'It's good to have you home.'

'It's good to *be* home.'

He left the land of cigar smoke and perfume and books and gentle light and ascended the stairs, talking, talking with

Edward. Edward pushed a door open, and there was the yellow brass bed and the old semaphore banners from college and a very musty raccoon coat which he stroked with muted affection. 'It's too much,' said the captain. 'I'm numb and I'm tired. Too much has happened today. I feel as if I'd been out in a pounding rain for forty-eight hours without an umbrella or a coat. I'm soaked to the skin with emotion.'

Edward slapped wide the snowy linens and flounced the pillows. He slid the window up and let the night-blooming jasmine float in. There was moonlight and the sound of distant dancing and whispering.

'So this is Mars,' said the captain, undressing.

'This is it.' Edward undressed in idle, leisurely moves, drawing his shirt off over his head, revealing golden shoulders and the good muscular neck.

The lights were out; they were in bed, side by side, as in the days how many decades ago? The captain lolled and was nourished by the scent of jasmine pushing the lace curtains in upon the dark air of the room. Among the trees, upon a lawn, someone had cranked up a portable phonograph and now it was playing softly, 'Always'.

The thought of Marilyn came to his mind.

'Is Marilyn here?'

His brother, lying straight out in the moonlight from the window, waited and then said, 'Yes. She's out of town. But she'll be here in the morning.'

The captain shut his eyes. 'I want to see Marilyn very much.'

The room was square and quiet except for their breathing.

'Good night, Ed.'

A pause. 'Good night, John.'

He lay peacefully, letting his thoughts float. For the first time the stress of the day was moved aside; he could think logically now. It had all been emotion. The bands playing, the familiar faces. But now . . .

How? he wondered. How was all this made? And why? For what purpose? Out of the goodness of some divine intervention? Was God, then, really that thoughtful of his children? How and why and what for?

He considered the various theories advanced in the first heat of the afternoon by Hinkston and Lustig. He let all kinds of new theories drop in lazy pebbles down through his mind, turning, throwing out dull flashes of light. Mom. Dad. Edward. Mars. Earth. Mars. Martians.

Who had lived here a thousand years ago on Mars? Martians? Or had this always been the way it was today?

Martians. He repeated the word idly, inwardly.

He laughed out loud almost. He had the most ridiculous theory quite suddenly. It gave him a kind of chill. It was really nothing to consider, of course. Highly improbable. Silly. Forget it. Ridiculous.

But, he thought, just *suppose* . . . Just suppose, now, that there were Martians living on Mars and they saw our ship coming and saw us inside our ship and hated us. Suppose, now, just for the hell of it, that they wanted to destroy us, as invaders, as unwanted ones, and they wanted to do it in a very clever way, so that we would be taken off guard. Well, what would the best weapon be that a Martian could use against Earth Men with atomic weapons?

The answer was interesting. Telepathy, hypnosis, memory, and imagination.

Suppose all of these houses aren't real at all, this bed not real, but only figments of my own imagination, given substance by telepathy and hypnosis through the Martians, thought Captain John Black. Suppose these houses are really some *other* shape, a Martian shape, but, by playing on my desires and wants, these Martians have made this seem like my old home town, my old house, to lull me out of my suspicions. What better way to fool a man, using his own mother and father as bait?

And this town, so old, from the year 1926, long before *any* of my men were born. From a year when I was six years old and there *were* records of Harry Lauder, and Maxfield Parrish paintings *still* hanging, and bead curtains, and 'Beautiful Ohio', and turn-of-the-century architecture. What if the Martians took the memories of a town *exclusively* from *my* mind? They say childhood memories are the clearest. And after they built the town from *my* mind, they populated it with the most-loved people from all the minds of the people on the rocket!

And suppose those two people in the next room, asleep, are not my mother and father at all. But two Martians, incredibly brilliant, with the ability to keep me under this dreaming hypnosis all of the time.

And that brass band today? What a startlingly wonderful plan it would be. First, fool Lustig, then Hinkston, then gather a crowd; and all the men in the rocket, seeing mothers, aunts, uncles, sweethearts, dead ten, twenty years ago, naturally, disregarding orders, rush out and abandon ship. What more natural? What more unsuspecting? What more simple? A man doesn't ask too many questions when his mother is suddenly brought back to life; he's much too happy. And here we all are tonight, in various houses, in various beds, with no weapons to protect us, and the rocket lies in the moonlight, empty. And wouldn't it be horrible and terrifying to discover that all of this was part of some great clever plan by the Martians to divide and conquer us, and kill us? Sometime during the night, perhaps, my brother here on this bed will change form, melt, shift, and become another thing, a terrible thing, a Martian. It would be very simple for him just to turn over in bed and put a knife into my heart. And in all those other houses down the street, a dozen other brothers or fathers suddenly melting away and taking knives and doing things to the unsuspecting, sleeping men of Earth . . .

His hands were shaking under the covers. His body was cold. Suddenly it was not a theory. Suddenly he was very afraid.

He lifted himself in bed and listened. The night was very quiet. The music had stopped. The wind had died. His brother lay sleeping beside him.

Carefully he lifted the covers, rolled them back. He slipped from bed and was walking softly across the room when his brother's voice said, 'Where are you going?'

'What?'

His brother's voice was quite cold. 'I said, where do you think you're going?'

'For a drink of water.'

'But you're not thirsty.'

'Yes, yes, I am.'

'No, you're not.'

Captain John Black broke and ran across the room. He screamed. He screamed twice.

He never reached the door.

In the morning the brass band played a mournful dirge. From every house in the street came little solemn processions bearing long boxes, and along the sun-filled street, weeping, came the grandmas and mothers and sisters and brothers and uncles and fathers, walking to the churchyard, where there were new holes freshly dug and new tombstones installed. Sixteen holes in all, and sixteen tombstones.

The mayor made a little sad speech, his face sometimes looking like the mayor, sometimes looking like something else.

Mother and Father Black were there, with Brother Edward, and they cried, their faces melting now from a familiar face into something else.

Grandpa and Grandma Lustig were there, weeping, their

faces shifting like wax, shimmering as all things shimmer on a hot day.

The coffins were lowered. Someone murmured about 'the unexpected and sudden deaths of sixteen fine men during the night —'

Earth pounded down on the coffin lids.

The brass band, playing 'Columbia, the Gem of the Ocean', marched and slammed back into town, and everyone took the day off.

The Silent Towns

There was a little white silent town on the edge of the dead Martian sea. The town was empty. No one moved in it. Lonely lights burned in the stores all day. The shop doors were wide, as if people had run off without using their keys. Magazines, brought from Earth on the silver rocket a month before, fluttered, untouched, burning brown, on wire racks fronting the silent drugstores.

The town was dead. Its beds were empty and cold. The only sound was the power hum of electric lines and dynamos, still alive, all by themselves. Water ran in forgotten bathtubs, poured out into living rooms, onto porches, and down through little garden plots to feed neglected flowers. In the dark theatres, gum under the many seats began to harden with tooth impressions still in it.

Across town was a rocket port. You could still smell the hard, scorched smell where the last rocket blasted off when it went back to Earth. If you dropped a dime in the telescope and pointed it at Earth, perhaps you could see the big war happening there. Perhaps you could see New York explode. Maybe London could be seen, covered with a new kind of fog. Perhaps then it might be understood why this small Martian town is abandoned. How quick was the evacuation? Walk in any store, bang the NO SALE key. Cash drawers jump out, all bright and jingly with coins. That war on Earth must be very bad . . .

Along the empty avenues of this town, now, whistling softly, kicking a tin can ahead of him in deepest concentration, came a tall, thin man. His eyes glowed with a dark, quiet look of loneliness. He moved his bony hands in his pockets, which were tinkling with new dimes. Occasionally he tossed a dime to the ground. He laughed temperately, doing this, and walked on, sprinkling bright dimes everywhere.

His name was Walter Gripp. He had a placer mine and a remote shack far up in the blue Martian hills and he walked to town once every two weeks to see if he could marry a quiet and intelligent woman. Over the years he had always returned to his shack, alone and disappointed. A week ago, arriving in town, he had found it this way!

That day he had been so surprised that he rushed to a delicatessen, flung wide a case, and ordered a triple-decker beef sandwich.

'Coming up!' he cried, a towel on his arm.

He flourished meats and bread baked the day before, dusted a table, invited himself to sit, and ate until he had to go find a soda fountain, where he ordered a bicarbonate. The druggist, being one Walter Gripp, was astoundingly polite and fizzed one right up for him!

He stuffed his jeans with money, all he could find. He loaded a boy's wagon with ten-dollar bills and ran licketysplit through town. Reaching the suburbs, he suddenly realized how shamefully silly he was. He didn't need money. He rode the ten-dollar bills back to where he'd found them, counted a dollar from his own wallet to pay for the sandwiches, dropped it in the delicatessen till, and added a quarter tip.

That night he enjoyed a hot Turkish bath, a succulent fillet carpeted with delicate mushrooms, imported dry sherry, and strawberries in wine. He fitted himself for a new blue flannel suit, and a rich grey Homburg which balanced oddly atop his gaunt head. He slid money into a juke box which played 'That Old Gang of Mine'. He dropped nickels in twenty boxes all over town. The lonely streets and the night were full of the sad music of 'That Old Gang of Mine' as he walked, tall and thin and alone, his new shoes clumping softly, his cold hands in his pockets.

But that was a week past. He slept in a good house on Mars Avenue, rose mornings at nine, bathed, and idled to town for ham and eggs. No morning passed that he didn't freeze a ton of meats, vegetables, and lemon cream pies, enough to last ten years, until the rockets came back from Earth, if they ever came.

Now, tonight, he drifted up and down, seeing the wax women in every colourful shop window, pink and beautiful. For the first time he knew how dead the town was. He drew a glass of beer and sobbed gently.

'Why,' he said. 'I'm all *alone*.'

He entered the Elite Theatre to show himself a film, to distract his mind from his isolation. The theatre was hollow, empty, like a tomb with phantoms crawling grey and black on the vast screen. Shivering, he hurried from the haunted place.

Having decided to return home, he was striking down the middle of a side street, almost running, when he heard the phone.

He listened.

'Phone ringing in someone's house.'

He proceeded briskly.

'Someone should answer that phone,' he mused.

He sat on a kerb to pick a rock from his shoe, idly.

'Someone!' he screamed, leaping. 'Me! Good Lord, what's wrong with me!' he shrieked. He whirled. Which house? That one!

He raced over the lawn, up the steps, into the house, down a dark hall.

He yanked up the receiver.

'Hello!' he cried.

Buzzzzzzzzzz.

'Hello, hello!'

They had hung up.

'Hello!' he shouted, and banged the phone. 'You stupid idiot!' he cried to himself. 'Sitting on that kerb, you fool! Oh, you damned and awful fool!' He squeezed the phone. 'Come on, ring again! Come *on*!'

He had never thought there might be others left on Mars. In the entire week he had seen no one. He had figured that all other towns were as empty as this one.

Now, staring at this terrible little black phone, he trembled. Interlocking dial systems connected every town on Mars. From which of the thirty cities had the call come?

He didn't know.

He waited. He wandered to the strange kitchen, thawed some iced huckleberries, ate them disconsolately.

'There wasn't anyone on the other end of that call,' he murmured. 'Maybe a pole blew down somewhere and the phone rang by itself.'

But hadn't he heard a click, which meant someone had hung up far away?

He stood in the hall the rest of the night. 'Not because of the phone,' he told himself. 'I just haven't anything else to do.'

He listened to his watch tick.

'She won't phone back,' he said. 'She won't *ever* call a number that didn't answer. She's probably dialling other houses in town *now*! And here I sit — Wait a minute!' He laughed. 'Why do I keep saying "she"?'

He walked out of the house and stood in the centre of the early, dim morning street.

He listened. Not a sound. No birds. No cars. Only his heart beating. Beat and pause and beat again. His face ached with strain. The wind blew gently, oh so gently, flapping his coat.

'Shh,' he whispered. '*Listen.*'

He swayed in a slow circle, turning his head from one silent house to another.

She'll phone more and more numbers, he thought. It must be a woman. Why? Only a woman would call and call. A man wouldn't. A man's independent. Did I phone anyone? No! Never thought of it. It must be a woman. It *has* to be, by God!

Listen.

Far away, under the stars, a phone rang.

He ran. He stopped to listen. The ringing, soft. He ran a few more steps. Louder. He raced down an alley. Louder still! He passed six houses, six more. Much louder! He chose a house and its door was locked.

The phone rang inside.

'Damn you!' He jerked the doorknob.

The phone screamed.

He heaved a porch chair through the parlour window, leaped in after it.

Before he even touched the phone, it was silent.

He stalked through the house then and broke mirrors, tore down drapes, and kicked in the kitchen stove.

Finally, exhausted, he picked up the thin directory which listed every phone on Mars. Fifty thousand names.

He started with number one.

Amelia Ames. He dialled her number in New Chicago, one hundred miles over the dead sea.

No answer.

Number two lived in New New York, five thousand miles across the blue mountains.

No answer.

He called three, four, five, six, seven, eight, his fingers jerking, unable to grip the receiver.

A woman's voice answered, 'Hello?'

Walter cried back at her, 'Hello, oh Lord, hello!'

'This is a recording,' recited the woman's voice. 'Miss Helen Arasumian is not home. Will you leave a message on the wire spool so she may call you when she returns? Hello?

This is a recording. Miss Arasumian is not home. Will you leave a message — ?'

He hung up.

He sat with his mouth twitching.

On second thought he redialled that number.

'When Miss Helen Arasumian comes home,' he said, 'tell her to go to hell.'

He phoned Mars Junction, New Boston, Arcadia, and Roosevelt City exchanges, theorizing that they would be logical places for persons to dial from; after that he contacted local city halls and other public institutions in each town. He phoned the best hotels. Leave it to a woman to put herself up in luxury.

Suddenly he stopped, clapped his hands sharply together, and laughed. Of course! He checked the directory and dialled a long-distance call through to the biggest beauty parlour in New Texas City. If ever there was a place where a woman would putter around, patting mud packs on her face and sitting under a drier, it would be a velvet-soft, diamond-gem beauty parlour!

The phone rang. Someone at the other end lifted the receiver.

A woman's voice said, 'Hello?'

'If this is a recording,' announced Walter Gripp, 'I'll come over and blow the place up.'

'This isn't a record,' said the woman's voice. 'Hello! Oh, hello, there *is* someone alive! Where *are* you?' She gave a delighted scream.

Walter almost collapsed. '*You!*' He stood up jerkily, eyes wild. 'Good Lord, what luck, what's your name?'

'Genevieve Selsor!' She wept into the receiver. 'Oh, I'm so glad to hear from you, whoever you are!'

'Walter Gripp!'

'Walter, hello, Walter!'

'Hello, Genevieve!'

'Walter. It's such a nice name. Walter, Walter!'

'Thank you.'

'Walter, where *are* you?'

Her voice was so kind and sweet and fine. He held the phone tight to his ear so she could whisper sweetly into it. He felt his feet drift off the floor. His cheeks burned.

'I'm in Marlin Village,' he said. 'I – '

Buzz.

'Hello?' he said.

Buzz.

He jiggled the hook. Nothing.

Somewhere a wind had blown down a pole. As quickly as she had come, Genevieve Selsor was gone.

He dialled, but the line was dead.

'I know where she is, anyway.' He ran out of the house. The sun was rising as he backed a beetle-car from the stranger's garage, filled its back seat with food from the house, and set out at eighty miles an hour down the highway, heading for New Texas City.

A thousand miles, he thought. Genevieve Selsor, sit tight, you'll hear from me!

He honked his horn on every turn out of town.

At sunset, after an impossible day of driving, he pulled to the roadside, kicked off his tight shoes, laid himself out in the seat, and slid the grey Homburg over his weary eyes. His breathing became slow and regular. The wind blew and the stars shone gently upon him in the new dusk. The Martian mountains lay all around, millions of years old. Starlight glittered on the spires of a little Martian town, no bigger than a game of chess, in the blue hills.

He lay in the half-place between awakeness and dreams. He whispered. Genevieve. *Oh, Genevieve, sweet Genevieve,* he sang softly, *the years may come, the years may go. But Genevieve, sweet Genevieve . . .* There was a warmth in him. He heard her quiet sweet cool voice sighing, *Hello, oh, hello, Walter! This is no record. Where are you, Walter, where are you?*

He sighed, putting up a hand to touch her in the moonlight. Long dark hair shaking in the wind; beautiful, it was. And her lips like red peppermints. And her cheeks like fresh-cut wet roses. And her body like a clear vaporous mist, while her soft cool sweet voice crooned to him once more the words to the old sad song, *Oh, Genevieve, sweet Genevieve, the years may come, the years may go . . .*

He slept.

He reached New Texas City at midnight.

He halted before the Deluxe Beauty Salon, yelling.

He expected her to rush out, all perfume, all laughter.

Nothing happened.

'She's asleep.' He walked to the door. 'Here I am!' he called. 'Hello, Genevieve!'

The town lay in double moonlit silence. Somewhere a wind flapped a canvas awning.

He swung the glass door wide and stepped in.

'Hey!' He laughed uneasily. 'Don't hide! I know you're here!'

He searched every booth.

He found a tiny handkerchief on the floor. It smelled so good he almost lost his balance. 'Genevieve,' he said.

He drove the car through the empty streets but saw nothing. 'If this is a practical joke . . .'

He slowed the car. 'Wait a minute. We were cut off. Maybe *she* drove to Marlin Village while I was driving here! She probably took the old Sea Road. We missed each other during the day. How'd she know I'd come get her? I didn't say I would. And she was so afraid when the phone died that she rushed to Marlin Village to find me! And here I am, by God, what a fool I am!'

Giving the horn a blow, he shot out of town.

He drove all night. He thought, What if she isn't in Marlin Village waiting, when I arrive?

He wouldn't think of that. She *must* be there. And he would run up and hold her and perhaps even kiss her, once, on the lips.

Genevieve, sweet Genevieve, he whistled, stepping it up to one hundred miles an hour.

Marlin Village was quiet at dawn. Yellow lights were still burning in several stores, and a juke box that had played steadily for one hundred hours finally, with a crackle of electricity, ceased, making the silence complete. The sun warmed the streets and warmed the cold and vacant sky.

Walter turned down Main Street, the car lights still on, honking the horn a double toot, six times at one corner, six times at another. He peered at the store names. His face was white and tired, and his hands slid on the sweaty steering wheel.

'Genevieve!' he called in the empty street.

The door to a beauty salon opened.

'Genevieve!' He stopped the car.

Genevieve Selsor stood in the open door of the salon as he ran across the street. A box of cream chocolates lay open in her arms. Her fingers, cuddling it, were plump and pallid. Her face, as she stepped into the light, was round and thick, and her eyes were like two immense eggs stuck into a white mess of bread dough. Her legs were as big around as the stumps of trees, and she moved with an ungainly shuffle. Her hair was an indiscriminate shade of brown that had been made and remade, it appeared, as a nest for birds. She had no lips at all and compensated this by stencilling on a large red, greasy mouth that now popped open in delight, now shut in sudden alarm. She had plucked her brows to thin antenna lines.

Walter stopped. His smile dissolved. He stood looking at her.

She dropped her candy box to the sidewalk.

'Are you — Genevieve Selsor?' His ears rang.

'Are you Walter Griff?' she asked.

'Gripp.'

'Gripp,' she corrected herself.

'How do you do,' he said with a restrained voice.

'How do you do.' She shook his hand.

Her fingers were sticky with chocolate.

'Well,' said Walter Gripp.

'What?' asked Genevieve Selsor.

'I just said, "Well",' said Walter.

'Oh.'

It was nine o'clock at night. They had spent the day picnicking, and for supper he had prepared a filet mignon which she didn't like because it was too rare, so he broiled it some more and it was too much broiled or fried or something. He laughed and said, 'We'll see a movie!' She said okay and put her chocolaty fingers on his elbow. But all she wanted to see was a fifty-year-old film of Clark Gable. 'Doesn't he just kill you?' She giggled. 'Doesn't he *kill* you, now?' The film ended. 'Run it off again,' she commanded. 'Again?' he asked. 'Again,' she said. And when he returned she snuggled up and put her paws all over him. 'You're not quite what I expected, but you're nice,' she admitted. 'Thanks,' he said, swallowing. 'Oh, that Gable,' she said, and pinched his leg. 'Ouch,' he said.

After the film they went shopping down the silent streets. She broke a window and put on the brightest dress she could find. Dumping a perfume bottle on her hair, she resembled a drowned sheep dog. 'How old are you?' he inquired. 'Guess.'

Dripping, she led him down the street. 'Oh, thirty,' he said. 'Well,' she announced stiffly, 'I'm only twenty-seven, so there!'

'Here's another candy store!' she said. 'Honest, I've led the life of Riley since everything exploded. I never liked my folks, they were fools. They left for Earth two months ago. I was supposed to follow on the last rocket, but I stayed on; you know why?'

'Why?'

'Because everyone picked on me. So I stayed where I could throw perfume on myself all day and drink ten thousand malts and eat candy without people saying, "Oh, that's full of calories!" So here I *am*!'

'Here you are.' Walter shut his eyes.

'It's getting late,' she said, looking at him.

'Yes.'

'I'm tired,' she said.

'Funny. I'm wide awake.'

'Oh,' she said.

'I feel like staying up all night,' he said. 'Say, there's a good record at Mike's. Come on, I'll play it for you.'

'I'm tired.' She glanced up at him with sly, bright eyes.

'I'm very alert,' he said. 'Strange.'

'Come back to the beauty shop,' she said. 'I want to show you something.'

She took him in through the glass door and walked him over to a large white box. 'When I drove from Texas City,' she said, 'I brought this with me.' She untied the pink ribbon. 'I thought: Well, here I am, the only lady on Mars, and here is the only man, and, well . . . ' She lifted the lid and folded back crisp layers of whispery pink tissue paper. She gave it a pat. 'There.'

Walter Gripp stared.

'What is it?' he asked, beginning to tremble.

'Don't you know, silly? It's all lace and all white and all fine and everything.'

'No, I don't know what it is.'

'It's a wedding dress, silly!'

'Is it?' His voice cracked.

He shut his eyes. Her voice was still soft and cool and sweet, as it had been on the phone. But when he opened his eyes and looked at her . . .

He backed up. 'How nice,' he said.

'Isn't it?'

'Genevieve.' He glanced at the door.

'Yes?'

'Genevieve, I've something to tell you.'

'Yes?' She drifted towards him, the perfume smell thick about her round white face.

'The thing I have to say to you is . . . ' he said.

'Yes?'

'Good-bye!'

And he was out the door and into his car before she could scream.

She ran and stood on the kerb as he swung the car about.

'Walter Griff, come back here!' she wailed, flinging up her arms.

'Gripp,' he corrected her.

'Gripp!' she shouted.

The car whirled away down the silent street, regardless of her stompings and shriekings. The exhaust from it fluttered the white dress she crumpled in her plump hands, and the stars shone bright, and the car vanished out on to the desert and away into blackness.

He drove all night and all day for three nights and days. Once he thought he saw a car following, and he broke into a shivering sweat and took another highway, cutting off across the lonely Martian world, past little dead cities, and he drove and drove for a week and a day, until he had put ten thousand miles between himself and Marlin Village. Then he pulled into a small town named Holtville Springs, where there were some tiny stores he could light up at night and restaurants to sit in, ordering meals. And he's lived there ever since, with two deep freezes packed with food to last him one hundred years, and enough cigars to last ten thousand days, and a good bed with a soft mattress.

And when once in a while over the long years the phone rings — he doesn't answer.

The Earth Men

Whoever was knocking at the door didn't want to stop.

Mrs Ttt threw the door open. 'Well?'

'You speak *English*!' The man standing there was astounded.

'I speak what I speak,' she said.

'It's wonderful *English*!' The man was in uniform. There were three men with him, in a great hurry, all smiling, all dirty.

'What do you want?' demanded Mrs Ttt.

'You are a *Martian*!' The man smiled. 'The word is not familiar to you, certainly. It's an Earth expression.' He nodded at his men. 'We are from Earth. I'm Captain Williams. We've landed on Mars within the hour. Here we are, the *Second* Expedition! There was a First Expedition, but we don't know what happened to it. But here we are, anyway. And you are the first Martian we've met!'

'Martian?' Her eyebrows went up.

'What I mean to say is, you live on the fourth planet from the sun. Correct?'

'Elementary,' she snapped, eyeing them.

'And *we*' — he pressed his chubby pink hand to his chest — 'we are from Earth. Right, men?'

'Right, sir!' A chorus.

'This is the planet Tyrr,' she said, 'if you want to use the proper name.'

'Tyrr, Tyrr.' The captain laughed exhaustedly. 'What a *fine* name! But, my good woman, how is it you speak such perfect English?'

'I'm not speaking, I'm thinking,' she said. 'Telepathy!

Good day!' And she slammed the door.

A moment later there was that dreadful knocking again.

She whipped the door open. 'What now?' she wondered.

The man was still there, trying to smile, looking bewildered. He put out his hands. 'I don't think you *understand* – '

'What?' she snapped.

The man gazed at her in surprise. 'We're from *Earth*!'

'I haven't time,' she said. 'I've a lot of cooking today and there's cleaning and sewing and all. You evidently wish to see Mr Ttt; he's upstairs in his study.'

'Yes,' said the Earth Man confusedly, blinking. 'By all means, let us see Mr Ttt.'

'He's busy.' She slammed the door again.

This time the knock on the door was most impertinently loud.

'See here!' cried the man when the door was thrust open again. He jumped in as if to surprise her. 'This is no way to treat visitors!'

'All over my clean floor!' she cried. 'Mud! Get out! If you come in my house, wash your boots first.'

The man looked in dismay at his muddy boots. 'This,' he said, 'is no time for trivialities. I think,' he said, 'we should be celebrating.' He looked at her for a long time, as if looking might make her understand.

'If you've made my crystal buns fall in the oven,' she exclaimed, 'I'll hit you with a piece of wood!' She peered into a little hot oven. She came back, red, steamy-faced. Her eyes were sharp yellow, her skin was soft brown, she was thin and quick as an insect. Her voice was metallic and sharp. 'Wait here. I'll see if I can let you have a moment with Mr Ttt. What was your business?'

The man swore luridly, as if she'd hit his hand with a hammer. 'Tell him we're from Earth and it's never been done before!'

'What hasn't?' She put her brown hand up. 'Never mind. I'll be back.'

The sound of her feet fluttered through the stone house.

Outside, the immense blue Martian sky was hot and still as warm deep sea water. The Martian desert lay broiling like a prehistoric mud pot, waves of heat rising and shimmering. There was a small rocket ship reclining upon a hilltop nearby. Large footprints came from the rocket to the door of this stone house.

Now there was a sound of quarrelling voices upstairs. The men within the door stared at one another, shifting on their boots, twiddling their fingers, and holding onto their hip belts. A man's voice shouted upstairs. The woman's voice replied. After fifteen minutes the Earth Men began walking in and out the kitchen door, with nothing to do.

'Cigarette?' said one of the men.

Somebody got out a pack and they lit up. They puffed slow streams of pale white smoke. They adjusted their uniforms, fixed their collars. The voices upstairs continued to mutter and chant. The leader of the men looked at his watch.

'Twenty-five minutes,' he said. 'I wonder what they're up to up there.' He went to a window and looked out.

'Hot day,' said one of the men.

'Yeah,' said someone else in the slow warm time of early afternoon. The voices had faded to a murmur and were now silent. There was not a sound in the house. All the men could hear was their own breathing.

An hour of silence passed. 'I hope we didn't cause any trouble,' said the captain. He went and peered into the living room.

Mrs Ttt was there, watering some flowers that grew in the centre of the room.

'I knew I had forgotten something,' she said when she saw the captain. She walked out to the kitchen. 'I'm sorry.' She handed him a slip of paper. 'Mr Ttt is much too busy.' She turned to her cooking. 'Anyway, it's not Mr Ttt you want to see; it's Mr Aaa. Take that paper over to the next farm, by the blue canal, and Mr Aaa'll advise you about whatever it is you want to know.'

'We don't want to know anything,' objected the captain, pouting out his thick lips. 'We already *know* it.'

'You have the paper, what more do you want?' she asked him straight out. And she would say no more.

'Well,' said the captain, reluctant to go. He stood as if waiting for something. He looked like a child staring at an empty Christmas tree. 'Well,' he said again. 'Come on, men.'

The four men stepped out into the hot silent day.

Half an hour later, Mr Aaa, seated in his library sipping a bit of electric fire from a metal cup, heard the voices outside in the stone causeway. He leaned over the window sill and gazed at the four uniformed men who squinted up at him.

'Are you Mr Aaa?' they called.

'I am.'

'Mr Ttt sent us to see you!' shouted the captain.

'Why did he do that?' asked Mr Aaa.

'He was busy!'

'Well, that's a shame,' said Mr Aaa sarcastically. 'Does he think I have nothing else to do but entertain people he's too busy to bother with?'

'That's not the important thing, sir,' shouted the captain.

'Well, it is to me. I have much reading to do. Mr Ttt is inconsiderate. This is not the first time he has been this thoughtless of me. Stop waving your hands, sir, until I finish. And pay attention. People usually listen to me when I talk. And you'll listen courteously or I won't talk at all.'

Uneasily the four men in the court shifted and opened their mouths, and once the captain, the veins on his face bulging, showed a few little tears in his eyes.

'Now,' lectured Mr Aaa, 'do you think it fair of Mr Ttt to

be so ill-mannered?'

The four men gazed up through the heat. The captain said, 'We're from Earth!'

'I think it very ungentlemanly of him,' brooded Mr Aaa.

'A rocket ship. We came on it. Over there!'

'Not the first time Ttt's been unreasonable, you know.'

'All the way from Earth.'

'Why, for half a mind, I'd call him up and tell him off.'

'Just the four of us; myself and these three men, my crew.'

'I'll call him up, yes, that's what I'll do!'

'Earth. Rocket. Men. Trip. Space.'

'Call him and give him a good lashing!' cried Mr Aaa. He vanished like a puppet from a stage. For a minute there were angry voices back and forth over some weird mechanism or other. Below, the captain and his crew glanced longingly back at their pretty rocket ship lying on the hillside, so sweet and lovely and fine.

Mr Aaa jerked up in the window, wildly triumphant. 'Challenged him to a duel, by the gods! A duel!'

'Mr Aaa – ' the captain started all over again, quietly.

'I'll shoot him dead, do you hear!'

'Mr Aaa, I'd like to *tell* you. We came sixty million miles.'

Mr Aaa regarded the captain for the first time. 'Where'd you say you were from?'

The captain flashed a white smile. Aside to his men he whispered. '*Now* we're getting someplace!' To Mr Aaa he called, 'We travelled sixty million miles. From Earth!'

Mr Aaa yawned. 'That's only *fifty* million miles this time of year.' He picked up a frightful-looking weapon. 'Well, I have to go now. Just take that silly note, though I don't know what good it'll do you, and go over that hill into the little town of Iopr and tell Mr Iii all about it. *He's* the man you want to see. Not Mr Ttt, he's an idiot; I'm going to kill him. Not me, because you're not in my line of work.'

'Line of work, line of work!' bleated the captain. 'Do you

have to be in a certain line of work to welcome Earth Men!'

'Don't be silly, everyone knows *that*!' Mr Aaa rushed downstairs. 'Good-bye!' And down the causeway he raced, like a pair of wild callipers.

The four travellers stood shocked. Finally the captain said, 'We'll find someone yet who'll listen to us.'

'Maybe we could go out and come in again,' said one of the men in a dreary voice. 'Maybe we should take off and land again. Give them time to organize a party.'

'That might be a good idea,' murmured the tired captain.

The little town was full of people drifting in and out of doors, saying hello to one another, wearing golden masks and blue masks and crimson masks for pleasant variety, masks with silver lips and bronze eyebrows, masks that smiled or masks that frowned, according to the owners' dispositions.

The four men, wet from their long walk, paused and asked a little girl where Mr Iii's house was.

'There.' The child nodded her head.

The captain got eagerly, carefully down on one knee, looking into her sweet young face. 'Little girl, I want to talk to you.'

He seated her on his knee and folded her small brown hands neatly in his own big ones, as if ready for a bedtime story which he was shaping in his mind slowly and with a great patient happiness in details.

'Well, here's how it is, little girl. Six months ago another rocket came to Mars. There was a man named York in it, and his assistant. Whatever happened to them, we don't know. Maybe they crashed. They came in a rocket. So did we. You should see it! A *big* rocket! So we're the *Second* Expedition, following up the First. And we came all the way from Earth . . . '

The little girl disengaged one hand without thinking about it, and clapped an expressionless golden mask over her face. Then she pulled forth a golden spider toy and dropped it to the ground while the captain talked on. The toy spider climbed back up to her knee obediently, while she speculated upon it coolly through the slits of her emotionless mask and the captain shook her gently and urged his story upon her.

'We're Earth Men,' he said. 'Do you believe me?'

'Yes.' The little girl peeped at the way she was wiggling her toes in the dust.

'Fine.' The captain pinched her arm, a little bit with joviality, a little bit with meanness to get her to look at him. 'We built our own rocket ship. Do you believe *that*?'

The little girl dug in her nose with a finger. 'Yes.'

'And — take your finger out of your nose, little girl — *I* am the captain, and — '

'Never before in history has anybody come across space in a big rocket ship,' recited the little creature, eyes shut.

'Wonderful! How did you know?'

'Oh, telepathy.' She wiped a casual finger on her knee.

'Well, aren't you just *ever* so excited?' cried the captain. 'Aren't you glad?'

'You just better go see Mr Iii right away.' She dropped her toy to the ground. 'Mr Iii will like talking to you.' She ran off, with the toy spider scuttling obediently after her.

The captain squatted there looking after her with his hand out. His eyes were watery in his head. He looked at his empty hands. His mouth hung open. The other three men stood with their shadows under them. They spat on the stone street . . .

Mr Iii answered his door. He was on his way to a lecture, but he had a minute, if they would hurry inside and tell him what they desired . . .

'A little attention,' said the captain, red-eyed and tired. 'We're from Earth, we have a rocket, there are four of us, crew and captain, we're exhausted, we're hungry, we'd like a place to sleep. We'd like someone to give us the key to the city or something like that, and we'd like somebody to shake our hands and say "Hooray" and say "Congratulations, old man!" That about sums it up.'

Mr Iii was a tall, vaporous, thin man with thick blind blue crystals over his yellowish eyes. He bent over his desk and brooded upon some papers, glancing now and again with extreme penetration at his guests.

'Well, I haven't the forms with me here, I don't *think*.' He rummaged through the desk drawers. 'Now, where *did* I put the forms?' He mused. 'Somewhere. Somewhere. Oh, *here* we are! Now!' He handed the papers over crisply. 'You'll have to sign these papers, of course.'

'Do we have to go through all this rigmarole?'

Mr Iii gave him a thick glassy look. 'You say you're from Earth, don't you? Well, then there's nothing for it but you sign.'

The captain wrote his name. 'Do you want my crew to sign also?'

Mr Iii looked at the captain, looked at the three others, and burst into a shout of derision. '*Them* sign! Ho! How marvellous! Them, oh, *them* sign!' Tears sprang from his eyes. He slapped his knee and bent to let his laughter jerk out of his gaping mouth. He held himself up with the desk. '*Them* sign!'

The four men scowled. 'What's funny?'

'*Them* sign!' sighed Mr Iii, weak with hilarity. 'So very funny. I'll have to tell Mr Xxx about this!' He examined the filled-out form, still laughing. 'Everything seems to be in order.' He nodded. 'Even the agreement for euthanasia if final decision on such a step is necessary.' He chuckled.

'Agreement for *what*?'

'Don't talk. I have something for you. Here. Take this key.'

The captain flushed. 'It's a great honour.'

'Not the key to the city, you fool!' snapped Mr Iii. 'Just a key to the House. Go down that corridor, unlock the big door, and go inside and shut the door tight. You can spend the night there. In the morning I'll send Mr Xxx to see you.'

Dubiously the captain took the key in hand. He stood looking at the floor. His men did not move. They seemed to be emptied of all their blood and their rocket fever. They were drained dry.

'What is it? What's wrong?' inquired Mr Iii. 'What are you waiting for? What do you want?' He came and peered up into the captain's face, stooping. 'Out with it, you!'

'I don't suppose you could even − ' suggested the captain. 'I mean, that is, try to, or think about . . . ' He hesitated. 'We've worked hard, we've come a long way, and maybe you could just shake our hands and say "Well done!" do you − think?' His voice faded.

Mr Iii stuck out his hand stiffly. 'Congratulations!' He smiled a cold smile. 'Congratulations.' He turned away. 'I must go now. Use that key.'

Without noticing them again, as if they had melted down through the floor, Mr Iii moved about the room packing a little manuscript case with papers. He was in the room another five minutes but never again addressed the solemn quartet that stood with heads down, their heavy legs sagging, the light dwindling from their eyes. When Mr Iii went out the door he was busy looking at his fingernails . . .

They straggled along the corridor in the dull, silent afternoon light. They came to a large burnished silver door, and the silver key opened it. They entered, shut the door, and turned.

They were in a vast sunlit hall. Men and women sat at tables and stood in conversing groups. At the sound of the door they regarded the four uniformed men.

One Martian stepped forward, bowing. 'I am Mr Uuu,' he said.

'And I am Captain Jonathan Williams, of New York City, on Earth,' said the captain without emphasis.

Immediately the hall exploded!

The rafters trembled with shouts and cries. The people, rushing forward, waved and shrieked happily, knocking down tables, swarming, rollicking, seizing the four Earth Men, lifting them swiftly to their shoulders. They charged about the hall six times, six times making a full and wonderful circuit of the room, jumping, bounding, singing.

The Earth Men were so stunned that they rode the toppling shoulders for a full minute before they began to laugh and shout at each other.

'Hey! This is more *like* it!'

'This is the life! Boy! Yay! Yow! Whoopee!'

They winked tremendously at each other. They flung up their hands to clap the air. 'Hey!'

'Hooray!' said the crowd.

They set the Earth Men on a table. The shouting died.

The captain almost broke into tears. 'Thank you. It's good, it's good.'

'Tell us about yourselves,' suggested Mr Uuu.

The captain cleared his throat.

The audience ohed and ahed as the captain talked. He introduced his crew; each made a small speech and was embarrassed by the thunderous applause.

Mr Uuu clapped the captain's shoulder. 'It's good to see another man from Earth. I am from Earth also.'

'How was that again?'

'There are many of us here from Earth.'

'You? From Earth?' The captain stared. 'But is that possible? Did you come by rocket? Has space travel been going on for centuries?' His voice was disappointed. 'What — what country are you from?'

'Tuiereol. I came by the spirit of my body, years ago.'

'Tuiereol.' The captain mouthed the word. 'I don't know

that country. What's this about spirit of body?'

'And Miss Rrr over here, she's from Earth, too, *aren't* you, Miss Rrr?'

Miss Rrr nodded and laughed strangely.

'And so is Mr Www and Mr Qqq and Mr Vvv!'

'I'm from Jupiter,' declared one man, preening himself.

'I'm from Saturn,' said another, eyes glinting slyly.

'Jupiter, Saturn,' murmured the captain, blinking.

It was very quiet now; the people stood around and sat at the tables which were strangely empty for banquet tables. Their yellow eyes were glowing, and there were dark shadows under their cheekbones. The captain noticed for the first time that there were no windows; the light seemed to permeate the walls. There was only one door. The captain winced. 'This is confusing. Where on Earth is this Tuiereol? Is it near America?'

'What is America?'

'You never heard of America! You say you're from Earth and yet you don't know!'

Mr Uuu drew himself up angrily. 'Earth is a place of seas and nothing but seas. There is no land. I am from Earth, and know.'

'Wait a minute.' The captain sat back. 'You look like a regular Martian. Yellow eyes. Brown skin.'

'Earth is a place of all *jungle*,' said Miss Rrr proudly. 'I am from Orri, on Earth, a civilization built of silver!'

Now the captain turned his head from them and then to Mr Uuu and then to Mr Www and Mr Zzz and Mr Nnn and Mr Hhh and Mr Bbb. He saw their yellow eyes waxing and waning in the light, focusing and unfocusing. He began to shiver. Finally he turned to his men and regarded them sombrely.

'Do you realize what this is?'

'What, sir?'

'This is no celebration,' replied the captain tiredly. 'This is no banquet. These aren't government representatives. This is no surprise party. Look at their eyes. Listen to them!'

Nobody breathed. There was only a soft white move of eyes in the close room.

'Now I understand' — the captain's voice was far away — 'why everyone gave us notes and passed us on, one from the other, until we met Mr Iii, who sent us down a corridor with a key to open a door and shut a door. And here we are . . . '

'Where are we, sir?'

The captain exhaled. 'In an insane asylum.'

It was night. The large hall lay quiet and dimly illumined by hidden light sources in the transparent walls. The four Earth Men sat around a wooden table, their bleak heads bent over their whispers. On the floors, men and women lay huddled. There were little stirs in the dark corners, solitary men and women gesturing their hands. Every half-hour one of the captain's men would try the silver door and return to the table. 'Nothing doing, sir. We're locked in proper.'

'They think we're really insane, sir?'

'Quite. That's why there was no hullabaloo to welcome us. They merely tolerated what, to them, must be a constantly recurring psychotic condition.' He gestured at the dark sleeping shapes all about them. 'Paranoids, every single one! What a welcome they gave us! For a moment there' — a little fire rose and died in his eyes — 'I thought we were getting our true reception. All the yelling and singing and speeches. Pretty nice, wasn't it — while it lasted?'

'How long will they keep us here, sir?'

'Until we prove we're not psychotics.'

'That should be easy.'

'I *hope* so.'

'You don't sound very certain, sir.'

'I'm not. Look in that corner.'

A man squatted alone in darkness. Out of his mouth issued

a blue flame which turned into the round shape of a small naked woman. It flourished on the air softly in vapours of cobalt light, whispering and sighing.

The captain nodded at another corner. A woman stood there, changing. First she was embedded in a crystal pillar, then she melted into a golden statue, finally a staff of polished cedar, and back to a woman.

All through the midnight hall people were juggling thin violet flames, shifting, changing, for night-time was the time of change and affliction.

'Magicians, sorcerers,' whispered one of the Earth Men.

'No, hallucination. They pass their insanity over into us so that we see their hallucinations too. Telepathy. Autosuggestion and telepathy.'

'Is that what worries you, sir?'

'Yes. If hallucinations can appear this "real" to us, to anyone, if hallucinations are catching and almost believable, it's no wonder they mistook us for psychotics. If that man can produce little blue fire women and that woman there melt into a pillar, how natural if normal Martians think *we* produce our rocket ship with *our* minds.'

'Oh,' said his men in the shadows.

Around them, in the vast hall, flames leaped blue, flared, evaporated. Little demons of red sand ran between the teeth of sleeping men. Women became oily snakes. There was a smell of reptiles and animals.

In the morning everyone stood around looking fresh, happy, and normal. There were no flames or demons in the room. The captain and his men waited by the silver door, hoping it would open.

Mr Xxx arrived after about four hours. They had a suspicion that he had waited outside the door, peering in at them for at least three hours before he stepped in, beckoned, and led them to his small office.

He was a jovial, smiling man, if one could believe the mask

he wore, for upon it was painted not one smile, but three. Behind it, his voice was the voice of a not so smiling psychologist. 'What seems to be the trouble?'

'You think we're insane, and we're not,' said the captain.

'Contrarily, I do not think *all* of you are insane.' The psychologist pointed a little wand at the captain. 'No. Just you, sir. The others are secondary hallucinations.'

The captain slapped his knee. 'So *that's* it! That's why Mr Iii laughed when I suggested my men sign the papers too!'

'Yes, Mr Iii told me.' The psychologist laughed out of the carved, smiling mouth. 'A good joke. Where was I? Secondary hallucinations, yes. Women come to me with snakes crawling from their ears. When I cure them, the snakes vanish.'

'We'll be glad to be cured. Go right ahead.'

Mr Xxx seemed surprised. 'Unusual. Not many people want to be cured. The cure is drastic, you know.'

'Cure ahead! I'm confident you'll find we're all sane.'

'Let me check your papers to be sure they're in order for a "cure".' He checked a file. 'Yes. You know, such cases as yours needs special "curing". The people in that hall are simpler forms. But once you've gone this far, I must point out, with primary, secondary, auditory, olfactory, and labial hallucinations, as well as tactile and optical fantasies, it is pretty bad business. We have to resort to euthanasia.'

The captain leaped up with a roar. 'Look here, we've stood quite enough! Test us, tap our knees, check our hearts, exercise us, ask questions!'

'You are free to speak.'

The captain raved for an hour. The psychologist listened.

'Incredible,' he mused. 'Most detailed dream fantasy I've ever heard.'

'God damn it, we'll show you the rocket ship!' screamed the captain.

'I'd like to see it. Can you manifest it in this room?'

'Oh, certainly. It's in that file of yours, under *R*.'

Mr Xxx peered seriously into his file. He went 'Tsk' and shut the file solemnly. 'Why did you tell me to look? The rocket isn't there.'

'Of course not, you idiot! I was joking. Does an insane man joke?'

'You find some odd senses of humour. Now, take me out to your rocket. I wish to see it.'

It was noon. The day was very hot when they reached the rocket.

'So.' The psychologist walked up to the ship and tapped it. It gonged softly. 'May I go inside?' he asked slyly.

'You may.'

Mr Xxx stepped in and was gone for a long time.

'Of all the silly, exasperating things.' The captain chewed a cigar as he waited. 'For two cents I'd go back home and tell people not to bother with Mars. What a suspicious bunch of louts.'

'I gather that a good number of their population are insane, sir. That seems to be their main reason for doubting.'

'Nevertheless, this is all so damned irritating.'

The psychologist emerged from the ship after half an hour of prowling, tapping, listening, smelling, tasting.

'*Now* do you believe!' shouted the captain, as if he were deaf.

The psychologist shut his eyes and scratched his nose. 'This is the most incredible example of sensual hallucination and hypnotic suggestion I've ever encountered. I went through your "rocket", as you call it.' He tapped the hull. 'I hear it. Auditory fantasy.' He drew a breath. 'I smell it. Olfactory hallucination, induced by sensual telepathy.' He kissed the ship. 'I taste it. Labial fantasy!'

He shook the captain's hand. 'May I congratulate you? You are a psychotic genius! You have done a most complete job! The task of projecting your psychotic image life into the mind of another via telepathy and keeping the hallucinations from becoming sensually weaker is almost impossible. Those people in the House usually concentrate on visuals or, at the most, visuals and auditory fantasies combined. You have balanced the whole conglomeration! Your insanity is beautifully complete!'

'My insanity.' The captain was pale.

'Yes, yes, what a lovely insanity. Metal, rubber, gravitizers, foods, clothing, fuel, weapons, ladders, nuts, bolts, spoons. Ten thousand separate items I checked on your vessel. Never have I seen such a complexity. There were even *shadows* under the bunks and under *everything*! Such concentration of will! And everything, no matter how or when tested, had a smell, a solidity, a taste, a sound! Let me embrace you!'

He stood back at last. 'I'll write this into my greatest monograph! I'll speak of it at the Martian Academy next month! *Look* at you! Why, you've even changed your eye colour from yellow to blue, your skin to pink from brown. And those clothes, and your hands having five fingers instead of six! Biological metamorphosis through psychological imbalance! And your three friends – '

He took out a little gun. 'Incurable, of course. You poor, wonderful man. You will be happier dead. Have you any last words?'

'Stop, for God's sake! Don't shoot!'

'You sad creature. I shall put you out of this misery which has driven you to imagine this rocket and these three men. It will be most engrossing to watch your friends and your rocket vanish once I have killed you. I will write a neat paper on the dissolvement of neurotic images from what I perceive here today.'

'I'm from Earth! My name is Jonathan Williams, and these – '

'Yes, I know,' soothed Mr Xxx, and fired his gun.

The captain fell with a bullet in his heart. The other three men screamed.

Mr Xxx stared at them. 'You continue to exist? This is superb! Hallucinations with time and spatial persistence!' He pointed the gun at them. 'Well, I'll scare you into dissolving.'

'No!' cried the three men.

'An auditory appeal, even with the patient dead,' observed Mr Xxx as he shot the three men down.

They lay on the sand, intact, not moving.

He kicked them. Then he rapped on the ship.

'*It* persists! *They* persist!' He fired his gun again and again at the bodies. Then he stood back. The smiling mask dropped from his face.

Slowly the little psychologist's face changed. His jaw sagged. The gun dropped from his fingers. His eyes were dull and vacant. He put his hands up and turned in a blind circle. He fumbled at the bodies, saliva filling his mouth.

'Hallucinations,' he mumbled frantically. 'Taste. Sight. Smell. Sound. Feeling.' He waved his hands. His eyes bulged. His mouth began to give off a faint froth.

'Go away!' he shouted at the bodies. 'Go away!' he screamed at the ship. He examined his trembling hands. 'Contaminated,' he whispered wildly. 'Carried over into me. Telepathy. Hypnosis. Now *I'm* insane. Now *I'm* contaminated. Hallucinations in all their sensual forms.' He stopped and searched around with his numb hands for the gun. 'Only one cure. Only one way to make them go away, vanish.'

A shot rang out. Mr Xxx fell.

The four bodies lay in the sun. Mr Xxx lay where he fell.

The rocket reclined on the little sunny hill and didn't vanish.

When the town people found the rocket at sunset they wondered what it was. Nobody knew, so it was sold to a junkman and hauled off to be broken up for scrap metal.

That night it rained all night. The next day was fair and warm.

The Off Season

Sam Parkhill motioned with the broom, sweeping away the blue Martian sand.

'Here we are,' he said. 'Yes, sir, look at that!' He pointed. 'Look at that sign. SAM'S HOT DOGS! Ain't that beautiful, Elma?'

'Sure, Sam,' said his wife.

'Boy, what a change for me. If the boys from the Fourth Expedition could see me now. Am I glad to be in business myself while all the rest of them guys're off soldiering around still. We'll make thousands, Elma, thousands.'

His wife looked at him for a long time, not speaking. 'Whatever happened to Captain Wilder?' she asked finally. 'That captain that killed that guy who thought he was going to kill off every other Earth Man, what was his name?'

'Spender, that nut. He was too damn particular. Oh, Captain Wilder? He's off on a rocket to Jupiter, I hear. They kicked him upstairs. I think he was a little batty about Mars too. Touchy, you know. He'll be back down from Jupiter and Pluto in about twenty years if he's lucky. That's what he gets for shooting off his mouth. And while he's freezing to death, look at me, look at this place!'

This was a crossroads where two dead highways came and went in darkness. Here Sam Parkhill had flung up this riveted aluminium structure, garish with white light, trembling with juke-box melody.

He stooped to fix a border of broken glass he had placed on the footpath. He had broken the glass from some old Martian buildings in the hills. 'Best hot dogs on two worlds! First man on Mars with a hot-dog stand! The best onions and chilli and mustard! You can't say I'm not alert. Here's the main high-ways, over there is the dead city and the mineral deposits. Those trucks from Earth Settlements 101 will have to pass here twenty-four hours a day! Do I know my locations, or don't I?'

His wife looked at her fingernails.

'You think those ten thousand new-type work rockets will come through to Mars?' she said at last.

'In a month,' he said loudly. 'Why you look so funny?'

'I don't trust those Earth people,' she said. 'I'll believe it when I see them ten thousand rockets arrive with the one hundred thousand Mexicans and Chinese on them.'

'Customers.' He lingered on the word. 'One hundred thousand hungry people.'

'If,' said his wife slowly, watching the sky, 'there's no atomic war. I don't trust no atom bombs. There's so many of them on Earth now, you never can tell.'

'Ah,' said Sam, and went on sweeping.

From the corners of his eyes he caught a blue flicker. Something floated in the air gently behind him. He heard his wife say, 'Sam. A friend of yours to see you.'

Sam whirled to see the mask seemingly floating in the wind.

'So you're back again!' And Sam held his broom like a weapon.

The mask nodded. It was cut from pale blue glass and was fitted above a thin neck, under which were blowing loose robes of thin yellow silk. From the silk two mesh silver hands appeared. The mask mouth was a slot from which musical sounds issued now as the robes, the mask, the hands increased to a height, decreased.

'Mr Parkhill, I've come back to speak to you again,' the voice said from behind the mask.

'I thought I told you I don't want you near here!' cried Sam. 'Go on, I'll give you the Disease!'

'I've already had the Disease,' said the voice. 'I was one of the few survivors. I was sick a long time.'

'Go on and hide in the hills, that's where you belong, that's where you've been. Why you come on down and bother *me*? Now, all of a sudden. Twice in one day.'

'We mean you no harm.'

'But I mean you harm!' said Sam, backing up. 'I don't like strangers. I don't like Martians. I never seen one before. It ain't natural. All these years you guys hide, and all of a sudden you pick on me. Leave me alone.'

'We come for an important reason,' said the blue mask.

'If it's about this land, it's mine. I built this hot-dog stand with my own hands.'

'In a way it *is* about the land.'

'Look here,' said Sam. 'I'm from New York City. Where I come from there's ten million others just like me. You Martians are a couple dozen left, got no cities, you wander around in the hills, no leaders, no laws, and now you come tell me about this land. Well, the old got to give way to the new. That's the law of give and take. I got a gun here. After you left this morning I got it out and loaded it.'

'We Martians are telepathic,' said the cold blue mask. 'We are in contact with one of your towns across the dead sea. Have you listened on your radio?'

'My radio's busted.'

'Then you don't know. There's big news. It concerns Earth – '

A silver hand gestured. A bronze tube appeared in it.

'Let me show you this.'

'A gun,' cried Sam Parkhill.

An instant later he had yanked his own gun from his hip holster and fired into the mist, the robe, the blue mask.

The mask sustained itself a moment. Then, like a small circus tent pulling up its stakes and dropping soft fold on fold, the silks rustled, the mask descended, the silver claws tinkled on the stone path. The mask lay on a small huddle of silent white bones and material.

Sam stood gasping.

His wife swayed over the huddled pile.

'That's no weapon,' she said, bending down. She picked up the bronze tube. 'He was going to show you a message. It's all written out in snake-script, all the blue snakes. I can't read it. Can you?'

'No, that Martian picture writing, it wasn't anything. Let it go!' Sam glanced hastily around. 'There may be others! We've got to get him out of sight. Get the shovel!'

'What're you going to do?'

'Bury him, of course!'

'You shouldn't have shot him.'

'It was a mistake. Quick!'

Silently she fetched him the shovel.

At eight o'clock he was back sweeping the front of the hot-dog stand self-consciously. His wife stood, arms folded, in the bright doorway.

'I'm sorry what happened,' he said. He looked at her, then away. 'You know it was purely the circumstances of Fate.'

'Yes,' said his wife.

'I hated like hell to see him take out that weapon.'

'What weapon?'

'Well, I thought it was one! I'm sorry, I'm sorry! How many times do I say it!'

'Ssh,' said Elma, putting one finger to her lips. 'Ssh.'

'I don't care,' he said. 'I got the whole Earth Settlements, Inc., back of me!' He snorted. 'These Martians won't dare –'

'Look,' said Elma.

He looked out onto the dead sea bottom. He dropped his broom. He picked it up and his mouth was open, a little free drop of saliva flew on the air, and he was suddenly shivering.

'Elma, Elma, Elma!' he said.

'Here they come,' said Elma.

Across the ancient sea floor a dozen tall, blue-sailed Martian sand ships floated, like blue ghosts, like blue smoke.

'Sand ships! But there aren't any more, Elma, no more sand ships.'

'Those seem to be sand ships,' she said.

'But the authorities confiscated all of them! They broke them up, sold some at auction! I'm the only one in this whole damn territory's got one and knows how to run one.'

'Not any more,' she said, nodding at the sea.

'Come on, let's get out of here!'

'Why?' she asked slowly, fascinated with the Martian vessels.

'They'll kill me! Get in our truck, quick!'

Elma didn't move.

He had to drag her around back of the stand where the two machines stood, his truck, which he had used steadily until a month ago, and the old Martian sand ship which he had bid for at auction, smiling, and which, during the last three weeks, he had used to carry supplies back and forth over the glassy sea floor. He looked at his truck now and remembered. The engine was out on the ground; he had been puttering with it for two days.

'The truck don't seem to be in running condition,' said Elma.

'The sand ship. Get in!'

'And let you drive me in a sand ship? Oh no.'

'Get in! I can do it!'

He shoved her in, jumped in behind her, and flapped the tiller, let the cobalt sail up to take the evening wind.

The stars were bright and the blue Martian ships were skimming across the whispering sands. At first his own ship would not move, then he remembered the sand anchor and yanked it in.

'There!'

The wind hurled the sand ship keening over the dead sea

bottom, over long-buried crystals, past upended pillars, past deserted docks of marble and brass, past dead white chess cities, past purple foothills, into distance. The figures of the Martian ships receded and then began to pace Sam's ship.

'Guess I showed them, by God!' cried Sam. 'I'll report to the Rocket Corporation. They'll give me protection! I'm pretty quick.'

'They could have stopped you if they wanted,' Elma said tiredly. 'They just didn't bother.'

He laughed. 'Come off it. Why should they let me get off? No, they weren't quick enough, is all.'

'Weren't they?' Elma nodded behind him.

He did not turn. He felt a cold wind blowing. He was afraid to turn. He felt something in the seat behind him, something as frail as your breath on a cold morning, something as blue as hickory-wood smoke at twilight, something like old white lace, something like a snowfall, something like the icy rime of winter on the brittle sedge.

There was a sound as of a thin plate of glass broken – laughter. Then silence. He turned.

The young woman sat at the tiller bench quietly. Her wrists were thin as icicles, her eyes as clear as the moons and as large, steady and white. The wind blew at her and, like an image on cold water, she rippled, silk standing out from her frail body in tatters of blue rain.

'Go back,' she said.

'No.' Sam was quivering, the fine, delicate fear-quivering of a hornet suspended in the air, undecided between fear and hate. 'Get off my ship!'

'This isn't your ship,' said the vision. 'It's old as our world. It sailed the sand seas ten thousand years ago when the seas were whispered away and the docks were empty, and you came and took it, stole it. Now turn it around, go back to the crossroad place. We have need to talk with you. Something important has happened.'

'Get off my ship!' said Sam. He took a gun from his holster with a creak of leather. He pointed it carefully. 'Jump off before I count three or —'

'Don't!' cried the girl. 'I won't hurt you. Neither will the others. We came in peace!'

'One,' said Sam.

'Sam!' said Elma.

'Listen to me,' said the girl.

'Two,' said Sam firmly, cocking the gun trigger.

'Sam!' cried Elma.

'Three,' said Sam.

'We only —' said the girl.

The gun went off.

In the sunlight, snow melts, crystals evaporate into a steam, into nothing. In the firelight, vapours dance and vanish. In the core of a volcano, fragile things burst and disappear. The girl, in the gunfire, in the heat, in the concussion, folded like a soft scarf, melted like a crystal figurine. What was left of her, ice, snowflake, smoke, blew away in the wind. The tiller seat was empty.

Sam holstered his gun and did not look at his wife.

'Sam,' she said after a minute more of travelling, whispering over the moon-coloured sea of sand, 'stop the ship.'

He looked at her and his face was pale. 'No, you don't. Not after all this time, you're not pulling out on me.'

She looked at his hand on his gun. 'I believe you would,' she said. 'You actually would.'

He jerked his head from side to side, hand tight on the tiller bar. 'Elma, this is crazy. We'll be in town in a minute, we'll be okay!'

'Yes,' said his wife, lying back cold in the ship.

'Elma, listen to me.'

'There's nothing to hear, Sam.'

'Elma!'

They were passing a little white chess city, and in his

frustration, in his rage, he sent six bullets crashing among the crystal towers. The city dissolved in a shower of ancient glass and splintered quartz. It fell away like carved soap, shattered. It was no more. He laughed and fired again, and one last tower, one last chess piece, took fire, ignited, and in blue flinders went up to the stars.

'I'll show them! I'll show everybody!'

'Go ahead, show us, Sam.' She lay in the shadows.

'Here comes another city!' Sam reloaded his gun. 'Watch me fix it!'

The blue phantom ships loomed up behind them, drawing steadily apace. He did not see them at first. He was only aware of a whistling and a high windy screaming, as of steel on sand, and it was the sound of the sharp razor prows of the sand ships preening the sea bottoms, their red pennants, blue pennants unfurled. In the blue light ships were blue dark images, masked men, men with silvery faces, men with blue stars for eyes, men with carved golden ears, men with tinfoil cheeks and ruby-studded lips, men with arms folded, men following him, Martian men.

One, two, three. Sam counted. The Martian ships closed in.

'Elma, Elma, I can't hold them all off!'

Elma did not speak or rise from where she had slumped.

Sam fired his gun eight times. One of the sand ships fell apart, the sail, the emerald body, the bronze hull points, the moon-white tiller, and all the separate images on it. The masked men, all of them, dug into the sand and separated out into orange and then smoke-flame.

But the other ships closed in.

'I'm outnumbered, Elma!' he cried. 'They'll kill me!'

He threw out the anchor. It was no use. The sail fluttered down, folding unto itself, sighing. The ship stopped. The wind stopped. Travel stopped. Mars stood still as the majestic vessels of the Martians drew around and hesitated over him.

'Earth Man,' a voice called from a high seat somewhere. A silverine mask moved. Ruby-rimmed lips glittered with the words.

'I didn't do anything!' Sam looked at all the faces, one hundred in all, that surrounded him. There weren't many Martians left on Mars – one hundred, one hundred and fifty, all told. And most of them were here now, on the dead seas, in their resurrected ships, by their dead chess cities, one of which had just fallen like some fragile vase hit by a pebble. The silverine masks glinted.

'It was all a mistake,' he pleaded, standing out of his ship, his wife slumped behind him in the deeps of the hold, like a dead woman. 'I came to Mars like any honest enterprising businessman. I took some surplus material from a rocket that crashed and I built me the finest little stand you ever saw right there on that land by the crossroads – you know where it is. You've got to admit it's a good job of building.' Sam laughed, staring around. 'And that Martian – I know he was a friend of yours – came. His death was an accident, I assure you. All I wanted to do was have a hot-dog stand, the only one on Mars, the first and most important one. You understand how it is? I was going to serve the best darned hot dogs there, with chilli and onions and orange juice.'

The silver masks did not move. They burned in the moonlight. Yellow eyes shone upon Sam. He felt his stomach clench in, wither, become a rock. He threw his gun in the sand.

'I give up.'

'Pick up your gun,' said the Martians in chorus.

'What?'

'Your gun.' A jewelled hand waved from the prow of a blue ship. 'Pick it up. Put it away.'

Unbelieving, he picked up the gun.

'Now,' said the voice. 'turn your ship and go back to your stand.'

'Now?'

'Now,' said the voice. 'We will not harm you. You ran away before we were able to explain. Come.'

Now the great ships turned as lightly as moon thistles. Their wing-sails flapped with a sound of soft applause on the air. The masks were coruscating, turning, firing the shadows.

'Elma!' Sam tumbled into the ship. 'Get up, Elma. We're going back.' He was excited. He almost gibbered with relief. 'They aren't going to hurt me, kill me, Elma. Get up, honey, get up.'

'What – what?' Elma blinked around and slowly, as the ship was sent into the wind again, she helped herself, as in a dream, back up to a seat and slumped there like a sack of stones, saying no more.

The sand slid under the ship. In half an hour they were back at the crossroads, the ships planted, all of them out of the ships.

The Leader stood before Sam and Elma, his mask beaten of polished bronze, the eyes only empty slits of endless blue-black, the mouth a slot out of which words drifted into the wind.

'Ready your stand,' said the voice. A diamond-gloved hand waved. 'Prepare the viands, prepare the foods, prepare the strange wines, for tonight is indeed a great night!'

'You mean,' said Sam, 'you'll let me stay on here?'

'Yes.'

'You're not mad at me?'

The mask was rigid and carved and cold and sightless.

'Prepare your place of food,' said the voice softly. 'And take this.'

'What is it?'

Sam blinked at the silver-foil scroll that was handed him, upon which, in hieroglyph, snake figures danced.

'It is the land grant to all of the territory from the silver mountains to the blue hills, from the dead salt sea there to the distant valleys of moonstone and emerald,' said the Leader.

'M-mine?' said Sam, incredulous.

'Yours.'

'One hundred thousand miles of territory?'

'Yours.'

'Did you hear that, Elma?'

Elma was sitting on the ground, leaning against the aluminium hot-dog stand, eyes shut.

'But why, why — why are you giving me all this?' asked Sam, trying to look into the metal slots of the eyes.

'That is not all. Here.' Six other scrolls were produced. The names were declared, the territories announced.

'Why, that's half of Mars! I own half of Mars!' Sam rattled the scrolls in his fists. He shook them at Elma, insane with laughing. 'Elma, did you hear?'

'I heard,' said Elma, looking at the sky.

She seemed to be watching for something. She was becoming a little more alert now.

'Thank you, oh, thank you,' said Sam to the bronze mask.

'Tonight is the night,' said the mask. 'You must be ready.'

'I will be. What is it — a surprise? Are the rockets coming through earlier than we thought, a month earlier from Earth? All ten thousand rockets, bringing the settlers, the miners, the workers and their wives, all hundred thousand of them? Won't that be swell, Elma? You see, I told you. I told you, that town there won't always have just one thousand people in it. There'll be fifty thousand more coming, and the month after that a hundred thousand more, and by the end of the year five million Earth Men. And me with the only hot-dog stand staked out on the busiest highway to the mines!'

The mask floated on the wind. 'We leave you. Prepare.

The land is yours.'

In the blowing moonlight, like metal petals of some ancient flower, like blue plumes, like cobalt butterflies immense and quiet, the old ships turned and moved over the shifting sands, the masks beaming and glittering, until the last shine, the last blue colour, was lost among the hills.

'Elma, why did they do it? Why didn't they kill me? Don't they know anything? What's wrong with them? Elma, do you understand?' He shook her shoulder. 'I own half of Mars!'

She watched the night sky, waiting.

'Come on,' he said. 'We've got to get the place fixed. All the hot dogs boiling, the buns warm, the chilli cooking, the onions peeled and diced, the relish laid out, the napkins in the clips, the place spotless! Hey!' He did a little wild dance, kicking his heels. 'Oh boy, I'm happy; yes, sir, I'm happy,' he sang, off key. 'This is my lucky day!'

He boiled the hot dogs, cut the buns, sliced the onions in a frenzy.

'Just think, that Martian said a surprise. That can only mean one thing, Elma. Those hundred thousand people coming in ahead of schedule, tonight, of all nights! We'll be flooded! We'll work long hours for days, what with tourists riding around seeing things, Elma. Think of the money!'

He went out and looked at the sky. He didn't see anything.

'In a minute, maybe,' he said, snuffling the cool air gratefully, arms up, beating his chest. 'Ah!'

Elma said nothing. She peeled potatoes for French fries quietly, her eyes always on the sky.

'Sam,' she said half an hour later. 'There it is. Look.'

He looked and saw it.

Earth.

It rose full and green, like a fine-cut stone, above the hills.

'Good old Earth,' he whispered lovingly. 'Good old wonderful Earth. Send me your hungry and your starved. Something, something — how does that poem go? Send me your hungry, old Earth. Here's Sam Parkhill, his hot dogs all boiled, his chilli cooking, everything neat as a pin. Come on, you Earth, send me your rockets!'

He went out to look at his place. There it sat, perfect as a fresh-laid egg on the dead sea bottom, the only nucleus of light and warmth in hundreds of miles of lonely wasteland. It was like a heart beating alone in a great dark body. He felt almost sorrowful with pride, gazing at it with wet eyes.

'It sure makes you humble,' he said among the cooking odours of wieners, warm buns, rich butter. 'Step up,' he invited the various stars in the sky. 'Who'll be the first to buy?'

'Sam,' said Elma.

Earth changed in the black sky.

It caught fire.

Part of it seemed to come apart in a million pieces, as if a gigantic jigsaw had exploded. It burned with an unholy dripping glare for a minute, three times normal size, then dwindled.

'What was that?' Sam looked at the green fire in the sky.

'Earth,' said Elma, holding her hands together.

'That can't be Earth, that's not Earth! No, that ain't Earth! It can't be.'

'You mean it couldn't be Earth,' said Elma, looking at him. 'That just isn't Earth. No, that's not Earth; is that what you mean?'

'Not Earth — oh no, it *couldn't* be,' he wailed.

He stood there, his hands at his sides, his mouth open, his eyes wide and dull, not moving.

'Sam.' She called his name. For the first time in days her eyes were bright. 'Sam?'

He looked up at the sky.

'Well,' she said. She glanced around for a minute or so in silence. Then briskly she flapped a wet towel over her arm. 'Switch on more lights, turn up the music, open the doors.

There'll be another batch of customers along in about a million years. Gotta be ready, yes, sir.'

Sam did not move.

'What a swell spot for a hot-dog stand,' she said. She reached over and picked a toothpick out of a jar and put it between her front teeth. 'Let you in on a little secret, Sam,' she whispered, leaning towards him. 'This looks like it's going to be an off season.'

The Million-Year Picnic

Somehow the idea was brought up by Mom that perhaps the whole family would enjoy a fishing trip. But they weren't Mom's words; Timothy knew that. They were Dad's words, and Mom used them for him somehow.

Dad shuffled his feet in a clutter of Martian pebbles and agreed. So immediately there was a tumult and a shouting, and very quickly the camp was tucked into capsules and containers, Mom slipped into travelling jumpers and blouse, Dad stuffed his pipe full with trembling hands, his eyes on the Martian sky, and the three boys piled yelling into the motorboat, none of them really keeping an eye on Mom and Dad, except Timothy.

Dad pushed a stud. The water boat sent a humming sound up into the sky. The water shook back and the boat nosed ahead, and the family cried, 'Hurrah!'

Timothy sat in the back of the boat with Dad, his small fingers atop Dad's hairy ones, watching the canal twist, leaving the crumbled place behind where they had landed in their small family rocket all the way from Earth. He remembered the night before they left Earth, the hustling and hurrying, the rocket that Dad had found somewhere, somehow, and the talk of a vacation on Mars. A long way to go for a vacation, but Timothy said nothing because of his younger brothers. They came to Mars and now, first thing, or so they said, they were going fishing.

Dad had a funny look in his eyes as the boat went up-canal. A look that Timothy couldn't figure. It was made of strong light and maybe a sort of relief. It made the deep wrinkles laugh instead of worry or cry.

So there went the cooling rocket, around a bend, gone.

'How far are we going?' Robert splashed his hand. It looked like a small crab jumping in the violet water.

Dad exhaled. 'A million years.'

'Gee,' said Robert.

'Look, kids.' Mother pointed one soft long arm. 'There's a dead city.'

They looked with fervent anticipation, and the dead city lay dead for them alone, drowsing in a hot silence of summer made on Mars by a Martian weatherman.

And Dad looked as if he was pleased that it was dead.

It was a futile spread of pink rocks sleeping on a rise of sand, a few tumbled pillars, one lonely shrine, and then the sweep of sand again. Nothing else for miles. A white desert around the canal and a blue desert over it.

Just then a bird flew up. Like a stone thrown across a blue pond, hitting, falling deep, and vanishing.

Dad got a frightened look when he saw it. 'I thought it was a rocket.'

Timothy looked at the deep ocean sky, trying to see Earth and the war and the ruined cities and the men killing each other since the day he was born. But he saw nothing. The war was as removed and far off as two flies battling to the death in the arch of a great high and silent cathedral. And just as senseless.

William Thomas wiped his forehead and felt the touch of his son's hand on his arm, like a young tarantula, thrilled. He beamed at his son. 'How goes it, Timmy?'

'Fine, Dad.'

Timothy hadn't quite figured out what was ticking inside the vast adult mechanism beside him. The man with the immense hawk nose, sunburnt, peeling – and the hot blue eyes like agate marbles you play with after school in summer back on Earth, and the long thick columnar legs in the loose riding breeches.

'What are you looking at so hard, Dad?'

'I was looking for Earthian logic, common sense, good government, peace, and responsibility.'

'All that up there?'

'No. I didn't find it. It's not there any more. Maybe it'll never be there again. Maybe we fooled ourselves that it was ever there.'

'Huh?'

'See the fish,' said Dad, pointing.

There rose a soprano clamour from all three boys as they rocked the boat in arching their tender necks to see. They *oohed* and *ahed*. A silver ring fish floated by them, undulating, and closing like an iris, instantly, around food particles, to assimilate them.

Dad looked at it. His voice was deep and quiet.

'Just like war. War swims along, sees food, contracts. A moment later — Earth is gone.'

'William,' said Mom.

'Sorry,' said Dad.

They sat still and felt the canal water rush cool, swift, and glassy. The only sound was the motor hum, the glide of water, the sun expanding the air.

'When do we see the Martians?' cried Michael.

'Quite soon, perhaps,' said Father. 'Maybe tonight.'

'Oh, but the Martians are a dead race now,' said Mom.

'No, they're not. I'll show you some Martians, all right,' Dad said presently.

Timothy scowled at that but said nothing. Everything was odd now. Vacations and fishing and looks between people.

The other boys were already engaged making shelves of their small hands and peering under them towards the seven-foot stone banks of the canal, watching for Martians.

'What do they look like?' demanded Michael.

'You'll know them when you see them.' Dad sort of

laughed, and Timothy saw a pulse beating time in his cheek.

Mother was slender and soft, with a woven plait of spun-gold hair over her head in a tiara, and eyes the colour of the deep cool canal water where it ran in shadow, almost purple, with flecks of amber caught in it. You could see her thoughts swimming around in her eyes, like fish – some bright, some dark, some fast, quick, some slow and easy, and sometimes, like when she looked up where Earth was, being nothing but colour and nothing else. She sat in the boat's prow, one hand resting on the side lip, the other on the lap of her dark blue breeches, and a line of sunburnt soft neck showing where her blouse opened like a white flower.

She kept looking ahead to see what was there, and, not being able to see it clearly enough, she looked backwards towards her husband, and through his eyes, reflected then, she saw what was ahead; and since he added part of himself to this reflection, a determined firmness, her face relaxed and she accepted it and she turned back, knowing suddenly what to look for.

Timothy looked too. But all he saw was a straight pencil line of canal going violet through a wide shallow valley penned by low, eroded hills, and on until it fell over the sky's edge. And this canal went on and on, through cities that would have rattled like beetles in a dry skull if you shook them. A hundred or two hundred cities dreaming hot summer-day dreams and cool summer-night dreams . . .

They had come millions of miles for this outing – to fish. But there had been a gun on the rocket. This was a vacation. But why all the food, more than enough to last them years and years, left hidden back there near the rocket? Vacation. Just behind the veil of the vacation was not a soft face of laughter, but something hard and bony and perhaps terrifying. Timothy could not lift the veil, and the two other boys were busy being ten and eight years old, respectively.

'No Martians yet. Nuts.' Robert put his V-shaped chin on

his hands and glared at the canal.

Dad had brought an atomic radio along, strapped to his wrist. It functioned on an old-fashioned principle: you held it against the bones near your ear and it vibrated singing or talking to you. Dad listened to it now. His face looked like one of those fallen Martian cities, caved in, sucked dry, almost dead.

Then he gave it to Mom to listen. Her lips dropped open.

'What – ' Timothy started to question, but never finished what he wished to say.

For at that moment there were two titanic, marrow-jolting explosions that grew upon themselves, followed by a half-dozen minor concussions.

Jerking his head up, Dad notched the boat speed higher immediately. The boat leaped and jounced and spanked. This shook Robert out of his funk and elicited yelps of frightened but ecstatic joy from Michael, who clung to Mom's legs and watched the water pour by his nose in a wet torrent.

Dad swerved the boat, cut speed, and ducked the craft into a little branch canal and under an ancient, crumbling stone wharf that smelled of crab flesh. The boat rammed the wharf hard enough to throw them all forward, but no one was hurt, and Dad was already twisted to see if the ripples on the canal were enough to map their route into hiding. Water lines went across, lapped the stones, and rippled back to meet each other, settling, to be dappled by the sun. It all went away.

Dad listened. So did everybody.

Dad's breathing echoed like fists beating against the cold wet wharf stones. In the shadow, Mom's cat eyes just watched Father for some clue to what next.

Dad relaxed and blew out a breath, laughing at himself.

'The rocket, of course. I'm getting jumpy. The rocket.'

Michael said, 'What happened, Dad, what happened?'

'Oh, we just blew up our rocket, is all,' said Timothy,

trying to sound matter-of-fact. 'I've heard rockets blown up before. Ours just blew.'

'Why did we blow up our rocket?' asked Michael. 'Huh, Dad?'

'It's part of the game, silly!' said Timothy.

'A game!' Michael and Robert loved the word.

'Dad fixed it so it would blow up and no one'd know where we landed or went! In case they ever came looking, see?'

'Oh boy, a secret!'

'Scared by my own rocket,' admitted Dad to Mom. 'I am nervous. It's silly to think there'll ever *be* any more rockets. Except *one*, perhaps, if Edwards and his wife get through with *their* ship.'

He put his tiny radio to his ear again. After two minutes he dropped his hand as you would drop a rag.

'It's over at last,' he said to Mom. 'The radio just went off the atomic beam. Every other world station's gone. They dwindled down to a couple in the last few years. Now the air's completely silent. It'll probably remain silent.'

'For how long?' asked Robert.

'Maybe — your great-grandchildren will hear it again,' said Dad. He just sat there, and the children were caught in the centre of his awe and defeat and resignation and acceptance.

Finally he put the boat out into the canal again, and they continued in the direction in which they had originally started.

It was getting late. Already the sun was down the sky, and a series of dead cities lay ahead of them.

Dad talked very quietly and gently to his sons. Many times in the past he had been brisk, distant, removed from them, but now he patted them on the head with just a word and they felt it.

'Mike, pick a city.'

'What, Dad?'

'Pick a city, Son. Any one of these cities we pass.'

'All right,' said Michael. 'How do I pick?'

'Pick the one you like the most. You, too, Robert and Tim. Pick the city you like best.'

'I want a city with Martians in it,' said Michael.

'You'll have that,' said Dad. 'I promise.' His lips were for the children, but his eyes were for Mom.

They passed six cities in twenty minutes. Dad didn't say anything more about the explosions; he seemed much more interested in having fun with his sons, keeping them happy, than anything else.

Michael liked the first city they passed, but this was vetoed because everyone doubted quick first judgments. The second city nobody liked. It was an Earth Man's settlement, built of wood and already rotting into sawdust. Timothy liked the third city because it was large. The fourth and fifth were too small and the sixth brought acclaim from everyone, including Mother, who joined in the Gees, Goshes, and Look-at-thats!

There were fifty or sixty huge structures still standing, streets were dusty but paved, and you could see one or two old centrifugal fountains still pulsing wetly in the plazas. That was the only life — water leaping in the late sunlight.

'This is the city,' said everybody.

Steering the boat to a wharf, Dad jumped out.

'Here we are. This is ours. This is where we live from now on!'

'From now on?' Michael was incredulous. He stood up, looking, and then turned to blink back at where the rocket used to be. 'What about the rocket? What about Minnesota?'

'Here,' said Dad.

He touched the small radio to Michael's blond head. 'Listen.'

Michael listened.

'Nothing,' he said.

'That's right. Nothing. Nothing at all any more. No more

Minneapolis, no more rockets, no more Earth.'

Michael considered the lethal revelation and began to sob little dry sobs.

'Wait a moment,' said Dad the next instant. 'I'm giving you a lot more in exchange, Mike!'

'What?' Michael held off the tears, curious, but quite ready to continue in case Dad's further revelation was as disconcerting as the original.

'I'm giving you this city, Mike. It's yours.'

'Mine?'

'For you and Robert and Timothy, all three of you, to own for yourselves.'

Timothy bounded from the boat. 'Look, guys, all for *us*! All of *that*!' He was playing the game with Dad, playing it large and playing it well. Later, after it was all over and things had settled, he could go off by himself and cry for ten minutes. But now it was still a game, still a family outing, and the other kids must be kept playing.

Mike jumped out with Robert. They helped Mom.

'Be careful of your sister,' said Dad, and nobody knew what he meant until later.

They hurried into the great pink-stoned city, whispering among themselves, because dead cities have a way of making you want to whisper, to watch the sun go down.

'In about five days,' said Dad quietly, 'I'll go back down to where our rocket was and collect the food hidden in the ruins there and bring it here; and I'll hunt for Bert Edwards and his wife and daughters there.'

'Daughters?' asked Timothy. 'How many?'

'Four.'

'I can see that'll cause trouble later.' Mom nodded slowly.

'Girls.' Michael made a face like an ancient Martian stone image. 'Girls.'

'Are they coming in a rocket, too?'

'Yes. If they make it. Family rockets are made for travel to the Moon, not Mars. We were lucky we got through.'

'Where did you get the rocket?' whispered Timothy, for the other boys were running ahead.

'I saved it. I saved it for twenty years, Tim. I had it hidden away, hoping I'd never have to use it. I suppose I should have given it to the government for the war, but I kept thinking about Mars . . .'

'And a picnic!'

'Right. This is between you and me. When I saw everything was finishing on Earth, after I'd waited until the last moment, I packed us up. Bert Edwards had a ship hidden, too, but we decided it would be safer to take off separately, in case anyone tried to shoot us down.'

'Why'd you blow up the rocket, Dad?'

'So we can't go back, ever. And so if any of those evil men ever come to Mars they won't know we're here.'

'Is that why you look up all the time?'

'Yes, it's silly. They won't follow us, ever. They haven't anything to follow with. I'm being too careful, is all.'

Michael came running back. 'Is this really *our* city, Dad?'

'The whole darn planet belongs to us, kids. The whole darn planet.'

They stood there, King of the Hill, Top of the Heap, Ruler of All They Surveyed, Unimpeachable Monarchs and Presidents, trying to understand what it meant to own a world and how big a world really was.

Night came quickly in the thin atmosphere, and Dad left them in the square by the pulsing fountain, went down to the boat, and came walking back carrying a stack of paper in his big hands.

He laid the papers in a clutter in an old courtyard and set them afire. To keep warm, they crouched around the blaze and laughed, and Timothy saw the little letters leap like frightened animals when the flames touched and engulfed them. The papers crinkled like an old man's skin, and the cremation surrounded innumerable words:

'GOVERNMENT BONDS; Business Graph, 1999; Religious Prejudice: An Essay; The Science of Logistics; Problems of the Pan-American Unity; Stock Report for July 3, 1998; The War Digest . . . '

Dad had insisted on bringing these papers for this purpose. He sat there and fed them into the fire, one by one, with satisfaction, and told his children what it all meant.

'It's time I told you a few things. I don't suppose it was fair, keeping so much from you. I don't know if you'll understand, but I have to talk, even if only part of it gets over to you.'

He dropped a leaf in the fire.

'I'm burning a way of life, just like that way of life is being burned clean of Earth right now. Forgive me if I talk like a politician. I am, after all, a former state governor, and I was honest and they hated me for it. Life on Earth never settled down to doing anything very good. Science ran too far ahead of us too quickly, and the people got lost in a mechanical wilderness, like children making over pretty things, gadgets, helicopters, rockets; emphasizing the wrong items, emphasizing machines instead of how to run the machines. Wars got bigger and bigger and finally killed Earth. That's what the silent radio means. That's what we ran away from.

'We were lucky. There aren't any more rockets left. It's time you knew this isn't a fishing trip at all. I put off telling you. Earth is gone. Interplanetary travel won't be back for centuries, maybe never. But that way of life proved itself wrong and strangled itself with its own hands. You're young. I'll tell you this again every day until it sinks in.'

He paused to feed more papers to the fire.

'Now we're alone. We and a handful of others who'll land in a few days. Enough to start over. Enough to turn away from all that back on Earth and strike out on a new line — '

The fire leaped up to emphasize his talking. And then all the papers were gone except one. All the laws and beliefs of Earth were burnt into small hot ashes which soon would be carried off in a wind.

Timothy looked at the last thing that Dad tossed in the fire. It was a map of the World, and it wrinkled and distorted itself hotly and went — flimpf — and was gone like a warm, black butterfly. Timothy turned away.

'Now I'm going to show you the Martians,' said Dad. 'Come on, all of you. Here, Alice.' He took her hand.

Michael was crying loudly, and Dad picked him up and carried him, and they walked down through the ruins towards the canal.

The canal. Where tomorrow or the next day their future wives would come up in a boat, small laughing girls now, with their father and mother.

The night came down around them, and there were stars. But Timothy couldn't find Earth. It had already set. That was something to think about.

A night bird called among the ruins as they walked. Dad said, 'Your mother and I will try to teach you. Perhaps we'll fail. I hope not. We've had a good lot to see and learn from. We planned this trip years ago, before you were born. Even if there hadn't been a war we would have come to Mars, I think, to live and form our own standard of living. It would have been another century before Mars would have been really poisoned by the Earth civilization. Now, of course — '

They reached the canal. It was long and straight and cool and wet and reflective in the night.

'I've always wanted to see a Martian,' said Michael. 'Where are they, Dad? You promised.'

'There they are,' said Dad, and he shifted Michael on his shoulder and pointed straight down.

The Martians were there. Timothy began to shiver.

The Martians were there — in the canal — reflected in the water. Timothy and Michael and Robert and Mom and Dad.

The Martians stared back up at them for a long, long silent time from the rippling water . . .

The Fox and the Forest

There were fireworks the very first night, things that you should be afraid of perhaps, for they might remind you of other more horrible things, but these were beautiful, rockets that ascended into the ancient soft air of Mexico and shook the stars apart in blue and white fragments. Everything was good and sweet, the air was that blend of the dead and the living, of the rains and the dusts, of the incense from the church, and the brass smell of the tuba on the bandstand which pulsed out vast rhythms of 'La Paloma'. The church doors were thrown wide and it seemed as if a giant yellow constellation had fallen from the October sky and lay breathing fire upon the church walls; a million candles sent their colour and fumes about. Newer and better fireworks scurried like tight-rope walking comets across the cool-tiled square, banged against adobe café walls, then rushed on hot wires to bash the high church tower, in which boys' naked feet alone could be seen kicking and re-kicking, clanging and tilting and re-tilting the monster bells into monstrous music. A flaming bull blundered about the plaza chasing laughing men and screaming children.

'The year is 1938,' said William Travis, standing by his wife on the edge of the yelling crowd, smiling. 'A good year.'

The bull rushed upon them. Ducking, the couple ran, with fire balls pelting them, past the music and riot, the church, the band, under the stars, clutching each other, laughing. The bull passed, carried lightly on the shoulders of a charging Mexican, a framework of bamboo and sulphurous gunpowder.

'I've never enjoyed myself so much in my life.' Susan

Travis had stopped for her breath.

'It's amazing,' said William.

'It will go on, won't it?'

'All night.'

'No, I mean our trip.'

He frowned and patted his breast pocket. 'I've enough traveller's cheques for a lifetime. Enjoy yourself. Forget it. They'll never find us.'

'Never?'

'Never.'

Now someone was setting off giant crackers, hurling them from the great bell-tolling tower of the church in a sputter of smoke, while the crowd below fell back under the threat and the crackers exploded in wonderful concussions among their dancing feet and flailing bodies. A wondrous smell of frying tortillas hung all about, and in the cafés men sat at tables looking out, mugs of beer in their brown hands.

The bull was dead. The fire was out of the bamboo tubes and he was expended. The labourer lifted the framework from his shoulders. Little boys clustered to touch the magnificent papier-mâché head, the real horns.

'Let's examine the bull,' said William.

As they walked past the café entrance Susan saw the man looking out at them, a white man in a salt-white suit, with a blue tie and blue shirt, and a thin, sunburned face. His hair was blond and straight and his eyes were blue, and he watched them as they walked.

She would never have noticed him if it had not been for the bottles at his immaculate elbow; a fat bottle of crème de menthe, a clear bottle of vermouth, a flagon of cognac, and seven other bottles of assorted liqueurs, and, at his finger tips, ten small half-filled glasses from which, without taking his eyes off the street, he sipped, occasionally squinting, pressing his thin mouth shut upon the savour. In his free hand a thin Havana cigar smoked, and on a chair stood twenty cartons of Turkish cigarettes, six boxes of cigars, and some packaged colognes.

'Bill — ' whispered Susan.

'Take it easy,' he said. 'He's nobody.'

'I saw him in the plaza this morning.'

'Don't look back, keep walking. Examine the papier-mâché bull here. That's it, ask questions.'

'Do you think he's from the Searchers?'

'They couldn't follow us!'

'They might!'

'What a nice bull,' said William to the man who owned it.

'He couldn't have followed us back through two hundred years, could he?'

'Watch yourself, for God's sake,' said William.

She swayed. He crushed her elbow tightly, steering her away.

'Don't faint.' He smiled, to make it look good. 'You'll be all right. Let's go right in that café, drink in front of him, so if he is what we think he is, he won't suspect.'

'No, I couldn't.'

'We've *got* to. Come on now. And so I said to David, that's ridiculous!' This last in a loud voice as they went up the café steps.

We are here, thought Susan. Who are we? Where are we going? What do we fear? Start at the beginning, she told herself, holding to her sanity, as she felt the adobe floor underfoot.

My name is Ann Kristen; my husband's name is Roger. We were born in year A.D. 2155. And we lived in a world that was evil. A world that was like a great black ship pulling away from the shore of sanity and civilization, roaring its black horn in the night, taking two billion people with it, whether they wanted to go or not, to death, to fall over the edge of the earth and the sea into radioactive flame and madness.

They walked into the café. The man was staring at them.

A phone rang.

The phone startled Susan. She remembered a phone ringing two hundred years in the future, on that blue April morning in 2155, and herself answering it.

'Ann, this is Rene! Have you heard? I mean about Travel in Time, Incorporated? Trips to Rome in 21 B.C., trips to Napoleon's Waterloo — any time, any place!'

'Rene, you're joking.'

'No. Clinton Smith left this morning for Philadelphia in 1776. Travel in Time, Inc., arranges everything. Costs money. But, *think* — to actually see the burning of Rome, Kubla Khan, Moses and the Red Sea! You've probably got an ad in your tube mail now.'

She had opened the suction mail tube and there was the metal foil advertisement:

ROME AND THE BORGIAS!
THE WRIGHT BROTHERS AT KITTY HAWK!

Travel in Time, Inc., can costume you, put you in a crowd during the assassination of Lincoln or Caesar! We guarantee to teach you any language you need to move freely in any civilization, in any year, without friction. Latin, Greek, ancient American colloquial. Take your vacation in *Time* as well as Place!

Rene's voice was buzzing on the phone. 'Tom and I leave for 1492 tomorrow. They're arranging for Tom to sail with Columbus. Isn't it amazing!'

'Yes,' murmured Ann, stunned. 'What does the Government say about this Time Machine company?'

'Oh, the police have an eye on it. Afraid people might evade the draft, run off and hide in the Past. Everyone has to leave a security bond behind, his house and belongings, to guarantee return. After all, the war's on.'

'Yes, the war,' murmured Ann. 'The war.'

Standing there, holding the phone, she had thought, Here is the chance my husband and I have talked and prayed over for so many years. We don't like this world of 2155. We want to run away from his work at the bomb factory, I from my position with disease-culture units. Perhaps there is a chance for us to escape, to run for centuries into a wild country of years where they will never find and bring us back to burn our books, censor our thoughts, scald our minds with fear, march us, scream at us with radios . . .

They were in Mexico in the year 1938.

She looked at the stained café wall.

Good workers for the Future State were allowed vacations into the Past to escape fatigue. And so she and her husband had moved back into 1938, a room in New York City, and enjoyed the theatres and the Statue of Liberty which still stood green in the harbour. And on the third day they had changed their clothes, their names, and had flown off to hide in Mexico!

'It *must* be him,' whispered Susan, looking at the stranger seated at the table. 'Those cigarettes, the cigars, the liquor. They give him away. Remember our first night in the Past?'

A month ago, their first night in New York, before their flight, drinking all the strange drinks, savouring and buying odd foods, perfumes, cigarettes of ten dozen rare brands, for they were rare in the Future, where war was everything. So they had made fools of themselves, rushing in and out of stores, salons, tobacconists, going up to their room to get wonderfully ill.

And now here was this stranger doing likewise, doing a thing that only a man from the Future would do who had been starved for liquors and cigarettes for many years.

Susan and William sat and ordered a drink.

The stranger was examining their clothes, their hair, their

jewellery — the way they walked and sat.

'Sit easily,' said William under his breath. 'Look as if you've worn this clothing style all your life.'

'We should never have tried to escape.'

'My God!' said William. 'He's coming over. Let me do the talking.'

The stranger bowed before them. There was the faintest tap of heels knocking together. Susan stiffened. That military sound! — unmistakable as that certain ugly rap on your door at midnight.

'Mr Roger Kristen,' said the stranger, 'you did not pull up your pant legs when you sat down.'

William froze. He looked at his hands lying on either leg, innocently. Susan's heart was beating swiftly.

'You've got the wrong person,' said William quickly. 'My name's not Krisler.'

'*Kristen*,' corrected the stranger.

'I'm William Travis,' said William. 'And I don't see what my pant legs have to do with you.'

'Sorry.' The stranger pulled up a chair. 'Let us say I thought I knew you because you did *not* pull your trousers up. *Everyone* does. If they don't, the trousers bag quickly. I am a long way from home, Mr — Travis, and in need of company. My name is Simms.'

'Mr Simms, we appreciate your loneliness, but we're tired. We're leaving for Acapulco tomorrow.'

'A charming spot. I was just there, looking for some friends of mine. They are somewhere. I shall find them yet. Oh, is the lady a bit sick?'

'Good night, Mr Simms.'

They started out the door, William holding Susan's arm firmly. They did not look back when Mr Simms called, 'Oh, just one other thing.' He paused and then slowly spoke the words:

'A.D. 2155.'

Susan shut her eyes and felt the earth falter under her. She kept going, into the fiery plaza, seeing nothing.

They locked the door of their hotel room. And then she was crying and they were standing in the dark, and the room tilted under them. Far away firecrackers exploded, and there was laughter in the plaza.

'What a damned, loud nerve,' said William. 'Him sitting there, looking us up and down like animals, smoking his damn cigarettes, drinking his drinks. I should have killed him then!' His voice was nearly hysterical. 'He even had the nerve to use his real name to us. The Chief of the Searchers. And the thing about my pant legs. My God, I should have pulled them up when I sat. It's an automatic gesture of this day and age. When I didn't do it, it set me off from the others; it made *him* think, Here's a man who never wore pants, a man used to breech uniforms and future styles. I could kill myself for giving us away!'

'No, no, it was my walk — these high heels — that did it. Our haircuts — so new, so fresh. Everything about us odd and uneasy.'

He turned on the light. 'He's still testing us. He's not positive of us — not completely. We can't run out on him, then. We can't make him certain. We'll go to Acapulco leisurely.'

'Maybe he *is* sure of us, but is just playing.'

'I wouldn't put it past him. He's got all the time in the world. He can dally here if he wants, and bring us back to the Future sixty seconds after we left it. He might keep us wondering for days, laughing at us.'

Susan sat on the bed, wiping the tears from her face, smelling the old smell of charcoal and incense.

'They won't make a scene, will they?'

'They won't dare. They'll have to get us alone to put us in that Time Machine and send us back.'

'There's a solution then,' she said. 'We'll never be alone; we'll always be in crowds. We'll make a million friends, visit markets, sleep in the Official Palaces in each town, pay the Chief of Police to guard us until we find a way to kill Simms and escape, disguise ourselves in new clothes, perhaps as Mexicans.'

Footsteps sounded outside their locked door.

They turned out the light and undressed in silence. The footsteps went away. A door closed.

Susan stood by the window looking down at the plaza in the darkness. 'So that building there is a church?'

'Yes.'

'I've often wondered what a church looked like. It's been so long since anyone saw one. Can we visit it tomorrow?'

'Of course. Come to bed.'

They lay in the dark room.

Half an hour later their phone rang. She lifted the receiver.

'Hello?'

'The rabbits may hide in the forest,' said a voice, 'but a fox can always find them.'

She replaced the receiver and lay back straight and cold in the bed.

Outside, in the year 1938, a man played three tunes upon a guitar, one following another.

During the night she put her hand out and almost touched the year 2155. She felt her fingers slide over cool space of time, as over a corrugated surface, and she heard the insistent thump of marching feet, a million bands playing a million military tunes, and she saw the fifty thousand rows of disease cultures in their aseptic glass tubes, her hand reaching out to them at her work in that huge factory in the Future; the tubes of leprosy, bubonic, typhoid, tuberculosis, and then the great explosion. She saw her hand burned to a wrinkled plum, felt it recoil from a concussion so immense that the world was lifted and let fall and all the buildings broke and people haemorrhaged and lay silent. Great volcanoes, machines, winds, avalanches slid down to silence and she awoke, sobbing, in the bed, in Mexico, many years away . . .

In the early morning, drugged with the single hour's sleep they had finally been able to obtain, they awoke to the sound of loud automobiles in the street. Susan peered down from the iron balcony at a small crowd of eight people only now emerging, chattering, yelling, from trucks and cars with red lettering on them. A crowd of Mexicans had followed the trucks.

'*Qué pasa?*' Susan called to a little boy.

The boy replied.

Susan turned back to her husband. 'An American motion-picture company, here on location.'

'Sounds interesting.' William was in the shower. 'Let's watch them. I don't think we'd better leave today. We'll try to lull Simms. Watch the films being made. They say the primitive film-making was something. Get our minds off ourselves.'

Ourselves, thought Susan. For a moment in the bright sun, she had forgotten that somewhere in the hotel, waiting, was a man smoking a thousand cigarettes, it seemed. She saw the eight loud happy Americans below and wanted to call to them: 'Save me, hide me, help me! Colour my hair, my eyes; clothe me in strange clothes. I need your help. I'm from the year 2155!'

But the words stayed in her throat. The functionaries of Travel in Time, Inc., were not foolish. In your brain, before you left on your trip, they placed a psychological block. You could tell no one your true time or birthplace, nor could you reveal any of the Future to those in the Past. The Past and the Future must be protected from each other. Only with this psychological block were people allowed to travel unguarded through the ages. The Future must be protected from any change brought about by her people travelling in the Past. Even if she wanted to with all her heart, she could not tell any of those happy people below in the plaza who she was, or what her predicament had become.

'What about breakfast?' said William.

Breakfast was being served in the immense dining room. Ham and eggs for everyone. The place was full of tourists. The film people entered, all eight of them — six men and two women, giggling, shoving chairs about. And Susan sat near them, feeling the warmth and protection they offered, even when Mr Simms came down the lobby stairs, smoking his Turkish cigarette with great intensity. He nodded at them from a distance, and Susan nodded back, smiling, because he couldn't do anything to them here, in front of eight film people and twenty other tourists.

'Those actors,' said William. 'Perhaps I could hire two of them, say it was a joke, dress them in our clothes, have them drive off in our car when Simms is in such a spot where he can't see their faces. If two people pretending to be us could lure him off for a few hours, we might make it to Mexico City. It'd take him years to find us there!'

'Hey!'

A fat man, with liquor on his breath, leaned on their table.

'American tourists!' he cried. 'I'm so sick of seeing Mexicans, I could kiss you!' He shook their hands. 'Come on, eat with us. Misery loves company. I'm Misery, this is Miss Gloom, and Mr and Mrs Do-We-Hate-Mexico! We all hate it. But we're here for some preliminary shots for a damn film. The rest of the crew arrives tomorrow. My name's Joe Melton. I'm a director. And if this ain't a hell of a country! Funerals in the streets, people dying. Come on, move over. Join the party; cheer us up!'

Susan and William were both laughing.

'Am I funny?' Mr Melton asked the immediate world.

'Wonderful!' Susan moved over.

Mr Simms was glaring across the dining room at them.

She made a face at him.

Mr Simms advanced among the tables.

'Mr and Mrs Travis,' he called. 'I thought we were break-fasting together, alone.'

'Sorry,' said William.

'Sit down, pal,' said Mr Melton. 'Any friend of theirs is a pal of mine.'

Mr Simms sat. The film people talked loudly, and while they talked, Mr Simms said quietly, 'I hope you slept well.'

'Did you?'

'I'm not used to spring mattresses,' replied Mr Simms wryly. 'But there are compensations. I stayed up half the night trying new cigarettes and foods. Odd, fascinating. A whole new spectrum of sensation, these ancient vices.'

'We don't know what you're talking about,' said Susan.

'Always the play acting,' Simms laughed. 'It's no use. Nor is this stratagem of crowds. I'll get you alone soon enough. I'm immensely patient.'

'Say,' Mr Melton broke in, his face flushed, 'is this guy giving you any trouble?'

'It's all right.'

'Say the word and I'll give him the bum's rush.'

Melton turned back to yell at his associates. In the laughter, Mr Simms went on: 'Let us come to the point. It took me a month of tracing you through towns and cities to find you, and all of yesterday to be sure of you. If you come with me quietly, I might be able to get you off with no punishment, if you agree to go back to work on the hydrogen-plus bomb.'

'Science this guy talks at breakfast!' observed Mr Melton, half listening.

Simms went on, imperturbably. 'Think it over. You can't escape. If you kill me, others will follow you.'

'We don't know what you're talking about.'

'Stop it!' cried Simms irritably. 'Use your intelligence! You know we can't let you get away with this escape. Other people in the year 2155 might get the same idea and do what you've done. We need people.'

'To fight your wars,' said William at last.

'Bill!'

'It's all right, Susan. We'll talk on his terms now. We can't escape.'

'Excellent,' said Simms. 'Really, you've both been incredibly romantic, running away from your responsibilities.'

'Running away from horror.'

'Nonsense. Only a war.'

'What are you guys talking about?' asked Mr Melton.

Susan wanted to tell him. But you could only speak in generalities. The psychological block in your mind allowed that. Generalities, such as Simms and William were now discussing.

'Only the war,' said William. 'Half the world dead of leprosy bombs!'

'Nevertheless,' Simms pointed out, 'the inhabitants of the Future resent you two hiding on a tropical isle, as it were, while they drop off the cliff into hell. Death loves death, not life. Dying people love to know that others die with them. It is a comfort to learn you are not alone in the kiln, in the grave. I am the guardian of their collective resentment against you two.'

'Look at the guardian of resentments!' said Mr Melton to his companions.

'The longer you keep me waiting, the harder it will go for you. We need you on the bomb project, Mr Travis. Return now – no torture. Later, we'll force you to work, and after you've finished the bomb, we'll try a number of complicated new devices on you, sir.'

'I've a proposition,' said William. 'I'll come back with you if my wife stays here alive, safe, away from that war.'

Mr Simms considered it. 'All right. Meet me in the plaza in ten minutes. Pick me up in your car. Drive me to a deserted country spot. I'll have the Travel Machine pick us up there.'

'Bill!' Susan held his arm tightly.

'Don't argue.' He looked over at her. 'It's settled.' To Simms: 'One thing. Last night you could have gotten in our room and kidnapped us. Why didn't you?'

'Shall we say that I was enjoying myself?' replied Mr Simms languidly, sucking his new cigar. 'I hate giving up this wonderful atmosphere, this sun, this vacation. I regret leaving behind the wine and the cigarettes. Oh, how I regret it. The plaza, then, in ten minutes. Your wife will be protected and may stay here as long as she wishes. Say your good-byes.'

Mr Simms arose and walked out.

'There goes Mr Big Talk!' yelled Mr Melton at the departing gentleman. He turned and looked at Susan. 'Hey. Someone's crying. Breakfast's no time for people to cry. Now *is* it?'

At nine-fifteen Susan stood on the balcony of their room, gazing down at the plaza. Mr Simms was seated there, his neat legs crossed, on a delicate bronze bench. Biting the tip from a cigar, he lit it tenderly.

Susan heard the throb of a motor, and far up the street, out of a garage and down the cobbled hill, slowly, came William in his car.

The car picked up speed. Thirty, now forty, now fifty miles an hour. Chickens scattered before it.

Mr Simms took off his white panama hat and mopped his pink forehead, put his hat back on, and then saw the car.

It was rushing sixty miles an hour, straight on for the plaza.

'William!' screamed Susan.

The car hit the low plaza kerb, thundering; it jumped up, sped across the tiles towards the green bench where Mr Simms now dropped his cigar, shrieked, flailed his hands, and was hit by the car. His body flew up and up in the air, and down and down, crazily, into the street.

On the far side of the plaza, one front wheel broken, the car stopped. People were running.

Susan went in and closed the balcony doors.

They came down the Official Palace steps together, arm in arm, their faces pale, at twelve noon.

'*Adiós, señor,*' said the Mayor behind them. '*Señora.*'

They stood in the plaza where the crowd was pointing at the blood.

'Will they want to see you again?' asked Susan.

'No, we went over and over it. It was an accident. I lost control of the car. I wept for them. God knows I had to get my relief out somewhere. I *felt* like weeping. I hated to kill him. I've never wanted to do anything like that in my life.'

'They won't prosecute you?'

'They talked about it, but no. I talked faster. They believe me. It was an accident. It's over.'

'Where will we go? Mexico City? Uruapan?'

'The car's in the repair shop. It'll be ready at four this afternoon. Then we'll get the hell out.'

'Will we be followed? Was Simms working alone?'

'I don't know. We'll have a little head start on them, I think.'

The film people were coming out of the hotel as they approached. Mr Melton hurried up, scowling. 'Hey I heard what happened. Too bad. Everything okay now? Want to get your minds off it? We're doing some preliminary shots up the street. You want to watch, you're welcome. Come on, do you good.'

They went.

They stood on the cobbled street while the film camera was being set up. Susan looked at the road leading down and away, and the highway going to Acapulco and the sea, past pyramids and ruins and little adobe towns with yellow walls, blue walls, purple walls, and flaming bougainvillea, and she thought, We shall take the roads, travel in clusters and crowds, in markets, in lobbies, bribe police to sleep near, keep double locks, but always the crowds, never alone again, always afraid the next person who passes may be another Simms. Never knowing if we've tricked and lost the Searchers. And always up ahead, in the Future, they'll wait for us to be brought back, waiting with their bombs to burn us and disease to rot us, and their police to tell us to roll over, turn around, jump through the hoop! And so we'll keep running through the forest, and we'll never ever stop or sleep well again in our lives.

A crowd gathered to watch the film being made. And Susan watched the crowd and the streets.

'Seen anyone suspicious?'

'No. What time is it?'

'Three o'clock. The car should be almost ready.'

The test film was finished at three forty-five. They all walked down to the hotel, talking. William paused at the garage. 'The car'll be ready at six,' he said, coming out, worried.

'But no later than that?'

'It'll be ready, don't worry.'

In the hotel lobby they looked around for other men travelling alone, men who resembled Mr Simms, men with new haircuts and too much cigarette smoke and cologne smell about them, but the lobby was empty. Going up the stairs, Mr Melton said, 'Well, it's been a long hard day. Who'd like to put a header on it? You folks? Martini? Beer?'

'Maybe one.'

The whole crowd pushed into Mr Melton's room and the drinking began.

'Watch the time,' said William.

Time, thought Susan. If only they had time. All she wanted was to sit in the plaza all of a long bright day in October, with not a worry or a thought, with the sun on her face and arms, her eyes closed, smiling at the warmth, and never move. Just sleep in the Mexican sun, and sleep warmly and easily and slowly and happily for many, many days . . .

Mr Melton opened the champagne.

'To a very beautiful lady, lovely enough for films,' he said, toasting Susan. 'I might even give you a test.'

She laughed.

'I mean it,' said Melton. 'You're very nice. I could make you a movie star.'

'And take me to Hollywood?' cried Susan.

'Get the hell out of Mexico, sure!'

Susan glanced at William and he lifted an eyebrow and nodded. It would be a change of scene, clothing, locale, name, perhaps; and they would be travelling with eight other people, a good shield against any interference from the Future.

'It sounds wonderful,' said Susan.

She was feeling the champagne now. The afternoon was slipping by; the party was whirling about her. She felt safe and good and alive and truly happy for the first time in many years.

'What kind of film would my wife be good for?' asked William, refilling his glass.

Melton appraised Susan. The party stopped laughing and listened.

'Well, I'd like to do a story of suspense,' said Melton. 'A story of a man and wife, like yourselves.'

'Go on.'

'Sort of a war story, maybe,' said the director, examining the colour of his drink against the sunlight.

Susan and William waited.

'A story about a man and wife, who live in a little house on a little street in the year 2155, maybe,' said Melton. 'This is ad lib, understand. But this man and wife are faced with a terrible war, super-plus hydrogen bombs, censorship, death in that year, and — here's the gimmick — they escape into the Past, followed by a man who they think is evil, but who is only trying to show them what their duty is.'

William dropped his glass to the floor.

Mr Melton continued: 'And this couple take refuge with a group of film people whom they learn to trust. Safety in numbers, they say to themselves.'

Susan felt herself slip down into a chair. Everyone was watching the director. He took a little sip of champagne. 'Ah, that's fine. Well, this man and woman, it seems, don't realize how important they are to the Future. The man, especially, is the keystone to a new bomb metal. So the Searchers, let's call them, spare no trouble or expense to find, capture, and take home the man and wife, once they get them totally alone, in a hotel room, where no one can see. Strategy. The Searchers work alone, or in groups of eight. One trick or another will do it. Don't you think it would make a wonderful film, Susan? Don't you, Bill?' He finished his drink.

Susan sat with her eyes straight ahead of her.

'Have a drink?' said Mr Melton.

William's gun was out and fired three times, and one of the men fell, and the others ran forward. Susan screamed. A hand was clamped to her mouth. Now the gun was on the floor and William was struggling, held.

Mr Melton said, 'Please,' standing there where he had stood, blood showing on his fingers. 'Let's not make matters worse.'

Someone pounded on the hall door.

'Let me in!'

'The manager,' said Mr Melton dryly. He jerked his head. 'Everyone, let's move!'

'Let me in! I'll call the police!'

Susan and William looked at each other quickly, and then at the door.

'The manager wishes to come in,' said Mr Melton. 'Quick!'

A camera was carried forward. From it shot a blue light which encompassed the room instantly. It widened out and the people of the party vanished, one by one.

'Quickly!'

Outside the window, in the instant before she vanished, Susan saw the green land and the purple and yellow and blue and crimson walls and the cobbles flowing down like a river, a man upon a burro riding into the warm hills, a boy drinking Orange Crush, she could feel the sweet liquid in her throat, a man standing under a cool plaza tree with a guitar, she could feel her hand upon the strings, and, far away, the sea, the blue and tender sea, she could feel it roll her over and take her in.

And then she was gone. Her husband was gone.

The door burst wide open. The manager and his staff rushed in.

The room was empty.

'But they were just here! I saw them come in, and now – gone!' cried the manager. 'The windows are covered with iron grating. They couldn't get out that way!'

In the late afternoon the priest was summoned and they opened the room again and aired it out, and had him sprinkle holy water through each corner and give it his blessing.

'What shall we do with these?' asked the charwoman.

She pointed to the closet, where there were 67 bottles of Chartreuse, cognac, crème de cacao, absinthe, vermouth, tequila, 106 cartons of Turkish cigarettes, and 198 yellow boxes of fifty-cent pure Havana-filler cigars . . .

Kaleidoscope

The first concussion cut the rocket up the side with a giant can opener. The men were thrown into space like a dozen wriggling silverfish. They were scattered into a dark sea; and the ship, in a million pieces, went on, a meteor swarm seeking a lost sun.

'Barkley, Barkley, where are you?'

The sound of voices calling like lost children on a cold night.

'Woode, Woode!'

'Captain!'

'Hollis, Hollis, this is Stone.'

'Stone, this is Hollis. Where are you?'

'I don't know. How can I? Which way is up? I'm falling. Good God, I'm falling.'

They fell. They fell as pebbles fall down wells. They were scattered as jack-stones are scattered from a gigantic throw. And now instead of men there were only voices — all kinds of voices, disembodied and impassioned, in varying degrees of terror and resignation.

'We're going away from each other.'

This was true. Hollis, swinging head over heels, knew this was true. He knew it with a vague acceptance. They were parting to go their separate ways, and nothing could bring them back. They were wearing their sealed-tight space suits with the glass tubes over their pale faces, but they hadn't had time to lock on their force units. With them they could be small lifeboats in space, saving themselves, saving others, collecting together, finding each other until they were an island of men with some plan. But without the force units snapped to their shoulders they were meteors, senseless, each going to a separate and irrevocable fate.

A period of perhaps ten minutes elapsed while the first terror died and a metallic calm took its place. Space began to weave its strange voices in and out, on a great dark loom, crossing, recrossing, making a final pattern.

'Stone to Hollis. How long can we talk by phone?'

'It depends on how fast you're going your way and I'm going mine.'

'An hour, I make it.'

'That should do it,' said Hollis, abstracted and quiet.

'What happened?' asked Hollis a minute later.

'The rocket blew up, that's all. Rockets do blow up.'

'Which way are you going?'

'It looks like I'll hit the Moon.'

'It's Earth for me. Back to old Mother Earth at ten thousand miles per hour. I'll burn like a match.' Hollis thought of it with a queer abstraction of mind. He seemed to be removed from his body, watching it fall down and down through space, as objective as he had been in regard to the first falling snowflakes of a winter season long gone.

The others were silent, thinking of the destiny that had brought them to this, falling, falling, and nothing they could do to change it. Even the captain was quiet, for there was no command or plan he knew that could put things back together again.

'Oh, it's a long way down. Oh, it's a long way down, a long, long, long way down,' said a voice. 'I don't want to die, I don't want to die, it's a long way down.'

'Who's that?'

'I don't know.'

'Stimson, I think. Stimson, is that you?'

'It's a long, long way and I don't like it. Oh, God, I don't like it.'

'Stimson, this is Hollis. Stimson, you hear me?'

A pause while they fell separate from one another.

'Stimson?'

'Yes.' He replied at last.

'Stimson, take it easy; we're all in the same fix.'

'I don't want to be here. I want to be somewhere else.'

'There's a chance we'll be found.'

'I must be, I must be,' said Stimson. 'I don't believe this; I don't believe any of this is happening.'

'It's a bad dream,' said someone.

'Shut up!' said Hollis.

'Come and make me,' said the voice. It was Applegate. He laughed easily, with a similar objectivity. 'Come and shut me up.'

Hollis for the first time felt the impossibility of his position. A great anger filled him, for he wanted more than anything at this moment to be able to do something to Applegate. He had wanted for many years to do something and now it was too late. Applegate was only a telephonic voice.

Falling, falling, falling . . .

Now, as if they had discovered the horror, two of the men began to scream. In a nightmare Hollis saw one of them float by, very near, screaming and screaming.

'Stop it!' The man was almost at his fingertips, screaming insanely. He would never stop. He would go on screaming for a million miles, as long as he was in radio range, disturbing all of them, making it impossible for them to talk to one another.

Hollis reached out. It was best this way. He made the extra effort and touched the man. He grasped the man's ankle and pulled himself up along the body until he reached the head. The man screamed and clawed frantically, like a drowning swimmer. The screaming filled the universe.

One way or the other, thought Hollis. The Moon or Earth or meteors will kill him, so why not now?

He smashed the man's glass mask with his iron fist. The screaming stopped. He pushed off from the body and let it spin away on its own course, falling.

Falling, falling down space Hollis and the rest of them went in the long, endless dropping and whirling of silence.

'Hollis, you still there?'

Hollis did not speak, but felt the rush of heat in his face.

'This is Applegate again.'

'All right, Applegate.'

'Let's talk. We haven't anything else to do.'

The captain cut in. 'That's enough of that. We've got to figure a way out of this.'

'Captain, why don't you shut up?' said Applegate.

'What!'

'You heard me, Captain. Don't pull your rank on me, you're ten thousand miles away by now, and let's not kid ourselves. As Stimson puts it, it's a long way down.'

'See here, Applegate!'

'Can it. This is a mutiny of one. I haven't a damn thing to lose. Your ship was a bad ship and you were a bad captain and I hope you break when you hit the Moon.'

'I'm ordering you to stop!'

'Go on, order me again.' Applegate smiled across ten thousand miles. The captain was silent. Applegate continued. 'Where were we, Hollis? Oh yes, I remember. I hate you too. But you know that. You've known it for a long time.'

Hollis clenched his fists, helplessly.

'I want to tell you something,' said Applegate. 'Make you happy. I was the one who blackballed you with the Rocket Company five years ago.'

A meteor flashed by. Hollis looked down and his left hand was gone. Blood spurted. Suddenly there was no air in his suit. He had enough air in his lungs to move his right hand over and twist a knob at his left elbow, tightening the joint and sealing the leak. It had happened so quickly that he was not surprised. Nothing surprised him any more. The air in the suit came back to normal in an instant now that the leak was sealed. And the blood that had flowed so swiftly was pressured as he fastened the knob yet tighter, until it made a tourniquet.

All this took place in a terrible silence on his part. And the other men chatted. That one man, Lespere, went on and on with his talk about his wife on Mars, his wife on Venus, his wife on Jupiter, his money, his wondrous times, his drunkenness, his gambling, his happiness. On and on, while they all fell. Lespere reminisced on the past, happy, while he fell to his death.

It was so very odd. Space, thousands of miles of space, and these voices vibrating in the centre of it. No one visible at all, and only the radio waves quivering and trying to quicken other men into emotion.

'Are you angry, Hollis?'

'No.' And he was not. The abstraction had returned and he was a thing of dull concrete, forever falling nowhere.

'You wanted to get to the top all your life, Hollis. You always wondered what happened. I put the black mark on you just before I was tossed out myself.'

'That isn't important,' said Hollis. And it was not. It was gone. When life is over it is like a flicker of bright film, an instant on the screen, all of its prejudices and passions condensed and illumined for an instant on space, and before you could cry out, 'There was a happy day, there a bad one, there an evil face, there a good one,' the film burned to a cinder, the screen went dark.

From this outer edge of his life, looking back, there was only one remorse, and that was only that he wished to go on living. Did all dying people feel this way, as if they had never lived? Did life seem that short, indeed, over and done before you took a breath? Did it seem this abrupt and impossible to everyone, or only to himself, here, now, with a few hours left to him for thought and deliberation?

One of the other men, Lespere, was talking. 'Well, I had me a good time: I had a wife on Mars, Venus, and Jupiter. Each of them had money and treated me swell. I got drunk and once I gambled away twenty thousand dollars.'

But you're here now, thought Hollis. I didn't have any of those things. When I was living I was jealous of you, Lespere; when I had another day ahead of me I envied you your women and your good times. Women frightened me and I went into space, always wanting them and jealous of you for having them, and money, and as much happiness as you could have in your own wild way. But now, falling here, with everything over, I'm not jealous of you any more, because it's over for you as it is for me, and right now it's like it never was. Hollis craned his face forward and shouted into the telephone.

'It's all over, Lespere!'

Silence.

'It's just as if it never was, Lespere!'

'Who's that?' Lespere's faltering voice.

'This is Hollis.'

He was being mean. He felt the meanness, the senseless meanness of dying. Applegate had hurt him; now he wanted to hurt another. Applegate and space had both wounded him.

'You're out here, Lespere. It's all over. It's just as if it had never happened, isn't it?'

'No.'

'When anything's over, it's just like it never happened. Where's your life any better than mine, now? Now is what counts. Is it any better? Is it?'

'Yes, it's better!'

'How!'

'Because I got my thoughts, I remember!' cried Lespere, far away, indignant, holding his memories to his chest with both hands.

And he was right. With a feeling of cold water rushing through his head and body, Hollis knew he was right. There were differences between memories and dreams. He had only dreams of things he had wanted to do, while Lespere had memories of things done and accomplished. And this knowledge began to pull Hollis apart, with a slow, quivering precision.

'What good does it do you?' he cried to Lespere. 'Now? When a thing's over it's not good any more. You're no better off than I.'

'I'm resting easy,' said Lespere. 'I've had my turn. I'm not getting mean at the end, like you.'

'Mean?' Hollis turned the word on his tongue. He had never been mean, as long as he could remember, in his life. He had never dared to be mean. He must have saved it all of these years for such a time as this. 'Mean.' He rolled the word into the back of his mind. He felt tears start into his eyes and roll down his face. Someone must have heard his gasping voice.

'Take it easy, Hollis.'

It was, of course, ridiculous. Only a minute before he had been giving advice to others, to Stimson; he had felt a braveness which he had thought to be the genuine thing, and now he knew that it had been nothing but shock and the objectivity possible in shock. Now he was trying to pack a lifetime of suppressed emotion into an interval of minutes.

'I know how you feel, Hollis,' said Lespere, now twenty thousand miles away, his voice fading. 'I don't take it personally.'

But aren't we equal? he wondered. Lespere and I? Here,

now? If a thing's over, it's done, and what good is it? You die anyway. But he knew he was rationalizing, for it was like trying to tell the difference between a live man and a corpse. There was a spark in one, and not in the other — an aura, a mysterious element.

So it was with Lespere and himself; Lespere had lived a good full life, and it made him a different man now, and he, Hollis, had been as good as dead for many years. They came to death by separate paths and, in all likelihood, if there were kinds of death, their kinds would be as different as night from day. The quality of death, like that of life, must be of an infinite variety, and if one has already died once, then what was there to look for in dying for good and all, as he was now?

It was a second later that he discovered his right foot was cut sheer away. It almost made him laugh. The air was gone from his suit again. He bent quickly, and there was blood, and the meteor had taken flesh and suit away to the ankle. Oh, death in space was most humorous. It cut you away, piece by piece, like a black and invisible butcher. He tightened the valve at the knee, his head whirling into pain, fighting to remain aware, and with the valve tightened, the blood retained, the air kept, he straightened up and went on falling, falling, for that was all there was left to do.

'Hollis?'

Hollis nodded sleepily, tired of waiting for death.

'This is Applegate again,' said the voice.

'Yes.'

'I've had time to think. I listened to you. This isn't good. It makes us bad. This is a bad way to die. It brings all the bile out. You listening, Hollis?'

'Yes.'

'I lied. A minute ago. I lied. I didn't blackball you. I don't know why I said that. Guess I wanted to hurt you. You seemed the one to hurt. We've always fought. Guess I'm getting old fast and repenting fast. I guess listening to you be mean made me ashamed. Whatever the reason, I want you to know I was an idiot too. There's not an ounce of truth in what I said. To hell with you.'

Hollis felt his heart begin to work again. It seemed as if it hadn't worked for five minutes, but now all of his limbs began to take colour and warmth. The shock was over, and the successive shocks of anger and terror and loneliness were passing. He felt like a man emerging from a cold shower in the morning, ready for breakfast and a new day.

'Thanks, Applegate.'

'Don't mention it. Up your nose, you bastard.'

'Hey,' said Stone.

'What?' Hollis called across space; for Stone, of all of them, was a good friend.

'I've got myself into a meteor swarm, some little asteroids.'

'Meteors?'

'I think it's the Myrmidone cluster that goes out past Mars and in towards Earth once every five years. I'm right in the middle. It's like a big kaleidoscope. You get all kinds of colours and shapes and sizes. God, it's beautiful, all that metal.'

Silence.

'I'm going with them,' said Stone. 'They're taking me off with them. I'll be damned.' He laughed.

Hollis looked to see, but saw nothing. There were only the great diamonds and sapphires and emerald mists and velvet inks of space, with God's voice mingling among the crystal fires. There was a kind of wonder and imagination in the thought of Stone going off in the meteor swarm, out past Mars for years and coming in towards Earth every five years, passing in and out of the planet's ken for the next million centuries. Stone and the Myrmidone cluster eternal and unending, shifting and shaping like the kaleidoscope colours when you were a child and held the long tube to the sun and gave it a twirl.

'So long, Hollis.' Stone's voice, very faint now. 'So long.'

'Good luck,' shouted Hollis across thirty thousand miles.

'Don't be funny,' said Stone, and was gone.

The stars closed in.

Now all the voices were fading, each on his own trajectory, some to Mars, others into farthest space. And Hollis himself . . . He looked down. He, of all the others, was going back to Earth alone.

'So long.'

'Take it easy.'

'So long, Hollis.' That was Applegate.

The many good-byes. The short farewells. And now the great loose brain was disintegrating. The components of the brain which had worked so beautifully and efficiently in the skull case of the rocket ship firing through space were dying one by one; the meaning of their life together was falling apart. And as a body dies when the brain ceases functioning, so the spirit of the ship and their long time together and what they meant to one another was dying. Applegate was now no more than a finger blown from the parent body, no longer to be despised and worked against. The brain was exploded, and the senseless, useless fragments of it were far scattered. The voices faded and now all of space was silent. Hollis was alone, falling.

They were all alone. Their voices had died like echoes of the words of God spoken and vibrating in the starred deep. There went the captain to the Moon; there Stone with the meteor swarm; there Stimson; there Applegate towards Pluto; there Smith and Turner and Underwood and all the rest, the shards of the kaleidoscope that had formed a thinking pattern for so long, hurled apart.

And I? thought Hollis. What can I do? Is there anything I can do now to make up for a terrible and empty life? If only I could do one good thing to make up for the meanness I collected all these years and didn't even know was in me! But there's no one here but myself and how can you do good all alone? You can't. Tomorrow night I'll hit Earth's atmosphere.

I'll burn, he thought, and be scattered in ashes all over the continental lands. I'll be put to use. Just a little bit, but ashes are ashes and they'll add to the land.

He fell swiftly, like a bullet, like a pebble, like an iron weight, objective, objective all of the time now, not sad or happy or anything, but only wishing he could do a good thing now that everything was gone, a good thing for just himself to know about.

When I hit the atmosphere, I'll burn like a meteor.

'I wonder,' he said, 'if anyone'll see me?'

The small boy on the country road looked up and screamed. 'Look, Mom, look! A falling star!'

The blazing white star fell down the sky of dusk in Illinois.

'Make a wish,' said his mother. 'Make a wish.'

The Rocket Man

The electrical fireflies were hovering above Mother's dark hair to light her path. She stood in her bedroom door looking out at me as I passed in the silent hall. 'You *will* help me keep him here this time, won't you?' she asked.

'I guess so,' I said.

'Please.' The fireflies cast moving bits of light on her white face. 'This time he mustn't go away again.'

'All right,' I said, after standing there a moment. 'But it won't do any good; it's no use.'

She went away, and the fireflies, on their electric circuits, fluttered after her like an errant constellation, showing her how to walk in darkness. I heard her say, faintly, 'We've got to try, anyway.'

Other fireflies followed me to my room. When the weight of my body cut a circuit in the bed, the fireflies winked out. It was midnight, and my mother and I waited, our rooms separated by darkness, in bed. The bed began to rock me and sing to me. I touched a switch; the singing and rocking stopped. I didn't want to sleep. I didn't want to sleep at all.

This night was no different from a thousand others in our time. We would wake nights and feel the cool air turn hot, feel the fire in the wind, or see the walls burned a bright colour for an instant, and then we knew *his* rocket was over our house — his rocket, and the oak trees swaying from the concussion. And I would lie there, eyes wide, panting, and Mother in her room. Her voice would come to me over the interroom radio?

'Did you feel it?'

And I would answer, 'That was him, all right.'

That was my father's ship passing over our town, a small town where space rockets never came, and we would lie awake for the next two hours, thinking. 'Now Dad's landed in Springfield, now he's on the tarmac, now he is signing the papers, now he's in the helicopter, now he's over the river, now the hills, now he's settling the helicopter in at the little airport at Green Village here . . . ' And the night would be half over when, in our separate cool beds, Mother and I would be listening, listening. 'Now he's walking down Bell Street. He always walks . . . never takes a cab . . . now across the park, now turning the corner of Oakhurst and *now* . . . '

I lifted my head from my pillow. Far down the street, coming closer and closer, smartly, quickly, briskly – footsteps. Now turning in at our house, up the porch steps. And we were both smiling in the cool darkness, Mom and I, when we heard the front door open in recognition, speak a quiet word of welcome, and shut, downstairs . . .

Three hours later I turned the brass knob to their room quietly, holding my breath, balancing in a darkness as big as the space between the planets, my hand out to reach the small black case at the foot of my parents' sleeping bed. Taking it, I ran silently to my room, thinking, He won't tell me, he doesn't want me to *know*.

And from the opened case spilled his black uniform, like a black nebula, stars glittering here or there, distantly, in the material. I kneaded the dark stuff in my warm hands; I smelled the planet Mars, an iron smell, and the planet Venus, a green ivy smell, and the planet Mercury, a scent of sulphur and fire; and I could smell the milky Moon and the hardness of the stars. I pushed the uniform into a centrifuge machine I'd built in my ninth-grade shop that year, set it whirling. Soon a fine powder precipitated into a retort. This I slid under a microscope. And while my parents slept unaware, and while our house was asleep, all the automatic bakers and servers and robot cleaners in an electric slumber, I stared down upon brilliant motes of meteor dust, comet tail, and loam from far Jupiter glistening like worlds themselves which drew me down the tube a billion miles into space, at terrific accelerations.

At dawn, exhausted with my journey and fearful of discovery, I returned the boxed uniform to their sleeping room.

Then I slept, only to waken at the sound of the horn of the dry-cleaning car which stopped in the yard below. They took the black uniform box with them. It's good I didn't wait, I thought. For the uniform would be back in an hour, clean of all its destiny and travel.

I slept again, with the little vial of magical dust in my pyjama pocket, over my beating heart.

When I came downstairs, there was Dad at the breakfast table, biting into his toast. 'Sleep good, Doug?' he said, as if he had been here all the time, and hadn't been gone for three months.

'All right,' I said.

'Toast?'

He pressed a button and the breakfast table made me four pieces, golden brown.

I remember my father that afternoon, digging and digging in the garden, like an animal after something, it seemed. There he was with his long dark arms moving swiftly, planting, tamping, fixing, cutting, pruning, his dark face always down to the soil, his eyes always down to what he was doing, never up to the sky, never looking at me, or Mother, even, unless we knelt with him to feel the earth soak up through the overalls at our knees, to put our hands into the black dirt and not look at the bright, crazy sky. Then he would glance to either side, to Mother or me, and give us a gentle wink, and go on, bent down, face down, the sky staring at his back.

That night we sat on the mechanical porch swing which swung us and blew a wind upon us and sang to us. It was summer and moonlight and we had lemonade to drink, and we held the cold glasses in our hands, and Dad read the stereo-newspapers inserted into the special hat you put on your head and which turned the microscopic page in front of the magnifying lens if you blinked three times in succession. Dad smoked cigarettes and told me about how it was when he was a boy in the year 1997. After a while he said, as he had always said, 'Why aren't you out playing kick-the-can, Doug?'

I didn't say anything, but Mom said, 'He does, on nights when you're not here.'

Dad looked at me and then, for the first time that day, at the sky. Mother always watched him when he glanced at the stars. The first day and night when he got home he wouldn't look at the sky much. I thought about him gardening and gardening so furiously, his face almost driven into the earth. But the second night he looked at the stars a little more. Mother wasn't afraid of the sky in the day so much, but it was the night stars that she wanted to turn off, and sometimes I could almost see her reaching for a switch in her mind, but never finding it. And by the third night maybe Dad'd be out here on the porch until way after we were all ready for bed, and then I'd hear Mom call him in, almost like she called me from the street at times. And then I would hear Dad fitting the electric-eye door lock in place, with a sigh. And the next morning at breakfast I'd glance down and see his little black case near his feet as he buttered his toast and Mother slept late.

'Well, be seeing you, Doug,' he'd say, and we'd shake hands.

'In about three months?'

'Right.'

And he'd walk away down the street, not taking a helicopter or beetle or bus, just walking with his uniform hidden in his small underarm case; he didn't want anyone to think he was vain about being a Rocket Man.

Mother would come out to eat breakfast, one piece of dry toast, about an hour later.

But now it was tonight, the first night, the good night, and he wasn't looking at the stars much at all.

'Let's go to the television carnival,' I said.

'Fine,' said Dad.

Mother smiled at me.

And we rushed off to town in a helicopter and took Dad through a thousand exhibits, to keep his face and head down with us and not looking anywhere else. And as we laughed at the funny things and looked serious at the serious ones, I thought, My father goes to Saturn and Neptune and Pluto, but he never brings me presents. Other boys' fathers who go into space bring back bits of ore from Callisto and hunks of black meteor or blue sand. But I have to get my own collection, trading from other boys, the Martian rocks and Mercurian sands which filled my room, but about which Dad would never comment.

On occasion, I remembered, he brought something for Mother. He planted some Martian sunflowers once in our yard, but after he was gone a month and the sunflowers grew large, Mom ran out one day and cut them all down.

Without thinking, as we paused at one of the three-dimensional exhibits, I asked Dad the question I always asked:

'What's it like, out in space?'

Mother shot me a frightened glance. It was too late.

Dad stood there for a full half-minute trying to find an answer, then he shrugged.

'It's the best thing in a lifetime of best things.' Then he caught himself. 'Oh, it's really nothing at all. Routine. You wouldn't like it.' He looked at me, apprehensively.

'But you always go back.'

'Habit.'

'Where're you going next?'

'I haven't decided yet. I'll think it over.'

He always thought it over. In those days rocket pilots were rare and he could pick and choose, work when he liked. On the third night of his homecoming you could see him picking and choosing among the stars.

'Come on,' said Mother, 'let's go home.'

It was still early when we got home. I wanted Dad to put on his uniform. I shouldn't have asked — it always made Mother unhappy — but I could not help myself. I kept at him, though he had always refused. I had never seen him in it, and at last he said, 'Oh, all right.'

We waited in the parlour while he went upstairs in the air flue. Mother looked at me dully, as if she couldn't believe that her own son could do this to her. I glanced away. 'I'm sorry,' I said.

'You're not helping at all,' she said. 'At all.'

There was a whisper in the air flue a moment later.

'Here I am,' said Dad quietly.

We looked at him in his uniform.

It was glossy black with silver buttons and silver rims to the heels of the black boots, and it looked as if someone had cut the arms and legs and body from a dark nebula, with little faint stars glowing through it. It fit as close as a glove fits to a slender long hand, and it smelled like cool air and metal and space. It smelled of fire and time.

Father stood, smiling awkwardly, in the centre of the room.

'Turn around,' said Mother.

Her eyes were remote, looking at him.

When he was gone, she never talked of him. She never said anything about anything but the weather or the condition of my neck and the need of a washcloth for it, or the fact that she didn't sleep nights. Once she said the light was too strong at night.

'But there's no moon this week,' I said.

'There's starlight,' she said.

I went to the store and bought her some darker, greener shades. As I lay in bed at night, I could hear her pull them down tight to the bottom of the windows. It made a long rustling noise.

Once I tried to mow the lawn.

'No.' Mom stood in the door. 'Put the mower away.'

So the grass went three months at a time without cutting. Dad cut it when he came home.

She wouldn't let me do anything else either, like repairing the electrical breakfast maker or the mechanical book reader. She saved everything up, as if for Christmas. And then I would see Dad hammering or tinkering, and always smiling at his work, and Mother smiled over him, happy.

No, she never talked of him when he was gone. And as for Dad, he never did anything to make a contact across the millions of miles. He said once, 'If I called you, I'd want to be with you. I wouldn't be happy.'

Once Dad said to me, 'Your mother treats me, sometimes, as if I weren't here — as if I were invisible.'

I had seen her do it. She would look just beyond him, over his shoulder, at his chin or hands, but never into his eyes. If she did look at his eyes, her eyes were covered with a film, like an animal going to sleep. She said yes at the right times, and smiled, but always a half second later than expected.

'I'm not there for her,' said Dad.

But other days she would be there and he would be there for her, and they would hold hands and walk around the block, or take rides, with Mom's hair flying like a girl's behind her, and she would cut off all the mechanical devices in the kitchen and bake him incredible cakes and pies and cookies, looking deep into his face, her smile a real smile. But at the end of such days when he was there to her, she would always cry. And Dad would stand helpless, gazing about the room as if to find the answer, but never finding it.

Dad turned slowly, in his uniform, for us to see.

'Turn around again,' said Mom.

The next morning Dad came rushing into the house with handfuls of tickets. Pink rocket tickets for California, blue tickets for Mexico.

'Come on!' he said. 'We'll buy disposable clothes and burn them when they're soiled. Look, we take the noon rocket to LA, the two-o'clock helicopter to Santa Barbara, the nine o'clock plane to Ensenada, sleep overnight!'

And we went to California and up and down the Pacific Coast for a day and a half, settling at last on the sands of Malibu to cook wieners at night. Dad was always listening or singing or watching things on all sides of him, holding on to things as if the world were a centrifuge going so swiftly that he might be flung off away from us at any instant.

The last afternoon at Malibu Mom was up in the hotel room. Dad lay on the sand beside me for a long time in the hot sun. 'Ah,' he sighed, 'this is it.' His eyes were gently closed; he lay on his back, drinking the sun. 'You *miss* this,' he said.

He meant 'on the rocket', of course. But he never said 'the rocket' or mentioned the rocket and all the things you couldn't have on the rocket. You couldn't have a salt wind on the rocket or a blue sky or a yellow sun or Mom's cooking. You couldn't talk to your fourteen-year-old boy on a rocket.

'Let's hear it,' he said at last.

And I knew that now we would talk, as we had always talked, for three hours straight. All afternoon we would murmur back and forth in the lazy sun about my school grades, how high I could jump, how fast I could swim.

Dad nodded each time I spoke and smiled and slapped my chest lightly in approval. We talked. We did not talk of

rockets or space, but we talked of Mexico, where we had
driven once in an ancient car, and of the butterflies we had
caught in the rain forests of green warm Mexico at noon,
seeing the hundred butterflies sucked to our radiator,
dying there, beating their blue and crimson wings,
twitching, beautiful, and sad. We talked of such things
instead of the things I wanted to talk about. And he listened
to me. That was the thing he did, as if he was trying to fill
himself up with all the sound he could hear. He listened to
the wind and the falling ocean and my voice, always with a
rapt attention, a concentration that almost excluded physical
bodies themselves and kept only the sounds. He shut his eyes
to listen. I would see him listening to the lawn mower as he
cut the grass by hand instead of using the remote-control
device, and I would see him smelling the cut grass as it
sprayed up at him behind the mower in a green fount.

'Doug,' he said, about five in the afternoon, as we were
picking up our towels and heading back along the beach near
the surf, 'I want you to promise me something.'

'What?'

'Don't ever be a Rocket Man.'

I stopped.

'I mean it,' he said. 'Because when you're out there you
want to be here, and when you're here you want to be out
there. Don't start that. Don't let it get hold of you.'

'But –'

'You don't know what it is. Every time I'm out there I
think, If I ever get back to Earth I'll stay there; I'll never go
out again. But I go out, and I guess I'll always go out.'

'I've thought about being a Rocket Man for a long time,' I
said.

He didn't hear me. 'I *try* to stay here. Last Saturday when I
got home I started trying so damned hard to *stay* here.'

I remembered him in the garden, sweating, and all the
travelling and doing and listening, and I knew that he did this

to convince himself that the sea and the towns and the land and his family were the only real things and the good things. But I knew where he would be tonight: looking at the jewellery in Orion from our front porch.

'Promise me you won't be like me,' he said.

I hesitated awhile. 'Okay,' I said.

He shook my hand. 'Good boy,' he said.

The dinner was fine that night. Mom had run about the kitchen with handfuls of cinnamon and dough and pots and pans tinkling, and now a great turkey fumed on the table, with dressing, cranberry sauce, peas, and pumpkin pie.

'In the middle of August?' said Dad, amazed.

'You won't be here for Thanksgiving.'

'So I won't.'

He sniffed it. He lifted each lid from each tureen and let the flavour steam over his sunburned face. He said 'Ah' to each. He looked at the room and his hands. He gazed at the pictures on the wall, the chairs, the table, me, and Mom. He cleared his throat. I saw him make up his mind. 'Lilly?'

'Yes?' Mom looked across her table which she had set like a wonderful silver trap, a miraculous gravy pit in which, like a struggling beast of the past caught in a tar pool, her husband might at last be caught and held, gazing out through a jail of wishbones, safe forever. Her eyes sparkled.

'Lilly,' said Dad.

Go on, I thought crazily. Say it quick: say you'll stay home this time, for good, and never go away; say it!

Just then a passing helicopter jarred the room and the windowpane shook with a crystal sound. Dad glanced at the window.

The blue stars of evening were there, and the red planet Mars was rising in the East.

Dad looked at Mars a full minute. Then he put his hand out blindly towards me. 'May I have some peas,' he said.

'Excuse me,' said Mother. 'I'm going to get some bread.'
She rushed out into the kitchen.
'But there's bread on the table,' I said.
Dad didn't look at me as he began his meal.

I couldn't sleep that night. I came downstairs at one in the morning and the moonlight was like ice on all the housetops, and dew glittered in a snow field on our grass. I stood in the doorway in my pyjamas, feeling the warm night wind, and then I knew that Dad was sitting in the mechanical porch swing, gliding gently. I could see his profile tilted back, and he was watching the stars wheel over the sky. His eyes were like grey crystal there, the Moon in each one.

I went out and sat beside him.

We glided awhile in the swing.

At last I said, 'How many ways are there to die in space?'

'A million.'

'Name some.'

'The meteors hit you. The air goes out of your rocket. Or comets take you along with them. Concussion. Strangulation. Explosion. Centrifugal force. Too much acceleration. Too little. The heat, the cold, the sun, the Moon, the stars, the planets, the asteroids, the planetoids, radiation . . .'

'And do they bury you?'

'They never find you.'

'Where do you go?'

'A billion miles away. Travelling graves, they call them. You become a meteor or a planetoid travelling forever through space.'

I said nothing.

'One thing,' he said later, 'it's quick in space. Death. It's over like that. You don't linger. Most of the time you don't even know it. You're dead and that's it.'

We went up to bed.

*   *   *

It was morning.

Standing in the doorway, Dad listened to the yellow canary singing in its golden cage.

'Well, I've decided,' he said. 'Next time I come home, I'm home to stay.'

'Dad!' I said.

'Tell your mother that when she gets up,' he said.

'You *mean* it!'

He nodded gravely. 'See you in about three months.'

And there he went off down the street, carrying his uniform in its secret box, whistling and looking at the tall green trees and picking chinaberries off the chinaberry bush as he brushed by, tossing them ahead of him as he walked away into the bright shade of early morning . . .

I asked Mother about a few things that morning after Father had been gone a number of hours. 'Dad said that sometimes you don't act as if you hear or see him,' I said.

And then she explained everything to me quietly.

'When he went off into space ten years ago, I said to myself, He's dead. Or as good as dead. So think of him dead. And when he comes back, three or four times a year, it's not him at all, it's only a pleasant little memory or a dream. And if a memory stops or a dream stops, it can't hurt half as much. So most of the time I think of him dead – '

'But other times – '

'Other times I can't help myself. I bake pies and treat him as if he were alive, and then it hurts. No, it's better to think he hasn't been here for ten years and I'll never see him again. It doesn't hurt as much.'

'Didn't he say next time he'd settle down?'

She shook her head slowly. 'No, he's dead. I'm very sure of that.'

'He'll come alive again, then,' I said.

'Ten years ago,' said Mother, 'I thought, What if he dies

on Venus? Then we'll never be able to see Venus again. What if he dies on Mars? We'll never be able to look at Mars again, all red in the sky, without wanting to go in and lock the door. Or what if he died on Jupiter or Saturn or Neptune? On those nights when those planets were high in the sky, we wouldn't want to have anything to do with the stars.'

'I guess not,' I said.

The message came the next day.

The messenger gave it to me and I read it standing on the porch. The sun was setting. Mom stood in the screen door behind me, watching me fold the message and put it in my pocket.

'Mom,' I said.

'Don't tell me anything I don't already know,' she said.

She didn't cry.

Well, it wasn't Mars, and it wasn't Venus, and it wasn't Jupiter or Saturn that killed him. We wouldn't have to think of him every time Jupiter or Saturn or Mars lit up the evening sky.

This was different.

His ship had fallen into the sun.

And the sun was big and fiery and merciless, and it was always in the sky and you couldn't get away from it.

So for a long time after my father died my mother slept through the days and wouldn't go out. We had breakfast at midnight and lunch at three in the morning, and dinner at the cold dim hour of 6 A.M. We went to all-night shows and went to bed at sunrise.

And, for a long while, the only days we ever went out to walk were the days when it was raining and there was no sun.

Marionettes, Inc.

They walked slowly down the street at about ten in the evening, talking calmly. They were both about thirty-five, both eminently sober.

'But why so early?' said Smith.

'Because,' said Braling.

'Your first night out in years and you go home at ten o'clock.'

'Nerves, I suppose.'

'What I wonder *is* how you ever managed it. I've been trying to get you out for ten years for a quiet drink. And now, on the one night, you insist on turning in early.'

'Mustn't crowd my luck,' said Braling.

'What did you do, put sleeping powder in your wife's coffee?'

'No, that would be unethical. You'll see soon enough.'

They turned a corner. 'Honestly, Braling, I hate to say this, but you *have* been patient with her. You may not admit it to me, but marriage has been awful for you, hasn't it?'

'I wouldn't say that.'

'It's got around, anyway, here and there, how she got you to marry her. That time back in 1979 when you were going to Rio — '

'Dear Rio. I never *did* see it after all my plans.'

'And how she tore her clothes and rumpled her hair and threatened to call the police unless you married her.'

'She always was nervous, Smith, understand.'

'It was more than unfair. You didn't love her. You told her as much, didn't you?'

'I recall that I was quite firm on the subject.'

'But you married her anyhow.'

'I had my business to think of, as well as my mother and father. A thing like that would have killed them.'

'And it's been ten years.'

'Yes,' said Braling, his grey eyes steady. 'But I think perhaps it might change now. I think what I've waited for has come about. Look here.'

He drew forth a long blue ticket.

'Why, it's a ticket for Rio on the Thursday rocket!'

'Yes, I'm finally going to make it.'

'But how wonderful! You *do* deserve it! But won't *she* object? Cause trouble?'

Braling smiled nervously. 'She won't know I'm gone. I'll be back in a month and no one the wiser, except you.'

Smith sighed. 'I wish I were going with you.'

'Poor Smith, *your* marriage hasn't exactly been roses, has it?'

'Not exactly, married to a woman who overdoes it. I mean, after all, when you've been married ten years, you don't expect a woman to sit on your lap for two hours every evening, call you at work twelve times a day and talk baby talk. And it seems to me that in the last month she's gotten worse. I wonder if perhaps she isn't a little simple-minded?'

'Ah, Smith, always the conservative. Well, here's my house. Now, would you like to know my secret? How I made it out this evening?'

'Will you really tell?'

'Look up, there!' said Braling.

They both stared up through the dark air.

In the window above them, on the second floor, a shade was raised. A man about thirty-five years old, with a touch of grey at either temple, sad grey eyes, and a small thin moustache looked down at them.

'Why, that's *you*!' cried Smith.

'Sh-h-h, not so loud!' Braling waved upwards. The man in

the window gestured significantly and vanished.

'I must be insane,' said Smith.

'Hold on a moment.'

They waited.

The street door of the apartment opened and the tall spare gentleman with the moustache and the grieved eyes came out to meet them.

'Hello, Braling,' he said.

'Hello, Braling,' said Braling.

They were identical.

Smith stared. 'Is this your twin brother? I never knew — '

'No, no,' said Braling quietly. 'Bend close. Put your ear to Braling Two's chest.'

Smith hesitated then leaned forward to place his head against the uncomplaining ribs.

Tick-tick-tick-tick-tick-tick-tick-tick.

'Oh no! It *can't* be!'

'It is.'

'Let me listen again.'

Tick-tick-tick-tick-tick-tick-tick-tick.

Smith staggered back and fluttered his eyelids, appalled. He reached out and touched the warm hands and the cheeks of the thing.

'Where'd you get him?'

'Isn't he excellently fashioned?'

'Incredible. Where?'

'Give the man your card, Braling Two.'

Braling Tow did a magic trick and produced a white card:

MARIONETTES, INC.

Duplicate self or friends; new humanoid plastic 1990 models, guaranteed against all physical wear. From $7,600 to our $15,000 de luxe model.

'No,' said Smith.

'Yes,' said Braling.

'Naturally,' said Braling Two.

'How long has this gone on?'

'I've had him for a month. I keep him in the cellar in a toolbox. My wife never goes downstairs, and I have the only lock and key to that box. Tonight I said I wished to take a walk to buy a cigar. I went down cellar and took Braling Two out of his box and sent him back up to sit with my wife while I came on out to see you, Smith.'

'Wonderful! He even *smells* like you: Bond Street and Melachrinos!'

'It may be splitting hairs, but I think it highly ethical. After all, what my wife wants most of all is *me*. This marionette *is* me to the hairiest detail. I've been home all evening. I shall be home with her for the next month. In the meantime another gentleman will be in Rio after ten years of waiting. When I return from Rio, Braling Two here will go back in his box.'

Smith thought that over a minute or two. 'Will he walk around without sustenance for a month?' he finally asked.

'For six months if necessary. And he's built to do everything — eat, sleep, perspire — everything, natural as natural is. You'll take good care of my wife, won't you, Braling Two?'

'Your wife is rather nice,' said Braling Two. 'I've grown rather fond of her.'

Smith was beginning to tremble. 'How long has Marionettes, Inc., been in business?'

'Secretly, for two years.'

'Could I — I mean, is there a possibility — ' Smith took his friend's elbow earnestly. 'Can you tell me where I can get one, a robot, a marionette, for myself? You *will* give me the address, won't you?'

'Here you are.'

Smith took the card and turned it round and round. 'Thank you,' he said. 'You don't know what this means. Just a little respite. A night or so, once a month even. My wife loves me so much she can't bear to have me gone an hour. I love her dearly, you know, but remember the old poem: "Love will fly if held too lightly, love will die if held too tightly." I just want her to relax her grip a little bit.'

'You're lucky, at least, that your wife loves you. Hate's my problem. Not so easy.'

'Oh, Nettie loves me madly. It will be my task to make her love me comfortably.'

'Good luck to you, Smith. Do drop around while I'm in Rio. It will seem strange, if you suddenly stop calling by, to my wife. You're to treat Braling Two, here, just like me.'

'Right! Good-bye. And thank you.'

Smith went smiling down the street. Braling and Braling Two turned and walked into the apartment hall.

On the crosstown bus Smith whistled softly, turning the white card in his fingers:

> Clients must be pledged to secrecy, for while an act is pending in Congress to legalize Marionettes, Inc., it is still a felony, if caught, to use one.

'Well,' said Smith.

> Clients must have a mould made of their body and a colour index check of their eyes, lips, hair, skin, etc. Clients must expect to wait for two months until their model is finished.

Not so long, thought Smith. Two months from now my ribs will have a chance to mend from the crushing they've taken. Two months from now my hand will heal from being so constantly held. Two months from now my bruised under-lip will begin to reshape itself. I don't mean to sound *ungrateful* . . . He flipped the card over.

> Marionettes, Inc., is two years old and has a fine record of satisfied customers behind it. Our motto is 'No Strings Attached'. Address: 43 South Wesley Drive.

The bus pulled to his stop; he alighted, and while humming up the stairs, he thought, Nettie and I have fifteen thousand in our joint bank account. I'll just slip eight thousand out as a business venture, you might say. The marionette will probably pay back my money, with interest, in many ways. Nettie needn't know. He unlocked the door and in a minute was in the bedroom. There lay Nettie, pale, huge, and piously asleep.

'Dear Nettie.' He was almost overwhelmed with remorse at her innocent face there in the semidarkness. 'If you were awake you would smother me with kisses and coo in my ear. Really, you make me feel like a criminal. You have been such a good, loving wife. Sometimes it is impossible for me to believe you married me instead of that Bud Chapman you once liked. It seems that in the last month you have loved me more widly than *ever* before.'

Tears came to his eyes. Suddenly he wished to kiss her, confess his love, tear up the card, forget the whole business. But as he moved to do this, his hand ached and his ribs cracked and groaned. He stopped, with a pained look in his eyes, and turned away. He moved out into the hall and through the dark rooms. Humming, he opened the kidney desk in the library and filched the bankbook. 'Just take eight thousand dollars is all,' he said. 'No more than that.' He stopped. 'Wait a minute.'

He rechecked the bankbook frantically. 'Hold on here!' he cried. 'Ten thousand dollars is missing!' He leaped up. 'There's only five thousand left! What's she done? What's

Nettie done with it? More hats, more clothes, more perfume! Or, wait — I know! She bought that little house on the Hudson she's been talking about for months, without so much as a by your leave!'

He stormed into the bedroom, righteous and indignant. What did she mean, taking their money like this? He bent over her. 'Nettie!' he shouted. 'Nettie, wake up!'

She did not stir. 'What've you done with my money!' he bellowed.

She stirred fitfully. The light from the street flushed over her beautiful cheeks.

There was something about her. His heart throbbed violently. His tongue dried. He shivered. His knees suddenly turned to water. He collapsed. 'Nettie, Nettie!' he cried. 'What've you done with my money!'

And then, the horrid thought. And then the terror and the loneliness engulfed him. And then the fever and disillusionment. For, without desiring to do so, he bent forward and yet forward again until his fevered ear was resting firmly and irrevocably upon her round pink bosom. 'Nettie!' he cried.

Tick-tick-tick-tick-tick-tick-tick-tick-tick-tick-tick.

As Smith walked away down the avenue in the night, Braling and Braling Two turned in at the door to the apartment. 'I'm glad he'll be happy too,' said Braling.

'Yes,' said Braling Two abstractedly.

'Well, it's the cellar box for you, B-Two.' Braling guided the other creature's elbow down the stairs to the cellar.

'That's what I want to talk to you about,' said Braling Two, as they reached the concrete floor and walked across it. 'The cellar. I don't like it. I don't like that toolbox.'

'I'll try and fix up something more comfortable.'

'Marionettes are made to move, not lie still. How would you like to lie in a box most of the time?'

'Well — '

'You wouldn't like it at all. I keep running. There's no way to shut me off. I'm perfectly alive and I have feelings.'

'It'll only be a few days now. I'll be off to Rio and you won't have to stay in the box. You can live upstairs.'

Braling Two gestured irritably. 'And when you come back from having a good time, back in the box I go.'

Braling said, 'They didn't tell me at the marionette shop that I'd get a difficult specimen.'

'There's a lot they don't know about us,' said Braling Two. 'We're pretty new. And we're sensitive. I hate the idea of you going off and laughing and lying in the sun in Rio while we're stuck here in the cold.'

'But I've wanted that trip all my life,' said Braling quietly.

He squinted his eyes and could see the sea and the mountains and the yellow sand. The sound of the waves was good to his inward mind. The sun was fine on his bared shoulders. The wine was most excellent.

'*I'll* never get to go to Rio,' said the other man. 'Have you thought of that?'

'No, I – '

'And another thing. Your wife.'

'What about her?' asked Braling, beginning to edge towards the door.

'I've grown quite fond of her.'

'I'm glad you're enjoying your employment.' Braling licked his lips nervously.

'I'm afraid you don't understand. I think – I'm in love with her.'

Braling took another step and froze. 'You're *what*?'

'And I've been thinking,' said Braling Two, 'how nice it is in Rio and how I'll never get there, and I've thought about your wife and – I think we could be very happy.'

'Th-that's nice.' Braling strolled as casually as he could to the cellar door. 'You won't mind waiting a moment, will you? I have to make a phone call.'

'To whom?' Braling Two frowned.

'No one important.'

'To Marionettes, Incorporated? To tell them to come get me?'

'No, no – nothing like that!' He tried to rush out the door.

A metal-firm grip seized his wrists. 'Don't run!'

'Take your hands off!'

'No.'

'Did my wife put you up to this?'

'No.'

'Did she guess? Did she talk to you? Does she know? Is *that* it?' He screamed. A hand clapped over his mouth.

'You'll never know, will you?' Braling Two smiled delicately. 'You'll never know.'

Braling struggled. 'She *must* have guessed; she *must* have affected you!'

Braling Two said, 'I'm going to put you in the box, lock it, and lose the key. Then I'll buy another Rio ticket for your wife.'

'Now, now, wait a minute. Hold on. Don't be rash. Let's talk this over!'

'Good-bye, Braling.'

Braling stiffened. 'What do you mean, "good-bye"?'

Ten minutes later Mrs Braling awoke. She put her hand to her cheek. Someone had just kissed it. She shivered and looked up. 'Why – you haven't done that in years,' she murmured.

'We'll see what we can do about that,' someone said.

No Particular Night
or Morning

He had smoked a packet of cigarettes in two hours.

'How far out in space are we?'

'A billion miles.'

'A billion miles from where?' said Hitchcock.

'It all depends,' said Clemens, not smoking at all. 'A billion miles from home, you might say.'

'Then say it.'

'Home. Earth. New York. Chicago. Wherever you were from.'

'I don't even remember,' said Hitchcock. 'I don't even believe there is an Earth now, do you?'

'Yes,' said Clemens. 'I dreamt about it this morning.'

'There is no morning in space.'

'During the night, then.'

'It's always night,' said Hitchcock quietly. 'Which night do you mean?'

'Shut up,' said Clemens irritably. 'Let me finish.'

Hitchcock lit another cigarette. His hand did not shake, but it looked as if, inside the sunburned flesh, it might be tremoring all to itself, a small tremor in each hand and a large invisible tremor in his body. The two men sat on the observation corridor floor, looking out at the stars. Clemens's eyes flashed, but Hitchcock's eyes focused on nothing; they were blank and puzzled.

'I woke up at 0500 hours myself,' said Hitchcock, as if he were talking to his right hand. 'And I heard myself screaming, "Where am I? where am I?" And the answer was "Nowhere!" And I said, "Where've I been?" And I said, "Earth!" "What's Earth?" I wondered. "Where I was born,"

I said. But it was nothing and worse than nothing. I don't believe in anything I can't see or hear or touch. I can't see Earth, so why should I believe in it? It's safer this way, not to believe.'

'There's Earth.' Clemens pointed, smiling. 'That point of light there.'

'That's not Earth; that's our sun. You can't see Earth from here.'

'I can see it. I have a good memory.'

'It's not the *same*, you fool,' said Hitchcock suddenly. There was a touch of anger in his voice. 'I mean *see* it. I've always been that way. When I'm in Boston, New York is dead. When I'm in New York, Boston is dead. When I don't *see* a man for a day, he's dead. When he comes walking down the street, my God, it's a resurrection. I do a dance, almost, I'm so glad to see him. I used to, anyway. I don't dance any more. I just look. And when the man walks off, he's dead again.'

Clemens laughed. 'It's simply that your mind works on a primitive level. You can't hold on to things. You've got no imagination, Hitchcock, old man. You've got to learn to hold on.'

'Why should I hold on to things I can't use?' said Hitchcock, his eyes wide, still staring into space. 'I'm practical. If Earth isn't here for me to walk on, you want me to walk on a memory? That *hurts*. Memories, as my father once said, are porcupines. To hell with them! Stay away from them. They make you unhappy. They ruin your work. They make you cry.'

'I'm walking on Earth right now,' said Clemens, squinting to himself, blowing smoke.

'You're kicking porcupines. Later in the day you won't be able to eat lunch, and you'll wonder why,' said Hitchcock in a dead voice. 'And it'll be because you've got a footful of quills aching in you. To hell with it! If I can't drink it, pinch it, punch it, or lie on it, then I say drop it in the sun. I'm dead to Earth. It's dead to me. There's no one in New York weeping for me tonight. Shove New York. There isn't any season here; winter and summer are gone. So is spring, and autumn. It isn't any particular night or morning; it's space and space. The only thing right now is you and me and this rocket ship. And the only thing I'm positive of is *me*. That's all of it.'

Clemens ignored this. 'I'm putting a dime in the phone slot right now,' he said, pantomiming it with a slow smile. 'And calling my girl in Evanston. Hello, Barbara!'

The rocket sailed on through space.

The lunch bell rang at 1305 hours. The men ran by on soft rubber sneakers and sat at the cushioned tables.

Clemens wasn't hungry.

'See, what did I tell you!' said Hitchcock. 'You and your damned porcupines! Leave them alone, like I told you. Look at me, shovelling away food.' He said this with a mechanical, slow, and unhumorous voice. 'Watch me.' He put a big piece of pie in his mouth and felt it with his tongue. He looked at the pie on his plate as if to see the texture. He moved it with his fork. He felt the fork handle. He mashed the lemon filling and watched it jet up between the tines. Then he touched a bottle of milk all over and poured out half a quart into a glass, listening to it. He looked at the milk as if to make it whiter. He drank the milk so swiftly that he couldn't have tasted it. He had eaten his entire lunch in a few minutes, cramming it in feverishly, and now he looked around for more, but it was gone. He gazed out the window of the rocket, blankly. 'Those aren't real either,' he said.

'What?' asked Clemens.

'The stars. Who's ever touched one? I can see them, sure, but what's the use of seeing a thing that's a million or a billion miles away? Anything that far off isn't worth bothering with.'

'Why did you come on this trip?' asked Clemens suddenly.

Hitchcock peered into his amazingly empty milk glass and clenched it tight, then relaxed his hand and clenched it again. 'I don't know.' He ran his tongue on the glass rim. 'I just had to, is all. How do you know why you do anything in this life?'

'You liked the idea of space travel? Going places?'

'I don't know. Yes. No. It wasn't going places. It was being between.' Hitchcock for the first time tried to focus his eyes upon something, but it was so nebulous and far off that his eyes couldn't make the adjustment, though he worked his face and hands. 'Mostly it was space. So much space. I liked the idea of nothing on top, nothing on the bottom, and a lot of nothing in between, and me in the middle of the nothing.'

'I never heard it put that way before.'

'*I* just put it that way; I hope you listened.'

Hitchcock took out his cigarettes and lit up and began to suck and blow smoke, again and again.

Clemens said, 'What sort of childhood did you have, Hitchcock?'

'I was never young. Whoever I was then is dead. That's more of your quills. I don't want a hideful, thanks. I've always figured it that you die each day and each day is a box, you see, all numbered and neat; but never go back and lift the lids, because you've died a couple of thousand times in your life, and that's a lot of corpses, each dead a different way, each with a worse expression. Each of those days is a different you, somebody you don't know or understand or want to understand.'

'You're cutting yourself off, that way.'

'Why should I have anything to do with that younger Hitchcock? He was a fool, and he was yanked around and taken advantage of and used. His father was no good, and he was glad when his mother died, because she was the same. Should I go back and see his face on that day and gloat over it? He was a fool.'

'We're all fools,' said Clemens, 'all the time. It's just we're a different kind each day. We think, I'm not a fool today. I've learned my lesson. I was a fool yesterday but not this morning. Then tomorrow we find out that, yes, we were a fool today too. I think the only way we can grow and get on in this world is to accept the fact that we're not perfect and live accordingly.'

'I don't want to remember imperfect things,' said Hitchcock. 'I can't shake hands with that younger Hitchcock, can I? Where is he? Can you find him for me? He's dead, so to hell with him! I won't shape what I do tomorrow by some lousy thing I did yesterday.'

'You've got it wrong.'

'Let me have it then.' Hitchcock sat, finished his meal, looking out the port. The other men glanced at him.

'Do meteors exist?' asked Hitchcock.

'You know damn well they do.'

'In our radar machines — yes, as streaks of light in space. No, I don't believe in anything that doesn't exist and act in my presence. Sometimes' — he nodded at the men finishing their food — 'sometimes I don't believe in anyone or anything but me.' He sat up. 'Is there an upstairs to this ship?'

'Yes.'

'I've got to see it immediately.'

'Don't get excited.'

'You wait here; I'll be right back.' Hitchcock walked out swiftly. The other men sat nibbling their food slowly. A moment passed. One of the men raised his head. 'How long's this been going on? I mean Hitchcock.'

'Just today.'

'He acted funny the other day too.'

'Yes, but it's worse today.'

'Has anyone told the psychiatrist?'

'We thought he'd come out of it. Everyone has a little touch of space the first time out. I've had it. You get wildly philosophical, then frightened. You break into a sweat, then you doubt your parentage, you don't believe in Earth, you get drunk, wake up with a hang-over, and that's it.'

'But Hitchcock don't get drunk,' said someone. 'I wish he would.'

'How'd he ever get past the examining board?'

'How'd we all get past? They need men. Space scares the hell out of most people. So the board lets a lot of borderlines through.'

'That man isn't a borderline,' said someone. 'He's a fall-off-a-cliff-and-no-bottom-to-hit.'

They waited for five minutes. Hitchcock didn't come back.

Clemens finally got up and went out and climbed the circular stair to the flight deck above. Hitchcock was there, touching the wall tenderly.

'It's here,' he said.

'Of course it is.'

'I was afraid it might not be.' Hitchock peered at Clemens. 'And you're alive.'

'I have been for a long time.'

'No,' said Hitchcock. 'Now, just now, this *instant*, while you're here with me, you're alive. A moment ago you weren't anything.'

'I was to me,' said the other.

'That's not important. You weren't here with me,' said Hitchcock. 'Only that's important. Is the crew down below?'

'Yes.'

'Can you prove it?'

'Look, Hitchcock, you'd better see Dr Edwards. I think you need a little servicing.'

'No, I'm all right. Who's the doctor, anyway? Can you prove he's on this ship?'

'I can. All I have to do is call him.'

'No. I mean, standing here, in this instant, you can't prove he's here, can you?'

'Not without moving, I can't.'

'You see. You have no mental evidence. That's what I want, a mental evidence I can *feel*. I don't want physical evidence, proof you have to go out and drag in. I want evidence that you can carry in your mind and always touch and smell and feel. But there's no way to do that. In order to believe in a thing you've got to carry it with you. You can't carry the Earth, or a man, in your pocket. I want a way to do that, carry things with me always, so I can believe in them. How clumsy to have to go to all the trouble of going out and bringing in something terribly physical to prove something. I hate physical things because they can be left behind and it becomes impossible to believe in them.'

'Those are the rules of the game.'

'I want to change them. Wouldn't it be fine if we could prove things with our mind, and know for certain that things are always in their place? I'd like to know what a place is *like* when I'm *not there*. I'd like to be *sure*.'

'That's not possible.'

'You know,' said Hitchcock, 'I first got the idea of coming out into space about five years ago. About the time I lost my job. Did you know I wanted to be a writer? Oh yes, one of those men who always talk about writing but rarely write. And too much temper. So I lost my good job and left the editorial business and couldn't get another job and went on down hill. Then my wife died. You see, nothing stays where you put it — you can't trust material things. I had to put my boy in an aunt's trust, and things got worse; then one day I had a story published with my name on it, but it wasn't me.'

'I don't get you.'

Hitchcock's face was pale and sweating.

'I can only say that I looked at the page with my name under the title. By Joseph Hitchcock. But it was some other man. There was no way to *prove* — actually *prove*, really prove

— that that man was me. The story was familiar — I knew I had written it — but that name on the paper still was not me. It was a symbol, a name. It was alien. And then I realized that even if I did become successful at writing, it would never mean a thing to me, because I couldn't identify myself with that name. It would be soot and ashes. So I didn't write any more. I was never sure, anyway, that the stories I had in my desk a few days later were mine, though I remembered typing them. There was always that gap of proof. That gap between doing and having done. What is done is dead and is not proof, for it is not an action. Only actions are important. And pieces of paper were remains of actions done and over and now unseen. The proof of doing was over and done. Nothing but memory remained, and I didn't trust my memory. Could I actually *prove* I'd written these stories? No. Can *any* author? I mean *proof*. I mean action as proof. No. Not really. Not unless someone sits in the room while you type, and then maybe you're doing it from memory. And once a thing is accomplished there is no proof, only memory. So then I began to find gaps between everything. I doubted I was married or had a child or ever had a job in my life. I doubted that I had been born in Illinois and had a drunken father and swinish mother. I couldn't prove anything. Oh yes, people could say, "You are thus-and-so and such-and-such," but that was nothing.'

'You should get your mind off stuff like that,' said Clemens.

'I can't. All the gaps and spaces. And that's how I got to thinking about the stars. I thought how I'd like to be in a rocket ship in space, in nothing, in *nothing*, going on into nothing with just a thin something, a thin eggshell of metal holding me, going on away from all the somethings with gaps in them that couldn't prove themselves. I knew then that the only happiness for me was space. When I get to Aldebaran II I'll sign up to return on the five-year journey to Earth and so go back and forth like a shuttlecock all the rest of my life.'

'Have you talked about this to the psychiatrist?'

'So he could try to mortar up the gaps for me, fill in the gulfs with noise and warm water and words and hands touching me, and all that? No, thanks.' Hitchcock stopped. 'I'm getting worse, aren't I? I thought so. This morning when I woke up I thought, I'm getting worse. Or is it better?' He paused again and cocked an eye at Clemens. 'Are you there? Are you *really* there? Go on, prove it.'

Clemens slapped him on the arm, hard.

'Yes,' said Hitchcock, rubbing his arm, looking at it very thoroughly, wonderingly, massaging it. 'You were there. For a brief fraction of an instant. But I wonder if you are – *now*.'

'See you later,' said Clemens. He was on his way to find the doctor. He walked away.

A bell rang. Two bells, three bells rang. The ship rocked as if a hand had slapped it. There was a sucking sound, the sound of a vacuum cleaner turned on. Clemens heard the screams and felt the air thin. The air hissed away about his ears. Suddenly there was nothing in his nose or lungs. He stumbled and then the hissing stopped.

He heard someone cry, 'A meteor!' Another said, 'It's patched!' And this was true. The ship's emergency spider, running over the outside of the hull had slapped a hot patch on the hole in the metal and welded it tight.

Someone was talking and talking and then beginning to shout at a distance. Clemens ran along the corridor through the freshening, thickening air. As he turned in at a bulkhead he saw the hole in the steel wall, freshly sealed; he saw the meteor fragments lying about the room like bits of a toy. He saw the captain and the members of the crew and a man lying on the floor. It was Hitchcock. His eyes were closed and he was crying. 'It tried to kill me,' he said, over and over. 'It tried to kill me.' They got him to his feet. 'It can't do that,' said Hitchcock. 'That's not how it should be. Things like that can't happen, can they? It came in after *me*. Why did it do that?'

'All right, all right, Hitchcock,' said the captain.

The doctor was bandaging a small cut on Hitchcock's arm. Hitchcock looked up, his face pale, and saw Clemens there looking at him. 'It tried to *kill* me,' he said.

'I know,' said Clemens.

Seventeen hours passed. The ship moved on in space.

Clemens stepped through a bulkhead and waited. The psychiatrist and the captain were there. Hitchcock sat on the floor with his legs drawn up to his chest, arms wrapped tight about them.

'Hitchcock,' said the captain.

No answer.

'Hitchcock, listen to me,' said the psychiatrist.

They turned to Clemens. 'You're his friend?'

'Yes.'

'Do you want to help us?'

'If I can.'

'It was that damned meteor,' said the captain. 'This might not have happened if it hadn't been for that.'

'It would've come anyway, sooner or later,' said the doctor. To Clemens: 'You might talk to him.'

Clemens walked quietly over and crouched by Hitchcock and began to shake his arm gently, calling in a low voice, 'Hey there, Hitchcock.'

No reply.

'Hey, it's me. Me, Clemens,' said Clemens. 'Look, I'm here.' He gave the arm a little slap. He massaged the rigid neck, gently, and the back of the bent-down head. He glanced at the psychiatrist, who sighed very softly. The captain shrugged.

'Shock treatment, Doctor?'

The psychiatrist nodded. 'We'll start within the hour.'

Yes, thought Clemens, shock treatment. Play a dozen jazz

records for him, wave a bottle of fresh green chlorophyll and dandelions under his nose, put grass under his feet, squirt Chanel on the air, cut his hair, clip his fingernails, bring him a woman, shout, bang and crash at him, fry him with electricity, fill the gap and the gulf, but where's your proof? You can't keep proving to him forever. You can't entertain a baby with rattles and sirens all night every night for the next thirty years. Sometime you've got to stop. When you do that, he's lost again. That is, if he pays any attention to you at all.

'Hitchcock!' he cried, as loud as he could, almost frantically, as if he himself were falling over a cliff. 'It's me. It's your pal! Hey!'

Clemens turned and walked away out of the silent room.

Twelve hours later another alarm bell rang.

After all of the running had died down, the captain explained: 'Hitchcock snapped out of it for a minute or so. He was alone. He climbed into a space suit. He opened an airlock. Then he walked out into space – alone.'

Clemens blinked through the immense glass port, where there was a blur of stars and distant blackness. 'He's out there now?'

'Yes. A million miles behind us. We'd never find him. First time I knew he was outside the ship was when his helmet radio came in on our control-room beam. I heard him talking to himself.'

'What did he say?'

'Something like "No more space ship now. Never was any. No people. No people in all the universe. Never were any. No plants. No stars." That's what he said. And then he said something about his hands and feet and legs. "No hands," he said. "I haven't any hands any more. Never had any. No feet. Never had any. Can't prove it. No body. Never had any. No lips. No face. No head. Nothing. Only space. Only space. Only the gap." '

The men turned quietly to look from the glass port out into the remote and cold stars.

Space, thought Clemens. The space that Hitchcock loved so well. Space, with nothing on top, nothing on the bottom; a lot of empty nothings between, and Hitchcock falling in the middle of nothing, on his way to no particular night and no particular morning . . .

The City

The city waited twenty thousand years.

The planet moved through space and the flowers of the fields grew up and fell away, and still the city waited; and the rivers of the planet rose and waned and turned to dust. Still the city waited. The winds that had been young and wild grew old and serene, and the clouds of the sky that had been ripped and torn were left alone to drift in idle whitenesses. Still the city waited.

The city waited with its windows and its black obsidian walls and its sky towers and its unpennanted turrets, with its untrod streets and its untouched doorknobs, with not a scrap of paper or a fingerprint upon it. The city waited while the planet arced in space, following its orbit about a blue-white sun, and the seasons passed from ice to fire and back to ice and then to green fields and yellow summer meadows.

It was on a summer afternoon in the middle of the twenty thousandth year that the city ceased waiting.

In the sky a rocket appeared.

The rocket soared over, turned, came back, and landed in the shale meadow fifty yards from the obsidian wall.

There were booted footsteps in the thin grass and calling voices from men within the rocket to men without.

'Ready?'

'All right, men. Careful! Into the city. Jensen, you and Hutchinson patrol ahead. Keep a sharp eye.'

The city opened secret nostrils in its black walls and a steady suction vent deep in the body of the city drew storms of air back through channels, through thistle filters and dust collectors, to a fine and tremblingly delicate series of coils and webs which glowed with silver light. Again and again the immense suctions occurred; again and again the odours from the meadow were borne upon warm winds into the city.

'Fire odour, the scent of a fallen meteor, hot metal. A ship has come from another world. The brass smell, the dusty fire smell of burned powder, sulphur, and rocket brimstone.'

This information, stamped on tapes which sprocketed into slots, slid down through yellow cogs into further machines.

Click-chakk-chakk-chakk.

A calculator made the sound of a metronome. Five, six, seven, eight, nine. Nine men! An instantaneous typewriter inked this message on tape which slithered and vanished.

Clickety-click-chakk-chakk.

The city awaited the soft tread of their rubberoid boots.

The great city nostrils dilated again.

The smell of butter. In the city air, from the stalking men, faintly, the aura which wafted to the great Nose broke down into memories of milk, cheese, ice cream, butter, the effluvia of a dairy economy.

Click-click.

'Careful, men!'

'Jones, get your gun out. Don't be a fool!'

'The city's dead; why worry?'

'You can't tell.'

Now, at the barking talk, the Ears awoke. After centuries of listening to winds that blew small and faint, of hearing leaves strip from trees and grass grow softly in the time of melting snows, now the Ears oiled themselves in a self-lubrication, drew taut, great drums upon which the heart-beat of the invaders might pummel and thud delicately as the tremor of a gnat's wing. The Ears listened and the Nose siphoned up great chambers of odour.

The perspiration of frightened men arose. There were islands of sweat under their arms, and sweat in their hands as they held their guns.

The Nose sifted and worried this air, like a connoisseur busy with an ancient vintage.

Chikk-chikk-chakk-click.

Information rotated down on parallel check tapes. Perspiration; chlorides such-and-such per cent; sulphates so-and-so; urea nitrogen, ammonia nitrogen, *thus*: creatinine, sugar, lactic acid, *there*!

Bells rang. Small totals jumped up.

The Nose whispered, expelling the tested air. The great Ears listened:

'I think we should go back to the rocket, Captain.'

'I give the orders, Mr Smith!'

'Yes, sir.'

'You, up there! Patrol! *See* anything?'

'Nothing, sir. Looks like it's been dead a long time!'

'You see, Smith? Nothing to fear.'

'I don't like it. I don't know why. You ever feel you've seen a place before? Well, this city's too familiar.'

'Nonsense. This planetary system's billions of miles from Earth; we couldn't possibly've been here ever before. Ours is the only light-year rocket in existence.'

'That's how I feel, anyway, sir. I think we should get out.'

The footsteps faltered. There was only the sound of the intruder's breath on the still air.

The Ear heard and quickened. Rotors glided, liquids glittered in small creeks through valves and blowers. A formula and a concoction – one followed another. Moments later, responding to the summons of the Ear and nose, through giant holes in the city walls a fresh vapour blew out over the invaders.

'Smell *that*, Smith? Ahh. Green grass. Ever smell anything better? By God, I just like to stand here and smell it.'

Invisible chlorophyll blew among the standing men.

'*Ahh!*'

The footsteps continued.

'Nothing wrong with *that*, eh, Smith? Come on!'

The Ear and Nose relaxed a billionth of a fraction. The countermove had succeeded. The pawns were proceeding forward.

Now the cloudy Eyes of the city moved out of fog and mist.

'Captain, the windows!'

'What?'

'Those house windows, there! I saw them move!'

'*I* didn't see it.'

'They shifted. They changed colour. From dark to light.'

'Look like ordinary square windows to me.'

Blurred objects focused. In the mechanical ravines of the city oiled shafts plunged, balance wheels dipped over into green oil pools. The window frames flexed. The windows gleamed.

Below, in the street, walked two men, a patrol, followed, at a safe interval, by seven more. Their uniforms were white, their faces as pink as if they had been slapped; their eyes were blue. They walked upright, upon hind legs, carrying metal weapons. Their feet were booted. They were males, with eyes, ears, mouths, noses.

The windows trembled. The windows thinned. They dilated imperceptibly, like the irises of numberless eyes.

'I tell you, Captain, it's the windows!'

'Get along.'

'I'm going back, sir.'

'What?'

'I'm going back to the rocket.'

'Mr Smith!'

'I'm not falling into any trap!'

'Afraid of an empty city?'

The others laughed, uneasily.

'Go on, laugh!'

The street was stone-cobbled, each stone three inches

wide, six inches long. With a move unrecognizable as such, the street settled. It weighed the invaders.

In a machine cellar a red wand touched a numeral: 178 pounds . . . 210, 154, 210, 198 — each man weighed, registered and the record spooled down into a correlative darkness.

Now the city was fully awake!

Now the vents sucked and blew air, the tobacco odour from the invaders' mouths, the green soap scent from their hands. Even their eyeballs had a delicate odour. The city detected it, and this information formed totals which scurried down to total other totals. The crystal windows glittered, the Ear tautened and skinned the drum of its hearing tight, tighter — all of the senses of the city swarming like a fall of unseen snow, counting the respiration and the dim hidden heartbeats of the men, listening, watching, tasting.

For the streets were like tongues, and where the men passed, the taste of their heels ebbed down through stone pores to be calculated on litmus. This chemical totality, so subtly collected, was appended to the now increasing sums waiting the final calculation among the whirling wheels and whispering spokes.

Footsteps. Running.

'Come back! Smith!'

'No, blast you!'

'Get him, men!'

Footsteps rushing.

A final test. The city, having listened, watched, tasted, felt, weighed, and balanced, must perform a final task.

A trap flung wide in the street. The captain, unseen by the others, running, vanished.

. Hung by his feet, a razor drawn across his throat, another down his chest, his carcass instantly emptied of its entrails, exposed upon a table under the street, in a hidden cell, the captain died. Great crystal microscopes stared at the red twines of muscle; bodiless fingers probed the still-pulsing heart. The flaps of his sliced skin were pinned to the table while hands shifted parts of his body like a quick and curious player of chess, using the red pawns and the red pieces.

Above on the street the men ran. Smith ran, men shouted. Smith shouted, and below in this curious room blood flowed into capsules, was shaken, spun, shoved on smear slides under further microscopes, counts made, temperatures taken, heart cut in seventeen sections, liver and kidneys expertly halved. Brain was drilled and scooped from bone socket, nerves pulled forth like the dead wires of a switchboard, muscles plucked for elasticity, while in the electric subterrene of the city the Mind at last totalled out its grandest total and all of the machinery ground to a monstrous and momentary halt.

The total.

These are men. These are men from a far world, a certain planet, and they have certain eyes, certain ears, and they walk upon legs in a specified way and carry weapons and think and fight, and they have particular hearts and all such organs as are recorded from long ago.

Above, men ran down the street towards the rocket.

Smith ran.

The total.

These are our enemies. These are the ones we have waited for twenty thousand years to see again. These are the men upon whom we waited to visit revenge. Everything totals. These are the men of a planet called Earth, who declared war upon Taollan twenty thousand years ago, who kept us in slavery and ruined us and destroyed us with a great disease. Then they went off to live in another galaxy to escape that disease which they visited upon us after ransacking our world. They have forgotten that war and that time, and they have forgotten us. But we have not forgotten them. These are our enemies. This is certain. Our waiting is done.

'Smith, come back!'

Quickly. Upon the red table, with the spread-eagled captain's body empty, new hands began a flight of motion. Into the wet interior were placed organs of copper, brass, silver, aluminium, rubber and silk; spiders spun gold web which was stung into the skin; a heart was attached, and into the skull case was fitted a platinum brain which hummed and fluttered small sparkles of blue fire, and the wires led down through the body to the arms and legs. In a moment the body was sewn tight, the incisions waxed, healed at neck and throat and about the skull – perfect, fresh, new.

The captain sat up and flexed his arms.

'Stop!'

On the street the captain reappeared, raised his gun and fired.

Smith fell, a bullet in his heart.

The other men turned.

The captain ran to them.

'That fool! Afraid of a city!'

They looked at the body of Smith at their feet.

They looked at their captain, and their eyes widened and narrowed.

'Listen to me,' said the captain. 'I have something important to tell you.'

Now the city which had weighed and tasted and smelled them, which had used all its powers save one, prepared to use its final ability, the power of speech. It did not speak with the rage and hostility of its massed walls or towers, nor with the bulk of its cobbled avenues and fortresses of machinery. It spoke with the quiet voice of one man.

'I am no longer your captain,' he said. 'Nor am I a man.'

The men moved back.

'I am the city,' he said, and smiled.

'I've waited two hundred centuries,' he said. 'I've waited

for the sons of the sons of the sons to return.'

'Captain, sir!'

'Let me continue. Who built me? The city. The men who died built me. The old race who once lived here. The people whom the Earth Men left to die of a terrible disease, a form of leprosy with no cure. And the men of that old race, dreaming of the day when Earth Men might return, built this city, and the name of this city was and is Revenge, upon the Planet of Darkness, near the shore of the Sea of Centuries, by the Mountains of the Dead; all very poetic. This city was to be a balancing machine, a litmus, an antenna to test all future space travellers. In twenty thousand years only two other rockets landed here. One from a distant galaxy called Ennt, and the inhabitants of that craft were tested, weighed, found wanting, and let free, unscathed, from the city. As were the visitors in the second ship. But today! At long last, you've come! The revenge will be carried out to the last detail. Those men have been dead two hundred centuries, but they left a city here to welcome you.'

'Captain, sir, you're not feeling well. Perhaps you'd better come back to the ship, sir.'

The city trembled.

The pavements opened and the men fell, screaming. Falling, they saw bright razors flash to meet them!

Time passed. Soon came the call:

'Smith?'

'Here!'

'Jensen?'

'Here!'

'Jones, Hutchinson, Springer?'

'Here!' 'Here!' 'Here!'

They stood by the door of the rocket.

'We return to Earth immediately.'

'Yes, sir!'

The incisions on their necks were invisible, as were their

hidden brass hearts and silver organs and the fine golden wire of their nerves. There was a faint electric hum from their heads.

'On the double!'

Nine men hurried the golden bombs of disease culture into the rocket.

'These are to be dropped on Earth.'

'Right, sir!'

The rocket valve slammed. The rocket jumped into the sky.

As the thunder faded, the city lay upon the summer meadow. Its glass eyes were dulled over. The Ear relaxed, the great nostril vents stopped, the streets no longer weighed or balanced, and the hidden machinery paused in its bath of oil.

In the sky the rocket dwindled.

Slowly, pleasurably, the city enjoyed the luxury of dying.

The Fire Balloons

Fire exploded over summer night lawns. You saw sparkling faces of uncles and aunts. Skyrockets fell up in the brown shining eyes of cousins on the porch, and the cold charred sticks thumped down in dry meadows far away.

The Very Reverend Father Joseph Daniel Peregrine opened his eyes. What a dream: he and his cousins with their fiery play at his grandfather's ancient Ohio home so many years ago!

He lay listening to the great hollow of the church, the other cells where others Fathers lay. Had they, too, on the eve of the flight of the rocket *Crucifix*, lain with memories of the Fourth of July? Yes. This was like those breathless Independence dawns when you waited for the first concussion and rushed out on the dewy sidewalks, your hands full of loud miracles.

So here they were, the Episcopal Fathers, in the breathing dawn before they pinwheeled off to Mars, leaving their incense through the velvet cathedral of space.

'Should we go at all?' whispered Father Peregrine. 'Shouldn't we solve our own sins on Earth? Aren't we running from our lives here?'

He arose, his fleshy body, with its rich look of strawberries, milk, and steak, moving heavily.

'Or is it sloth?' he wondered. 'Do I dread the journey?'

He stepped into the needle-spray shower.

'But I shall take you to Mars, body.' He addressed himself. 'Leaving old sins here. And on to Mars to find *new* sins?' A delightful thought, almost. Sins no one had ever thought of. Oh, he himself had written a little book: *The Problem of Sin on Other Worlds,* ignored as somehow not serious enough by his Episcopal brethren.

Only last night, over a final cigar, he and Father Stone had talked of it.

'On Mars sin might appear as virtue. We must guard against virtuous acts there that, later, might be found to be sins!' said Father Peregrine, beaming. 'How exciting! It's been centuries since so much adventure has accompanied the prospect of being a missionary!'

'*I* will recognize sin,' said Father Stone bluntly, '*even* on Mars.'

'Oh, we priests pride ourselves on being litmus paper, changing colour in sin's presence,' retorted Father Peregrine, 'but what if Martian chemistry is such we do not colour *at all*! If there are new senses on Mars, you must admit the possibility of unrecognizable sin.'

'If there is no malice aforethought, there is no sin or punishment for same − the Lord assures us that,' Father Stone replied.

'On Earth, yes. But perhaps a Martian sin might inform the subconscious of its evil, telepathically, leaving the conscious mind of man free to act, seemingly without malice! What *then*?'

'What *could* there be in the way of new sins?'

Father Peregrine leaned heavily forward. 'Adam *alone* did not sin. Add Eve and you add temptation. Add a second man and you make adultery possible. With the addition of sex or people, you add sin. If men were armless they could not strangle with their hands. You would not have that particular sin of murder. Add arms, and you add the possibility of a new violence. Amoebas cannot sin because they reproduce by fission. They do not covet wives or murder each other. Add sex to amoebas, add arms and legs, and you would have murder and adultery. Add an arm or leg or person, or take away each, and you add or subtract possible evil. On Mars, what if there are five new senses, organs, invisible limbs we can't conceive of − then mightn't there be five *new sins?*'

Father Stone gasped. 'I think you *enjoy* this sort of thing!'

'I keep my mind alive, Father; just alive, is all.'

'Your mind's always juggling, isn't it? − mirrors, torches, plates.'

'Yes. Because sometimes the Church seems like those posed circus tableaux where the curtain lifts and men, white, zinc-oxide, talcum-powder statues, freeze to represent abstract Beauty. Very wonderful. But I hope there will always be room for me to dart about among the statues, don't you, Father Stone?'

Father Stone had moved away. 'I think we'd better go to bed. In a few hours we'll be jumping up to see your *new* sins, Father Peregrine.'

The rocket stood ready for the firing.

The Fathers walked from their devotions in the chilly morning, many a fine priest from New York or Chicago or Los Angeles − the Church was sending its best − walking across town to the frosty field. Walking, Father Peregrine remembered the Bishop's words:

'Father Peregrine, you will captain the missionaries, with Father Stone at your side. Having chosen you for this serious task, I find my reasons deplorably obscure, Father, but your pamphlet on planetary sin did not go unread. You are a flexible man. And Mars is like that uncleaned closet we have neglected for millenniums. Sin has collected there like bric-a-brac. Mars is twice Earth's age and has had double the number of Saturday nights, liquor baths, and eye-poppings at women as naked as white seals. When we open that closet door, things will fall on us. We need a quick, flexible man − one whose mind can dodge. Anyone a little too dogmatic might break in two. I feel you'll be resilient. Father, the job is yours.'

The Bishop and the Fathers knelt.

The blessing was said and the rocket given a little shower of holy water. Arising, the Bishop addressed them:

'I know you will go with God, to prepare the Martians for the reception of His Truth. I wish you all a *thoughtful* journey.'

They filed past the Bishop, twenty men, robes whispering, to deliver their hands into his kind hands before passing into the cleansed projectile.

'I wonder,' said Father Peregrine, at the last moment, 'if Mars is Hell? Only waiting for our arrival before it bursts into brimstone and fire.'

'Lord, be with us,' said Father Stone.

The rocket moved.

Coming out of space was like coming out of the most beautiful cathedral they had ever seen. Touching Mars was like touching the ordinary pavement outside the church five minutes after having *really* known your love for God.

The Fathers stepped gingerly from the steaming rocket and knelt upon Martian sand while Father Peregrine gave thanks.

'Lord, we thank Thee for the journey through Thy rooms. And, Lord, we have reached a new land, so we must have new eyes. We shall hear new sounds and must needs have new ears. And there will be new sins, for which we ask the gift of better and firmer and purer hearts. Amen.'

They arose.

And here was Mars like a sea under which they trudged in the guise of submarine biologists, seeking life. Here the territory of hidden sin. Oh, how carefully they must all balance, like grey feathers, in this new element, afraid that walking *itself* might be sinful; or breathing, or simple fasting!

And here was the mayor of First Town come to meet them with outstretched hand. 'What can I do for you, Father Peregrine?'

'We'd like to know about the Martians. For only if we know about them can we plan our church intelligently. Are they ten feet tall? We will build large doors. Are their skins blue or red or green? We must know when we put human figures in the stained glass so we may use the right skin colour. Are they heavy? We will build sturdy seats for them.'

'Father,' said the mayor, 'I don't think you should worry about the Martians. There are two races. One of them is pretty well dead. A few are in hiding. And the second race — well, they're not quite human.'

'Oh?' Father Peregrine's heart quickened.

'They're round luminous globes of light, Father, living in those hills. Man or beast, who can say? But they act intelligently, I hear.' The mayor shrugged. 'Of course, they're not men, so I don't think you'll care —'

'On the contrary,' said Father Peregrine swiftly. 'Intelligent, you say?'

'There's a story. A prospector broke his leg in those hills and would have died there. The blue spheres of light came at him. When he woke, he was down on a highway, and didn't know how he got there.'

'Drunk,' said Father Stone.

'That's the story,' said the mayor. 'Father Peregrine, with most of the Martians dead, and only these blue spheres, I frankly think you'd be better off in First City. Mars is opening up. It's a frontier now, like in the old days on Earth, out West, and in Alaska. Men are pouring up here. There's a couple thousand black Irish mechanics and miners and day labourers in First Town who need saving, because there're too many wicked women came with them, and too much ten-century-old Martian wine — '

Father Peregrine was gazing into the soft blue hills.

Father Stone cleared his throat. 'Well, Father?'

Father Peregrine did not hear. 'Spheres of blue *fire*?'

'Yes, Father.'

'Ah,' Father Peregrine sighed.

'Blue balloons.' Father Stone shook his head. 'A circus!'

Father Peregrine felt his wrists pounding. He saw the little frontier town with raw, fresh-built sin, and he saw the hills, old with the oldest and yet perhaps an even newer (to him) sin.

'Mayor, could your black Irish labourers cook one more day in hellfire?'

'I'd turn and baste them for you, Father.'

Father Peregrine nodded to the hills. 'Then that's where we'll go.'

There was a murmur from everyone.

'It would be so simple,' explained Father Peregrine, 'to go into town. I prefer to think that if the Lord walked here and people said, "Here is the beaten path," He would reply, "Show me the weeds. I will *make* a path." '

'But —'

'Father Stone, think how it would weigh upon us if we passed sinners by and did not extend our hands.'

'But globes of fire!'

'I imagine man looked funny to other animals when we first appeared. Yet he has a soul, for all his homeliness. Until we prove otherwise, let us assume that these fiery spheres have souls.'

'All right,' agreed the mayor, 'but you'll be back to town.'

'We'll see. First, some breakfast. Then you and I, Father Stone, will walk alone into the hills. I don't want to frighten those fiery Martians with machines or crowds. Shall we have breakfast?'

The Fathers ate in silence.

At nightfall Father Peregrine and Father Stone were high in the hills. They stopped and sat upon a rock to enjoy a moment of relaxation and waiting. The Martians had not as yet appeared and they both felt vaguely disappointed.

'I wonder — ' Father Peregrine mopped his face. 'Do you think if we called "Hello!" they might answer?'

'Father Peregrine, won't you ever be serious?'

'Not until the good Lord is. Oh, don't look so terribly shocked, please. The Lord is not serious. In fact, it is a little hard to know just what else He is except loving. And love has to do with humour, doesn't it? For you cannot love someone unless you put up with him, can you? And you cannot put up with someone constantly unless you can laugh at him. Isn't that true? And certainly we are ridiculous little animals wallowing in the fudge bowl, and God must love us all the more because we appeal to His humour.'

'*I* never thought of God as humorous,' said Father Stone.

'The Creator of the platypus, the camel, the ostrich, and man? Oh, come now!' Father Peregrine laughed.

But at this instant, from among the twilight hills, like a series of blue lamps lit to guide their way, came the Martians.

Father Stone saw them first. 'Look!'

Father Peregrine turned and the laughter stopped in his mouth.

The round blue globes of fire hovered among the twinkling stars, distantly trembling.

'Monsters!' Father Stone leaped up. But Father Peregrine caught him. 'Wait!'

'We should've gone to town!'

'No, listen, look!' pleaded Father Peregrine.

'I'm afraid!'

'Don't be. This is God's work!'

'The devil's!'

'No, now, quiet!' Father Peregrine gentled him and they crouched with the soft blue light on their upturned faces as the fiery orbs drew near.

And again, Independence Night, thought Father Peregrine, tremoring. He felt like a child back in those July Fourth evenings, the sky blowing apart, breaking into powdery stars and burning sound, the concussions jingling house windows like the ice on a thousand thin ponds. The aunts, uncles, cousins crying, 'Ah!' as to some celestial physician. The summer sky colours. And the Fire Balloons, lit by an indulgent grandfather, steadied in his massively tender hands. Oh, the memory of those lovely Fire Balloons, softly lighted, warmly billowed bits of tissue, like insect wings, lying like folded wasps in boxes and, last of all, after the day of riot and fury, at long last from their boxes, delicately unfolded, blue, red, white, patriotic — the Fire Balloons! He saw the dim faces of dear relatives long dead and mantled with moss as Grandfather lit the tiny candle and let the warm air breathe up to form the balloon plumply luminous in his hands, a shining vision which they held, reluctant to let it go; for, once released, it was yet another year gone from life, another Fourth, another bit of Beauty vanished. And then up, up, still up through the warm summer night constellations, the Fire Balloons had drifted, while red-white-and-blue eyes followed them, wordless, from family porches. Away into deep Illinois country, over night rivers and sleeping mansions the Fire Balloons dwindled, forever gone . . .

Father Peregrine felt tears in his eyes. Above him the Martians, not one but a *thousand* whispering Fire Balloons, it seemed, hovered. Any moment he might find his long-dead and blessed grandfather at his elbow, staring up at Beauty.

But it was Father Stone.

'Let's go, please, Father!'

'I must speak to them.' Father Peregrine rustled forward, not knowing what to say, for what had he ever said to the Fire Balloons of time past except with his mind: *you are beautiful, you are beautiful*, and that was not enough now. He could only lift his heavy arms and call upwards, as he had often wished to call after the enchanted Fire Balloons, 'Hello!'

But the fiery spheres only burned like images in a dark

mirror. They seemed fixed, gaseous, miraculous, forever.

'We come with God,' said Father Peregrine to the sky.

'Silly, silly, silly.' Father Stone chewed the back of his hand. 'In the name of God, Father Peregrine, stop!'

But now the phosphorescent spheres blew away into the hills. In a moment they were gone.

Father Peregrine called again, and the echo of his last cry shook the hills above. Turning, he saw an avalanche shake out dust, pause, and then, with a thunder of stone wheels, crash down the mountain upon them.

'Look what you've done!' cried Father Stone.

Father Peregrine was almost fascinated, then horrified. He turned, knowing they could run only a few feet before the rocks crushed them into ruins. He had time to whisper, *Oh, Lord!* and the rocks fell!

'Father!'

They were separated like chaff from wheat. There was a blue shimmering of globes, a shift of cold stars, a roar, and then they stood upon a ledge two hundred feet away watching the spot where their bodies should have been buried under tons of stone.

The blue light evaporated.

The two Fathers clutched each other. 'What happened?'

'The blue fires lifted us!'

'We ran, *that* was it!'

'No, the globes saved us.'

'They couldn't!'

'They *did*.'

The sky was empty. There was a feel as if a great bell had just stopped tolling. Reverberations lingered in their teeth and marrow.

'Let's get away from here. You'll have us killed.'

'I haven't feared death for a good many years, Father Stone.'

'We've proved nothing. Those blue lights ran off at the first cry. It's useless.'

'No.' Father Peregrine was suffused with a stubborn wonder. 'Somehow, they saved us. That proves they have souls.'

'It proves only that they *might* have saved us. Everything was confused. We might have escaped, ourselves.'

'They are not animals, Father Stone. Animals do not save lives, especially of strangers. There is mercy and compassion here. Perhaps, tomorrow, we may prove more.'

'Prove what? How?' Father Stone was immensely tired now; the outrage to his mind and body showed on his stiff face. 'Follow them in helicopters, reading chapter and verse? They're not human. They haven't eyes or ears or bodies like ours.'

'But I feel something about them,' replied Father Peregrine. 'I know a great revelation is at hand. They saved us. They *think*. They had a choice; let us live or die. That proves free will!'

Father Stone set to work building a fire, glaring at the sticks in his hands, choking on the grey smoke. 'I myself will open a convent for nursling geese, a monastery for sainted swine, and I shall build a miniature apse in a microscope so that paramecium can attend services and tell their beads with their flagella.'

'Oh, Father Stone.'

'I'm sorry.' Father Stone blinked redly across the fire. 'But this is like blessing a crocodile before he chews you up. You're risking the entire missionary expedition. We belong in First Town, washing liquor from men's throats and perfume off their hands!'

'Can't you recognize the human in the inhuman?'

'I'd much rather recognize the inhuman in the human.'

'But if I prove these things sin, know sin, know a moral

life, have free will and intellect, Father Stone?'

'That will take much convincing.'

The night grew rapidly cold and they peered into the fire to find their wildest thoughts, while eating biscuits and berries, and soon they were bundled for sleep under the chiming stars. And just before turning over one last time Father Stone, who had been thinking for many minutes to find something to bother Father Peregrine about, stared into the soft pink charcoal bed and said, 'No Adam and Eve on Mars. No Original Sin. Maybe the Martians live in a state of God's grace. Then we can go back down to town and start work on the Earth Men.'

Father Peregrine reminded himself to say a little prayer for Father Stone, who got so mad and who was now being vindictive, God help him. 'Yes, Father Stone, but the Martians killed some of our settlers. That's sinful. There must have been an Original Sin and a Martian Adam and Eve. We'll find them. Men are men, unfortunately, no matter what their shape, and inclined to sin.'

But Father Stone was pretending sleep.

Father Peregrine did not shut his eyes.

Of course they couldn't let these Martians go to Hell, could they? With a compromise to their consciences, could they go back to the new colonial towns, those towns so full of sinful gullets and women with scintilla eyes and white oyster bodies rollicking in beds with lonely labourers? Wasn't that the place for the Fathers? Wasn't this trek into the hills merely a personal whim? Was he really thinking of God's Church, or was he quenching the thirst of a spongelike curiosity? Those blue round globes of St Anthony's fire — how they burned in his mind! What a challenge, to find the man behind the mask, the human behind the inhuman. Wouldn't he be proud if he could say, even to his secret self, that he had converted a rolling huge pool table full of fiery spheres! What a sin of pride! Worth doing penance for! But then one did many prideful things out of Love, and he loved the Lord so much and was so happy at it that he wanted everyone else to be happy too.

The last thing he saw before sleep was the return of the blue fires, like a flight of burning angels silently singing him to his worried rest.

The blue round dreams were still there in the sky when Father Peregrine awoke in the early morning.

Father Stone slept like a stiff bundle, quietly. Father Peregrine watched the Martians floating and watching him. They were human — he *knew* it. But he must prove it or face a dry-mouthed, dry-eyed Bishop telling him kindly to step aside.

But how to prove humanity if they hid in the high vaults of the sky? How to bring them nearer and provide answers to the many questions?

'They saved us from the avalanche.'

Father Peregrine arose, moved off among the rocks, and began to climb the nearest hill until he came to a place where a cliff dropped sheerly to a floor two hundred feet below. He was choking from his vigorous climb in the frosty air. He stood, getting his breath.

'If I fell from here, it would surely kill me.'

He let a pebble drop. Moments later it clicked on the rocks below.

'The Lord would never forgive me.'

He tossed another pebble.

'It wouldn't be suicide, would it, if I did it out of Love . . . ?'

He lifted his gaze to the blue spheres. 'But first, another try.' He called to them: 'Hello, hello!'

The echoes tumbled upon each other, but the blue fires did not blink or move.

He talked to them for five minutes. When he stopped, he peered down and saw Father Stone, still indignantly asleep, below in the little camp.

'I must prove everything.' Father Peregrine stepped to the cliff rim. 'I am an old man. I am not afraid. Surely the Lord will understand that I am doing this for Him?'

He drew a deep breath. All his life swam through his eyes and he thought, In a moment shall I die? I am afraid that I love living much too much. But I love other things more.

And, thinking thus, he stepped off the cliff.

He fell.

'Fool!' he cried. He tumbled end over end. 'You were wrong!' The rocks rushed up at him and he saw himself dashed on them and sent to glory. 'Why did I do this thing?' But he knew the answer, and an instant later was calm as he fell. The wind roared around him and the rocks hurtled to meet him.

And then there was a shift of stars, a glimmering of blue light, and he felt himself surrounded by blueness and suspended. A moment later he was deposited, with a gentle bump, upon the rocks, where he sat a full moment, alive, and touching himself, and looking up at those blue lights that had withdrawn instantly.

'You saved me!' he whispered. 'You wouldn't let me die. You knew it was wrong.'

He rushed over to Father Stone, who still lay quietly asleep. 'Father, Father, wake up!' He shook him and brought him round. 'Father, they saved me!'

'Who saved you?' Father Stone blinked and sat up.

Father Peregrine related his experience.

'A dream, a nightmare; go back to sleep,' said Father Stone irritably. 'You and your circus balloons.'

'But I was awake!'

'Now, now, Father, calm yourself. There now.'

'You don't believe me? Have you a gun? Yes, there, let me have it.'

'What are you going to do?' Father Stone handed over the small pistol they had brought along for protection against snakes or other similar and unpredictable animals.

Father Peregrine seized the pistol. 'I'll prove it!'

He pointed the pistol at his own hand and fired.

'Stop!'

There was a shimmer of light, and before their eyes the bullet stood upon the air, poised an inch from his open palm. It hung for a moment, surrounded by a blue phosphorescence. Then it fell, hissing, into the dust.

Father Peregrine fired the gun three times – at his hand, at his leg, at his body. The three bullets hovered, glittering, and, like dead insects, fell at their feet.

'You see?' said Father Peregrine, letting his arm fall, and allowing the pistol to drop after the bullets. 'They know. They understand. They are not animals. They think and judge and live in a moral climate. What animal would save me from myself like this? There is no animal would do that. Only another man, Father. Now, do you believe?'

Father Stone was watching the sky and the blue lights, and now, silently, he dropped to one knee and picked up the warm bullets and cupped them in his hand. He closed his hand tight.

The sun was rising behind them.

'I think we had better go down to the others and tell them of this and bring them back up here,' said Father Peregrine.

By the time the sun was up, they were well on their way back to the rocket.

Father Peregrine drew the round circle in the centre of the blackboard.

'This is Christ, the Son of the Father.'

He pretended not to hear the other Fathers' sharp intake of breath.

'This is Christ, in all His Glory,' he continued.

'It looks like a geometry problem,' observed Father Stone.

'A fortunate comparison, for we deal with symbols here. Christ is *no* less Christ, you must admit, in being represented by a circle or a square. For centuries the cross has symbolized His love and agony. So this circle will be the Martian Christ. This is how we shall bring Him to Mars.'

The Fathers stirred fretfully and looked at each other.

'You, Brother Mathias, will create, in glass, a replica of this circle, a globe, filled with bright fire. It will stand upon the altar.'

'A cheap magic trick,' muttered Father Stone.

Father Peregrine went on patiently: 'On the contrary. We are giving them God in an understandable image. If Christ had come to us on Earth as an octopus, would we have accepted Him readily?' He spread his hands. 'Was it then a cheap magic trick of the Lord's to bring us Christ through Jesus, in man's shape? After we bless the church we build here and sanctify its altar and this symbol, do you think Christ would refuse to inhabit the shape before us? You know in your hearts He would not refuse.'

'But the body of a soulless animal!' said Brother Mathias.

'We're already gone over that, many times since we returned this morning, Brother Mathias. These creatures saved us from the avalanche. They realized that self-destruction was sinful, and prevented it, time after time. Therefore we must build a church in the hills, live with them, to find their own special ways of sinning, the alien ways, and help them to discover God.'

The Fathers did not seem pleased at the prospect.

'Is it because they are so odd to the eye?' wondered Father Peregrine. 'But what is a shape? Only a cup for the blazing soul that God provides us all. If tomorrow I found that sea lions suddenly possessed free will, intellect, knew when not to sin, knew what life was and tempered justice with mercy and life with love, then I would build an undersea cathedral. And if the sparrows should, miraculously, with God's will, gain everlasting souls tomorrow, I would freight a church with helium and take after them, for all souls, in any shape, if they have free will and are aware of their sins, will burn in Hell unless given their rightful communions. I would not let a Martian sphere burn in Hell either, for it is a sphere only in mine eyes. When I close my eyes it stands before me, an intelligence, a love, a soul — and I must not deny it.'

'But that glass globe you wish placed on the altar,' protested Father Stone.

'Consider the Chinese,' replied Father Peregrine imperturbably. 'What sort of Christ do Christian Chinese worship? An oriental Christ, naturally. You've all seen oriental Nativity scenes. How is Christ dressed? In Eastern robes. Where does He walk? In Chinese settings of bamboo and misty mountain and crooked tree. His eyelids taper, His cheekbones rise. Each country, each race adds something to Our Lord. I am reminded of the Virgin of Guadalupe, to whom all Mexico pays its love. Her skin? Have you noticed the paintings of her? A dark skin, like that of her worshippers. Is this blasphemy? Not at all. It is not logical that men should accept a God, no matter how real, of another colour. I often wonder why our missionaries do well in Africa, with a snow-white Christ. Perhaps because white is a sacred colour, in albino, or any other form, to the African tribes. Given time, mightn't Christ darken there too? The form does not matter. Content is everything. We cannot expect these Martians to accept an alien form. We shall give them Christ in their own image.'

'There's a flaw in your reasoning, Father,' said Father Stone. 'Won't the Martians suspect us of hypocrisy? They will realize that *we* don't worship a round, globular Christ, but a man with limbs and a head. How do we explain the difference?'

'By showing there is none. Christ will fill any vessel that is offered. Bodies or globes, He is there, and each will worship the same thing in a different guise. What is more, we must *believe* in this globe we give the Martians. We must believe in a shape which is meaningless to us as to form. This spheroid *will* be Christ. And we must remember that we ourselves, and the shape of our Earth Christ, would be meaningless, ridiculous, a squander of material to these Martians.'

Father Peregrine laid aside his chalk. 'Now let us go into the hills and build our church.'

The Fathers began to pack their equipment.

The church was not a church but an area cleared of rocks, a plateau on one of the low mountains, its soil smoothed and brushed, and an altar established whereon Brother Mathias placed the fiery globe he had constructed.

At the end of six days of work the 'church' was ready.

'What shall we do with this?' Father Stone tapped an iron bell they had brought along. 'What does a bell mean to *them*?'

'I imagine I brought it for our own comfort,' admitted Father Peregrine. 'We need a few familiarities. This church seems so little like a church. And we feel somewhat absurd here — even I; for it is something new, this business of converting the creatures of another world. I feel like a ridiculous play actor at times. And then I pray to God to lend me strength.'

'Many of the Fathers are unhappy. Some of them joke about all this, Father Peregrine.'

'I know. We'll put this bell in a small tower for their comfort, anyway.'

'What about the organ?'

'We'll play it at the first service, tomorrow.'

'But, the Martians — '

'I know. But again, I suppose, for our own comfort, our own music. Later we may discover theirs.'

They arose very early on Sunday morning and moved through the coldness like pale phantoms, rime tinkling on their habits; covered with chimes they were, shaking down showers of silver water.

'I wonder if it *is* Sunday here on Mars?' mused Father Peregrine, but seeing Father Stone wince, he hastened on, 'It might be Tuesday or Thursday — who knows? But no matter. My idle fancy. It's Sunday to *us*. Come.'

The Fathers walked into the flat wide area of the 'church' and knelt, shivering and blue-lipped.

Father Peregrine said a little prayer and put his cold fingers to the organ keys. The music went up like a flight of pretty birds. He touched the keys like a man moving his hands among the weeds of a wild garden, startling up great soarings of Beauty into the hills.

The music calmed the air. It smelled the fresh smell of morning. The music drifted into the mountains and shook down mineral powders in a dusty rain.

The Fathers waited.

'Well, Father Peregrine.' Father Stone eyed the empty sky where the sun was rising, furnace-red. 'I don't see our friends.'

'Let me try again.' Father Peregrine was perspiring.

He built an architecture of Bach, stone by exquisite stone, raising a music cathedral so vast that its furthest chancels were in Nineveh, its furthest dome at St Peter's left hand. The music stayed and did not crash in ruin when it was over, but partook of a series of white clouds and was carried away among other lands.

The sky was still empty.

'They'll come!' But Father Peregrine felt the panic in his chest, very small, growing. 'Let us pray. Let us ask them to come. They read minds; they *know*.'

The Fathers lowered themselves yet again, in rustlings and whispers. They prayed.

And to the East, out of the icy mountains of seven o'clock on Sunday morning or perhaps Thursday morning or maybe Monday morning on Mars, came the soft fiery globes.

They hovered and sank and filled the area around the shivering priests. 'Thank you; oh, thank you, Lord.' Father Peregrine shut his eyes tight and played the music, and when it was done he turned and gazed upon his wondrous congregation.

And a voice touched his mind, and the voice said:

'We have come for a little while.'

'You may stay,' said Father Peregrine.

'For a little while only,' said the voice quietly. 'We have come to tell you certain things. We should have spoken sooner. But we had hoped that you might go on your way if left alone.'

Father Peregrine started to speak, but the voice hushed him.

'We are the Old Ones,' the voice said, and it entered him like a blue gaseous flare and burned in the chambers of his head. 'We are the old Martians, who left our marble cities and went into the hills, forsaking the material life we had lived. So very long ago we became these things that we are now. Once we were men, with bodies and legs and arms such as yours. The legend has it that one of us, a good man, discovered a way to free man's soul and intellect, to free him of bodily ills and melancholies, of deaths and transfigurations, of ill humours and senilities, and so we took on the look of lightning and blue fire and have lived in the winds and skies and hills forever after that, neither prideful nor arrogant, neither rich nor poor, passionate nor cold. We have lived apart from those we left behind, those other men of this world, and how we came to be has been forgotten, the process lost; but we shall never die, nor do harm. We have put away the sins of the body and live in God's grace. We covet no other property; we have no property. We do not steal, nor kill, nor lust, nor hate. We live in happiness. We cannot reproduce; we do not eat or drink or make war. All the sensualities and childishness and sins of the body were stripped away when our bodies were put aside. We have left sin behind, Father Peregrine, and it is burned like the leaves in the autumn, and it is gone like the soiled snow of an evil winter, and it is gone like the sexual flowers of a red-and-yellow spring, and it is gone like the panting nights of hottest summer, and our season is temperate and our clime is rich in thought.'

Father Peregrine was standing now, for the voice touched him at such a pitch that it almost shook him from his senses. It was an ecstasy and a fire washing through him.

'We wish to tell you that we appreciate your building this place for us, but we have no need of it, for each of us is a temple unto himself and needs no place wherein to cleanse himself. Forgive us for not coming to you sooner, but we are separate and apart and have talked to no one for ten thousand years, nor have we interfered in any way with the life of this planet. It has come into your mind now that we are the lilies of the field; we toil not, neither do we spin. You are right. And so we suggest that you take the parts of this temple into your own new cities and there cleanse others. For, rest assured, we are happy and at peace.'

The Fathers were on their knees in the vast blue light, and Father Peregrine was down, too, and they were weeping, and it did not matter that their time had been wasted; it did not matter to them at all.

The blue spheres murmured and began to rise once more, on a breath of cool air.

'May I' — cried Father Peregrine, not daring to ask, eyes closed — 'may I come again, someday, that I may learn from you?'

The blue fires blazed. The air trembled.

Yes. Someday he might come again. Someday.

And then the Fire Balloons blew away and were gone, and he was like a child, on his knees, tears streaming from his eyes, crying to himself, 'Come back, come back!' And at any moment Grandfather might lift him and carry him upstairs to his bedroom in a long-gone Illinois town . . .

They filed down out of the hills at sunset. Looking back, Father Peregrine saw the blue fires burning. No, he thought, we couldn't build a church for the likes of you. You're beauty itself. What church could compete with the fireworks of the pure soul?

Father Stone moved in silence beside him. At last he spoke:

'The way I see it is there's a Truth on every planet. All parts of the Big Truth. On a certain day they'll fit together like the pieces of a jigsaw. This has been a shaking experience. I'll never doubt again, Father Peregrine. For this Truth here is as true as Earth's Truth, and they lie side by side. And we'll go on to other worlds, adding the sum of the parts of the Truth until one day the whole Total will stand before us like the light of a new day.'

'That's a lot, coming from you, Father Stone.'

'I'm sorry now, in a way, we're going down to the town to handle our own kind. Those blue lights now. When they settled about us, and that *voice* . . . ' Father Stone shivered.

Father Peregrine reached out to take the other's arm. They walked together.

'And you know,' said Father Stone finally, fixing his eyes on Brother Mathias, who strode ahead with the glass sphere tenderly carried in his arms, that glass sphere with the blue phosphorous light glowing forever inside it, 'you know, Father Peregrine, that globe there – '

'Yes?'

'It's Him. It *is* Him, after all.'

Father Peregrine smiled, and they walked down out of the hills towards the new town.

The Last Night
of the World

'What would you do if you knew that this was the last night of the world?'

'What would I do? You mean seriously?'

'Yes, seriously.'

'I don't know. I hadn't thought.'

He poured some coffee. In the background the two girls were playing blocks on the parlour rug in the light of the green hurricane lamps. There was an easy, clean aroma of the brewed coffee in the evening air.

'Well, better start thinking about it,' he said.

'You don't mean it!'

He nodded.

'A war?'

He shook his head.

'Not the hydrogen or atom bomb?'

'No.'

'Or germ warfare?'

'None of those at all,' he said, stirring his coffee slowly. 'But just, let's say, the closing of a book.'

'I don't think I understand.'

'No, nor do I, really; it's just a feeling. Sometimes it frightens me, sometimes I'm not frightened at all but at peace.' He glanced in at the girls and their yellow hair shining in the lamplight. 'I didn't say anything to you. It first happened about four nights ago.'

'What?'

'A dream I had. I dreamed that it was all going to be over, and a voice said it was; not any kind of voice I can remember, but a voice anyway, and it said things would stop here on

Earth. I didn't think too much about it the next day, but then I went to the office and caught Stan Willis looking out the window in the middle of the afternoon, and I said, A penny for your thoughts, Stan, and he said, I had a dream last night, and before he even told me the dream I knew what it was. I could have told him, but he told me and I listened to him.'

'It was the same dream?'

'The same. I told Stan I had dreamed it too. He didn't seem surprised. He relaxed, in fact. Then we started walking through the office, for the hell of it. It wasn't planned. We didn't say, Let's walk around. We just walked on our own, and everywhere we saw people looking at their desks or their hands or out windows. I talked to a few. So did Stan.'

'And they all had dreamed?'

'All of them. The same dream, with no difference.'

'Do you believe in it?'

'Yes. I've never been more certain.'

'And when will it stop? The world, I mean.'

'Sometime during the night for us, and then as the night goes on around the world, that'll go too. It'll take twenty-four hours for it all to go.'

They sat awhile not touching their coffee. Then they lifted it slowly and drank, looking at each other.

'Do we deserve this?' she said.

'It's not a matter of deserving; it's just that things didn't work out. I notice you didn't even argue about this. Why not?'

'I guess I've a reason,' she said.

'The same one everyone at the office had?'

She nodded slowly. 'I didn't want to say anything. It happened last night. And the women on the block talked about it, among themselves, today. They dreamed. I thought it was only a coincidence.' She picked up the evening paper. 'There's nothing in the paper about it.'

'Everyone knows, so there's no need.'

He sat back in his chair, watching her. 'Are you afraid?'

'No. I always thought I would be, but I'm not.'

'Where's that spirit called self-preservation they talk so much about?'

'I don't know. You don't get too excited when you feel things are logical. This is logical. Nothing else but this could have happened from the way we've lived.'

'We haven't been too bad, have we?'

'No, nor enormously good. I suppose that's the trouble — we haven't been very much of anything except us, while a big part of the world was busy being lots of quite awful things.'

The girls were laughing in the parlour.

'I always thought people would be screaming in the streets at a time like this.'

'I guess not. You don't scream about the real thing.'

'Do you know, I won't miss anything but you and the girls. I never liked cities or my work or anything except you three. I won't miss a thing except perhaps the change in the weather, and a glass of ice water when it's hot, and I might miss sleeping. How can we sit here and talk this way?'

'Because there's nothing else to do.'

'That's it, of course; for if there were, we'd be doing it. I suppose this is the first time in the history of the world that everyone has known just what they were going to do during the night.'

'I wonder what everyone else will do now, this evening, for the next few hours.'

'Go to a show, listen to the radio, watch television, play cards, put the children to bed, go to bed themselves, like always.'

'In a way that's something to be proud of — like always.'

They sat a moment and then he poured himself another coffee. 'Why do you suppose it's tonight?'

'Because.'

'Why not some other night in the last century, or five centuries ago, or ten?'

'Maybe because it was never October 19, 1969, ever before in history, and now it is and that's it; because this date means more than any other date ever meant; because it's the year when things are as they are all over the world and that's why it's the end.'

'There are bombers on their schedules both ways across the ocean tonight that'll never see land.'

'That's part of the reason why.'

'Well,' he said, getting up, 'what shall it be? Wash the dishes?'

They washed the dishes and stacked them away with special neatness. At eight-thirty the girls were put to bed and kissed good night and the little lights by their beds turned on and the door left open just a trifle.

'I wonder,' said the husband, coming from the bedroom and glancing back, standing there with his pipe for a moment.

'What?'

'If the door will be shut all the way, or if it'll be left just a little ajar so some light comes in.'

'I wonder if the children know.'

'No, of course not.'

They sat and read the papers and talked and listened to some radio music and then sat together by the fireplace watching the charcoal embers as the clock struck ten-thirty and eleven and eleven-thirty. They thought of all the other people in the world who had just spent their evening, each in his own special way.

'Well,' he said at last.

He kissed his wife for a long time.

'We've been good for each other, anyway.'

'Do you want to cry?' he asked.

'I don't think so.'

They moved through the house and turned out the lights and went into the bedroom and stood in the night cool darkness undressing and pushing back the covers. 'The sheets are so clean and nice.'

'I'm tired.'

'We're *all* tired.'

They got into bed and lay back.

'Just a moment,' she said.

He heard her get out of bed and go into the kitchen. A moment later, she returned. 'I left the water running in the kitchen sink,' she said.

Something about this was so very funny that he had to laugh.

She laughed with him, knowing what it was that she had done that was funny. They stopped laughing at last and lay in their cool night bed, their hands clasped, their heads together.

'Good night,' he said, after a moment.

'Good night,' she said.

The Veldt

'George, I wish you'd look at the nursery.'

'What's wrong with it?'

'I don't know.'

'Well, then.'

'I just want you to look at it, is all, or call a psychologist in to look at it.'

'What would a psychologist want with a nursery?'

'You know very well what he'd want.' His wife paused in the middle of the kitchen and watched the stove busy humming to itself, making supper for four.

'It's just that the nursery is different now than it was.'

'All right, let's have a look.'

They walked down the hall of their soundproofed Happy-life Home, which had cost them thirty thousand dollars installed, this house which clothed and fed and rocked them to sleep and played and sang and was good to them. Their approach sensitized a switch somewhere and the nursery light flicked on when they came within ten feet of it. Similarly, behind them, in the halls, lights went on and off as they left them behind, with a soft automaticity.

'Well,' said George Hadley.

They stood on the thatched floor of the nursery. It was forty feet across by forty feet long and thirty feet high; it had cost half again as much as the rest of the house. 'But nothing's too good for our children,' George had said.

The nursery was silent. It was empty as a jungle glade at hot high noon. The walls were blank and two-dimensional. Now, as George and Lydia Hadley stood in the centre of the room, the walls began to purr and recede into crystalline distance, it seemed, and presently an African veldt appeared, in three dimensions; on all sides, in colours reproduced to the final pebble and bit of straw. The ceiling above them became a deep sky with a hot yellow sun.

George Hadley felt the perspiration start on his brow.

'Let's get out of the sun,' he said. 'This is a little too real. But I don't see anything wrong.'

'Wait a moment, you'll see,' said his wife.

Now the hidden odorophonics were beginning to blow a wind of odour at the two people in the middle of the baked veldtland. The hot straw smell of lion grass, the cool green smell of the hidden water hole, the great rusty smell of animals, the smell of dust like a red paprika in the hot air. And now the sounds: the thump of distant antelope feet on grassy sod, the papery rustling of vultures. A shadow passed through the sky. The shadow flickered on George Hadley's upturned, sweating face.

'Filthy creatures,' he heard his wife say.

'The vultures.'

'You see, there are the lions, far over, that way. Now they're on their way to the water hole. They've just been eating,' said Lydia. 'I don't know what.'

'Some animal.' George Hadley put his hand up to shield off the burning light from his squinted eyes. 'A zebra or a baby giraffe, maybe.'

'Are you sure?' His wife sounded peculiarly tense.

'No, it's a little late to be *sure*,' he said, amused. 'Nothing over there I can see but cleaned bone, and the vultures dropping for what's left.'

'Did you hear that scream?' she asked.

'No.'

'About a minute ago?'

'Sorry, no.'

The lions were coming. And again George Hadley was filled with admiration for the mechanical genius who had conceived this room. A miracle of efficiency selling for an absurdly low price. Every home should have one. Oh, occasionally they frightened you with their clinical accuracy, they startled you, gave you a twinge, but most of the time what fun for everyone, not only your own son and daughter, but for yourself when you felt like a quick jaunt to a foreign land, a quick change of scenery. Well, here it was!

And here were the lions now, fifteen feet away, so real, so feverishly and startlingly real that you could feel the prickling fur on your hand, and your mouth was stuffed with the dusty upholstery smell of their heated pelts, and the yellow of them was in your eyes like the yellow of an exquisite French tapestry, the yellows of lions and summer grass, and the sound of matted lion lungs exhaling on the silent noontide, and the smell of meat from the panting, dripping mouths.

The lions stood looking at George and Lydia Hadley with terrible green-yellow eyes.

'Watch out!' screamed Lydia.

The lions came running at them.

Lydia bolted and ran. Instinctively, George sprang after her. Outside, in the hall, with the door slammed, he was laughing and she was crying and they both stood appalled at the other's reaction.

'George!'

'Lydia! Oh, my dear poor sweet Lydia!'

'They almost got us!'

'Walls, Lydia, remember; crystal walls, that's all they are. Oh, they look real, I must admit — Africa in your parlour — but it's all dimensional superactionary, supersensitive colour film and mental tape film behind glass screens. It's all odorophonics and sonics, Lydia. Here's my handkerchief.'

'I'm afraid.' She came to him and put her body against him and cried steadily. 'Did you see? Did you *feel*? It's too real.'

'Now, Lydia . . . '

'You've got to tell Wendy and Peter not to read any more on Africa.'

'Of course — of course.' He patted her.

'Promise?'

'Sure.'

'And lock the nursery for a few days until I get my nerves settled.'

'You know how difficult Peter is about that. When I punished him a month ago by locking the nursery for even a few hours — the tantrum he threw! And Wendy too. They *live* for the nursery.'

'It's got to be locked, that's all there is to it.'

'All right.' Reluctantly he locked the huge door. 'You've been working too hard. You need a rest.'

'I don't know — I don't know,' she said, blowing her nose, sitting down in a chair that immediately began to rock and comfort her. 'Maybe I don't have enough to do. Maybe I have time to think too much. Why don't we shut the whole house off for a few days and take a vacation?'

'You mean you want to fry my eggs for me?'

'Yes.' She nodded.

'And darn my socks?'

'Yes.' A frantic, watery-eyed nodding.

'And sweep the house?'

'Yes, yes — oh, yes!'

'But I thought that's why we bought this house, so we wouldn't have to do anything?'

'That's just it. I feel like I don't belong here. The house is wife and mother now and nursemaid. Can I compete with an African veldt? Can I give a bath and scrub the children as efficiently or quickly as the automatic scrub bath can? I cannot. And it isn't just me. It's you. You've been awfully nervous lately.'

'I suppose I have been smoking too much.'

'You look as if you don't know what to do with yourself in

this house, either. You smoke a little more every morning and drink a little more every afternoon and need a little more sedative every night. You're beginning to feel unnecessary too.'

'Am I?' He paused and tried to feel into himself to see what was really there.

'Oh, George!' She looked beyond him, at the nursery door. 'Those lions can't get out of there, can they?'

He looked at the door and saw it tremble as if something had jumped against it from the other side.

'Of course not,' he said.

At dinner they ate alone, for Wendy and Peter were at a special plastic carnival across town and had televised home to say they'd be late, to go ahead eating. So George Hadley, bemused, sat watching the dining-room table produce warm dishes of food from its mechanical interior.

'We forgot the ketchup,' he said.

'Sorry,' said a small voice within the table, and ketchup appeared.

As for the nursery, thought George Hadley, it won't hurt for the children to be locked out of it awhile. Too much of anything isn't good for anyone. And it was clearly indicated that the children had been spending a little too much time on Africa. That *sun*. He could feel it on his neck, still, like a hot paw. And the *lions*. And the smell of blood. Remarkable how the nursery caught the telepathic emanations of the children's minds and created life to fill their every desire. The children thought lions, and there were lions. The children thought zebras, and there were zebras. Sun — sun. Giraffes — giraffes. Death and death.

That *last*. He chewed tastelessly on the meat that the table had cut for him. Death thoughts. They were awfully young, Wendy and Peter, for death thoughts. Or, no, you were never too young, really. Long before you knew what death was you were wishing it on someone else. When you were two years old you were shooting people with cap pistols.

But this — the long, hot African veldt — the awful death in the jaws of a lion. And repeated again and again.

'Where are you going?'

He didn't answer Lydia. Preoccupied, he let the lights glow softly on ahead of him, extinguish behind him as he padded to the nursery door. He listened against it. Far away, a lion roared.

He unlocked the door and opened it. Just before he stepped inside, he heard a faraway scream. And then another roar from the lions, which subsided quickly.

He stepped into Africa. How many times in the last year had he opened this door and found Wonderland, Alice, the Mock Turtle, or Aladdin and his Magical Lamp, or Jack Pumpkinhead of Oz, or Dr Doolittle, or the cow jumping over a very real-appearing moon — all the delightful contraptions of a make-believe world. How often had he seen Pegasus flying in the ceiling, or seen fountains of red fireworks, or heard angel voices singing. But now, this yellow hot Africa, this bake oven with murder in the heat. Perhaps Lydia was right. Perhaps they needed a little vacation from the fantasy which was growing a bit too real for ten-year-old children. It was all right to exercise one's mind with gymnastic fantasies, but when the lively child mind settled on *one* pattern . . . ? It seemed that, at a distance, for the past month, he had heard lions roaring, and smelled their strong odour seeping as far away as his study door. But, being busy, he had paid it no attention.

George Hadley stood on the African grassland alone. The lions looked up from their feeding, watching him. The only flaw to the illusion was the open door through which he could see his wife, far down the dark hall, like a framed picture, eating her dinner abstractedly.

'Go away,' he said to the lions.

They did not go.

He knew the principle of the room exactly. You sent out your thoughts. Whatever you thought would appear.

'Let's have Aladdin and his lamp,' he snapped.

The veldtland remained; the lions remained.

'Come on, room! I demand Aladdin!' he said.

Nothing happend. The lions mumbled in their baked pelts.

'Aladdin!'

He went back to dinner. 'The fool room's out of order,' he said. 'It won't respond.'

'Or – '

'Or what?'

'Or it *can't* respond,' said Lydia, 'because the children have thought about Africa and lions and killing so many days that the room's in a rut.'

'Could be.'

'Or Peter set it to remain that way.'

'*Set* it?'

'He may have got into the machinery and fixed something.'

'Peter doesn't know machinery.'

'He's a wise one for ten. That I.Q. of his – '

'Nevertheless – '

'Hello, Mom. Hello, Dad.'

The Hadleys turned. Wendy and Peter were coming in the front door, cheeks like peppermint candy, eyes like bright blue agate marbles, a smell of ozone on their jumpers from their trip in the helicopter.

'You're just in time for supper,' said both parents.

'We're full of strawberry ice cream and hot dogs,' said the children, holding hands. 'But we'll sit and watch.'

'Yes, come tell us about the nursery,' said George Hadley.

The brother and sister blinked at him and then at each other. 'Nursery?'

'All about Africa and everything,' said the father with false joviality.

'I don't understand,' said Peter.

'Your mother and I were just travelling through Africa with rod and reel; Tom Swift and his Electric Lion,' said George Hadley.

'There's no Africa in the nursery,' said Peter simply.

'Oh, come now, Peter. We know better.'

'I don't remember any Africa,' said Peter to Wendy. 'Do you?'

'No.'

'Run and see and come tell.'

She obeyed.

'Wendy, come back here!' said George Hadley, but she was gone. The house lights followed her like a flock of fireflies. Too late, he realized he had forgotten to lock the nursery door after his last inspection.

'Wendy'll look and come tell us,' said Peter.

'She doesn't have to tell *me*. I've seen it.'

'I'm sure you're mistaken, Father.'

'I'm not, Peter. Come along now.'

But Wendy was back. 'It's not Africa,' she said breathlessly.

'We'll see about this,' said George Hadley, and they all walked down the hall together and opened the nursery door.

There was a green, lovely forest, a lovely river, a purple mountain, high voices singing, and Rima, lovely and mysterious, lurking in the trees with colourful flights of butterflies, like animated bouquets, lingering in her long hair. The African veldtland was gone. The lions were gone. Only Rima was there now, singing a song so beautiful that it brought tears to your eyes.

George Hadley looked in at the changed scene. 'Go to bed,' he said to the children.

They opened their mouths.

'You heard me,' he said.

They went off to the air closet, where a wind sucked them like brown leaves up the flue to their slumber rooms.

George Hadley walked through the singing glade and picked up something that lay in the corner near where the lions had been. He walked slowly back to his wife.

'What is that?' she asked.

'An old wallet of mine,' he said.

He showed it to her. The smell of hot grass was on it and the smell of a lion. There were drops of saliva on it, it had been chewed, and there were blood smears on both sides.

He closed the nursery door and locked it, tight.

In the middle of the night he was still awake and he knew his wife was awake. 'Do you think Wendy changed it?' she said at last, in the dark room.

'Of course.'

'Made it from a veldt into a forest and put Rima there instead of lions?'

'Yes.'

'Why?'

'I don't know. But it's staying locked until I find out.'

'How did your wallet get there?'

'I don't know anything,' he said, 'except that I'm beginning to be sorry we bought that room for the children. If children are neurotic at all, a room like that — '

'It's supposed to help them work off their neuroses in a healthful way.'

'I'm starting to wonder.' He stared at the ceiling.

'We've given the children everything they ever wanted. Is this our reward — secrecy, disobedience?'

'Who was it said, "Children are carpets, they should be stepped on occasionally!" We've never lifted a hand. They're insufferable — let's admit it. They come and go when they like; they treat us as if *we* were offspring. They're spoiled and we're spoiled.'

'They've been acting funny ever since you forbade them to take the rocket to New York a few months ago.'

'They're not old enough to do that alone, I explained.'

'Nevertheless, I've noticed they've been decidedly cool towards us since.'

'I think I'll have David McClean come tomorrow morning to have a look at Africa.'

'But it's not Africa now, it's Green Mansions country and Rima.'

'I have a feeling it'll be Africa again before then.'

A moment later they heard the screams.

Two screams. Two people screaming from downstairs. And then a roar of lions.

'Wendy and Peter aren't in their rooms,' said his wife.

He lay in his bed with his beating heart. 'No,' he said. 'They've broken into the nursery.'

'Those screams – they sound familiar.'

'Do they?'

'Yes, awfully.'

And although their beds tried very hard, the two adults couldn't be rocked to sleep for another hour. A smell of cats was in the night air.

'Father?' said Peter.

'Yes.'

Peter looked at his shoes. He never looked at his father any more, nor at his mother. 'You aren't going to lock up the nursery for good, are you?'

'That all depends.'

'On what?' snapped Peter.

'On you and your sister. If you intersperse this Africa with a little variety – oh, Sweden perhaps, or Denmark or China – '

'I thought we were free to play as we wished.'

'You are, within reasonable bounds.'

'What's wrong with Africa, Father?'

'Oh, so now you admit you have been conjuring up Africa, do you?'

'I wouldn't want the nursery locked up,' said Peter coldly. 'Ever.'

'Matter of fact, we're thinking of turning the whole house off for about a month. Live sort of a carefree one-for-all existence.'

'That sounds dreadful! Would I have to tie my own shoes instead of letting the shoe tier do it? And brush my own teeth and comb my hair and give myself a bath?'

'It would be fun for a change, don't you think?'

'No, it would be horrid. I didn't like it when you took out the picture painter last month.'

'That's because I wanted you to learn to paint all by yourself, Son.'

'I don't want to do anything but look and listen and smell; what else *is* there to do?'

'All right, go play in Africa.'

'Will you shut off the house sometime soon?'

'We're considering it.'

'I don't think you'd better consider it any more, Father.'

'I won't have any threats from my son!'

'Very well.' And Peter strolled off to the nursery.

'Am I on time?' said David McClean.

'Breakfast?' asked George Hadley.

'Thanks, had some. What's the trouble?'

'David, you're a psychologist.'

'I should hope so.'

'Well, then, have a look at our nursery. You saw it a year ago when you dropped by; did you notice anything peculiar about it then?'

'Can't say I did; the usual violences, a tendency towards a slight paranoia here or there, usual in children because they feel persecuted by parents constantly, but, oh, really nothing.'

They walked down the hall. 'I locked the nursery up,' explained the father, 'and the children broke back into it during the night. I let them stay so they could form the patterns for you to see.'

There was a terrible screaming from the nursery.

'There it is,' said George Hadley. 'See what you make of it.'

They walked in on the children without rapping.

The screams had faded. The lions were feeding.

'Run outside a moment, children,' said George Hadley. 'No, don't change the mental combination. Leave the walls as they are. Get!'

With the children gone, the two men stood studying the lions clustered at a distance, eating with great relish whatever it was they had caught.

'I wish I knew what it was,' said George Hadley. 'Sometimes I can almost see. Do you think if I brought high-powered binoculars here and — '

David McClean laughed dryly. 'Hardly.' He turned to study all four walls. 'How long has this been going on?'

'A little over a month.'

'It certainly doesn't *feel* good.'

'I want facts, not feelings.'

'My dear George, a psychologist never saw a fact in his life. He only hears about feelings; vague things. This doesn't feel good, I tell you. Trust my hunches and my instincts. I have a nose for something bad. This is very bad. My advice to you is to have the whole damn room torn down and your children brought to me every day during the next year for treatment.'

'Is it that bad?'

'I'm afraid so. One of the original uses of these nurseries

was so that we could study the patterns left on the walls by the child's mind, study at our leisure, and help the child. In this case, however, the room has become a channel towards — destructive thoughts, instead of a release away from them.'

'Didn't you sense this before?'

'I sensed only that you had spoiled your children more than most. And now you're letting them down in some way. What way?'

'I wouldn't let them go to New York.'

'What else?'

'I've taken a few machines from the house and threatened them, a month ago, with closing up the nursery unless they did their homework. I did close it for a few days to show I meant business.'

'Ah, ha!'

'Does that mean anything?'

'Everything. Where before they had a Santa Claus now they have a Scrooge. Children prefer Santas. You've let this room and this house replace you and your wife in your children's affections. This room is their mother and father, far more important in their lives than their real parents. And now you come along and want to shut it off. No wonder there's hatred here. You can feel it coming out of the sky. Feel that sun. George, you'll have to change your life. Like too many others, you've built it around creature comforts. Why, you'd starve tomorrow if something went wrong in your kitchen. You wouldn't know how to tap an egg. Nevertheless, turn everything off. Start new. It'll take time. But we'll make good children out of bad in a year, wait and see.'

'But won't the shock be too much for the children, shutting the room up abruptly, for good?'

'I don't want them going any deeper into this, that's all.'

The lions were finished with their red feast.

The lions were standing on the edge of the clearing

watching the two men.

'Now *I'm* feeling persecuted,' said McClean. 'Let's get out of here. I never have cared for these damned rooms. Make me nervous.'

'The lions look real, don't they?' said George Hadley. 'I don't suppose there's any way — '

'What?'

' — that they could *become* real?'

'Not that I know.'

'Some flaw in the machinery, a tampering or something?'

'No.'

They went to the door.

'I don't imagine the room will like being turned off,' said the father.

'Nothing ever likes to die — even a room.'

'I wonder if it hates me for wanting to switch it off?'

'Paranoia is thick around here today,' said David McClean. 'You can follow it like a spoor. Hello.' He bent and picked up a bloody scarf. 'This yours?'

'No.' George Hadley's face was rigid. 'It belongs to Lydia.'

They went to the fuse box together and threw the switch that killed the nursery.

The two children were in hysterics. They screamed and pranced and threw things. They yelled and sobbed and swore and jumped at the furniture.

'You can't do that to the nursery, you can't!'

'Now, children.'

The children flung themselves onto a couch, weeping.

'George,' said Lydia Hadley, 'turn on the nursery, just for a few moments. You can't be so abrupt.'

'No.'

'You can't be so cruel.'

'Lydia, it's off, and it stays off. And the whole damn house dies as of here and now. The more I see of the mess we've put ourselves in, the more it sickens me. We've been contemplating our mechanical, electronic navels for too long. My God, how we need a breath of honest air!'

And he marched about the house turning off the voice clocks, the stoves, the heaters, the shoe shiners, the shoe lacers, the body scrubbers and swabbers and massagers, and every other machine he could put his hand to.

The house was full of dead bodies, it seemed. It felt like a mechanical cemetery. So silent. None of the humming hidden energy of machines waiting to function at the tap of a button.

'Don't let them do it!' wailed Peter at the ceiling, as if he was talking to the house, the nursery. 'Don't let Father kill everything.' He turned to his father. 'Oh, I hate you!'

'Insults won't get you anywhere.'

'I wish you were dead!'

'We were, for a long while. Now we're going to really start living. Instead of being handled and massaged, we're going to *live*.'

Wendy was still crying and Peter joined her again. 'Just a moment, just one moment, just another moment of nursery,' they wailed.

'Oh, George,' said his wife, 'it can't hurt.'

'All right — all right, if they'll only just shut up. One minute, mind you, and then off forever.'

'Daddy, Daddy, Daddy!' sang the children, smiling with wet faces.

'And then we're going on a vacation. David McClean is coming back in half an hour to help us move out and get to the airport. I'm going to dress. You turn the nursery on for a minute, Lydia, just a minute, mind you.'

And the three of them went babbling off while he let himself be vacuumed upstairs through the air flue and set about dressing himself. A minute later Lydia appeared.

'I'll be glad when we get away,' she sighed.

'Did you leave them in the nursery?'

'I wanted to dress too. Oh, that horrid Africa. What can they see in it?'

'Well, in five minutes we'll be on our way to Iowa. Lord, how did we ever get in this house? What prompted us to buy a nightmare?'

'Pride, money, foolishness.'

'I think we'd better get downstairs before those kids get engrossed with those damned beasts again.'

Just then they heard the children calling, 'Daddy, Mommy, come quick — quick!'

They went downstairs in the air flue and ran down the hall. The children were nowhere in sight. 'Wendy? Peter!'

They ran into the nursery. The veldtland was empty save for the lions waiting, looking at them. 'Peter, Wendy?'

The door slammed.

'Wendy, Peter!'

George Hadley and his wife whirled and ran back to the door.

'Open the door!' cried George Hadley, trying the knob. 'Why, they've locked it from the outside! Peter!' He beat at the door. 'Open up!'

He heard Peter's voice outside, against the door.

'Don't let them switch off the nursery and the house,' he was saying.

Mr and Mrs George Hadley beat at the door. 'Now, don't be ridiculous, children. It's time to go. Mr McClean'll be here in a minute and . . . '

And then they heard the sounds.

The lions on three sides of them, in the yellow veldt grass, padding through the dry straw, rumbling and roaring in their throats.

The lions.

Mr Hadley looked at his wife and they turned and looked

back at the beasts edging slowly forward, crouching, tails stiff.

Mr and Mrs Hadley screamed.

And suddenly they realized why those other screams had sounded familiar.

'Well, here I am,' said David McClean in the nursery doorway. 'Oh, hello.' He stared at the two children seated in the centre of the open glade eating a little picnic lunch. Beyond them was the water hole and the yellow veldtland; above was the hot sun. He began to perspire. 'Where are your father and mother?'

The children looked up and smiled. 'Oh, they'll be here directly.'

'Good, we must get going.' At a distance Mr McClean saw the lions fighting and clawing and then quieting down to feed in silence under the shady trees.

He squinted at the lions with his hand up to his eyes.

Now the lions were done feeding. They moved to the water hole to drink.

A shadow flickered over Mr McClean's hot face. Many shadows flickered. The vultures were dropping down the blazing sky.

'A cup of tea?' asked Wendy in the silence.

The Long Rain

The rain continued. It was a hard rain, a perpetual rain, a sweating and steaming rain; it was a mizzle, a downpour, a fountain, a whipping at the eyes, an undertow at the ankles; it was a rain to drown all rains and the memory of rains. It came by the pound and the ton, it hacked at the jungle and cut the trees like scissors and shaved the grass and tunnelled the soil and molted the bushes. It shrank men's hands into the hands of wrinkled apes; it rained a solid glassy rain, and it never stopped.

'How much farther, Lieutenant?'

'I don't know. A mile, ten miles, a thousand.'

'Aren't you sure?'

'How can I be sure?'

'I don't like this rain. If we only knew how far it is to the Sun Dome, I'd feel better.'

'Another hour or two from here.'

'You really think so, Lieutenant?'

'Of course.'

'Or are you lying to keep us happy?'

'I'm lying to keep you happy. Shut up!'

The two men sat together in the rain. Behind them sat two other men who were wet and tired and slumped like clay that was melting.

The lieutenant looked up. He had a face that once had been brown and now the rain had washed it pale, and the rain had washed the colour from his eyes and they were white, as were his teeth, and as was his hair. He was all white. Even his uniform was beginning to turn white, and perhaps a little green with fungus.

The lieutenant felt the rain on his cheeks. 'How many million years since the rain stopped raining here on Venus?'

'Don't be crazy,' said one of the two other men. 'It never stops raining on Venus. It just goes on and on. I've lived here for ten years and I never saw a minute, a second, when it wasn't pouring.'

'It's like living under water,' said the lieutenant, and rose up, shrugging his guns into place. 'Well, we'd better get going. We'll find that Sun Dome yet.'

'Or we won't find it,' said the cynic.

'It's an hour or so.'

'Now you're lying to me, Lieutenant.'

'No, now I'm lying to myself. This is one of those times when you've got to lie. I can't take much more of this.'

They walked down the jungle trail, now and then looking at their compasses. There was no direction anywhere, only what the compass said. There was a grey sky and rain falling and jungle and a path, and, far back behind them somewhere, a rocket in which they had ridden and fallen. A rocket in which lay two of their friends, dead and dripping rain.

They walked in single file, not speaking. They came to a river which lay wide and flat and brown, flowing down to the great Single Sea. The surface of it was stippled in a billion places by the rain.

'All right, Simmons.'

The lieutenant nodded and Simmons took a small packet from his back which, with a pressure of hidden chemical, inflated into a large boat. The lieutenant directed the cutting of wood and the quick making of paddles and they set out into the river, paddling swiftly across the smooth surface in the rain.

The lieutenant felt the cold rain on his cheeks and on his neck and on his moving arms. The cold was beginning to seep into his lungs. He felt the rain on his ears, on his eyes, on his legs.

'I didn't sleep last night,' he said.

'Who could? Who has? When? How many nights *have* we slept? Thirty nights, thirty days! Who can sleep with rain slamming their head, banging away . . . I'd give anything for a hat. Anything at all, just so it wouldn't hit my head any more. I get headaches. My head is sore; it hurts all the time.'

'I'm sorry I came to China,' said one of the others.

'First time I ever heard Venus called China.'

'Sure, China. Chinese water cure. Remember the old torture? Rope you against a wall. Drop one drop of water on your head every half hour. You go crazy waiting for the next one. Well, that's Venus, but on a big scale. We're not made for water. You can't sleep, you can't breathe right, and you're crazy from just being soggy. If we'd been ready for a crash, we'd have brought waterproofed uniforms and hats. It's this beating rain on your head gets you, most of all. It's so heavy. It's like BB shot. I don't know how long I can take it.'

'Boy, me for the Sun Dome! The man who thought *them* up, thought of something.'

They crossed the river, and in crossing they thought of the Sun Dome, somewhere ahead of them, shining in the jungle rain. A yellow house, round and bright as the sun. A house fifteen feet high by one hundred feet in diameter, in which were warmth and quiet and hot food and freedom from rain. And in the centre of the Sun Dome, of course, was a sun. A small floating free globe of yellow fire, drifting in a space at the top of the building where you could look at it from where you sat, smoking or reading a book or drinking your hot chocolate crowned with marshmallow dollops. There it would be, the yellow sun, just the size of the Earth sun, and it was warm and continuous, and the rain world of Venus would be forgotten as long as they stayed in that house and idled their time.

The lieutenant turned and looked back at the three men using their oars and gritting their teeth. They were as white as mushrooms, as white as he was. Venus bleached everything away in a few months. Even the jungle was an immense cartoon nightmare, for how could the jungle be green with no sun, with always rain falling and always dusk? The white, white jungle with the pale cheese-coloured leaves, and the earth carved of wet Camembert, and the tree boles like immense toadstools — everything black and white. And how often could you see the soil itself? Wasn't it mostly a creek, a stream, a puddle, a pool, a lake, a river, and then, at last, the sea?

'Here we are!'

They leaped out on the farther shore, splashing and sending up showers. The boat was deflated and stored in a cigarette packet. Then, standing on the rainy shore, they tried to light up a few smokes for themselves, and it was five minutes or so before, shuddering, they worked the inverted lighter and, cupping their hands, managed a few drags upon cigarettes that all too quickly were limp and beaten away from their lips by a sudden slap of rain.

They walked on.

'Wait just a moment,' said the lieutenant. 'I thought I saw something ahead.'

'The Sun Dome?'

'I'm not sure. The rain closed in again.'

Simmons began to run. 'The Sun Dome!'

'Come back, Simmons!'

'The Sun Dome!'

Simmons vanished in the rain. The others ran after him.

They found him in a little clearing, and they stopped and looked at him and what he had discovered.

The rocket ship.

It was lying where they had left it. Somehow they had circled back and were where they had started. In the ruin of the ship green fungus was growing up and out of the mouths of the two dead men. As they watched, the fungus took flower, the petals broke away in the rain, and the fungus died.

'How did we do it?'

'An electrical storm must be nearby. Threw our compasses off. That explains it.'

'You're right.'

'What'll we do now?'

'Start out again.'

'Good Lord, we're not any closer to anywhere!'

'Let's try to keep calm about it, Simmons.'

'Calm, calm! This rain's driving me wild!'

'We've enough food for another two days if we're careful.'

The rain danced on their skin, on their wet uniforms; the rain streamed from their noses and ears, from their fingers and knees. They looked like stone fountains frozen in the jungle, issuing forth water from every pore.

And, as they stood, from a distance they heard a roar.

And the monster came out of the rain.

The monster was supported upon a thousand electric blue legs. It walked swiftly and terribly. It struck down a leg with a driving blow. Everywhere a leg struck a tree fell and burned. Great whiffs of ozone filled the rainy air, and smoke blew away and was broken up by the rain. The monster was a half-mile wide and a mile high and it felt of the ground like a great blind thing. Sometimes, for a moment, it had no legs at all. And then, in an instant, a thousand whips would fall out of its belly, white-blue whips, to sting the jungle.

'There's the electrical storm,' said one of the men. 'There's the thing ruined our compasses. And it's coming this way.'

'Lie down, everyone,' said the lieutenant.

'Run!' cried Simmons.

'Don't be a fool. Lie down. It hits the highest points. We may get through unhurt. Lie down about fifty feet from the rocket. It may very well spend its force there and leave us be. Get down!'

The men flopped.

'Is it coming?' they asked each other, after a moment.

'Coming.'

'Is it nearer?'

'Two hundred yards off.'

'Nearer?'

'Here she is!'

The monster came and stood over them. It dropped down ten blue bolts of lightning which struck the rocket. The rocket flashed like a beaten gong and gave off a metal ringing. The monster let down fifteen more bolts which danced about in a ridiculous pantomime, feeling of the jungle and the watery soil.

'No, no!' One of the men jumped up.

'Get down, you fool!' cried the lieutenant.

'No!'

The lightning struck the rocket another dozen times. The lieutenant turned his head on his arm and saw the blue blazing flashes. He saw trees split and crumple into ruin. He saw the monstrous dark cloud turn like a black disc overhead and hurl down a hundred other poles of electricity.

The man who had leaped up was now running, like someone in a great hall of pillars. He ran and dodged between the pillars and then at last a dozen of the pillars slammed down and there was the sound a fly makes when landing upon the grill wires of an exterminator. The lieutenant remembered this from his childhood on a farm. And there was a smell of a man burned to a cinder.

The lieutenant lowered his head. 'Don't look up,' he told the others. He was afraid that he too might run at any moment.

The storm above them flashed down another series of bolts and then moved on away. Once again there was only the rain, which rapidly cleared the air of the charred smell, and in a moment the three remaining men were sitting and waiting for the beat of their hearts to subside into quiet once more.

They walked over to the body, thinking that perhaps they could still save the man's life. They couldn't believe that there wasn't some way to help the man. It was the natural act of men who have not accepted death until they have touched it and turned it over and made plans to bury it or leave it there for the jungle to bury in an hour of quick growth.

The body was twisted steel, wrapped in burned leather. It looked like a wax dummy that had been thrown into an incinerator and pulled out after the wax had sunk to the charcoal skeleton. Only the teeth were white, and they shone like a strange white bracelet dropped half through a clenched black fist.

'He shouldn't have jumped up.' They said it almost at the same time.

Even as they stood over the body it began to vanish, for the vegetation was edging in upon it, little vines and ivy and creepers, and even flowers for the dead.

At a distance the storm walked off on blue bolts of lightning and was gone.

They crossed a river and a creek and a stream and a dozen other rivers and creeks and streams. Before their eyes rivers appeared, rushing, new rivers, while old rivers changed their courses − rivers the colour of mercury, rivers the colour of silver and milk.

They came to the sea.

The Single Sea. There was only one continent on Venus. This land was three thousand miles long by a thousand miles wide, and about this island was the Single Sea, which covered the entire raining planet. The Single Sea, which lay upon the pallid shore with little motion . . .

'This way.' The lieutenant nodded south. 'I'm sure there are two Sun Domes down that way.'

'While they were at it, why didn't they build a hundred more?'

'There're a hundred and twenty of them now, aren't there?'

'One hundred and twenty-six, as of last month. They tried to push a bill through Congress back on Earth a year ago to provide for a couple dozen more, but oh no, you know how *that* is. They'd rather a few men went crazy with the rain.'

They started south.

The lieutenant and Simmons and the third man, Pickard, walked in the rain, in the rain that fell heavily and lightly, heavily and lightly; in the rain that poured and hammered and did not stop falling upon the land and the sea and the walking people.

Simmons saw it first. 'There it is!'

'There's what?'

'The Sun Dome!'

The lieutenant blinked the water from his eyes and raised his hands to ward off the stinging blows of the rain.

At a distance there was a yellow glow on the edge of the jungle, by the sea. It was, indeed, the Sun Dome.

The men smiled at each other.

'Looks like you were right, Lieutenant.'

'Luck.'

'Brother, that puts muscle in me, just seeing it. Come on! Last one there's a son-of-a-bitch!' Simmons began to trot. The others automatically fell in with this, gasping, tired, but keeping pace.

'A big pot of coffee for me,' panted Simmons, smiling. 'And a pan of cinnamon buns, by God! And just lie there and let the old sun hit you. The guy that invented the Sun Domes, he should have got a medal!'

They ran faster. The yellow glow grew brighter.

'Guess a lot of men went crazy before they figured out the

cure. Think it'd be obvious! Right off.' Simmons panted the words in cadence to his running. 'Rain, rain! Years ago. Found a friend. Of mine. Out in the jungle. Wandering around. In the rain. Saying over and over, "Don't know enough, to come in, outta the rain. Don't know enough, to come in, outta the rain. Don't know enough – " On and on. Like that. Poor crazy bastard.'

'Save your breath.'

They ran.

They all laughed. They reached the door of the Sun Dome, laughing.

Simmons yanked the door wide. 'Hey!' he yelled. 'Bring on the coffee and buns!'

There was no reply.

They stepped through the door.

The Sun Dome was empty and dark. There was no synthetic yellow sun floating in a high gaseous whisper at the centre of the blue ceiling. There was no food waiting. It was cold as a vault. And through a thousand holes which had been newly punctured in the ceiling water streamed, the rain fell down, soaking into the thick rugs and the heavy modern furniture and splashing on the glass tables. The jungle was growing up like a moss in the room, on top of the bookcases and the divans. The rain slashed through the holes and fell upon the three men's faces.

Pickard began to laugh quietly.

'Shut up, Pickard!'

'Ye gods, look what's here for us – no food, no sun, nothing. The Venusians – they did it! Of course!'

Simmons nodded, with the rain funnelling down on his face. The water ran in his silvered hair and on his white eyebrows. 'Every once in a while the Venusians come up out of the sea and attack a Sun Dome. They know if they ruin the Sun Domes they can ruin us.'

'But aren't the Sun Domes protected with guns?'

'Sure.' Simmons stepped aside to a place that was relatively dry. 'But it's been five years since the Venusians tried anything. Defence relaxes. They caught this Dome unawares.'

'Where are the bodies?'

'The Venusians took them all down into the sea. I hear they have a delightful way of drowning you. It takes about eight hours to drown the way they work it. Really delightful.'

'I bet there isn't any food here at all.' Pickard laughed.

The lieutenant frowned at him, nodded at him so Simmons could see. Simmons shook his head and went back to a room at one side of the oval chamber. The kitchen was strewn with soggy loaves of bread, and meat that had grown a faint green fur. Rain came through a hundred holes in the kitchen roof.

'Brilliant.' The lieutenant glanced up at the holes. 'I don't suppose we can plug up all those holes and get snug here.'

'Without food, sir?' Simmons snorted. 'I notice the sun machine's torn apart. Our best bet is to make our way to the next Sun Dome. How far is that from here?'

'Not far. As I recall, they built two rather close together here. Perhaps if we waited here, a rescue mission from the other might – '

'It's probably been here and gone already, some days ago. They'll send a crew to repair this place in about six months, when they get the money from Congress. I don't think we'd better wait.'

'All right then, we'll eat what's left of our rations and get on to the next Dome.'

Pickard said, 'If only the rain wouldn't hit my head, just for a few minutes. If I could only remember what it's like not to be bothered.' He put his hands on his skull and held it tight. 'I remember when I was in school a bully used to sit in back of me and pinch me and pinch me and pinch me every five minutes, all day long. He did that for weeks and months. My arms were sore and black and blue all the time. And I thought I'd go crazy from being pinched. One day I must have gone a little mad from being hurt and hurt, and I turned around and took a metal trisquare I used in mechanical drawing and I almost killed that bastard. I almost cut his lousy head off. I almost took his eye out before they dragged me out of the room, and I kept yelling, "Why don't he leave me alone? why don't he leave me alone?" Brother!' His hands clenched the bone of his head, shaking, tightening, his eyes shut. 'But what do I do *now*? Who do I hit, who do I tell to lay off, stop bothering me, this damn rain, like the pinching, always *on* you, that's all you hear, that's all you feel!'

'We'll be at the other Sun Dome by four this afternoon.'

'Sun Dome? Look at this one! What if all the Sun Domes on Venus are gone? What then? What if there are holes in all the ceilings, and the rain coming in!'

'We'll have to chance it.'

'I'm tired of chancing it. All I want is a roof and some quiet. I want to be alone.'

'That's only eight hours off, if you hold on.'

'Don't worry, I'll hold on all right.' And Pickard laughed, not looking at them.

'Let's eat,' said Simmons, watching him.

They set off down the coast, soutward again. After four hours they had to cut inland to go around a river that was a mile wide and so swift it was not navigable by boat. They had to walk inland six miles to a place where the river boiled out of the earth, suddenly, like a mortal wound. In the rain, they walked on solid ground and returned to the sea.

'I've got to sleep,' said Pickard at last. He slumped. 'Haven't slept in four weeks. Tried, but couldn't. Sleep here.'

The sky was getting darker. The night of Venus was

setting in and it was so completely black that it was dangerous to move. Simmons and the lieutenant fell to their knees also, and the lieutenant said, 'All right, we'll see what we can do. We've tried it before, but I don't know. Sleep doesn't seem one of the things you can get in this weather.'

They lay out full, propping their heads up so the water wouldn't come to their mouths, and they closed their eyes. The lieutenant twitched.

He did not sleep.

There were things that crawled on his skin. Things grew upon him in layers. Drops fell and touched other drops and they became streams that trickled over his body, and while these moved down his flesh, the small growths of the forest took root in his clothing. He felt the ivy cling and make a second garment over him; he felt the small flowers bud and open and petal away, and still the rain pattered on his body and on his head. In the luminous night — for the vegetation glowed in the darkness — he could see the other two men outlined, like logs that had fallen and taken upon themselves velvet coverings of grass and flowers. The rain hit his face. He covered his face with his hands. The rain hit his neck. He turned over on his stomach in the mud, on the rubbery plants, and the rain hit his back and hit his legs.

Suddenly he leaped up and began to brush the water from himself. A thousand hands were touching him and he no longer wanted to be touched. He no longer could stand being touched. He floundered and struck something else and knew that it was Simmons, standing up in the rain, sneezing moisture, coughing and choking. And then Pickard was up, shouting, running about.

'Wait a minute, Pickard!'

'Stop it, stop it!' Pickard screamed. He fired off his gun six times at the night sky. In the flashes of powdery illumination they could see armies of raindrops, suspended as in a vast motionless amber, for an instant, hesitating as if shocked by the explosion, fifteen billion droplets, fifteen billion tears, fifteen billion ornaments, jewels standing out against a white velvet viewing board. And then, with the light gone, the drops which had waited to have their pictures taken, which had suspended their downward rush, fell upon them, stinging, in an insect cloud of coldness and pain.

'Stop it! Stop it!'

'Pickard!'

But Pickard was only standing now, alone. When the lieutenant switched on a small hand lamp and played it over Pickard's wet face, the eyes of the man were dilated, and his mouth was open, his face turned up, so the water hit and splashed on his tongue, and hit and drowned the wide eyes, and bubbled in a whispering froth on the nostrils.

'Pickard!'

The man would not reply. He simply stood there for a long while with the bubbles of rain breaking out in his whitened hair and manacles of rain jewels dripping from his wrists and neck.

'Pickard! We're leaving. We're going on. Follow us.'

The rain dripped from Pickard's ears.

'Do you hear me, Pickard!'

It was like shouting down a well.

'Pickard!'

'Leave him alone,' said Simmons.

'We can't go on without him.'

'What'll we do, carry him?' Simmons spat. 'He's no good to us or himself. You know what he'll do? He'll just stand here and drown.'

'What?'

'You ought to know that by now. Don't you know the story? He'll just stand here with his head up and let the rain come in his nostrils and his mouth. He'll breathe water.'

'No.'

'That's how they found General Mendt that time. Sitting

on a rock with his head back, breathing the rain. His lungs were full of water.'

The lieutenant turned the light back to the unblinking face. Pickard's nostrils gave off a tiny whispering wet sound.

'Pickard!' The lieutenant slapped his face.

'He can't even feel you,' said Simmons. 'A few days in this rain and you don't have any face or any legs or hands.'

The lieutenant looked at his own hand in horror. He could no longer feel it.

'But we can't leave Pickard here.'

'I'll show you what we can do.' Simmons fired his gun.

Pickard fell into the raining earth.

Simmons said, 'Don't move, Lieutenant. I've got my gun ready for you too. Think it over; he would only have stood or sat there and drowned. It's quicker this way.'

The lieutenant blinked at the body. 'But you killed him.'

'Yes, because he'd have killed us by being a burden. You saw his face. Insane.'

After a moment the lieutenant nodded. 'All right.'

They walked off into the rain.

It was dark and their hand lamps threw a beam that pierced the rain for only a few feet. After a half hour they had to stop and sit through the rest of the night, aching with hunger, waiting for the dawn to come; when it did come it was grey and continually raining as before, and they began to walk again.

'We've miscalculated,' said Simmons.

'No. Another hour.'

'Speak louder. I can't hear you.' Simmons stopped and smiled. 'By Christ,' he said, and touched his ears. 'My ears. They've gone out on me. All the rain pouring finally numbed me right down to the bone.'

'Can't you hear anything?' said the lieutenant.

'What?' Simmons's eyes were puzzled.

'Nothing. Come on.'

'I think I'll wait here. You go on ahead.'

'You can't do that.'

'I can't hear you. You go on. I'm tired. I don't think the Sun Dome is down this way. And, if it is, it's probably got holes in the roof, like the last one. I think I'll just sit here.'

'Get up from there!'

'So long, Lieutenant.'

'You can't give up now.'

'I've got a gun here that says I'm staying. I just don't give a damn any more. I'm not crazy yet, but I'm the next thing to it. I don't want to go out that way. As soon as you get out of sight I'm going to use this gun on myself.'

'Simmons!'

'You said my name. I can read that much off your lips.'

'Simmons.'

'Look, it's a matter of time. Either I die now or in a few hours. Wait'll you get to that next Dome, if you ever get there, and find rain coming in through the roof. Won't that be nice?'

The lieutenant waited and then splashed off in the rain. He turned and called back once, but Simmons was only sitting there with the gun in his hands, waiting for him to get out of sight. He shook his head and waved the lieutenant on.

The lieutenant didn't even hear the sound of the gun.

He began to eat the flowers as he walked. They stayed down for a time, and weren't poisonous; neither were they particularly sustaining, and he vomited them up, sickly, a minute or so later.

Once he took some leaves and tried to make himself a hat, but he had tried that before; the rain melted the leaves from his head. Once picked, the vegetation rotted quickly and fell away into grey masses in his fingers.

'Another five minutes,' he told himself. 'Another five minutes and then I'll walk into the sea and keep walking. We weren't made for this; no Earth Man was or ever will be able to take it. Your nerves, your nerves.'

He floundered his way through a sea of slush and foliage and came to a small hill.

At a distance there was a faint yellow smudge in the cold veils of water.

The next Sun Dome.

Through the trees, a long round yellow building, far away. For a moment he only stood, swaying, looking at it.

He began to run and then he slowed down, for he was afraid. He didn't call out. What if it's the same one? What if it's the dead Sun Dome, with no sun in it? he thought.

He slipped and fell. Lie here, he thought; it's the wrong one. Lie here. It's no use. Drink all you want.

But he managed to climb to his feet again and crossed several creeks, and the yellow light grew very bright, and he began to run again, his feet crashing into mirrors and glass, his arms flailing at diamonds and precious stones.

He stood before the yellow door. The printed letters over it said THE SUN DOME. He put his numb hand up to feel it. Then he twisted the doorknob and stumbled in.

He stood for a moment looking about. Behind him the rain whirled at the door. Ahead of him, upon a low table, stood a silver pot of hot chocolate, steaming, and a cup, full, with a marshmallow in it. And beside that, on another tray, stood thick sandwiches of rich chicken meat and fresh-cut tomatoes and green onions. And on a rod just before his eyes was a great thick green Turkish towel, and a bin in which to throw wet clothes, and, to his right, a small cubicle in which heat rays might dry you instantly. And upon a chair, a fresh change of uniform, waiting for anyone – himself, or any lost one – to make use of it. And farther over, coffee in steaming copper urns, and a phonograph from which music was playing quietly, and books bound in red and brown leather. And near the books a cot, a soft deep cot upon which one might lie, exposed and bare, to drink in the rays of the one great bright thing which dominated the long room.

He put his hands to his eyes. He saw other men moving towards him, but said nothing to them. He waited, and opened his eyes, and looked. The water from his uniform pooled at his feet, and he felt it drying from his hair and his face and his chest and his arms and his legs.

He was looking at the sun.

It hung in the centre of the room, large and yellow and warm. It made not a sound, and there was no sound in the room. The door was shut and the rain only a memory to his tingling body. The sun hung very high in the blue sky of the room, warm, hot, yellow, and very fine.

He walked forward, tearing off his clothes as he went.

The Great Fire

The morning the great fire started, nobody in the house could put it out. It was Mother's niece, Marianne, living with us while her parents were in Europe, who was all aflame. So nobody could smash the little window in the red box at the corner and pull the trigger to bring the gushing hoses and the hatted firemen. Blazing like so much ignited cellophane, Marianne came downstairs, plumped herself with a loud cry or moan at the breakfast table, and refused to eat enough to fill a tooth cavity.

Mother and Father moved away, the warmth in the room being excessive.

'Good morning, Marianne.'

'What?' Marianne looked beyond people and spoke vaguely. 'Oh, good morning.'

'Did you sleep well last night, Marianne?'

But they knew she hadn't slept. Mother gave Marianne a glass of water to drink, and everyone wondered if it would evaporate in her hand. Grandma, from her table chair, surveyed Marianne's fevered eyes. 'You're sick, but it's no microbe,' she said. 'They couldn't find it under a microscope.'

'What?' said Marianne.

'Love is godmother to stupidity,' said Father detachedly.

'She'll be all right,' Mother said to Father. 'Girls only seem stupid because when they're in love they can't hear.'

'It affects the semicircular canals,' said Father. 'Making many girls fall right into a fellow's arms. I *know*. I was almost crushed to death once by a falling woman, and let me tell you – '

'Hush.' Mother frowned, looking at Marianne.

'She can't hear what we're saying; she's cataleptic right now.'

'He's coming to pick her up this morning,' whispered Mother to Father, as if Marianne wasn't even in the room. 'They're going riding in his jalopy.'

Father patted his mouth with a napkin. 'Was our daughter like this, Mama?' he wanted to know. 'She's been married and gone so long, I've forgotten. I don't recall she was so foolish. One would never know a girl had an ounce of sense at a time like this. That's what fools a man. He says, Oh, what a lovely brainless girl, she loves me, I think I'll marry her. He marries her and wakes up one morning and all the dreaminess is gone out of her and her intellect has returned, unpacked, and is hanging up undies all about the house. The man begins running into ropes and lines. He finds himself on a little desert isle, a little living room alone in the midst of a universe, with a honeycomb that has turned into a bear trap, with a butterfly metamorphosed into a wasp. He then immediately takes up a hobby: stamp collecting, lodge meetings, or —'

'How you *do* run on,' cried Mother. 'Marianne, tell us about this young man. What was his name again? Was it Isak Van Pelt?'

'What? Oh — Isak, yes.' Marianne had been roving about her bed all night, sometimes flipping poetry books and reading incredible lines, sometimes lying flat on her back, sometimes on her tummy looking out at dreaming moonlit country. The smell of jasmine had touched the room all night and the excessive warmth of early spring (the thermometer read fifty-five degrees) had kept her awake. She looked like a dying moth, if anyone had peeked through the keyhole.

This morning she had clapped her hands over her head in the mirror and come to breakfast, remembering just in time to put on a dress.

Grandma laughed quietly all during breakfast. Finally she said, 'You must eat, child, you *must*.' So Marianne played with her toast and got half a piece down. Just then there was a loud honk outside. That was Isak! In his jalopy!

'Whoop!' cried Marianne, and ran upstairs quickly.

The young Isak Van Pelt was brought in and introduced around.

When Marianne was finally gone, Father sat down, wiping his forehead. 'I don't know. This is too much.'

'You were the one who suggested she start going out,' said Mother.

'And I'm sorry I suggested it,' he said. 'But she's been visiting us for six months now, and six more months to go. I thought if she met some nice young man – '

'And they were married,' husked Grandma darkly, 'why, Marianne might move out almost immediately – is *that* it?'

'Well,' said Father.

'Well,' said Grandma.

'But now it's worse than before,' said Father. 'She floats around singing with her eyes shut, playing those infernal love records and talking to herself. A man can stand so much. She's getting so she laughs all the time, too. Do eighteen-year-old girls often wind up in the booby hatch?'

'He seems a nice young man,' said Mother.

'Yes, we can always pray for that,' said Father, taking out a little shot glass. 'Here's to an early marriage.'

The second morning Marianne was out of the house like a fireball when first she heard the jalopy horn. There was no time for the young man even to come to the door. Only Grandma saw them roar off together, from the parlour window.

'She almost knocked me down.' Father brushed his moustache. 'What's *that*? Brained eggs? Well.'

In the afternoon, Marianne, home again, drifted about the

living room to the phonograph records. The needle hiss filled the house. She played 'That Old Black Magic' twenty-one times, going 'la la la' as she swam with her eyes closed in the room.

'I'm afraid to go in my own parlour,' said Father. 'I retired from business to smoke cigars and enjoy living, not to have a limp relative humming about under the parlour chandelier.'

'Hush,' said Mother.

'This is a crisis,' announced Father, 'in my life. After all, she's just visiting.'

'You know how visiting girls are. Away from home they think they're in Paris, France. She'll be gone in October. It's not so dreadful.'

'Let's see,' figured Father slowly. 'I'll have been buried just about one hundred and thirty days out at Green Lawn Cemetery by then.' He got up and threw his paper down into a little white tent on the floor. 'By George, Mother, I'm talking to her right *now*!'

He went and stood in the parlour door, peering through it at the waltzing Marianne. 'La,' she sang to the music.

Clearing his throat, he stepped through.

'Marianne,' he said.

' "That old black magic . . . " ' sang Marianne. 'Yes?'

He watched her hands swinging in the air. She gave him a sudden fiery look as she danced by.

'I want to talk to you.' He straightened his tie.

'Dah dum dee dum dum dee dum dee dum dum,' she sang.

'Did you *hear* me?' he demanded.

'He's *so* nice,' she said.

'Evidently.'

'Do you know, he bows and opens doors like a doorman and plays a trumpet like Harry James and brought me daisies this morning?'

'I wouldn't doubt.'

'His eyes are blue.' She looked at the ceiling.

He could find nothing at all on the ceiling to look at.

She kept looking, as she danced, at the ceiling as he came over and stood near her, looking up, but there wasn't a rain spot or a settling crack there, and he sighed, 'Marianne.'

'And we ate lobster at that river café.'

'Lobster. I know, but we don't want you breaking down, getting weak. One day, tomorrow, you must stay home and help your aunt Math make her doilies – '

'Yes, sir.' She dreamed around the room with her wings out.

'Did you *hear* me?' he demanded.

'Yes,' she whispered. 'Yes.' Her eyes shut. 'Oh yes, yes.' Her skirts whished around. 'Uncle,' she said, her head back, lolling.

'You'll help your aunt with her doilies?' he cried.

' – with her doilies,' she murmured.

'There!' He sat down in the kitchen, plucking up the paper. 'I guess *I* told her!'

But next morning he was on the edge of his bed when he heard the hotrod's thunderous muffler and heard Marianne fall downstairs, linger two seconds in the dining room for breakfast, hesitate by the bathroom long enough to consider whether she would be sick, and then the slam of the front door, the sound of the jalopy banging down the street, two people singing off-key in it.

Father put his head in his hands. 'Doilies,' he said.

'What?' said Mother.

'Dooley's,' said Father. 'I'm going down to Dooley's for a morning visit.'

'But Dooley's isn't open until ten.'

'I'll wait,' decided Father, eyes shut.

That night and seven other wild nights the porch swing sang a little creaking song, back and forth, back and forth. Father, hiding in the living room, could be seen in fierce relief whenever he draughted his ten-cent cigar and the cherry light illumined his immensely tragic face. The porch swing creaked. He waited for another creak. He heard little butter-fly-soft sounds from outside, little palpitations of laughter and sweet nothings in small ears. 'My porch,' said Father. 'My swing,' he whispered to his cigar, looking at it. 'My house.' He listened for another creak. 'My God,' he said.

He went to the tool shed and appeared on the dark porch with a shiny oil can. 'No, don't get up. Don't bother. There, and there.' He oiled the swing joints. It was dark. He couldn't see Marianne; he could smell her. The perfume almost knocked him off into the rosebush. He couldn't see her gentleman friend, either. 'Good night,' he said. He went in and sat down and there was no more creaking. Now all he could hear was something that sounded like the mothlike flutter of Marianne's heart.

'He must be very nice,' said Mother in the kitchen door, wiping a dinner dish.

'That's what I'm hoping,' whispered Father. 'That's why I let them have the porch every night!'

'So many days in a row,' said Mother. 'A girl doesn't go with a nice young man that many times unless he's serious.'

'Maybe he'll propose tonight!' was Father's happy thought.

'Hardly so soon. And she is so young.'

'Still,' he ruminated, 'it might happen. It's *got* to happen, by the Lord Harry.'

Grandma chuckled from her corner easy chair. It sounded like someone turning the pages of an ancient book.

'What's so funny?' said Father.

'Wait and see,' said Grandma. 'Tomorrow.'

Father stared at the dark, but Grandma would say no more.

'Well, well,' said Father at breakfast. He surveyed his eggs with a kindly, paternal eye. 'Well, well, by gosh, last night, on the porch, there was *more whispering*. What's his name? Isak? Well, now, if I'm any judge at all, I think he proposed to Marianne last night; yes, I'm positive of it!'

'It would be nice,' said Mother. 'A spring marriage. But it's so *soon*.'

'Look,' said Father with full-mouthed logic. 'Marianne's the kind of girl who marries quick and young. We can't stand in her way, can we?'

'For once I think you're right,' said Mother. 'A marriage would be fine. Spring flowers, and Marianne looking nice in that gown I saw at Haydecker's last week.'

They all peered anxiously at the stairs, waiting for Marianne to appear.

'Pardon me,' rasped Grandma, sighting up from her morning toast. 'But I wouldn't talk of getting rid of Marianne just yet if I were you.'

'And why not?'

'Because.'

'Because why?'

'I hate to spoil your plans,' rustled Grandma, chuckling. She gestured with her little vinegary head. 'But while you people were worrying about getting Marianne married, I've been keeping tabs on her. Seven days now I've been watching this young fellow each day he came in his car and honked his horn outside. He must be an actor or a quick-change artist or something.'

'What?' asked Father.

'Yep,' said Grandma. 'Because one day he was a young blond fellow, and next day he was a tall dark fellow, and Wednesday he was a chap with a brown moustache, and Thursday he had wavy red hair, and Friday he was shorter, with a Chevrolet stripped down instead of a Ford.'

Mother and Father sat for a moment as if hit with a hammer right behind the left ear.

At last Father, his face exploding with colour, shouted,

'Do you mean to *say*! You *sat* there, woman, you say; all those men, and you – '

'You were always hiding,' snapped Grandma. 'So you wouldn't spoil things. If you'd come out in the open you'd have seen the same as I. I never said a word. She'll simmer down. It's just her time of life. Every woman goes through it. It's hard, but they can survive. A new man every day does wonders for a girl's ego!'

'You, you, you, you, *you*!' Father choked on it, eyes wild, throat gorged too big for his collar. He fell back in his chair, exhausted. Mother sat, stunned.

'Good morning, everyone!' Marianne raced downstairs and popped into a chair. Father stared at her.

'You, you, you, you, you,' he accused Grandma.

I shall run down the street shouting, thought Father wildly, and break the fire-alarm window and pull the lever and bring the fire engines and the hoses. Or perhaps there will be a late snowstorm and I shall set Marianne out in it to cool.

He did neither. The heat in the room being excessive, according to the wall calendar, everyone moved out onto the cool porch while Marianne sat looking at her orange juice.

The Wilderness

'Oh, the Good Time has come at last – '

It was twilight, and Janice and Leonora packed steadily in their summer house, singing songs, eating little, and holding to each other when necessary. But they never glanced at the window where the night gathered deep and the stars came out bright and cold.

'Listen!' said Janice.

A sound like a steamboat down the river, but it was a rocket in the sky. And beyond that – banjos playing? No, only the summer-night crickets in this year 2003. Ten thousand sounds breathed through the town and the weather. Janice, head bent, listened. Long, long ago, 1849, this very street had breathed the voices of ventriloquists, preachers, fortunetellers, fools, scholars, gamblers, gathered at this selfsame Independence, Missouri. Waiting for the moist earth to bake and the great tidal grasses to come up heavy enough to hold the weight of their carts, their wagons, their indiscriminate destinies, and their dreams.

> *'Oh, the Good Time has come at last,*
> *To Mars we are a-going, sir,*
> *Five Thousand Women in the sky,*
> *That's quite a springtime sowing, sir!'*

'That's an old Wyoming song,' said Leonora. 'Change the words and it's fine for 2003.'

Janice lifted a matchbox of food pills, calculating the totals of things carried in those high-axled, tall-bedded wagons.

For each man, each woman, incredible tonnages! Hams, bacon slabs, sugar, salt, flour, dried fruits, 'pilot' bread, citric acid, water, ginger, pepper — a list as big as the land! Yet here, today, pills that fit in a wristwatch fed you not from Fort Laramie to Hangtown, but all across a wilderness of stars.

Janice threw wide the closet door and almost screamed. Darkness and night and all the spaces between the stars looked out at her.

Long years ago two things had happened. Her sister had locked her, shrieking, in a closet. And, at a party, playing hide-and-seek, she had run through the kitchen and into a long dark hall. But it wasn't a hall. It was an unlit stairwell, a swallowing blackness. She had run out upon empty air. She had pedalled her feet, screamed, and fallen! Fallen in midnight blackness. Into the cellar. It took a long while, a heartbeat, to fall. And she had smothered in that closet a long, long time without daylight, without friends, no one to hear her screamings. Away from everything, locked in darkness. Falling in darkness. Shrieking!

The two memories.

Now, with the closet door wide, with darkness like a velvet shroud hung before her to be stroked by a trembling hand, with the darkness like a black panther breathing there, looking at her with unlit eyes, the two memories rushed out. Space and a falling. Space and being locked away, screaming. She and Leonora working steadily, packing, being careful not to glance out the window at the frightening Milky Way and the vast emptiness. Only to have the long-familiar closet, with its private night, remind them at last of their destiny.

This was how it would be, out there, sliding towards the stars, in the night, in the great hideous black closet, screaming, but no one to hear. Falling forever among meteor clouds and godless comets. Down the elevator shaft. Down the nightmare coal chute into nothingness.

She screamed. None of it came out of her mouth. It collided upon itself in her chest and head. She screamed. She slammed the closet door! She lay against it! She felt the darkness breathe and yammer at the door and she held it tight, eyes watering. She stood there a long time, until the trembling vanished, watching Leonora work. And the hysteria, thus ignored, drained away and away, and at last was gone. A wristwatch ticked, with a clean sound of normality, in the room.

'Sixty *million* miles.' She moved at last to the window as if it were a deep well. 'I can't believe that men on Mars, tonight, are building towns, waiting for us.'

'The only thing to believe is catching our Rocket tomorrow.'

Janice raised a white gown like a ghost in the room.

'Strange, strange. To marry — on another world.'

'Let's get to bed.'

'No! The call comes at midnight. I couldn't sleep, thinking how to tell Will I've decided to take the Mars Rocket. Oh, Leonora, think of it, my voice travelling sixty million miles on the light-phone to him. I changed my mind so quick — I'm scared!'

'Our *last* night on Earth.'

Now they really knew and accepted it; now the knowledge had found them out. They were going away, and they might never come back. They were leaving the town of Independence in the state of Missouri on the continent of North America, surrounded by one ocean which was the Atlantic and another the Pacific, none of which could be put in their travelling cases. They had shrunk from this final knowledge. Now it was facing them. And they were struck numb.

'Our children, they won't be Americans, or Earth people at all. We'll all be Martians, the rest of our lives.'

'I don't want to go!' cried Janice suddenly.

The panic froze her.

'I'm afraid! The space, the darkness, the Rocket, the meteors! *Everything* gone! Why should I go out there?'

Leonora took hold of her shoulders and held her close, rocking her. 'It's a new world. It's like the old days. The men first and the women after.'

'Why, why should I go, tell me!'

'Because,' said Leonora at last, quietly, seating her on the bed, 'Will is up there.'

His name was good to hear. Janice quieted.

'These men make it so hard,' said Leonora. 'Used to be if a woman ran two hundred miles for a man it was something. Then they made it a thousand miles. And now they put a whole universe between us. But that can't stop us, can it?'

'I'm afraid I'll be a fool on the Rocket.'

'I'll be a fool with you.' Leonora got up. 'Now, let's walk around town, let's see everything one last time.'

Janice stared out at the town. 'Tomorrow night this'll all be here, but we won't. People'll wake up, eat, work, sleep, wake again, but we won't know it, and they'll never miss us.'

Leonora and Janice moved around each other as if they couldn't find the door.

'Come on.'

They opened the door, switched off the lights, stepped out, and shut the door behind them.

In the sky there was a great coming-in and coming-in. Vast flowering motions, huge whistlings and whirlings, snow-storms falling. Helicopters, white flakes, dropping quietly. From west and east and north and south the women were arriving, arriving. Through all of the night sky you saw helicopters blizzard down. The hotels were full, private homes were making accommodations, tent cities rose in meadows and pastures like strange, ugly flowers, and the town and the country were warm with more than summer tonight. Warm with women's pink faces and the sunburnt faces of new men watching the sky. Beyond the hills rockets tried their fire, and a sound like a giant organ, all its keys pressed upon at once, shuddered every crystal window and every hidden bone. You felt it in your jaw, your toes, your fingers, a shivering.

Leonora and Janice sat in the drugstore among unfamiliar women.

'You ladies look very pretty, but you sure look sad,' said the soda-fountain man.

'Two chocolate malteds.' Leonora smiled for both of them, as if Janice were mute.

They gazed at the chocolate drink as if it were a rare museum painting. Malts would be scarce for many years on Mars.

Janice fussed in her purse and took out an envelope reluctantly and laid it on the marble counter.

'This is from Will to me. It came in the Rocket mail two days ago. It was this that made up my mind for me, made me decide to go. I didn't tell you. I want you to see it now. Go ahead, read the note.'

Leonora shook the note out of the envelope and read it aloud: '*Dear Janice: this is* our *house if you decide to come to Mars. Will.*'

Leonora tapped the envelope again, and a colour photograph dropped out, glistening, on the counter. It was a picture of a house, a dark, mossy, ancient, caramel-brown, comfortable house with red flowers and green cool ferns bordering it, and a disreputably hairy ivy on the porch.

'But, Janice!'

'What?'

'This is a picture of *your* house, here on Earth, here on Elm Street!'

'No. Look close.'

And they looked again, together, and on both sides of the

comfortable dark house and behind it was scenery that was not Earth scenery. The soil was a strange colour of violet, and the grass was the faintest bit red, and the sky glowed like a grey diamond, and a strange crooked tree grew to one side, looking like an old woman with crystals in her white hair.

'That's the house Will's built for me,' said Janice, 'on Mars. It helps to look at it. All yesterday, when I had the chance, alone, and was most afraid and panicky, I took out this picture and looked at it.'

They both gazed at the dark comfortable house sixty million miles away, familiar but unfamiliar, old but new, a yellow light shining in the right front parlour window.

'That man Will,' said Leonora, nodding her head, 'knows just what he's doing.'

They finished their drinks. Outside, a vast warm crowd of strangers wandered by and the 'snow' fell steadily in the summer sky.

They bought many silly things to take with them, bags of lemon candy, glossy women's magazines, fragile perfumes; and then they walked out into the town and rented two belted jackets that refused to recognize gravity and imitated only the moth, touched the delicate controls, and felt themselves whispered like white blossom petals over the town. 'Anywhere,' said Leonora, 'anywhere at all.'

They let the wind blow them where it would; they let the wind take them through the night of summer apple trees and the night of warm preparation, over the lovely town, over the houses of childhood and other days, over schools and avenues, over creeks and meadows and farms so familiar that each grain of wheat was a golden coin. They blew as leaves must blow before the threat of a fire-wind, with warning whispers and summer lightning crackling among the folded hills. They saw the milk-dust country roads where not so long ago they had drifted in moonlit helicopters in great whorls of sound spiralling down to touch beside cool night streams with the young men who were now gone.

They floated in an immense sigh above a town already made remote by the little space between themselves and the earth, a town receding behind them in a black river and coming up in a tidal wave of lights and colour ahead, untouchable and a dream now, already smeared in their eyes with nostalgia, with a panic of memory that began before the thing itself was gone.

Blown quietly, eddying, they gazed secretly at a hundred faces of dear friends they were leaving behind, the lamplit people held and framed by windows which slid by on the wind, it seemed; all of Time breathing them along. There was no tree they did not examine for old confessions of love carved and whittled there, no sidewalk they did not skim across as over fields of mica-snow. For the first time they knew their town was beautiful and the lonely lights and the ancient bricks beautiful, and they both felt their eyes grow large with the beauty of this feast they were giving themselves. All floated upon an evening carousel, with fitful drifts of music wafting up here and there, and voices calling and murmuring from houses that were whitely haunted by television.

The two women passed like needles, sewing one tree to the next with their perfume. Their eyes were too full, and yet they kept putting away each detail, each shadow, each solitary oak and elm, each passing car upon the small snaking streets below, until not only their eyes but their heads and then their hearts were too full.

I feel like I'm dead, thought Janice, and in the graveyard on a spring night and everything alive but me and everyone moving and ready to go on with life without me. It's like I felt each spring when I was sixteen, passing the graveyard and weeping for them because they were dead and it didn't seem fair, on nights as soft as that, that I was alive. I was guilty of living. And now, here, tonight, I feel they have taken me from the graveyard and let me go above the town just once more to see what it's like to be living, to be a town and a people, before they slam the black door on me again.

Softly, softly, like two white paper lanterns on a night wind, the women moved over their lifetime and their past, and over the meadows where the tent cities glowed and the highways where supply trucks would be clustered and running until dawn. They hovered above it all for a long time.

The courthouse clock was booming eleven forty-five when they came like spider webs floating from the stars, touching on the moonlit pavement before Janice's old house. The city was asleep, and Janice's house waited for them to come in searching for *their* sleep, which was not there.

'Is this *us*, here?' asked Janice. 'Janice Smith and Leonora Holmes, in the year 2003?'

'Yes.'

Janice licked her lips and stood straight. 'I wish it was some other year.'

'1492? 1612?' Leonora sighed, and the wind in the trees sighed with her, moving away. 'It's always Columbus Day or Plymouth Rock Day, and I'll be darned if I know what we women can do about it.'

'Be old maids.'

'Or do just what we're doing.'

They opened the door of the warm night house, the sounds of the town dying slowly in their ears. As they shut the door, the phone began to ring.

'The call!' cried Janice, running.

Leonora came into the bedroom after her and already Janice had the receiver up and was saying, 'Hello, hello!' And the operator in a far city was readying the immense apparatus which would tie two worlds together, and the two women waited, one sitting and pale, the other standing, but just as pale, bent towards her.

There was a long pause, full of stars and time, a waiting pause not unlike the last three years for all of them. And now the moment had arrived, and it was Janice's turn to phone through millions upon millions of miles of meteors and comets, running away from the yellow sun which might boil or burn her words or scorch the meaning from them. But her voice went like a silver needle through everything, in stitches of talking, across the big night, reverberating from the moons of Mars. And then her voice found its way to a man in a room in a city there on another world, five minutes by radio away. And her message was this:

'Hello, Will. This is Janice!'

She swallowed.

'They say I haven't much time. A minute.'

She closed her eyes.

'I want to talk slow, but they say talk fast and get it all in. So I want to say — I've decided. I will come up there. I'll go on the Rocket tomorrow. I *will* come up there to you, after all. And I love you. I hope you can hear me. I love you. It's been so long . . . '

Her voice motioned on its way to that unseen world. Now, with the message sent, the words said, she wanted to call them back, to censor, to rearrange them, to make a prettier sentence, a fairer explanation of her soul. But already the words were hung between planets and if, by some cosmic radiation, they could have been illuminated, caught fire in vaporous wonder there, her love would have lit a dozen worlds and startled the night side of Earth into a premature dawn, she thought. Now the words were not hers at all, they belonged to space, they belonged to no one until they arrived, and they were travelling at one hundred and eighty-six thousand miles a second to their destination.

What will he say to me? What will he say back in *his* minute of time? she wondered. She fussed with and twisted the watch on her wrist, and the light-phone receiver on her ear crackled and space talked to her with electrical jigs and dances and audible auroras.

'Has he answered?' whispered Leonora.

'Shhh!' said Janice, bending, as if sick.

Then his voice came through space.

'I hear him!' cried Janice.

'What does he say?'

The voice called out from Mars and took itself through the places where there was no sunrise or sunset, but always the night with a sun in the middle of the blackness. And somewhere between Mars and Earth everything of the message was lost, perhaps in a sweep of electrical gravity rushing by on the flood tides of a meteor, or interfered with by a rain of silver meteors. In any event, the small words and the unimportant words of the message were washed away. And his voice came through saying only one word:

' . . . love . . . '

After that there was the huge night again and the sound of stars turning and suns whispering to themselves and the sound of her heart, like another world in space, filling her earphones.

'Did you *hear* him?' asked Leonora.

Janice could only nod.

'What did he say, what did he say?' cried Leonora.

But Janice could not tell anyone; it was much too good to tell. She sat listening to that one word again and again, as her memory played it back. She sat listening, while Leonora took the phone away from her without her knowing it and put it down upon its hook.

Then they were in bed and the lights out and the night wind blowing through the rooms a smell of the long journey in darkness and stars, and their voices talking of tomorrow, and the days after tomorrow which would not be days at all, but day-nights of timeless Time; their voices faded away into sleep or wakeful thinking, and Janice lay alone in her bed.

Is this how it was over a century ago, she wondered, when the women, the night before, lay ready for sleep, or not ready, in the small towns of the East, and heard the sound of horses in the night and the creak of the Conestoga wagons ready to go, and the brooding of oxen under the trees, and the cry of children already lonely before their time? All the sounds of arrivals and departures into the deep forests and fields, the blacksmiths working in their own red hells through midnight? And the smell of bacons and hams ready for the journeying, and the heavy feel of the wagons like ships foundering with goods, with water in the wooden kegs to tilt and slop across prairies, and the chickens hysterical in their slung-beneath-the-wagon crates, and the dogs running out to the wilderness ahead and, fearful, running back with a look of empty space in their eyes? Is this, then, how it was so long ago? On the rim of the precipice, on the edge of the cliff of stars? In their time the smell of buffalo, and in our time the smell of the Rocket? Is this, then, how it was?

And she decided, as sleep assumed the dreaming for her, that yes, yes indeed, very much so, irrevocably, this was as it had always been and would forever continue to be.

A Sound of Thunder

The sign on the wall seemed to quaver under a film of sliding warm water. Eckels felt his eyelids blink over his stare, and the sign burned in this momentary darkness:

TIME SAFARI, INC.
SAFARIS TO ANY YEAR IN THE PAST.
YOU NAME THE ANIMAL.
WE TAKE YOU THERE.
YOU SHOOT IT.

A warm phlegm gathered in Eckels' throat; he swallowed and pushed it down. The muscles around his mouth formed a smile as he put his hand slowly out upon the air, and in that hand waved a cheque for ten thousand dollars at the man behind the desk.

'Does this safari guarantee I come back alive?'

'We guarantee nothing,' said the official, 'except the dinosaurs.' He turned. 'This is Mr Travis, your Safari Guide in the Past. He'll tell you what and where to shoot. If he says no shooting, no shooting. If you disobey instructions, there's a stiff penalty of another ten thousand dollars, plus possible government action, on your return.'

Eckels glanced across the vast office at a mass and tangle, a snaking and humming of wires and steel boxes, at an aurora that flickered now orange, now silver, now blue. There was a sound like a gigantic bonfire burning all of Time, all the years and all the parchment calendars, all the hours piled high and set aflame.

A touch of the hand and this burning would, on the

instant, beautifully reverse itself. Eckels remembered the wording in the advertisements to the letter. Out of chars and ashes, out of dust and coals, like golden salamanders, the old years, the green years, might leap; roses sweeten the air, white hair turn Irish-black, wrinkles vanish; all, everything fly back to seed, flee death, rush down to their beginnings, suns rise in western skies and set in glorious easts, moons eat themselves opposite to the custom, all and everything cupping one in another like Chinese boxes, rabbits into hats, all and everything returning to the fresh death, the seed death, the green death, to the time before the beginning. A touch of a hand might do it, the merest touch of a hand.

'Hell and damn,' Eckels breathed, the light of the Machine on his thin face. 'A real Time Machine.' He shook his head. 'Makes you think. If the election had gone badly yesterday, I might be here now running away from the results. Thank God Keith won. He'll make a fine President of the United States.'

'Yes,' said the man behind the desk. 'We're lucky. If Deutscher had gotten in, we'd have the worst kind of dictatorship. There's an anti-everything man for you, a militarist, anti-Christ, anti-human, anti-intellectual. People called us up, you know, joking but not joking. Said if Deutscher became President they wanted to go live in 1492. Of course it's not our business to conduct Escapes, but to form Safaris. Anyway, Keith's President now. All you got to worry about is – '

'Shooting my dinosaur.' Eckels finished it for him.

'A *Tyrannosaurus rex*. The Thunder Lizard, the damndest monster in history. Sign this release. Anything happens to you, we're not responsible. Those dinosaurs are hungry.'

Eckels flushed angrily. 'Trying to scare me!'

'Frankly, yes. We don't want anyone going who'll panic at the first shot. Six Safari leaders were killed last year, and a dozen hunters. We're here to give you the damndest thrill a *real* hunter ever asked for. Travelling you back sixty million years to bag the biggest damned game in all Time. Your personal cheque's still there. Tear it up.

Mr Eckels looked at the cheque for a long time. His fingers twitched.

'Good luck,' said the man behind the desk. 'Mr Travis, he's all yours.'

They moved silently across the room, taking their guns with them, towards the Machine, towards the silver metal and the roaring light.

First a day and then a night and then a day and then a night, then it was day-night-day-night-day. A week, a month, a year, a decade. A.D. 2055, A.D. 2019. 1999! 1957! Gone! the Machine roared.

They put on their oxygen helmets and tested the intercoms.

Eckels swayed on the padded seat, his face pale, his jaw stiff. He felt the trembling in his arms and he looked down and found his hands tight on the new rifle. There were four other men in the Machine. Travis, the Safari leader, his assistant, Lesperance, and two other hunters, Billings and Kramer. They sat looking at each other, and the years blazed around them.

'Can these guns get a dinosaur cold?' Eckels felt his mouth saying.

'If you hit them right,' said Travis on the helmet radio. 'Some dinosaurs have two brains, one in the head, another far down the spinal column. We stay away from those. That's stretching luck. Put your first two shots into the eyes, if you can, blind them, and go back into the brain.'

The Machine howled. Time was a film run backwards. Suns fled and ten million moons fled after them. 'Good God,' said Eckels. 'Every hunter that ever lived would envy us today. This makes Africa seem like Illinois.'

The Machine slowed; its scream fell to a murmur. The Machine stopped.

The sun stopped in the sky.

The fog that had enveloped the Machine blew away and they were in an old time, a very old time indeed, three hunters and two Safari Heads with their blue metal guns across their knees.

'Christ isn't born yet,' said Travis. 'Moses has not gone to the mountain to talk with God. The Pyramids are still in the earth, waiting to be cut and put up. *Remember* that. Alexander, Caesar, Napoleon, Hitler — none of them exists.'

The men nodded.

'That' — Mr Travis pointed — 'is the jungle of sixty million two thousand and fifty-five years before President Keith.'

He indicated a metal path that struck off into green wilderness, over steaming swamp, among giant ferns and palms.

'And that,' he said, 'is the Path, laid by Time Safari for your use. It floats six inches above the earth. Doesn't touch so much as one grass blade, flower, or tree. It's an anti-gravity metal. Its purpose is to keep you from touching this world of the past in any way. Stay on the Path. Don't go off it. I repeat. *Don't go off.* For *any* reason! If you fall off, there's a penalty. And don't shoot any animal we don't okay.'

'Why?' asked Eckels.

They sat in the ancient wilderness. Far birds' cries blew on a wind, and the smell of tar and an old salt sea, moist grasses, and flowers the colour of blood.

'We don't want to change the Future. We don't belong here in the Past. The government doesn't *like* us here. We have to pay big graft to keep our franchise. A Time Machine is damn finicky business. Not knowing it, we might kill an important animal, a small bird, a roach, a flower even, thus destroying an important link in a growing species.'

'That's not clear,' said Eckels.

'All right,' Travis continued, 'say we accidentally kill one mouse here. That means all the future families of this one particular mouse are destroyed, right?'

'Right.'

'And all the families of the families of the families of that one mouse! With a stamp of your foot, you annihilate the first one, then a dozen, then a thousand, a million, a *billion* possible mice!'

'So they're dead,' said Eckels. 'So what?'

'So what?' Travis snorted quietly. 'Well, what about the foxes that'll need those mice to survive? For want of ten mice, a fox dies. For want of ten foxes, a lion starves. For want of a lion, all manner of insects, vultures, infinite billions of life forms are thrown into chaos and destruction. Eventually it all boils down to this: fifty-nine million years later, a cave man, one of a dozen on the *entire world*, goes hunting wild boar or sabre-tooth tiger for food. But you, friend, have *stepped* on all the tigers in that region. By stepping on *one* single mouse. So the cave man starves. And the cave man, please note, is not just *any* expendable man, no! He is an *entire future nation*. From his loins would have sprung ten sons. From *their* loins one hundred sons, and thus onward to a civilization. Destroy this one man, and you destroy a race, a people, an entire history of life. It is comparable to slaying some of Adam's grandchildren. The stamp of your foot, on one mouse, could start an earthquake, the effects of which could shake our Earth and destinies down through Time, to their very foundations. With the death of that one cave man, a billion others yet unborn are throttled in the womb. Perhaps Rome never rises on its seven hills. Perhaps Europe is forever a dark forest, and only Asia waxes healthy and teeming. Step on a mouse and you crush the Pyramids. Step on a mouse and you leave your print, like a Grand Canyon, across Eternity. Queen Elizabeth might never be born, Washington might not cross the Delaware, there might never be a United States at all. So be careful. Stay on the Path. *Never* step off!'

'I see,' said Eckels. 'Then it wouldn't pay for us even to touch the *grass*?'

'Correct. Crushing certain plants could add up infinitesimally. A little error here would multiply in sixty million years, all out of proportion. Of course maybe our theory is wrong. Maybe Time *can't* be changed by us. Or maybe it can be changed only in little subtle ways. A dead mouse here makes an insect imbalance there, a population disproportion later, a bad harvest further on, a depression, mass starvation, and, finally, a change in *social* temperament in far-flung countries. Something much more subtle, like that. Perhaps only a soft breath, a whisper, a hair, pollen on the air, such a slight, slight change that unless you looked close you wouldn't see it. Who knows? Who really can say he knows? We don't know. We're guessing. But until we do know for certain whether our messing around in Time *can* make a big roar or a little rustle in History, we're being damned careful. This Machine, this Path, your clothing and bodies, were sterilized, as you know, before the journey. We wear these oxygen helmets so we can't introduce our bacteria into an ancient atmosphere.'

'How do we know which animals to shoot?'

'They're marked with red paint,' said Travis. 'Today, before our journey, we sent Lesperance here back with the Machine. He came to this particular era and followed certain animals.'

'Studying them?'

'Right,' said Lesperance. 'I track them through their entire existence, noting which of them lives longest. Not long. How many times they mate. Not often. Life's short. When I find one that's going to die when a tree falls on him, or one that drowns in a tar pit, I note the exact hour, minute, and second. I shoot a paint bomb. It leaves a red patch on his hide. We can't miss it. Then I correlate our arrival in the Past so that we meet the Monster not more than two minutes before he would have died anyway. This way, we kill only animals with no future, that are never going to mate again. You see how *careful* we are?'

'But if you came back this morning in Time,' said Eckels eagerly, 'you must've bumped into *us*, our Safari! How did it turn out? Was it successful? Did all of us get through — *alive*?'

Travis and Lesperance gave each other a look.

'That'd be a paradox,' said the latter. 'Time doesn't permit that sort of mess — a man meeting himself. When such occasions threaten, Time steps aside. Like an aeroplane hitting an air pocket. You felt the Machine jump just before we stopped? That was us passing ourselves on the way back to the Future. We saw nothing. There's no way of telling *if* this expedition was a success, *if* we got our Monster, or whether all of us — meaning *you*, Mr Eckels — got out alive.'

Eckels smiled palely.

'Cut that,' said Travis sharply. 'Everyone on his feet!'

They were ready to leave the Machine.

The jungle was high and the jungle was broad and the jungle was the entire world forever and forever. Sounds like music and sounds like flying tents filled the sky, and those were pterodactyls soaring with cavernous grey wings, gigantic bats out of a delirium and a night fever. Eckels, balanced on the narrow Path, aimed his rifle playfully.

'Stop that!' said Travis. 'Don't even aim for fun, damn it! If your gun should go off — '

Eckels flushed. 'Where's our *Tyrannosaurus*?'

Lesperance checked his wristwatch. 'Up ahead. We'll bisect his trail in sixty seconds. Look for the red paint, for Christ's sake. Don't shoot till we give the word. Stay on the Path. *Stay on the Path!*'

They moved forward in the wind of morning.

'Strange,' murmured Eckels. 'Up ahead, sixty million years, Election Day over. Keith made President. Everyone celebrating. And here we are, a million years lost, and they don't exist. The things we worried about for months, a lifetime, not even born or thought about yet.'

'Safety catches off, everyone!' ordered Travis. 'You, first shot, Eckels. Second, Billings. Third, Kramer.'

'I've hunted tiger, wild boar, buffalo, elephant, but Jesus, this is *it*,' said Eckels. 'I'm shaking like a kid.'

'Ah,' said Travis.

Everyone stopped.

Travis raised his hand. 'Ahead,' he whispered. 'In the mist. There he is. There's His Royal Majesty now.'

The jungle was wide and full of twitterings, rustlings, murmurs, and sighs.

Suddenly it all ceased, as if someone had shut a door.

Silence.

A sound of thunder.

Out of the mist, one hundred yards away, came *Tyranno-saurus rex*.

'Jesus God,' whispered Eckels.

'Shh!'

It came on great oiled, resilient, striding legs. It towered thirty feet above half of the trees, a great evil god, folding its delicate watchmaker's claws close to its oily reptilian chest. Each lower leg was a piston, a thousand pounds of white bone, sunk in thick ropes of muscle, sheathed over in a gleam of pebbled skin like the mail of a terrible warrior. Each thigh was a ton of meat, ivory, and steel mesh. And from the great breathing cage of the upper body, those two delicate arms dangled out front, arms with hands which might pick up and examine men like toys, while the snake neck coiled. And the head itself, a ton of sculptured stone, lifted easily upon the sky. Its mouth gaped, exposing a fence of teeth like daggers.

Its eyes rolled, ostrich eggs, empty of all expression save hunger. It closed its mouth in a death grin. It ran, its pelvic bones crushing aside trees and bushes, its taloned feet clawing damp earth, leaving prints six inches deep wherever it settled its weight. It ran with a gliding ballet step, far too poised and balanced for its ten tons. It moved into a sunlit arena warily, its beautifully reptile hands feeling the air.

'My God!' Eckels twitched his mouth. 'It could reach up and grab the Moon.'

'Shh!' Travis jerked angrily. 'He hasn't seen us yet.'

'It can't be killed.' Eckels pronounced this verdict quietly, as if there could be no argument. He had weighed the evidence and this was his considered opinion. The rifle in his hands seemed a cap gun. 'We were fools to come. This is impossible.'

'Shut up!' hissed Travis.

'Nightmare.'

'Turn around,' commanded Travis. 'Walk quietly to the Machine. We'll remit one-half your fee.'

'I didn't realize it would be this *big*,' said Eckels. 'I miscalculated, that's all. And now I want out.'

'It *sees* us!'

'There's the red paint on its chest!'

The Thunder Lizard raised itself. Its armoured flesh glittered like a thousand green coins. The coins, crusted with slime, steamed. In the slime, tiny insects wriggled, so that the entire body seemed to twitch and undulate, even while the Monster itself did not move. It exhaled. The stink of raw flesh blew down the wilderness.

'Get me out of here,' said Eckels. 'It was never like this before. I was always sure I'd come through alive. I had good guides, good safaris, and safety. This time, I figured wrong. I've met my match and admit it. This is too much for me to get hold of.'

'Don't run,' said Lesperance. 'Turn around. Hide in the Machine.'

'Yes.' Eckels seemed to be numb. He looked at his feet as if trying to make them move. He gave a grunt of helplessness.

'Eckels!'

He took a few steps, blinking, shuffling.

'Not *that* way!'

The Monster, at the first motion, lunged forward with a terrible scream. It covered one hundred yards in four seconds. The rifles jerked up and blazed fire. A windstorm from the beast's mouth engulfed them in the stench of slime and old blood. The Monster roared, teeth glittering with sun.

Eckels, not looking back, walked blindly to the edge of the Path, his gun limp in his hand, stepped off the Path, and walked, not knowing it, in the jungle. His feet sank into green moss. His legs moved him, and he felt alone and remote from the events behind.

The rifles cracked again. Their sound was lost in shriek and lizard thunder. The great lever of the reptile's tail swung up, lashed sideways. Trees exploded in clouds of leaf and branch. The Monster twitched its jeweller's hands down to fondle at the men, to twist them in half, to crush them like berries, to cram them into its teeth and its screaming throat. Its boulder-stone eyes levelled with the men. They saw themselves mirrored. They fired at the metallic eyelids and the blazing black iris.

Like a stone idol, like a mountain avalanche, *Tyrannosaurus* fell. Thundering, it clutched trees, pulled them with it. It wrenched and tore the metal Path. The men flung themselves back and away. The body hit, ten tons of cold flesh and stone. The guns fired. The Monster lashed its armoured tail, twitched its snake jaws, and lay still. A fount of blood spurted from its throat. Somewhere inside, a sac of fluids burst. Sickening gushes drenched the hunters. They stood, red and glistening.

The thunder faded.

The jungle was silent. After the avalanche, a green peace. After the nightmare, morning.

Billings and Kramer sat on the pathway and threw up. Travis and Lesperance stood with smoking rifles, cursing steadily.

In the Time Machine, on his face, Eckels lay shivering. He had found his way back to the Path, climbed into the Machine.

Travis came walking, glanced at Eckels, took cotton gauze from a metal box, and returned to the others, who were sitting on the Path.

'Clean up.'

They wiped the blood from their helmets. They began to curse too. The Monster lay, a hill of solid flesh. Within, you could hear the sighs and murmurs as the furthest chambers of it died, the organs malfunctioning, liquids running a final instant from pocket to sac to spleen, everything shutting off, closing up forever. It was like standing by a wrecked locomotive or a steam shovel at quitting time, all valves being released or levered tight. Bones cracked; the tonnage of its own flesh, off-balance, dead weight, snapped the delicate forearms, caught underneath. The meat settled, quivering.

Another cracking sound. Overhead, a gigantic tree branch broke from its heavy moorings, fell. It crashed upon the dead beast with finality.

'There.' Lesperance checked his watch. 'Right on time. That's the giant tree that was scheduled to fall and kill this animal originally.' He glanced at the two hunters. 'You want the trophy picture?'

'What?'

'We can't take a trophy back to the Future. The body has to stay right here where it would have died originally, so the insects, birds, and bacteria can get at it, as they were intended to. Everything in balance. The body stays. But we *can* take a picture of you standing near it.'

The two men tried to think, but gave up, shaking their heads.

They let themselves be led along the metal Path. They sank wearily into the Machine cushions. They gazed back at the ruined Monster, the stagnating mound, where already strange reptilian birds and golden insects were busy at the steaming armour.

A sound on the floor of the Time Machine stiffened them. Eckels sat there, shivering.

'I'm sorry,' he said at last.

'Get up!' cried Travis.

Eckels got up.

'Go out on that Path alone,' said Travis. He had his rifle pointed. 'You're not coming back in the Machine. We're leaving you here!'

Lesperance seized Travis's arm. 'Wait – '

'Stay out of this!' Travis shook his hand away. 'This son of a bitch nearly killed us. But it isn't *that* so much. Hell, no. It's his *shoes*! Look at them! He ran off the Path. My God, that *ruins* us! Christ knows how much we'll forfeit! Tens of thousands of dollars of insurance! We guarantee no one leaves the Path. He left it. Oh, the damn fool! I'll have to report to the government. They might revoke our licence to travel. God knows *what* he's done to Time, to History!'

'Take it easy, all he did was kick up some dirt.'

'How do we *know*? cried Travis. 'We don't know anything! It's all a damn mystery! Get out there, Eckels!'

Eckels fumbed his shirt. 'I'll pay anything. A hundred thousand dollars!'

Travis glared at Eckels' cheque book and spat. 'Go out there. The Monster's next to the Path. Stick your arms up to your elbows in his mouth. Then you can come back with us.'

'That's unreasonable!'

'The Monster's dead, you yellow bastard. The bullets! The bullets can't be left behind. They don't belong in the Past; they might change something. Here's my knife. Dig them out!'

The jungle was alive again, full of the old tremorings and bird cries. Eckels turned slowly to regard that primeval garbage dump, that hill of nightmares and terror. After a long time, like a sleepwalker, he shuffled out along the Path.

He returned, shuddering, five minutes later, his arms soaked and red to the elbows. He held out his hands. Each held a number of steel bullets. Then he fell. He lay where he fell, not moving.

'You didn't have to make him do that,' said Lesperance.

'Didn't I? It's too early to tell.' Travis nudged the still body. 'He'll live. Next time he won't go hunting game like this. Okay.' He jerked his thumb wearily at Lesperance. 'Switch on. Let's go home.'

1492. 1776. 1812.

They cleaned their hands and faces. Their changed their caking shirts and pants. Eckels was up and around again, not speaking. Travis glared at him for a full ten minutes.

'Don't look at me,' cried Eckels. 'I haven't done anything.'

'Who can tell?'

'Just ran off the Path, that's all, a little mud on my shoes — what do you want me to do — get down and pray?'

'We might need it. I'm warning you, Eckels, I might kill you yet. I've got my gun ready.'

'I'm innocent. I've done nothing!'

1999. 2000. 2055.

The Machine stopped.

'Get out,' said Travis.

The room was there as they had left it. But not the same as they had left it. The same man sat behind the same desk. But the same man did not quite sit behind the same desk.

Travis looked around swiftly. 'Everything okay here?' he snapped.

'Fine. Welcome home!'

Travis did not relax. He seemed to be looking at the very atoms of the air itself, at the way the sun poured through the one high window.

'Okay, Eckels, get out. Don't ever come back.'

Eckels could not move.

'You heard me,' said Travis. 'What're you *staring* at?'

Eckels stood smelling of the air, and there was a thing to the air, a chemical taint so subtle, so slight, that only a faint cry of his subliminal senses warned him it was there. The colours, white, grey, blue, orange, in the wall, in the furniture, in the sky beyond the window, were . . . were . . . And there was a *feel*. His flesh twitched. His hands twitched. He stood drinking the oddness with the pores of his body. Somewhere, someone must have been screaming one of those whistles that only a dog can hear. His body screamed silence in return. Beyond this room, beyond this wall, beyond this man who was not quite the same man seated at this desk that was not quite the same desk . . . lay an entire world of streets and people. What sort of world it was now, there was no telling. He could feel them moving there, beyond the walls, almost, like so many chess pieces blown in a dry wind . . .

But the immediate thing was the sign painted on the office wall, the same sign he had read earlier today on first entering. Somehow, the sign had changed:

TYME SEFARI INC.
SEFARIS TU ANY YEER EN THE PAST.
YU NAIM THE ANIMALL.
WEE TAEK YU THAIR.
YU SHOOT ITT.

Eckels felt himself fall into a chair. He fumbled crazily at the thick slime on his boots. He held up a clod of dirt, trembling. 'No, it *can't* be. Not a *little* thing like that. No!'

Embedded in the mud, glistening green and gold and black, was a butterfly, very beautiful, and very dead.

'Not a little thing like *that*! Not a butterfly!' cried Eckels.

It fell to the floor, an exquisite thing, a small thing that could upset balances and knock down a line of small dominoes and then big dominoes and then gigantic dominoes, all down the years across Time. Eckels' mind whirled. It *couldn't* change things. Killing one butterfly couldn't be *that* important! Could it?

His face was cold. His mouth trembled, asking: 'Who — who won the presidential election yesterday?'

The man behind the desk laughed. 'You joking? You know damn well. Deutscher, of course! Who else? Not that damn weakling Keith. We got an iron man now, a man with guts, by God!' The official stopped. 'What's wrong?'

Eckels moaned. He dropped to his knees. He scrabbled at the golden butterfly with shaking fingers. 'Can't we,' he pleaded to the world, to himself, to the officials, to the Machine, 'can't we take it *back*, can't we *make* it alive again? Can't we start over? Can't we — '

He did not move. Eyes shut, he waited, shivering. He heard Travis breathe loud in the room; he heard Travis shift his rifle, click the safety catch, and raise the weapon.

There was a sound of thunder.

The Murderer

Music moved with him in the white halls. He passed an office
door: 'The Merry Widow Waltz'. Another door: *Afternoon of
a Faun*. A third: 'Kiss Me Again'. He turned into a cross-
corridor: 'The Sword Dance' buried him in cymbals, drums,
pots, pans, knives, forks, thunder, and tin lightning. All
washed away as he hurried through an anteroom where a
secretary sat nicely stunned by Beethoven's Fifth. He moved
himself before her eyes like a hand; she didn't see him.

His wrist radio buzzed.

'Yes?'

'This is Lee, Dad. Don't forget about my allowance.'

'Yes, Son, yes. I'm busy.'

'Just didn't want you to forget, Dad,' said the wrist radio.
Tchaikovsky's *Romeo and Juliet* swarmed about the voice
and flushed into the long halls.

The psychiatrist moved in the beehive of offices, in the
cross-pollination of themes, Stravinsky mating with Bach,
Haydn unsuccessfully repulsing Rachmaninoff, Schubert
slain by Duke Ellington. He nodded to the humming
secretaries and the whistling doctors fresh to their morning
work. At his office he checked a few papers with his steno-
grapher, who sang under her breath, then phoned the police
captain upstairs. A few minutes later a red light blinked, a
voice said from the ceiling:

'Prisoner delivered to Interview Chamber Nine.'

He unlocked the chamber door, stepped in, heard the door
lock behind him.

'Go away,' said the prisoner, smiling.

The psychiatrist was shocked by that smile. A very sunny,

pleasant warm thing, a thing that shed bright light upon the room. Dawn among the dark hills. High noon at midnight, that smile. The blue eyes sparkled serenely above that display of self-assured dentistry.

'I'm here to help you,' said the psychiatrist, frowning. Something was wrong with the room. He had hesitated the moment he entered. He glanced around. The prisoner laughed. 'If you're wondering why it's so quiet in here, I just kicked the radio to death.'

Violent, thought the doctor.

The prisoner read this thought, smiled, put out a gentle hand. 'No, only to machines that yak-yak-yak.'

Bits of the wall radio's tubes and wires lay on the grey carpeting. Ignoring these, feeling that smile upon him like a heat lamp, the psychiatrist sat across from his patient in the unusual silence which was like the gathering of a storm.

'You're Mr Albert Brock, who calls himself The Murderer?'

Brock nodded pleasantly. 'Before we start . . .' He moved quietly and quickly to detach the wrist radio from the doctor's arm. He tucked it in his teeth like a walnut, gritted, heard it crack, handed it back to the appalled psychiatrist as if he had done them both a favour. 'That's better.'

The psychiatrist stared at the ruined machine. 'You're running up quite a damage bill.'

'I don't care,' smiled the patient. 'As the old song goes: "Don't Care What Happens to Me!" He hummed it.

The psychiatrist said: 'Shall we start?'

'Fine. The first victim, or one of the first, was my telephone. Murder most foul. I shoved it in the kitchen Insink-erator! Stopped the disposal unit in mid-swallow. Poor thing strangled to death. After that I shot the television set!'

The psychiatrist said, 'Mmm.'

'Fired six shots right through the cathode. Made a beautiful tinkling crash, like a dropped chandelier.'

'Nice imagery.'

'Thanks, I always dreamt of being a writer.'

'Suppose you tell me when you first began to hate the telephone.'

'It frightened me as a child. Uncle of mine called it the Ghost Machine. Voices without bodies. Scared the living hell out of me. Later in life I was never comfortable. Seemed to me a phone was an impersonal instrument. If it *felt* like it, it let your personality go through its wires. If it didn't *want* to, it just drained your personality away until what slipped through at the other end was some cold fish of a voice, all steel, copper, plastic, no warmth, no reality. It's easy to say the wrong thing on telephones; the telephone changes your meaning on you. First thing you know, you've made an enemy. Then, of course, the telephone's such a *convenient* thing; it just sits there and *demands* you call someone who doesn't want to be called. Friends were always calling, calling, calling me. Hell, I hadn't any time of my own. When it wasn't the telephone it was the television, the radio, the phonograph. When it wasn't the television or radio or the phonograph it was motion pictures at the corner theatre, motion pictures projected, with commercials on low-lying cumulus clouds. It doesn't rain rain any more, it rains soapsuds. When it wasn't High-Fly Cloud advertisements, it was music by Mozzek in every restaurant; music and commercials on the buses I rode to work. When it wasn't music, it was interoffice communications, and my horror chamber of a radio wristwatch on which my friends and my wife phoned every five minutes. What is there about such "conveniences" that makes them so *temptingly* convenient? The average man thinks, Here I am, time on my hands, and there on my wrist is a wrist telephone, so why not just buzz old Joe up, eh? "Hello, *hello*!" I love my friends, my wife, humanity, very much, but when one minute my wife calls to say, "Where are you *now*, dear?" and a friend calls and says, "Got the best off-colour joke to tell you. Seems there was a guy —" And a stranger calls and cries out, "This is the Find-Fax Poll. What gum are you chewing at this very *instant*?" Well!'

'How did you feel during the week?'

'The fuse lit. On the edge of the cliff. That same afternoon I did what I did at the office.'

'Which was?'

'I poured a paper cup of water into the intercommunications system.'

The psychiatrist wrote on his pad.

'And the system shorted?'

'Beautifully! The Fourth of July on wheels! My God, stenographers ran around looking *lost*! What an uproar!'

'Felt better temporarily, eh?'

'Fine! Then I got the idea at noon of stamping my wrist radio on the sidewalk. A shrill voice was just yelling out of it at me, "This is People's Poll Number Nine. What did you eat for lunch?" when I kicked the Jesus out of the wrist radio!'

'Felt even *better*, eh?'

'It *grew* on me!' Brock rubbed his hands together. 'Why didn't I start a solitary revolution, deliver man from certain "conveniences"? "Convenient for who?" I cried. Convenient for friends: "Hey, Al, thought I'd call you from the locker room out here at Green Hills. Just made a sockdolager hole in one! A hole in one, Al! A *beautiful* day. Having a shot of whisky now. Thought you'd want to know, Al!" Convenient for my office, so when I'm in the field with my radio car there's no moment when I'm not in touch. *In touch! There's* a slimy phrase. Touch, hell. *Gripped*! Pawed, rather. Mauled and massaged and pounded by FM voices. You can't leave your car without checking in: "Have stopped to visit gas-station men's room." "Okay, Brock, step on it!" "Brock, what *took* you so long?" "Sorry, sir." "Watch it next time, Brock." "*Yes*, sir!" So, do you know what I did, Doctor? I bought a quart of French chocolate ice cream and spooned it into the car radio transmitter.'

'Was there any *special* reason for selecting French chocolate ice cream to spoon into the broadcasting unit?'

Brock thought about it and smiled. 'It's my favourite flavour.'

'Oh,' said the doctor.

'I figured, hell, what's good enough for me is good enough for the radio transmitter.'

'What made you think of spooning *ice cream* into the radio?'

'It was a hot day.'

The doctor paused.

'And what happened next?'

'Silence happened next. God, it was *beautiful*. That car radio cackling all day, "Brock go here, Brock go there, Brock check in, Brock check out, okay Brock, hour lunch, Brock, lunch over, Brock, Brock, Brock." Well, that silence was like putting ice cream in my ears.'

'You seem to like ice cream a lot.'

'I just rode around feeling of the silence. It's a big bolt of the nicest, softest flannel ever made. Silence. A whole hour of it. I just sat in my car, smiling, feeling of that flannel with my ears. I felt *drunk* with Freedom!'

'Go on.'

'Then I got the idea of the portable diathermy machine. I rented one, took it on the bus going home that night. There sat all the tired commuters with their wrist radios, talking to their wives, saying, "Now I'm at Forty-third, now I'm at Forty-fourth, here I am at Forty-ninth, now turning at Sixty-first." One husband cursing, "Well, get *out* of that bar, damn it, and get home and get dinner started, I'm at Seventieth!" And the transit-system radio playing "Tales from the Vienna Woods," a canary singing words about a first-rate wheat cereal. Then — I switched on my diathermy! Static! Interference! All wives cut off from husbands grousing about a hard day at the office. All husbands cut off from wives who had just seen their children break a window! The "Vienna Woods" chopped down, the canary mangled. *Silence!* A terrible, unexpected silence. The bus inhabitants faced with having to converse with each other. Panic! Sheer, animal panic!'

'The police seized you?'

'The bus *had* to stop. After all, the music *was* being scrambled, husbands and wives *were* out of touch with reality. Pandemonium, riot, and chaos. Squirrels chattering in cages! A trouble unit arrived, triangulated on me instantly, had me reprimanded, fined, and home, minus my diathermy machine, in jig time.'

'Mr Brock, may I suggest that so far your whole pattern here is not very – practical? If you didn't like transit radios or office radios or car business radios, why didn't you join a fraternity of radio haters, start petitions, get legal and constitutional rulings? After all, this *is* a democracy.'

'And I,' said Brock, 'am that thing best called a minority. I *did* join fraternities, picket, pass petitions, take it to court. Year after year I protested. Everyone laughed. Everyone else *loved* bus radios and commercials. *I* was out of step.'

'Then you should have taken it like a good soldier, don't you think? The majority rules.'

'But they went too far. If a little music and "keeping in touch" was charming, they figured a lot would be ten times as charming. I went *wild*! I got home to find my wife hysterical. *Why?* Because she had been completely out of touch with me for half a day. Remember, I did a dance on my wrist radio? Well, that night I laid plans to murder my house.'

'Are you *sure* that's how you want me to write it down?'

'That's semantically accurate. Kill it dead. It's one of those talking, singing, humming, weather-reporting, poetry-reading, novel-reciting, jingle-jangling, rockaby-crooning-when-you-go-to-bed houses. A house that screams opera to you in the shower and teaches you Spanish in your sleep. One of those blathering caves where all kinds of electronic Oracles make you feel a trifle larger than a thimble, with stoves that say, "I'm apricot pie, and I'm *done*," or 'I'm prime roast beef, so *baste* me!" and other nursery gibberish like that. With beds that rock you to sleep and *shake* you awake. A house that *barely* tolerates humans, I tell you. A front door that barks: "You've mud on your feet, sir!" And an electronic vacuum hound that snuffles around after you from room to room, inhaling every fingernail or ash you drop. Jesus God, *I* say, Jesus God!'

'Quietly,' suggested the psychiatrist.

'Remember that Gilbert and Sullivan song – "I've Got It on My List, It Never Will Be Missed"? All night I listed grievances. Next morning early I bought a pistol. I *purposely* muddied my feet! Wipe your feet! Please be *neat*!" I shot the damn thing in its keyhole! I ran to the kitchen, where the stove was just whining, "Turn me *over*!" In the middle of a mechanical omelet I did the stove to death. Oh, how it sizzled and screamed, "I'm *shorted*!" Then the telephone rang like a spoiled brat. I shoved it down the Insinkerator. I must state here and now I have *nothing* whatever against the Insinkerator; it was an innocent bystander. I feel sorry for it now, a practical device indeed, which never said a word, purred like a sleepy lion most of the time, and digested our leftovers. I'll have it restored. Then I went in and shot the televisor, that insidious beast, that Medusa, which freezes a billion people to stone every night, staring fixedly, that Siren which called and sang and promised so much and gave, after all, so little, but myself always going back, going back, hoping and waiting until – bang! Like a headless turkey, gobbling, my wife whooped out the front door. The police came. Here I *am*!'

He sat back happily and lit a cigarette.

'And did you realize, in committing these crimes, that the wrist radio, the broadcasting transmitter, the phone, the bus radio, the office intercoms, all were rented or were someone else's property?'

'I would do it all over again, so help me God.'

The psychiatrist sat there in the sunshine of that beatific smile.

'You don't want any further help from the Office of Mental Health? You're ready to take the consequences?'

'This is only the beginning,' said Mr Brock. 'I'm the vanguard of the small public which is tired of noise and being taken advantage of and pushed around and yelled at, every moment music, every moment in touch with some voice somewhere, do this, do that, quick, quick, now here, now there. You'll *see*. The revolt begins. My name will go down in history!'

'Mmm.' The psychiatrist seemed to be thinking.

'It'll take time, of course. It was all so enchanting at first. The very *idea* of these things, the practical uses, was wonderful. They were almost toys, to be played with, but the people got too involved, went too far, and got wrapped up in a pattern of social behaviour and couldn't get out, couldn't admit they were *in*, even. So they rationalized their nerves as something else. "Our modern age," they said. "Conditions," they said. 'High-strung," they said. But mark my words, the seed has been sown. I got world-wide coverage on TV, radio, films; *there's* an irony for you. That was five days ago. A billion people know about me. Check your financial columns. Any day now. Maybe today. Watch for a sudden spurt, a rise in sales for French chocolate ice cream!'

'I see,' said the psychiatrist.

'Can I go back to my nice private cell now, where I can be alone and quiet for six months?'

'Yes,' said the psychiatrist quietly.

'Don't worry about me,' said Mr Brock, rising. 'I'm just going to sit around for a long time stuffing that nice soft bolt of quiet material in both ears.'

'Mmm,' said the psychiatrist, going to the door.

'Cheers,' said Mr Brock.

'Yes,' said the psychiatrist.

He pressed the code signal on a hidden button, the door opened, he stepped out, the door shut and locked. Alone, he moved in the offices and corridors. The first twenty yards of his walk were accompanied by 'Tambourin chinois'. Then it was 'Tzigane', Bach's Passacaglia and Fugue in something Minor, 'Tiger Rag', 'Love Is Like a Cigarette'. He took his broken wrist radio from his pocket like a dead praying mantis. He turned in at his office. A bell sounded; a voice came out of the ceiling, 'Doctor?'

'Just finished with Brock,' said the psychiatrist.

'Diagnosis?'

'Seems completely disoriented, but convivial. Refuses to accept the simplest realities of his environment and work *with* them.'

'Prognosis?'

'Indefinite. Left him enjoying a piece of invisible material.'

Three phones rang. A duplicate wrist radio in his desk drawer buzzed like a wounded grasshopper. The intercom flashed a pink light and click-clicked. Three phones rang. The drawer buzzed. Music blew in through the open door. The psychiatrist, humming quietly, fitted the new wrist radio to his wrist, flipped the intercom, talked a moment, picked up one telephone, talked, picked up another telephone; talked, picked up the third telephone, talked, touched the wrist-radio button, talked calmly and quietly, his face cool and serene, in the middle of the music and the lights flashing, the phones ringing again, and his hands moving, and his wrist radio buzzing, and the intercoms talking, and voices speaking from the ceiling. And he went on quietly this way through the remainder of a cool, air-conditioned, and long afternoon; telephone, wrist radio, intercom, telephone, wrist radio, intercom, telephone, wrist radio, intercom, telephone, wrist radio, intercom, telephone, wrist radio, intercom, telephone, wrist radio . . .

The April Witch

Into the air, over the valleys, the stars, above a river, a pond, a road, flew Cecy. Invisible as new spring winds, fresh as the breath of clover rising from twilight fields, she flew. She soared in doves as soft as white ermine, stopped in trees and lived in blossoms, showering away in petals when the breeze blew. She perched in a lime-green frog, cool as mint by a shining pool. She trotted in a brambly dog and barked to hear echoes from the sides of distant barns. She lived in new April grasses, in sweet clear liquids rising from the musky earth.

It's spring, thought Cecy. I'll be in every living thing in the world tonight.

Now she inhabited neat crickets on the tar-pool roads, now prickled in dew on an iron gate. Hers was an adaptably quick mind flowing unseen upon Illinois winds on this one evening of her life when she was just seventeen.

'I want to be in love,' she said.

She had said it at supper. And her parents had widened their eyes and stiffened back in their chairs. 'Patience,' had been their advice. 'Remember, you're remarkable. Our whole Family is odd and remarkable. We can't mix or marry with ordinary folk. We'd lose our magical powers if we did. You wouldn't want to lose *your* ability to "travel" by magic, would you? Then be careful. Be careful!'

But in her high bedroom, Cecy had touched perfume to her throat and stretched out, trembling and apprehensive, on her four-poster, as a moon the colour of milk rose over Illinois country, turning rivers to cream and roads to platinum.

'Yes,' she sighed. 'I'm one of an odd family. We sleep days

and fly nights like black kites on the wind. If we want, we can sleep in moles through the winter, in the warm earth. I can live in anything at all — a pebble, a crocus, or a praying mantis. I can leave my plain, bony body behind and send my mind far out for adventure. Now!'

The wind whipped her away over fields and meadows.

She saw the warm spring lights of cottages and farms glowing with twilight colours.

If I can't be in love, myself, because I'm plain and odd, then I'll be in love through someone else, she thought.

Outside a farmhouse in the spring night a dark-haired girl, no more than nineteen, drew up water from a deep stone well. She was singing.

Cecy fell — a green leaf — into the well. She lay in the tender moss of the well, gazing up through dark coolness. Now she quickened in a fluttering invisible amoeba. Now in a water droplet! At last, within a cold cup, she felt herself lifted to the girl's warm lips. There was a soft night sound of drinking.

Cecy looked out from the girl's eyes.

She entered into the dark head and gazed from the shining eyes at the hands pulling the rough rope. She listened through the shell ears to this girl's world. She smelled a particular universe through these delicate nostrils, felt this special heart beating, beating. Felt this strange tongue move with singing.

Does she know I'm here? thought Cecy.

The girl gasped. She stared into the night meadows.

'Who's there?'

No answer.

'Only the wind,' whispered Cecy.

'Only the wind.' The girl laughed at herself, but shivered.

It was a good body, this girl's body. It held bones of finest slender ivory hidden and roundly fleshed. This brain was like a pink tea rose, hung in darkness, and there was cider-wine in this mouth. The lips lay firm on the white, white teeth and the brows arched neatly at the world, and the hair blew soft and fine on her milky neck. The pores knit small and close. The nose tilted at the moon and the cheeks glowed like small fires. The body drifted with feather-balances from one motion to another and seemed always singing to itself. Being in this body, this head, was like basking in a hearth fire, living in the purr of a sleeping cat, stirring in warm creek waters that flowed by night to the sea.

I'll like it here, thought Cecy.

'What?' asked the girl, as if she'd heard.

'What's your name?' asked Cecy carefully.

'Ann Leary.' The girl twitched. 'Now why should I say *that* out loud?'

'Ann, Ann,' whispered Cecy. 'Ann, you're going to be in love.'

As if to answer this, a great roar sprang from the road, a clatter and a ring of wheels on gravel. A tall man drove up in a rig, holding the reins high with his monstrous arms, his smile glowing across the yard.

'Ann!'

'Is that you, Tom?'

'Who else?' Leaping from the rig, he tied the reins to the fence.

'I'm not speaking to you!' Ann whirled, the bucket in her hands slopping.

'No!' cried Cecy.

Ann froze. She looked at the hills and the first spring stars. She stared at the man named Tom. Cecy made her drop the bucket.

'Look what you've done!'

Tom ran up.

'Look what you *made* me do!'

He wiped her shoes with a kerchief, laughing.

'Get away!' She kicked at his hands, but he laughed again,

and gazing down on him from miles away, Cecy saw the turn of his head, the size of his skull, the flare of his nose, the shine of his eye, the girth of his shoulder, and the hand strength of his hands doing this delicate thing with the handkerchief. Peering down from the secret attic of this lovely head, Cecy yanked a hidden copper ventriloquist's wire and the pretty mouth popped wide: 'Thank you!'

'Oh, so you *have* manners?' The smell of leather on his hands, the smell of the horse rose from his clothes into the tender nostrils, and Cecy, far, far away over night meadows and flowered fields, stirred as with some dream in her bed.

'Not for you, no!' said Ann.

'Hush, speak gently,' said Cecy. She moved Ann's fingers out towards Tom's head. Ann snatched them back.

'I've gone mad!'

'You have.' He nodded, smiling but bewildered. 'Were you going to touch me then?'

'I don't know. Oh, go away!' Her cheeks glowed with pink charcoals.

'Why don't you run? I'm not stopping you.' Tom got up. 'Have you changed your mind? Will you go to the dance with me tonight? It's special. Tell you why later.'

'No,' said Ann.

'Yes!' cried Cecy. 'I've never danced. I want to dance. I've never worn a long gown, all rustly. I want that. I want to dance all night. I've never known what it's like to be in a woman, dancing; Father and Mother would never permit it. Dogs, cats, locusts, leaves, everything else in the world at one time or another I've known, but never a woman in the spring, never on a night like this. Oh, please — we *must* go to that dance!'

She spread her thought like the fingers of a hand within a new glove.

'Yes,' said Ann Leary, 'I'll go. I don't know why, but I'll go to the dance with you tonight, Tom.'

'Now inside, quick!' cried Cecy. 'You must wash, tell your folks, get your gown ready, out with the iron, into your room!'

'Mother,' said Ann, 'I've changed my mind!'

The rig was galloping off down the pike, the rooms of the farmhouse jumped to life, water was boiling for a bath, the coal stove was heating an iron to press the gown, the mother was rushing about with a fringe of hairpins in her mouth. 'What's come over you, Ann? You don't like Tom!'

'That's true.' Ann stopped amidst the great fever.

But it's spring! thought Cecy.

'It's spring,' said Ann.

And it's a fine night for dancing, thought Cecy.

' . . . for dancing,' murmured Ann Leary.

Then she was in the tub and the soap creaming on her white seal shoulders, small nests of soap beneath her arms, and the flesh of her warm breasts moving in her hands and Cecy moving the mouth, making the smile, keeping the actions going. There must be no pause, no hesitation, or the entire pantomime might fall in ruins! Ann Leary must be kept moving, doing, acting, wash here, soap there, now out! Rub with a towel! Now perfume and powder!

'You!' Ann caught herself in the mirror, all whiteness and pinkness like lilies and carnations. '*Who* are you tonight?'

'I'm a girl seventeen.' Cecy gazed from her violet eyes. 'You can't see me. Do you know I'm here?'

Ann Leary shook her head. 'I've rented my body to an April witch, for sure.'

'*Close*, very close!' laughed Cecy. 'Now, on with your dressing.'

The luxury of feeling good clothes move over an ample body! And then the halloo outside.

'Ann, Tom's back!'

'Tell him to wait.' Ann sat down suddenly. 'Tell him I'm

not going to that dance.'

'What?' said her mother, in the door.

Cecy snapped back into attention. It had been a fatal relaxing, a fatal moment of leaving Ann's body for only an instant. She had heard the distant sound of horses' hoofs and the rig rambling through moonlit spring country. For a second she thought, I'll go find Tom and sit in his head and see what it's like to be a man of twenty-two on a night like this. And so she had started quickly across a heather field, but now, like a bird to a cage, flew back and rustled and beat about in Ann Leary's head.

'Ann!'

'Tell him to go away!'

'Ann!' Cecy settled down and spread her thoughts.

But Ann had the bit in her mouth now. 'No, no, I hate him!'

I shouldn't have left — even for a moment. Cecy poured her mind into the hands of the young girl, into the heart, into the head, softly, softly. *Stand up*, she thought.

Ann stood.

Put on your coat!

Ann put on her coat.

Now, march!

No! thought Ann Leary.

March!

'Ann,' said her mother, 'don't keep Tom waiting another minute. You get on out there now and no nonsense. What's come over you?'

'Nothing, Mother. Good night. We'll be home late.'

Ann and Cecy ran together into the spring evening.

A room full of softly dancing pigeons ruffling their quiet, trailing feathers, a room full of peacocks, a room full of rainbow eyes and lights. And in the centre of it, around, around, around, danced Ann Leary.

'Oh, it *is* a fine evening,' said Cecy.

'Oh, it's a fine evening,' said Ann.

'You're odd,' said Tom.

The music whirled them in dimness, in rivers of song; they floated, they bobbed, they sank down, they arose for air, they gasped, they clutched each other like drowning people and whirled on again, in fan motions, in whispers and sighs, to 'Beautiful Ohio.'

Cecy hummed. Ann's lips parted and the music came out.

'Yes, I'm odd,' said Cecy.

'You're not the same,' said Tom.

'No, not tonight.'

'You're not the Ann Leary I knew.'

'No, not at all, at all,' whispered Cecy, miles and miles away. 'No, not at all,' said the moved lips.

'I've the funniest feeling,' said Tom.

'What about?'

'About you.' He held her back and danced her and looked into her glowing face, watching for something. 'Your eyes,' he said, 'I can't figure it.'

'Do you see *me*?' asked Cecy.

'Part of you's here, Ann, and part of you's not.' Tom turned her carefully, his face uneasy.

'Yes.'

'Why did you come with me?'

'I didn't want to come,' said Ann.

'Why, then?'

'Something made me.'

'What?'

'I don't know.' Ann's voice was faintly hysterical.

'Now, now, hush, hush,' whispered Cecy. 'Hush, that's it. Around, around.'

They whispered and rustled and rose and fell away in the dark room, with the music moving and turning them.

'But you *did* come to the dance,' said Tom.

'I did,' said Cecy.

'Here.' And he danced her lightly out an open door and walked her quietly away from the hall and the music and the people.

They climbed up and sat together in the rig.

'Ann,' he said, taking her hands, trembling. 'Ann.' But the way he said her name it was as if it wasn't her name. He kept glancing into her pale face, and now her eyes were open again. 'I used to love you, you know that,' he said.

'I know.'

'But you've always been fickle and I didn't want to be hurt.'

'It's just as well, we're very young,' said Ann.

'No, I mean to say, I'm sorry,' said Cecy.

'What *do* you mean?' Tom dropped her hands and stiffened.

The night was warm and the smell of the earth shimmered up all about them where they sat, and the fresh trees breathed one leaf against another in a shaking and rustling.

'I don't know,' said Ann.

'Oh, but *I* know,' said Cecy. 'You're tall and you're the finest-looking man in all the world. This is a good evening; this is an evening I'll always remember, being with you.' She put out the alien cold hand to find his reluctant hand again and bring it back, and warm it and hold it very tight.

'But,' said Tom, blinking, 'tonight you're here, you're there. One minute one way, the next minute another. I wanted to take you to the dance tonight for old times' sake. I meant nothing by it when I first asked you. And then, when we were standing at the well, I knew something had changed, really changed, about you. You were different. There was something new and soft, something . . . ' He groped for a word. 'I don't know, I can't say. The way you looked. Something about your voice. And I know I'm in love with you again.'

'No,' said Cecy. 'With me, with *me*.'

'And I'm afraid of being in love with you,' he said. 'You'll hurt me again.'

'I might,' said Ann.

No, no, I'd love you with all my heart! thought Cecy. Ann, say it to him, say it for me. Say you'd love him with all your heart.

Ann said nothing.

Tom moved quietly closer and put his hand up to hold her chin. 'I'm going away. I've got a job a hundred miles from here. Will you miss me?'

'Yes,' said Ann and Cecy.

'May I kiss you good-bye, then?'

'Yes,' said Cecy before anyone else could speak.

He placed his lips to the strange mouth. He kissed the strange mouth and he was trembling.

Ann sat like a white statue.

'Ann!' said Cecy. 'Move your arms, *hold* him!'

She sat like a carved wooden doll in the moonlight.

Again he kissed her lips.

'I do love you,' whispered Cecy. 'I'm here, it's me you saw in her eyes, it's me, and I love you if she never will.'

He moved away and seemed like a man who had run a long distance. He sat beside her. 'I don't know what's happening. For a moment there . . . '

'Yes?' asked Cecy.

'For a moment I thought — ' He put his hands to his eyes. 'Never mind. Shall I take you home now?'

'Please,' said Ann Leary.

He clucked to the horse, snapped the reins tiredly, and drove the rig away. They rode in the rustle and slap and motion of the moonlit rig in the still early, only eleven o'clock spring night, with the shining meadows and sweet fields of clover gliding by.

And Cecy, looking at the fields and meadows, thought, It

would be worth it, it would be worth everything to be with him from this night on. And she heard her parents' voices again, faintly, 'Be careful. You wouldn't want to lose your magical powers, would you — married to a mere mortal? Be careful. You wouldn't want that.'

Yes, yes, thought Cecy, even that I'd give up, here and now, if he would have me. I wouldn't need to roam the spring nights then, I wouldn't need to live in birds and dogs and cats and foxes, I'd need only to be with him. Only him. Only him.

The road passed under, whispering.

'Tom,' said Ann at last.

'What?' He stared coldly at the road, the horse, the trees, the sky, the stars.

'If you're ever, in years to come, at any time, in Mellin Town, Illinois, a few miles from here, will you do me a favour?'

'Perhaps.'

'Will you do me the favour of stopping and seeing a friend of mine?' Ann Leary said this haltingly, awkwardly.

'Why?'

'She's a good friend. I've told her of you. I'll give you her address. Just a moment.' When the rig stopped at her farm she drew forth a pencil and paper from her small purse and wrote in the moonlight, pressing the paper to her knee. 'There it is. Can you read it?'

He glanced at the paper and nodded bewilderedly.

'Cecy Elliott, 12 Willow Street, Mellin Town, Illinois,' he said.

'Will you visit her someday?' asked Ann.

'Someday,' he said.

'Promise?'

'What has this to do with us?' he cried savagely. 'What do I want with names and papers?' He crumpled the paper into a tight ball and shoved it in his coat.

'Oh, please promise!' begged Cecy.

' . . . promise . . . ' said Ann.

'All right, all right, now let me be!' he shouted.

I'm tired, thought Cecy. I can't stay. I have to go home. I'm weakening. I've only the power to stay a few hours out like this in the night, travelling, travelling. But before I go . . .

' . . . before I go,' said Ann.

She kissed Tom on the lips.

'This is *me* kissing you,' said Cecy.

Tom held her off and looked at Ann Leary and looked deep, deep inside. He said nothing, but his face began to relax slowly, very slowly, and the lines vanished away, and his mouth softened from its hardness, and he looked deep again into the moonlit face held here before him.

Then he put her off the rig and without so much as good night was driving swiftly down the road.

Cecy let go.

Ann Leary, crying out, released from prison, it seemed, raced up the moonlit path to her house and slammed the door.

Cecy lingered for only a little while. In the eyes of a cricket she saw the spring night world. In the eyes of a frog she sat for a lonely moment by a pool. In the eyes of a night bird she looked down from a tall, moon-haunted elm and saw the lights go out in two farmhouses, one here, one a mile away. She thought of herself and her Family, and her strange power, and the fact that no one in the Family could ever marry any one of the people in this vast world out here beyond the hills.

'Tom?' Her weakening mind flew in a night bird under the trees and over deep fields of wild mustard. 'Have you still got the paper, Tom? Will you come by someday, some year, sometime, to see me? Will you know me then? Will you look in my face and remember then where it was you saw me last and know that you love me as I love you, with all my heart for all time?

She paused in the cool night air, a million miles from towns and people, above farms and continents and rivers and hills. 'Tom?' Softly.

Tom was asleep. It was deep night; his clothes were hung on chairs or folded neatly over the end of the bed. And in one silent, carefully upflung hand upon the white pillow, by his head, was a small piece of paper with writing on it. Slowly, slowly, a fraction of an inch at a time, his fingers closed down upon and held it tightly. And he did not even stir or notice when a blackbird, faintly, wondrously, beat softly for a moment against the clear moon crystals of the windowpane, then, fluttering quietly, stopped and flew away towards the east, over the sleeping earth.

Invisible Boy

She took the great iron spoon and mummified frog and gave it a bash and made dust of it, and talked to the dust while she ground it in her stony fists quickly. Her beady grey bird-eyes flickered at the cabin. Each time she looked, a head in the small thin window ducked as if she'd fired off a shotgun.

'Charlie!' cried Old Lady. 'You come outa there! I'm fixing a lizard magic to unlock that rusty door! You come out now and I won't make the earth shake or the trees go up in fire or the sun set at high noon!'

The only sound was the warm mountain light on the high turpentine trees, a tufted squirrel chittering around and around on a green-furred log, the ants moving in a fine brown line at Old Lady's bare, blue-veined feet.

'You been starving in there two days, darn you!' she panted, chiming the spoon against a flat rock, causing the plump grey miracle bag to swing at her waist. Sweating sour, she rose and marched at the cabin, bearing the pulverized flesh. 'Come out, now!' She flicked a pinch of powder inside the lock. 'All right, I'll come get you!' she wheezed.

She spun the knob with one walnut-coloured hand, first one way, then the other. 'O Lord,' she intoned, 'fling this door wide!'

When nothing flung, she added yet another philtre and held her breath. Her long blue untidy skirt rustled as she peered into her bag of darkness to see if she had any scaly monsters there, any charm finer than the frog she'd killed months ago for such a crisis as this.

She heard Charlie breathing against the door. His folks had pranced off into some Ozark town early this week, leaving him, and he'd run almost six miles to Old Lady for company — she was by way of being an aunt or cousin or some such, and he didn't mind her fashions.

But then, two days ago, Old Lady, having gotten used to the boy around, decided to keep him for convenient company. She pricked her thin shoulder bone, drew out three blood pearls, spat wet over her right elbow, tramped on a crunch-cricket, and at the same instant clawed her left hand at Charlie, crying, 'My son you are, you are my son, for all eternity!'

Charlie, bounding like a startled hare, had crashed off into the bush, heading for home.

But Old Lady, skittering quick as a gingham lizard, cornered him in a dead end, and Charlie holed up in this old hermit's cabin and wouldn't come out, no matter how she whammed door, window, or knothole with amber-coloured fist or trounced her ritual fires, explaining to him that he was certainly her son *now*, all right.

'Charlie, you *there*?' she asked, cutting holes in the door planks with her bright little slippery eyes.

'I'm all of me here,' he replied firmly, very tired.

Maybe he would fall out on the ground any moment. She wrestled the knob hopefully. Perhaps a pinch too much frog powder had grated the lock wrong. She always overdid or underdid her miracles, she mused angrily, never doing them just *exact*, Devil take it!

'Charlie, I only wants someone to night-prattle to, someone to warm hands with at the fire. Someone to fetch kindling for me mornings, and fight off the spunks that come creeping of early fogs! I ain't got no fetchings on you for myself, son, just for your company.' She smacked her lips. 'Tell you what, Charlie, you come out and I *teach* you things!'

'What things?' he suspicioned.

'Teach you how to buy cheap, sell high. Catch a snow

weasel, cut off its head, carry it warm in your hind pocket. There!'

'Aw,' said Charlie.

She made haste. 'Teach you to make yourself shot-proof. So if anyone bangs at you with a gun, nothing happens.'

When Charlie stayed silent, she gave him the secret in a high fluttering whisper. 'Dig and stitch mouse-ear roots on Friday during full moon, and wear 'em around your neck in a white silk.'

'You're *crazy*,' Charlie said.

'Teach you how to stop blood or make animals stand frozen or make blind horses see, all them things I'll teach you! Teach you to cure a swelled-up cow and unbewitch a goat. Show you how to make yourself invisible!'

'Oh,' said Charlie.

Old Lady's heart beat like a Salvation tambourine.

The knob turned from the other side.

'You,' said Charlie, 'are funning me.'

'No, I'm not,' exclaimed Old Lady. 'Oh, Charlie, why, I'll make you like a window, see right through you. Why, child, you'll be surprised!'

'Real invisible?'

'Real invisible!'

'You won't fetch onto me if I walk out?'

'Won't touch a bristle of you, son.'

'Well,' he drawled reluctantly, 'all right.'

The door opened. Charlie stood in his bare feet, head down, chin against chest. 'Make me invisible,' he said.

'First we got to catch us a bat,' said Old Lady. 'Start lookin'!'

She gave him some jerky beef for his hunger and watched him climb a tree. He went high up and high up and it was nice seeing him there and it was nice having him here and all about after so many years alone with nothing to say good morning to but bird-droppings and silvery snail tracks.

   Pretty soon a bat with a broken wing fluttered down out of the tree. Old Lady snatched it up, beating warm and shrieking between its porcelain white teeth, and Charlie dropped down after it, hand upon clenched hand, yelling.

That night, with the moon nibbling at the spiced pine cones, Old Lady extracted a long silver needle from under her wide blue dress. Gumming her excitement and secret anticipation, she sighted up the dead bat and held the cold needle steady-steady.

   She had long ago realized that her miracles, despite all perspirations and salts and sulphurs, failed. But she had always dreamt that one day the miracles might start functioning, might spring up in crimson flowers and silver stars to prove that God had forgiven her for her pink body and her pink thoughts and her warm body and her warm thoughts as a young miss. But so far God had made no sign and said no word, but nobody knew this except Old Lady.

   'Ready?' she asked Charlie, who crouched cross-kneed, wrapping his pretty legs in long goose-pimpled arms, his mouth open, making teeth. 'Ready,' he whispered, shivering.

   'There!' She plunged the needle deep in the bat's right eye. 'So!'

   'Oh!' screamed Charlie, wadding up his face.

   'Now I wrap it in gingham, and here, put it in your pocket, keep it there, bat and all. Go on!'

   He pocketed the charm.

   'Charlie!' she shrieked fearfully. 'Charlie, where *are* you? I can't *see* you, child!'

   'Here!' He jumped so the light ran in red streaks up his body. 'I'm here, Old Lady!' He stared wildly at his arms, legs, chest, and toes. 'I'm here!'

   Her eyes looked as if they were watching a thousand

fireflies crisscrossing each other in the wild night air.

'Charlie, oh, you went *fast*! Quick as a hummingbird! Oh, Charlie, come *back* to me!'

'But I'm *here*!' he wailed.

'Where?'

'By the fire, the fire! And — I can see myself. I'm not invisible at all!'

Old Lady rocked on her lean flanks. 'Course *you* can see *you*! Every invisible person knows himself. Otherwise, how could you eat, walk, or get around places? Charlie, touch me. Touch me so I *know* you.'

Uneasily he put out a hand.

She pretended to jerk, startled, at his touch. '*Ah*!'

'You mean to say you can't *find* me?' he asked. 'Truly?'

'Not the least half-rump of you!'

She found a tree to stare at, and stared at it with shining eyes, careful not to glance at him. 'Why, I sure *did* a trick *that* time!' She sighed with wonder. 'Whooeee. Quickest invisible I *ever* made! Charlie. Charlie, how you *feel*?'

'Like creek water — all stirred.'

'You'll settle.'

Then after a pause, she added, 'Well, what you going to do now, Charlie, since you're invisible?'

All sorts of things shot through his brain, she could tell. Adventures stood up and danced like hell-fire in his eyes, and his mouth, just hanging, told what it meant to be a boy who imagined himself like the mountain winds. In a cold dream, he said, 'I'll run across wheat fields, climb snow mountains, steal white chickens off'n farms. I'll kick pink pigs when they ain't looking. I'll pinch pretty girls' legs when they sleep, snap their garters in schoolrooms.' Charlie looked at Old Lady, and from the shiny tips of her eyes she saw something wicked shape his face. 'And other things I'll do, I'll do, I will,' he said.

'Don't try nothing on me,' warned Old Lady. 'I'm brittle as spring ice and I don't take handling.' Then: 'What about your folks?'

'My folks?'

'You can't fetch yourself home looking like that. Scare the inside ribbons out of them. Your mother'd faint straight back like timber falling. Think they want you about the house to stumble over and your ma have to call you every three minutes, even though you're in the room next her elbow?'

Charlie had not considered it. He sort of simmered down and whispered out a little 'Gosh' and felt of his long bones carefully.

'You'll be mighty lonesome. People looking through you like a water glass, people knocking you aside because they didn't reckon you to be underfoot. And women, Charlie, *women* – '

He swallowed. 'What about women?'

'No woman will be giving you a second stare. And no woman wants to be kissed by a boy's mouth they can't even *find*!'

Charlie dug his bare toe in the soil contemplatively. He pouted. 'Well, I'll stay invisible, anyway, for a spell. I'll have me some fun. I'll just be pretty careful, is all. I'll stay out from in front of wagons and horses and Pa. Pa shoots at the nariest sound.' Charlie blinked. 'Why, with me invisible, someday Pa might just up and fill me with buckshot, thinkin' I was a hill squirrel in the dooryard. Oh . . . . '

Old Lady nodded at a tree. 'That's likely.'

'Well,' he decided slowly, 'I'll stay invisible for tonight, and tomorrow you can fix me back all whole again, Old Lady.'

'Now if that ain't just like a critter, always wanting to be what he can't be,' remarked Old Lady to a beetle on a log.

'What you mean?' said Charlie.

'Why,' she explained, 'it was real hard work, fixing you

up. It'll take a little *time* for it to wear off. Like a coat of paint wears off, boy.'

'You!' he cried. 'You did this to me! Now you make me back, you make me seeable!'

'Hush,' she said. 'It'll wear off, a hand or a foot at a time.'

'How'll it look, me around the hills with just one hand showing!'

'Like a five-winged bird hopping on the stones and bramble.'

'Or a foot showing!'

'Like a small pink rabbit jumping thicket.'

'Or my head floating!'

'Like a hairy balloon at the carnival!'

'How long before I'm *whole*?' he asked.

She deliberated that it might pretty well be an entire year.

He groaned. He began to sob and bite his lips and make fists. 'You magicked me, you did this, you did this thing to me. Now I won't be able to run home!'

She winked. 'But you *can* stay here, child, stay with me real comfort-like, and I'll keep you fat and saucy.'

He flung it out: 'You did this on purpose! You mean old hag, you want to keep me here!'

He ran off through the shrubs on the instant.

'Charlie, come back!'

No answer but the pattern of his feet on the soft dark turf, and his wet choking cry which passed swiftly off and away.

She waited and then kindled herself a fire. 'He'll be back,' she whispered. And thinking inward on herself, she said, 'And now I'll have me my company through spring and into late summer. Then, when I'm tired of him and want a silence, I'll send him home.'

Charlie returned noiselessly with the first grey of dawn, gliding over the rimed turf to where Old Lady sprawled like a bleached stick before the scattered ashes.

chase invisible boys, so she sat down, scowling, sputtering, and tried to fry more bacon. But every fresh strip she cut he would steal bubbling off the fire and run away far. Finally, cheeks burning, she cried, 'I know where you are! Right *there*! I hear you run!' She pointed to one side of him, not too accurate. He ran again. 'Now you're there!' she shouted. 'There, and there!' pointing to all the places he was in the next five minutes. 'I hear you press a grass blade, knock a flower, snap a twig. I got fine shell ears, delicate as roses. They can hear the stars moving!'

Silently he galloped off among the pines, his voice trailing back, 'Can't hear me when I'm set on a rock. I'll just *set*!'

All day he sat on an observatory rock in the clear wind, motionless and sucking his tongue.

Old Lady gathered wood in the deep forest, feeling his eyes weaselling on her spine. She wanted to babble: 'Oh, I see you, I see you! I was only fooling about invisible boys! You're right there!' But she swallowed her gall and gummed it tight.

The following morning he did the spiteful things. He began leaping from behind trees. He made toad-faces, frog-faces, spider-faces at her, clenching down his lips with his fingers, popping his raw eyes, pushing up his nostrils so you could peer in and see his brain thinking.

Once she dropped her kindling. She pretended it was a blue jay startled her.

He made a motion as if to strangle her.

She trembled a little.

He made another move as if to bang her shins and spit on her cheek.

These motions she bore without a lid-flicker or a mouth-twitch.

He stuck out his tongue, making strange bad noises. He wiggled his loose ears so she wanted to laugh, and finally she did laugh and explained it away quickly by saying, 'Sat on a salamander! Whew, how it poked!'

By high noon the whole madness boiled to a terrible peak.

For it was at that exact hour that Charlie came racing down the valley stark boy-naked!

Old Lady nearly fell flat with shock!

'Charlie!' she almost cried.

Charlie raced naked up one side of a hill and naked down the other — naked as day, naked as the moon, raw as the sun and a newborn chick, his feet shimmering and rushing like the wings of a low-skimming hummingbird.

Old Lady's tongue locked in her mouth. What could she say? Charlie, go dress? For *shame*? *Stop* that? *Could* she? Oh, Charlie, Charlie, God! Could she say that now? *Well?*'

Upon the big rock, she witnessed him dancing up and down, naked as the day of his birth, stamping bare feet, smacking his hands on his knees and sucking in and out his white stomach like blowing and deflating a circus balloon.

She shut her eyes tight and prayed.

After three hours of this she pleaded, 'Charlie, Charlie, come here! I got something to *tell* you!'

Like a fallen leaf he came, dressed again, praise the Lord.

'Charlie,' she said, looking at the pine trees, 'I see your right toe. *There* it is.'

'You do?' he said.

'Yes,' she said very sadly. 'There it is like a horny toad on the grass. And there, up there's your left ear hanging on the air like a pink butterfly.'

Charlie danced. 'I'm forming in, I'm forming in!'

Old Lady nodded. 'Here comes your ankle!'

'Gimme *both* my feet!' ordered Charlie.

'You got 'em.'

'How about my hands?'

'I see one crawling on your knee like a daddy longlegs.'

'How about the other one?'

'It's crawling too.'

'I got a body?'

'Shaping up fine.'

'I'll need my head to go home, Old Lady.'

To go home, she thought wearily. 'No!' she said, stubborn and angry. 'No, you ain't got no head. No head at all,' she cried. She'd leave that to the very last. 'No head, no head,' she insisted.

'No head?' he wailed.

'Yes, oh my God, yes, yes, you got your blamed head!' she snapped, giving up. 'Now , fetch me back my bat with the needle in his eye!'

He flung it at her. 'Haaaa-yoooo!' His yelling went all up the valley, and long after he had run towards home she heard his echoes, racing.

Then she plucked up her kindling with a great dry weariness and started back towards her shack, sighing, talking. And Charlie followed her all the way, *really* invisible now, so she couldn't see him, just hear him, like a pine cone dropping or a deep underground stream trickling, or a squirrel clambering a bough; and over the fire at twilight she and Charlie sat, him so invisible, and her feeding him bacon he wouldn't take, so she ate it herself, and then she fixed some magic and fell asleep with Charlie, made out of sticks and rags and pebbles, but still warm and her very own son, slumbering and nice in her shaking mother arms . . . and they talked about golden things in drowsy voices until dawn made the fire slowly, slowly wither out . . .

The Golden Kite,
the Silver Wind

'In the shape of a *pig*?' cried the Mandarin.

'In the shape of a pig,' said the messenger, and departed.

'Oh, what an evil day in an evil year,' cried the Mandarin. 'The town of Kwan-Si, beyond the hill, was very small in my childhood. Now it has grown so large that at last they are building a wall.'

'But why should a wall two miles away make my good father sad and angry all within the hour?' asked his daughter quietly.

'They build their wall,' said the Mandarin, 'in the shape of a pig! Do you see? Our own city wall is built in the shape of an orange. That pig will devour us, greedily!'

'Ah.'

They both sat thinking.

Life was full of symbols and omens. Demons lurked everywhere. Death swam in the wetness of an eye, the turn of a gull's wing meant rain, a fan held *so*, the tilt of a roof, and, yes, even a city wall was of immense importance. Travellers and tourists, caravans, musicians, artists, coming upon these two towns, equally judging the portents, would say, 'The city shaped like an orange? No! I will enter the city shaped like a pig and prosper, eating all, growing fat with good luck and prosperity!'

The Mandarin wept. 'All is lost! These symbols and signs terrify. Our city will come on evil days.'

'Then,' said the daughter, 'call in your stonemasons and temple builders. I will whisper from behind the silken screen and you will know the words.'

The old man clapped his hands despairingly. 'Ho, stonemasons! Ho, builders of towns and palaces!'

The men who knew marble and granite and onyx and quartz came quickly. The Mandarin faced them most uneasily, himself waiting for a whisper from the silken screen behind his throne. At last the whisper came.

'I have called you here,' said the whisper.

'I have called you here,' said the Mandarin aloud, 'because our city is shaped like an orange, and the vile city of Kwan-Si has this day shaped theirs like a ravenous pig — '.

Here the stonemasons groaned and wept. Death rattled his cane in the outer courtyard. Poverty made a sound like a wet cough in the shadows of the room.

'And so,' said the whisper, like the Mandarin, 'you raisers of walls must go bearing trowels and rocks and change the shape of *our* city!'

The architects and masons gasped. The Mandarin himself gasped at what he had said. The whisper whispered. The Mandarin went on: 'And you will change our walls into a club which may beat the pig and drive it off!'

The stonemasons rose up, shouting. Even the Mandarin, delighted at the words from his mouth, applauded, stood down from his throne. 'Quick!' he cried. 'To work!'

When his men had gone, smiling and bustling, the Mandarin turned with great love to the silken screen. 'Daughter,' he whispered, 'I will embrace you.' There was no reply. He stepped around the screen, and she was gone.

Such modesty, he thought. She has slipped away and left me with a triumph, as if it were mine.

The news spread through the city; the Mandarin was acclaimed. Everyone carried stone to the walls. Fireworks were set off and the demons of death and poverty did not linger, as all worked together. At the end of the month the wall had been changed. It was now a mighty bludgeon with which to drive pigs, boars, even lions, far away. The Mandarin slept like a happy fox every night.

'I would like to see the Mandarin of Kwan-Si when the news is learned. Such pandemonium and hysteria; he will likely throw himself from a mountain! A little more of that wine, oh Daughter-who-thinks-like-a-son.'

But the pleasure was like a winter flower; it died swiftly. That very afternoon, the messenger rushed into the courtroom. 'Oh Mandarin, disease, early sorrow, avalanches, grasshopper plagues, and poisoned well water!'

The Mandarin trembled.

'The town of Kwan-Si,' said the messenger, 'which was built like a pig and which animal we drove away by changing our walls to a mighty stick, has now turned triumph to winter ashes. They have built their city's walls like a great bonfire to burn our stick!'

The Mandarin's heart sickened within him, like an autumn fruit upon the ancient tree. 'Oh, gods! Travellers will spurn us. Tradesmen, reading the symbols, will turn from the stick, so easily destroyed, to the fire, which conquers all!'

'No,' said a whisper like a snowflake from behind the silken screen.

'No,' said the startled Mandarin.

'Tell my stonemasons,' said the whisper that was a falling drop of rain, 'to build our walls in the shape of a shining lake.'

The Mandarin said this aloud, his heart warmed.

'And with this lake of water,' said the whisper and the old man, 'we will quench the fire and put it out forever!'

The city turned out in joy to learn that once again they had been saved by the magnificent Emperor of ideas. They ran to the walls and built them nearer to this new vision, singing, not as loudly as before, of course, for they were tired, and not as quickly, for since it had taken a month to rebuild the wall the first time, they had had to neglect business and crops and therefore were somewhat weaker and poorer.

There then followed a succession of horrible and wonderful days, one in another like a nest of frightening boxes.

'Oh, Emperor,' cried the messenger, 'Kwan-Si has rebuilt their walls to resemble a mouth with which to drink all our lake!'

'Then,' said the Emperor, standing very close to his silken screen, 'build our walls like a needle to sew up that mouth!'

'Emperor!' screamed the messenger. 'They make their walls like a sword to break your needle!'

The Emperor held, trembling, to the silken screen. 'Then shift the stones to form a scabbard to sheathe that sword!'

'Mercy,' wept the messenger the following morn, 'they have worked all night and shaped their walls like lightning which will explode and destroy that sheath!'

Sickness spread in the city like a pack of evil dogs. Shops closed. The population, working now steadily for endless months upon the changing of the walls, resembled Death himself, clattering his white bones like musical instruments in the wind. Funerals began to appear in the streets, though it was the middle of summer, a time when all should be tending and harvesting. The Mandarin fell so ill that he had his bed drawn up by the silken screen and there he lay, miserably giving his architectural orders. The voice behind the screen was weak now, too, and faint, like the wind in the eaves.

'Kwan-Si is an eagle. Then our walls must be a net for that eagle. They are a sun to burn our net. Then we build a moon to eclipse their sun!'

Like a rusted machine, the city ground to a halt.

At last the whisper behind the screen cried out:

'In the name of the gods, send for Kwan-Si!'

Upon the last day of summer the Mandarin of Kwan-Si, very ill and withered away, was carried into our Mandarin's courtroom by four starving footmen. The two mandarins were propped up, facing each other. Their breaths fluttered like winter winds in their mouths. A voice said:

'Let us put an end to this.'

The old men nodded.

'This cannot go on,' said the faint voice. 'Our people do nothing but rebuild our cities to a different shape every day, every hour. They have no time to hunt, to fish, to love, to be good to their ancestors and their ancestors' children.'

'This I admit,' said the mandarins of the towns of the Cage, the Moon, the Spear, the Fire, the Sword and this, that, and other things.

'Carry us into the sunlight,' said the voice.

The old men were borne out under the sun and up a little hill. In the late summer breeze a few very thin children were flying dragon kites in all the colours of the sun, and frogs and grass, the colour of the sea and the colour of coins and wheat.

The first Mandarin's daughter stood by his bed.

'See,' she said.

'Those are nothing but kites,' said the two old men.

'But what is a kite on the ground?' she said. 'It is nothing. What does it need to sustain it and make it beautiful and truly spiritual?'

'The wind, of course!' said the others.

'And what do the sky and wind need to make *them* beautiful?'

'A kite, of course – many kites, to break the monotony, the sameness of the sky. Coloured kites, flying!'

'So,' said the Mandarin's daughter. 'You, Kwan-Si, will make a last rebuilding of your town to resemble nothing more nor less than the wind. And we shall build like a golden kite. The wind will beautify the kite and carry it to wondrous heights. And the kite will break the sameness of the wind's existence and give it purpose and meaning. One without the other is nothing. Together, all will be beauty and co-operation and a long and enduring life.'

Whereupon the two mandarins were so overjoyed that they

took their first nourishment in days, momentarily were given strength, embraced, and lavished praise upon each other, called the Mandarin's daughter a boy, a man, a stone pillar, a warrior, and a true and unforgettable son. Almost immediately they parted and hurried to their towns, calling out and singing, weakly but happily.

And so, in time, the towns became the Town of the Golden Kite and the Town of the Silver Wind. And harvestings were harvested and business tended again, and the flesh returned, and disease ran off like a frightened jackal. And on every night of the year the inhabitants in the Town of the Kite could hear the good clear wind sustaining them. And those in the Town of the Wind could hear the kite singing, whispering, rising, and beautifying them.

'So be it,' said the Mandarin in front of his silken screen.

The Fog Horn

Out there in the cold water, far from land, we waited every night for the coming of the fog, and it came, and we oiled the brass machinery and lit the fog light up in the stone tower. Feeling like two birds in the grey sky, McDunn and I sent the light touching out, red, then white, then red again, to eye the lonely ships. And if they did not see our light, then there was always our Voice, the great deep cry of our Fog Horn shuddering through the rags of mist to startle the gulls away like decks of scattered cards and make the waves turn high and foam.

'It's a lonely life, but you're used to it now, aren't you?' asked McDunn.

'Yes,' I said. 'You're a good talker, thank the Lord.'

'Well, it's your turn on land tomorrow,' he said, smiling, 'to dance the ladies and drink gin.'

'What do you think, McDunn, when I leave you out here alone?'

'On the mysteries of the sea.' McDunn lit his pipe. It was a quarter past seven of a cold November evening, the heat on, the light switching its tail in two hundred directions, the Fog Horn bumbling in the high throat of the tower. There wasn't a town for a hundred miles down the coast, just a road which came lonely through dead country to the sea, with few cars on it, a stretch of two miles of cold water out to our rock, and rare few ships.

'The mysteries of the sea,' said McDunn thoughtfully. 'You know, the ocean's the biggest damned snowflake ever? It rolls and swells a thousand shapes and colours, no two alike. Strange. One night, years ago, I was here alone, when all of the fish of the sea surfaced out there. Something made them swim in and lie in the bay, sort of trembling and staring up at the tower light going red, white, red, white across them so I could see their funny eyes. I turned cold. They were like a big peacock's tail, moving out there until midnight. Then, without so much as a sound, they slipped away, the million of them was gone. I kind of think maybe, in some sort of way, they came all those miles to worship. Strange. But think how the tower must look to them, standing seventy feet above the water, the God-light flashing out from it, and the tower declaring itself with a monster voice. They never came back, those fish, but don't you think for a while they thought they were in the Presence?'

I shivered. I looked out at the long grey lawn of the sea stretching away into nothing and nowhere.

'Oh, the sea's full.' McDunn puffed his pipe nervously, blinking. He had been nervous all day and hadn't said why. 'For all our engines and so-called submarines, it'll be ten thousand centuries before we set foot on the real bottom of the sunken lands, in the fairy kingdoms there, and know *real* terror. Think of it, it's still the year 300,000 Before Christ down under there. While we've paraded around with trumpets, lopping off each other's countries and heads, they have been living beneath the sea twelve miles deep and cold in a time as old as the beard of a comet.'

'Yes, it's an old world.'

'Come on. I got something special I been saving up to tell you.'

We ascended the eighty steps, talking and taking our time. At the top, McDunn switched off the room lights so there'd be no reflection in the plate glass. The great eye of the light was humming, turning easily in its oiled socket. The Fog Horn was blowing steadily, once every fifteen seconds.

'Sounds like an animal, don't it?' McDunn nodded to

himself. 'A big lonely animal crying in the night. Sitting here on the edge of ten billion years calling out to the Deeps, I'm here, I'm here, I'm here. And the Deeps *do* answer, yes, they do. You been here now for three months, Johnny, so I better prepare you. About this time of year,' he said, studying the murk and fog, 'something comes to visit the lighthouse.'

'The swarms of fish like you said?'

'No, this is something else. I've put off telling you because you might think I'm daft. But tonight's the latest I can put it off, for if my calendar's marked right from last year, tonight's the night it comes. I won't go into detail, you'll have to see it yourself. Just sit down there. If you want, tomorrow you can pack your duffel and take the motorboat in to land and get your car parked there at the dinghy pier on the cape and drive on back to some little inland town and keep your lights burning nights, I won't question or blame you. It's happened three years now, and this is the only time anyone's been here with me to verify it. You wait and watch.'

Half an hour passed with only a few whispers between us. When we grew tired waiting, McDunn began describing some of his ideas to me. He had some theories about the Fog Horn itself.

'One day many years ago a man walked along and stood in the sound of the ocean on a cold sunless shore and said, "We need a voice to call across the water, to warn ships; I'll make one. I'll make a voice like all of time and all of the fog that ever was; I'll make a voice that is like an empty bed beside you all night long, and like an empty house when you open the door, and like trees in autumn with no leaves. A sound like the birds flying south, crying, and a sound like November wind and the sea on the hard, cold shore. I'll make a sound that's so alone that no one can miss it, that whoever hears it will weep in their souls, and hearths will seem warmer, and being inside will seem better to all who hear it in the distant towns. I'll make me a sound and an apparatus and they'll call it a Fog Horn and whoever hears it will know the sadness of eternity and the briefness of life." '

The Fog Horn blew.

'I made up that story,' said McDunn quietly, 'to try to explain why this thing keeps coming back to the lighthouse every year. The Fog Horn calls it, I think, and it comes . . . '

'But — ' I said.

'Sssst!' said McDunn. 'There!' He nodded out to the Deeps.

Something was swimming towards the lighthouse tower.

It as a cold night, as I have said; the high tower was cold, the light coming and going, and the Fog Horn calling and calling through the ravelling mist. You couldn't see far and you couldn't see plain, but there was the deep sea moving on its way about the night earth, flat and quiet, the colour of grey mud, and here were the two of us alone in the high tower, and there, far out at first, was a ripple, followed by a wave, a rising, a bubble, a bit of froth. And then, from the surface of the cold sea came a head, a large head, dark-coloured, with immense eyes, and then a neck. And then — not a body — but more neck and more! The head rose a full forty feet above the water on a slender and beautiful dark neck. Only then did the body, like a little island of black coral and shells and crayfish, drip up from the subterranean. There was a flicker of tail. In all, from head to tip of tail, I estimated the monster at ninety or a hundred feet.

I don't know what I said. I said something.

'Steady, boy, steady,' whispered McDunn.

'It's impossible!' I said.

'No, Johnny, *we're* impossible. *It's* like it always was ten million years ago. *It* hasn't changed. It's *us* and the land that've changed, become impossible. *Us!*'

It swam slowly and with a great dark majesty out in the icy waters, far away. The fog came and went about it, momentarily erasing its shape. One of the monster eyes caught and held and flashed back our immense light, red, white, red, white, like a disc held high and sending a message in primeval code. It was as silent as the fog through which it swam.

'It's a dinosaur of some sort!' I crouched down, holding to the stair rail.

'Yes, one of the tribe.'

'But they died out!'

'No, only hid away in the Deeps. Deep, deep down in the deepest Deeps. Isn't *that* a word now, Johnny, a real word, it says so much: the Deeps. There's all the coldness and dark- ness and deepness in the world in a word like that.'

'What'll we do?'

'Do? We got our job, we can't leave. Besides, we're safer here than in any boat trying to get to land. That thing's as big as a destroyer and almost as swift.'

'But here, why does it come *here*?'

The next moment I had my answer.

The Fog Horn blew.

And the monster answered.

A cry came across a million years of water and mist. A cry so anguished and alone that it shuddered in my head and my body. The monster cried out at the tower. The Fog Horn blew. The monster roared again. The Fog Horn blew. The monster opened its great toothed mouth and the sound that came from it was the sound of the Fog Horn itself. Lonely and vast and far away. The sound of isolation, a viewless sea, a cold night, apartness. That was the sound.

'Now,' whispered McDunn, 'do you know why it comes here?'

I nodded.

'All year long, Johnny, that poor monster there lying far out, a thousand miles at sea, and twenty miles deep maybe, biding its time, perhaps it's a million years old, this one creature. Think of it, waiting a million years; could *you* wait that long? Maybe it's the last of its kind. I sort of think that's true. Anyway, here come men on land and build this light-house, five years ago. And set up their Fog Horn and sound it and sound it, out towards the place where you bury yourself in sleep and sea memories of a world where there were thousands like yourself, but now you're alone, all alone in a world not made for you, a world where you have to hide.

'But the sound of the Fog Horn comes and goes, comes and goes, and you stir from the muddy bottom of the Deeps, and your eyes open like the lenses of two-foot cameras and you move, slow, slow, for you have the ocean sea on your shoulders, heavy. But that Fog Horn comes through a thousand miles of water, faint and familiar, and the furnace in your belly stokes up, and you begin to rise, slow, slow. You feed yourself on great slakes of cod and minnow, on rivers of jellyfish, and you rise slow through the autumn months, through September when the fogs started, through October with more fog and the horn still calling you on, and then, late in November, after pressurizing yourself day by day, a few feet higher every hour, you are near the surface and still alive. You've got to go slow; if you surfaced all at once you'd explode. So it takes you all of three months to surface, and then a number of days to swim through the cold waters to the lighthouse. And there you are, out there, in the night, Johnny, the biggest damn monster in creation. And here's the lighthouse calling to you, with a long neck like your neck sticking way up out of the water, and a body like your body, and, most important of all, a voice like your voice. Do you understand now, Johnny, do you understand?'

The Fog Horn blew.

The monster answered.

I saw it all, I knew it all — the million years of waiting alone, for someone to come back who never came back. The million years of isolation at the bottom of the sea, the insanity of time there, while the skies cleared of reptile-birds, the swamps dried on the continental lands, the sloths and sabertooths had their day and sank in tar pits, and men ran like white ants upon the hills.

The Fog Horn blew.

'Last year,' said McDunn, 'that creature swam round and round, round and round, all night. Not coming too near, puzzled, I'd say. Afraid, maybe. And a bit angry after coming all this way. But the next day, unexpectedly, the fog lifted, the sun came out fresh, the sky was as blue as a painting. And the monster swam off away from the heat and the silence and didn't come back. I suppose it's been brooding on it for a year now, thinking it over from every which way.'

The monster was only a hundred yards off now, it and the Fog Horn crying at each other. As the lights hit them, the monster's eyes were fire and ice, fire and ice.

'That's life for you,' said McDunn. 'Someone always waiting for someone who never comes homes. Always someone loving some thing more than that thing loves them. And after a while you want to destroy whatever that thing is, so it can't hurt you no more.'

The monster stopped and froze. Its great lantern eyes The Fog Horn blew.

'Let's see what happens,' said McDunn.

He switched the Fog Horn off.

The ensuing minute of silence was so intense that we could hear our hearts pounding in the glassed area of the tower, could hear the slow greased turn of the light.

The monster stopped and froze. Its great lantern eyes blinked. Its mouth gaped. It gave a sort of rumble, like a volcano. It twitched its head this way and that, as if to seek the sounds now dwindled off into the fog. It peered at the lighthouse. It rumbled again. Then its eyes caught fire. It reared up, threshed the water, and rushed at the tower, its eyes filled with angry torment.

'McDunn!' I cried. 'Switch on the horn!'

McDunn fumbled with the switch. But even as he flicked it on, the monster was rearing up. I had a glimpse of its gigantic paws, fishskin flittering in webs between the finger-like projections, clawing at the tower. The huge eye on the right side of its anguished head glittered before me like a cauldron into which I might drop, screaming. The tower shook. The Fog Horn cried; the monster cried. It seized the tower and gnashed the glass, which shattered in upon us.

McDunn seized my arm. 'Downstairs!'

The tower rocked, trembled, and started to give. The Fog Horn and the monster roared. We stumbled and half fell down the stairs. 'Quick!'

We reached the bottom as the tower buckled down towards us. We ducked under the stairs into the small stone cellar. There were a thousand concussions as the rocks rained down; the Fog Horn stopped abruptly. The monster crashed upon the tower. The tower fell. We knelt together, McDunn and I, holding tight, while our world exploded.

Then it was over, and there was nothing but darkness and the wash of the sea on the raw stones.

That and the other sound.

'Listen,' said McDunn quietly. 'Listen.'

We waited a moment. And then I began to hear it. First a great vacuumed sucking of air, and then the lament, the bewilderment, the loneliness of the great monster, folded over and upon us, so that the sickening reek of its body filled the air, a stone's thickness away from our cellar. The monster gasped and cried. The tower was gone. The light was gone. The thing that had called to it across a million years was gone. And the monster was opening its mouth and sending out great sounds. The sounds of a Fog Horn, again and again. And ships far at sea, not finding the light, not seeing anything, but passing and hearing late that night, must've thought: There it is, the lonely sound, the Lonesome Bay horn. All's well. We've rounded the cape.

And so it went for the rest of that night.

The sun was hot and yellow the next afternoon when the rescuers came out to dig us from our stoned-under cellar.

'It fell apart, is all,' said Mr McDunn gravely. 'We had a few bad knocks from the waves and it just crumbled.' He pinched my arm.

There was nothing to see. The ocean was calm, the sky blue. The only thing was a great algaic stink from the green matter that covered the fallen tower stones and the shore rocks. Flies buzzed about. The ocean washed empty on the shore.

The next year they built a new lighthouse, but by that time I had a job in the little town and a wife and a good small warm house that glowed yellow on autumn nights, the doors locked, the chimney puffing smoke. As for McDunn, he was master of the new lighthouse, built to his own specifications, out of steel-reinforced concrete. 'Just in case,' he said.

The new lighthouse was ready in November. I drove down alone one evening late and parked my car and looked across the grey waters and listened to the new horn sounding, once, twice, three, four times a minute far out there, by itself.

The monster?

It never came back.

'It's gone away,' said McDunn. 'It's gone back to the Deeps. It's learned you can't love anything too much in this world. It's gone into the deepest Deeps to wait another million years. Ah, the poor thing! Waiting out there, and waiting out there, while man comes and goes on this pitiful little planet. Waiting and waiting.'

I sat in my car, listening. I couldn't see the lighthouse or the light standing out in Lonesome Bay. I could only hear the Horn, the Horn, the Horn. It sounded like the monster calling.

I sat there wishing there was something I could say.

The Big Black and
White Game

The people filled the stands behind the wire screen, waiting. Us kids, dripping from the lake, ran between the white cottages, past the resort hotel, screaming, and sat on the bleachers, making wet bottom marks. The hot sun beat down through the tall oak trees around the baseball diamond. Our fathers and mothers, in golf pants and light summer dresses, scolded us and made us sit still.

We looked towards the hotel and the back door of the vast kitchen, expectantly. A few coloured women began walking across the shade-freckled area between, and in ten minutes the far left section of the bleachers was mellow with the colour of their fresh-washed faces and arms. After all these years, whenever I think back on it, I can still hear the sounds they made. The sound on the warm air was like a soft moving of dove voices each time they talked among themselves.

Everybody quickened into amusement, laughter rose right up into the clear blue Wisconsin sky, as the kitchen door flung wide and out ran the big and little, the dark and high-yellar uniformed Negro waiters, janitors, bus boys, boatmen, cooks, bottle washers, soda jerks, gardeners, and golf-links tenders. They came capering, showing their fine white teeth, proud of their new red-striped uniforms, their shiny shoes rising and coming down on the green grass as they skirted the bleachers and drifted with lazy speed out on the field, calling to everybody and everything.

Us kids squealed. There was Long Johnson, the lawn-cutting man, and Cavanaugh, the soda-fountain man, and Shorty Smith and Pete Brown and Jiff Miller!

And *there* was Big Poe! Us kids shouted, applauded!

Big Poe was the one who stood so tall by the popcorn machine every night in the million-dollar dance pavilion farther down beyond the hotel on the lake rim. Every night I bought popcorn from Big Poe and he poured lots of butter all over it for me.

I stamped and yelled, 'Big Poe! Big Poe!'

And he looked over at me and stretched his lips to bring out his teeth, waved, and shouted a laugh.

And Mama looked to the right, to the left, and back of us with worried eyes and nudged my elbow. 'Hush,' she said. 'Hush.'

'Land, land,' said the lady next to my mother, fanning herself with a folded paper. 'This is quite a day for the coloured servants, ain't it? Only time of year they break loose. They look forward all summer to the big Black and White game. But this ain't nothing. You seen their Cakewalk Jamboree?'

'We got tickets for it,' said Mother. 'For tonight at the pavilion. Cost us a dollar each. That's pretty expensive, I'd say.'

'But I always figure,' said the woman, 'once a year you got to spend. And it's really something to watch them dance. They just naturally got . . . '

'Rhythm,' said Mother.

'That's the word,' said the lady. 'Rhythm. That's what they got. Land, you should see the coloured maids up at the hotel. They been buying satin yardage in at the big store in Madison for a month now. And every spare minute they sit sewing and laughing. And I seen some of the feathers they bought for their hats. Mustard and wine ones and blue ones and violet ones. Oh, it'll be a sight!'

'They been airing out their tuxedos,' I said. 'I saw them hanging on lines behind the hotel all last week!'

'Look at them prance,' said Mother. 'You'd think they thought they were going to win the game from our men.'

The coloured men ran back and forth and yelled with their high, fluting voices and their low, lazy interminable voices. Way out in centre field you could see the flash of teeth, their upraised naked black arms swinging and beating their sides as they hopped up and down and ran like rabbits, exuberantly.

Big Poe took a double fistful of bats, bundled them on his huge bull shoulder, and strutted along the first-base line, head back, mouth smiling wide open, his tongue moving, singing:

> ' — *gonna dance out both of my shoes,*
> *When they play those Jelly Roll Blues;*
> *Tomorrow night at the Dark Town Strutters' Ball!'*

Up went his knees and down and out, swinging the bats like musical batons. A burst of applause and soft laughter came from the left-hand grandstands, where all the young, ripply coloured girls with shiny brown eyes sat eager and easy. They made quick motions that were graceful and mellow because, maybe, of their rich colouring. Their laughter was like shy birds; they waved at Big Poe, and one of them with a high voice cried, 'Oh, Big Poe! Oh, Big Poe!'

The white section joined politely in the applause as Big Poe finished his cakewalk. 'Hey, Big Poe!' I yelled again.

'Stop that, Douglas!' said Mother, straight at me.

Now the white men came running between the trees with their uniforms on. There was a great thunder and shouting and rising up in our grandstand. The white men ran across the green diamond, flashing white.

'Oh, there's Uncle George!' said Mother. 'My, doesn't he look nice?' And there was my Uncle George toddling along in his outfit which didn't quite fit because Uncle has a potbelly, and jowls that sit out over any collar he puts on. He was hurrying along, trying to breathe and smile at the same time, lifting up his pudgy little legs. 'My, they look *so* nice,' enthused Mother.

I sat there, watching their movements. Mother sat beside me, and I think she was comparing and thinking, too, and what she saw amazed and disconcerted her. How easily the dark people had come running first, like those slow-motion deer and buck antelopes in those African moving pictures, like things in dreams. They came like beautiful brown, shiny animals that didn't know they were alive, but lived. And when they ran and put their easy, lazy, timeless legs out and followed them with their big, sprawling arms and loose fingers and smiled in the blowing wind, their expressions didn't say, 'Look at *me* run, look at *me* run!' No, not at all. Their faces dreamily said, 'Lord, but it's sure nice to run. See the ground swell soft under me? Gosh, I feel good. My muscles are moving like oil on my bones and it's the best pleasure in the world to run.' And they ran. There was no purpose to their running but exhilaration and living.

The white men worked at their running as they worked at everything. You felt embarrassed for them because they were alive too much in the wrong way. Always looking from the corners of their eyes to see if you were watching. The Negroes didn't care if you watched or not; they went on living, moving. They were so sure of playing that they didn't have to think about it any more.

'My, but our men look so nice,' said my mother, repeating herself rather flatly. She had seen, compared the teams. Inside, she realized how laxly the coloured men hung swaying in their uniforms, and how tensely, nervously, the white men were crammed, shoved, and belted into *their* outfits.

I guess the tenseness began then.

I guess everybody saw what was happening. They saw how the white men looked like senators in sun suits. And they admired the graceful unawareness of the coloured men. And, as is always the case, that admiration turned to envy, to jealousy, to irritation. It turned to conversation like:

'That's my husband, Tom, on third base. Why doesn't he pick up his feet? He just *stands* there.'

'Never you mind, never you mind. He'll pick 'em up when the time comes!'

'That's what *I* say! Now, take my Henry, for instance. Henry mightn't be active all the time, but when there's a crisis — just you *watch* him. Uh — I do wish he'd wave or something, though. Oh, *there*! Hello, Henry!'

'Look at that Jimmi Cosner playing around out there!'

I looked. A medium-sized white man with a freckled face and red hair was clowning on the diamond. He was balancing a bat on his forehead. There was laughter from the white grandstand. But it sounded like the kind of laughter you laugh when you're embarrassed for someone.

'Play ball!' said the umpire.

A coin was flipped. The coloured men batted first.

'Darn it,' said my mother.

The coloured men ran in from the field happily.

Big Poe was first to bat. I cheered. He picked up the bat in one hand like a toothpick and idled over to the plate and laid the bat on his thick shoulder, smiling along its polished surface towards the stands where the coloured women sat with their fresh flowery cream dresses stirring over their legs, which hung down between the seat intervals like crisp new sticks of ginger; their hair was all fancily spun and hung over their ears. Big Poe looked in particular at the little dainty-as-a-chicken-bone shape of his girl friend Katherine. She was the one who made the beds at the hotel and cottages every morning, who tapped on your door like a bird and politely asked if you was done dreaming, 'cause if you was she'd clean away all them old nightmares and bring in a fresh batch — please use them *one* at a time, thank yoah. Big Poe shook his head, looking at her, as if he couldn't believe she was there. Then he turned, one hand balancing the bat, his left hand dangling free at his side, to await the trial pitches. They hissed past, spatted into the open mouth of the catcher's mitt, were hurled back. The umpire grunted. The next pitch was the starter.

Big Poe let the first ball go by him.

'Stee-rike!' announced the umpire. Big Poe winked good-naturedly at the white folks. Bang! 'Stee-rike two!' cried the umpire.

The ball came for the third time.

Big Poe was suddenly a greased machine pivoting; the dangling hand swept up to the butt end of the bat, the bat swivelled, connected with the ball – *Whack!* The ball shot up into the sky, away down towards the wavering line of oak trees, down towards the lake, where a white sailboat slid silently by. The crowd yelled, me loudest! There went Uncle George, running on his stubby, wool-stockinged legs, getting smaller with distance.

Big Poe stood for a moment watching the ball go. Then he began to run. He went around the bases, loping, and on the way home from third base he waved to the coloured girls naturally and happily and they waved back, standing on their seats and shrilling.

Ten minutes later, with the bases loaded and run after run being driven in, and Big Poe coming to bat again, my mother turned to me. 'They're the most inconsiderate people,' she said.

'But that's the game,' I said. 'They've only got two outs.'

'But the score's seven to nothing,' my mother protested.

'Well, just you wait until *our* men come to bat,' said the lady next to my mother, waving away a fly with a pale blue-veined hand. 'Those Negroes are too big for their britches.'

'Stee-rike two!' said the umpire as Big Poe swung.

'All the past week at the hotel,' said the woman next to my mother, staring out at Big Poe steadily, 'the hotel service has been simply terrible. Those maids don't talk about a thing save the Cakewalk Jamboree, and whenever you want ice water it takes them half an hour to fetch it, they're so busy sewing.'

'Ball one!' said the umpire.

The woman fussed. 'I'll be glad when this week's over, that's what I got to say,' she said.

'Ball two!' said the umpire to Big Poe.

'Are they going to *walk* him?' asked my mother of me. 'Are they *crazy*?' To the woman next to her: 'That's right. They been acting funny all week. Last night I had to tell Big Poe twice to put extra butter on my popcorn. I guess he was trying to save money or something.'

'Ball three!' said the umpire.

The lady next to my mother cried out suddenly and fanned herself furiously with her newspaper. 'Land, I just *thought*! Wouldn't it be awful if they *won* the game? They *might*, you know. They might do it.'

My mother looked at the lake, at the trees, at her hands. 'I don't know why Uncle George had to play. Make a fool of himself. Douglas, you run tell him to quit right now. Its bad on his heart.'

'You're out!' cried the umpire to Big Poe.

'Ah,' sighed the grandstand.

The side was retired. Big Poe laid down his bat gently and walked along the base line. The white men pattered in from the field looking red and irritable, with big islands of sweat under their armpits. Big Poe looked over at me. I winked at him. He winked back. Then I knew he wasn't so dumb.

He'd struck out on purpose.

Long Johnson was going to pitch for the coloured team.

He ambled out to the rubber, worked his fingers around in his fists to limber them up.

First white man to bat was a man named Kodimer, who sold suits in Chicago all year round.

Long Johnson fed them over the plate with tired, un-assuming controlled accuracy.

Mr Kodimer chopped. Mr Kodimer swatted. Finally Mr Kodimer bunted the ball down the third-base line.

'Out at first base,' said the umpire, an Irishman named Mahoney.

Second man up was a young Swede named Moberg. He hit a high fly to centre field which was taken by a little plump Negro who didn't look fat because he moved around like a smooth, round glob of mercury.

Third man up was a Milwaukee truck driver. He whammed a line drive to centre field. It was good. Except that he tried to stretch it into a two-bagger. When he pulled up at second base, there was Emancipated Smith with a white pellet in his dark, dark hand, waiting.

My mother sank back in her seat, exhaling. 'Well, I *never!*'

'It's getting hotter,' said the lady elbow-next. 'Think I'll go for a stroll by the lake soon. It's too hot to sit and watch a silly game today. Mightn't you come along with me, missus?' she asked Mother.

It went on that way for five innings.

It was eleven to nothing and Big Poe had struck out three times on purpose, and in the last half of the fifth was when Jimmie Cosner came to bat for our side again. He'd been trying all afternoon, clowning, giving directions, telling everybody just where he was going to blast that pill once he got hold of it. He swaggered up towards the plate now, confident and bugle-voiced. He swung six bats in his thin hands, eyeing them critically with his shiny green little eyes. He chose one, dropped the others, ran to the plate, chopping out little islands of green fresh lawn with his cleated heels. He pushed his cap back on his dusty red hair. 'Watch this!' he called out loud to the ladies. 'You watch me show these dark boys! Ya-hah!'

Long Johnson on the mound did a slow serpentine

windup. It was like a snake on a limb of a tree, uncoiling, suddenly darting at you. Instantly Johnson's hand was in front of him, open, like black fangs, empty. And the white pill slashed across the plate with a sound like a razor.

'Stee-rike!'

Jimmie Cosner put his bat down and stood glaring at the umpire. He said nothing for a long time. Then he spat deliberately near the catcher's foot, took up the yellow maple bat again, and swung it so the sun glinted the rim of it in a nervous halo. He twitched and sidled it on his thin-boned shoulder, and his mouth opened and shut over his long nicotined teeth.

Clap! went the catcher's mitt.

Cosner turned, stared.

The catcher, like a black magician, his white teeth gleaming, opened up his oily glove. There, like a white flower glowing, was the baseball.

'Stee-rike two!' said the umpire, far away in the heat.

Jimmie Cosner laid his bat across the plate and hunched his freckled hands on his hips. 'You mean to tell me that was a strike?'

'That's what I said,' said the umpire. 'Pick up the bat.'

'To hit you on the head with,' said Cosner sharply.

'Play ball or hit the showers!'

Jimmie Cosner worked his mouth to collect enough saliva to spit, then angrily swallowed it, swore a bitter oath instead. Reaching down, he raised the bat, poised it like a musket on his shoulder.

And here came the ball! It started out small and wound up big in front of him. Powie! An explosion off the yellow bat. The ball spiralled up and up. Jimmie lit out for first base. The ball paused, as if thinking about gravity up there in the sky. A wave came in on the shore of the lake and fell down. The crowd yelled. Jimmie ran. The ball made its decision, came down. A lithe high-yellar was under it, fumbled it. The ball spilled to the turf, was plucked up, hurled to first base.

Jimmie saw he was going to be out. So he jumped feet-first at the base.

Everyone saw his cleats go into Big Poe's ankle. Everybody saw the red blood. Everybody heard the shout, the shriek, saw the heavy clouds of dust rising.

'I'm safe!' protested Jimmie two minutes later.

Big Poe sat on the ground. The entire dark team stood around him. The doctor bent down, probed Big Poe's ankle, saying, 'Mmmm,' and 'Pretty bad. Here.' And he swabbed medicine on it and put a white bandage on it.

The umpire gave Cosner the cold-water eye. 'Hit the showers!'

'Like hell!' said Cosner. And he stood on that first base, blowing his cheeks out and in, his freckled hands swaying at his side. 'I'm safe. I'm staying right here, by God! No nigger put *me* out.'

'No,' said the umpire. 'A white man did. *Me. Get!*'

'He dropped the ball! Look up the rules! I'm safe!'

The umpire and Cosner stood glaring at each other.

Big Poe looked up from having his swollen ankle tended. His voice was thick and gentle and his eyes examined Jimmie Cosner gently.

'Yes, he's safe, Mr Umpire. Leave him stay. He's safe.'

I was standing right there. I heard the whole thing. Me and some other kids had run out on the field to see. My mother kept calling me to come back to the stands.

'Yes, he's safe,' said Big Poe again.

All the coloured men let out a yell.

'What'sa matter with you, black boy? You get hit in the head?'

'You heard me,' replied Big Poe quietly. He looked at the doctor bandaging him. 'He's safe. Leave him stay.'

The umpire swore.

'Okay, okay. So he's safe!'

The umpire stalked off, his back stiff, his neck red.

Big Poe was helped up. 'Better not walk on that,' cautioned the doctor.

'I can walk,' whispered Big Poe carefully.

'Better not play.'

'I can play,' said Big Poe gently, certainly, shaking his head, wet streaks drying under his white eyes. 'I'll play *good*.' He looked no place at all. 'I'll play plenty good.'

'Oh,' said the second-base coloured man. It was a funny sound.

All the coloured men looked at each other, at Big Poe, then at Jimmie Cosner, at the sky, at the lake, the crowd. They walked off quietly to take their places. Big Poe stood with his bad foot hardly touching the ground, balanced. The doctor argued. But Big Poe waved him away.

'Batter up!' cried the umpire.

We got settled in the stands again. My mother pinched my leg and asked me why I couldn't sit still. It got warmer. Three or four more waves fell on the shore line. Behind the wire screen the ladies fanned their wet faces and the men inched their rumps forwards on the wooden planks, held papers over their scowling brows to see Big Poe standing like a redwood tree out there on first base, Jimmie Cosner standing in the immense shade of that dark tree.

Young Moberg came up to bat for our side.

'Come on, Swede, come on, Swede!' was the cry, a lonely cry, like a dry bird, from out on the blazing green turf. It was Jimmie Cosner calling. The grandstand stared at him. The dark heads turned on their moist pivots in the outfield; the black faces came in his direction, looking him over, seeing his thin, nervously arched back. He was the centre of the universe.

'Come on, Swede! Let's show these black boys!' laughed Cosner.

He trailed off. There was a complete silence. Only the

wind came through the high, glittering trees.

'Come on, Swede, hang one on that old pill . . . '

Long Johnson, on the pitcher's mound, cocked his head. Slowly, deliberately, he eyed Cosner. A look passed between him and Big Poe, and Jimmie Cosner saw the look and shut up and swallowed, hard.

Long Johnson took his time with his windup.

Cosner took a lead off base.

Long Johnson stopped loading his pitch.

Cosner skipped back to the bag, kissed his hand, and patted the kiss dead centre of the plate. Then he looked up and smiled around.

Again the pitcher coiled up his long, hinged arm, curled loving dark fingers on the leather pellet, drew it back and – Cosner danced off first base. Cosner jumped up and down like a monkey. The pitcher did not look at him. The pitcher's eyes watched him secretively, slyly, amusedly, sidewise. Then, snapping his head, the pitcher scared Cosner back to the plate. Cosner stood and jeered.

The third time Long Johnson made as if to pitch, Cosner was far off the plate and running towards second.

Snap went the pitcher's hand. *Bom* went the ball in Big Poe's glove at first base.

Everything was sort of frozen. Just for a second.

There was the sun in the sky, the lake and the boats on it, the grandstands, the pitcher on his mound standing with his hand out and down after tossing the ball; there was Big Poe with the ball in his mighty black hand; there was the infield staring, crouching in at the scene, and there was Jimmie Cosner running, kicking up the dirt, the only moving thing in the entire summer world.

Big Poe leaned forward, sighted towards second base, drew back his mighty right hand, and hurled that white baseball straight down along the line until it reached Jimmie Cosner's head.

Next instant, the spell was broken.

Jimmie Cosner lay flat on the burning grass. People boiled out of the grandstands. There was swearing, and women screaming, a clattering of wood as the men rushed down the wooden boards of the bleachers. The coloured team ran in from the field. Jimmie Cosner lay there. Big Poe, no expression on his face, limped off the field, pushing white men away from him like clothespins when they tried stopping him. He just picked them up and threw them away.

'Come on, Douglas!' shrieked Mother, grabbing me. 'Let's get home! They might have razors! Oh!'

That night, after the near riot of the afternoon, my folks stayed home reading magazines. All the cottages around us were lighted. Everybody was home. Distantly I heard music. I slipped out the back door into the ripe summer-night darkness and ran towards the dance pavilion. All the lights were on, and music played.

But there were no white people at the tables. Nobody had come to the Jamboree.

There were only coloured folks. Women in bright red and blue satin gowns and net stockings and soft gloves, with wine-plume hats, and men in glossy tuxedos. The music crashed out, up, down, and around the floor. And laughing and stepping high, flinging their polished shoes out and up in the cakewalk, were Long Johnson and Cavanaugh and Jiff Miller and Pete Brown, and — limping — Big Poe and Katherine, his girl, and all the other lawn-cutters and boatmen and janitors and chambermaids, all on the floor at one time.

It was so dark all around the pavilion; the stars shone in the black sky, and I stood outside, my nose against the window, looking in for a long, long time, silently.

I went to bed without telling anyone what I'd seen.

I just lay in the dark smelling the ripe apples in the dimness and hearing the lake at night and listening to that distant, faint and wonderful music. Just before I slept I heard those last strains again:

> ' – *gonna dance out both of my shoes,*
> *When they play those Jelly Roll Blues;*
> *Tomorrow night at the Dark Town Strutters' Ball!*'

Embroidery

The dark porch air in the late afternoon was full of needle
flashes, like a movement of gathered silver insects in the
light. The three women's mouths twitched over their work.
Their bodies lay back and then imperceptibly forwards, so
that the rocking chairs tilted and murmured. Each woman
looked to her own hands, as if quite suddenly she had found
her heart beating there.

'What time is it?'

'Ten minutes to five.'

'Got to get up in a minute and shell those peas for dinner.'

'But — ' said one of them.

'Oh yes, I forgot. How foolish of me . . . ' The first
woman paused, put down her embroidery and needle, and
looked through the open porch door, through the warm
interior of the quiet house, to the silent kitchen. There upon
the table, seeming more like symbols of domesticity than
anything she had ever seen in her life, lay the mound of
fresh-washed peas in their neat, resilient jackets, waiting for
her fingers to bring them into the world.

'Go hull them if it'll make you feel good,' said the second
woman.

'No,' said the first. 'I won't. I just won't.'

The third woman sighed. She embroidered a rose, a leaf, a
daisy on a green field. The embroidery needle rose and
vanished.

The second woman was working on the finest, most
delicate piece of embroidery of them all, deftly poking, finding, and returning the quick needle upon innumerable
journeys. Her quick black glance was on each motion. A

flower, a man, a road, a sun, a house; the scene grew under her hand, a miniature beauty, perfect in every threaded detail.

'It seems at times like this that it's always your hands you turn to,' she said, and the others nodded enough to make the rockers rock again.

'I believe,' said the first lady, 'that our souls are in our hands. For we do *everything* to the world with our hands. Sometimes I think we don't use our hands half enough; it's certain we don't use our heads.'

They all peered more intently at what their hands were doing. 'Yes,' said the third lady, 'when you look back on a whole lifetime, it seems you don't remember faces so much as hands and what they did.'

They recounted to themselves the lids they had lifted, the doors they had opened and shut, the flowers they had picked, the dinners they had made, all with slow or quick fingers, as was their manner or custom. Looking back, you saw a flurry of hands, like a magician's dream, doors popping wide, taps turned, brooms wielded, children spanked. The flutter of pink hands was the only sound; the rest was a dream without voices.

'No supper to fix tonight or tomorrow night or the next night after that,' said the third lady.

'No windows to open or shut.'

'No coal to shovel in the basement furnace next winter.'

'No papers to clip cooking articles out of.'

And suddenly they were crying. The tears rolled softly down their faces and fell into the material upon which their fingers twitched.

'This won't help things,' said the first lady at last, putting the back of her thumb to each under-eyelid. She looked at her thumb and it was wet.

'Now look what I've done!' cried the second lady, exasperated. The others stopped and peered over. The second lady held out her embroidery. There was the scene, perfect except that while the embroidered yellow sun shone down upon the embroidered green field, and the embroidered brown road curved towards an embroidered pink house, the man standing on the road had something wrong with his face.

'I'll just have to rip out the whole pattern, practically, to fix it right,' said the second lady.

'What a shame.' They all stared intently at the beautiful scene with the flaw in it.

The second lady began to pick away at the thread with her little deft scissors flashing. The pattern came out thread by thread. She pulled and yanked, almost viciously. The man's face was gone. She continued to seize at the threads.

'What are you *doing*?' asked the other woman.

They leaned and saw what she had done.

The man was gone from the road. She had taken him out entirely.

They said nothing but returned to their own tasks.

'What time is it?' asked someone.

'Five minutes to five.'

'Is it supposed to happen at five o'clock?'

'Yes.'

'And they're not sure what it'll do to anything, really, when it happens?'

'No, not sure.'

'Why didn't we stop them before it got this far and this big?'

'It's twice as big as ever before. No, ten times, maybe a thousand.'

'This isn't like the first one or the dozen later ones. This is different. Nobody knows what it might do when it comes.'

They waited on the porch in the smell of roses and cut grass. 'What time is it now?'

'One minute to five.'

The needles flashed silver fire. They swam like a tiny

school of metal fish in the darkening summer air.

Far away a mosquito sound. Then something like a tremor of drums. The three women cocked their heads, listening.

'We won't hear anything, will we?'

'They say not.'

'Perhaps we're foolish. Perhaps we'll go right on, after five o'clock, shelling peas, opening doors, stirring soups, washing dishes, making lunches, peeling oranges . . . '

'My, how we'll laugh to think we were frightened by an old experiment!' They smiled a moment at each other.

'It's five o'clock.'

At these words, hushed, they all busied themselves. Their fingers darted. Their faces were turned down to the motions they made. They made frantic patterns. They made lilacs and grass and trees and houses and rivers in the embroidered cloth. They said nothing, but you could hear their breath in the silent porch air.

Thirty seconds passed.

The second woman sighed finally and began to relax.

'I think I just *will* go shell those peas for supper,' she said. 'I – '

But she hadn't time even to lift her head. Somewhere, at the side of her vision, she saw the world brighten and catch fire. She kept her head down, for she knew what it was. She didn't look up, nor did the others, and in the last instant their fingers were flying; they didn't glance about to see what was happening to the country, the town, this house, or even this porch. They were only staring down at the design in their flickering hands.

The second woman watched an embroidered flower go. She tried to embroider it back in, but it went, and then the road vanished, and the blades of grass. She watched a fire, in slow motion, almost, catch upon the embroidered house and unshingle it, and pull each threaded leaf from the small green tree in the hoop, and she saw the sun itself pulled apart in the design. Then the fire caught upon the moving point of the needle while still it flashed; she watched the fire come along her fingers and arms and body, untwisting the yarn of her being so painstakingly that she could see it in all its devilish beauty, yanking out the pattern from the material at hand. What it was doing to the other women or the furniture or the elm tree in the yard, she never knew. For now, yes now! it was plucking at the white embroidery of her flesh, the pink thread of her cheeks, and at last it found her heart, a soft red rose sewn with fire, and it burned the fresh, embroidered petals away, one by delicate one . . .

The Golden Apples
of the Sun

'South,' said the captain.

'But,' said his crew, 'there simply *aren't* any directions out here in space.'

'When you travel on down towards the sun,' replied the captain, 'and everything gets yellow and warm and lazy, then you're going in one direction only.' He shut his eyes and thought about the smouldering, warm, faraway land, his breath moving gently in his mouth. 'South.' He nodded slowly to himself. 'South.'

Their rocket was the *Copa de Oro*, also named the *Prometheus* and the *Icarus*, and their destination in all reality was the blazing noonday sun. In high good spirits they had packed along two thousand sour lemonades and a thousand white-capped beers for this journey to the wide Sahara. And now as the sun boiled up at them they remembered a score of verses and quotations:

'The golden apples of the sun"?'

'Yeats.'

' "Fear no more the heat of the sun"?'

'Shakespeare, of course!'

'*Cup of Gold*? Steinbeck. *The Crock of Gold*? Stephens. And what about the pot of gold at the rainbow's end? *There's* a name for our trajectory, by God. Rainbow!'

'Temperature?'

'One thousand degrees Fahrenheit!'

The captain stared from the huge dark-lensed port, and there indeed was the sun, and to go to that sun and touch it and steal part of it forever away was his quiet and single idea. In this ship were combined the coolly delicate and the coldly practical. Through corridors of ice and milk-frost, ammoniated winter and storming snowflakes blew. Any spark from that vast hearth burning out there beyond the callous hull of this ship, any small firebreath that might seep through would find winter, slumbering here like all the coldest hours of February.

The audio-thermometer murmured in the arctic silence: 'Temperature: two thousand degrees!'

Falling, thought the captain, like a snowflake into the lap of June, warm July, and the sweltering dog-mad days of August.

'Three thousand degrees Fahrenheit!'

Under the snow fields engines raced, refrigerants pumped ten thousand miles per hour in rimed boa-constrictor coils.

'Four thousand degrees Fahrenheit.'

Noon. Summer. July.

'Five thousand Fahrenheit!'

And at last the captain spoke with all the quietness of the journey in his voice:

'Now, we are touching the sun.'

Their eyes, thinking it, were melted gold.

'Seven thousand degrees!'

Strange how a mechanical thermometer could sound excited, though it possessed only an emotionless steel voice.

'What *time* is it?' asked someone.

Everyone had to smile.

For now there was only the sun and the sun and the sun. It was every horizon, it was every direction. It burned the minutes, the seconds, the hourglasses, the clocks; it burned all time and eternity away. It burned the eyelids and the serum of the dark world behind the lids, the retina, the hidden brain; and it burned sleep and the sweet memories of sleep and cool nightfall.

'Watch it!'

'Captain!'

Bretton, the first mate, fell flat to the winter deck. His protective suit whistled where, burst open, his warmness, his oxygen, and his life bloomed out in a frosted steam.

'Quick!'

Inside Bretton's plastic face-mask, milk crystals had already gathered in blind patterns. They bent to see.

'A structural defect in his suit, Captain. Dead.'

'Frozen.'

They stared at that other thermometer which showed how winter lived in this snowing ship. One thousand degrees below zero. The captain gazed down upon the frosted statue and the twinkling crystals that iced over it as he watched. Irony of the coolest sort, he thought; a man afraid of fire and killed by frost.

The captain turned away. 'No time. No time. Let him lie.' He felt his tongue move. 'Temperature?'

The dials jumped four thousand degrees.

'Look. Will you look? Look.'

Their icicle was melting.

The captain jerked his head to look at the ceiling.

As if a motion-picture projector had jammed a single clear memory frame in his head, he found his mind focused ridiculously on a scene whipped out of childhood.

Spring mornings as a boy he had leaned from his bedroom window into the snow-smelling air to see the sun sparkle the last icicle of winter. A dripping of white wine, the blood of cool but warming April fell from that clear crystal blade. Minute by minute, December's weapon grew less dangerous. And then at last the icicle fell with the sound of a single chime to the gravelled walk below.

'Auxiliary pump's broken, sir. Refrigeration. We're losing our ice!'

A shower of warm rain shivered down upon them. The captain jerked his head right and left. 'Can you see the trouble? Christ, don't stand there, we haven't time!'

The men rushed; the captain bent in the warm rain, cursing, felt his hands run over the cold machine, felt them burrow and search, and while he worked he saw a future which was removed from them by the merest breath. He saw the skin peel from the rocket beehive, men, thus revealed, running, running, mouths shrieking, soundless. Space was a black mossed well where life drowned its roars and terrors. Scream a big scream, but space snuffed it out before it was half up your throat. Men scurried, ants in a flaming matchbox; the ship was dripping lava, gushing steam, nothing!

'Captain?'

The nightmare flicked away.

'Here.' He worked in the soft warm rain that fell from the upper decks. He fumbled at the auxiliary pump. 'Damn it!' He jerked the feed line. When it came, it'd be the quickest death in the history of dying. One moment, yelling; a warm flash later only the billion billion tons of space-fire would whisper, unheard, in space. Popped like strawberries in a furnace, while their thoughts lingered on the scorched air a long breath after their bodies were charred roast and fluorescent gas.

'Damn!' He stabbed the auxiliary pump with a screwdriver. 'Jesus!' He shuddered. The complete annihilation of it. He clamped his eyes tight, teeth tight. God, he thought, we're used to more leisurely dyings, measured in minutes and hours. Even twenty seconds now would be a slow death compared to this hungry idiot thing waiting to eat us!

'Captain, do we pull out or stay?'

'Get the Cup ready. Take over, finish this. Now!'

He turned and put his hand to the working mechanism of the huge Cup; shoved his fingers into the robot Glove. A twitch of his hand here moved a gigantic hand, with gigantic metal fingers, from the bowels of the ship. Now, now, the great metal hand slid out holding the huge *Copa de Oro*, breathless, into the iron furnace, the bodiless body and the fleshless flesh of the sun.

A million years ago, thought the captain, quickly, quickly, as he moved the hand and the Cup, a million years ago a naked man on a lonely northern trail saw lightning strike a tree. And while his clan fled, with bare hands he plucked a limb of fire, broiling the flesh of his fingers, to carry it, running in triumph, shielding it from the rain with his body, to his cave, where he shrieked out a laugh and tossed it full on a mound of leaves and gave his people summer. And the tribe crept at last, trembling, near the fire, and they put out their flinching hands and felt the new season in their cave, this small yellow spot of changing weather, and they, too, at last, nervously, smiled. And the gift of fire was theirs.

'Captain!'

It took all of four seconds for the huge hand to push the empty Cup to the fire. So here we are again, today, on another trail, he thought, reaching for a cup of precious gas and vacuum, a handful of different fire with which to run back up cold space, lighting our way, and take to Earth a gift of fire that might burn forever. Why?

He knew the answer before the question.

Because the atoms we work with our hands, on Earth, are pitiful; the atomic bomb is pitiful and small and our knowledge is pitiful and small, and only the sun really knows what we want to know, and only the sun has the secret. And besides, it's fun, it's a chance, it's a great thing coming here, playing tag, hitting and running. There is no reason, really, except the pride and vanity of little insect men hoping to sting the lion and escape the maw. My God, we'll say, we *did* it! And here is our cup of energy, fire, vibration, call it what you will, that may well power our cities and sail our ships and light our libraries and tan our children and bake our daily breads and simmer the knowledge of our universe for us for a thousand years until it is well done. Here, from this cup, all good men of science and religion: drink! Warm yourselves against the night of ignorance, the long snows of superstition, the cold winds of disbelief, and from the great fear of darkness in each man. So: we stretch out our hand with the beggar's cup . . .

'Ah.'

The Cup dipped into the sun. It scooped up a bit of the flesh of God, the blood of the universe, the blazing thought, the blinding philosophy that set out and mothered a galaxy, that idled and swept planets in their fields and summoned or laid to rest lives and livelihoods.

'Now, *slow*,' whispered the captain.

'What'll happen when we pull it inside? That extra heat now, at this time, Captain?'

'God knows.'

'Auxiliary pump all repaired, sir.'

'Start it!'

The pump leaped on.

'Close the lid of the Cup and inside now, slow, slow.'

The beautiful hand outside the ship trembled, a tremendous image of his own gesture, sank with oiled silence into the ship body. The Cup, lid shut, dripped yellow flowers and white stars, slid deep. The audio-thermometer screamed. The refrigerator system kicked; ammoniated fluids banged the walls like blood in the head of a shrieking idiot.

He shut the outer air-lock door.

'Now.'

They waited. The ship's pulse ran. The heart of the ship rushed, beat, rushed, the Cup of Gold in it. The cold blood raced around about down through, around about down through.

The captain exhaled slowly.

The ice stopped dripping from the ceiling. It froze again.

'Let's get out of here.'

The ship turned and ran.

'Listen!'

The heart of the ship was slowing, slowing. The dials spun on down through the thousands; the needles whirred, invisible. The thermometer voice chanted the change of seasons. They were all thinking now, together: Pull away and away from the fire and the flame, the heat and the melting, the yellow and the white. Go on out now to cool and dark. In twenty hours perhaps they might even dismantle some refrigerators, let winter die. Soon they would move in night so cold it might be necessary to use the ship's new furnace, draw heat from the shielded fire they carried now like an unborn child.

They were going home.

They were going home and there was some little time, even as he tended to the body of Bretton lying in a bank of white winter snow, for the captain to remember a poem he had written many years before:

> *Sometimes I see the sun a burning Tree,*
> *Its golden fruit swung bright in airless air,*
> *Its apples wormed with man and gravity,*
> *Their worship breathing from them everywhere,*
> *As man sees Sun as burning Tree . . .*

The captain sat for a long while by the body, feeling many separate things. I feel sad, he thought, and I feel good, and I feel like a boy coming home from school with a handful of dandelions.

'Well,' said the captain, sitting, eyes shut, sighing. 'Well, where do we go now, eh, where are we going?' He felt his men sitting or standing all about him, the terror dead in them, their breathing quiet. 'When you've gone a long, long way down to the sun and touched it and lingered and jumped around and streaked away from it, where are you going then?

When you go away from the heat and the noonday light and the laziness, where do you go?'

His men waited for him to say it out. They waited for him to gather all of the coolness and the whiteness and the welcome and refreshing climate of the word in his mind, and they saw him settle the word, like a bit of ice cream, in his mouth, rolling it gently.

'There's only one direction in space from here on out,' he said at last:

They waited. They waited as the ship moved swiftly into cold darkness away from the light.

'North,' murmured the captain. 'North.'

And they all smiled, as if a wind had come up suddenly in the middle of a hot afternoon.

Powerhouse

The horses moved gently to a stop, and the man and his wife gazed down into a dry, sandy valley. The woman sat lost in her saddle; she hadn't spoken for hours, didn't know a good word *to* speak. She was trapped somewhere between the hot, dark pressure of the storm-clouded Arizona sky and the hard, granite pressure of the wind-blasted mountains. A few drops of cool rain fell on her trembling hands.

She looked over at her husband wearily. He sat his dusty horse easily, with a firm quietness. She closed her eyes and thought of how she had been all of these mild years until today. She wanted to laugh at the mirror she was holding up to herself, but there was no way of doing even that; it would be somewhat insane. After all, it might just be the pushing of this dark weather, or the telegram they had taken from the messenger on horseback this morning, or the long journey now to town.

There was still an empty world to cross, and she was cold.

'I'm the lady who was never going to need religion,' she said quietly, her eyes shut.

'What?' Berty, her husband, glanced over at her.

'Nothing,' she whispered, shaking her head. In all the years, how *certain* she had been. Never, never would she have need of a church. She had heard fine people talk on and on of religion and waxed pews and calla lilies in great bronze buckets and vast bells of churches in which the preacher rang like a clapper. She had heard the shouting kind and the fervent, whispery kind, and they were all the same. Hers was simply not a pew-shaped spine.

'I just never had a reason ever to sit in a church,' she had told people. She wasn't vehement about it. She just walked around and lived and moved her hands that were pebble-smooth and pebble-small. Work had polished the nails of those hands with a polish you could never buy in a bottle. The touching of children had made them soft, and the raising of children had made them temperately stern, and the loving of a husband had made them gentle.

And now, death made them tremble.

'Here,' said her husband. And the horses dusted down the trail to where an odd brick building stood beside a dry wash. The building was all glazed green windows, blue machinery, red tile, and wires. The wires ran off on high-tension towers to the farthest directions of the desert. She watched them go, silently, and, still held by her thoughts, turned her gaze back to the strange storm-green windows and the burning-coloured bricks.

She had never slipped a ribbon in a Bible at a certain significant verse, because though her life in this desert was a life of granite, sun, and the steaming away of the waters of her flesh, there had never been a threat in it to her. Always things had worked out before the necessity had come for sleepless dawns and wrinkles in the forehead. Somehow, the very poisonous things of life had passed her by. Death was a remote storm-rumour beyond the farthest range.

Twenty years had blown in tumbleweeds, away, since she'd come West, worn this lonely trapping man's gold ring, and taken the desert as a third, and constant, partner to their living. None of their four children had ever been fearfully sick or near death. She had never had to get down on her knees except for the scrubbing of an already well-scrubbed floor.

Now all that was ended. Here they were riding towards a remote town because a simple piece of yellow paper had come and said very plainly that her mother was dying.

And she could not imagine it – no matter how she turned

her head to see or turned her mind to look in on itself. There were no rungs anywhere to hold to, going either up *or* down, and her mind, like a compass left out in a sudden storm of sand, was suddenly blown free of all its once-clear directions, all points of reference worn away, the needle spinning without purpose, around, around. Even with Berty's arms on her back it wasn't enough. It was like the end of a good play and the beginning of an evil one. Someone she loved was actually going to die. This was impossible!

'I've got to stop,' she said, not trusting her voice at all, so she made it sound irritated to cover her fear.

Berty knew her as no irritated woman, so the irritation did not carry over and fill him up. He was a capped jug; the contents there for sure. Rain on the outside didn't stir the brew. He side-ran his horse to her and took her hand gently. 'Sure,' he said. He squinted at the eastern sky. 'Some clouds piling up black there. We'll wait a bit. It might rain. I wouldn't want to get caught in it.'

Now she was irritated at her own irritation, one fed upon the other, and she was helpless. But rather than speak and risk the cycle's commencing again, she slumped forward and began to sob, allowing the horse to be led until it stood and tramped its feet softly beside the red brick building.

She slid down like a parcel into his arms, and he held her as she turned in on his shoulder; then he set her down and said, 'Don't look like there's people here.' He called, 'Hey, there!' and looked at the sign on the door: DANGER. BUREAU OF ELECTRIC POWER.

There was a great insect humming all through the air. It sang in a ceaseless, bumbling tone, rising a bit, perhaps falling just a bit, but keeping the same pitch. Like a woman humming between pressed lips as she makes a meal in the warm twilight over a hot stove. They could see no movement within the building: there was only the gigantic humming. It was the sort of noise you would expect the sun-shimmer to make rising from hot railroad ties on a blazing summer day, when there is that flurried silence and you see the air eddy and whorl and ribbon, and expect a sound from the process but get nothing but an arched tautness of the eardrums and the tense quiet.

The humming came up through her heels, into her medium-slim legs, and thence to her body. It moved to her heart and touched it, as the sight of Berty just sitting on a top rail of the corral often did. And then it moved on to her head and slenderest niches in the skull and set up a singing, as love songs and good books had done once on a time.

The humming was everywhere. It was as much a part of the soil as the cactus. It was as much a part of the air as the heat.

'What is it?' she asked, vaguely perplexed, looking at the building.

'I don't know much about it except it's a powerhouse,' said Berty. He tried the door. 'It's open,' he said, surprised. 'I wish someone was around.' The door swung wide and the pulsing hum came out like a breath of air over them, louder.

They entered together into the solemn, singing place. She held him tightly, arm in arm.

It was a dim undersea place, smooth and clean and polished, as if something or other was always coming through and coming through and nothing ever stayed, but always there was motion and motion, invisible and stirring and never settling. On each side of them as they advanced were what first appeared to be people standing quietly, one after the other, in a double line. But these resolved into round, shell-like machines from which the humming sprang. Each black and grey and green machine gave forth golden cables and lime-coloured wires, and there were silver metal pouches with crimson tabs and white lettering, and a pit like a wash-tub in which something whirled as if rinsing unseen materials at invisible speeds. The centrifuge raced so fast it stood still.

Immense snakes of copper looped down from the twilight ceiling, and vertical pipes webbed up from cement floor to fiery brick wall. And the whole of it was as clean as a bolt of green lightning and smelled similarly. There was a crackling, eating sound, a dry rustling as of paper; flickers of blue fire shuttled, snapped, sparked, hissed where wires joined porcelain bobbins and green glass insulation.

Outside, in the real world, it began to rain.

She didn't want to stay in this place; it was no place to stay, with its people that were not people but dim machines and its music like an organ caught and pressed on a low note and a high note. But the rain washed every window and Berty said, 'Looks like it'll last. Might have to stay the night here. It's late, anyhow. I'd better get the stuff in.'

She said nothing. She wanted to be getting on. Getting on to what thing in what place, there was really no way of knowing. But at least in town she would hold on to the money and buy the tickets and hold them tight in her hand and hold on to a train which would rush and make a great noise, and get off the train, and get on another horse, or get into a car hundreds of miles away and ride again, and stand at last by her dead or alive mother. It all depended on time and breath. There were many places she would pass through, but none of them would offer a thing to her except ground for her feet, air for her nostrils, food for her numb mouth. And these were worse than nothing. Why go to her mother at all, say words, and make gestures? she wondered. What would be the use?

The floor was clean as a solid river under her. When she moved forwards on it, it sent echoes cracking back and forth like small, faint gunshots through the room. Any word that was spoken came back as from a granite cavern.

Behind her, she heard Berty setting down the equipment. He spread two grey blankets and put out a little collection of tinned foods.

*   *   *

Powerhouse 473

It was night. The rain still streamed on the high green-glazed windows, rinsing and making patterns of silk that flowed and intermingled in soft clear curtains. There were occasional thunderclaps which fell and broke upon themselves in avalanches of cold rain and wind hitting sand and stone.

Her head lay upon a folded cloth, and no matter how she turned it, the humming of the immense powerhouse worked up through the cloth into her head. She shifted, shut her eyes, and adjusted herself, but it went on and on. She sat up, patted the cloth, lay back down.

But the humming was there.

She knew without looking, by some sense deep in herself, that her husband was awake. There was no year she could remember when she hadn't know. It was some subtle difference in his breathing. It was the absence of sound, rather; no sound of breathing at all, save at long, carefully thought-out intervals. She knew then that he was looking at her in the rainy darkness, concerned with her, taking great care of his breath.

She turned in the darkness. 'Berty?'

'Yes?'

'I'm awake too,' she said.

'I know,' he said.

They lay, she very straight, very rigid, he in a half curl, like a hand relaxed, half bent inward. She traced this dark, easy curve and was filled with incomprehensible wonder.

'Berty,' she asked, and paused a long while, 'how . . . how are you like you are?'

He waited a moment. 'How do you mean?' he said.

'How do you *rest?*' She stopped. It sounded very bad. It sounded so much like an accusation, but it was not, really. She knew him to be a man concerned with all things, a man who could see in darknesses and who was not conceited because of his ability. He was worried for her now, and for her mother's life or death, but he had a way of worrying that seemed indifferent and irresponsible. It was neither of the two. His concern was all in him, deep; but it lay side by side with some faith, some belief that accepted it, made it welcome, and did not fight it. Something in him took hold of the sorrow first, got acquainted with it, knew each of its traceries before passing the message on to all of his waiting body. His body held a faith like a maze, and the sorrow that struck into him was lost and gone before it finally reached where it wanted to hurt him. Sometimes this faith drove her into a senseless anger, from which she recovered quickly, knowing how useless it was to criticize something as contained as a stone in a peach.

'Why didn't I ever catch it from you?' she said at last.

He laughed a little bit, softly. 'Catch what?'

'I caught everything else. You shook me up and down in other ways. I didn't know anything but what you taught me.' She stopped. It was hard to explain. Their life had been like the warm blood in a person passing through tissues quietly, both ways.

'Everything but religion,' she said. 'I never caught that from you.'

'It's not a catching thing,' he said. 'Someday you just relax. And there it is.'

Relax, she thought. Relax what? The body. But how to relax the mind? Her fingers twitched beside her. Her eyes wandered idly about the vast interior of the powerhouse. The machines stood over her in dark silhouettes with little sparkles crawling on them. The humming-humming-humming crept along her limbs.

Sleepy. Tired. She drowsed. Her eyes lidded and opened and lidded and opened. The humming-humming filled her marrow as if small hummingbirds were suspended in her body and in her head.

She traced the half-seen tubing up and up into the ceiling, and she saw the machines and heard the invisible whirlings.

She suddenly became very alert in her drowsiness. Her eyes moved swiftly up and up and then down and across, and the humming-singing of the machines grew louder and louder, and her eyes moved, and her body relaxed; and on the tall, green windows she saw the shadows of the high-tension wires rushing off into the raining night.

Now the humming was in her, her eyes jerked, she felt herself yanked violently upright. She felt seized by a whirling dynamo, around, around in a whirl, out, out, into the heart of whirling invisibilities, fed into, accepted by a thousand copper wires, and shot, in an instant, over the earth!

She was everywhere at once!

Streaking along high monster towers in instants, sizzling between high poles where small glass knobs sat like crystal-green birds holding the wires in their non-conductive beaks, branching in four directions, eight secondary directions, finding towns, hamlets, cities, racing on to farms, ranches, haciendas, she descended gently like a widely filamented spider web upon a thousand square miles of desert!

The earth was suddenly more than many separate things, more than houses, rocks, concrete roads, a horse here or there, a human in a shallow, boulder-topped grave, a prickling of cactus, a town invested with its own light surrounded by night, a million apart things. Suddenly it all had one pattern encompassed and held by the pulsing electric web.

She spilled out swiftly into rooms where life was rising from a slap on a naked child's back, into rooms where life was leaving bodies like the light fading from an electric bulb — the filament glowing, fading, finally colourless. She was in every town, every house, every room, making light-patterns over hundreds of miles of land; seeing, hearing everything, not alone any more, but one of thousands of people, each with his ideas and his faiths.

Her body lay, a lifeless reed, pale and trembling. Her mind, in all its electric tensity, was flung about this way, that, down vast networks of powerhouse tributary.

Everything balanced. In one room she saw life wither; in another, a mile away, she saw wineglasses lifted to a new-born, cigars passed, smiles, handshakes, laughter. She saw the pale, drawn faces of people at white deathbeds, heard how they understood and accepted death, saw their gestures, felt their feelings, and saw that they, too, were lonely in themselves, with no way to get to the world to see the balance, see it as she was seeing it now.

She swallowed. Her eyelids flickered and her throat burned under her upraised fingers.

She was not alone.

The dynamo had whirled and flung her with centrifugal force out along a thousand lines into a million glass capsules screwed into ceilings, plucked into light by a pull of a cord or a twist of a knob or a flick of a switch.

The light could be in *any* room; all that was needed was to touch the switch. All rooms were dark until light came. And here she was, in all of them at once. And she was not alone. Her grief was but one part of a vast grief, her fear only one of countless others. And this grief was only a half thing. There was the other half; of things born, of comfort in the shape of a new child, of food in the warmed body, of colours for the eye and sounds in the awakened ear, and spring wild flowers for the smelling.

Whenever a light blinked out, life threw another switch; rooms were illumined afresh.

She was with those named Clark and those named Gray and the Shaws and Martins and Hanfords, the Fentons, the Drakes, the Shattucks, the Hubbells, and the Smiths. Being alone was not alone, except in the mind. You had all sorts of peekholes in your head. A silly, strange way to put it, per-haps, but there were the holes; the ones to see through and see that the world was there and people in it, as hard put to and uneasy as yourself; and there were the holes for hearing, and the one for speaking out your grief and getting rid of it, and the holes for knowing the changes of season through the scents of summer grain or winter ice or autumn fires. They were there to be used so that one was not alone. Loneliness was a shutting of the eyes. Faith was a simple opening.

The light-net fell upon all the world she had known for twenty years, herself blended with every line. She glowed and pulsed and was gentled in the great easy fabric. It lay across the land, covering each mile like a gentle, warm, and humming blanket. She was everywhere.

In the powerhouse the turbines whirled and hummed and the electric sparks, like little votive candles, jumped and clustered upon bent elbows of electric piping and glass. And the machines stood like saints and choruses, haloed now yellow, now red, now green, and a massed singing beat along the roof hollows and echoed down in endless hymns and chants. Ouside, the wind clamoured at the brick walls and drenched the glazed windows with rain; inside, she lay upon her small pillow and suddenly began to cry.

Whether it was with understanding, acceptance, joy, resignation, she couldn't know. The singing went on, higher and higher, and she was everywhere. She put out her hand, caught hold of her husband, who was still awake, his eyes fixed at the ceiling. Perhaps he had run everywhere, too, in this instant, through the network of light and power. But then, he had always been everywhere at once. He felt himself a unit of a whole and therefore he was stable; to her, unity was new and shaking. She felt his arms suddenly around her and she pressed her face into his shoulder for a long while, hard, while the humming and the humming climbed higher, and she cried freely, achingly, against him . . .

In the morning the desert sky was very clear. They walked from the powerhouse quietly, saddled their horses, cinched on all of the equipment, and mounted.

She settled herself and sat there under the blue sky. And slowly she was aware of her back, and her back was straight, and she looked at her alien hands on the reins, and they had ceased trembling. And she could see the far mountains; there was no blur nor a running-of-colour to things. All was solid stone touching stone, and stone touching sand, and sand touching wild flower, and wild flower touching the sky in one continuous clear flow, everything definite and of a piece.

'Wope!' cried Berty, and the horses walked slowly off, away from the brick building, through the cool sweet morning air.

She rode handsomely and she rode well, and in her, like a stone in a peach, was a peacefulness. She called to her husband as they slowed on a rise, 'Berty!'

'Yes?'

'Can we . . . ' she asked.

'Can we what?' he said, not hearing the first time.

'Can we come here again sometime?' she asked, nodding back towards the powerhouse. 'Once in a while? Some Sunday?'

He looked at her and nodded slowly. 'I reckon. Yes. Sure. I reckon so.'

And as they rode on into town she was humming, humming a strange soft tune, and he glanced over and listened to it, and it was the sound you would expect to hear from sun-warmed railroad ties on a hot summer day when the air rises in a shimmer, flurried and whorling; a sound in one key, one pitch, rising a little, falling a little, humming, humming, but constant, peaceful, and wondrous to hear.

Hail and Farewell

But of course he was going away, there was nothing else to do, the time was up, the clock had run out, and he was going very far away indeed. His suitcase was packed, his shoes were shined, his hair was brushed, he had expressly washed behind his ears, and it remained only for him to go down the stairs, out the front door, and up the street to the small-town station where the train would make a stop for him alone. Then Fox Hill, Illinois, would be left far off in his past. And he would go on, perhaps to Iowa, perhaps to Kansas, perhaps even to California; a small boy, twelve years old, with a birth certificate in his valise to show he had been born forty-three years ago.

'Willie!' called a voice downstairs.

'Yes!' He hoisted his suitcase. In his bureau mirror he saw a face made of June dandelions and July apples and warm summer-morning milk. There, as always, was his look of the angel and the innocent, which might never, in the years of his life, change.

'Almost time,' called the woman's voice.

'All right!' And he went down the stairs, grunting and smiling. In the living room sat Anna and Steve, their clothes painfully neat.

'Here I am!' cried Willie in the parlour door.

Anna looked like she was going to cry. 'Oh, good lord, you can't really be leaving us, can you, Willie?'

'People are beginning to talk,' said Willie quietly. 'I've been here three years now. But when people begin to talk, I know it's time to put on my shoes and buy a railroad ticket.'

'It's all so strange. I don't understand. It's so sudden,'

Anna said. 'Willie, we'll miss you.'

'I'll write you every Christmas, so help me. Don't you write me.'

'It's been a great pleasure and satisfaction,' said Steve, sitting there, his words the wrong size in his mouth. 'It's a shame it had to stop. It's a shame you had to tell us about yourself. It's an awful shame you can't stay on.'

'You're the nicest folks I ever had,' said Willie, four feet high, in no need of a shave, the sunlight on his face.

And then Anna *did* cry. 'Willie, Willie.' And she sat down and looked as if she wanted to hold him but was afraid to hold him now; she looked at him with shock and amazement and her hands empty, not knowing what to do with him now.

'It's not easy to go,' said Willie. 'You get used to things. You want to stay. But it doesn't work. I tried to stay on once after people began to suspect. "How horrible!" people said. "All these years, playing with our innocent children," they said, "and us not guessing! Awful!" they said. And finally I had to just leave town one night. It's not easy. You know darned well how much I love both of you. Thanks for three swell years.'

They all went to the front door. 'Willie, where're you going?'

'I don't know. I just start travelling. When I see a town that looks green and nice, I settle in.'

'Will you ever come back?'

'Yes,' he said earnestly with his high voice. 'In about twenty years it should begin to show in my face. When it does, I'm going to make a grand tour of all the mothers and fathers I've ever had.'

They stood on the cool summer porch, reluctant to say the last words. Steve was looking steadily at an elm tree. 'How many other folks've you stayed with, Willie? How many adoptions?'

Willie figured it, pleasantly enough. 'I guess it's about five towns and five couples and over twenty years gone by since I started my tour.'

'Well, we can't holler,' said Steve. 'Better to've had a son thirty-six months than none whatever.'

'Well,' said Willie, and kissed Anna quickly, seized at his luggage, and was gone up the street in the green noon light, under the trees, a very young boy indeed, not looking back, running steadily.

The boys were playing on the green park diamond when he came by. He stood a little while among the oak-tree shadows, watching them hurl the white, snowy baseball into the warm summer air, saw the baseball shadow fly like a dark bird over the grass, saw their hands open like mouths to catch this swift piece of summer that now seemed most especially important to hold on to. The boys' voices yelled. The ball lit on the grass near Willie.

Carrying the ball forward from under the shade trees, he thought of the last three years now spent to the penny, and the five years before that, and so on down the line to the year when he was really eleven and twelve and fourteen and the voices saying: 'What's wrong with Willie, missus?' 'Mrs B, is Willie late a-growin'?' 'Willie, you smokin' *cigars* lately?' The echoes died in summer light and colour. His mother's voice: 'Willie's twenty-one today!' And a thousand voices saying: 'Come back, son, when you're fifteen; *then* maybe we'll give you a job.'

He stared at the baseball in his trembling hand, as if it were his life, an interminable ball of years strung around and around and around, but always leading back to his twelfth birthday. He heard the kids walking towards him; he felt blot out the sun, and they were older, standing around him.

'Willie! Where you goin'?' They kicked his suitcase.

How tall they stood to the sun. In the last few months it seemed the sun had passed a hand above their heads, beckoned, and they were warm metal drawn melting upwards; they were golden taffy pulled by an immense gravity to the sky, thirteen, fourteen years old, looking down upon Willie, smiling, but already beginning to neglect him. It had started four months ago:

'Choose up sides! Who wants Willie?'

'Aw, Willie's too little; we don't play with "kids".'

And they raced ahead of him, drawn by the moon and the sun and the turning seasons of leaf and wind, and he was twelve years old and not of them any more. And the other voices beginning again on the old, the dreadfully familiar, the cool refrain: 'Better feed that boy vitamins, Steve.' 'Anna, does shortness *run* in your family?' And the cold fist kneading at your heart again and knowing that the roots would have to be pulled up again after so many good years with the 'folks.'

'Willie, where you goin'?'

He jerked his head. He was back among the towering, shadowing boys who milled around him like giants at a drinking fountain bending down.

'Goin' a few days visitin' a cousin of mine.'

'Oh.' There was a day, a year ago, when they would have cared very much indeed. But now there was only curiosity for his luggage, their enchantment with trains and trips and far places.

'How about a coupla fast ones?' said Willie.

They looked doubtful, but, considering the circumstances, nodded. He dropped his bag and ran out; the white baseball was up in the sun, away to their burning white figures in the far meadow, up in the sun again, rushing, life coming and going in a pattern. Here, *there*! Mr and Mrs Robert Hanlon, Creek Bend, Wisconsin, 1932, the first couple, the first year! Here, there! Henry and Alice Boltz, Limeville, Iowa, 1935! The baseball flying. The Smiths, the Eatons, the Robinsons! 1939! 1945! Husband and wife, husband and wife, husband and wife, no children, no children, no children! A knock on this door, a knock on that.

'Pardon me. My name is William. I wonder if – '

'A sandwich? Come in, sit down. Where you *from*, son?'

The sandwich, a tall glass of cold milk, the smiling, the nodding, the comfortable, leisurely talking.

'Son, you look like you been travelling. You run *off* from somewhere?'

'No.'

'Boy, are you an orphan?'

Another glass of milk.

'We always wanted kids. It never worked out. Never knew why. One of those things. Well, well. It's getting late, son. Don't you think you better hit for home?'

'Got no home.'

'A boy like you? Not dry behind the ears? Your mother'll be worried.'

'Got no home and no folks anywhere in the world. I wonder if – I wonder – could I sleep here tonight?'

'Well, now, son, I don't just *know*. We never considered taking in – ' said the husband.

'We got chicken for supper tonight,' said the wife, 'enough for extras, enough for company . . . '

And the years turning and flying away, the voices, and the faces, and the people, and always the same first conversations. The voice of Emily Robinson, in her rocking chair, in summer-night darkness, the last night he stayed with her, the night she discovered his secret, her voice saying:

'I look at all the little children's faces going by. And I sometimes think, What a shame, what a shame, that all these flowers have to be cut, all these bright fires have to be put out. What a shame these, all of these you see in schools or running by, have to get tall and unsightly and wrinkle and turn grey or get bald, and finally, all bone and wheeze, be dead and buried off away. When I hear them laugh I can't believe they'll ever go the road I'm going. Yet here they *come*!

I still remember Wordsworth's poem: "When all at once I saw a crowd, A host of golden daffodils; Beside the lake, beneath the trees, Fluttering and dancing in the breeze." That's how I think of children, cruel as they sometimes are, mean as I know they can be, but not yet showing the meanness around their eyes or *in* their eyes, not yet full of tiredness. They're so eager for everything! I guess that's what I miss most in older folks, the eagerness gone nine times out of ten, the freshness gone, so much of the drive and life down the drain. I like to watch school let out each day. It's like someone threw a bunch of flowers out the school front doors. How does it feel, Willie? How does it feel to be young forever? To look like a silver dime new from the mint? Are you happy? Are you as fine as you *seem*?'

The baseball whizzed from the blue sky, stung his hand like a great pale insect. Nursing it, he heard his memory say:

'I worked with what I had. After my folks died, after I found I couldn't get man's work anywhere, I tried carnivals, but they only laughed. "Son," they said, "you're not a midget, and even if you are, you look like a *boy*! We want midgets with midgets' *faces*! Sorry, son, sorry." So I left home, started out, thinking: What *was* I? A boy. I looked like a boy, sounded like a boy, so I might as well go on being a boy. No use fighting it. No use screaming. So what could I do? What job was handy? And then one day I saw this man in a restaurant looking at another man's pictures of his children. "Sure wish I had kids," he said. "Sure wish I had kids." He kept shaking his head. And me sitting a few seats away from him, a hamburger in my hands. I sat there, *frozen*! At that very instant I knew what my job would be for all the rest of my life. There *was* work for me, after all. Making lonely people happy. Keeping myself busy. Playing forever. I knew I had to play forever. Deliver a few papers, run a few errands, mow a few lawns, maybe. But *hard* work? No. All I had to do was be a mother's son and a father's pride. I turned to the man down the counter from me. "I beg your pardon," I said. I *smiled* at him . . . '

'But, Willie,' said Mrs Emily long ago, 'didn't you ever get lonely? Didn't you ever want — *things* — that grownups wanted?'

'I fought that out alone,' said Willie. 'I'm a boy, I told myself, I'll have to live in a boy's world, read boys' books, play boys' games, cut myself off from everything else. I can't be both. I got to be only one thing — young. And so I played that way. Oh, it wasn't easy. There were times — ' He lapsed into silence.

'And the family you lived with, they never knew?'

'No. Telling them would have spoiled everything. I told them I was a runaway; I let them check through official channels, police. Then, when there was no record, let them put in to adopt me. That was best of all; as long as they never guessed. But then, after three years, or five years, they guessed, or a travelling man came through, or a carnival man saw me, and it was over. It always had to end.'

'And you're *very* happy and it's *nice* being a child for over forty years?'

'It's a living, as they say. And when you make other people happy, then you're almost happy too. I got my job to do and I do it. And anyway, in a few years now I'll be in my second childhood. All the fevers will be out of me and all the unfulfilled things and most of the dreams. Then I can relax, maybe, and play the role all the way.'

He threw the baseball one last time and broke the reverie. Then he was running to seize his luggage. Tom, Bill, Jamie, Bob, Sam — their names moved on his lips. They were embarrassed at his shaking hands.

'After all, Willie, it ain't as if you're going to China or Timbuktu.'

'That's right, isn't it?' Willie did not move.

'So long, Willie. See you next week!'

'So long, so long!'

And he was walking off with his suitcase again, looking at the trees, going away from the boys and the street where he had lived, and as he turned the corner a train whistle screamed, and he began to run.

The last thing he saw and heard was a white ball tossed at a high roof, back and forth, back and forth, and two voices crying out as the ball pitched now up, down, and back through the sky, 'Annie, annie, over! Annie, annie, over!' like the crying of birds flying off to the far south.

In the early morning, with the smell of the mist and the cold metal, with the iron smell of the train around him and a full night of travelling shaking his bones and his body, and a smell of the sun beyond the horizon, he awoke and looked out upon a small town just arising from sleep. Lights were coming on, soft voices muttered, a red signal bobbed back and forth, back and forth in the cold air. There was that sleeping hush in which echoes are dignified by clarity, in which echoes stand nakedly alone and sharp. A porter moved by, a shadow in shadows.

'Sir,' said Willie.

The porter stopped.

'What town's this?' whispered the boy in the dark.

'Valleyville.'

'How many people?'

'Ten thousand. Why? This your stop?'

'It looks green.' Willie gazed out at the cold morning town for a long time. 'It looks nice and quiet,' said Willie.

'Son,' said the porter, 'you know where you *going*?'

'Here,' said Willie, and got up quietly in the still, cool, iron-smelling morning, in the train dark, with a rustling and stir.

'I hope you know what you're doing, boy,' said the porter.

'Yes, sir,' said Willie. 'I know what I'm doing.' And he was down the dark aisle, luggage lifted after him by the porter, and out in the smoking, steaming-cold, beginning-to-lighten morning. He stood looking up at the porter and the black metal train against the few remaining stars. The train gave a great wailing blast of whistle, the porters cried out all along the line, the cars jolted, and his special porter waved and smiled down at the boy there, the small boy there with the big luggage who shouted up to him, even as the whistle screamed again.

'What?' shouted the porter, hand cupped to ear.

'Wish me luck!' cried Willie.

'Best of luck, son,' called the porter, waving, smiling. 'Best of luck, boy!'

'Thanks!' said Willie, in the great sound of the train, in the steam and roar.

He watched the black train until it was completely gone away and out of sight. He did not move all the time it was going. He stood quietly, a small boy twelve years old, on the worn wooden platform, and only after three entire minutes did he turn at last to face the empty streets below.

Then, as the sun was rising, he began to walk very fast, so as to keep warm, down into the new town.

The Great Wide
World over There

It was a day to be out of bed, to pull curtains and fling open windows. It was a day to make your heart bigger with warm mountain air.

Cora, feeling like a young girl in a wrinkled old dress, sat up in bed.

It was early, the sun barely on the horizon, but already the birds were stirring from the pines and ten billion red ants milled free from their bronze hills by the cabin door. Cora's husband Tom slept like a bear in a snowy hibernation of bedclothes beside her. Will my heart wake him up? she wondered.

And then she knew why this seemed a special day.

'Benjy's coming!'

She imagined him far off, leaping green meadows, fording streams where spring was pushing itself in cool colours of moss and clear water towards the sea. She saw his great shoes dusting and flicking the stony roads and paths. She saw his freckled face high in the sun looking giddily down his long body at his distant hands flying out and back behind him.

Benjy, come on! she thought, opening a window swiftly. Wind blew her hair like a grey spider web about her cold ears. Now Benjy's at Iron Bridge, now at Meadow Pike, now up Creek Path, over Chesley's Field . . .

Somewhere in those Missouri mountains was Benjy. Cora blinked. Those strange high hills beyond which twice a year she and Tom drove their horse and wagon to town, and through which, thirty years ago, she had wanted to run forever, saying, 'Oh, Tom, let's just drive and drive until we reach the sea.' But Tom had looked at her as if she had slapped his face, and he had turned the wagon around and driven on home, talking to the mare. And if people lived by shores where the sea came like a storm, now louder, now softer, every day, she did not know it. And if there were cities where neons were like pink ice and green mint and red fireworks each evening, she didn't know that either. Her horizon, north, south, east, west, was this valley, and had never been anything else.

But now, today, she thought, Benjy's coming from that world out there; he's seen it, heard it, smelt it; he'll tell me about it. And he can write. She looked at her hands. He'll be here a whole month and teach me. Then I can write out into that world and bring it here to the mailbox I'll make Tom build today. 'Get up, Tom! You *hear*?'

She put her hand out to push the bank of sleeping snow.

By nine o'clock the valley was full of grasshoppers flinging themselves through the blue, piny air, while smoke curled into the sky.

Cora, singing into her pots and pans as she polished them, saw her wrinkled face bronzed and freshened in the copper bottoms. Tom was grumbling the sounds of a sleepy bear at his mush breakfast, while her singing moved all about him, like a bird in a cage.

'*Someone's* mighty happy,' said a voice.

Cora made herself into a statue. From the corners of her eyes she saw a shadow cross the room.

'Mrs Brabbam?' asked Cora of her scouring cloth.

'That's who it is!' And there stood the Widow Lady, her gingham dress dragging the warm dust, her letters in her chickeny hand. 'Morning! I just been to my mailbox. Got me a real beauty of a letter from my uncle George in Springfield.' Mrs Brabbam fixed Cora with a gaze like a silver needle. 'How long since you got a letter from *your* uncle, missus?'

'My uncles are all dead.' It was not Cora herself, but her tongue, that lied. When the time came, she knew; it would be her tongue alone that must take communion and confess earthly sinning.

'It's certainly *nice*, getting mail.' Mrs Brabbam waved her letters in a straight flush on the morning air.

Always twisting the knife in the flesh. How many years, thought Cora, had this run on, Mrs Brabbam and her smily eyes, talking loud of how she got mail; implying that nobody else for miles around could read? Cora bit her lip and almost threw the pot, but set it down, laughing. 'I forgot to tell you. My nephew Benjy's coming; his folks are poorly, and he's here for the summer today. He'll teach me to write. And Tom's building us a postal box, aren't you, Tom?'

Mrs Brabbam clutched her letters. 'Well, isn't that fine! You *lucky* lady.' And suddenly the door was empty. Mrs Brabbam was gone.

But Cora was after her. For in that instant she had seen something like a scarecrow, something like a flicker of pure sunlight, something like a brook trout jumping upstream, leap a fence in the yard below. She saw a huge hand wave and birds flush in terror from a crab-apple tree.

Cora was rushing, the world rushing back of her, down the path. 'Benjy!'

They ran at each other like partners in a Saturday dance, linked arms, collided, and waltzed, jabbering. 'Benjy!'

She glanced swiftly behind his ear.

Yes, *there* was the yellow pencil.

'Benjy, welcome!'

'Why, ma'am!' He held her off at arm's length. 'Why, ma'am, you're *crying*.'

'Here's my nephew,' said Cora.

Tom scowled up from spooning his corn-meal mush.

'Mighty glad,' smiled Benjy.

Cora held his arm tight so he couldn't vanish. She felt faint, wanting to sit, stand, run, but she only beat her heart fast and laughed at strange times. Now, in an instant, the far

countries were brought near; here was this tall boy, lighting
up the room like a pine torch, this boy who had seen cities
and seas and been places when things had been better for his
parents.

'Benjy, I got peas, corn, bacon, mush, soup, and beans for
breakfast.'

'Hold on!' said Tom.

'Hush, Tom, the boy's down to the bone with walking.'
She turned to the boy. 'Benjy, tell me all about yourself. You
did go to school?'

Benjy kicked off his shoes. With one bare foot he traced a
word in the hearth ashes.

Tom scowled. 'What's it say?'

'It says,' said Benjy, '*c* and *o* and *r* and *a*. *Cora*.'

'*My* name, Tom, see it! Oh, Benjy, it's good you really
write, child. We had one cousin here, long ago, claimed he
could spell upside down and backwards. So we fattened him
up and he wrote letters and we never got answers. Come to
find out he knew just enough spelling to mail letters to the
dead-letter office. Lord, Tom knocked two months' worth of
vittles out of that boy, batting him up the road with a piece of
fence.'

They laughed anxiously.

'I write fine,' said the serious boy.

'That's all we want to know.' She shoved a cut of berry pie
at him. 'Eat.'

By ten-thirty, with the sun riding higher, after watching
Benjy devour heaped platters of food, Tom thundered from
the cabin, jamming his cap on. 'I'm going out, by God, and
cut down half the forest!' he said angrily.

But no one heard. Cora was seated in a breathless spell. She
was watching the pencil behind Benjy's peach-fuzz ear. She
saw him finger it casually, lazily, indifferently. Oh, not so
casual, Benjy, she thought. Handle it like a spring robin's

egg. She wanted to touch the pencil, but hadn't touched one in years because it made her feel foolish and then angry and then sad. Her hand twitched in her lap.

'You got some paper?' asked Benjy.

'Oh, land, I never thought,' she wailed, and the room walls darkened. 'What'll we do?'

'Just happens I brought some.' He fetched a tablet from his little bag. 'You want to write a letter somewhere?'

She smiled outrageously. 'I want to write a letter to . . . to . . . ' Her face fell apart. She looked around for someone in the distance. She looked at the mountains in the morning sunshine. She heard the sea rolling off on yellow shores a thousand miles away. The birds were coming north over the valley, on their way to multitudes of cities indifferent to her need at this instant.

'Benjy, why, I never thought until this moment. I don't know anybody in all that world out there. Nobody but my aunt. And if I wrote her it'd make her feel bad, a hundred miles from here, to have to find someone else to read the letter to her. She's got a whale-boned-corset sort of pride. Make her nervous the next ten years, that letter setting in her house on the mantel. No, no letter to her.' Cora's eyes moved from the hills and the unseen ocean. 'Who then? Where? Someone. I just've got to get me some letters.'

'Hold on.' Benjy fished a dime magazine from his coat. It had a red cover of an undressed lady screaming away from a green monster. 'All sorts of addresses in here.'

They leafed the pages together. 'What's *this*?' Cora tapped an ad.

' "Here's your *Power Plus* Free Muscle Chart. Send name, address," ' read Benjy, ' "to Department M-3 for Free Health Map!" '

'And what about *this* one?'

' "Detectives make secret investigations. Particulars free. Write: G.D.M. Detective School —" '

'Everything's free. Well, Benjy.' She looked at the pencil
in his hand. He drew up his chair. She watched him turn the
pencil in his fingers, making minor adjustments. She saw
him bite his tongue softly. She saw him squint his eyes. She
held her breath. She bent forward. She squinted her own
eyes and clamped her tongue.

Now, now Benjy raised his pencil, licked it, and set it
down to the paper.

There it is, thought Cora.

The first words. They formed themselves slowly on the
incredible paper.

Dear Power Plus Muscle Company
   Sirs, [he wrote].

The morning blew away on a wind, the morning flowed down
the creek, the morning flew off with some ravens, and the sun
burned on the cabin roof. Cora didn't turn when she heard a
shuffle at the blazing, sun-filled door. Tom was there, but
not there; nothing was before her but a series of filled pages, a
whispering pencil, and Benjy's careful Palmer Penmanship
hand. Cora moved her head around, around, with each *o*,
each *l*, with each small hill of an *m;* each tiny dot made her
head peck like a chicken; each crossed *t* made her tongue lick
across her upper lip.

'It's noon and I'm hungry!' said Tom almost behind her.

But Cora was a statue now, watching the pencil as one
watches a snail leaving an exceptional trail across a flat stone
in the early morning.

'It's noon!' cried Tom again.

Cora glanced up, stunned.

'Why, it seems only a moment ago we wrote to that Philadelphia Coin Collecting Company, ain't that right, Benjy?'
Cora smiled a smile much too dazzling for a woman fifty-five
years old. 'While you wait for your vittles, Tom, just can't

you build that mailbox? Bigger than Mrs Brabbam's, please?'

'I'll nail up a shoe box.'

'Tom Gibbs.' She rose pleasantly. Her smile said, Better run, better work, better *do*! I want a big, pretty mailbox. All white, for Benjy to paint our name on in black spelling. I won't have any shoe box for my very first real letter.'

And it was done.

Benjy lettered the finished mailbox; MRS CORA GIBBS, while Tom stood grumbling behind him.

'What's it say?'

' "Mr Tom Gibbs," ' said Benjy quietly, painting.

Tom blinked at it for a minute, quietly, and then said, 'I'm *still* hungry. Someone light the fire.'

There were no stamps. Cora turned white. Tom was made to hitch up the horse and drive to Green Fork to buy some red ones, a green, and ten pink stamps with dignified gentlemen printed on them. But Cora rode along to be certain Tom didn't hurl these first letters in the creek. When they rode home, the first thing Cora did, face glowing, was poke in the new mailbox.

'You crazy?' said Tom.

'No harm looking.'

That afternoon she visited the mailbox six times. On the seventh, a woodchuck jumped out. Tom stood laughing in the door, pounding his knees. Cora chased him out of the house, still laughing.

Then she stood in the window looking down at her mailbox right across from Mrs Brabbam's. Ten years ago the Widow Lady had plunked her letter box right under Cora's nose, almost, when she could as easily have built it up nearer her own cabin. But it gave Mrs Brabbam an excuse to float like a flower on a river down the hill path, flip the box wide with a great coughing and rustling, from time to time spying up to see if Cora was watching. Cora always was. When caught, she pretended to sprinkle flowers with an empty watering can, or pick mushrooms in the wrong season.

Next morning Cora was up before the sun had warmed the strawberry patch or the wind had stirred the pines.

Benjy was sitting up in his cot when Cora returned from the mailbox. 'Too early,' he said. 'Postmen won't drive by yet.'

'*Drive* by?'

'They come in cars this far out.'

'Oh.' Cora sat down.

'You sick, Aunt Cora?'

'No, no.' She blinked. 'It's just, I don't recall in twenty years *seeing* no mail truck whistle by here. It just came to me. All this time, I never seen no mailman at all.'

'Maybe he comes when you're not around.'

'I'm up with the fog spunks, down with the chickens. I never really gave it a thought, of course, but – ' She turned to look out the window, up at Mrs Brabbam's house. 'Benjy, I got a kind of sneaking hunch.' She stood up and walked straight out of the cabin, down the dust path, Benjy following, across the thin road to Mrs Brabbam's mailbox. A hush was on the fields and hills. It was so early it made you whisper.

'Don't break the law, Aunt Cora!'

'Shh! Here.' She opened the box, put her hand in like someone fumbling in a gopher hole. 'And here, and here.' She rattled some letters into his cupped hands.

'Why, these been opened already! You open these, Aunt Cora?'

'Child, I never touched them.' Her face was stunned. 'This is the first time in my life I ever even let my shadow touch this box.'

Benjy turned the letters around and around, cocking his head. 'Why, Aunt Cora, these letters, they're ten years old!'

'What!' Cora grabbed at them.

'Aunt Cora, that lady's been getting the same mail every day for years. And they're not even addressed to Mrs Brabbam, they're to some woman named Ortega in Green Fork.'

'Ortega, the Mexican grocery woman! All these years,' whispered Cora, staring at the worn mail in her hands. 'All these years.'

They gazed up at Mrs Brabbam's sleeping house in the cool quiet morning.

'Oh, that sly woman, making a commotion with her letters, making me feel small. All puffed out she was, swishing along, reading her mail.'

Mrs Brabbam's front door opened.

'Put them back, Aunt Cora!'

Cora slammed the mailbox shut with time to spare.

Mrs Brabbam drifted down the path, stopping here or there, quietly, to peer at the opening wild flowers.

'Morning,' she said sweetly.

'Mrs Brabbam, this is my nephew Benjy.'

'How nice.' Mrs Brabbam, with a great swivel of her body, a flourish of her flour-white hands, rapped the mailbox as if to shake the letters loose inside, flipped the lid, and extracted the mail, covering her actions with her back. She made motions, and spun about merrily, winking. 'Wonderful! Why, just look at this letter from dear Uncle George!'

'Well, ain't that *nice*!' said Cora.

Then the breathless summer days of waiting. The butterflies jumping orange and blue on the air, the flowers nodding about the cabin, and the hard, constant sound of Benjy's pencil scribbling through the afternoons. Benjy's mouth was always packed with food, and Tom was always stamping in, to find lunch or supper late, cold, or both, or none at all.

Benjy handled the pencil with a delicious spread of his

bony hands, lovingly inscribing each vowel and consonant as Cora hovered about him, making up words, rolling them on her tongue, delighted each time she saw them roll out on the paper. But she wasn't learning to write. 'It's so much fun watching you write, Benjy. Tomorrow I'll start learning. Now take another letter!'

They worked their way through ads about Asthma, Trusses, and Magic, they joined the Rosicrucians, or at least sent for a free Sealed Book all about the Knowledge that had been damned to oblivion, Secrets from hidden ancient temples and buried sanctuaries. Then there were free packets of Giant Sunflower seeds, and something about HEARTBURN. They had worked back to page 127 of *Quarter Murder Magazine* on a bright summer morning when . . .

'Listen!' said Cora.

They listened.

'A car,' said Benjy.

And up the blue hills and through the tall fiery green pines and along the dusty road, mile by mile, came the sound of a car riding along and along, until finally, at the bend, it came full thundering, and in an instant Cora was out the door running, and as she ran she heard and saw and felt many things. First, from the corner of her eye, she saw Mrs Brabbam gliding down the road from the other direction. Mrs Brabbam froze when she saw the bright green car boiling on the grade, and there was the whistle of a silver whistle and the old man in the car leaned out just before Cora arrived and said, 'Mrs Gibbs?' 'Yes!' she cried. 'Mail for you, ma'am,' he said, and held it towards her. She put out her hand, then drew it back, remembering. 'Oh,' she said, 'please, would you mind, would you put it, please . . . in my mailbox?' The old man squinted at her, at the mailbox, back at her, and laughed. 'Don't mind,' he said, and did just that, put the mail in the box.

Mrs Brabbam stood where she was, not moving, eyes wild.

'Any mail for Mrs Brabbam?' asked Cora.

'That's all.' And the car dusted away down the road.

Mrs Brabbam stood with her hands clenched together. Then, without looking in her own letter box, turned and rustled swiftly up her path, out of sight.

Cora walked around her mailbox twice, not touching it for a long time. 'Benjy, I've got me some letters!' She reached in delicately and took them out and turned them over. She put them quietly in his hand. 'Read them to me. Is my name on the front?'

'Yes'm.' He opened the first letter with due carefulness and read it aloud in the summer morning.

'Dear Mrs Gibbs . . . '

He stopped and let her savour it, her eyes half shut, her mouth moving the words. He repeated it for artistic emphasis and then went on: ' "We are sending you our free folder, enclosed, from the Intercontinental Mailing Schools concerning full particulars on how you, too, can take our Correspondence Course in Sanitary Engineering – " '

'Benjy, Benjy, I'm so happy! Start over again!'

' "Dear Mrs Gibbs," ' he read.

After that the mailbox was never empty. The world came rushing and crowding in, all the places she had never seen or heard about or been to. Travel folders, spicecake recipes, and even a letter from an elderly gentleman who wished for a lady ' – fifty years old, gentle disposition, money; object matrimony.' Benjy wrote back. 'I am already married, but thank you for your kind and thoughtful consideration. Yours truly, Cora Gibbs.'

And the letters continued to pour across the hills, coin collectors' catalogues, Dime Novelty books, Magic List Numbers, Arthritis Charts, Flea Killer Samples. The world filled up her letter box, and suddenly she was not alone or remote from people. If a man wrote a form letter to Cora about the Mysteries of Ancient Maya Revealed, he was likely as not to receive three letters from Cora in the next week, budding out their formal meeting into a warm friendship. After one particularly hard day of writing. Benjy was forced to soak his hand in Epsom salts.

By the end of the third week Mrs Brabbam no longer came down to her mailbox. She didn't even come out the front door of her cabin to get the air, for Cora was always down at the road, leaning out, smiling for the mailman.

All too quickly the summer was at an end, or, at least, that part of the summer that counted most, anyway: Benjy's visit. There was his red bandanna handkerchief on the cabin table, sandwiches folded fresh and oniony in it, tied with a mint sprig to keep it clean to the smell; there on the floor, freshly polished, were his shoes to get into, and there on the chair, with his pencil which had once been long and yellow but was now stubby and chewed, sat Benjy. Cora took hold of his chin and tilted his head, as if she were testing a summer squash of an unfamiliar variety.

'Benjy, I owe you an apology. I don't think I looked at your face once in all this time. Seems I know every wart on your hand, every hangnail, every bump and every crinkle, but I might pass your face in a crowd and miss you.'

'It's no face to look at,' said Benjy shyly.

'But I'd know that hand in a million hands,' Cora said. 'Let anyone shake my hand in a dark room, a thousand people, and out of all those I'd say, "Well, *this* one's Benjy." ' She smiled quietly and walked away to the open door. 'I been thinking.' She looked up at the distant cabin. 'Ain't seen Mrs Brabbam, in weeks. Stays in all the time now. I've got a guilty feeling. I've done a prideful thing, a thing more sinful than she ever done me. I took the bottom out of her life. It was a mean and spiteful thing and I'm ashamed.' She gazed up the hill towards that silent, locked place. 'Benjy, would you do me one last favour?'

'Yes'm.'

'Write a letter for Mrs Brabbam.'

'Ma'am?'

'Yes, write one of those companies for a free chart, a sample, something, and sign Mrs Brabbam's name.'

'All right,' said Benjy.

'That way, in a week or a month the postman'll come by and whistle, and I'll tell him to go up to her door, special, and deliver it. And I'll be sure and be out in my front yard where I can see and Mrs Brabbam can see I see. And I'll wave my letters to her and she'll wave her letters to me, and everybody'll smile.'

'Yes'm,' said Benjy.

He wrote three letters, licked the envelopes carefully, stuck them in his pocket. 'I'll mail them when I get to St Louis.'

'It's been a fine summer,' she said.

'It sure has.'

'But, Benjy, I didn't learn to write, did I? I was after the letters and made you write late nights, and we were so busy sending labels and getting samples, land, it seemed there wasn't time to learn. And that means . . . '

He knew what it meant. He shook her hand. They stood in the cabin door. 'Thanks,' she said, 'for everything.'

Then he was running off. He ran as far as the meadow fence, leaped it easily, and the last she saw of him he was still running, waving the special letters, off into the great world over the hills.

The letters kept coming for some six months after Benjy went away. There would be the postman's little green car and the sharp ice-rimed shout of good morning, or the whistle, as he clapped two or three pink or blue envelopes into that fine mailbox.

And there was that special day when Mrs Brabbam,

received her first real letter.

After that the letters were spaced a week apart, then a month, and finally the postman didn't say hello at all, there was no sound of a car coming up that lonely mountain road. First a spider moved into the mailbox, then a sparrow.

And Cora, while the letters still lasted, would clutch them in her bewildered hands, staring at them quietly until the pressure of her face muscles squeezed clear round shiny drops of water from her eyes. She'd hold up one blue envelope. 'Who's this from?'

'Don't know,' said Tom.

'What's it say?' she wailed.

'Don't know,' said Tom.

'What's going on in that world out there, oh, I'll never know, I'll never know now,' she said. 'And this letter, and this one, and *this*!' She tumbled the stacks and stacks of letters that had come since Benjy ran off. 'All the world and all the people and all the happenings, and me not knowing. All that world and people waiting to hear from us, and us not writing, and them not ever writing back!'

And at last the day came when the wind blew the mailbox over. In the mornings again, Cora would stand at the open door of her cabin, brushing her grey hair with a slow brush, not speaking, looking at the hills. And in all the years that followed she never passed the fallen mailbox without stooping aimlessly to fumble inside and take her hand out with nothing in it before she wandered on again into the fields.

The Playground

A thousand times before and after his wife's death Mr Charles Underhill ignored the Playground on his way to and from his commuters' limited train. He neither liked nor disliked the Playground; he hardly knew it existed.

Bu only this morning his sister Carol, who had occupied the empty space across the breakfast table from him each day for six months, quietly broached the subject.

'Jim's almost three years old now,' she said. 'So tomorrow I'm going to start him at the Playground.'

'Playground?' said Mr Underhill.

At his office, he underlined a memorandum with black ink: *Look at Playground.*

That afternoon, the thunder of the train subsiding in his body, Underhill struck up through town on his usual path home, newspaper tucked crisply under arm to prevent reading himself past the park. So it was, at five-ten in the late day, that he came to the cool iron fence and open gate of the Playground, and stood for a long, long time, frozen there, gazing at it all . . .

At first there seemed absolutely nothing whatever to see. And then as he adjusted his attention outward from his usual interior monologue, the scene before him, a grey, blurred television image, came to a slow focus.

Primarily, he was aware of dim voices, faint underwater cries emerging from a series of vague streaks and zigzag lines and shadows. Then, as if someone had kicked the machine, screams jumped at him in full throat, visions leaped clear. Now he saw the children! They were dashing across the Playground meadow, fighting, pummelling, scratching falling, every wound bleeding or about to bleed or freshly caked over. A dozen cats thrown among sleeping dogs could not have shrieked as loud. With incredible clarity, Mr Underhill saw the tiniest cuts and scabs on knees and faces.

He weathered the first blast of sound, blinking. His nostrils took over when his eyes and ears retired in panic.

He sniffed the cutting odours of salve, raw adhesive, camphor, and pink Mercurochrome, so strong it lay bitter on his tongue. An iodine wind blew through the steel fence wires which glinted dully in the grey light of the overcast day. The rushing children were hell cut loose in a vast pinball table, colliding, and banging, a totalling of hits and misses, thrusts and plungings to a grand and as yet unforeseen total of brutalities.

And was he mistaken or was the light within the Playground of a peculiar intensity? Every child seemed to possess four shadows: one dark, three faint penumbras which made it strategically impossible to tell which way their swift bodies were racing until they bashed their targets. Yes, the oblique, pressing light made the Playground seem deep, far away, and remote from his touching. Or perhaps it was the hard steel wire fence, not unlike those barriers in zoos, beyond which *anything* might happen.

A pen of misery, thought Underhill. Why do children insist on making life horrible for each other? Oh, the continual torture. He heard himself sigh with immense relief. Thank God, childhood was over and done for him. No more pinchings, bruisings, senseless passions and shattered dreams.

A gust of wind tore the paper from his hand. He ran after it down the Playground steps. Clutching the paper, he retreated hastily. For in that one brief instant, stranded in the Playground's atmosphere, he had felt his hat grow too large, his coat too cumbersome, his belt too loose, his shoes too big; he had felt like a small boy playing businessman in his father's clothes; the gate behind him had loomed impossibly tall, while the sky pressed a huge weight of greyness at his eyes, and the scent of iodine, like a tiger's breath exhaled upon him, blew his hair. He tipped and almost fell, running back.

He stood outside the Playground, like someone who has just emerged, in shock, from a terrible cold sea.

'Hello, Charlie!'

He heard the voice and turned to see who had called him. There on top of a metal slide, a boy of some nine years was waving. 'Hello, Charlie . . . !'

Mr Charles Underhill raised a hand. But I don't *know* that boy, he thought. And why should he call me by my first name?

The boy was smiling high in the misty air, and now, jostled by other yelling children, rushed shrieking down the slide.

Underhill stood bemused by what he saw. Now the Playground was an immense iron industry whose sole products were pain, sadism, and sorrow. If you watched half an hour there wasn't a face in the entire enclosure that didn't wince, cry, redden with anger, pale with fear, one moment or another. Really! Who said Childhood was the best time of life? when in reality it was the most terrible, the most merciless era, the barbaric time when there were no police to protect you, only parents preoccupied with themselves and their taller world. No, if he had his way, he touched the cold fence with one hand, they'd nail a new sign here: TORQUEMADA'S GREEN.

And as for that boy, the one who had called out to him, who was he? There was something familiar there, perhaps in the hidden bones, an echo of some old friend; probably the son of a successfully ulcered father.

So this is the Playground where my son will play, thought Mr Underhill. So this is it.

Hanging his hat in the hall, checking his lean image in the watery mirror, Underhill felt wintry and tired. When his sister appeared, and his son came tapping on mouse feet, he greeted them with something less than full attention. The boy clambered thinly over him, playing King of the Hill. And the father, fixing his gaze to the end of the cigar he was slowly lighting, finally cleared his throat and said, 'I've been thinking about that Playground, Carol.'

'I'm taking Jim over tomorrow.'

'Not really? *That* Playground?'

His mind rebelled. The smell and look of the place were still vivid. That writhing world with its atmosphere of cuts and beaten noses, the air as full of pain as a dentist's office, and those horrid ticktacktoes and frightening hopscotches under his feet as he picked up his newspaper, horrid and frightening for no reason he could see.

'What's wrong with *that* Playground?' asked Carol.

'Have you seen it?' He paused in confusion. 'Damn it, I mean, the children there. It's a Black Hole.'

'All the children are from well-to-do families.'

'Well, they shove and push like little Gestapos, said Underhill. 'It'd be like sending a boy to a flour mill to be crushed into meal by a couple of two-ton grinders! Every time I think of Jim playing in that barbaric pit, I freeze.'

'You know very well it's the only convenient park for miles around.'

'I don't care about that. All I care is I saw a dozen kinds of bats and clubs and air guns. By the end of the first day, Jim would be in splinters. They'd have him barbecued, with an orange in his mouth.

She was beginning to laugh. 'How you exaggerate.'

'I'm serious!'

'You can't live Jim's life for him. He has to learn the hard way. He's got to take a little beating and beat others up; boys are like that.'

'I don't *like* boys like that.'

'It's the happiest time of life.'

'Nonsense. I used to look back on childhood with great nostalgia. But now I realize I was a sentimental fool. It was nothing but screaming and running in a nightmare and coming home drenched with terror, from head to foot. If I could possibly save Jim from that, I would.'

'That's impractical and, thank God, impossible.'

'I won't have him near that place, I tell you. I'll have him grow up a neurotic recluse first.'

'Charlie!'

'I will! Those little beasts, you should've seen them. Jim's *my* son, he is; he's not yours, remember.' He felt the boy's thin legs about his shoulders, the boy's delicate fingers rumpling his hair. 'I won't have him butchered.'

'He'll get it in school. Better to let him take a little shoving about now, when he's three, so he's prepared for it.'

'I've thought of that, too.' Mr Underhill held fiercely to his son's ankles which dangled like warm, thin sausages on either lapel. 'I might even get a private tutor for him.'

'Oh, Charles!'

They did not speak during dinner.

After dinner, he took Jim for a brief walk while his sister was washing the dishes. They strolled past the Playground under the dim street lamps. It was a cooling September night, with the first dry spice of autumn in it. Next week, and the children would be raked in off the fields like so many leaves and set to burning in the schools, using their fire and energy for more constructive purposes. But they would be here after school, ramming about, making projectiles of themselves, crashing and exploding, leaving wakes of misery behind every miniature war.

'Want to go in,' said Jim, leaning against the high wire fence, watching the late-playing children beat each other and run.

'No, Jim, you don't want that.'

'Play,' said Jim, his eyes shining with fascination as he saw a large boy kick a small boy and the small boy kick a smaller boy to even things up.

'Play, Daddy.'

'Come along, Jim, you'll never get in that mess if *I* can help it.' Underhill tugged the small arm firmly.

'I want to play.' Jim was beginning to blubber now. His eyes were melting out of his face and his face was becoming a wrinkled orange of colour.

Some of the children heard the crying and glanced over. Underhill had the terrible sense of watching a den of foxes suddenly startled and looking up from the white, hairy ruin of a dead rabbit. The mean yellow-glass eyes, the conical chins, the sharp white teeth, the dreadful wiry hair, the brambly sweaters, the iron-coloured hands covered with a day's battle stains. Their breath moved out to him, dark licorice and mint and Juicy Fruit so sickeningly sweet, so combined as to twist his stomach. And over this the hot mustard smell of someone tolerating an early chest cold; the greasy stink of flesh smeared with hot camphorous salves cooking under a flannel sheath. All these cloying and some-how depressing odours of pencils, chalks, grass and slate-board erasers, real or imagined, summoned old memory in an instant. Popcorn mortared their teeth, and green jelly showed in their sucking, blowing nostrils. God! God!

They saw Jim, and he was new to them. They said not a word, but as Jim cried louder and Underhill, by main force, dragged him like a cement bag along the walk, the children followed with their glowing eyes. Underhill felt like pushing his fist at them and crying, 'You little beasts, you won't get *my* son!'

And then, with beautiful irrelevance, the boy at the top of the blue metal slide, so high he seemed almost in a mist, far away, the boy with the somehow familar face, called out to him, waving and waving.

'Hello Charlie . . . !'

Underhill paused and Jim stopped crying.

'See you later, Charlie . . . !'

And the face of the boy way up there on that high and very lonely slide was suddenly like the face of Thomas Marshall, an old business friend who lived just around the block, but whom he hadn't seen in months.

'See you later, Charlie.'

Later, later? What did the fool boy mean?

'I know *you*, Charlie!' called the boy. 'Hi!'

'What?' gasped Underhill.

'Tomorrow night, Charlie, hey!' And the boy fell off the slide and lay choking for breath, face like a white cheese from the fall, while children jumped him and tumbled over.

Underhill stood undecided for five seconds or more, until Jim thought to cry again, and then, with the golden fox eyes upon them, in the first chill of autumn, he dragged Jim all the way home.

The next afternoon Mr Underhill finished at the office early and took the three o'clock train, arriving out in Green Town at three twenty-five, in plenty of time to drink in the brisk rays of the autumnal sun. Strange how one day it is suddenly autumn, he thought. One day it is summer and the next, how could you measure or tell it? Something about the temperature or the smell? Or the sediment of age knocked loose from your bones during the night and circulating in your blood and heart, giving you a slight tremble and a chill? A year older, a year dying, was *that* it?

He walked up towards the Playground, planning the future. It seemed you did more planning in autumn than any other season. This had to do with dying, perhaps. You thought of death and you automatically planned. Well, then, there was to be a tutor for Jim, *that* was positive; none of

those horrible schools for him. It would pinch the bank
account a bit, but Jim would at least grow up a happy boy.
They would pick and choose his friends. Any slam-bang
bullies would be thrown out as soon as they so much as
touched Jim. And as for this Playground? Completely out of
the question!

'Oh hello, Charles.'

He looked up suddenly. Before him, at the entrance to the
wire enclosure, stood his sister. He noted instantly that she
called him Charles, instead of Charlie. Last night's un-
pleasantness had not quite evaporated. 'Carol, what're you
doing *here*?'

She flushed guiltily and glanced in through the fence.

'You didn't,' he said.

His eyes sought among the scrabbling, running, screaming
children. 'Do you mean to say . . . ?'

His sister nodded, half amused. 'I thought I'd bring him
early –'

'Before I got home, so I wouldn't know, is *that* it?'

That was it.

'Good God, Carol, where *is* he?'

'I just came to see.'

'You mean you left him there all afternoon?'

'Just for five minutes while I shopped.'

'And you *left* him. Good God!' Underhill seized her wrist.
'Well, come on, find him, get him out of there!'

They peered in together past the wire to where a dozen
boys charged about, girls slapped each other, and a squab-
bling heap of children took turns at getting off, making a
quick run, and crashing one against another.

'That's where he is, I *know* it!' said Underhill.

Just then, across the field, sobbing and wailing, Jim ran,
six boys after him. He fell, got up, ran, fell again, shrieking,
and the boys behind shot beans through metal blowers.

'I'll stuff those blowers up their noses!' said Underhill.

'Run, Jim! Run!'

Jim made it to the gate. Underhill caught him. It was like catching a rumpled, drenched wad of material. Jim's nose was bleeding, his pants were ripped, he was covered with grime.

'*There's* your Playground,' said Underhill, on his knees, staring up from his son, holding him, at his sister. '*There* are your sweet, happy innocents, your well-to-do piddling Fascists. Let me catch this boy here again and there'll be hell to pay. Come on, Jim, all right, you little bastards, get back there!' he shouted.

'We didn't do nothing,' said the children.

'What's the world coming to?' Mr Underhill questioned the universe.

'Hi! Charlie!' said the strange boy, standing to one side. He waved casually and smiled.

'Who's that?' asked Carol.

'How in hell do *I* know?' said Underhill.

'Be seeing you, Charlie. So long,' called the boy, fading off.

Mr Underhill marched his sister and his son home.

'Take your hand off my elbow!' said Carol.

He was trembling; absolutely, continually trembling with rage when he got to bed. He had tried some coffee, but nothing stopped it. He wanted to beat their pulpy little brains out, those gross Cruikshank children; yes, that phrase fit them, those fox-fiend, melancholy Cruikshank children, with all the guile and poison and slyness in their cold faces. In the name of all that was decent, what manner of chidl was this new generation! A bunch of cutters and hangers and bangers, a drove of bleeding, moronic thumbscrewers, with the sewage of neglect running in their veins? He lay violently jerking his head from one side of his hot pillow to the other, and at last got up and lit a cigarette, but it wasn't enough. He

and Carol had had a huge battle when they got home. He had
yelled at her and she had yelled back, peacock and peahen
shrieking in a wilderness where law and order were insanities
laughed at and quite forgotten.

He was ashamed. You didn't fight violence with violence,
not if you were a gentleman. You talked very calmly. But
Carol didn't give you a chance, damn it! She wanted the boy
put in a vice and squashed. She wanted him reamed and
punctured and given the laying on of hands. To be beaten
from playground to kindergarten, to grammar school, to
junior high, to high school. If he was lucky, in high school,
the beatings and sadisms would refine themselves, the sea of
blood and spittle would drain back down the shore of years
and Jim would be left upon the edge of maturity, with God
knows what outlook to the future, with a desire, perhaps, to
be a wolf among wolves, a dog among dogs, a fiend among
fiends. But there was enough of that in the world already.
The very thought of the next ten or fifteen years of torture
was enough to make Mr Underhill cringe; he felt his own
flesh impaled with BB shot, stung, burned, fisted,
scrounged, twisted, violated, and bruised. He quivered, like
a jellyfish hurled violently into a concrete mixer. Jim would
never survive it. Jim was too delicate for this horror.

Underhill walked in the midnight rooms of his house
thinking of all this, of himself, of the son, the Playground,
the fear; there was no part of it he did not touch and turn over
with his mind. How much, he asked himself, how much of
this is being alone, how much due to Ann's dying, how much
to my need, and how much is the reality of the Playground
itself, and the children? How much rational and how much
nonsense? He twitched the delicate weights upon the scale
and watched the indicator glide and fix and glide again, back
and forth, softly, between midnight and dawn, between
black and white, between raw sanity and naked insanity. He
should not hold so tight, he should let his hands drop away

from the boy. And yet — there was no hour that looking into Jim's small face he did not see Ann there, in the eyes, in the mouth, in the turn of the nostrils, in the warm breathing, in the glow of blood moving just under the thin shell of flesh. I have a right, he thought, to be afraid. I have every right. When you have two precious bits of porcelain and one is broken and the other, the last one, remains, where can you find the time to be objective, to be immensely calm, to be anything else but concerned?

No, he thought, walking slowly in the hall, there seems to be nothing I can do except go on being afraid and being afraid of being afraid.

'You needn't prowl the house at night,' his sister called from her bed, as she heard him pass her open door. 'You needn't be childish. I'm sorry if I seem dictatorial or cold. But you've got to make up your mind. Jim simply cannot have a private tutor. Ann would have wanted him to go to a regular school. And he's got to go back to that Playground tomorrow and keep going back until he's learned to stand on his own two feet and until he's familiar to all the children; then they won't pick on him so much.'

Underhill said nothing. He got dressed quietly, in the dark, and, downstairs, opened the front door. It was about five minutes to midnight as he walked swiftly down the street in the shadows of the tall elms and oaks and maples, trying to outdistance his rage and outrage. He knew Carol was right, of course. This was the world, you lived in it, you accepted it. But that was the very trouble! He had been through the mill already, he knew what it was to be a boy among lions; his own childhood had come rushing back to him in the last few hours, a time of terror and violence, and now he could not bear to think of Jim's going through it all, those long years, especially if you were a delicate child, through no fault of your own, your bones thin, your face pale, what could you expect but to be harried and chased?

He stopped by the Playground, which was still lit by one great overhead lamp. The gate was locked for the night, but that one light remained on until twelve. He wanted to tear the contemptible place down, rip up the steel fences, obliterate the slides, and say to the children, 'Go home! Play in your back yards!'

How ingenious, the cold, deep Playground. You never knew where anyone lived. The boy who knocked your teeth out, who was *he*? Nobody knew. Where did he live? Nobody knew. How to find him? Nobody knew. Why, you could come here one day, beat the living tar out of some smaller child, and run on the next day to some *other* Playground. They would never find you. From Playground to Playground, you could take your criminal tricks, with everyone forgetting you, since they never knew you. You could return to this Playground a month later, and if the little child whose teeth you knocked out was there and recognized you, you could deny it. 'No, I'm not the one. Must be some other kid. This is my first time here! No, not me!' And when his back is turned, knock him over. And run off down nameless streets, a nameless person.

What can I possibly do? thought Underhill. Carol's been more than generous with her time; she's been good for Jim, no doubt of it. A lot of the love she would have put into a marriage has gone to him this year. I can't fight her forever on this, and I can't tell her to leave. Perhaps moving to the country might help. No, no, impossible; the money. But I can't leave Jim here, either.

'Hello, Charlie,' said a quiet voice.

Underhill snapped about. Inside the Playground fence, seated in the dirt, making diagrams with one finger in the cool dust, was the solemn nine-year-old boy. He didn't glance up. He said, 'Hello, Charlie,' just sitting there, easily, in that world beyond the hard steel fence.

Underhill said, 'How do you know my name?'

'I know it.' The boy crossed his legs, comfortably, smiling quietly. 'You're having lots of trouble.'

'How'd you get in there so late? Who are you?'

'My name's Marshall.'

'Of course! Tom Marshall's son Tommy! I *thought* you looked familiar.'

'More familiar than you think.' The boy laughed gently.

'How's your father, Tommy?'

'Have you seen him lately?' the boy asked.

'On the street, briefly, two months ago.'

'How did he look?'

'What?'

'How did Mr Marshall *look*?' asked the boy. It seemed strange he refused to say 'my father'.

'He looked all right. Why?'

'I guess he's happy,' said the boy. Mr Underhill saw the boy's arms and legs and they were covered with scabs and scratches.

'Aren't you going home, Tommy?'

'I sneaked out to see you. I just knew you'd come. You're afraid.'

Mr Underhill didn't know what to say.

'Those little monsters,' he said at last.

'Maybe I can help you.' The boy made a dust triangle.

It was ridiculous. 'How?'

'You'd give anything, wouldn't you, if you could spare Jim all this? You'd trade places with him if you could?'

Mr Underhill nodded, frozen.

'Well, you come down here tomorrow afternoon at four. Then I can help you.'

'How do you mean, help?'

'I can't tell you outright,' said the boy. 'It has to do with the Playground. Any place where there's lots of evil, that makes power. You can feel it, can't you?'

A kind of warm wind stirred off the bare field under the one high light. Underhill shivered. Yes, even now, at midnight, the Playground seemed evil, for it was used for evil things. 'Are all Playgrounds like this?'

'Some. Maybe this is the only one like this. Maybe it's just how *you* look at it, Charlie. Things *are* what you *want* them to be. A lot of people think this is a *swell* Playground. They're right, too. It's how you look at it, maybe. What I wanted to say, though, is that Tom Marshall was like you. He worried about Tommy Marshall and the Playground and the kids, too. He wanted to save Tommy the trouble and the hurt, also.

This business of talking about people as if they were remote made Mr Underhill uncomfortable.

'So we made a bargain,' said the boy.

'Who with?'

'With the Playground, I guess, or whoever runs it.'

'Who runs it?'

'I've never seen him. There's an office over there under the grandstand. A light burns in it all night. It's a bright, blue light, kind of funny. There's a desk there with no papers in it and an empty chair. The sign says MANAGER, but nobody ever sees the man.'

'He must be around.'

'That's right,' said the boy. 'Or I wouldn't be where I am, and someone else wouldn't be where they are.'

'You certainly talk grown-up.'

The boy was pleased. 'Do you want to know who I really am? I'm not Tommy Marshall at all. I'm Tom Marshall the father.' He sat there in the dust, not moving, late at night, under the high and faraway light, with the late wind blowing his shirt collar gently under his chin, blowing the cool dust. 'I'm Tom Marshall, the father. I know it'll be hard for you to believe. But it *is* true. I was afraid for Tommy. I was the way you are now about Jim. So I made this deal with the Playground. Oh, there are others who did the same, here. If you look close, you'll see them among the other children, by the expression in their eyes.'

Underhill blinked. 'You'd better run home to bed.'

'You want to believe me. You want it to be true. I saw your eyes just then! If you could trade places with Jim, you would. You'd like to save him all that torture, let him be in your place, grown-up, the real work over and done.'

'Any decent parent sympathizes with his children.'

'You, more than most. You feel every bite and kick. Well, you come here tomorrow. You can make a deal, too.'

'Trade places?' It was an incredible, an amusing, but an oddly satisfying thought. 'What would I have to do?'

'Just make up your mind.'

Underhill tried to make his next question sound very casual, a joke, but his mind was in a rage again. 'What would I pay?'

'Nothing. You'd just have to play in the Playground.'

'All day?'

'And go to school, of course.'

'And grow up again?'

'Yes, and grow up again. Be here at four tomorrow afternoon.'

'I have to work in the city tomorrow.'

'Tomorrow,' said the boy.

'You'd better get home to bed, Tommy.'

'My name is *Tom* Marshall.' The boy sat there.

The Playground lights went out.

Mr Underhill and his sister did not speak at breakfast. He usually phoned her at noon to chat about this or that, but he did not phone. But at one-thirty, after a bad lunch, he dialled the house number. When Carol answered he hung up. Five minutes later he phoned again.

'Charlie, was that you called five minutes ago?'

'Yes,' he said.

'I thought I heard you breathing before you hung up. What'd you call about, dear?' She was being sensible again.

'Oh, just called.'

'It's been a bad two days, hasn't it? You *do* see what I mean, don't you, Charlie? Jim *must* go to the Playground and get a few knocks.'

'A few knocks, yes.'

He saw the blood and the hungry foxes and the torn rabbits.

'And learn to give and take,' she was saying, 'and fight if he has to.'

'Fight if he has to,' he murmured.

'I knew you'd come around.'

'Around,' he said. 'You're right. No way out. He must be sacrificed.'

'Oh, Charlie, you *are* odd.'

He cleared his throat. 'Well, that's settled.'

'Yes.'

I wonder what it would be like?' he thought.

'Everything else okay,' he asked the phone.

He thought of the diagrams in the dust, the boy seated there with the hidden bones in his face.

'Yes,' she said.

'I've been thinking,' he said.

'Speak up.'

'I'll be home at three,' he said, slowly, piecing out the words like a man hit in the stomach, gasping for breath. 'We'll take a walk, you and Jim and I,' he said, eyes shut.

'Wonderful!'

'To the Playground,' he said and hung up.

It was really autumn now, the real chill, the real snap; overnight the trees burnt red and snapped free of their leaves, which spiralled about Mr Underhill's face as he walked up the front steps, and there were Carol and Jim bundled up against the sharp wind, waiting for him.

'Hello!' they cried to one another, with much embracing and kissing. 'There's Jim down there!' 'There's Daddy up there!' They laughed and he felt paralysed and in terror of the late day. It was almost four. He looked at the leaden sky, which might pour down molten silver any moment, a sky of lava and soot and a wet wind blowing out of it. He held his sister's arm very tightly as they walked. 'Aren't you friendly, though?' she smiled.

'It's ridiculous, of course,' he said, thinking of something else.

'What?'

They were at the Playground gate.

'Hello, Charlie. Hi!' Far away, atop the monstrous slide stood the Marshall boy, waving, not smiling now.

'You wait here,' said Mr Underhill to his sister. 'I'll be only a moment, I'll just take Jim in.'

'All right.'

He grasped the small boy's hand. 'Here we go, Jim. Stick close to Daddy.'

They stepped down the hard concrete steps and stood in the flat dust. Before them, in a magical sequence, stood the diagrams, the gigantic ticktacktoes, the monstrous hop-scotches, the amazing numerals and triangles and oblongs the children had scrabbled in the incredible dust.

The sky blew a huge wind upon him and he was shivering. He grasped the little boy's hand still tighter and turned to his sister. 'Good-bye,' he said. For he was believing it. He was in the Playground and believing it, and it was for the best. Nothing too good for Jim. Nothing at all in this outrageous world! And now his sister was laughing back at him, 'Charlie, you idiot!'

Then they were running, running across the dirt Playground floor, at the bottom of a stony sea that pressed and blew upon them. Now Jim was crying, 'Daddy, Daddy!' and the children racing to meet them, the boy on the slide yelling, the ticktacktoe and the hopscotchers whirling, a sense of bodiless terror gripping him, but he knew what he must do and what must be done and what would happen. Far across the field footballs sailed, baseballs whizzed, bats flew, fists flashed up, and the door of the Manager's office stood open, the desk empty, the seat empty, a lone light burning over it.

Underhill stumbled, shut his eyes and fell, crying out, his body clenched by a hot pain, mouthing strange words, everything in turmoil.

'There you are, Jim,' said a voice.

And he was climbing, climbing, eyes closed, climbing metal-ringing ladder rungs, screaming, yelling, his throat raw.

Mr. Underhill opened his eyes.

He was on top of the slide. The gigantic, blue metal slide which seemed ten thousand feet high. Children crushed at his back, children beat him to go on, slide! Slide!

And he looked, and there, going off across the field, was a man in a black overcoat. And there, at the gate, was a woman waving and the man standing there with the woman, both of them looking in at him, waving, and their voices calling, 'Have a good time! Have a good time, Jim!'

He screamed. He looked at his hands, in a panic of realization. The small hands, the thin hands. He looked at the earth far below. He felt his nose bleeding and there was the Marshall boy next to him. 'Hi!' cried the other, and bashed him in the mouth. 'Only twelve years here!' cried the other in the uproar.

Twelve years! thought Mr Underhill, trapped. And time is different to children. A year is like ten years. No, not twelve years of childhood ahead of him, but a century, a century of *this*.

'Slide!'

Behind him the stink of Musterole, Vicks VapoRub,

peanuts, chewed hot tar, spearmint gum and blue fountain-pen ink, the smell of kite twine and glycerin soap, a pumpkin smell of Halloween and a papier-mâché fragrance of skull masks, and the smell of dry scabs, as he was pinched, pummelled, shoved. Fists rose and fell, he saw the fox faces and beyond, at the fence, the man and woman standing there, waving. He shrieked, he covered his face, he felt himself pushed, bleeding, to the rim of nothingness. Headfirst, he careened down the slide, screeching, with ten thousand monsters behind. One thought jumped through his mind a moment before he hit bottom in a nauseous mound of claws.

This is hell, he thought, *this is hell!*'

And no one in the hot, milling heap contradicted him.

Skeleton

It was past time for him to see the doctor again. Mr Harris turned palely in at the stairwell, and on his way up the flight saw Dr Burleigh's name gilded over a pointing arrow. Would Dr Burleigh sigh when he walked in? After all, this would make the tenth trip so far this year. But Burleigh shouldn't complain; he was paid for the examinations!

The nurse looked Mr Harris over and smiled, a bit amusedly, as she tiptoed to the glazed glass door, opened it, and put her head in. Harris thought he heard her say, 'Guess who's here, Doctor.' And didn't the doctor's voice reply, faintly, 'Oh, my God, *again*?' Harris swallowed uneasily.

When Harris walked in, Dr Burleigh snorted. 'Aches in your bones again! Ah!!' He scowled and adjusted his glasses. 'My dear Harris, you've been curried with the finest-tooth combs and bacteria-brushes known to science. You're just nervous. Let's see your fingers. Too many cigarettes. Let's smell your breath. Too much protein. Let's see your eyes. Not enough sleep. My response? Go to bed, stop the protein, no smoking. Ten dollars, please.'

Harris stood sulking.

The doctor glanced up from his papers. '*You* still here? You're a hypochondriac! That's *eleven* dollars, now.'

'But why should my bones ache?' asked Harris.

Dr Burleigh spoke as to a child. 'You ever had a sore muscle, and kept irritating it, fussing with it, rubbing it? It gets worse, the more you bother it. Then you leave it alone and the pain vanishes. You realize you caused most of the soreness yourself. Well, son, that's what's with you. Leave yourself alone. Take a dose of salts. Get out of here and take that trip to Phoenix you've stewed about for months. Do you good to travel!'

Five minutes later, Mr Harris riffled through a classified phone directory at the corner druggist's. A fine lot of sympathy one got from blind fools like Burleigh! He passed his finger down a list of Bone Specialists, found one named M Munigant. Munigant lacked an MD, or any other academic lettering behind his name, but his office was conveniently near. Three blocks down, one block over . . .

M Munigant, like his office, was small and dark. Like his office, he smelled of iodoform, iodine, and the other odd things. He was a good listener, though, and listened with eager shiny moves of his eyes, and when he talked to Harris, his accent was such that he softly whistled each word; undoubtedly because of imperfect dentures.

Harris told all.

M Munigant nodded. He had seen cases like this before. The bones of the body. Man was not aware of his bones. Ah, yes, the bones. The skeleton. Most difficult. Something concerning an imbalance, an unsympathetic co-ordination between soul, flesh, and skeleton. Very complicated, softly whistled M Munigant. Harris listened, fascinated. Now, *here* was a doctor who understood his illness! Psychological, said M Munigant. He moved swiftly, delicately to a dingy wall and slashed down half a dozen X-rays to haunt the room with their look of things found floating in an ancient tide. Here, here! The skeleton surprised! Here luminous portraits of the long, the short, the large, the small bones. Mr Harris must be aware of his position, his problem! M Munigant's hand tapped, rattled, whispered, scratched at faint nebulae of flesh in which hung ghosts of cranium, spinal cord, pelvis, lime, calcium, marrow, here, there, this, that, these, those, and others! Look!

Harris shuddered. The X-rays and the paintings blew in a

green and phosphorescent wind from a land peopled by the monsters of Dali and Fuseli.

M Munigant whistled quietly. Did Mr Harris wish his bones – treated?

'That depends,' said Harris.

Well, M Munigant could not help Harris unless Harris was in the proper mood. Psychologically, one had to *need* help, or the doctor was useless. But (shrugging) M Munigant would 'try'.

Harris lay on a table with his mouth open. The lights were switched off, the shades drawn. M Munigant approached his patient.

Something touched Harris's tongue.

He felt his jawbones forced out. They creaked and made faint cracking noises. One of those skeleton charts on the dim wall seemed to quiver and jump. A violent shudder seized Harris. Involuntarily, his mouth snapped shut.

M Munigant shouted. His nose had almost been bitten off! No use, no use! Now was not the time! M Munigant whispered the shades up, dreadfully disappointed. When Mr Harris felt he could co-operate psychologically, when Mr Harris really *needed* help and trusted M Munigant to help him, then maybe something could be done. M Munigant held out his little hand. In the meantime, the fee was only two dollars. Mr Harris must begin to think. Here was a sketch for Mr Harris to take home and study. It would acquaint him with his body. He must be tremblingly aware of himself. He must be on guard. Skeletons were strange, unwieldy things. M Munigant's eyes glittered. Good day to Mr Harris. Oh, and would he care for a breadstick? M Munigant proffered a jar of long hard salty breadsticks to Harris, taking one himself, saying that chewing breadsticks kept him in – ah – practice. Good day, good day to Mr Harris! Mr Harris went home.

The next day, Sunday, Mr Harris discovered innumerable

fresh aches and pains in his body. He spent the morning, his eyes fixed, staring with new interest at the small, anatomically perfect painting of a skeleton M Munigant had given him.

His wife, Clarisse, startled him at dinner when she cracked her exquisitely thin knuckles, one by one, until he clapped his hands to his ears and cried, 'Stop!'

The rest of the afternoon he quarantined himself in his room. Clarisse played bridge in the parlour laughing and chatting with three other ladies while Harris, hidden away, fingered and weighed the limbs of his body with growing curiosity. After an hour he suddenly rose and called:

'Clarisse!'

She had a way of dancing into any room, her body doing all sorts of soft, agreeable things to keep her feet from ever quite touching the nap of a rug. She excused herself from her friends and came to see him now, brightly. She found him re-seated in a far corner and she saw that he was staring at the anatomical sketch. 'Are you still brooding, sweet?' she asked. 'Please don't.' She sat upon his knees.

Her beauty could not distract him now in his absorption. He juggled her lightness, he touched her kneecap, suspiciously. It seemed to move under her pale, glowing skin. 'Is it supposed to do that?' he asked, sucking in his breath.

'Is it supposed to do what?' she laughed. 'You mean my kneecap?'

'Is it supposed to run around on top of your knee that way?'

She experimented. 'So it *does*,' she marvelled.

'I'm glad yours slithers, too,' he sighed. 'I was beginning to worry.'

'About what?'

He patted his ribs. 'My ribs don't go all the way down, they stop *here*. And I found some confounded ones that dangle in midair!'

Beneath the curve of her small breasts, Clarisse clasped her hands.

'Of course, silly. Everybody's ribs stop at a given point. And those funny short ones are floating ribs.'

'I hope they don't float around too much.' The joke was most uneasy. Now, above all, he wished to be alone. Further discoveries, newer and stranger archaeological diggings, lay within reach of his trembling hands, and he did not wish to be laughed at.

'Thanks for coming in, dear,' he said.

'Any time.' She rubbed her small nose softly against his.

'Wait! Here, now . . . ' He put his finger to touch his nose and hers. 'Did you realize? The nose-bone grows down only *this* far. From there on a lot of gristly tissue fills out the rest!'

She wrinkled hers. 'Of course, darling!' And she danced from the room.

Now, sitting alone, he felt the perspiration rise from the pools and hollows of his face, to flow in a thin tide down his cheeks. He licked his lips and shut his eyes. Now . . . now . . . next on the agenda, what . . . ? The spinal cord, yes. Here. Slowly, he examined it, in the same way he operated the many push-buttons in his office, thrusting them to summon secretaries, messengers. But now, in these pushings of his spinal column, fears and terrors answered, rushed from a million doors in his mind to confront and shake him! His spine felt horribly — unfamiliar. Like the brittle shards of a fish, freshly eaten, its bones left strewn on a cold china platter. He seized the little rounded knobbins. 'Lord! Lord!'

His teeth began to chatter. God All-Mighty! he thought, why haven't I realized it all these years? All these years I've gone around with a — *skeleton* — inside me! How is it we take ourselves for granted? How is it we never question our bodies and our being?

A skeleton. One of those jointed, snowy, hard things, one of those foul, dry, brittle, gouge-eyed, skull-faced, shake-fingered, rattling things that sway from neck-chains in abandoned webbed closets, one of those things found on the desert all long and scattered like dice!

He stood upright, because he could not bear to remain seated. Inside me now, he grasped his stomach, his head, inside my head is a – a skull. One of those curved carapaces which holds my brain like an electrical jelly, one of those cracked shells with the holes in front like two holes shot through it by a double-barrelled shotgun! With its grottoes and caverns of bone, its revetments and placements for my flesh, my smelling, my seeing, my hearing, my thinking! A skull, encompassing my brain, allowing it exit through its brittle windows to see the outside world!

He wanted to dash into the bridge party, upset it, a fox in a chickenyard, the cards fluttering all around like chicken feathers burst upwards in clouds! He stopped himself only with a violent, trembling effort. Now, now, man, control yourself. This is a revelation, take it for what it's worth, understand it, savour it. But a *skeleton*! screamed his subconscious. I won't stand for it. It's vulgar, it's terrible, it's frightening. Skeletons are horrors; they clink and tinkle and rattle in old castles, hung from oaken beams, making long, indolently rustling pendulums on the wind . . .

'Darling, will you come meet the ladies?' His wife's clear, sweet voice called from far away.

Mr Harris stood. His *skeleton* held him up! This thing inside, this invader this horror, was supporting his arms, legs, and head! It was like feeling someone just behind you who shouldn't be there. With every step, he realized how dependent he was on this other Thing.

'Darling, I'll be with you in a moment,' he called weakly. To himself he said, Come on, brace up! You've got to go back to work tomorrow. Friday you must make that trip to Phoenix. It's a long drive. Hundreds of miles. Must be in shape for that trip or you won't get Mr Creldon to invest in your ceramics business. Chin up, now!

A moment later he stood among the ladies, being introduced to Mrs Withers, Mrs Abblematt, and Miss Kirthy, all of whom had skeletons inside them, but took it very calmly, because nature had carefully clothed the bare nudity of clavicle, tibia, and femur with breasts, thighs, calves, with coiffure and eyebrow satanic, with bee-stung lips and – *Lord!* shouted Mr Harris inwardly – when they talk or eat, part of their skeleton shows – their *teeth*! I never thought of that. 'Excuse me,' he gasped, and ran from the room only in time to drop his lunch among the petunias over the garden balustrade.

That night, seated on the bed as his wife undressed, he pared his toenails and fingernails scrupulously. These parts, too, were where his skeleton was showing, indignantly growing out. He must have muttered part of this theory, because next thing he knew his wife, in negligee, was on the bed, her arms about his neck, yawning, 'Oh, my darling, fingernails are *not* bone, they're only hardened epidermis!'

He threw the scissors down. 'Are you certain? I hope so. I'd feel better.' He looked at the curve of her body, marvelling. 'I hope all people are made the same way.'

'If you aren't the darndest hypochondriac!' She held him at arm's length. 'Come on. What's wrong? Tell mama.'

'Something inside me,' he said. 'Something – I ate.'

The next morning and all afternoon at hs downtown office, Mr Harris sorted out the sizes, shapes, and construction of various bones in his body with displeasure. At ten a.m. he asked to feel Mr Smith's elbow one moment. Mr Smith obliged, but scowled suspiciously. And after lunch Mr Harris asked to touch Miss Laurel's shoulder blade and she immediately pushed herself back against him, purring like a kitten and shutting her eyes.

'Miss Laurel!' he snapped. 'Stop that!'

Alone, he pondered his neuroses. The war was just over, the pressure of his work, the uncertainty of the future, probably had much to do with his mental outlook. He wanted to leave the office, get into business for himself. He had more than a little talent for ceramics and sculpture. As soon as possible he'd head for Arizona, borrow that money from Mr Creldon, build a kiln and set up shop. It was a worry. What a case he was. But luckily he had contacted M Munigant, who seemed eager to understand and help him. He would fight it out with himself, not go back to either Munigant or Dr Burleigh unless he was forced to. The alien feeling would pass. He sat staring into space.

The alien feeling did not pass. It grew.

On Tuesday and Wednesday it bothered him terrifically that his epidermis, hair and other appendages were of a high disorder, while the integumented skeleton of himself was a slick clean structure of efficient organization. Sometimes, in certain lights with his lips drawn morosely down, weighted with melancholy, he imagined he saw his skull grinning at him behind the flesh.

Let go! he cried. Let go of me! My lungs! Stop!

He gasped convulsively, as if his ribs were crushing the breath from him.

My brain — stop squeezing it!

And terrifying headaches burnt his brain to a blind cinder.

My insides, let them be, for God's sake! Stay away from my heart!

His heart cringed from the fanning motion of ribs like pale spiders crouched and fiddling with their prey.

Drenched with sweat, he lay upon the bed one night while Clarisse was out attending a Red Cross meeting. He tried to gather his wits but only grew more aware of the conflict between his dirty exterior and this beautiful cool clean calciumed thing inside.

His complexion: wasn't it oily and lined with worry?

Observe the flawless, snow-white perfection of the skull.

His nose: wasn't it too large?

Then observe the tiny bones of the skull's nose before that monstrous nasal cartilage begins forming the lopsided proboscis.

His body: wasn't it plump?

Well, consider the skeleton; slender, svelte, economical of line and contour. Exquisitely carved oriental ivory! Perfect, thin as a white praying mantis!

His eyes: weren't they protuberant, ordinary, numblooking?

Be so kind as to note the eye-sockets of the skull; so deep and rounded, sombre, quiet pools, all-knowing, eternal. Gaze deep and you never touch the bottom of their dark understanding. All irony, all life, all everything is there in the cupped darkness.

Compare. Compare. Compare.

He raged for hours. And the skeleton, ever the frail and solemn philosopher, hung quietly inside, saying not a word, suspended like a delicate insect within a crysalis, waiting and waiting.

Harris sat slowly up.

'Wait a minute. Hold on!' he exclaimed. 'You're helpless, too. I've got you, too. I can make you do anything I want! You can't prevent it! I say move your carpals, metacarpals, and phalanges and — sswtt — up they go, as I wave to someone!' He laughed. 'I order the fibula and femur to locomote and *Hunn* two three four, *Hunn* two three four — we walk around the block. There!'

Harris grinned.

'It's a fifty-fifty fight. Even-Stephen. And we'll fight it out, we two! After all, I'm the part that *thinks*! Yes, by God! yes. Even if I didn't have you, I could still think!'

Instantly, a tiger's jaw snapped shut, chewing his brain in half. Harris screamed. The bones of his skull grabbed hold and gave him nightmares. Then slowly, while he shrieked, nuzzled and ate the nightmares one by one, until the last one was gone and the light went out . . .

At the end of the week he postponed the Phoenix trip because of his health. Weighing himself on a penny scale he saw the slow gliding red arrow point to: 165.

He groaned. Why, I've weighed 175 for years. I can't have lost 10 pounds! He examined his cheeks in the fly-dotted mirror. Cold, primitive fear rushed over him in odd little shivers. You, you! I know what you're about, *you*!

He shook his fist at his bony face, particularly addressing his remarks to his superior maxillary, his inferior maxillary, to his cranium and to his cervical vertebrae.

'You damn thing, you! Think you can starve me, make me lose weight, eh? Peel the flesh off, leave nothing, but skin on bone. Trying to ditch me, so you can be supreme, ah? No, no!'

He fled into a cafeteria.

Turkey, dressing, creamed potatoes, four vegetables, three desserts, he could eat none of it, he was sick to his stomach. He forced himself. His teeth began to ache. Bad teeth, is it? he thought angrily. I'll eat in spite of every tooth clanging and banging and rattling so they fall in my gravy.

His head blazed, his breath jerked in and out of a constricted chest, his teeth raged with pain, but he knew one small victory. He was about to drink milk when he stopped and poured it into a vase of nasturtiums. No calcium for you, my boy, no calcium for you. Never again shall I eat foods with calcium or other bone-fortifying minerals. I'll eat for one of us, not both, my lad.

'One hundred and fifty pounds,' he said the following week to his wife. 'Do you *see* how I've changed?'

'For the better,' said Clarisse. 'You were always a little plump for your height, darling.' She stroked his chin. 'I like your face. It's so much nicer; the lines of it are so firm and strong now.'

'They're not *my* lines, they're his, damn him! You mean to say you like him better than you like me?'

'Him? Who's "*him*"?'

In the parlour mirror, beyond Clarisse, his skull smiled back at him behind his fleshy grimace of hatred and despair.

Fuming, he popped malt tablets into his mouth. This was one way of gaining weight when you couldn't keep other foods down. Clarisse noticed the malt pellets.

'But, darling, really, you don't have to regain the weight for me,' she said.

Oh, shut up! he felt like saying.

She made him lie with his head in her lap. 'Darling,' she said, 'I've watched you lately. You're so − badly off. You don't say anything, but you look − hunted. You toss in bed at night. Maybe you should go to a psychiatrist. But I think I can tell you everything he would say. I've put it all together from hints you've let escape you. I can tell you that you and your skeleton are one and the same, one nation, indivisible, with liberty and justice for all. United you stand, divided you fall. If you two fellows can't get along like an old married couple in the future, go back and see Dr Burleigh. But, first, relax. You're in a vicious circle; the more you worry, the more your bones stick out, the more you worry. After all, who picked this fight − you or that anonymous entity you claim is lurking around behind your alimentary canal?'

He closed his eyes. 'I did. I guess I did. Go on, Clarisse, keep talking.'

'You rest now,' she said softly. 'Rest and forget.'

Mr Harris felt buoyed up for half a day, then he began to sag. It was all very well to blame his imagination, but this particular skeleton, by God, was fighting back.

Harris set out for M Munigant's office late in the day. Walking for half an hour until he found the address, he caught sight of the name M MUNIGANT initialled in ancient, flaking gold on a glass plate outside the building. Then, his bones seemed to explode from their moorings, blasted and erupted with pain. Blinded, he staggered away. When he opened his eyes again he had rounded a corner. M Munigant's office was out of sight.

The pains ceased.

M Munigant was the man to help him. If the sight of his name would cause so titanic a reaction, of course M Munigant *must* be just the man.

But, not today. Each time he tried to return to that office, the terrible pains took hold. Perspiring, he had to give up and swayed into a cocktail bar.

Moving across the dim lounge, he wondered briefly if a lot of blame couldn't be put on M Munigant's shoulders. After all, it was Munigant who'd first drawn specific attention to his skeleton, and let the psychological impact of it slam home! Could M Munigant be using him for some nefarious purpose? But what purpose? Silly to suspect him. Just a little doctor. Trying to be helpful. Munigant and his jar of breadsticks. Ridiculous. M Munigant was okay, okay . . .

There was a sight within the cocktail lounge to give him hope. A large, fat man, round as a butterball, stood drinking consecutive beers at the bar. Now *there* was a successful man. Harris repressed a desire to go up, clap the fat man's shoulder, and inquire as to how he'd gone about impounding his bones. Yes, the fat man's skeleton was luxuriously closeted. There were pillows of fat here, resilient bulges of it there, with several round chandeliers of fat under his chin. The poor skeleton was lost; it could never fight clear of that blubber. It might have tried once — but not now, overwhelmed, not a bony echo of the fat man's supporter remained.

Not without envy, Harris approached the fat man as one might cut across the bow of an ocean liner. Harris ordered a drink, drank it, and then dared to address the fat man:

'Glands?'

'You talking to me?' asked the fat man.

'Or is there a special diet?' wondered Harris. 'I beg your pardon, but, as you see, I'm down. Can't seem to put on any weight. I'd like a stomach like that one of yours. Did you grow it because you were afraid of something?'

'You,' announced the fat man, 'are drunk. But — I like drunkards.' He ordered more drinks. 'Listen close, I'll tell you. Layer by layer,' said the fat man, 'twenty years, man and boy, I built this.' He held his vast stomach like a globe of the world, teaching his audience its gastronomical geography. 'It was no overnight circus. The tent was not raised before dawn on the wonders installed within. I have cultivated my inner organs as if they were thoroughbred dogs, cats, and other animals. My stomach is a fat pink Persian tom slumbering, rousing at intervals to purr, mew, growl, and cry for chocolate titbits. I feed it well, it will 'most sit up for me. And, my dear fellow, my intestines are the rarest pure-bred Indian anacondas you ever viewed in the sleekest, coiled, fine and ruddy health. Keep 'em in prime, I do, all my pets. For fear of something? Perhaps.'

This called for another drink for everyone.

'Gain weight?' The fat man savoured the words on his tongue. 'Here's what you do: get yourself a quarrelling bird of a wife, a baker's dozen of relatives who can flush a covey of troubles out from behind the veriest molehill. Add to these a sprinkling of business associates whose prime motivation is snatching your last lonely quid, and you are well on your way to getting fat. How so? In no time you'll begin subconsciously building fat betwixt yourself and them. A buffer epidermal state, a cellular wall. You'll soon find that eating is the only fun on earth. But one needs to be bothered by outside sources. Too many people in this world haven't enough to worry about, then they begin picking on themselves, and they lose weight. Meet all of the vile, terrible people you can possibly meet, and pretty soon you'll be adding the good old fat!'

And with that advice, the fat man launched himself out into the dark tide of night, swaying mightily and wheezing.

'That's exactly what Dr Burleigh told me, slightly changed,' said Harris thoughtfully. 'Perhaps that trip to Phoenix, now, at this time — '

The trip from Los Angeles to Phoenix was a sweltering one, crossing, as it did, the Mojave Desert on a broiling yellow day. Traffic was thin and inconstant, and for long stretches there would not be a car on the road for miles ahead or behind. Harris twitched his fingers on the steering wheel. Whether or not Creldon, in Phoenix, lent him the money he needed to start his business, it was still a good thing to get away, to put distance behind.

The car moved in the hot sluice of desert wind. The one Mr H sat inside the other Mr H. Perhaps both perspired. Perhaps both were miserable.

On a curve, the inside Mr H suddenly constricted the outer flesh, causing him to jerk forward on the hot steering wheel.

The car plunged off the road into boiling sand and turned half over.

Night came, a wind rose, the road was lonely and silent. The few cars that passed went swiftly on their way, their view obstructed. Mr Harris lay unconscious, until very late he heard a wind rising out of the desert, felt the sting of little sand needles on his cheeks, and opened his eyes.

Morning found him gritty-eyed and wandering in thoughtless senseless circles, having, in his delirium, got away from the road. At noon he sprawled in the poor shade of a bush. The sun struck him with a keen sword edge, cutting through to his — bones. A vulture circled.

Harris's parched lips cracked open. 'So that's it?' he whispered, red-eyed, bristle-cheeked. 'One way or another you'll walk me, starve me, thirst me, kill me.' He swallowed dry burrs of dust. 'Sun cook off my flesh so you can peek out. Vultures lunch off me, and there you'll lie, grinning. Grinning with victory. Like a bleached xylophone strewn and played by vultures with an ear for odd music. You'd like that. Freedom.'

He walked on through a landscape that shivered and bubbled in the direct pour of sunlight; stumbling, falling flat, lying to feed himself little mouths of fire. The air was blue alcohol flame, and vultures roasted and steamed and glittered as they flew in glides and circles. Phoenix. The road. Car. Water. Safety.

'Hey!'

Someone called from way off in the blue alcohol flame.

Mr Harris propped himself up.

'Hey!'

The call was repeated. A crunching of footsteps, quick.

With a cry of unbelievable relief, Harris rose, only to collapse again into the arms of someone in a uniform with a badge.

The car tediously hauled, repaired, Phoenix reached, Harris found himself in such an unholy state of mind that the business transaction was a numb pantomime. Even when he got the loan and held the money in his hand, it meant nothing. This Thing within him like a hard white sword in a scabbard tainted his business, his eating, coloured his love for Clarisse, made it unsafe to trust an automobile; all in all this Thing had to be put in its place. The desert incident had brushed too close. Too near the bone, one might say with an ironic twist of one's mouth. Harris heard himself thanking Mr Creldon, dimly, for the money. Then he turned his car and motored back across the long miles, this time cutting across to San Diego, so he would miss that desert stretch between El Centro and Beaumont. He drove north along the coast. He didn't trust that desert. But — careful! Salt waves boomed, hissing on the beach outside Laguna. Sand, fish and crustacea would cleanse his bones as swiftly as vultures. Slow down on the curves over the surf.

Damn, he was sick!

Where to turn? Clarisse? Burleigh? Munigant? Bone specialist. Munigant. Well?

'Darling!' Clarisse kissed him. He winced at the solidness of the teeth and jaw behind the passionate exchange.

'Darling,' he said, slowly, wiping his lips with his wrist, trembling.

'You look thinner; oh, darling, the business deal — ?'

'It went through. I guess. Yes, it did.'

She kissed him again. They ate a slow, falsely cheerful dinner, with Clarisse laughing and encouraging him. He studied the phone; several times he picked it up indecisively, then laid it down.

His wife walked in, putting on her coat and hat. 'Well, sorry, but I have to leave.' She pinched him on the cheek. 'Come on now, cheer up! I'll be back from Red Cross in three hours. You lie around and snooze. I simply *have* to go.'

When Clarisse was gone, Harris dialled the phone, nervously.

'M Munigant?'

The explosions and the sickness in his body after he set the phone down were unbelievable. His bones were racked with every kind of pain, cold and hot, he had ever thought of or experienced in wildest nightmare. He swallowed all the aspirin he could find, in an effort to stave off the assault; but when the doorbell finally rang an hour later, he could not move; he lay weak and exhausted, panting, tears streaming down his cheeks.

'Come in! Come in, for God's sake!'

M Munigant came in. Thank God the door was unlocked.

Oh, but Mr Harris looked terrible. M Munigant stood in the centre of the living room, small and dark. Harris nodded. The pains rushed through him, hitting him with large iron hammers and hooks. M Munigant's eyes glittered as he saw Harris's protuberant bones. Ah, he saw that Mr Harris was now psychologically prepared for aid. Was it not so? Harris nodded again, feebly, sobbing. M Munigant still whistled when he talked; something about his tongue and the whistling. No matter. Through his shimmering eyes Harris seemed to see M Munigant shrink, get smaller. Imagination, of course. Harris sobbed out his story of the Phoenix trip. M Munigant sympathized. This skeleton was a — a traitor! They would fix him for once and for all!

'M Munigant,' sighed Harris, faintly, 'I — I never noticed before. Your tongue. Round, tubelike. Hollow? My eyes. Delirious. What do I do?'

M Munigant whistled softly, appreciatively, coming closer. If Mr Harris would relax in his chair, and open his mouth? The lights were switched off. M Munigant peered into Harris's dropped jaw. Wider, please? It had been so hard, that first visit, to help Harris, with both body and bone in revolt. Now, he had co-operation from the flesh of the man, anyway, even if the skeleton protested. In the darkness, M Munigant's voice got small, small, tiny, tiny. The whistling became high and shrill. Now. Relax, Mr Harris, NOW!

Harris felt his jaw pressed violently in all directions, his tongue depressed as with a spoon, his throat clogged. He gasped for breath. Whistle. He couldn't breathe! Something squirmed, corkscrewed his cheeks out, bursting his jaws. Like a hot-water douche, something squirted into his sinuses, his ears clanged! 'Ahhhh!' shrieked Harris, gagging. His head, its carapaces riven, shattered, hung loose. Agony shot fire through his lungs.

Harris could breathe again, momentarily. His watery eyes sprang wide. He shouted. His ribs, like sticks picked up and bundled, were loosened in him. Pain! He fell to the floor, wheezing out his hot breath.

Lights flickered in his senseless eyeballs, he felt his limbs swiftly cast loose and free. Through streaming eyes he saw the parlour.

The room was empty.

'M Munigant? In God's name, where are you, M Munigant? Come help me!'

M Munigant was gone.

'Help!'

Then he heard it.

Deep down in the subterannean fissures of his body, the minute, unbelievable noises; little smackings and twistings and little dry chippings and grindings and nuzzling sounds – like a tiny hungry mouse down in the red-blooded dimness, gnawing ever so earnestly and expertly at what might have been, but was not, a submerged timber . . . !

Clarisse, walking along the sidewalk, held her head high and marched straight towards her house on St James Place. She was thinking of the Red Cross as she turned the corner and almost ran into this little dark man who smelled of iodine.

Clarisse would have ignored him if it were not for the fact that as she passed, he took something long, white and oddly familiar from his coat and proceeded to chew on it, as on a peppermint stick. Its end devoured, his extraordinary tongue darted within the white confection, sucking out the filling, making contented noises. He was still crunching his goody as she proceeded up the sidewalk to her house, turned the doorknob and walked in.

'Darling?' she called, smiling around. 'Darling, where are you?' she shut the door, walked down the hall and into the living room. 'Darling . . .'

She stared at the floor for twenty seconds, trying to understand.

She screamed.

Outside in the sycamore darkness, the little man pierced a long white stick with intermittent holes; then, softly, sighing, his lips puckered, played a little sad tune upon the improvised instrument to accompany the shrill and awful singing of Clarisse's voice as she stood in the living room.

Many times as a little girl Clarisse had run on the beach sands, stepped on a jellyfish and screamed. It was not so bad, finding an intact, gelatine-skinned jellyfish in one's living room. One could step back from it.

It was when the jellyfish *called you by name* . . .

The Man Upstairs

He remembered how carefully and expertly Grandmother would fondle the cold cut guts of the chicken and withdraw the marvels therein; the wet shining loops of meat-smelling intestine, the muscled lump of heart, the gizzard with the collection of seeds in it. How neatly and nicely Grandma would slit the chicken and push her fat little hand in to deprive it of its medals. These would be segregated, some in pans of water, others in paper to be thrown to the dog later, perhaps. And then the ritual of taxidermy, stuffing the bird with watered, seasoned bread, and performing surgery with a swift, bright needle, stitch after pulled-tight stitch.

This was one of the prime thrills of Douglas's eleven-year-old life span.

Altogether, he counted twenty knives in the various squeaking drawers of the magic kitchen table from which Grandma, a kindly, gentle-faced, white-haired old witch, drew paraphernalia for her miracles.

Douglas was to be quiet. He could stand across the table from Grandma, his freckled nose tucked over the edge, watching, but any loose boy-talk might interfere with the spell. It was a wonder when Grandma brandished silver shakers over the bird, supposedly sprinkling showers of mummy-dust and pulverized Indian bones, muttering mystical verses under her toothless breath.

'Grammy,' said Douglas at last, breaking the silence. 'Am I like that inside?' He pointed at the chicken.

'Yes,' said Grandma. 'A little more orderly and presentable, but just about the same . . . '

'And more *of* it!' added Douglas, proud of his guts.

'Yes,' said Grandma. 'More of it.'

'Grandpa has lots more'n me. His sticks out in front so he can rest his elbows on it.'

Grandma laughed and shook her head.

Douglas said, 'And Lucie Williams, down the street, she . . . '

'Hush, child!' cried Grandma.

'But she's got . . . '

'Never you mind what she's got! That's different.'

'But why is *she* different?'

'A darning-needle dragon-fly is coming by some day and sew up your mouth,' said Grandma firmly.

Douglas waited, then asked, 'How do you know I've got insides like that, Grandma?'

'Oh, go 'way, now!'

The front doorbell rang.

Through the front-door glass as he ran down the hall, Douglas saw a straw hat. The bell jangled again and again. Douglas opened the door.

'Good morning, child, is the landlady at home?'

Cold grey eyes in a long, smooth, walnut-coloured face gazed upon Douglas. The man was tall, thin, and carried a suitcase, a briefcase, an umbrella under one bent arm, gloves rich and thick and grey on his thin fingers, and wore a horribly new straw hat.

Douglas backed up. 'She's busy.'

'I wish to rent her upstairs room, as advertised.'

'We've got ten boarders, and it's already rented; go away!'

'Douglas!' Grandma was behind him suddenly. 'How do you do?' she said to the stranger. 'Never mind this child.'

Unsmiling, the man stepped stiffly in. Douglas watched them ascend out of sight up the stairs, heard Grandma detailing the conveniences of the upstairs room. Soon she hurried down to pile linens from the linen closet on Douglas and send him scooting up with them.

Douglas paused at the room's threshold. The room was changed oddly, simply because the stranger had been in it a moment. The straw hat lay brittle and terrible upon the bed, the umbrella leaned stiff against one wall like a dead bat with dark wings folded.

Douglas blinked at the umbrella.

The stranger stood in the centre of the changed room, tall, tall.

'Here!' Douglas littered the bed with supplies. 'We eat at noon sharp, and if you're late coming down the soup'll get cold. Grandma fixes it so it will, every time!'

The tall strange man counted out ten new copper pennies and tinkled them in Douglas's blouse pocket. 'We shall be friends,' he said, grimly.

It was funny, the man having nothing but pennies. Lots of them. No silver at all, no dimes, no quarters. Just new copper pennies.

Douglas thanked him glumly. 'I'll drop these in my dime bank when I get them changed into a dime. I got six dollars and fifty cents in dimes all ready for my camp trip in August.'

'I must wash now,' said the tall strange man.

Once, at midnight, Douglas had wakened to hear a storm rumbling outside — the cold hard wind shaking the house, the rain driving against the window. And then a lightning bolt had landed outside the window with a silent, terrific concussion. He remembered that fear of looking about at his room, seeing it strange and awful in the instantaneous light.

So it was, now, in this room. He stood looking up at the stranger. This room was no longer the same, but changed indefinably because this man, quick as a lightning bolt, had shed his light about it. Douglas backed up slowly as the stranger advanced.

The door closed in his face.

The wooden fork went up with mashed potatoes, came down

empty. Mr Koberman, for that was his name, had brought the wooden fork and wooden knife and spoon with him when Grandma called lunch.

'Mrs Spaulding,' he said, quietly, 'my own cutlery; please use it. I will have lunch today, but from tomorrow on, only breakfast and supper.'

Grandma bustled in and out, bearing steaming tureens of soup and beans and mashed potatoes to impress her new boarder, while Douglas sat rattling his silverware on his plate, because he had discovered it irritated Mr Koberman.

'I know a trick,' said Douglas. 'Watch.' He picked a fork-tine with his fingernail. He pointed at various sectors of the table, like a magician. Wherever he pointed, the sound of the vibrating fork-tine emerged, like a metal elfin voice. Simply done, of course. He pressed the fork handle on the table-top, secretly. The vibration came from the wood like a sounding board. It looked quite magical. 'There, there, and *there*!' exclaimed Douglas, happily plucking the fork again. He pointed at Mr Koberman's soup and the noise came from it.

Mr Koberman's walnut-coloured face became hard and firm and awful. He pushed the soup bowl away violently, his lips twisting. He fell back in his chair.

Grandma appeared. 'Why, what's wrong, Mr Koberman?'

'I cannot eat this soup.'

'Why?'

'Because I am full and can eat no more. Thank you.'

Mr Koberman left the room, glaring.

'What did you do, just then?' asked Grandma at Douglas, sharply.

'Nothing, Grandma, why does he eat with *wooden* spoons?'

'Yours not to question! When do you go back to school, anyway?'

'Seven weeks.'

'Oh, my land!' said Grandma.

Mr Koberman worked nights. Each morning at eight he arrived mysteriously home, devoured a very small breakfast, and then slept soundlessly in his room all through the dreaming hot daytime, until the huge supper with all the other boarders at night.

Mr Koberman's sleeping habits made it necessary for Douglas to be quiet. This was unbearable. So, whenever Grandma visited down the street, Douglas stamped up and down stairs beating a drum, bouncing golf balls, or just screaming for three minutes outside Mr Koberman's door, or flushing the toilet seven times in succession.

Mr Koberman never moved. His room was silent, dark. He did not complain. There was no sound. He slept on and on. It was very strange.

Doulgas felt a pure white flame of hatred burn inside himself with a steady, unflickering beauty. Now that room was Koberman Land. Once it had been flowery bright when Miss Sadlowe lived there. Now it was stark, bare, cold, clean, everything in its place, alien and brittle.

Douglas climbed upstairs on the fourth morning.

Halfway to the second floor was a large sun-filled window, framed by six-inch panes of orange, purple, blue, red and burgundy glass. In the enchanted early mornings when the sun fell through to strike the landing and slide down the stair banister, Douglas stood entranced at this window peering at the world through the multi-coloured panes.

Now a blue world, a blue sky, blue people, blue streetcars and blue trotting dogs.

He shifted panes. Now – an amber world! Two lemonish women glided by, resembling the daughters of Fu Manchu! Douglas giggled. This pane made even the sunlight more purely golden.

It was eight A.M. Mr Koberman strolled by below, on the

sidewalk, returning from his night's work, his umbrella looped over his elbow, straw hat glued to his head with patent oil.

Douglas shifted panes again. Mr Koberman was a red man walking through a red world with red trees and red flowers and — something else.

Something about — Mr Koberman.

Douglas squinted.

The red glass *did* things to Mr Koberman. His face, his suit, his hands. The clothes seemed to melt away. Douglas almost believed, for one terrible instant, that he could see *inside* Mr Koberman. And what he saw made him lean wildly against the small red pane, blinking.

Mr Koberman glanced up just then, saw Douglas, and raised his umbrella angrily, as if to strike. He ran swiftly across the red lawn to the front door.

'Young man!' he cried, running up the stairs. 'What were you doing?'

'Just looking,' said Douglas numbly.

'That's all, is it?' cried Mr Koberman.

'Yes, sir. I look through all the glasses. All kinds of worlds. Blue ones, red ones, yellow ones. All different.'

'All kinds of worlds, is it!' Mr Koberman glanced at the little panes of glass, his face pale. He got hold of himself. He wiped his face with a handkerchief and pretended to laugh. 'Yes. All kinds of worlds. All different.' He walked to the door of his room. 'Go right ahead; play,' he said.

The door closed. The hall was empty. Mr Koberman had gone in.

Douglas shrugged and found a new pane.

'Oh, everything's violet!'

Half an hour later, while playing in his sandbox behind the house, Douglas heard the crash and the shattering tinkle. He leaped up.

A moment later, Grandma appeared on the back porch, the old razor strop trembling in her hand.

'Douglas! I told you time and time again never fling your basketball against the house! Oh, I could just cry!'

'I been sitting right here,' he protested.

'Come see what you've done, you nasty boy!'

The great coloured window panes lay shattered in a rainbow chaos on the upstairs landing. His basketball lay in the ruins.

Before he could even begin telling his innocence, Douglas was struck a dozen stinging blows upon his rump. Wherever he landed, screaming, the razor strop struck again.

Later, hiding his mind in the sandpile like an ostrich, Douglas nursed his dreadful pains. He knew who'd thrown that basketball. A man with a straw hat and a stiff umbrella and a cold, grey room. Yeah, yeah, yeah. He dribbled tears. Just wait. Just *wait*.

He heard Grandma sweeping up the broken glass. She brought it out and threw it in the trash bin. Blue, pink, yellow meteors of glass dropped brightly down.

When she was gone, Douglas dragged himself, whimpering, over to save out three pieces of the incredible glass. Mr Koberman disliked the coloured windows. These — he clinked them in his fingers — would be worth saving.

Grandfather arrived from his newspaper office each night, shortly ahead of the other boarders, at five o'clock. When a slow, heavy tread filled the hall, and a thick, mahogany cane thumped in the cane-rack, Douglas ran to embrace the large stomach and sit on Grandpa's knee while he read the evening paper.

'Hi, Grampa!'

'Hello, down there!'

'Grandma cut chickens again today. It's fun watching,' said Douglas.

Grandpa kept reading. 'That's twice this week, chickens. She's the chickenist woman. You like to watch her cut 'em, eh? Cold-blooded little pepper! Ha!'

'I'm just curious.'

'You are,' rumbled Grandpa, scowling. 'Remember that day when that young lady was killed at the rail station? You just walked over and looked at her, blood and all.' He laughed. 'Queer duck. Stay that way. Fear nothing, ever in your life. I guess you get it from your father, him being a military man and all, and you so close to him before you came here to live last year.' Grandpa returned to his paper.

A long pause. 'Gramps?'

'Yes?'

'What if a man didn't have a heart or lungs or stomach but still walked around, alive?'

'That,' rumbled Gramps, 'would be a miracle.'

'I don't mean a — a miracle. I mean, what if he was all *different* inside? Not like me.'

'Well, he wouldn't be quite human then, would he, boy?'

'Guess not, Gramps. Gramps, you got a heart and lungs?'

Gramps chuckled. 'Well, tell the truth, I don't *know*. Never seen them. Never had an X-ray, never been to a doctor. Might as well be potato-solid for all I know.'

'Have *I* got a stomach?'

'You certainly have!' cried Grandma from the parlour entry. ''Cause I feed it! And you've lungs, you scream loud enough to wake the crumblees. And you've dirty hands, go wash them! Dinner's ready. Grandpa, come on. Douglas, git!'

In the rush of boarders streaming downstairs, Grandpa, if he intended questioning Douglas further about the weird conversation, lost his opportunity. If dinner delayed an instant more, Grandma and the potatoes would develop simultaneous lumps.

The boarders, laughing and talking at the table — Mr Koberman silent and sullen among them — were silenced when Grandfather cleared his throat. He talked politics a few minutes and then shifted over into the intriguing topic of recent peculiar deaths in the town.

'It's enough to make an old newspaper editor prick up his ears,' he said, eyeing them all. 'That young Miss Larson, lived across the ravine, now. Found her dead three days ago for no reason, just funny kinds of tattoos all over her, and a facial expression that would make Dante cringe. And that other young lady, what was her name? Whitely? She disappeared and *never did* come back.'

'Them things happen alla time,' said Mr Britz, the garage mechanic, chewing. 'Ever peek inna Missing Peoples Bureau file? It's *that* long.' He illustrated. 'Can't tell *what* happens to most of 'em.'

'Anyone want more dressing?' Grandma ladled liberal portions from the chicken's interior. Douglas watched, thinking about how that chicken had had two kinds of guts — God-made and Man-made.

Well, how about *three* kinds of guts?

Eh?

Why not?

Conversation continued about the mysterious death of so-and-so, and, oh, yes, remember a week ago, Marion Barsumian died of heart failure, but maybe that didn't connect up? or did it? you're crazy! forget it, why talk about it at the dinner table? So.

'Never can tell,' said Mr Britz. 'Maybe we got a vampire in town.'

Mr Koberman stopped eating.

'In the year 1927?' said Grandma. 'A vampire? Oh go on, now.'

'Sure,' said Mr Britz. 'Kill 'em with silver bullets. Anything silver for that matter. Vampires *hate* silver. I read it in a book somewhere, once. Sure, I did.'

Douglas looked at Mr Koberman who ate with wooden knives and forks and carried only new copper pennies in his pocket.

'It's poor judgment,' said Grandpa, 'to call anything by a name. We don't know what a hobgoblin or a vampire or a troll is. Could be lots of things. You can't heave them into categories with labels and say they'll act one way or another. That'd be silly. They're people. People who do things. Yes, that's the way to put it: people who *do* things.'

'Excuse me,' said Mr Koberman, who got up and went out for his evening walk to work.

The stars, the moon, the wind, the clock ticking, and the chiming of the hours into dawn, the sun rising, and here it was another morning, another day, and Mr Koberman coming along the sidewalk from his night's work. Douglas stood off like a small mechanism whirring and watching with carefully microscopic eyes.

At noon, Grandma went to the store to buy groceries.

As was his custom every day when Grandma was gone, Douglas yelled outside Mr Koberman's door for a full three minutes. As usual, there was no response. The silence was horrible.

He ran downstairs, got the pass-key, a silver fork, and the three pieces of coloured glass he had saved from the shattered window. He fitted the key to the lock and swung the door slowly open.

The room was in half light, the shades drawn. Mr Koberman lay atop his bedcovers, in slumber clothes, breathing gently, up and down. He didn't move. His face was motionless.

'Hello, Mr Koberman!'

The colourless walls echoed the man's regular breathing.

'Mr Koberman, hello!'

Bouncing a golf ball, Douglas advanced. He yelled. Still no answer. 'Mr Koberman!'

Bending over Mr Koberman, Douglas picked the tines of the silver fork in the sleeping man's face.

Mr Koberman winced. He twisted. He groaned bitterly.

Response. Good. Swell.

Douglas drew a piece of blue glass from his pocket. Looking through the blue glass fragment he found himself in a blue room, in a blue world different from the world he knew. As different as was the red world. Blue furniture, blue bed, blue ceiling and walls, blue wooden eating utensils atop the blue bureau, and the sullen dark blue of Mr Koberman's face and arms and his blue chest rising, falling. Also . . .

Mr Koberman's eyes were wide, staring at him with a hungry darkness.

Douglas fell back, pulled the blue glass from his eyes.

Mr Koberman's eyes were shut.

Blue glass again – open. Blue glass away – shut. Blue glass again – open. Away – shut. Funny. Douglas experimented, trembling. Through the glass the eyes seemed to peer hungrily, avidly, through Mr Koberman's closed lids. Without the blue glass they seemed tightly shut.

But it was the rest of Mr Koberman's body . . .

Mr Koberman's bedclothes dissolved off him. The blue glass had something to do with it. Or perhaps it was the clothes themselves, just being *on* Mr Koberman. Douglas cried out.

He was looking through the wall of Mr Koberman's stomach, right *inside* him!

Mr Koberman was solid.

Or, nearly so, anyway.

There were strange shapes and sizes within him.

Douglas must have stood amazed for five minutes, thinking about the blue worlds, the red worlds, the yellow worlds side by side, living together like glass panes around the big white stair window. Side by side, the coloured panes, the different worlds; Mr Koberman had said so himself.

So this was why the coloured window had been broken.

'Mr Koberman, wake up!'

No answer.

'Mr Koberman, where do you work at night? Mr Koberman, where do you work?'

A little breeze stirred the blue window shade.

'In a red world or a green world or a yellow one, Mr Koberman?'

Over everything was a blue glass silence.

'Wait there,' said Douglas.

He walked down to the kitchen, pulled open the great squeaking drawer and picked out the sharpest, biggest knife.

Very calmly he walked into the hall, climbed back up the stairs again, opened the door to Mr Koberman's room, went in, and closed it, holding the sharp knife in one hand.

Grandma was busy fingering a piecrust into a pan when Douglas entered the kitchen to place something on the table.

'Grandma, what's this?'

She glanced up briefly, over her glasses. 'I don't know.'

It was square, like a box, and elastic. It was bright orange in colour. It had four square tubes, coloured blue, attached to it. It smelled funny.

'Ever see anything like it, Grandma?'

'No.'

'That's what *I* thought.'

Douglas left it there, went from the kitchen. Five minutes later he returned with something else. 'How about *this*?'

He laid down a bright pink linked chain with a purple triangle at one end.

'Don't bother me,' said Grandma. 'It's only a chain.'

Next time he returned with two hands full. A ring, a square, a triangle, a pyramid, a rectangle, and — other shapes. All of them were pliable, resilient, and looked as if they were made of gelatin. 'This isn't all,' said Douglas, putting them down. 'There's more where this came from.'

Grandma said, 'Yes, yes,' in a far-off tone, very busy.

'You were wrong, Grandma.'

'About what?'

'About all people being the same inside.'

'Stop talking nonsense.'

'Where's my piggy-bank?'

'On the mantel, where you left it.'

'Thanks.'

He tramped into the parlour, reached up for his piggy-bank.

Grandpa came home from the office at five.

'Grandpa, come upstairs.'

'Sure, son. Why?'

'Something to show you. It's not nice; but it's interesting.'

Grandpa chuckled, following his grandson's feet up to Mr Koberman's room.

'Grandma mustn't know about this; she wouldn't like it,' said Douglas. He pushed the door wide open. 'There.'

Grandfather gasped.

Douglas remembered the next few hours all the rest of his life. Standing over Mr Koberman's naked body, the coroner and his assistants. Grandma, downstairs, asking somebody, 'What's going on up there?' and Grandpa saying, shakily, 'I'll take Douglas away on a long vacation so he can forget this whole ghastly affair. Ghastly, ghastly affair!'

Douglas said, 'Why should it be bad? I don't see anything bad. I don't feel bad.'

The coroner shivered and said. 'Koberman's dead, all right.'

His assistant sweated. 'Did you see those *things* in the pans of water and in the wrapping paper?'

'Oh, my God, my God, yes, I saw them.'

'Christ.'

The coroner bent over Mr Koberman's body again. 'This better be kept secret, boys. It wasn't murder. It was a mercy the boy acted. God knows what might have happened if he hadn't.'

'What was Koberman? A vampire? A monster?'

'Maybe. I don't know. Something — not human.' The coroner moved his hands deftly over the suture.

Douglas was proud of his work. He'd gone to much trouble. He had watched Grandmother carefully and remembered. Needle and thread and all. All in all, Mr Koberman was as neat a job as any chicken ever popped into hell by Grandma.

'I heard the boy say that Koberman lived even after all those *things* were taken out of him.' The coroner looked at the triangles and chains and pyramids floating in the pans of water. 'Kept on *living*. God.'

'Did the boy say that?'

'He did.'

'Then, what *did* kill Koberman?'

The coroner drew a few strands of sewing thread from their bedding.

'This . . . ' he said.

Sunlight blinked coldly off a half-revealed treasure trove; six dollars and sixty cents' worth of silver dimes inside Mr Koberman's chest.

'I think Douglas made a wise investment,' said the coroner, sewing the flesh back up over the 'dressing' quickly.

Touched with Fire

They stood in the blazing sunlight for a long while, looking at the bright faces of their old-fashioned railroad watches, while the shadows tilted beneath them, swaying, and the perspiration ran out under their porous summer hats. When they uncovered their heads to mop their lined and pinkened brows, their hair was white and soaked through, like something that had been out of the light for years. One of the men commented that his shoes felt like two loaves of baked bread and then, sighing warmly, added:

'Are you positive this is the right tenement?'

The second old man, Foxe by name, nodded, as if any quick motion might make him catch fire by friction alone. 'I saw this woman every day for three days. She'll show up. If she's still alive, that is. Wait till you *see* her, Shaw. Lord! what a case.'

'Such an odd business,' said Shaw. 'If people knew they'd think us Peeping Toms, doddering old fools. Lord, I feel self-conscious standing here.'

Foxe leaned on his cane. 'Let me do all the talking if — hold on! There she is!' He lowered his voice. 'Take a slow look as she comes out.'

The tenement front door slammed viciously. A dumpy woman stood at the top of the thirteen porch steps glancing this way and that with angry jerkings of her eyes. Jamming a plump hand in her purse, she seized some crumpled dollar bills, plunged down the steps brutally, and set off down the street in a charge. Behind her, several heads peered from apartment windows above, summoned by her crashing of the door.

'Come on,' whispered Foxe. 'Here we go to the butcher's.'

The woman flung open a butchershop door, rushed in. The two old men had a glimpse of a mouth sticky with raw lipstick. Her eyebrows were like moustaches over her squinting, always suspicious eyes. Abreast of the butchershop, they heard her voice already screaming inside.

'I want a good cut of meat. Let's see what you got hidden to take home for yourself!'

The butcher stood silently in his bloody-fingerprinted frock, his hands empty. The two old men entered behind the woman and pretended to admire a pink loaf of fresh-ground sirloin.

'Them lambchops look sickly!' cried the woman. 'What's the price on brains?'

The butcher told her in a low dry voice.

'Well, weigh me a pound of liver!' said the woman. 'Keep your thumbs off!'

The butcher weighed it out, slowly.

'Hurry up!' snapped the woman.

The butcher now stood with his hands out of sight below the counter.

'Look,' whispered Foxe. Shaw leaned back a trifle to peer below the case.

In one of the butcher's bloody hands, empty before, a silvery meat axe was now clenched tightly, relaxed, clenched tightly, relaxed. The butcher's eyes were blue and dangerously serene above the white porcelain counter while the woman yelled into those eyes and that pink self-contained face.

'Now do you believe?' whispered Foxe. 'She really needs our help.'

They stared at the raw cube-steaks for a long time, noticing all the little dents and marks where it had been hit, ten dozen times, by a steel mallet.

The braying continued at the grocer's and the dime store,

with the two old men following at a respectful distance.

'Mrs Death-Wish,' said Mr Foxe quietly. 'It's like watching a two-year-old run out on a battlefield. Any moment, you say, she'll hit a mine; bang! Get the temperature just right, too much humidity, everyone itching, sweating, irritable. Along'll come this fine lady, whining, shrieking. And so good-bye. Well, Shaw, do we start business?'

'You mean just walk up to her?' Shaw was stunned by his own suggestion. 'Oh, but we're not really going to do this, are we? I thought it was sort of a hobby. People, habits, customs, et cetera. It's been fun. But actually mixing in — ? We've better things to do.'

'Have we?' Foxe nodded down the street to where the woman ran out in front of cars, making them stop with a great squall of brakes, horn-blowing, and cursing. 'Are we Christians? Do we let her feed herself subconsciously to the lions? Or do we convert her?'

'Convert her?'

'To love, to serenity, to a longer life. Look at her. Doesn't want to live any more. Deliberately aggravates people. One day soon, someone'll favour her, with a hammer, or strychnine. She's been going down for the third time a long while now. When you're drowning, you get nasty, grab at people, scream. Let's have lunch and lend a hand, eh? Otherwise, our victim will run on until she finds her murderer.'

Shaw stood with the sun driving him into the boiling white sidewalk, and it seemed for a moment the street tilted vertically, became a cliff down which the woman fell towards a blazing sky. At last he shook his head.

'You're right,' he said. 'I wouldn't want her on my conscience.'

The sun burnt the paint from the tenement fronts, bleached the air raw and turned the gutter-waters to vapour by mid-afternoon when the old men, numbed and evaporated, stood in the inner passageway of a house that funnelled bakery air from front to back in a searing torrent. When they spoke it was the submerged, muffled talk of men in steam rooms, preposterously tired and remote.

The front door opened. Foxe stopped a boy who carried a well-mangled loaf of bread. 'Son, we're looking for the woman who gives the door an *awful* slam when she goes out.'

'Oh, *her*?' The boy ran upstairs, calling back. 'Mrs Shrike!'

Foxe grabbed Shaw's arm. 'Lord, Lord! It can't be true!'

'I want to go home,' said Shaw.

'But there it is!' said Foxe, incredulous, tapping his cane on the room-index in the lobby. 'Mr and Mrs Albert Shrike, 331 upstairs! Husband's a longshoreman, big hulking brute, comes home dirty. Saw them out on Sunday, her jabbering, him never speaking, never looking at her. Oh, come *on*, Shaw.'

'It's no use,' said Shaw. 'You can't help people like her unless they want to be helped. That's the first law of mental health. You know it, I know it. If you get in her way, she'll trample you. Don't be a fool.'

'But who's to speak for her — and people like her? Her husband? Her friends? The grocer, the butcher? They'd sing at her wake! Will they tell her she needs a psychiatrist? Does she know it? No. Who knows it? We do. Well, then, you don't keep vital information like that from the victim, do you?'

Shaw took off his sopping hat and gazed bleakly into it. 'Once, in biology class, long ago, our teacher asked if we thought we could remove a frog's nervous system, intact, with a scalpel. Take out the whole delicate antennalike structure, with all its little pink thistles and half-invisible ganglions. Impossible, of course. The nervous system's so much a part of the frog there's no way to pull it like a hand from a green glove. You'd destroy the frog, doing it. Well, that's Mrs Shrike. There's no way to operate on a souring ganglion. Bile is in the vitreous humour of her mad little elephant eyes. You might as well try to get all the saliva out of her mouth forever. It's very sad. But I think we've gone too far already.'

'True,' said Foxe patiently, earnestly, nodding. 'But all I want to do is post a warning. Drop a little seed in her subconscious. Tell her, "You're a murderee, a victim looking for a place to happen." One tiny seed I want to plant in her head and hope it'll sprout and flower. A very faint, very poor hope that before it's too late, she'll gather her courage and go see a psychiatrist!'

'It's too hot to talk.'

'All the more reason to act! More murders are committed at ninety-two degrees Fahrenheit than any other temperature. Over one hundred, it's too hot to move. Under ninety, cool enough to survive. But right *at* ninety-two degrees lies the apex of irritability, everything is itches and hair and sweat and cooked pork. The brain becomes a rat rushing around a red-hot maze. The least thing, a word, a look, a sound, the drop of a hair and — irritable murder. *Irritable murder*, there's a pretty and terrifying phrase for you. Look at that hall thermometer, eighty-nine degrees. Crawling up towards ninety, itching up towards ninety-one, sweating towards ninety-two an hour, two hours from now. Here's the first flight of stairs. We can rest on each landing. Up we *go*!'

The two old men moved in the third-floor darkness.

'Don't check the numbers,' said Foxe. 'Let's guess which apartment is hers.'

Behind the last door a radio exploded, the ancient paint shuddered and flaked softly onto the worn carpet at their feet. The men watched the entire door jitter with vibration in its grooves.

They looked at each other and nodded grimly.

Another sound cut like an axe through the panelling; a woman, shrieking to someone across town on a telephone.

'No phone necessary. She should just open her window and yell.'

Foxe rapped.

The radio blasted out the rest of its song, the voice bellowed. Foxe rapped again, and tested the knob. To his horror the door got free of his grasp and floated swiftly inwards, leaving them like actors trapped on-stage when a curtain rises too soon.

'Oh, no!' cried Shaw.

They were buried in a flood of sound. It was like standing in the spillway of a dam and pulling the gate-lever. Instinctively, the old men raised their hands, wincing as if the sound were pure blazing sunlight that burnt their eyes.

The woman (it was indeed Mrs Shrike!) stood at a wall phone, saliva flying from her mouth at an incredible rate. She showed all of her large white teeth, chunking off her monologue, nostrils flared, a vein in her wet forehead ridged up, pumping, her free hand flexing and unflexing itself. Her eyes were clenched shut as she yelled:

'Tell that damned son-in-law of mine I won't see him, he's a lazy bum!'

Suddenly the woman snapped her eyes wide, some animal instinct having felt rather than heard or seen an intrusion. She continued yelling into the phone, meanwhile piercing her visitors with a glance forged of the coldest steel. She yelled for a full minute longer, then slammed down the receiver and said, without taking a breath: 'Well?'

The two men moved together for protection. Their lips moved.

'Speak up!' cried the woman.

'Would you mind,' said Foxe, 'turning the radio down?'

She caught the word 'radio' by lip reading. Still glaring at them out of her sunburnt face, she slapped the radio without looking at it, as one slaps a child that cries all day every day and has become an unseen pattern in life. The radio subsided.

'I'm not buyin' anything!'

She ripped a dog-eared packet of cheap cigarettes like it was a bone with meat on it, snapped one of the cigarettes in her smeared mouth and lit it, sucking greedily on the smoke, jetting it through her thin nostrils until she was a feverish dragon confronting them in a fire-clouded room. 'I got work to do. Make your pitch!'

They looked at the magazines spilled like great catches of bright-coloured fish on the linoleum floor, the unwashed coffee cup near the broken rocking chair, the tilted, greasy thumb-marked lamps, the smudged windowpanes, the dishes piled in the sink under the steadily dripping, dripping faucet, the cobwebs floating like dead skin in the ceiling corners, and over all of it the thickened smell of life lived too much, too long, with the window down.

They saw the wall thermometer.

Temperature: ninety degrees Fahrenheit.

They gave each other a half-startled look.

'I'm Mr Foxe, this is Mr Shaw. We're retired insurance salesmen. We still sell occasionally, to supplement our retirement fund. Most of the time, however, we're taking it easy and – '

'You tryin' to sell me insurance!' She cocked her head at them through the cigarette smoke.

'There's no money connected with this, no.'

'Keep talking,' she said.

'I hardly know how to begin. May we sit down?' He looked about and decided there wasn't a thing in the room he would trust himself to sit on. 'Never mind.' He saw she was about to bellow again, so went on swiftly. 'We retired after forty years

of seeing people from nursery to cemetery gate, you might
say. In that time we'd formulated certain opinions. Last year,
sitting in the park talking, we put two and two together. We
realized that many people didn't have to die so young. With
the correct investigation, a new type of Customer's Information might be provided as a sideline by insurance
companies . . . '

'I'm not sick,' said the woman.

'Oh, but you *are*!' cried Mr Foxe, and then put two fingers
to his mouth in dismay.

'Don't tell *me* what I am!' she cried.

Foxe plunged headlong. 'Let me make it clear. People die
every day, psychologically speaking. Some part of them gets
tired. And that small part tries to kill off the entire person.
'For example — ' He looked about and seized on his first
evidence with what amounted to a vast relief. 'There! That
light bulb in your bathroom, hung right over the tub on
frayed wire. Someday you'll slip, make a grab and — pfft!'

Mrs Albert J. Shrike squinted at the light bulb in the
bathroom. 'So?'

'People — ' Mr Foxe warmed to his subject, while Mr Shaw
fidgeted, his face now flushed, now dreadfully pale, edged
towards the door — 'people, like cars, need their brakes
checked; their emotional brakes, do you see? Their lights,
their batteries, their approaches and responses to life.'

Mrs Shrike snorted. 'Your two minutes are up. I haven't
learned a damned thing.'

Mr Foxe blinked, first at her, then at the sun burning
mercilessly through the dusty windowpanes. Perspiration
was running in the soft lines of his face. He chanced a look at
the wall thermometer.

'Ninety-one,' he said.

'What's eating you, pop?' asked Mrs Shrike.

'I beg your pardon.' He stared in fascination at the red-hot
line of mercury firing up the small glass vent across the room.

'Sometimes — sometimes we all make wrong turnings. Our choice of marriage partners. A wrong job. No money. Illness. Migraine headaches. Glandular deficiencies. Dozens of little prickly, irritable things. Before you know it, you're taking it out on everyone everywhere.'

She was watching his mouth as if he were talking a foreign language; she scowled, she squinted, she tilted her head, her cigarette smouldering in one plump hand.

'We run about screaming, making enemies.' Foxe swallowed and glanced away from her. 'We make people want to see us — gone — sick — dead, even. People want to hit us, knock us down, shoot us. It's all unconscious, though. You *see*?'

God, it's hot in here, he thought. If there were only one window open. Just one. Just one window open.

Mrs Shrike's eyes were widening, as if to allow in everything he said.

'Some people are not only accident-prones, which means they want to punish themselves physically, for some crime, usually a petty immorality they think they've long forgotten. But their subconscious puts them in dangerous situations, makes them jaywalk, makes them — ' He hesitated and the sweat dripped from his chin. 'Makes them ignore frayed electric cords over bathtubs — they're potential victims. It is marked on their faces, hidden like — like tattoos, you might say, on the inner rather than the outer skin. A murderer passing one of these accident-prones, these wishers-after-death, would see the invisible markings, turn, and follow them, instinctively, to the nearest alley. With luck, a potential victim might not happen to cross the tracks of a potential murderer for fifty years. Then — one afternoon — fate! These people, these death-prones, touch all the wrong nerves in passing strangers; they brush the murder in all our breasts.'

Mrs Shrike mashed her cigarette in a dirty saucer, very slowly.

Foxe shifted his cane from one trembling hand to the other. 'So it was that a year ago we decided to try to find people who needed help. These are always the people who don't even know they need help, who'd never dream of going to a psychiatrist. At first, I said, we'll make dry runs. Shaw was always against it, save as a hobby, a harmless little quiet thing between ourselves. I suppose you'd say I'm a fool. Well, we've just completed a year of dry runs. We watched two men, studied their environmental factors, their work, marriages, at a discreet distance. None of our business, you say? But each time, the men came to a bad end. One killed in a bar-room. Another pushed out a window. A woman we studied, run down by a streetcar. Coincidence? What about that old man accidentally poisoned? Didn't turn on the bathroom light one night. What was there in his mind that wouldn't let him turn the light on? What made him move in the dark and drink medicine in the dark and die in the hospital next day, protesting he wanted nothing but to live? Evidence, evidence, we have it, we have it. Two dozen cases. Coffins nailed to a good half of them in that little time. No more dry runs; it's time for action, preventative use of data. Time to work *with* people, make friends before the undertaker slips in the side door.'

Mrs Shrike stood as if he had struck her on the head, quite suddenly, with a large weight. Then just her blurred lips moved. 'And you came *here*?'

'Well — '

'You've been watching *me*?'

'We only — '

'Following *me*?'

'In order to — '

'Get out!' she said.

'We can – '

'Get out!' she said.

'If you'll only listen – '

'Oh, I *said* this would happen,' whispered Shaw, shutting his eyes.

'Dirty old men, get out!' she shouted.

'There's no money involved.'

'I'll throw you out, I'll throw you out!' she shrieked, clenching her fists, gritting her teeth. Her face coloured insanely. 'Who are you, dirty old grandmas, coming here, spying, you old cranks!' she yelled. She seized the straw hat from Mr Foxe's head; he cried out; she tore the lining from it, cursing. 'Get out, get out, get out, get out!' She hurled it to the floor. She crunched one heel through the middle. She kicked it. 'Get out, get out!'

'Oh, but you *need* us!' Foxe stared in dismay at the hat as she swore at him in a language that turned corners, blazing, that flew in the air like great searing torches. The woman knew every language and every word in every language. She spoke with fire and alcohol and smoke.

'Who do you think you are? God? God and the Holy Ghost, passing on people, snooping, prying, you old jerks, you old dirty-minded grandmas! You, you – ' She gave them further names, names that forced them towards the door in shock, recoiling. She gave them a long vile list of names without pausing for breath. Then she stopped, gasped, trembled, heaved in a great suction of air, and started a further list of ten dozen even viler names.

'See here!' said Foxe, stiffening.

Shaw was out the door, pleading with his partner to come along, it was over and done, it was as he expected, they were fools, they were everything she said they were, oh, how embarrassing!

'Old maid!' shouted the woman.

'I'll thank you to keep a civil tongue.'

'Old maid, old maid!'

Somehow this was worse than all the really vile names.

Foxe swayed, his mouth clapped open, shut, open, shut.

'Old woman!' she cried. 'Woman, woman, woman!'

He was in a blazing yellow jungle. The room was drowned in fire, it clenched upon him, the furniture seemed to shift and whirl about, the sunlight shot through the rammed-shut windows, firing the dust, which leaped up from the rug in angry sparks when a fly buzzed a crazy spiral from nowhere; her mouth, a feral red thing, licked the air with all the obscenities collected just behind it in a lifetime, and beyond her on the baked brown wallpaper the thermometer said ninety-two, and he looked again and it said ninety-two, and still the woman screamed like the wheels of a train scraping around a vast iron curve of track; fingernails down a black-board, and steel across marble. 'Old maid! Old maid! Old maid!'

Foxe drew his arm back, cane clenched in fist, very high, and struck.

'No!' cried Shaw in the doorway.

But the woman had slipped and fallen aside, gibbering, clawing the floor. Foxe stood over her with a look of positive disbelief on his face. He looked at his arm and his wrist and his hand and his fingers, each in turn, through a great invisible glaring hot wall of crystal that enclosed him. He looked at the cane as if it was an easily seen and incredible exclamation point come out of nowhere to the centre of the room. His mouth stayed open, the dust fell in silent embers, dead. He felt the blood drop from his face as if a small door had banged wide into his stomach. 'I – '

She frothed.

Scrabbling about, every part of her seemed a separate animal. Her arms and legs, her hands, her head, each was a lopped-off bit of some creature wild to return to itself, but blind to the proper way of making that return. Her mouth still gushed out her sickness with words and sounds that were not even faintly words. It had been in her a long time, a long long time. Foxe looked upon her, in a state of shock, himself. Before today, she had spat her venom out, here, there, another place. Now he had loosed the flood of a lifetime and he felt in danger of drowning here. He sensed someone pulling him by his coat. He saw the door sills pass on either side. He heard the cane fall and rattle like a thin bone far away from his hand, which seemed to have been stung by some terrible unseen wasp. And then he was out, walking mechanically, down through the burning tenement, between the scorched walls. Her voice crashed like a guillotine down the stair. 'Get out! Get out! Get *out!*'

Fading like the wail of a person dropped down an open well into darkness.

At the bottom of the last flight, near the street door, Foxe turned himself loose from this other man here, and for a long moment leaned against the wall, his eyes wet, able to do nothing but moan. His hands, while he did this, moved in the air to find the lost cane, moved on his head, touched at his moist eyelids, amazed, and fluttered away. They sat on the bottom hall step for ten minutes in silence, drawing sanity into their lungs with every shuddering breath. Finally Mr Foxe looked over at Mr Shaw, who had been staring at him in wonder and fright for the full ten minutes.

'Did you *see* what I did? Oh, oh, that was close. Close. Close.' He shook his head. 'I'm a fool. That poor, poor woman. She was right.'

'There's nothing to be done.'

'I see that now. It had to fall on me.'

'Here, wipe your face. That's better.'

'Do you think she'll tell Mr Shrike about us?'

'No, no.'

'Do you think we could — '

'Talk to *him?*'

They considered this and shook their heads. They opened the front door to a gush of furnace heat and were almost knocked down by a huge man who strode between them.

'Look where you're going!' he cried.

They turned and watched the man move ponderously, in fiery darkness, one step at a time, up into the tenement house, a creature with the ribs of a mastodon and the head of an unshorn lion, with great beefed arms, irritably hairy, painfully sunburnt. The face they had seen briefly as he shouldered past was a sweating, raw, sunblistered pork face, salt droplets under the red eyes, dripping from the chin; great smears of perspiration stained the man's armpits, colouring his tee-shirt to the waist.

They shut the tenement door gently.

'That's him,' said Mr Foxe. 'That's the husband.'

They stood in the little store across from the tenement. It was five-thirty, the sun tilting down the sky, the shadows the colour of hot summer grapes under the rare few trees and in the alleys.

'What was it, hanging out of the husband's back pocket?'

'Longshoreman's hook. Steel. Sharp, heavy-looking. Like those claws one-armed men used to wear on the end of their stumps, years ago.'

Mr Foxe did not speak.

'What's the temperature?' asked Mr Foxe, a minute later, as if he were too tired to turn his head to look.

'Store thermometer still reads ninety-two. Ninety-two right on the nose.'

Foxe sat on a packing crate, making the least motion to hold an orange soda bottle in his fingers. 'Cool off,' he said. 'Yes, I need an orange pop very much, right now.'

They sat there in the furnace, looking up at one special tenement window for a long time, waiting, waiting . . .

The Emissary

Martin knew it was autumn again, for Dog ran into the house bringing wind and frost and a smell of apples turned to cider under trees. In dark clock-springs of hair, Dog fetched goldenrod, dust of farewell-summer, acorn-husk, hair of squirrel, feather of departed robin, sawdust from fresh-cut cordwood, and leaves like charcoals shaken from a blaze of maple trees. Dog jumped. Showers of brittle fern, black-berry vine, marsh-grass sprang over the bed where Martin shouted. No doubt, no doubt of it at all, this incredible beast was October!

'Here, boy, here!'

And Dog settled to warm Martin's body with all the bonfires and subtle burnings of the season, to fill the room with soft or heavy, wet or dry odours of far-travelling. In spring, he smelled of lilac, iris, lawn-mowered grass; in summer, ice-cream-moustached, he came pungent with firecracker, Roman candle, pinwheel, baked by the sun. But autumn! Autumn!

'Dog, what's it like outside?'

And lying there, Dog told as he always told. Lying there, Martin found autumn as in the old days before sickness bleached him white on his bed. Here was his contact, his carry-all, the quick-moving part of himself he sent with a yell to run and return, circle and scent, collect and deliver the time and texture of worlds in town, country, by creek, river, lake, down-cellar, up-attic, in closet or coal-bin. Ten dozen times a day he was gifted with sunflower seed, cinder-path, milkweed, horse-chestnut, or full flame-smell of pumpkin. Through the loomings of the universe Dog shuttled; the design was hid in his pelt. Put out your hand, it was there . . .

'And where did you go this morning?'

But he knew without hearing where Dog had rattled down hills where autumn lay in cereal crispness, where children lay in funeral pyres, in rustling heaps, the leaf-buried but watchful dead, as Dog and the world blew by. Martin trembled as his fingers searched the thick fur, read the long journey. Through stubbled fields, over glitters of ravine creek, down marbled spread of cemetery yard, into woods. In the great season of spices and rare incense, now Martin ran through his emissary, around, about, and home!

The bedroom door opened.

'That dog of yours is in trouble again.'

Mother brought in a tray of fruit salad, cocoa, and toast, her blue eyes snapping.

'Mother . . . '

'Always digging places. Dug a hole in Miss Tarkin's garden this morning. She's spittin' mad. That's the fourth hole he's dug there this week.'

'Maybe he's looking for something.'

'Fiddlesticks, he's too darned curious. If he doesn't behave he'll be locked up.'

Martin looked at this woman as if she were a stranger. 'Oh, you wouldn't do that! How would I learn anything? How would I find things out if Dog didn't tell me?'

Mom's voice was quieter. 'Is that what he does — tell you things?'

'There's nothing I don't know when he goes out and around and back, *nothing* I can't find out from him!'

They both sat looking at Dog and the dry strewings of mould and seed over the quilt.

'Well, if he'll just stop digging where he shouldn't, he can run all he wants,' said Mother.

'Here, boy, here!'

And Martin snapped a tin note to the dog's collar:

MY OWNER IS MARTIN SMITH – TEN YEARS OLD –
SICK IN BED – VISITORS WELCOME.

Dog barked. Mother opened the downstairs door and let him out.

Martin sat listening.

Far off and away you could hear Dog run in the quiet autumn rain that was falling now. You could hear the barking-jingling fade, rise, fade again as he cut down alley, over lawn, to fetch back Mr Holloway and the oiled metallic smell of the delicate snowflake-interiored watches he repaired in his home shop. Or maybe he would bring Mr Jacobs, the grocer, whose clothes were rich with lettuce, celery, tomatoes, and the secret tinned and hidden smell of the red demons stamped on cans of devilled ham. Mr Jacobs and his unseen pink-meat devils waved often from the yard below. Or Dog brought Mr Jackson, Mrs Gillespie, Mr Smith, Mrs Holmes, *any* friend or near-friend, encountered, cornered, begged, worried, and at last shepherded home for lunch, or tea-and-biscuits.

Now, listening, Martin heard Dog below, with footsteps moving in a light rain behind him. The downstairs bell rang, Mom opened the door, light voices murmured. Martin sat forward, face shining. The stair treads creaked. A young woman's voice laughed quietly. Miss Haight, of course, his teacher from school!

The bedroom door sprang open.

Martin had company.

Morning, afternoon, evening, dawn and dusk, sun and moon circled with Dog, who faithfully reported temperatures of turf and air, colour of earth and tree, consistency of mist or rain, but — most important of all — brought back again and again and again — Miss Haight.

On Saturday, Sunday and Monday she baked Martin orange-iced cupcakes, brought him library books about dinosaurs and cave men. On Tuesday, Wednesday and Thursday somehow he beat her at dominoes, somehow she lost at checkers, and soon, she cried, he'd defeat her handsomely at chess. On Friday, Saturday and Sunday they talked and never stopped talking, and she was so young and laughing and handsome and her hair was a soft, shining brown like the season outside the window, and she walked clear, clean and quick, a heartbeat warm in the bitter afternoon when he heard it. Above all, she had the secret of signs, and could read and interpret Dog and the symbols she searched out and plucked forth from his coat with her miraculous fingers. Eyes shut, softly laughing, in a gypsy's voice, she divined the world from the treasures in her hands.

And on Monday afternoon, Miss Haight was dead.

Martin sat up in bed, slowly.

'Dead?' he whispered.

Dead, said his mother, yes, dead, killed in an auto accident a mile out of town. Dead, yes dead, which meant cold to Martin, which meant silence and whiteness and winter come long before its time. Dead, silent, cold, white. The thoughts circled round, blew down, and settled in whispers.

Martin held Dog, thinking; turned to the wall. The lady with the autumn-coloured hair. The lady with the laughter that was very gentle and never made fun and the eyes that watched your mouth to see everything you ever said. The-other-half-of-autumn-lady, who told what was left untold by Dog, about the world. The heartbeat at the still centre of grey afternoon. The heartbeat fading . . .

'Mom? What do they do in the graveyard, Mom, under the ground? Just lay there?'

'*Lie* there.'

'Lie there? Is that *all* they do? It doesn't sound like much fun.'

'For goodness sake, it's not made out to be fun.'

'Why don't they jump up and run around once in a while if they get tired lying there? God's pretty silly — '

'Martin!'

'Well, you'd think He'd treat people better than to tell them to lie still for keeps. That's impossible. Nobody can do it! I tried once. Dog tries. I tell him, "Dead Dog!" He plays dead awhile, then gets sick and tired and wags his tail or opens one eye and looks at me, bored. Boy, I bet sometimes those graveyard people do the same, huh, Dog?'

Dog barked.

'Be still with that kind of talk!' said Mother.

Martin looked off into space.

'Bet that's exactly what they do,' he said.

Autumn burnt the trees bare and ran Dog still farther around, fording creek, prowling graveyard as was his custom, and back in the dusk to fire off volleys of barking that shook windows wherever he turned.

In the late last days of October, Dog began to act as if the wind had changed and blew from a strange country. He stood quivering on the porch below. He whined, his eyes fixed at the empty land beyond town. He brought no visitors for Martin. He stood for hours each day, as if leashed, trembling, then shot away straight, as if someone had called. Each night he returned later, with no one following. Each night, Martin sank deeper and deeper in his pillow.

'Well, people are busy,' said Mother. 'They haven't time to notice the tag Dog carries. Or they mean to come visit, but forget.'

But there was more to it than that. There was the fevered

shining in Dog's eyes, and his whimpering tic late at night, in some private dream. His shivering in the dark, under the bed. The way he sometimes stood half the night, looking at Martin as if some great and impossible secret was his and he knew no way to tell it save by savagely thumping his tail, or tunring in endless circles, never to lie down, spinning and spinning again.

On October thirtieth, Dog ran out and didn't come back at all, even when after supper Martin heard his parents call and call. The hour grew late, the streets and sidewalks stood empty, the air moved cold about the house and there was nothing, nothing.

Long after midnight, Martin lay watching the world beyond the cool, clear glass windows. Now there was not even autumn, for there was no Dog to fetch it in. There would be no winter, for who could bring the snow to melt in your hands? Father? Mother? No, not the same. They couldn't play the game with its special secrets and rules, its sounds and pantomimes. No more seasons. No more time. The go-between, the emissary, was lost to the wild throng-ings of civilization, poisoned, stolen, hit by a car, left somewhere in a culvert . . .

Sobbing, Martin turned his face to his pillow. The world was a picture under glass, untouchable. The world was dead.

Martin twisted in bed and in three days the last Hallowe'en pumpkins were rotting in trash cans, papier-mâché skulls and witches were burnt on bonfires, and ghosts were stacked on shelves with other linens until next year.

To Martin, Hallowe'en had been nothing more than one evening when tin horns cried off in the cold autumn stars, children blew like goblin leaves along the flinty walks, flinging their heads, or cabbages, at porches, soap-writing names or similar magic symbols on icy windows. All of it as distant, unfathomable, and nightmarish as a puppet show seen from so many miles away that there is no sound or meaning.

For three days in November, Martin watched alternate light and shadow sift across his ceiling. The fire-pageant was over forever; autumn lay in cold ashes. Martin sank deeper, yet deeper in white marble layers of bed, motionless, listening always listening . . .

Friday evening, his parents kissed him goodnight and walked out of the house into the hushed cathedral weather towards a motion-picture show. Miss Tarkin from next door stayed on in the parlour below until Martin called down he was sleepy, then took her knitting off home.

In silence, Martin lay following the great move of stars down a clear and moonlit sky, remembering nights such as this when he'd spanned the town with Dog ahead, behind, around about, tracking the green-plush ravine, lapping slumbrous streams gone milky with the fullness of the moon, leaping cemetery tombstones while whispering the marble names; on, quickly on, through shaved meadows where the only motion was the off-on quivering of stars, to streets where shadows would not stand aside for you but crowded all the sidewalks for mile on mile. Run now run! chasing, being chased by bitter smoke, fog, mist, wind, ghost of mind, fright of memory; home, safe, sound, snug-warm, asleep . . .

Nine o'clock.

Chime. The drowsy clock in the deep stairwell below. Chime.

Dog, come home, and run the world with you. Dog, bring a thistle with frost on it, or bring nothing else but the wind. Dog, where *are* you? Oh, listen, now, I'll call.

Martin held his breath.

Way off somewhere — a sound.

Martin rose up, trembling.

There, again — the sound.

So small a sound, like a sharp needle-point brushing the sky long miles and many miles away.

The dreamy echo of a dog — barking.

The sound of a dog crossing fields and farms, dirt roads and rabbit paths, running, running, letting out great barks of steam, cracking the night. The sound of a circling dog which came and went, lifted and faded, opened up, shut in, moved forward, went back, as if the animal were kept by someone on a fantastically long chain. As if the dog were running and someone whistled under the chestnut trees, in mould-shadow, tar-shadow, moon-shadow, walking, and the dog circled back and sprang out again towards home.

Dog! Martin thought. Oh Dog, come home, boy! Listen, oh listen, where you *been*? Come on, boy, make tracks!

Five, ten, fifteen minutes; near, very near, the bark, the sound. Martin cried out, thrust his feet from the bed, leaned to the window. Dog! Listen, boy! Dog! Dog! He said it over and over. Dog! Dog! Wicked Dog, run off and gone all these days! Bad Dog, good Dog, home, boy, hurry, and bring what you can!

Near now, near, up the street, barking, to knock clap-board housefronts with sound, whirl iron cocks on rooftops in the moon, firing off volleys — Dog! now at the door below . . .

Martin shivered.

Should he run — let Dog in, or wait for Mom and Dad? Wait? Oh, God, wait? But what if Dog ran off again? No, he'd go down, snatch the door wide, yell, grab Dog in, and run upstairs so fast, laughing, crying, holding tight, that . . .

Dog stopped barking.

Hey! Martin almost broke the window, jerking to it.

Silence. As if someone had told Dog to hush now, hush, hush.

A full minute passed. Martin clenched his fists.

Below, a faint whimpering.

Then, slowly, the downstairs front door opened. Someone was kind enough to have opened the door for Dog. Of course! Dog had brought Mr Jacobs or Mr Gillespie or Miss Tarkin, or . . .

The downstairs door shut.

Dog raced upstairs, whining, flung himself on the bed.

'Dog, Dog, where've you *been*, what've you *done*! Dog, Dog!'

And he crushed Dog hard and long to himself, weeping. Dog, Dog. He laughed and shouted. Dog! But after a moment he stopped laughing and crying, suddenly.

He pulled back away. He held the animal and looked at him, eyes widening.

The odour coming from Dog was different.

It was a smell of strange earth. It was a smell of night within night, the smell of digging down deep in shadow through earth that had lain cheek by jowl with things that were long hidden and decayed. A stinking and rancid soil fell away in clods of dissolution from Dog's muzzle and paws. He had dug deep. He had dug very deep indeed. That *was* it, wasn't it? wasn't it? *wasn't it*!

What kind of message was this from Dog? What could such a message mean? The stench — the ripe and awful cemetery earth.

Dog was a bad dog, digging where he shouldn't. Dog was a good dog, always making friends. Dog loved people. Dog brought them home.

And now, moving up the dark hall stairs, at intervals, came the sound of feet, one foot dragged after the other, painfully, slowly, slowly, slowly.

Dog shivered. A rain of strange night earth fell seething on the bed.

Dog turned.

The bedroom door whispered in.
Martin had company.

The Jar

It was one of those things they keep in a jar in the tent of a sideshow on the outskirts of a little, drowsy town. One of those pale things drifting in alcohol plasma, forever dreaming and circling, with its peeled, dead eyes staring out at you and never seeing you. It went with the noiselessness of late night, and only the crickets chirping, the frogs sobbing off in the moist swampland. One of those things in a big jar that makes your stomach jump as it does when you see a preserved arm in a laboratory vat.

Charlie stared back at it for a long time.

A long time, his big, raw hands, hairy on the roofs of them, clenching the rope that kept back curious people. He had paid his dime and now he stared.

It was getting late. The merry-go-round drowsed down to a lazy mechanical tinkle. Tent-peggers back of a canvas smoked and cursed over a poker game. Lights switched out, putting a summer gloom over the carnival. People streamed homeward in cliques and queues. Somewhere, a radio flared up, then cut, leaving the Louisiana sky wide and silent with stars.

There was nothing in the world for Charlie but that pale thing sealed in its universe of serum. Charlie's loose mouth hung open in a pink weal, teeth showing; his eyes were puzzled, admiring, wondering.

Someone walked in the shadows behind him, small beside Charlie's gaunt tallness. 'Oh,' said the shadow, coming into the light-bulb glare. 'You still here, bud?'

'Yeah,' said Charlie, like a man in his sleep.

The carny-boss appreciated Charlie's curiosity. He

nodded at his old acquaintance in the jar. 'Everybody likes it; in a peculiar kinda way, I mean.'

Charlie rubbed his long jawbone. 'You – uh – ever consider sellin' it?'

The carny-boss's eyes dilated, then closed. He snorted. 'Naw. It brings customers. They like seeing stuff like that. Sure.'

Charlie made a disappointed, 'Oh.'

'Well,' considered the carny-boss, 'if a guy had money, maybe – '

'How much money?'

'If a guy had – ' The carny-boss estimated, counting fingers, watching Charlie as he tacked it out one finger after another. 'If a guy had three, four, say, maybe seven or eight – '

Charlie nodded with each motion, expectantly. Seeing this, the carny-boss raised his total, ' – maybe ten dollars or maybe fifteen – '

Charlie scowled, worried. The carny-boss retreated. 'Say a guy has *twelve* dollars – '

Charlie grinned. 'Why he could buy that thing in that jar,' concluded the carny-boss.

'Funny thing,' said Charlie. 'I got just twelve bucks in my denims. And I been reckoning how looked-up-to I'd be back down at Wilder's Hollow if I brung home something like this to set on my shelf over the table. Folks would sure look up to me then, I bet.'

'*Well*, now, listen here – ' said the carny-boss.

The sale was completed with the jar put on the back seat of Charlie's wagon. The horse skittered his hoofs when he saw the jar, and whinnied.

The carny-boss glanced up with an expression of, almost, relief. 'I was tired of seeing that damn thing around, anyway. Don't thank me. Lately I been thinking things about it, funny things – but, hell, I'm a big-mouthed so-and-so. S'long, farmer!'

Charlie drove off. The naked blue light bulbs withdrew like dying stars, the open, dark country night of Louisiana swept in around wagon and horse. There was just Charlie, the horse timing his grey hoofs, and the crickets.

And the jar behind the high seat.

It sloshed back and forth, back and forth. Sloshed wet. And the cold grey thing drowsily slumped against the glass, looking out, looking out, but seeing nothing, nothing.

Charlie leaned back to pet the lid. Smelling of strange liquor his hand returned, changed and cold and trembling, excited. *Yes, sir!* he thought to himself, *Yes, sir!*

Slosh, slosh, slosh . . .

In the Hollow, numerous grass-green and blood-red lanterns tossed dusty light over men huddled, murmuring, spitting, sitting on General Store property.

They knew the creak-bumble of Charlie's wagon and did not shift their raw, drab-haired skulls as he rocked to a halt. Their cigars were glowworms, their voices were frog mutterings on summer nights.

Charlie leaned down eagerly. 'Hi, Clem! Hi, Milt!'

''Lo, Charlie. 'Lo, Charlie,' they murmured. The political conflict continued. Charlie cut it down the seam:

'I got somethin' here. I got somethin' you might wanna see!'

Tom Carmody's eyes glinted, green in the lamplight, from the General Store porch. It seemed to Charlie that Tom Carmody was forever installed under porches in shadow, or under trees in shadow, or if in a room, then in the farthest niche shining his eyes out at you from the dark. You never knew what his face was doing, and his eyes were always funning you. And every time they looked at you they laughed a different way.

'You ain't got nothin' we wants to see, baby-doll.'

Charlie made a fist and looked at it. 'Somethin' in a jar,' he went on. 'Looks kine a like a brain, kine a like a pickled jellyfish, kine a like — well, come see yourself!'

Someone snicked a cigar into a fall of pink ash and ambled over to look. Charlie grandly elevated the jar lid, and in the uncertain lantern light the man's face changed. 'Hey, now, what in hell *is* this — ?'

It was the first thaw of the evening. Others shifted lazily upright, leaned forward; gravity pulled them into walking. They made no effort, except to put one shoe before the other to keep from collapsing upon their unusual faces. They circled the jar and contents. And Charlie, for the first time in his life, seized on some hidden strategy and crashed the glass lid shut.

'You want to see more, drop aroun' my house! It'll be there,' he declared, generously.

Tom Carmody spat from out his porch eyrie. 'Ha!'

'Lemme see that again!' cried Gramps Medknowe. 'Is it a octopus?'

Charlie flapped the reins; the horse stumbled into action.

'Come on aroun'! You're welcome!'

'What'll your wife say?'

'She'll kick the tar off'n our heels!'

But Charlie and wagon were gone over the hill. The men stood, all of them, chewing their tongues, squinting up the road in the dark. Tom Carmody swore softly from the porch . . .

Charlie climbed the steps of his shack and carried the jar to its throne in the living room, thinking that from now on this lean-to would be a palace, with an 'emperor' — that was the word! 'emperor' — all cold and white and quiet drifting in his private pool, raised, elevated upon a shelf over a ramshackle table.

The jar, as he watched, burnt off the cold mist that hung over this place on the rim of the swamp.

'What you got there?'

Thedy's thin soprano turned him from his awe. She stood in the bedroom door glaring out, her thin body clothed in faded blue gingham, her hair drawn to a drab knot behind red ears. Her eyes were faded like the gingham. 'Well,' she repeated. 'What is it?'

'What's it look like to you, Thedy?'

She took a thin step forward, making a slow, indolent pendulum of hips, her eyes intent upon the jar, her lips drawn back to show feline milk teeth.

The dead pale thing hung in its serum.

Thedy snapped a dull-blue glance at Charlie, then back to the jar, once more at Charlie, once more to the jar, then she whirled quickly:

'It — it looks — looks just like *you*, Charlie!' she cried.

The bedroom door slammed.

The reverberation did not disturb the jar's contents. But Charlie stood there, longing after his wife, heart pounding frantically. Much later, when his heart slowed, he talked to the thing in the jar.

'I work the bottom land to the butt-bone every year, and she grabs the money and runs off down home visitin' her folks nine weeks at a stretch. I can't keep hold of her. Her and the men from the store, they make fun of me. I can't help it if I don't know a way to hold on to her! Damn, but I *try*!'

Philosophically, the contents of the jar gave no advice.

'Charlie?'

Someone stood in the front-yard door.

Charlie turned, startled, then broke out in a grin.

It was some of the men from the General Store.

'Uh — Charlie — we — we thought — well — we came up to have a look at that — stuff — you got in that there jar — '

July passed warm and it was August.

For the first time in years, Charlie was happy as tall corn

growing after a drought. It was gratifying of an evening to hear boots shushing through the tall grass, the sound of men spitting into the ditch prior to setting foot on the porch, the sound of heavy bodies creaking the boards, and the groan of the house as yet another shoulder leaned against its frame door and another voice said, as a hairy wrist wiped a mouth clean:

'Kin I come in?'

With elaborate casualness, Charlie'd invite the arrivals in. There'd be chairs, soapboxes for all, or at least carpets to squat on. And by the time crickets were itching their legs into a summertime humming and frogs were throat-swollen like ladies with goitres shouting in the great night, the room would be full to bursting with people from all the bottom lands.

At first nobody would say anything. The first half-hour of such an evening, while people came in and got settled, was spent in carefully rolling cigarettes. Putting tobacco neatly into the rut of brown paper, loading it, tamping it, as they loaded and tamped and rolled their thoughts and fears and amazement for the evening. It gave them time to think. You could see their brains working behind their eyes as they fingered the cigarettes into smoking order.

It was kind of a rude church gathering. They sat, squatted, leaned on plaster walls, and one by one, with reverent awe, they stared at the jar upon its shelf.

They wouldn't stare sudden-like. No, they kind of did it slow, casual, as if they were glancing around the room — letting their eyes fumble over just *any* old object that happened into their consciousness.

And — just by accident, of course — the focus of their wandering eyes would occur always at the same place. After a while all eyes in the room would be fastened to it, like pins stuck in some incredible pincushion. And the only sound would be someone sucking a corncob. Or the children's barefooted scurry on the porch planks outside. Maybe some woman's voice would come, 'You kids git away, now! Git!' And with a giggle like soft, quick water, the bare feet would rush off to scare the bullfrogs.

Charlie would be up front, naturally, on his rocking chair, a plaid pillow under his lean rump, rocking slow, enjoying the fame and looked-up-to-ness that came with keeping the jar.

Thedy, she'd be seen way back of the room with the womenfolk in a bunch, all grey and quiet, abiding their men.

Thedy looked like she was ripe for jealous screaming. But she said nothing, just watched men tramp into her living room and sit at the feet of Charlie, staring at this here Holy Grail-like thing, and her lips were set cold and hard and she spoke not a civil word to anybody.

After a period of proper silence, someone, maybe old Gramps Medknowe from Crick Road, would clear the phlegm from a deep cave somewhere inside himself, lean forward, blinking, wet his lips, maybe, and there'd be a curious tremble in his calloused fingers.

This would cue everyone to get ready for the talking to come. Ears were primed. People settled like sows in the warm mud after a rain.

Gramps looked a long while, measured his lips with a lizard tongue, then settled back and said, like always, in a high, thin, old-man's tenor:

'Wonder what it is? Wonder if it's a he or a she or just a plain old *it*? Sometimes I wake up nights, twist on my corn-mattin', think about that jar settin' here in the long dark. Think about it hangin' in liquid, peaceful and pale like an animal oyster. Sometimes I wake Maw and we both think on it . . . '

While talking, Gramps moved his fingers in a quavering pantomime. Everybody watched his thick thumb weave, and the other heavy-nailed fingers undulate.

' . . . We both lay there, thinkin'. And we shivers. Maybe a hot night, trees sweatin', mosquitoes too hot to fly, but we shivers jest the same, and turn over, tryin' to sleep . . . '

Gramps lapsed back into silence, as if his speech was enough from him, let some other voice talk the wonder, awe, and strangeness.

Juke Marmer, from Willow Sump, wiped sweat off his palms on the round of his knees and softly said:

'I remember when I was a runnel-nosed kid. We had a cat who was all the time makin' kittens. Lordamighty, she'd a litter any time she jumped around and skipped a fence — ' Juke spoke in a kind of holy softness, benevolent. 'Well, we give the kittens away, but when this one particular litter busted out, everybody within walkin' distance had one-two our cats by gift, already.

'So Ma busied on the back porch with a big two-gallon glass jar, fillin' it to the top with water. Ma said, "Juke, you drown them kittens!" I 'member I stood there; the kittens mewed, runnin' 'round, blind, small, helpless, and funny — just beginnin' to get their eyes open. I looked at Ma, I said, "Not *me*, Ma! *You* do it!" But Ma turned pale and said it had to be done and I was the only one handy. And she went off to stir gravy and fix chicken. I — I picked up one — kitten. I held it. It was warm. It made a mewin' sound, I felt like runnin' away, not ever comin' back.'

Juke nodded his head now, eyes bright, young, seeing into the past, making it new, shaping it with words, smoothing it with his tongue.

'I dropped the kitten in the water. The kitten closed his eyes, opened his mouth, tryin' for air. I 'member how the little white fangs showed, the pink tongue came out, and bubbles with it, in a line to the top of the water!

'I know to this day the way that kitten floated after it was all over, driftin' aroun', slow and not worryin', lookin' out at me, not condemnin' me for what I done. But not likin' me, neither. Ahhhh . . . '

Hearts jumped quick. Eyes swivelled from Juke to the shelved jar, back down, up again apprehensively.

A pause.

Jahdoo, the black man from Heron Swamp, tossed his ivory eyeballs, like a dusky juggler, in his head. His dark knuckles knotted and flexed – grasshoppers alive.

'You know what that is? You know, you *know*? I tells you. That be the centre of Life, sure 'nuff! Lord believe me, it so!'

Swaying in a tree-like rhythm, Jahdoo was blown by a swamp wind no one could see, hear or feel, save himself. His eyeballs went around again, as if cut free to wander. His voice needled a dark thread pattern, picking up each person by the lobes of their ears and sewing them into one unbreathing design:

'From that, lyin' back in the Middibamboo Sump, all sort o'thing crawl. It put out hand, it put out feet, it put out tongue an' horn an' it grow. Little bitty amoeba, perhap. Then a frog with a bulge-throat fit ta bust! Yah!' He cracked knuckles. 'It slobber on up to its gummy joints and it – it *am human*! That am the centre of creation! That am Middibamboo Mamma, from which we all come ten thousand year ago. Believe it!'

'Ten thousand year ago!' whispered Granny Carnation.

'It am old! Looky it! It donn worra no more. It know betta. It hang like pork chop in fryin' fat. It got eye to see with, but it donn blink 'em, they donn look fretted, does they? No, man! It know betta. It know that we done come *from* it, and we is goin' back to it.'

'What colour eyes it got?'

'Grey.'

'Naw, *green*!'

'What colour hair? Brown?'

'Black!'

'Red!'

'No, *grey*!'

Then Charlie would give his drawling opinion. Some nights he'd say the same thing, some nights not. It didn't matter. When you said the same thing night after night in the deep summer, it always sounded different. The crickets changed it. The frogs changed it. The thing in the jar changed it. Charlie said:

'What if an old man went back into the swamp, or maybe a young kid, and wandered aroun' for years and years lost in all that drippin', on the trails and gullies, in them old wet ravines in the nights, skin a-turnin' pale, and makin' cold and shrivellin' up. Bein' away from the sun he'd keep witherin' away up and up and finally sink into a muck-hole and lay in a kind of — scum — like the maggot 'skeeters sleepin' in sump-water. Why, why — for all we can tell, this might be someone we *know*! Someone we passed words with once on a time. For all we know — '

A hissing from among the womenfolk back in the shadow. One woman standing, eyes shining black, fumbled for words. Her name was Mrs Tridden, and she murmured:

'Lots of little kids run stark naked to the swamp ever' year. They runs around and never comes back. I almost got lost maself. I — I lost my little boy, Foley, that way. You — you *don't suppose*!!!'

Breath was snatched through nostrils, constricted, tightened. Mouths turned down at corners, bent by hard, clinching muscle. Heads turned on celery-stalk necks, and eyes read her horror and hope. It was in Mrs Tridden's body, wire-taut, holding to the wall back of her with straight fingers stiff.

'My baby,' she whispered. She breathed it out. 'My baby. My Foley. Foley! Foley, is that you? Foley! Foley, tell me, baby, is that YOU!'

Everybody held their breath, turning to see the jar.

The thing in the jar said nothing. It just stared blind-white out upon the multitude. And deep in rawboned bodies a secret fear-juice ran like a spring thaw, and their resolute calmness and belief and easy humbleness was gnawed and eaten by that juice and melted away in a torrent! Someone screamed.

'It moved!'

'No, no, it didn' move. Just your eyes playin' tricks!'

'Hones' ta God!' cried Juke. 'I saw it shift slow like a dead kitten!'

'Hush up, now. It's been dead a long, long time. Maybe since before you was born!'

'He made a sign!' screamed Mrs Tridden. 'That's my Foley! My baby you got there! Three-year-old he was! My baby lost and gone in the swamp!'

The sobbing broke from her.

'Now, Mrs Tridden. There now. Set yourself down, stop shakin'. Ain't no more your child'n mine. There, there.'

One of the womenfolk held her and faded out the sobbing into jerked breathing and a fluttering of her lips in butterfly quickness as the breath stroked over them, afraid.

When all was quiet again, Granny Carnation, with a withered pink flower in her shoulder-length grey hair, sucked the pipe in her trap mouth and talked around it, shaking her head to make the hair dance in the light:

'All this talkin' and shovin' words. Like as not we'll never find out, never know what it is. Like as not if we found out we wouldn't *want* to know. It's like magic tricks magicians do at shows. Once you find the fake, ain't no more fun'n the innards of a jackbob. We come collectin' around here every ten nights or so, talkin', social-like, with somethin', always somethin', to talk about. Stands to reason if we spied out what the damn thing is there'd be nothin' to chew about, so there!'

'Well, damn it to hell!' rumbled a bull voice. 'I don't think it's nothin'!'

Tom Carmody.

Tom Carmody standing, as always, in shadow. Out on the porch, just his eyes staring in, his lips laughing at you dimly, mocking. His laughter got inside Charlie like a hornet sting. Thedy had put him up to it. Thedy was trying to kill Charlie's new life, she was!

'Nothin',' repeated Carmody, harshly, 'in that jar but a bunch of old jellyfish from Sea Cove, a-rottin' and stinkin' fit to whelp!'

'You mightn't be jealous, Cousin Carmody?' asked Charlie, slow.

'Haw!' snorted Carmody. 'I just come aroun' ta watch you dumb fools jaw about nuthin'. You notice I never set foot inside or took part. I'm goin' home right now. Anybody wanna come along with me?'

He got no offer of company. He laughed again, as if this were a bigger joke, how so many people could be so far gone, and Thedy was raking her palms with her fingernails away back in a corner of the room. Charlie saw her mouth twitch and was cold and could not speak.

Carmody, still laughing, rapped off the porch with his high-heeled boots and the sound of crickets took him away.

Granny Carnation gummed her pipe. 'Like I was sayin' before the storm: that thing on the shelf, why couldn't it be sort of — all things? Lots of things. All kinds of life — death — I don't know. Mix rain and sun and muck and jelly, all that together. Grass and snakes and children and mist and all the nights and days in the dead canebrake. Why's it have to be *one* thing? Maybe it's *lots*.'

And the talking ran soft for another hour, and Thedy slipped away into the night on the track of Tom Carmody, and Charlie began to sweat. They were up to something, those two. They were planning something. Charlie sweated warm all the rest of the evening . . .

The meeting broke up late, and Charlie bedded down with mixed emotions. The meeting had gone off well, but what about Thedy and Tom?

Very late, with certain star coveys shuttled down the sky marking the time as after midnight, Charlie heard the slushing of the tall grass parted by her penduluming hips. Her heels tacked soft across the porch, into the house, into the bedroom.

She lay soundlessly in bed, cat eyes staring at him. He couldn't see them, but he could feel them staring.

'Charlie?'

He waited.

Then he said, 'I'm awake.'

Then she waited.

'Charlie?'

'What?'

'Bet you don't know where I been; bet you don't know where I been.' It was a faint, derisive singsong in the night.

He waited.

She waited again. She couldn't bear waiting, long, though, and continued:

'I been to the carnival over in Cape City. Tom Carmody drove me. We — we talked to the carny-boss, Charlie, we did, we did, we *sure* did!' And she sort of giggled to herself, secretly.

Charlie was ice-cold. He stirred upright on an elbow.

She said, 'We found out what it is in your jar, Charlie — ' insinuatingly.

Charlie flumped over, hands to ears. 'I dont wanna hear!'

'Oh, but you gotta hear, Charlie. It's a good joke. Oh, it's rare, Charlie,' she hissed.

'Go away,' he said.

'Unh-unh! No, no, sir, Charlie. Why, no, Charlie —

honey. Not until I tell!'

'Git!' he said.

'Let me tell! We talked to that carny-boss, and he — he liked to die laughin'. He said he sold that jar and what was in it to some, some — hick — for twelve bucks. And it ain't worth more'n two bucks at most!'

Laughter bloomed in the dark, right out of her mouth, an awful kind of laughter.

She finished it, quick:

'It's just junk, Charlie! Rubber, papier-mâché, silk, cotton, boric acid! That's all! Got a metal frame inside! That's all it is, Charlie. That's all!' she shrilled.

'No, no!'

He sat up swiftly, ripping sheets apart in big fingers, roaring.

'I don't wanna hear! Don't wanna hear!' he bellowed over and over.

She said, 'Wait'll everyone hears how fake it is! Won't they laugh! Won't they flap their lungs!'

He caught her wrists. 'You ain't gonna tell them?'

'Wouldn't wan me known as a liar, would you, Charlie?'

He flung her off and away.

'Whyncha leave me alone? You dirty! Dirty jealous mean of ever'thing I do. I took shine off your nose when I brung the jar home. You didn' sleep right 'til you ruined things!'

She laughed. 'Then I won't tell anybody,' she said.

He stared at her. 'You spoiled *my* fun. That's all that counted. It don't matter if you tell the rest. *I* know. And I'll never have no more fun. You and that Tom Carmody. I wish I could stop him laughin'. He's been laughin' for years at me! Well, you just go tell the rest, the other people, now — might as well have your fun — !'

He strode angrily, grabbed the jar so it sloshed, and would have flung it on the floor, but he stopped trembling, and let it down softly on the spindly table. He leaned over it, sobbing.

If he lost this, the world was gone. And he was losing Thedy, too. Every month that passed she danced further away, sneering at him, funning him. For too many years her hips had been the pendulum by which he reckoned the time of his living. But other men, Tom Carmody, for one, were reckoning time from the same source.

Thedy stood waiting for him to smash the jar. Instead, he petted and stroked and gradually quieted himself over it. He thought of the long, good evenings in the past month, those rich evenings of friends and talk, moving about the room. That, at least, was good, if nothing else.

He turned slowly to Thedy. She was lost forever to him.

'Thedy, you didn't go to the carnival.'

'Yes, I did.'

'You're lyin',' he said, quietly.

'No, I'm not!'

'This — this jar *has* to have somethin' in it. Somethin' besides the junk you say. Too many people believe there's somethin' in it, Thedy. You can't change that. The carny-boss, if you talked with him, he lied.' Charlie took a deep breath and then said, 'Come here, Thedy.'

'What you want?' she asked, sullenly.

'Come over here.'

He took a step towards her. 'Come here.'

'Keep away from me, Charlie.'

'Just want to show you somethin', Thedy.' His voice was soft, low, and insistent. 'Here, kittie. Here, kittie, kittie, kittie — *HERE KITTIE!*'

It was another night, about a week later. Gramps Medknowe and Granny Carnation came, followed by young Juke and Mrs Tridden and Jahdoo, the black man. Followed by all the others, young and old, sweet and sour, creaking into chairs, each with his or her thought, hope, fear, and wonder in mind. Each not looking at the shrine, but saying hello softly to Charlie.

They waited for the others to gather. From the shine of their eyes one could see that each saw something different in the jar, something of the life and the pale life after life, and the life in death and the death in life, each with his story, his cue, his lines, familiar, old but new.

Charlie sat alone.

'Hello, Charlie.' Somebody peered into the empty bedroom. 'Your wife gone off again to visit her folks?'

'Yeah, she run for Tennessee. Be back in a couple weeks. She's the darndest one for runnin'. You know Thedy.'

'Great one for jumpin' around, that woman.'

Soft voices talking, getting settled, and then, quite suddenly, walking on the dark porch and shining his eyes in at the people — Tom Carmody.

Tom Carmody standing outside the door, knees sagging and trembling, arms hanging and shaking at his side, staring into the room. Tom Carmody not daring to enter. Tom Carmody with his mouth open, but not smiling. His lips wet and slack, not smiling. His face pale as chalk, as if it had been sick for a long time.

Gramps looked up at the jar, cleared his throat and said, 'Why I never noticed so definite before. It's got *blue* eyes.'

'It always had blue eyes,' said Granny Carnation.

'No,' whined Gramps. 'No, it didn't. They was brown last time we was here,' He blinked upwards. 'And another thing — it's got brown hair. Didn't have brown hair *before*!'

'Yes, yes, it did,' sighed Mrs Tridden.

'No, it didn't!'

'Yes, it did!'

Tom Carmody, shivering in the summer night, staring in at the jar. Charlie, glancing up at it, rolling a cigarette, casually, all peace and calm, very certain of his life and thoughts. Tom Carmody, alone, seeing things about the jar he never saw before. *Everybody* seeing what he wanted to see; all thoughts running in a fall of quick rain:

My baby. My little baby, thought Mrs Tridden.

A brain! thought Gramps.

The black man jigged his fingers. Middibamboo Mama!

A fisherman pursed his lips. Jellyfish!

Kitten. Here kittie, kittie, kittie! The thoughts drowned clawing in Juke's eyes. Kitten!

Everything and anything! shrilled Granny's weazened thought. The night, the swamp, death, the pale things, the wet things from the sea!

Silence. And then Gramps whispered, 'I wonder. Wonder if it's a he — or a she — or just a plain old *it*?'

Charlie glanced up, satisfied, tamping his cigarette, shaping it to his mouth. Then he looked at Tom Carmody, who would never smile again, in the door. 'I reckon we'll never know. Yeah, I reckon we won't.' Charlie shook his head slowly and settled down with his guests, looking, looking.

It was just one of those things they keep in a jar in the tent of a sideshow on the outskirts of a little, drowsy town. One of those pale things drifting in alcohol plasma, forever dreaming and circling, with its peeled dead eyes staring out at you and never seeing you . . .

The Small Assassin

Just when the idea occurred to her that she was being murdered she could not tell. There had been little subtle signs, little suspicions for the past month; things as deep as sea tides in her, looking at a perfectly calm stretch of tropic water, wanting to bathe in it and finding, just as the tide takes your body, that monsters dwell just under the surface, things unseen, bloated, many-armed, sharp-finned, malignant and inescapable.

A room floated around her in an effluvium of hysteria. Sharp instruments hovered and there were voices, and people in sterile white masks.

My name, she thought, what is it?

Alice Leiber. It came to her. David Leiber's wife. But it gave her no comfort. She was alone with these silent, whispering white people and there was great pain and nausea and death-fear in her.

I am being murdered before their eyes. These doctors, these nurses don't realize what hidden thing has happened to me. David doesn't know. Nobody knows except me and — the killer, the little murderer, the small assassin.

I am dying, and I can't tell them now. They'd laugh and call me one in delirium. They'll see the murderer and hold him and never think him responsible for my death. But here I am, in front of God and man, dying, no one to believe my story, everyone to doubt me, comfort me with lies, bury me in ignorance, mourn me and salvage my destroyer.

Where is David? she wondered. In the waiting room, smoking one cigarette after another, listening to the long tickings of the very slow clock?

Sweat exploded from all of her body at once, and with it an angonized cry. Now. Now! Try and kill me, she screamed. Try, try, but I won't die! I won't!

There was a hollowness. A vacuum. Suddenly the pain fell away. Exhaustion, and dusk came around. It was over. Oh, God! She plummeted down and struck a black nothingness which gave way to nothingness and nothingness and another and still another . . .

Footsteps. Gentle, approaching footsteps.

Far away, a voice said, 'She's asleep. Don't disturb her.'

An odour of tweeds, a pipe, a certain shaving lotion. David was standing over her. And beyond him the immaculate smell of Dr Jeffers.

She did not open her eyes. 'I'm awake,' she said, quietly. It was a surprise, a relief to be able to speak, to not be dead.

'Alice,' someone said, and it was David beyond her closed eyes, holding her tired hands.

Would you like to meet the murderer, David? she thought. I hear your voice asking to see him, so there's nothing but for me to point him out to you.

David stood over her. She opened her eyes. The room came into focus. Moving a weak hand, she pulled aside a coverlet.

The murderer looked up at David Leiber with a small, red-faced, blue-eyed calm. Its eyes were deep and sparkling.

'Why!' cried David Leiber, smiling. 'He's a *fine* baby!'

Dr Jeffers was waiting for David Leiber the day he came to take his wife and new child home. He motioned Leiber to a chair in his office, gave him a cigar, lit one for himself, sat on the edge of his desk, puffing solemnly for a long moment. Then he cleared his throat, looked David Leiber straight on and said, 'Your wife doesn't like her child, Dave.'

'What!'

'It's been a hard thing for her. She'll need a lot of love this next year. I didn't say much at the time, but she was hysterical in the delivery room. The strange things she said — I won't repeat them. All I'll say is that she feels alien to the child. Now, this may simply be a thing we can clear up with one or two questions.' He sucked on his cigar another moment, then said, 'Is this child a "wanted" child, Dave?'

'Why do you ask?'

'It's vital.'

'Yes. Yes, it is a "wanted" child. We planned it together. Alice was so happy, a year ago, when — '

'Mmmm — that makes it more difficult. Because if the child was unplanned, it would be a simple case of a woman hating the idea of motherhood. That doesn't fit Alice.' Dr Jeffers took his cigar from his lips, rubbed his hand across his jaw. 'It must be something else, then. Perhaps something buried in her childhood that's coming out now. Or it might be the simple temporary doubt and distrust of any mother who's gone through the unusual pain and near-death that Alice has. If so, then a little time should heal that. I thought I'd tell you, though, Dave. It'll help you be easy and tolerant with her if she says anything about — well — about wishing the child had been born dead. And if things don't go well, the three of you drop in on me. I'm always glad to see old friends, eh? Here, take another cigar along for — ah — for the baby.'

It was a bright spring afternoon. Their car hummed along wide, tree-lined boulevards. Blue sky, flowers, a warm wind. David talked a lot, lit his cigar, talked some more. Alice answered directly, softly, relaxing a bit more as the trip progressed. But she held the baby not tightly or warmly or motherly enough to satisfy the queer ache in Dave's mind. She seemed to be merely carrying a porcelain figurine.

'Well,' he said, at last, smiling. 'What'll we name him?'

Alice Leiber watched green trees slide by. 'Let's not

decide yet. I'd rather wait until we get an exceptional name for him. Don't blow smoke in his face.' Her sentences ran together with no change of tone. The last statement held no motherly reproof, no interest, no irritation. She just mouthed it and it was said.

The husband, disquieted, dropped the cigar from the window. 'Sorry,' he said.

The baby rested in the crook of his mother's arm, shadows of sun and tree changing his face. His blue eyes opened like fresh blue spring flowers. Moist noises came from the tiny, pink, elastic mouth.

Alice gave her baby a quick glance. Her husband felt her shiver against him.

'Cold?' he asked.

'A chill. Better raise the window, David.'

It was more than a chill. He rolled the window slowly up.

Suppertime.

Dave had brought the child from the nursery, propped him at a tiny, bewildered angle, supported by many pillows, in a newly purchased high chair.

Alice watched her knife and fork move. 'He's not high-chair size,' she said.

'Fun having him here, anyway,' said Dave, feeling fine. 'Everything's fun. At the office, too. Orders up to my nose. If I don't watch myself I'll make another fifteen thousand this year. Hey, look at Junior, will you? Drooling all down his chin!' He reached over to wipe the baby's mouth with his napkin. From the corner of his eye he realized that Alice wasn't even watching. He finished the job.

'I guess it wasn't very interesting,' he said, back again at his food. 'But one would think a mother'd take some interest in her own child!'

Alice jerked her chin up. 'Dont speak that way! Not in front of him! Later, if you must.'

'Later?' he cried. 'In front of, in back of, what's the difference?' He quieted suddenly, swallowed, was sorry. 'All right. Okay. I know how it is.'

After dinner she let him carry the baby upstairs. She didn't tell him to; she *let* him.

Coming down, he found her standing by the radio, listening to music she didn't hear. Her eyes were closed, her whole attitude one of wondering, self-questioning. She started when he appeared.

Suddenly, she was at him, against him, soft, quick; the same. Her lips found him, kept him. He was stunned. Now that the baby was gone, upstairs, out of the room, she began to breathe again, live again. She was free. She was whispering, rapidly, endlessly.

'Thank you, thank you, darling. For being yourself, always. Dependable, so very dependable!'

He had to laugh. 'My father told me, "Son, provide for your family!" '

Wearily, she rested her dark, shining hair against his neck. 'You've overdone it. Sometimes I wish we were just the way we were when we were first married. No responsibilities, nothing but ourselves. No — no babies.'

She crushed his hand in hers, a supernatural whiteness in her face.

'Oh, Dave, once it was just you and me. We protected each other, and now we protect the baby, but get no protection from it. Do you understand? Lying in the hospital I had time to think a lot of things. The world is evil — '

'Is it?'

'Yes. It is. But laws protect us from it. And when there aren't laws, then love does the protecting. You're protected from my hurting you, by my love. You're vulnerable to me, of all people, but love shields you. I feel no fear of you, because love cushions all your irritations, unnatural instincts, hatreds and immaturities. But — what about the baby? It's too young to know love, or a law of love, or anything, until we teach it. And in the meantime be vulnerable to it.'

'Vulnerable to a baby?' He held her away and laughed gently.

'Does a baby know the difference between right and wrong?' she asked.

'No. But it'll learn.'

'But a baby is so new, so amoral, so conscience-free.' She stopped. Her arms dropped from him and she turned swiftly. 'That noise? What was it?'

Leiber looked around the room. 'I didn't hear — '

She stared at the library door. 'In there,' she said, slowly.

Leiber crossed the room, opened the door and switched the library lights on and off. 'Not a thing.' He came back to her. 'You're worn out. To bed with you — right now.'

Turning out the lights together, they walked slowly up the soundless hall stairs, not speaking. At the top she apologized. 'My wild talk, darling. Forgive me. I'm exhausted.'

He understood, and said so.

She paused, undecided, by the nursery door. Then she fingered the brass knob sharply, walked in. He watched her approach the crib much too carefully, look down, and stiffen as if she'd been struck in the face. 'David!'

Leiber stepped forward, reached the crib.

The baby's face was bright red and very moist; his small pink mouth opened and shut, opened and shut; his eyes were a fiery blue. His hands leapt about on the air.

'Oh,' said Dave, 'he's just been crying.'

'Has he?' Alice Leiber sized the crib-railing to balance herself. 'I didn't hear him.'

'The door was closed.'

'Is that why he breathes so hard, why his face is red?'

'Sure. Poor little guy. Crying all alone in the dark. He can sleep in our room tonight, just in case he cries.'

'You'll spoil him,' his wife said.

Leiber felt her eyes follow as he rolled the crib into their bedroom. He undressed silently, sat on the edge of the bed. Suddenly he lifted his head, swore under his breath, snapped his fingers. 'Damn it! Forgot to tell you. I must fly to Chicago Friday.'

'Oh, David.' Her voice was lost in the room.

'I've put this trip off for two months, and now it's so critical I just *have* to go.'

'I'm afraid to be alone.'

'We'll have the new cook by Friday. She'll be here all the time. I'll only be gone a few days.'

'I'm afraid. I don't know of what. You wouldn't believe me if I told you. I guess I'm crazy.'

He was in bed now. She darkened the room; he heard her walk around the bed, throw back the cover, slide in. He smelled the warm woman-smell of her next to him. He said, 'If you want me to wait a few days, perhaps I could – '

'No,' she said, unconvinced. 'You go. I know it's important. It's just that I keep thinking about what I told you. Laws of love and protection. Love protects you from me. But, the baby – ' She took a breath. 'What protects you from him, David?'

Before he could answer, before he could tell her how silly it was, speaking so of infants, she switched on the bed light, abruptly.

'Look,' she said, pointing.

The baby lay wide awake in its crib, staring straight at him, with deep, sharp blue eyes.

The lights went out again. She trembled against him.

'It's not nice being afraid of the thing you birthed.' Her whisper lowered, became harsh, fierce, swift. 'He tried to kill me! He lies there, listens to us talking, waiting for you to go away so he can try to kill me again! I swear it!' Sobs broke from her.

'Please,' he kept saying, soothing her. 'Stop it, stop it. Please.'

She cried in the dark for a long time. Very late she relaxed, shakingly, against him. Her breathing came soft, warm, regular, her body twitched its worn reflexes and she slept.

He drowsed.

And just before his eyes lidded wearily down, sinking him into deeper and yet deeper tides, he heard a strange little sound of awareness and awakeness in the room.

The sound of small, moist, pinkly elastic lips.

The baby.

And then — sleep.

In the morning, the sun blazed. Alice smiled.

David Leiber dangled his watch over the crib. 'See, baby? Something bright. Something pretty. Sure. Sure. Something bright. Something pretty.'

Alice smiled. She told him to go ahead, fly to Chicago, she'd be very brave, no need to worry. She'd take care of baby. Oh, yes, she'd take care of him, all right.

The aeroplane went east. There was a lot of sky, a lot of sun and clouds and Chicago running over the horizon. Dave was dropped into the rush of ordering, planning, banqueting, telephoning, arguing in conference. But he wrote letters each day and sent telegrams to Alice and the baby.

On the evening of his sixth day away from home he received the long-distance phone call. Los Angeles.

'Alice?'

'No, Dave. This is Jeffers speaking.'

'Doctor!'

'Hold on to yourself, son. Alice is sick. You'd better get the next plane home. It's pneumonia. I'll do everything I can, boy. If only it wasn't so soon after the baby. She needs strength.'

Leiber dropped the phone into its cradle. He got up, with

no feet under him, and no hands and no body. The hotel room blurred and fell apart.

'Alice,' he said, blindly, starting for the door.

The propellers spun about, whirled, fluttered, stopped; time and space were put behind. Under his hand, David felt the doorknob turn; under his feet the floor assumed reality, around him flowed the walls of a bedroom, and in the late-afternoon sunlight Dr Jeffers stood, turning from a window, as Alice lay waiting in her bed, something carved from a fall of winter snow. Then Dr Jeffers was talking, talking continuously, gently, the sound rising and falling through the lamplight, a soft flutter, a white murmur of voice.

'Your wife's too good a mother, Dave. She worried more about the baby than herself . . . '

Somewhere in the paleness of Alice's face, there was a sudden constriction which smoothed itself out before it was realized. Then, slowly, half-smiling, she began to talk and she talked as a mother should about this, that, and the other thing, the telling detail, the minute-by-minute and hour-by-hour report of a mother concerned with a dollhouse world and the miniature life of that world. But she could not stop; the spring was wound tight, and her voice rushed on to anger, fear and the faintest touch of revulsion, which did not change Dr Jeffers' expression, but caused David's heart to match the rhythm of this talk that quickened and could not stop:

'The baby wouldn't sleep. I thought he was sick. He just lay, staring, in his crib, and late at night he'd cry. So loud, he'd cry, and he'd cry all night and all night. I couldn't quiet him, and I couldn't rest.'

Dr Jeffers' head nodded slowly, slowly. 'Tired herself right into pneumonia. But she's full of sulpha now and on the safe side of the whole damn thing.'

Dave felt ill. 'The baby, what about the baby?'

'Fit as a fiddle; cock of the walk!'

'Thanks, Doctor.'

The doctor walked off away and down the stairs, opened the front door faintly, and was gone.

'David!'

He turned to her frightened whisper.

'It was the baby again.' She clutched his head. 'I try to lie to myself and say that I'm a fool, but the baby knew I was weak from the hospital, so he cried all night every night, and when he wasn't crying he'd be much too quiet. I knew if I switched on the light he'd be there, staring up at me.'

David felt his body close in on itself like a fist. He remembered seeing the baby, feeling the baby, awake in the dark, awake very late at night when babies should be asleep. Awake and lying there, silent as thought, not crying, but watching from its crib. He thrust the thought aside. It was insane.

Alice went on. 'I was going to kill the baby. Yes, I was. When you'd been gone only a day on your trip I went to his room and put my hands about his neck; and I stood there, for a long time, thinking, afraid. Then I put the covers up over his face and turned him over on his face and pressed him down and left him that way and ran out of the room.'

He tried to stop her.

'No, let me finish,' she said, hoarsely, looking at the wall. 'When I left his room I thought, It's simple. Babies smother every day. No one'll ever know. But when I came back to see him dead, David, he was alive! Yes, alive, turned over on his back, alive and smiling and breathing. And I couldn't touch him again after that. I left him there and I didn't come back, not to feed him or look at him or do anything. Perhaps the cook tended to him. I don't know. All I know is that his crying kept me awake, and I thought all through the night, and walked around the rooms and now I'm sick.' She was almost finished now. 'The baby lies there and thinks of ways to kill me. Simple ways. Because he knows I know so much about him. I have no love for him; there is no protection between us; there never will be.'

She was through. She collapsed inward on herself and finally slept. David Leiber stood for a long time over her, not able to move. His blood was frozen in his body, not a cell stirred anywhere, anywhere at all.

The next morning there was only one thing to do. He did it. He walked into Dr Jeffers' office and told him the whole thing, and listened to Jeffers' tolerant replies:

'Let's take this thing slowly, son. It's quite natural for mothers to hate their children, sometimes. We have a label for it — ambivalence. The ability to hate, while loving. Lovers hate each other, frequently. Children detest their mothers — '

Leiber interuppted. 'I never hated my mother.'

'You won't admit it, naturally. People don't enjoy admitting hatred for their loved ones.'

'So Alice hates her baby.'

'Better say she has an obsession. She's gone a step further than plain, ordinary ambivalence. A Caesarian operation brought the child into the world and almost took Alice out of it. She blames the child for her near-death and her pneumonia. She's projecting her troubles, blaming them on the handiest object she can use as a source of blame. We *all* do it. We stumble into a chair and curse the furniture, not our own clumsiness. We miss a golf-stroke and damn the turf or our club, or the make of ball. If our business fails we blame the gods, the weather, our luck. All I can tell you is what I told you before. Love her. Finest medicine in the world. Find little ways of showing your affection, give her security. Find ways of showing her how harmless and innocent the child is. Make her feel that the baby was worth the risk. After a while, she'll settle down, forget about death, and begin to love the child. If she doesn't come around in the next month or so, ask me. I'll recommend a good psychiatrist. Go on along, now, and take that look off your face.'

When summer came, things seemed to settle, become easier. Dave worked, immersed himself in office details, but found much time for his wife. She, in turn, took long walks, gained strength, played an occasional light game of badminton. She rarely burst out any more. She seemed to have rid herself of her fears.

Except on one certain midnight when a sudden summer wind swept around the house, warm and swift, shaking the trees like so many shining tambourines. Alice wakened, trembling, and slid over into her husband's arms, and let him console her, and ask her what was wrong.

She said, 'Something's here in the room, watching us.'

He switched on the light. 'Dreaming again,' he said. 'You're better, though. Haven't been troubled for a long time.'

She sighed as he clicked off the light again, and suddenly she slept. He held her, considering what a sweet, weird creature she was, for about half an hour.

He heard the bedroom door sway open a few inches.

There was nobody at the door. No reason for it to come open. The wind had died.

He waited. It seemed like an hour he lay silently, in the dark.

Then, far away, wailing like some small meteor dying in the vast inky gulf of space, the baby began to cry in his nursery.

It was a small, lonely sound in the middle of the stars and the dark and the breathing of this woman in his arms and the wind beginning to sweep through the trees again.

Leiber counted to one hundred, slowly. The crying continued.

Carefully disengaging Alice's arm he slipped from bed, put

on his slippers, robe, and moved quietly from the room.

He'd go downstairs, he thought, fix some warm milk, bring it up, and —

The blackness dropped out from under him. His foot slipped and plunged. Slipped on something soft. Plunged into nothingness.

He thrust his hands out, caught frantically at the railing. His body stopped falling. He held. He cursed.

The 'something soft' that caused his feet to slip rustled and thumped down a few steps. His head rang. His heart hammered at the base of his throat, thick and shot with pain.

Why do careless people leave things strewn about a house? He groped carefully with his fingers for the object that had almost spilled him headlong down the stairs.

His hand froze, startled. His breath went in. His heart held one or two beats.

The thing he held in his hand was a toy. A large cumbersome, patchwork doll he had bought as a joke, for —

For the baby.

Alice drove him to work the next day.

She slowed the car halfway downtown, pulled to the kerb and stopped it. Then she turned on the seat and looked at her husband.

'I want to go away on a vacation. I don't know if you can make it now, darling, but if not, please let me go alone. We can get someone to take care of the baby, I'm sure. But I just have to get away. I thought I was growing out of this — this *feeling*. But I haven't. I can't stand being in the room with him. He looks up at me as if he hates me, too. I can't put my finger on it; all I know is I want to get away before something happens.'

He got out on his side of the car, came around, motioned to her to move over, got in. 'The only thing you're going to do is see a good psychiatrist. And if he suggests a vacation, well, okay. But this can't go on; my stomach's in knots all the time.' He started the car. 'I'll drive the rest of the way.'

Her head was down; she was trying to keep back tears. She looked up when they reached his office building. 'All right. Make the appointment. I'll go talk to anyone you want, David.'

He kissed her. 'Now, you're talking sense, lady. Think you can drive home okay?'

'Of course, silly.'

'See you at supper, then. Drive carefully.'

'Don't I always? 'Bye.'

He stood on the kerb, watching her drive off, the wind taking hold of her long, dark, shining hair. Upstairs, a minute later, he phoned Jeffers and arranged an appointment with a reliable neuro-psychiatrist.

The day's work went uneasily. Things fogged over; and in the fog he kept seeing Alice lost and calling his name. So much of her fear had come over to him. She actually had him convinced that the child was in some ways not quite natural.

He dictated long, uninspired letters. He checked some shipments downstairs. Assistants had to be questioned, and kept going. At the end of the day he was exhausted, his head throbbed, and he was very glad to go home.

On the way down in the elevator he wondered, What if I told Alice about the toy — that patchwork doll — I slipped on on the stairs last night? Lord, wouldn't *that* back her off? No, I won't ever tell her. Accidents are, after all, accidents.

Daylight lingered in the sky as he drove home in a taxi. In front of the house he paid the driver and walked slowly up the cement walk, enjoying the light that was still in the sky and the trees. The white colonial front of the house looked unnaturally silent and uninhabited, and then, quietly, he remembered this was Thursday, and the hired help they were able to obtain from time to time were all gone for the day.

He took a deep breath of air. A bird sang behind the house.

Traffic moved on the boulevard a block away. He twisted the key in the door. The knob turned under his fingers, oiled, silent.

The door opened. He stepped in, put his hat on the chair with his briefcase, started to shrug out of his coat, when he looked up.

Late sunlight streamed down the stairwell from the window near the top of the hall. Where the sunlight touched it took on the bright colour of the patchwork doll sprawled at the bottom of the stairs.

But he paid no attention to the toy.

He could only look, and not move, and look again at Alice.

Alice lay in a broken, grotesque, pallid gesturing and angling of her thin body, at the bottom of the stairs, like a crumpled doll that doesn't want to play any more, ever.

Alice was dead.

The house remained quiet, except for the sound of his heart.

She was dead.

He held her head in his hands, he felt her fingers. He held her body. But she wouldn't live. She wouldn't even try to live. He said her name, out loud, many times, and he tried, once again, by holding her to him, to give her back some of the warmth she had lost, but that didn't help.

He stood up. He must have made a phone call. He didn't remember. He found himself, suddenly, upstairs. He opened the nursery door and walked inside and stared blankly at the crib. His stomach was sick. He couldn't see very well.

The baby's eyes were closed, but his face was red, moist with perspiration, as if he'd been crying long and hard.

'She's dead,' said Leiber to the baby. 'She's dead.'

Then he started laughing low and soft and continuously for a long time until Dr Jeffers walked in out of the night and slapped him again and again across the face.

'Snap out of it! Pull yourself together!'

'She fell down the stairs, Doctor. She tripped on a patch-work doll and fell. I almost slipped on it the other night, myself. And now —'

The doctor shook him.

'Doc, Doc, Doc,' said Dave, hazily. 'Funny thing. Funny. I — I finally thought of a name for the baby.'

The doctor said nothing.

Leiber put his head back in his trembling hands and spoke the words. 'I'm going to have him christened next Sunday. Know what name I'm giving him? I'm going to call him Lucifer.'

It was eleven at night. A lot of strange people had come and gone through the house, taking the essential flame with them — Alice.

David Leiber sat across from the doctor in the library.

'Alice wasn't crazy,' he said, slowly. 'She had good reason to fear the baby.'

Jeffers exhaled. 'Don't follow after her! She blamed the child for her sickness, now you blame it for her death. She stumbled on a toy, remember that. You can't blame the child.'

'You mean Lucifer?'

'Stop calling him that!'

Leiber shook his head. 'Alice heard things at night, moving in the halls. You want to know what made those noises, Doctor? They were made by the baby. Four months old, moving in the dark, listening to us talk. Listening to every word!' He held to the sides of the chair. 'And if I turned the lights on, a baby is so small. It can hide behind furniture, a door, against a wall — below eye-level.'

'I want you to stop this!' said Jeffers.

'Let me say what I think or I'll go crazy. When I went to

Chicago, who was it kept Alice awake, tiring her into pneumonia? The baby! And when Alice didn't die, then he tried killing me. It was simple; leave a toy on the stairs, cry in the night until your father goes downstairs to fetch your milk, and stumbles. A crude trick, but effective. It didn't get me. But it killed Alice dead.'

David Leiber stopped long enough to light a cigarette. 'I should have caught on. I'd turn on the lights in the middle of the night, many nights, and the baby'd be lying there, eyes wide. Most babies sleep all the time. Not this one. He stayed awake, thinking.'

'Babies don't think.'

'He stayed awake doing whatever he *could* do with his brain, then. What in hell do we know about a baby's mind? He had every reason to hate Alice; she suspected him for what he was — certainly not a normal child. Something — different. What do you know of babies, Doctor? The general run, yes. You know, of course, how babies kill their mothers at birth. Why? Could it be resentment at being forced into a lousy world like this one?'

Leiber leaned towards the doctor, tiredly. 'It all ties up. Suppose that a few babies out of all the millions born are instantaneously able to move, see, hear, think, like many animals and insects can. Insects are born self-sufficient. In a few weeks most mammals and birds adjust. But children take years to speak and learn to stumble around on their weak legs.'

'But suppose one child in a billion is — strange? Born perfectly aware, able to think, instinctively. Wouldn't it be a perfect setup, a perfect blind for anything the baby might want to do? He could pretend to be ordinary, weak, crying, ignorant. With just a *little* expenditure of energy he could crawl about a darkened house, listening. And how easy to place obstacles at the top of stairs. How easy to cry all night and tire a mother into pneumonia. How easy, right at birth, to be so close to the mother that *a few deft manoeuvres might cause peritonitis!*'

'For God's sake!' Jeffers was on his feet. 'That's a repulsive thing to say!'

'It's a repulsive thing I'm speaking of. How many mothers have died at the birth of their children? How many have suckled strange little improbabilities who cause death one way or another? Strange, red little creatures with brains that work in a bloody darkness we can't even guess at. Elemental little brains, warm with racial memory, hatred, and raw cruelty, with no more thought than self-preservation. And self-preservation in this case consisted of eliminating a mother who realized what a horror she had birthed. I ask you, Doctor, what is there in the world more selfish than a baby? Nothing!'

Jeffers scowled and shook his head, helplessly.

Leiber dropped his cigarette down. 'I'm not claiming any great strength for the child. Just enough to crawl around a little, a few months ahead of schedule. Just enough to listen all the time. Just enough to cry late at night. That's enough, more than enough.'

Jeffers tried to ridicule. 'Call it murder, then. But murder must be motivated. What motive had the child?'

Leiber was ready with the answer. 'What is more at peace, more dreamfully content, at ease, at rest, fed, comforted, unbothered, than an unborn child? Nothing. It floats in a sleepy, timeless wonder of nourishment and silence. Then, suddenly, it is asked to give up its berth, is forced to vacate, rushed out into a noisy, uncaring, selfish world where it is asked to shift for itself, to hunt, to feed from the hunting, to seek after a vanishing love that once was its unquestionable right, to meet confusion instead of inner silence and conservative slumber! And the child *resents* it! Resents the cold air, the huge spaces, the sudden departure from familiar things.

And in the tiny filament of brain the only thing the child knows is selfishness and hatred because the spell has been rudely shattered. Who is responsible for this disenchantment, this rude breaking of the spell? The mother. So here the new child has someone to hate with all its unreasoning mind. The mother has cast it out, rejected it. And the father is no better, kill him, too! He's responsible in *his* way!'

Jeffers interrupted. 'If what you say is true, then every woman in the world would have to look on her baby as something to dread, something to wonder about.'

'And why not? Hasn't the child a perfect alibi? A thousand years of accepted medical belief protects him. By all natural accounts he is helpless, not responsible. The child is born hating. And things grow worse, instead of better. At first the baby gets a certain amount of attention and mothering. But then as time passes, things change. When very new, a baby has the power to make parents do silly things when it cries or sneezes, jump when it makes a noise. As the years pass, the baby feels that small power slip rapidly, forever away, never to return. Why shouldn't it grasp all the power it can have? Why shouldn't it jockey for position while it has all the advantages? In later years it would be too late to express its hatred. *Now* would be the time to strike.'

Leiber's voice was very soft, very low.

'My little boy baby, lying in his crib nights, his face moist and red and out of breath. From crying? No. From climbing slowly out of his crib, from crawling long distances through darkened hallways. My little boy baby. I want to kill him.'

The doctor handed him a water glass and some pills. 'You're not killing anyone. You're going to sleep for twenty-four hours. Sleep'll change your mind. Take this.'

Leiber drank down the pills and let himself be led upstairs to his bedroom, crying, and felt himself being put to bed. The doctor waited until he was moving deep into sleep, then left the house.

Leiber, alone, drifted down, down.

He heard a noise. 'What's — what's *that*?' he demanded, feebly.

Something moved in the hall.

David Leiber slept.

Very early the next morning, Dr Jeffers drove up to the house. It was a good morning, and he was here to drive Leiber to the country for a rest. Leiber would still be asleep upstairs. Jeffers had given him enough sedative to knock him out for at least fifteen hours.

He rang the doorbell. No answer. The servants were probably not up. Jeffers tried the front door, found it open, stepped in. He put his medical kit on the nearest chair.

Something white moved out of sight at the top of the stairs. Just a suggestion of a movement. Jeffers hardly noticed it.

The smell of gas was in the house.

Jeffers ran upstairs, crashed into Leiber's bedroom.

Leiber lay motionless on the bed, and the room billowed with gas, which hissed from a released jet at the base of the wall near the door. Jeffers twisted it off, then forced up all the windows and ran back to Leiber's body.

The body was cold. It had been dead quite a few hours.

Coughing violently, the doctor hurried from the room, eyes watering. Leiber hadn't turned on the gas himself. He *couldn't* have. Those sedatives had knocked him out, he wouldn't have wakened until noon. It wasn't suicide. Or was there the faintest possibility?

Jeffers stood in the hall for five minutes. Then he walked to the door of the nursery. It was shut. He opened it. He walked inside and to the crib.

The crib was empty.

He stood swaying by the crib for half a minute, then he said something to nobody in particular.

'The nursery door blew shut. You couldn't get back into

your crib where it was safe. You didn't plan on the door blowing shut. A little thing like a slammed door can ruin the best of plans. I'll find you somewhere in the house, hiding, pretending to be somewhere you are not.' The doctor looked dazed. He put his hand to his head and smiled palely. 'Now I'm talking like Alice and David talked. But, I can't take any chances. I'm not sure of anything, but I can't take chances.'

He walked downstairs, opened his medical bag on the chair, took something out of it and held it in his hands.

Something rustled down the hall. Something very small and very quiet. Jeffers turned rapidly.

I had to operate to bring you into this world, he thought. Now I guess I can operate to take you out of it . . .

He took half a dozen slow, sure steps forward into the hall. He raised his hand into the sunlight.

'See, baby! Something bright — something pretty!'

A scalpel.

The Next in Line

It was a little caricature of a town square. In it were the following fresh ingredients: a candy-box of a bandstand where men stood on Thursday and Sunday nights exploding music; fine, green-patinated bronze-copper benches all scrolled and flourished; fine blue and pink tiled walks — blue as women's newly lacquered eyes, pink as women's hidden wonders; and fine French-clipped trees in the shape of exact hatboxes. The whole, from your hotel window, had the fresh ingratiation and unbelievable fantasy one might expect of a French villa in the nineties. But not, this was Mexico! and this was a plaza in a small colonial Mexican town, with a fine State Opera House (in which movies were shown for two pesos admission: *Rasputin and the Empress, The Big House, Madame Curie, Love Affair, Mama Loves Papa*).

Joseph came out on the sun-heated balcony in the morning and knelt by the grille, pointing his little box Brownie. Behind him, in the bath, the water was running and Marie's voice came out:

'What're you doing?'

He muttered ' — a picture.' She asked again. He clicked the shutter, stood up, wound the spool inside, squinting, and said, 'Took a picture of the town square. God, didn't those men shout last night? I didn't sleep until two-thirty. We would have to arrive when the local Rotary's having its wingding.'

'What're our plans for today?' she asked.

'We're going to see the mummies,' he said.

'Oh,' she said. There was a long silence.

He came in, set the camera down, and lit himself a cigarette.

'I'll go up and see them alone,' he said, 'if you'd rather.'

'No,' she said, not very loud. 'I'll go along. But I wish we could forget the whole thing. It's such a lovely little town.'

'Look here!' he cried, catching a movement from the corner of his eyes. He hurried to the balcony, stood there, his cigarette smoking and forgotten in his fingers. 'Come quick, Marie!'

'I'm drying myself,' she said.

'Please, hurry,' he said, fascinated, looking down into the street.

There was movement behind him, and then the odour of soap and water-rinsed flesh, wet towel, fresh cologne; Marie was at his elbow. 'Stay right there,' she cautioned him, 'so I can look without exposing myself. I'm stark. What *is* it?'

'Look!' he cried.

A procession travelled along the street. One man led it, with a package on his head. Behind him came women in black rebozos, chewing away the peels of oranges and spitting them on the cobbles; little children at their elbows, men ahead of them. Some ate sugar cane, gnawing away at the outer bark until it split down and they pulled it off in great hunks to get at the succulent pulp and the juicy sinews on which to suck. In all, there were fifty people.

'Joe,' said Marie behind him, holding his arm.

It was no ordinary package the first man in the procession carried on his head, balanced delicately as a chicken-plume. It was covered with silver satin and silver fringe and silver rosettes. And he held it gently with one brown hand, the other hand swinging free.

This was a funeral and the little package was a coffin.

Joseph glanced at his wife.

She was the colour of fine, fresh milk. The pink colour of

the bath was gone. Her heart had sucked it all down to some hidden vacuum in her. She held fast to the French doorway and watched the travelling people go, watched them eat fruit, heard them talk gently, laugh gently. She forgot she was naked.

He said, 'Some little girl or boy gone to a happier place.'

'Where are they taking — her?'

She did not think it unusual, her choice of the feminine pronoun. Already she had identified herself with that tiny fragment parcelled like an unripe variety of fruit. Now, in this moment, she was being carried up the hill within compressing darkness, a stone in a peach, silent and terrified, and touch of the father against the coffin material outside; gentle and noiseless and firm inside.

'To the graveyard, naturally; that's where they're taking her,' he said, the cigarette making a filter of smoke across his casual face.

'Not *the* graveyard?'

'There's only one cemetery in these towns, you know that. They usually hurry it. That little girl has probably been dead only a few hours.'

'A few hours — '

She turned away, quite ridiculous, quite naked, with only the towel supported by her limp, untrying hands. She walked towards the bed. 'A few hours ago she was alive, and now — '

He went on: 'Now they're hurrying her up the hill. The climate isn't kind to the dead. It's hot, there's no embalming. They have to finish it quickly.'

'But to *that* graveyard, that horrible place,' she said, with a voice from a dream.

'Oh, the mummies,' he said. 'Don't let that bother you.'

She sat on the bed, again and again stroking the towel laid across her lap. Her eyes were blind as the brown paps of her breasts. She did not see him or the room. She knew that if he snapped his fingers or coughed, she wouldn't even look up.

'They were eating fruit at her funeral, and laughing,' she said.

'It's a long climb to the cemetery.'

She shuddered, a convulsive motion, like a fish trying to free itself from a deep-swallowed hook. She lay back and he looked at her as one examines a poor sculpture; all criticism, all quiet and easy and uncaring. She wondered idly just how much his hands had had to do with the broadening and flattening and changement of her body. Certainly this was not the body he'd started with. It was past saving now. Like clay which the sculptor has carelessly impregnated with water, it was impossible to shape again. In order to shape clay you warm it with your hands, evaporate the moisture with heat. But there was no more of that fine summer weather between them. There was no warmth to bake away the ageing moisture that collected and made pendant now her breasts and body. When the heat is gone, it is marvellous and unsettling to see how quickly a vessel stores self-destroying water in its cells.

'I don't feel well,' she said. She lay there, thinking it over. 'I don't feel well,' she said again, when he made no response. After another minute or two she lifted herself. 'Let's not stay here another night, Joe.'

'But it's a wonderful town.'

'Yes, but we've seen everything.' She got up. She knew what came next. Gayness, blitheness, encouragement, everything quite false and hopeful. 'We could go on to Pátzcuaro. Make it in no time. You won't have to pack, I'll do it all myself, darling! We can get a room at the Don Posada there. They say it's a beautiful little town —'

'This,' he remarked, 'is a beautiful little town.'

'Bougainvillea climb all over the buildings — ' she said.

'These — ' he pointed to some flowers at the window ' — are bougainvillea.'

' — and we'd fish, you like fishing,' she said in bright haste.

'And I'd fish, too, I'd learn, yes I would, I've always *wanted* to learn! And they say the Tarascan Indians there are almost Mongoloid in feature, and don't speak much Spanish, and from there we could go to Parícutin, that's near Uruapan, and they have some of the finest lacquered boxes there, oh, it'll be fun, Joe. I'll pack. You just take it easy, and –'

'Marie.'

He stopped her with one word as she ran to the bathroom door.

'Yes?'

'I thought you said you didn't feel well?'

'I didn't. I don't. But, thinking of all those swell places – '

'We haven't seen one tenth of this town,' he explained logically. 'There's that statue of Morelos on the hill, I want a shot of that, and some of that French architecture up the street . . . we've travelled three hundred miles and we've been here one day and now you want to rush off somewhere else. I've already paid the rent for another night . . . '

'You can get it back,' she said.

'Why do you want to run away?' he said, looking at her with an attentive simplicity. 'Don't you like the town?'

'I simply adore it,' she said, her cheeks white, smiling. 'It's so green and pretty.'

'Well, then,' he said. 'Another day. You'll love it. That's settled.'

She started to speak.

'Yes?' he asked.

'Nothing.'

She closed the bathroom door. Behind it she rattled open a medicine box. Water rushed into a tumbler. She was taking something for her stomach.

He came to the bathroom door.

'Marie, the mummies don't bother you, do they?'

'Unh-unh,' she said.

'Was it the funeral, then?'

'Unh.'

'Because, if you were really afraid, I'd pack in a moment, you know that, darling.'

He waited.

'No, I'm not afraid,' she said.

'Good girl,' he said.

The graveyard was enclosed by a thick adobe wall, and at its four corners small stone angels tilted out on stony wings, their grimy heads capped with bird droppings, their hands gifted with amulets of the same substance, their faces unquestionably freckled.

In the warm smooth flow of sunlight which was like a depthless, tideless river, Joseph and Marie climbed up the hill, their shadows slanting blue behind them. Helping one another, they made the cemetery gate, swung back the Spanish blue iron grille and entered.

It was several mornings after the celebratory fiesta of *El Día de los Muertos*, the Day of the Dead, and ribbons and ravels of tissue and sparkle-tape still clung like insane hair to the raised stones, to the hand-carved, love-polished cruci-fixes, and to the above-ground tombs which resembled marble jewel-cases. There were statues frozen in angelic postures over gravel mounds, and intricately carved stones tall as men with angels spilling all down their rims, and tombs as big and ridiculous as beds put out to dry in the sun after some nocturnal accident. And within the four walls of the yard, inserted into square mouths and slots, were coffins, walled in, plated in by marble plates and plaster, upon which names were struck and upon which hung tin pictures, cheap peso portraits of the inserted dead. Thumb-tacked to the different pictures were trinkets they'd loved in life, silver charms, silver arms, legs, bodies, silver cups, silver dogs, silver church medallions, bits of red crepe and blue ribbon. On some places were painted slats of tin showing the dead rising to heaven in oil-tinted angels' arms.

Looking at the graves again, they saw the remnants of the Death Fiesta. The little tablets of tallow splashed over the stones by the lighted festive candles, the wilted orchid blossoms lying like crushed red-purple tarantulas against the milky stones, some of them looking horridly sexual, limp and withered. There were loop-frames of cactus leaves, bamboo, reeds, and wild, dead morning-glories. There were circles of gardenias and sprigs of bougainvillea, desiccated. The entire floor of the yard seemed a ballroom after a wild dancing, from which the participants have fled; the tables askew, confetti, candles, ribbons and deep dreams left behind.

They stood, Marie and Joseph, in the warm silent yard, among the stones, between the walls. Far over in one corner a little man with high cheekbones, the milk colour of the Spanish infiltration, thick glasses, a black coat, a grey hat and grey, unpressed pants and neatly laced shoes, moved about among the stones, supervising something or other that another man in overalls was doing to a grave with a shovel. The little man with glasses carried a thrice-folded newspaper under his left arm and had his hands in his pockets.

'*Buenos días, señora y señor!*' he said, when he finally noticed Joseph and Marie and came to see them.

'Is this the place of *las momias?*' asked Joseph. 'They do exist, do they not?'

'*Sí* the mummies,' said the man. 'They exist and are here. In the catacombs.'

'*Por favor,*' said Joseph. '*Yo quiero veo las momias, si?*'

'*Sí, señor.*'

'*Me Español es mucho estúpido, es muy malo,*' apologized Joseph.

'No, no, *señor.* You speak well! This way, please.'

He led them between the flowered stones to a tomb near the wall shadows. It was a large flat tomb, flush with the gravel, with a thin kindling door flat on it, padlocked. It was unlocked and the wooden door flung back rattling to one side. Revealed was a round hole the circled interior of which contained steps which screwed into the earth.

Before Joseph could move, his wife had set her foot on the first step. 'Here,' he said. 'Me first.'

'No. That's all right,' she said, and went down and around in a darkening spiral until the earth vanished her. She moved carefully, for the steps were hardly enough to contain a child's feet. It got dark and she heard the caretaker stepping after her, at her ears, and then it got light again. They stepped out into a long whitewashed hall twenty feet under the earth, dimly lit by a few small gothic windows high in the arched ceiling. The hall was fifty yards long, ending on the left in a double door in which were set tall crystal panes and a sign forbidding entrance. On the right end of the hall was a large stack of white rods and round white stones.

'The soldiers who fought for Father Morelos,' said the caretaker.

They walked to the vast pile. They were neatly put in place, bone on bone, like firewood, and on top was a mound of a thousand dry skulls.

'I don't mind skulls and bones,' said Marie. 'There's nothing even vaguely human to them. I'm not scared of skulls and bones. They're like something insectile. If a child was raised and didn't know he had a skeleton in him, he wouldn't think anything of bones, would he? That's how it is with me. Everything human has been scraped off *these*. There's nothing familiar left to be horrible. In order for a thing to be horrible it has to suffer a change you can recognize. This isn't changed. They're still skeletons, like they always were. The part that changed is gone, and so there's nothing to show for it. Isn't that interesting?'

Joseph nodded.

She was quite brave now.

'Well,' she said, 'let's see the mummies.'

'Here, *señora*, said the caretaker.

He took them far down the hall away from the stack of bones and when Joseph paid him a peso he unlocked the forbidden crystal doors and opened them wide and they looked into an even longer, dimly lighted hall in which stood the people.

They waited inside the door in a long line under the arch-roofed ceiling, fifty-five of them against one wall, on the left, fifty-five of them against the right wall, and five of them way down at the very end.

'Mister Interlocutor!' said Joseph, briskly.

They resembled nothing more than those preliminary erections of a sculptor, the wire frame, the first tendons of clay, the muscles, and a thin lacquer of skin. They were unfinished, all one hundred and fifteen of them.

They were parchment-coloured and the skin was stretched as if to dry, from bone to bone. The bodies were intact, only the watery humours had evaporated from them.

'The climate,' said the caretaker. 'It preserves them. Very dry.'

'How long have they been here?' asked Joseph.

'Some one year, some five, señor, some ten, some seventy.'

There was an embarrassment of horror. You started with the first man on your right, hooked and wired upright against the wall, and he was not good to look upon, and you went on to the woman next to him who was unbelievable and then to a man who was horrendous and then to a woman who was very sorry she was dead and in such a place as this.

'What are they doing here?' asked Joseph.

'Their relatives did not pay the rent upon their graves.'

'Is there a rent?'

'*Sí, señor*. Twenty pesos a year. Or, if they desire the permanent interment, one hundred seventy pesos. But our people, they are very poor, as you must know, and one hundred seventy pesos is as much as many of them make in two years. So they carry their dead here and place them into the earth for one year, and the twenty pesos are paid, with fine intentions of paying each year and each year, but each year and each year after the first year they have a burro to buy or a new mouth to feed, or maybe three new mouths, and the dead, after all, are not hungry, and the dead, after all, can pull no ploughs; or there is a new wife or there is a roof in need of mending, and the dead, remember, can be in no beds with a man, and the dead, you understand, can keep no rain off one, and so it is the dead are not paid up upon their rent.'

'*Then* what happens? Are you listening, Marie?' asked Joseph.

Marie counted the bodies. One, two, three, four, five, six, seven, eight. 'What?' she said, quietly.

'Are you listening?'

'I think so. What? Oh, yes! I'm listening.'

Eight, nine, ten, eleven, twelve, thirteen.

'Well, then,' said the little man. 'I call a *trabajador* and with his delicate shovel at the end of the first year he does dig and dig and dig down. How deep do you think we dig, *señor?*'

'Six feet. That's the usual depth.'

'Ah, no, ah, no. There, *señor*, you would be wrong. Knowing that after the first year the rent is liable not to be paid, we bury the poorest two feet down. It is less work, you understand? Of course, we must judge by the family who own a body. Some of them we bury sometimes three, sometimes four feet deep, sometimes five, sometimes six, depending on how rich the family is, depending on what the chances are we won't have to dig him from out his place a year later. And, let me tell you, *señor*, when we bury a man the whole six feet deep we are very certain of his staying. We have never dug up a six-foot-buried one yet, that is the accuracy with which we know the money of the people.'

Twenty-one, twenty-two, twenty-three. Mare's lips

moved with a small whisper.

'And the bodies which are dug up are placed down here against the wall with other *compañeros*.'

'Do the relatives know the bodies are here?'

'*Sí.*' The small man pointed. 'This one, *vea usted*? It is new. It has been here but one year. His *madre y padre* know him to be here. But have they money? Ah no.'

'Isn't that rather gruesome for his parents?'

The little man was earnest. 'They never think of it,' he said.

'Did you hear that, Marie?'

'What?' Thirty, thirty-one, thirty-two, thirty-three, thirty-four. 'Yes. They never think of it.'

'What if the rent is paid again, after a lapse?' inquired Joseph.

'In that time,' said the caretaker, 'the bodies are reburied for as many years as are paid.'

'Sounds like blackmail,' said Joseph.

The little man shrugged, hands in pockets. 'We must live.'

'You are certain no one can pay the one hundred seventy pesos all at once,' said Joseph. 'So in this way you get them for twenty pesos a year, year after year, for maybe thirty years. If they don't pay, you threaten to stand *mamacita* or little *niño* in the catacomb.'

'We must live,' said the little man.

Fifty-one, fifty-two, fifty-three.

Marie counted in the centre of the long corridor, the standing dead on all sides of her.

They were screaming.

They looked as if they had leaped, snapped upright in their graves, clutched hands over their shrivelled bosoms and screamed, jaws wide, tongues out, nostrils flared.

And been frozen that way.

All of them had open mouths. Theirs was a perpetual screaming. They were dead and they knew it. In every raw fibre and evaporated organ they knew it.

She stood listening to them scream.

They say dogs hear sounds humans never hear, sounds so many decibels higher than normal hearing that they seem nonexistent.

The corridor swarmed with screams. Screams poured from terror-yawned lips and dry tongues, screams you couldn't hear because they were so high.

Joseph walked up to one standing body.

'Say "ah," ' he said.

Sixty-five, sixty-six, sixty-seven, counted Marie, among the screams.

'Here is an interesting one,' said the proprietor.

They saw a woman with arms flung to her head, mouth wide, teeth intact, whose hair was wildly flourished, long and shimmery on her head. Her eyes were small pale white-blue eggs in her skull.

'Sometimes, this happens. This woman, she is a cataleptic. One day she falls down upon the earth, but is really not dead, for, deep in her, the little drum of her heart beats and beats, so dim one cannot hear. So she was buried in the graveyard in a fine inexpensive box . . . '

'Didn't you know she was cataleptic?'

'Her sisters knew. But this time they thought her at last dead. And funerals are hasty things in this warm town.'

'She was buried a few hours after her "death"?'

'*Sí*, the same. All of this, as you see here, we would never have known, if a year later her sisters, having other things to buy, had not refused the rent on her burial. So we dug very quietly down and loosed the box and took it up and opened the top of her box and laid it aside and looked in upon her — '

Marie stared.

This woman had wakened under the earth. She had torn, shrieked, clubbed at the box-lid with her fists, died of suffocation, in this attitude, hands flung over her gaping face, horror-eyed, hair wild.

'Be pleased, *señor*, to find that difference between *her* hands and these other ones,' said the caretaker. 'Their peaceful fingers at their hips, quiet as little roses. Hers? Ah, hers! are jumped up, very wildly, as if to pound the lid free!'

'Couldn't rigor mortis do that?'

'Believe me, *señor*, rigor mortis pounds upon no lids. Rigor mortis screams not like this, nor twists nor wrestles to rip free nails, *señor*, or prise boards loose hunting for air, *señor*. All these others are open mouth, *sí*, because they were not injected with the fluids of embalming, but theirs is a simple screaming of muscles, *señor*. This *señorita*, here, hers is the *muerte horrible*.'

Marie walked, scuffling her shoes, turning first this way, then that. Naked bodies. Long ago the clothes had whispered away. The fat women's breasts were lumps of yeasty dough left in the dust. The men's loins were indrawn, withered orchids.

'Mr Grimace and Mr Gape,' said Joseph.

He pointed his camera at two men who seemed in conversation, mouths in mid-sentence, hands gesticulant and stiffened over some long-dissolved gossip.

Joseph clicked the shutter, rolled the film, focused the camera on another body, clicked the shutter, rolled the film, walked on to another.

Eighty-one, eighty-two, eighty-three. Jaws down, tongues out like jeering children, eyes pale brown-irised in up-clenched sockets. Hairs, waxed and prickled by sunlight, each sharp as quills embedded on the lips, the cheeks, the eyelids, the brows. Little beards on chins and bosoms and loins. Flesh like drumheads and manuscripts and crisp bread dough. The women, huge ill-shaped tallow things, death-melted. The insane hair of them, like nests made and unmade and remade. Teeth, each single, each fine, each perfect, in

jaw. Eighty-six, eighty-seven, eighty-eight. A rushing of
Marie's eyes. Down the corridor, flicking. Counting,
rushing, never stopping. On! Quick! Ninety-one, ninety-
two, ninety-three! Here was a man, his stomach open, like a
tree hollow where you dropped your child love letters when
you were eleven! Her eyes entered the hole in the space under
his ribs. She peeked in. He looked like an Erector set inside.
The spine, the pelvic plates. The rest was tendon, parchment,
bone, eye, beardy jaw, ear, stupefied nostril. And this ragged
eaten cicatrix in his navel into which a pudding might be
spooned. Ninety-seven, ninety-eight! Names, places, dates,
things!

'This woman died in childbirth!'

Like a little hungry doll, the prematurely born child was
wired, dangling, to her wrist.

'This was a soldier. His uniform still half on him – '

Marie's eyes slammed the furthest wall after a back-forth,
back-forth swinging from horror to horror, from skull to
skull, beating from rib to rib, staring with hypnotic fascination at paralysed, loveless, fleshless loins, at men made
into women by evaporation, at women made into dugged
swine. The fearful ricochet of vision, growing, growing,
taking impetus from swollen breast to raving mouth, wall to
wall, wall to wall, again, again, like a ball hurled in a game,
caught in the incredible teeth, spat in a scream across the
corridor to be caught in claws, lodged between thin teats, the
whole standing chorus invisibly chanting the game on, on,
the wild game of sight recoiling, rebounding, reshuttling on
down the inconceivable procession, through a montage of
erected horrors that ended finally and for all time when vision
crashed against the corridor ending with one last scream from
all present!

Marie turned and shot her vision far down to where the
spiral steps walked up into sunlight. How talented was death.
How many expressions and manipulations of hand, face,

body, no two alike. They stood like the naked pipes of a vast derelict calliope, their mouths cut into frantic vents. And now the great hand of mania descended upon all keys at once, and the long calliope screamed upon one hundred-throated, unending scream.

Click went the camera and Joseph rolled the film. Click went the camera and Joseph rolled the film.

Moreno, Morelos, Cantine, Gómez, Gutiérrez, Villanousul, Ureta, Licón, Navarro, Iturbi, Jorge, Filomena, Nena, Manuel, José, Tomás, Ramona. This man walked and this man sang and this man had three wives; and this man died of this, and that of that, and the third from another thing, and the fourth was shot, and the fifth was stabbed and the sixth fell straight down dead; and the seventh drank deep and died dead, and the eighth died in love, and the ninth fell from his horse, and the tenth coughed blood, and the eleventh stopped his heart, and the twelfth used to laugh much, and the thirteenth was a dancing one, and the fourteenth was most beautiful of all, the fifteenth had ten children and the sixteenth is one of those children as is the seventeenth; and the eighteenth was Tomás and did well with his guitar; the next three cut maize in their fields, had three lovers each; the twenty-second was never loved; the twenty-third sold tortillas, patting and shaping them each at the kerb before the Opera House with her little charcoal stove; and the twenty-fourth beat his wife and now she walks proudly in the town and is merry with new men and here he stands bewildered by this unfair thing, and the twenty-fifth drank several quarts of river with his lungs and was pulled forth in a net, and the twenty-sixth was a great thinker and his brain now sleeps like a burnt plum in his skull.

'I'd like a colour shot of each, and his or her name and how he or she died,' said Joseph. 'It would be an amazing, an ironical book to publish. The more you think, the more it grows on you. Their life histories and then a picture of each of them standing here.'

He tapped each chest, softly. They gave off hollow sounds, like someone rapping on a door.

Marie pushed her way through screams that hung net-wise across her path. She walked evenly, in the corridor centre, now slow, but not too fast, towards the spiral stair, not looking to either side. Click went the camera behind her.

'You have room down here for more?' said Joseph.

'*Sí, Señor*. Many more.'

'Wouldn't want to be next in line, next on your waiting list.'

'Ah, no, *señor*, one would not wish to be next.'

'How are chances of buying one of these?'

'Oh, no, no, *señor*. Oh, no, no. Oh, no, *señor*.

'I'll pay you fifty pesos.'

'Oh, no *señor*, no, no, *señor*.'

In the market, the remainder of candy skulls from the Death Fiesta were sold from flimsy little tables. Women hung with black rebozos sat quietly, now and then speaking one word to each other, the sweet sugar skeletons, the saccharine corpses and white candy skulls at their elbows. Each skull had a name on top in gold candy curlicue: José or Carmen or Ramón or Tena or Guillermo or Rosa. They sold cheap. The Death Festival was gone. Joseph paid a peso and got two candy skulls.

Marie stood in the narrow street. She saw the candy skulls and Joseph and the dark ladies who put the skulls in a bag.

'Not *really*,' said Marie.

'Why not?' said Joseph.

'Not after just *now*,' she said.

'In the catacombs?'

She nodded.

He said, 'But these are good.'

'They look poisonous.'

'Just because they're skull-shaped?'

'No. The sugar itself looks raw, how do you know what kind of people made them, they might have the colic.'

'My dear Marie, all people in Mexico have colic,' he said.

'You can eat them both,' she said.

'Alas, poor Yorick,' he said, peeking into the bag.

They walked along a street that was held between high buildings in which were yellow window frames and blue iron grilles and the smell of tamales came from them and the sound of lost fountains splashing on hidden tiles and little birds clustering and peeping in bamboo cages and someone playing Chopin on a piano.

'Chopin, here,' said Joseph. 'How strange and swell.' He looked up. 'I like that bridge. Hold this.' He handed her the candy bag while he clicked a picture of a red bridge spanning two white buildings with a man walking on it, a red serape on his shoulder. 'Fine,' said Joseph.

Marie walked looking at Joseph, looking away from him and then back at him, her lips moving but not speaking, her eyes fluttering, a little neck muscle under her chin like a wire, a little nerve in her brow ticking. She passed the candy bag from one hand to the other. She stepped up a kerb, leaned back somehow, gestured, said something to restore balance, and dropped the bag.

'For Christ's sake.' Joseph snatched up the bag. 'Look what you've done! Clumsy!'

'I should have broken my ankle,' she said, 'I suppose.'

'These were the best skulls; both of them smashed; I wanted to save them for friends up home.'

'I'm sorry,' she said, vaguely.

'For God's sake, oh, damn it to hell!' He scowled into the bag. 'I might not find any more good as these. Oh, I don't know, I give up!'

The wind blew and they were alone in the street, he staring down into the shattered debris in the bag, she with the street shadows all around her, sun on the other side of the street, nobody about, and the world far away, the two of them alone, two thousand miles from anywhere, on a street in a false town which was nothing and around which was nothing but blank desert and circling hawks. On top the State Opera House, a block down, the golden Greek statues stood sun-bright and high, and in a beer place a shouting phonograph cried *ay! marimba . . . corazón . . .* and all kinds of alien words which the wind stirred away.

Joseph twisted the bag shut, stuck it furiously in his pocket.

They walked back to the two-thirty lunch at the hotel.

He sat at the table with Marie, sipping *albóndiga* soup from his moving spoon, silently. Twice she commented cheerfully upon the wall murals and he looked at her steadily and sipped. The bag of cracked skulls lay on the table . . .

'*Señora . . .*'

The soup plates were cleared by a brown hand. A large plate of enchiladas was set down.

Marie looked at the plate.

There were sixteen enchiladas.

She put her fork and knife out to take one and stopped. She put her fork and knife down at each side of her plate. She glanced at the walls and then at her husband and then at the sixteen enchiladas.

Sixteen. One by one. A long row of them, crowded together.

She counted them.

One, two, three, four, five, six.

Joseph took one on his plate and ate it.

Six, seven, eight, nine, ten, eleven.

She put her hands on her lap.

Twelve, thirteen, fourteen, fifteen, sixteen. She finished counting.

'I'm not hungry,' she said.

He placed another enchilada before himself. It had an interior clothed in a papyrus of corn tortilla. It was slender and it was one of many he cut and placed in his mouth and she chewed it for him in her mind's mouth, and squeezed her eyes tight.

'Eh?' he asked.

'Nothing,' she said.

Thirteen enchiladas remained, like tiny bundles, like scrolls.

He ate five more.

'I don't feel well,' she said.

'Feel better if you ate,' he said.

'No.'

He finished, then opened the sack and took out one of the half-demolished skulls.

'Not *here*?' she said.

'Why not?' And he put one sugar socket to his lips, chewing. 'Not bad,' he said, thinking the taste. He popped in another section of skull. 'Not bad at all.'

She looked at the name on the skull he was eating.

Marie, it said.

It was tremendous, the way she helped him pack. In those newsreels you see men leap off diving-boards into pools, only, a moment later when the reel is reversed, to jump back up in airy fantasy to alight once more safe on the diving-board. Now, as Joseph watched, the suits and dresses flew into their boxes and cases, the hats were like birds darting, clapped into round, bright hatboxes, the shoes seemed to run across the floor like mice to leap into valises. The suitcases banged shut, the hasps clicked, the keys turned.

'There!' she cried. 'All packed! Oh, Joe, I'm so glad you let me change your mind.'

She started for the door.

'Here, let me help,' he said.

'They're not heavy,' she said.

'But you never carry suitcases. You never have. I'll call a boy.'

'Nonsense,' she said, breathless with the weight of the valises.

A boy seized the cases outside the door. '*Señora, por favor!*'

'Have we forgotten anything?' He looked under the two beds, he went out on the balcony and gazed at the plaza, came in, went to the bathroom, looked in the cabinet and on the washbowl. 'Here,' he said, coming out and handing her something. 'You forgot your wristwatch.'

'Did I?' She put it on and went out the door.

'I don't know,' he said. 'It's damn late in the day to be moving out.'

'It's only three-thirty,' she said. 'Only three-thirty.'

'I don't know,' he said, doubtfully.

He looked around the room, stepped out, closed the door, locked it, went downstairs, jingling the keys.

She was outside in the car already, settled in, her coat folded on her lap, her gloved hands folded on the coat. He came out, supervised the loading of what luggage remained into the trunk receptacle, came to the front door and tapped on the window. She unlocked it and let him in.

'Well, here we *go!*' she cried with a laugh, her face rosy, her eyes frantically bright. She was leaning forward as if by this movement she might set the car rolling merrily down the hill. 'Thank you, darling, for letting me get the refund on the money you paid for our room tonight. I'm sure we'll like it much better in Guadalajara tonight. Thank you!'

'Yeah,' he said.

Inserting the ignition keys he stepped on the starter.

Nothing happened.

He stepped on the starter again. Her mouth twitched.

'It needs warming,' she said. 'It was a cold night last night.'

He tried it again. Nothing.

Marie's hands tumbled on her lap.

He tried it six more times. 'Well,' he said, lying back, ceasing.

'Try it again, next time it'll work,' she said.

'It's no use,' he said. 'Something's wrong.'

'Well, you've got to try it once more.'

He tried it once more.

'It'll work, I'm sure,' she said. 'Is the ignition on?'

'Is the ignition on,' he said. 'Yes, it's *on*.'

'It doesn't look like it's on,' she said.

'It's on.' He showed her by twisting the key.

'*Now*, try it,' she said.

'There,' he said, when nothing happened. 'I *told* you.'

'You're not doing it right; it almost caught that time,' she cried.

'I'll wear out the battery, and God knows where you can buy a battery here.'

'Wear it out, then. I'm sure it'll start next time!'

'Well, if you're so good, you try it.' He slipped from the car and beckoned her over behind the wheel. 'Go ahead!'

She bit her lips and settled behind the wheel. She did things with her hands that were like a little mystic ceremony; with moves of hands and body she was trying to overcome gravity, friction and every other natural law. She patted the starter with her toeless shoe. The car remained solemnly quiet. A little squeak came out of Marie's tightened lips. She rammed the starter home and there was a clear smell in the air as she fluttered the choke.

'You've flooded it,' he said. 'Fine! Get back over on your side, will you?'

He got three boys to push and they started the car downhill. He jumped in to steer. The car rolled swiftly, bumping and rattling. Marie's face glowed expectantly. 'This'll start it!' she said.

Nothing started. They rolled quietly into the filling station at the bottom of the hill, bumping softly on the cobbles, and stopped by the tanks.

She sat there, saying nothing, and when the attendant came from the station her door was locked, the window up, and he had to come around on the husband's side to make his query.

The mechanic arose from the car engine, scowled at Joseph and they spoke together in Spanish, quietly.

She rolled the window down and listened.

'What's he say?' she demanded.

The two men talked on.

'What's he say?' she demanded.

The dark mechanic waved at the engine. Joseph nodded and they conversed.

'What's wrong?' Marie wanted to know.

Joseph frowned over at her. 'Wait a moment, will you? I can't listen to both of you.'

The mechanic took Joseph's elbow. They said many words.

'What's he saying now?' she asked.

'He says — ' said Joseph, and was lost as the Mexican took him over to the engine and bent him down in earnest discovery.

'How much will it cost?' she cried, out the window, around at their bent backs.

The mechanic spoke to Joseph.

'Fifty pesos,' said Joseph.

'How long will it take?' cried his wife.

Joseph asked the mechanic. The man shrugged and they argued for five minutes.

'How long will it take?' said Marie.

The discussion continued.

The sun went down the sky. She looked at the sun upon

the trees that stood high by the cemetery yard. The shadows rose and rose until the valley was enclosed and only the sky was clear and untouched and blue.

'Two days, maybe three,' said Joseph, turning to Marie.

'Two days! Can't he fix it so we can just go on to the next town and have the rest done there?'

Joseph asked the man. The man replied.

Joseph said to his wife. 'No, he'll have to do the entire job.'

'Why, that's silly, it's so silly, he doesn't either, he doesn't really have to do it all. You tell him that, Joe, tell him that, he can hurry and fix it — '

The two men ignored her. They were talking earnestly again.

This time it was all in very slow motion. The unpacking of the suitcases. He did his own, she left hers by the door.

'I don't need anything,' she said, leaving it locked.

'You'll need your nightgown,' he said.

'I'll sleep naked,' she said.

'Well, it isn't my fault,' he said. 'That damned car.'

'You can go down and watch them work on it, later,' she said. She sat on the edge of the bed. They were in a new room. She had refused to return to their old room. She said she couldn't stand it. She wanted a new room so it would seem they were in a new hotel in a new city. So this was a new room, but it still had a view of the plaza and the drum-box trees. 'You go down and supervise the work, Joe. If you don't, you know they'll take weeks!' She looked at him. 'You should be down there now, instead of standing around.'

'I'll go down,' he said.

'I'll go down with you. I want to buy some magazines.'

'You won't find any American magazines in a town like this.'

'I can look, can't I?'

'Besides, we haven't much money,' he said. 'I don't want

to have to wire my bank. It takes a god-awful time and it's not worth the bother.'

'I can at least have my magazines,' she said.

'Maybe one or two,' he said.

'As many as I want,' she said, feverishly, on the bed.

'For God's sake, you've got a million magazines in the car now. *Posts, Collier's, Mercury, Atlantic Monthlys, Barnaby, Superman!* You haven't read half of the articles.

'But they're not new,' she said. 'They're not new, I've *looked* at them and after you've looked at a thing, I don't know —'

'Try reading them instead of looking at them,' he said.

As they came downstairs night was in the plaza.

'Give me a few pesos,' she said, and he gave her some. 'Teach me to say about magazines in Spanish,' she said.

'*Quiero una publicación americana*,' he said, walking swiftly.

She repeated it, stumblingly, and laughed. 'Thanks.'

He went on ahead to the mechanic's shop, and she turned in at the nearest *farmacia botica*, and all the magazines racked before her there were alien colours and alien names. She read the titles with swift moves of her eyes and looked at the old man behind the counter. 'Do you have American magazines?' she asked, in English, embarrassed to use the Spanish words.

The old man stared at her.

'*Habla inglés?*' she asked.

'No, *señorita*.'

She tried to think of the right words. '*Quiero* — no!' She stopped. She started again. '*Americano* — uh — *magg-ah-zeen-as?*'

'Oh, no, *señorita!*'

Her hands opened wide at her waist, then closed, like mouths. Her mouth opened and closed. The shop had a veil over it, in her eyes. Here she was and here were these small baked adobe people to whom she could say nothing and from whom she could get no words she understood, and she was in a town of people who said no words to her and she said no words to them except in blushing confusion and bewilderment. And the town was circled by desert and time, and home was far away, far away in another life.

She whirled and fled.

Shop following shop she found no magazines save those giving bullfights in blood on their covers or murdered people or lace-confection priests. But at last three poor copies of the *Post* were bought with much display and loud laughter and she gave the vendor of this small shop a handsome tip.

Rushing out with the *Posts* eagerly on her bosom in both hands she hurried along the narrow walk, took a skip over the gutter, ran across the street, sang la-la, jumped onto the further walk, made another little scamper with her feet, smiled an inside smile, moving along swiftly, pressing the magazines tightly to her, half-closing her eyes, breathing the charcoal evening air, feeling the wind watering past her ears.

Starlight tinkled in golden nuclei off the highly perched Greek figures atop the State Opera House. A man shambled by in the shadow, balancing upon his head a basket. The basket contained bread loaves.

She saw the man and the balanced basket and suddenly she did not move and there was no inside smile, nor did her hands clasp tight the magazines. She watched the man walk, with one hand of his gently poised up to tap the basket any time it unbalanced, and down the street he dwindled, while the magazines slipped from Marie's fingers and scattered on the walk.

Snatching them up, she ran into the hotel and almost fell going upstairs.

She sat in the room. The magazines were piled on each side of her and in a circle at her feet. She had made a little castle with

portcullises of words and into this she was withdrawn. All
about her were the magazines she had bought and bought and
looked at and looked at on other days, and these were the
outer barrier and upon the inside of the barrier, upon her lap,
as yet unopened, but her hands were trembling to open them
and read and read and read again with hungry eyes, were the
three battered *Post* magazines. She opened to the first page.
She would go through them page by page, line by line, she
decided. Not a line would go unnoticed, a comma unread,
every little ad and every colour would be fixed by her. And –
she smiled with discovery – in those other magazines at her
feet were still advertisements and cartoons she had neglected
– there would be little morsels of stuff for her to reclaim and
utilize later.

She would read this first *Post* tonight, yes tonight she
would read this first delicious *Post*. Page on page she would
eat it and tomorrow night, if there was going to be a
tomorrow night, but maybe there wouldn't be a tomorrow
night here, maybe the motor would start and there'd be
odours of exhaust and round hum of rubber tyre on road and
wind riding in the window and pennanting her hair – but,
suppose, just suppose there would *be* a tomorrow night here,
in this room. Well, then, there would be two more *Posts*, one
for tomorrow night, and the next for the next night. How
neatly she said it to herself with her mind's tongue. She
turned the first page.

She turned the second page. Her eyes moved over it and
over it and her fingers unknown to her slipped under the next
page and flickered it in preparation for turning, and the
watch ticked on her wrist, and time passed and she sat
turning pages, turning pages, hungrily seeing the framed
people in the pictures, people who lived in another land in
another world where neons bravely held off the night with
crimson bars and the smells were home smells and the people
talked good fine words and here she was turning the pages,

and all the lines went across and down and the pages flew under her hands, making a fan. She threw down the first *Post*, seized on and riffled through the second in half an hour, threw that down, took up the third, threw that down a good fifteen minutes later and found herself breathing, breathing stiffly and swiftly in her body and out of her mouth. She put her hand up to the back of her beck.

Somewhere, a soft breeze was blowing.

The hairs along the back of her neck slowly stood upright.

She touched them with one pale hand as one touches the nape of a dandelion.

Outside, in the plaza, the street lights rocked like crazy flashlights on a wind. Papers ran through the gutters in sheep flocks. Shadows pencilled and slashed under the bucketing lamps now this way, now that, here a shadow one instant, there a shadow next, now no shadows, all cold light, now no light, all cold blue-black shadow. The lamps creaked on their high metal hasps.

In the room her hands began to tremble. She saw them tremble. Her body began to tremble. Under the bright bright print of the brightest, loudest skirt she could find to put on especially for tonight, in which she had whirled and cavorted feverishly before the coffin-sized mirror, beneath the rayon skirt the body was all wire and tendon and excitation. Her teeth chattered and fused and chattered. Her lipstick smeared, one lip crushing another.

Joseph knocked on the door.

They got ready for bed. He had returned with the news that something had been done to the car and it would take time, he'd go watch them tomorrow.

'But don't knock on the door,' she said, standing before the mirror as she undressed.

'Leave it unlocked then,' he said.

'I want it locked. But don't rap. Call.'

'What's wrong with rapping?' he said.

'It sounds funny,' she said.

'What do you mean, funny?'

She wouldn't say. She was looking at herself in the mirror and she was naked, with her hands at her sides, and there were her breasts and her hips and her entire body, and it moved, it felt the floor under it and the walls and air around it, and the breasts could know hands if hands were put there, and the stomach would make no hollow echo if touched.

'For God's sake,' he said, 'don't stand there admiring yourself.' He was in bed. 'What are you doing?' he said. 'What're you putting your hands up that way for, over your face?'

He put the lights out.

She could not speak to him for she knew no words that he knew and he said nothing to her that she understood, and she walked to her bed and slipped into it and he lay with his back to her in his bed and he was like one of these brown-baked people of this faraway town upon the moon, and the real earth was off somewhere where it would take a star-flight to reach it. If only he could speak with her and she to him tonight, how good the night might be, and how easy to breathe and how lax the vessels of blood in her ankles and in her wrists and the under-arms, but there was no speaking and the night was ten thousand tickings and ten thousand twistings of the blankets, and the pillow was like a tiny white warm stove under-cheek, and the blackness of the room was a mosquito netting draped all about so that a turn entangled her in it. If only there was one word, one word between them. But there was no word and the veins did not rest easy in the wrists and the heart was a bellows forever blowing upon a little coal of fear, forever illumining and making it into a cherry light, again, pulse, and again, an ingrown light which her inner eyes stared upon with unwanting fascination. The lungs did not rest but were exercised as if she were a drowned person and she herself performing artificial respiration to keep the last life going. And all of these things were lubricated by the sweat of her glowing body, and she was glued fast between the heavy blankets like something pressed, smashed, redolently moist between the white pages of a heavy book.

And as she lay this way the long hours of midnight came when again she was a child. She lay, now and again thumping her heart in tambourine hysteria, then, quieting, the slow sad thoughts of bronze childhood when everything was sun on green trees and sun on water and sun on blond child hair. Faces flowed by on merry-go-rounds of memory, a face rushing to meet her, facing her, and away to the right; another, whirling it from the left, a quick fragment of lost conversation, and out to the right. Around and round. Oh, the night was very long. She consoled herself by thinking of the car starting tomorrow, the throttling sound and the power sound and the road moving under, and she smiled in the dark with pleasure. But then, suppose the car did *not* start? She crumpled in the dark, like a burning, withering paper. All the folds and corners of her clenched in about her and tick tick tick went the wristwatch, tick tick tick and another tick to wither on . . .

Morning. She looked at her husband lying straight and easy on his bed. She let her hand laze down at the cool space between the beds. All night her hand had hung in that cold empty interval between. Once she had put her hand out towards him, stretching, but the space was just a little too long, she couldn't reach him. She had snapped her hand back, hoping he hadn't heard the movement of her silent reaching.

There he lay now. His eyes gently closed, the lashes softly interlocked like clasped fingers. Breathing so quietly you could scarce see his ribs move. As usual, by this time of morning, he had worked out of his pyjamas. His naked chest was revealed from the waist up. The rest of him lay under cover. His head lay on the pillow, in thoughtful profile.

There was a beard stubble on his chin.

The morning light showed the white of her eyes. They were the only things in the room in motion, in slow starts and stops, tracing the anatomy of the man across from her.

Each little hair was perfect on the chin and cheeks. A tiny hole of sunlight from the window-shade lay on his chin and picked out, like the spikes of a music-box cylinder, each little hair on his face.

His wrists on either side of him had little curly black hairs, each perfect, each separate and shiny and glittering.

The hair on his head was intact, strand by dark strand, down to the roots. The ears were beautifully carved. The teeth were intact behind the lips.

'Joseph!' she screamed.

'Joseph!' she screamed again, flailing up in terror.

Bong! Bong! Bong! went the bell thunder across the street, from the great tiled cathedral!

Pigeons rose in a papery white whirl, like so many magazines fluttered past the window! The pigeons circled the plaza, spiralling up. Bong! went the bells! Honk went a taxi horn! Far away down an alley a music box played 'Cielito Lindo'.

All these faded into the dripping of the faucet in the bath sink.

Joseph opened his eyes.

His wife sat on her bed, staring at him.

'I thought —' he said. He blinked. 'No.' He shut his eyes and shook his head. 'Just the bells.' A sigh. 'What time is it?'

'I don't know. Yes, I do. Eight o'clock.'

'Good God,' he murmured, turning over. 'We can sleep three more hours.'

'You've got to get up!' she cried.

'Nobody's up. They won't be to work at the garage until

ten, you know that, you can't rush these people; keep quiet now.'

'But you've got to get up,' she said.

He half-turned. Sunlight prickled black hairs into bronze on his upper lip. '*Why?* Why, in Christ's name, do I *have* to get up?'

'You need a shave!' she almost screamed.

He moaned. 'So I have to get up and lather myself at eight in the morning because I need a shave.'

'Well, you do need one.'

'I'm not shaving again till we reach Texas.'

'You can't go around looking like a tramp!'

'I can and I will. I've shaved every morning for thirty goddamn mornings and put on a tie and had a crease in my pants. From now on, no pants, no ties, no shaving, no nothing.'

He yanked the covers over his ears so violently that he pulled the blankets off one of his naked legs.

He leg hung upon the rim of the bed, warm white in the sunlight, each little black hair — perfect.

Her eyes widened, focused, stared upon it.

She put her hand over her mouth, tight.

He went in and out of the hotel all day. He did not shave. He walked along the plaza tiles below. He walked so slowly she wanted to throw a lightning bolt out of the window and hit him. He paused and talked to the hotel manager below, under a drum-cut tree, shifting his shoes on the pale blue plaza tiles. He looked at birds on trees and saw how the State Opera House statues were dressed in fresh morning gilt, and stood on the corner, watching the traffic carefully. There was no traffic! He was standing there on purpose, taking his time, not looking back at her. Why didn't he run, lope down the alley, down the hill to the garage, pound on the doors, threaten the mechanics, lift them by their pants, shove them into the car motor! He stood instead, watching the ridiculous traffic pass. A hobbled swine, a man on a bike, a 1927 Ford, and three half-nude children. Go, go, go, she screamed silently, and almost smashed the window.

He sauntered across the street. He went around the corner. All the way down to the garage he'd stop at windows, read signs, look at pictures, handle pottery. Maybe he'd stop in for a beer. God, yes, a beer.

She walked in the plaza, took the sun, hunted for more magazines. She cleaned her fingernails, burnished them, took a bath, walked again in the plaza, ate very little, and returned to the room to feed upon her magazines.

She did not lie down. She was afraid to. Each time she did she fell into a half-dream, half-drowse in which all her childhood was revealed in a helpless melancholy. Old friends, children she hadn't seen or thought of in twenty years filled her mind. And she thought of things she wanted to do and had never done. She had meant to call Lila Holdridge for the past eight years since college, but somehow she never had. What friends they had been! Dear Lila! She thought, lying down, of all the books, the fine new and old books, she had meant to buy and might never buy now and read. How she loved books and the smell of books. She thought of a thousand old sad things. She'd wanted to own the Oz books all her life, yet had never bought them. Why *not*? while yet there was life! The first thing she'd do would be to buy them when she got back to New York! And she'd call Lila immediately! And she'd see Bert and Jimmy and Helen and Louise, and go back to Illinois and walk around in her childhood place and see the things to be seen there. If she got back to the States. If. Her heart beat painfully in her, paused, held on to itself, and beat again. *If* she ever got back.

She lay listening to her heart, critically.

Thud and a thud and a thud. Pause. Thud and a thud and a thud. Pause.

What if it should stop while she was listening?

There!

Silence inside her.

'Joseph!'

She leaped up. She grabbed at her breasts as if to squeeze, to pump to start the silent heart again!

It opened in her, closed, rattled and beat nervously, twenty rapid, shotlike times!

She sank onto the bed. What if it should stop again and not start? What would she think? What would there be to do? She'd die of fright, that's what. A joke; it was very humorous. Die of fright if you heard your heart stop. She would have to listen to it, keep it beating. She wanted to go home and see Lila and buy the books and dance again and walk in Central Park and — listen —

Thud and a thud and a thud. Pause.

Joseph knocked on the door. Joseph knocked on the door and the car was not repaired and there would be another night; and Joseph did not shave and each little hair was perfect on his chin, and the magazine shops were closed and there were no more magazines, and they ate supper, a little bit anyway for her, and he went out in the evening to walk in the town.

She sat once more in the chair and slow erections of hair rose as if a magnet were passed over her neck. She was very weak and could not move from the chair, and she had no body, she was only a heart-beat, a huge pulsation of warmth and ache between four walls of the room. Her eyes were hot and pregnant, swollen with child of terror behind the bellied, tautened lips.

Deeply inside herself, she felt the first little cog slip. Another night, another night, another night, she thought. And this will be longer than the last. The first little cog slipped, the pendulum missed a stroke. Followed by the second and third interrelated cogs. The cogs interlocked, a small with a little larger one, the little larger one with a bit larger one, the bit larger one with a large one, the large one with a huge one, the huge one with an immense one, the immense one with a titanic one . . .

A red ganglion, no bigger than a scarlet thread, snapped and quivered; a nerve, no greater than a red linen fibre twisted. Deep in her one little mesh was gone and the entire machine, imbalanced, was about to steadily shake itself to bits.

She didn't fight it. She let it quake and terrorize her and knock the sweat off her brow and jolt down her spine and flood her mouth with horrible wine. She felt as if a broken gyro tilted now this way, now that, and blundered and trembled and whined in her. The colour fell from her face like light leaving a clicked-off bulb, the crystal cheeks of the bulb vessel showing veins and filaments all colourless . . .

Joseph was in the room, he had come in, but she didn't even hear him. He was in the room but it made no difference, he changed nothing with his coming. He was getting ready for bed and said nothing as he moved about and she said nothing but fell into the bed while he moved around in a smoke-filled space beyond her and once he spoke but she didn't hear him.

She timed it. Every five minutes she looked at her watch and the watch shook and time shook and the five fingers were fifteen moving, reassembling into five. The shaking never stopped. She called for water. She turned and turned upon the bed. The wind blew outside, cocking the lights and spilling bursts of illumination that hit buildings glancing sidelong blows, causing windows to glitter like opened eyes and shut swiftly as the light tilted in yet another direction. Downstairs, all was quiet after the dinner, no sounds came up into their silent room. He handed her a water glass.

'I'm cold, Joseph,' she said, lying deep in folds of cover.

'You're all right,' he said.

'No, I'm not. I'm not well. I'm afraid.'

'There's nothing to be afraid of.'

'I want to get on the train for the United States.'

'There's a train in León, but none here,' he said, lighting a new cigarette.

'Let's drive there.'

'In these taxis, with these drivers, and leave our car here?'

'Yes, I want to go.'

'You'll be all right in the morning.'

'I know I won't be. I'm not well.'

He said, 'It would cost hundreds of dollars to have the car shipped home.'

'I don't care. I have two hundred dollars in the bank home. I'll pay for it. But, please, let's go home.'

'When the sun shines tomorrow you'll feel better, it's just that the sun's gone now.'

'Yes, the sun's gone and the wind's blowing,' she whispered, closing her eyes, turning her head, listening. 'Oh, what a lonely wind. Mexico's a strange land. All the jungles and deserts and lonely stretches, and here and there a little town, like this, with a few lights burning you could put out with a snap of your fingers . . . '

'It's pretty big country,' he said.

'Don't these people ever get lonely?'

'They're used to it this way.'

'Don't they ever get afraid, then?'

'They have a religion for that.'

'I wish *I* had a religion.'

'The minute you get a religion you stop thinking,' he said. 'Believe in one thing too much and you have no room for new ideas.'

'Tonight,' she said, faintly, 'I'd like nothing more than to have no more room for new ideas, to stop thinking, to believe in one thing so much it leaves me no time to be afraid.'

'You're not afraid,' he said.

'If I had a religion,' she said, ignoring him, 'I'd have a lever with which to lift myself. But I haven't a lever now and I don't know how to lift myself.'

'Oh, for God's – ' he mumbled to himself, sitting down.

'I used to have a religion,' she said.

'Baptist.'

'No, that was when I was twelve. I got over that. I mean – *later*.'

'You never told me.'

'You should have known,' she said.

'What religion? Plaster saints in the sacristy? Any special saint you liked to tell your beads to?'

'Yes.'

'And did he answer your prayers?'

'For a little while. Lately, no, never. Never any more. Not for years now. But I keep praying.'

'Which saint is this?'

'Saint Joseph.'

'Saint Joseph.' He got up and poured himself a glass of water from the glass pitcher, and it was a lonely trickling sound in the room. 'My name.'

'Coincidence,' she said.

They looked at one another for a few moments.

He looked away. 'Plaster saints,' he said, drinking the water down.

After a while she said, 'Joseph?' He said, 'Yes?' and she said, 'Come hold my hand, will you?' 'Women,' he sighed. He came and held her hand. After a minute she drew her hand away, hid it under the blanket, leaving his hand empty behind. With her eyes closed she trembled the words, 'Never mind. It's not as nice as I can imagine it. It's really nice the way I can make you hold my hand in my hand.' 'Gods,' he said, and went into the bathroom. She turned off the light. Only the small crack of light under the bathroom door showed. She listened to her heart. It beat one hundred and fifty times a minute, steadily, and the little whining tremor was still in her marrow, as if each bone of her body had a blue-bottle fly imprisoned in it, hovering, buzzing, shaking, quivering deep, deep, deep. Her eyes reversed into herself, to watch the secret heart of herself pounding itself to pieces against the side of her chest.

Water ran in the bathroom. She heard him washing his teeth.

'Joseph!'

'Yes,' he said, behind the shut door.

'Come here.'

'What do you want?'

'I want you to promise me something, please, oh, please.'

'What is it?'

'Open the door, first.'

'What *is* it?' he demanded, behind the closed door.

'Promise me,' she said, and stopped.

'Promise you what?' he asked, after a long pause.

'Promise me,' she said, and couldn't go on. She lay there. He said nothing. She heard the watch and her heart pounding together. A lantern creaked on the hotel exterior. 'Promise me, if anything — happens,' she heard herself say, muffled and paralysed, as if she were on one of the surrounding hills talking at him from the distance, ' — if anything happens to me, you won't let me be buried here in the graveyard over those terrible catacombs!'

'Don't be foolish,' he said, behind the door.

'Promise me?' she said, eyes wide in the dark.

'Of all the foolish things to talk about.'

'Promise, *please* promise?'

'You'll be all right in the morning,' he said.

'Promise so I can sleep. I can sleep if only you'd say you wouldn't let me be put there. I don't want to be put there.'

'Honestly,' he said, out of patience.

'Please,' she said.

'Why should I promise anything so ridiculous?' he said. 'You'll be fine tomorrow. And besides, if you died, you'd look very pretty in the catacomb standing between Mr Grimace and Mr Gape, with a sprig of morning-glory in your hair.' And he laughed sincerely.

Silence. She lay there in the dark.

'Don't you think you'll look pretty there?' he asked, laughingly, behind the door.

She said nothing in the dark room.

'*Don't* you?' he said.

Somebody walked down below in the plaza, faintly, fading away.

'Eh?' he asked her, brushing his teeth.

She lay there, staring up at the ceiling, her breasts rising and falling faster, faster, faster, the air going in and out, in and out her nostrils, a little trickle of blood coming from her clenched lips. Her eyes were very wide, her hands blindly constricted the bedclothes.

'Eh?' he said again behind the door.

She said nothing.

'Sure,' he talked to himself. 'Pretty as hell,' he murmured, under the flow of tap water. He rinsed his mouth. 'Sure,' he said.

Nothing from her in the bed.

'Women are funny,' he said to himself in the mirror.

She lay in bed.

'Sure,' he said. He gargled with some antiseptic, spat it down the drain. 'You'll be all right in the morning,' he said.

Not a word from her.

'We'll get the car fixed.'

She didn't say anything.

'Be morning before you know it.' He was screwing caps on things now, putting freshener on his face. 'And the car fixed tomorrow, maybe, at the very latest the next day. You won't mind another night here will you?'

She didn't answer.

'*Will* you?' he asked.

No reply.

The light blinked out under the bathroom door.

'Marie?'

He opened the door.

'Asleep?'

She lay with eyes wide, breasts moving up and down.

'Asleep,' he said. 'Well, good night, lady.'

He climbed into his bed. 'Tired,' he said.

No reply.

'Tired,' he said.

The wind tossed the lights outside; the room was oblong and black and he was in his bed dozing already.

She lay, eyes wide, the watch ticking on her wrist, breasts moving up and down.

It was a fine day coming through the Tropic of Cancer. The automobile pushed along the turning road leaving the jungle country behind, heading for the United States, roaring between the green hills, taking every turn, leaving behind a faint vanishing trail of exhaust smoke. And inside the shiny automobile sat Joseph with his pink, healthy face and his Panama hat, and a little camera cradled on his lap as he drove; a swathe of black silk pinned around the left upper arm of his tan coat. He watched the country slide by and absent-mindedly made a gesture to the seat beside him, and stopped.

He broke into a little sheepish smile and turned once more to the window of his car, humming a tuneless tune, his right hand slowly reaching over to touch the seat beside him . . .

Which was empty.

Jack-in-the-Box

He looked through the cold morning windows with the Jack-in-the-Box in his hands, prying the rusted lid. But no matter how he struggled, the Jack would not jump to the light with a cry, or slap its velvet mittens on the air, or bob in a dozen directions with a wild and painted smile. Crushed under the lid, in its jail, it stayed crammed tight coil on coil. With your ear to the box, you felt pressure beneath, the fear and panic of the trapped toy. It was like holding someone's heart in your hand. Edwin could not tell if the box pulsed or if his own blood beat against the lid.

He threw the box down and looked to the window. Outside the window the trees surrounded the house which surrounded Edwin. He could not see beyond the trees. If he tried to find another World beyond them, the trees wove themselves thick with the wind, to still his curiosity, to stop his eyes.

'Edwin!' Behind him, Mother's waiting, nervous breath as she drank her breakfast coffee. 'Stop staring. Come eat.'

'No,' he whispered.

'What?' A stiffened rustle. She must have turned. 'Which is more important, breakfast or that window?'

'The window . . .' he whispered and sent his gaze running the paths and trails he had tried for thirteen years. Was it true that the trees flowed on ten thousand miles to nothingness? He could not say. His sight returned defeated, to the lawn, the steps, his hands trembling on the pane.

He turned to eat his tasteless apricots, alone with his mother in the vast and echoing breakfast room. Five thousand mornings at this table, this window, and no movement beyond the trees.

The two of them ate silently.

She was the pale woman that no one but the birds saw in old country houses in fourth-floor cupola windows, each morning at six, each afternoon at four, each evening at nine, and also passing by one minute after midnight, there she would be, in her tower, silent and white, high and alone and quiet. It was like passing a deserted greenhouse in which one last wild white blossom lifted its head to the moonlight.

And her child, Edwin, was the thistle that one breath of wind might unpod in a season of thistles. His hair was silken and his eyes were of a constant blue and feverish temperature. He had a haunted look, as if he slept poorly. He might fly apart like a packet of ladyfinger firecrackers if a certain door slammed.

His mother began to talk, slowly and with great caution, then more rapidly, and then angrily, and then almost spitting at him.

'Why must you disobey every morning? I don't like your staring from the window, do you hear? What do you want? Do you want to see them?' she cried, her fingers twitching. She was blazingly lovely, like an angry white flower. 'Do you want to see the Beasts that run down paths and crush people like strawberries?'

Yes, he thought, I'd like to see the Beasts, horrible as they are.

'Do you want to go out there,' she cried, 'like your father did before you were born, and be killed as he was killed, struck down by one of those Terrors on the road, would you like that?'

'No . . .'

'Isn't it enough they murdered your father? Why should you even think of those Beasts?' She motioned towards the forest. 'Well, if you really want to die that much, go ahead!'

She quieted, but her fingers kept opening and closing on

the tablecloth. 'Edwin, Edwin, your father built every part of this World, it was beautiful for him, it should be for you. There's nothing, nothing, beyond those trees but death; I won't have you near it! This *is* the World. There's no other worth bothering with.'

He nodded miserably.

'Smile now, and finish your toast,' she said.

He ate slowly, with the window reflected in secret on his silver spoon.

'Mom . . . ?' He couldn't say it. 'What's . . . dying? You talk about it. Is it a feeling?'

'To those who must live on after someone else, a bad feeling, yes.' She stood up suddenly. 'You're late for school! Run!'

He kissed her as he grabbed his books. 'Bye!'

'Say hello to Teacher!'

He fled from her like a bullet from a gun. Up endless stair-cases, through passages, halls, past windows that poured down dark gallery panels like white waterfalls. Up, up through the layer-cake Worlds with the thick frostings of Oriental rug between, and bright candles on top.

From the highest stair he gazed down through four intervals of Universe.

Lowlands of kitchen, dining room, parlour. Two Middle Countries of music, games, pictures, and locked, forbidden rooms. And here – he whirled – the Highlands of picnics, adventure, and learning. Here he roamed, idled, or sat singing lonely child songs on the winding journey to school.

This, then, was the Universe. Father (or God, as Mother often called him) had raised its mountains of wallpapered plaster long ago. This was Father-God's creation, in which stars blazed at the flick of a switch. And the sun was Mother, and Mother was the sun, about which all the Worlds swung, turning. And Edwin, a small dark meteor, spun up around through the dark carpets and shimmering tapestries of space. You saw him rise to vanish on vast comet staircases, on hikes and explorations.

Sometimes he and Mother picnicked in the Highlands, spread cool snow linens on red-tuffed, Persian lawns, on crimson meadows in a rarefied plateau at the summit of the Worlds where flaking portraits of sallow strangers looked meanly down on their eating and their revels. They drew water from silver taps in hidden tiled niches, smashed the tumblers on hearthstones, shrieking. Played hide-and-seek in enchanged Upper Countries, in unknown, wild, and hidden lands, where she found him rolled like a mummy in a velvet window drape or under sheeted furniture like a rare plant protected from some wind. Once, lost, he wandered for hours in insane foothills of dust and echoes, where the hooks and hangers in closets were hung only with night. But she found him and carried him weeping down through the levelling Universe to the parlour where dust motes, exact and familiar, fell in showers of sparks on the sunlit air.

He ran up a stair.

Here he knocked a thousand thousand doors, all locked and forbidden. Here Picasso ladies and Dali gentlemen screamed silently from canvas asylums, their gold eyes burning when he dawdled.

'Those Things live *out there*,' his mother had said, pointing to the Dali-Picasso families.

Now running quickly past, he stuck out his tongue at them.

He stopped running.

One of the forbidden doors stood open.

Sunlight slanted warm through it, exciting him.

Beyond the door, a spiral stair screwed around up in sun and silence.

He stood, gasping. Year after year he had tried the doors that were always found locked. What would happen now if he shoved this one full open and climbed the stair? Was some Monster hiding at the top?

'Hello!'

His voice leapt up around the spiralled sunlight. 'Hello . . . ' whispered a faint, far lazy echo, high, high, and gone.

He moved through the door.

'Please, please, don't hurt me,' he whispered to the high sunlit place.

He climbed, pausing with each step to wait for his punishment, eyes shut like a penitent. Faster now, he leapt around and around and up until his knees ached and his breath fountained in and out and his head banged like a bell and at last he reached the terrible summit of the climb and stood in an open, sun-drenched tower.

The sun struck his eyes a blow. Never, never so much sun! He stumbled to the iron rail.

'It's here!' His mouth opened from one direction to another. 'It's there!' He ran in a circle. 'There!'

He was above the sombre tree barrier. For the first time he stood high over the windy chestnuts and elms and as far as he could see was green grass, green trees, and white ribbons on which beetles ran, and the other half of the World was blue and endless, with the sun lost and dropping away in an incredible deep blue room so vast he felt himself fall with it, screamed, and clutched the tower ledge, and beyond the trees, beyond the white ribbons where the beetles ran he saw things like fingers sticking up, but he saw no Dali-Picasso Terrors, he saw only some small red-and-white-and-blue handkerchiefs fluttering high on great white poles.

He was suddenly sick; he was sick again.

Turning, he almost fell flat down the stairs.

He slammed the forbidden door, fell against it.

'You'll go blind.' He crushed his hands to his eyes. 'You shouldn't have seen, you shouldn't, you shouldn't!'

He fell to his knees, he lay on the floor twisted tight, covered up. He need wait but a moment – the blindness would come.

Five minutes later he stood at an ordinary Highlands window, looking out at his own familiar Garden World.

He saw once more the elms and hickory trees and the stone wall, and that forest which he had taken to be an endless wall itself, beyond which lay nothing but nightmare nothingness, mist, rain, and eternal night. Now it was certain, the Universe did not end with the forest. There were other Worlds than those contained in Highland or Lowland.

He tried the forbidden door again. Locked.

Had he really gone up? Had he really discovered those half-green, half-blue vastnesses? Had God seen him? Edwin trembled. God. God, who smoked mysterious black pipes and wielded magical walking sticks. God who might be watching even now!

Edwin murmured, touching his cold face.

'I can still see. Thank you, thank you. I can *still* see!'

At nine-thirty, half an hour late, he rapped on the school door.

'Good morning, Teacher!'

The door swung open. Teacher waited in her tall, grey, thick-clothed monk's robe, the cowl hiding her face. She wore her usual silver spectacles. Her grey-gloved hands beckoned.

'You're late.'

Beyond her the land of books burned in bright colours from the hearth. There were walls bricked with encyclopedias, and a fireplace in which you could stand without bumping your head. A log blazed fiercely.

The door closed, and there was a warm quiet. Here was the desk, where God had once sat, he'd walked this carpet, stuffing his pipe with rich tobacco, and scowled out that vast, stained-glass window. The room smelled of God, rubbed wood, tobacco, leather, and silver coins. Here, Teacher's voice sang like a solemn harp, telling of God, the old days, and the World when it had shaken with God's determination, trembled at his wit, when the World was abuilding under God's hand, a blueprint, a cry, and timber rising. God's fingerprints still lay like half-melted snowflakes on a dozen sharpened pencils in a locked glass display. They must never never be touched lest they melt away forever.

Here, here in the Highlands, to the soft sound of Teacher's voice running on, Edwin learned what was expected of him and his body. He was to grow into a Presence, he must fit the odours and the trumpet voice of God. He must some day stand tall and burning with pale fire at this high window to shout dust off the beams of the Worlds; he must be God himself! Nothing must prevent it. Not the sky or the trees or the Things beyond the trees.

Teacher moved like a vapour in the room.

'Why are you late, Edwin?'

'I don't know.'

'I'll ask you again. Edwin, why are you late?'

'One — one of the forbidden doors was open . . . '

He heard the hiss of Teacher's breath. He saw her slowly slide back and sink into the large hand-carved chair, swallowed by darkness, her glasses flashing light before they vanished. He felt her looking out at him from shadow and her voice was numbed and so like a voice he heard at night, his own voice crying just before he woke from some nightmare. 'Which door? Where?' she said. 'Oh, it must be locked!'

'The door by the Dali-Picasso people,' he said, in panic. He and Teacher had always been friends. Was that finished now? Had he spoiled things? 'I climbed the stair. I had to, I had to! I'm sorry, I'm sorry. Please, don't tell Mother!'

Teacher sat lost in the hollow chair, in the hollow cowl. Her glasses made faint firefly glitters in the well where she moved alone. 'And what did you *see* up there?' she murmured.

'A big blue room!'

'Did you?'

'And a green one, and ribbons with bugs running on them, but I didn't, I didn't stay long, I swear, I swear!'

'Green room, ribbons, yes ribbons, and the little bugs running along them, yes,' she said, and her voice made him sad.

He reached out for her hand, but it fell away to her lap and groped back, in darkness, to her breast. 'I came right down, I locked the door, I won't go look again, ever!' he cried.

Her voice was so faint he could hardly hear what she said. 'But now you've seen, and you'll want to see more, and you'll always be curious now.' The cowl moved slowly back and forth. Its deepness turned towards him, questioning. 'Did you – *like* what you saw?'

'I was scared. It was big.'

'Big, yes, too big. Large, large, so large, Edwin. Not like *our* World. Big, large, uncertain. Oh, why did you do this! You knew it was wrong!'

The fire bloomed and withered on the hearth while she waited for his answer and finally when he could not answer she said, as if her lips were barely moving, 'Is it your mother?'

'I dont know!'

'Is she nervous, is she mean, does she snap at you, does she hold too tight, do you want time alone, is that it, is that it, is that it?'

'Yes, yes!' he sobbed, wildly.

'Is that why you ran off, she demands all your time, all your thoughts?' Lost and sad, her voice. 'Tell me . . . '

His hands had gone sticky with tears. 'Yes!' He bit his fingers and the backs of his hands. 'Yes!' It was wrong to admit such things, but he didn't have to say them now, she said them, she said them, and all he must do is agree, shake his head, bite his knuckles, cry out between sobs.

Teacher was a million years old.

'We learn,' she said, wearily. Rousing from her chair, she moved with a slow swaying of grey robes to the desk where her gloved hand searched a long time to find pen and paper. 'We learn, Oh God, but slowly, and with pain, we learn. We think we do right, but all the time, all the time, we kill the Plan . . .' She hissed her breath, jerked her head up suddenly. The cowl looked completely empty, shivering.

She wrote words on the paper.

'Give this to your mother. It tells her you must have two full hours every afternoon to yourself, to prowl where you wish. Anywhere. Except *out there*. Are you listening, child?'

'Yes.' He dried his face. 'But – '

'Go on.'

'Did Mother lie to me about *out there*, and the Beasts?'

'Look at me,' she said. 'I've been your friend, I've never beaten you, as your mother sometimes must. We're both here to help you understand and grow so you won't be destroyed as God was.'

She arose, and in rising, turned the cowl such a way that colour from the hearth washed over her face. Swiftly, the firelight erased her many wrinkles.

Edwin gasped. His heart gave a jolting thump. 'The fire!'

Teacher froze.

'The fire!' Edwin looked at the fire and back to her face. The cowl jerked away from his gaze, the face vanished in the deep well, gone. 'Your face,' said Edwin numbly. 'You look like Mother!'

She moved swiftly to the books, seized one down. She talked to the shelves in her high, singing monotonous voice.

'Women look alike, you know that! Forget it! Here, here!' And she brought him the book. 'Read the first chapter! Read the diary!'

Edwin took the book but did not feel its weight in his hands. The fire rumbled and sucked itself brilliantly up the flue as he began to read and as he read Teacher sank back down and settled and quieted and the more he read the more the grey cowl nodded and became serene, the hidden face like a clapper gone solemn in its bell. Firelight ignited the gold animal lettering of the shelved books as he read and he spoke the words but was really thinking of these books from which pages had been razored, and clipped, certain lines erased, certain pictures torn, the leather jaws of some books glued tight, others like mad dogs, muzzled in hard bronze straps to keep him away. All this he thought while his lips moved through the fire-quiet.

'In the Beginning was God, who created the Universe, and the Worlds within the Universe, the Continents within the Worlds and the Lands within the Continents, and shaped from his mind and hand his loving wife and a child who in time would be God himself . . . '

Teacher nodded slowly. The fire fell softly away to slumbering coals. Edwin read on.

Down the banister, breathless, he slid into the parlour. 'Mom, Mom!'

She lay in a plump maroon chair, breathless, as if she, too, had run a great way.

'Mom, Mom, you're soaking wet!'

'Am I?' she said, as if it was his fault she'd been rushing about. 'So I am, so I am.' She took a deep breath and sighed. Then she took his hands and kissed each one. She looked at him steadily, her eyes dilating. 'Well now, listen here, I've a surprise! Do you know what's coming tomorrow? You can't guess! Your birthday!'

'But it's only been ten months!'

'Tomorrow it is! Do us wonders, I say. And anything I *say* is so is *really* so, my dear.'

She laughed.

'And we open another secret room?' He was dazed.

'The fourteenth room, yes! Fifteenth room next year, sixteenth, seventeenth, and so on and on till your twenty-first birthday, Edwin! Then, oh, then we'll open up the triple-locked doors to the most important room and you'll be Man of the House, Father, God, Ruler of the Universe!'

'Hey,' he said. 'And, 'Hey!' He tossed his books straight up in the air. They exploded like a great burst of doves, whistling. He laughed. She laughed. Their laughter flew and fell with the books. He ran to scream down the banister again.

At the bottom of the stairs, she waited, arms wide, to catch him.

Edwin lay on his moonlit bed and his fingers pried at the Jack-in-the-Box, but the lid stayed shut; he turned it in his hands, blindly, but did not look down at it. Tomorrow, his birthday — but why? Was he *that* good? No. Why then, should the birthday come so soon? Well, simply because things had gotten, what word could you use? Nervous? Yes, things had begun to shimmer by day as well as by night. He saw the white tremor, the moonlight sifting down and down on an invisible snow in his mother's face. It would take yet another of his birthdays to quiet her again.

'My birthdays,' he said to the ceiling, 'will you come quicker from now on. I know, I know. Mom laughs so loud, so much, and her eyes are funny . . . '

Would Teacher be invited to the party? No. Mother and Teacher had never met. 'Why not?' 'Because,' said Mom. 'Don't you *want* to meet Mom, Teacher?' 'Some day,' said Teacher, faintly, blowing off like cobwebs in the hall.

'Some . . . day . . . '

And where did Teacher go at night? Did she drift through all those secret mountain countries high up near the moon where the chandeliers were skinned blind with dust, or did she wander out beyond the trees that lay beyond the trees that lay beyond the trees? No, hardly that!

He twisted the toy in his sweating hands. Last year, when things began to tremble and quiver, hadn't Mother advanced his birthday several months, too? Yes, oh, yes, yes.

Think of something else. God. God building cold midnight cellar, sunbaked attic, and all miracles between. Think of the hour of his death, crushed by some monstrous beetle beyond the wall. Oh, how the Worlds must have rocked with his passing!

Edwin moved the Jack-in-the-Box to his face, whispered against the lid. 'Hello! Hello! Hello, hello . . . '

No answer save the sprung-tight coiled-in tension there.

I'll get you out, thought Edwin. Just wait, just wait. It may hurt, but there's only one way. Here, here . . .

And he moved from bed to window and leaned far out, looking down to the marbled walk in the moonlight. He raised the box high, felt the sweat trickle from his armpit, felt his fingers clench, felt his arm jerk. He flung the box out, shouting. The box tumbled in the cold air, down. It took a long time to strike the marble pavement.

Edwin bent still further over, gasping.

'Well?' he cried. 'Well?' and again, 'You there!' and 'You!'

The echoes faded. The box lay in the forest shadows. He could not see if the crash had broken it wide. He could not see if the Jack had risen, smiling, from its hideous jail or if it bobbed upon the wind now this way, that, this way, that, its silver bells jingling softly. He listened. He stood by the window for an hour staring, listening, and at last went back to bed.

Morning. Bright voices moved near and far, in and out the Kitchen World and Edwin opened his eyes. Whose voices, now whose could they be? Some of God's workmen? The Dali people? But Mother hated them; no. The voices faded in a humming roar. Silence. And from a great distance, a running, running, grew louder and still louder until the door burst open.

'Happy Birthday!'

They danced, they ate frosted cookies, they bit lemon ices, they drank pink wines, and there stood his name on a snow-powdered cake as Mother chorded the piano into an avalanche of sound and opened her mouth to sing, then whirled to seize him away to more strawberries, more wines, more laughter that shook chandeliers into trembling rain. Then, a silver key flourished, they raced to unlock the fourteenth forbidden door.

'Ready! Hold on!'

The door whispered into the wall.

'Oh,' said Edwin.

For, disappointingly enough, this fourteenth room was nothing at all but a dusty dull-brown closet. It promised nothing as had the rooms given him on other anniversaries! His sixth birthday present, now, had been the schoolroom in the Highlands. On his seventh birthday he had opened the playroom in the Lowlands. Eighth, the music room; ninth, the miraculous hell-fired kitchen! Tenth was the room where phonographs hissed in a continuous exhalation of ghosts singing on a gentle wind. Eleventh was the vast green diamond room of the garden with a carpet that had to be cut instead of swept!

'Oh, don't be disappointed; move!' Mother, laughing, pushed him in the closet. 'Wait till you see how magical! Shut the door!'

She thrust a red button flush with the wall.

Edwin shrieked. 'No!'

For the room was quivering, working, like a mouth that held them in iron jaws; the room moved, the wall slid away below.

'Oh, hush now, darling,' she said. The door drifted down through the floor, and a long insanely vacant wall slithered by like an endlessly rustling snake to bring another door and another door with it that did not stop but travelled on while Edwin screamed and clutched his mother's waist. The room whined and cleared its throat somewhere; the trembling ceased, the room stood still. Edwin stared at a strange new door and heard his mother say go on, open it, there, now, there. And the new door gaped upon still further mystery. Edwin blinked.

'The Highlands! This is the Highlands! How did we get here? Where's the parlour, Mom, where's the parlour?'

She fetched him out through the door. 'We jumped straight up, and we flew. Once a week, you'll fly to school instead of running the long way around!'

He still could not move, but only stood looking at the mystery of Land exchanged for Land, of Country replaced by higher and further Country.

'Oh, Mother, Mother . . . ' he said.

It was a sweet long time in the deep grass of the garden where they idled most deliciously, sipped huge cupfuls of apple cider with their elbows on crimson silk cushions, their shoes kicked off, their toes bedded in sour dandelions, sweet clover. Mother jumped twice when she heard Monsters roar beyond the forest. Edwin kissed her cheek. 'It's all right,' he said, 'I'll protect you.'

'I know you will,' she said, but she turned to gaze at the pattern of trees, as if any moment the chaos out there might smash the forest with a blow and stamp its Titan's foot down and grind them to dust.

Late in the long blue afternoon, they saw a chromium bird

thing fly through a bright rift in the trees, high and roaring. They ran for the parlour, heads bent as before a green storm of lightning and rain, feeling the sound pour blinding showers to drench them.

Crackle, crackle — the birthday burnt away to cellophane nothingness. At sunset, in the dim soft Parlour Country, Mother inhaled champagne with her tiny seedling nostrils and her pale summer-rose mouth, then, drowsy wild, herded Edwin off to his room and shut him in.

He undressed in slow-pantomimed wonder, thinking, this year, next year, and which room two years, three years, from today? What about the Beasts, the Monsters? And being mashed and God killed? What was killed? What was Death? Was Death a feeling? Did God enjoy it so much he never came back? Was Death a journey then?

In the hall, on her way downstairs, Mother dropped a champagne bottle. Edwin heard and was cold, for the thought that jumped through his head was, that's how Mother'd sound. If she fell, if she broke, you'd find a million fragments in the morning. Bright crystal and clear wine on the parquet flooring, that's all you'd see at dawn.

Morning was the smell of vines and grapes and moss in his room, a smell of shadowed coolness. Downstairs, breakfast was in all probability, at this instant, manifesting itself in a fingersnap on the wintry tables.

Edwin got up to wash and dress and wait, feeling fine. Now things would be fresh and new for at least a month. Today, like all days, there'd be breakfast, school, lunch, songs in the music room, an hour or two at the electrical games, then — tea in the Outlands, on the luminous grass. Then up to school again for a late hour or so, where he and Teacher might prowl the censored library together and he'd puzzle with words and thoughts about the World *out there* that had been censored from his eyes.

He had forgotten Teacher's note. Now, he must give it to Mother.

He opened the door. The hall was empty. Down through the deeps of the Worlds, a soft mist floated, through a silence which no footsteps broke; the hills were quiet; the silver fonts did not pulse in the first sunlight, and the banister, coiling up from the mists, was a prehistoric monster peering into his room. He pulled away from this creature, looking to find Mother, like a white boat, drifted by the dawn tides and vapours below.

She was not there. He hurried down through the hushed lands, calling, 'Mother!'

He found her in the parlour, collapsed on the floor in her shiny green-gold party dress, a champagne goblet in one hand, the carpet littered with broken glass.

She was obviously asleep, so he sat at the magical breakfast table. He blinked at the empty white cloth and the gleaming plates. There was no food. All his life wondrous foods had awaited him here. But not today.

'Mother, wake up!' He ran to her. 'Shall I go to school? Where's the food? Wake up!'

He ran up the stairs.

The Highlands were cold and shadowed, and the white glass suns no longer glowed from the ceilings in this day of sullen fog. Down dark corridors, through dim continents of silence, Edwin rushed. He rapped and rapped at the school door. It drifted in, whining, by itself.

The school lay empty and dark. No fire roared on the hearth to toss shadows on the beamed ceiling. There was not a crackle or a whisper.

'Teacher?'

He poised in the centre of the flat, cold room.

'Teacher!' he screamed.

He slashed the drapes aside; a faint shaft of sunlight fell through the stained glass.

Edwin gestured. He commanded the fire to explode like a popcorn kernel on the hearth. He commanded it to bloom to life! He shut his eyes, to give Teacher time to appear. He opened his eyes and was stupefied at what he saw on her desk.

Neatly folded was the grey cowl and robe, atop which gleamed her silver spectacles, and one grey glove. He touched them. One grey glove was gone. A piece of greasy cosmetic chalk lay on the robe. Testing it, he made dark lines on his hands.

He drew back, staring at Teacher's empty robe, the glasses, the greasy chalk. His hand touched a knob of a door which had always been locked. The door swung slowly wide. He looked into a small brown closet.

'Teacher!'

He ran in, the door crashed shut, he pressed a red button. The room sank down, and with it sank a slow mortal coldness. The World was silent, quiet, and cool. Teacher gone and Mother – sleeping. Down fell the room, with him in its iron jaws.

Machinery clashed. A door slid open. Edwin ran out.

The parlour!

Behind was not a door, but a tall oak panel from which he had emerged.

Mother lay uncaring, asleep. Folded under her, barely showing as he rolled her over, was one of Teacher's soft grey gloves.

He stood near her, holding the incredible glove, for a long time. Finally, he began to whimper.

He fled back to the Highlands. The hearth was cold, the room empty. He waited. Teacher did not come. He ran down again to the solemn Lowlands, commanded the table to fill with steaming dishes! Nothing happened. He sat by his mother, talking and pleading with her and touching her, and her hands were cold.

The clock ticked and the light changed in the sky and still she did not move, and he was hungry and the silent dust dropped down on the air through all the Worlds. He thought of Teacher and knew that if she was in none of the hills and mountains above, then there was only one place she could be. She had wandered, by error, into the Outlands, lost until someone found her. And so he must go out, call after her, bring her back to wake Mother, or she would lie here forever with the dust falling in the great darkened spaces.

Through the kitchen, out back, he found late afternoon sun and the Beasts hooting faintly beyond the rim of the World. He clung to the garden wall, not daring to let go, and in the shadows, at a distance, saw the shattered box he had flung from the window. Freckles of sunlight quivered on the broken lid and touched tremblingly over and over the face of the Jack jumped out and sprawled with its arms overhead in an eternal gesture of freedom. The doll smiled and did not smile, smiled and did not smile, as the sun winked on the mouth, and Edwin stood, hypnotized, above and beyond it. The doll opened its arms towards the path that led off between the secret trees, the forbidden path smeared with oily droppings of the Beasts. But the path lay silent and the sun warmed Edwin and he heard the wind blow softly in the trees. At last, he let go of the garden wall.

'Teacher?'

He edged along the path a few feet.

'Teacher!'

His shoes slipped on the animal droppings and he stared far down the motionless tunnel, blindly. The path moved under, the trees moved over him.

'Teacher!'

He walked slowly but steadily. He turned. Behind him lay his World and its very new silence. It was diminished, it was small! How strange to see it less than it had been. It had always and forever seemed so large. He felt his heart stop. He stepped back. But then, afraid of that silence in the World, he turned to face the forest path ahead.

Everything before him was new. Odours filled his nostrils, colours, odd shapes, incredible sizes filled his eyes.

If I run beyond the trees I'll die, he thought, for that's what Mother said. You'll die, you'll die.

But what's dying? Another room? A blue room, a green room, far larger than all the rooms that ever were! But where's the key? There, far ahead, a large half-open iron door, a wrought-iron gate. Beyond a room as large as the sky, all coloured green with trees and grass! Oh, Mother, Teacher . . .

He rushed, stumbled, fell, got up, ran again, his numb legs under him were left behind as he fell down and down the side of a hill, the path gone, wailing, crying, and then not wailing or crying any more, but making new sounds. He reached the great rusted, screaming iron gate, leapt through; the Universe dwindled behind, he did not look back at his old Worlds, but ran as they withered and vanished.

The policeman stood at the kerb, looking down the street. 'These kids. I'll never be able to figure them.'

'How's that?' asked the pedestrian.

The policeman thought it over and frowned. 'Couple seconds ago a little kid ran by. He was laughing and crying, crying and laughing, both. He was jumping up and down and touching things. Things like lampposts, the telephone poles, fire hydrants, dogs, people. Things like sidewalks, fences, gates, cars, plateglass windows, barber poles. Hell, he even grabbed hold and looked at me, and looked at the sky, you should have seen the tears, and all the time he kept yelling and yelling something funny.'

'What did he yell?' asked the pedestrian.

'He kept yelling, "I'm dead, I'm dead, I'm glad I'm dead, I'm dead, I'm dead, I'm glad I'm dead, I'm dead, I'm dead, it's *good* to be dead!" ' The policeman scratched his chin slowly. 'One of them new kid games, I guess.'

The Leave-Taking

She was a woman with a broom or a dustpan or a washrag or a mixing spoon in her hand. You saw her cutting piecrust in the morning, humming to it, or you saw her setting out the baked pies at noon or taking them in, cool, at dusk. She rang porcelain cups like a Swiss bell ringer, to their place. She glided through the halls as steadily as a vacuum machine, seeking, finding, and setting to rights. She made mirrors of every window, to catch the sun. She strolled but twice through any garden, trowel in hand, and the flowers raised their quivering fires upon the warm air in her wake. She slept quietly and turned no more than three times in a night, as relaxed as a white glove to which, at dawn, a brisk hand will return. Waking, she touched people like pictures, to set their frames straight.

But, now . . . ?

'Grandma,' said everyone. 'Great-grandma.'

Now it was as if a huge sum in arithmetic were finally drawing to an end. She had stuffed turkeys, chickens, squabs, gentlemen, and boys. She had washed ceilings, walls, invalids, and children. She had laid linoleum, repaired bicycles, wound clocks, stoked furnaces, swabbed iodine on ten thousand grievous wounds. Her hands had flown all around about and down, gentling this, holding that, throwing baseballs, swinging bright croquet mallets, seeding black earth, or fixing covers over dumplings, ragouts, and children wildly strewn by slumber. She had pulled down shades, pinched out candles, turned switches, and – grown old. Looking back on thirty billions of things started, carried, finished and done, it all summed up, totalled out; the last decimal was placed, the final zero swung slowly into line. Now, chalk in hand, she stood back from life a silent hour before reaching for the eraser.

'Let me see now,' said Great-grandma. 'Let me see . . . '

With no fuss or further ado, she travelled the house in an ever-circling inventory, reached the stairs at last, and, making no special announcement, she took herself up three flights to her room where, silently, she laid herself out like a fossil imprint under the snowing cool sheets of her bed and began to die.

Again the voices:

'Grandma! Great-grandma!'

The rumour of what she was doing dropped down the stairwell, hit, and spread ripples through the rooms, out doors and windows and along the street of elms to the edge of the green ravine.

'Here, now, here!'

The family surrounded her bed.

'Just let me lie,' she whispered.

Her ailment could not be seen in any microscope; it was a mild but ever-deepening tiredness, a dim weighing of her sparrow body; sleepy, sleepier, sleepiest.

As for her children and her children's children – it seemed impossible that with such a simple act, the most leisurely act in the world, she could cause such apprehension.

'Great-grandma, now listen – what you're doing is no better than breaking a lease. This house will fall down without you. You must give us at least a year's notice!'

Great-grandma opened one eye. Ninety years gazed calmly out at her physicians like a dust-ghost from a high cupola window in a fast-emptying house. 'Tom . . . ?'

The boy was sent, alone, to her whispering bed.

'Tom,' she said, faintly, far away, 'in the Southern Seas

there's a day in each man's life when he knows it's time to shake hands with all his friends and say good-bye and sail away, and he does, and it's natural — it's just his time. That's how it is today. I'm so like you sometimes, sitting through Saturday matinees until nine at night when we send your dad to bring you home. Tom, when the time comes that the same cowboys are shooting the same Indians on the same mountaintop, then it's best to fold back the seat and head for the door, with no regrets and no walking backward up the aisle. So, I'm leaving while I'm still happy and still entertained.'

Douglas was summoned next to her side.

'Grandma, who'll shingle the roof next spring?'

Every April for as far back as there were calendars, you thought you heard woodpeckers tapping the housetop. But no, it was Great-grandma, somehow transported, singing, pounding nails, replacing shingles, high in the sky!

'Douglas,' she whispered, 'don't ever let anyone do the shingles unless it's fun for them.'

'Yes'm.'

'Look around come April, and say, "Who'd like to fix the roof?" And whichever face lights up is the face you want, Douglas. Because up there on that roof you can see the whole town going towards the country and the country going towards the edge of the earth and the river shining, and the morning lake, and birds on the trees down under you, and the best of the wind all around above. Any one of those should be enough to make a person climb a weather vane some spring sunrise. It's a powerful hour, if you give it half a chance . . . '

Her voice sank to a soft flutter.

Douglas was crying.

She roused herself again. 'Now, why are you doing that?'

'Because,' he said, 'you won't be here tomorrow.'

She turned a small hand-mirror from herself to the boy. He

'It's all right,' whispered Great-grandma, as the dream floated her. 'Like everything else in this life, it's fitting.'

And the sea moved her back down the shore.

Exorcism

She came out of the bathroom putting iodine on her finger where she had almost lopped it off cutting herself a chunk of coconut cake. Just then the mailman came up the porch steps, opened the door, and walked in. The door slammed. Elmira Brown jumped a foot.

'Sam!' she cried. She waved her iodined finger on the air to cool it. 'I'm still not used to my husband being a postman. Every time you just walk in, it scares the life out of me!'

Sam Brown stood there with the mail pouch half empty, scratching his head. He looked back out the door as if a fog had suddenly rolled in on a calm sweet summer morn.

'Sam, you're home early,' she said.

'Can't stay,' he said in a puzzled voice.

'Spit it out, what's wrong?' She came over and looked into his face.

'Maybe nothing, maybe lots. I just delivered some mail to Clara Goodwater up the street . . . '

'Clara Goodwater!'

'Now don't get your dander up. Books it was, from the Johnson-Smith Company, Racine, Wisconsin. Title of one book . . . let's see now.' He screwed up his face, then unscrewed it. '*Albertus Magnus* — that's it. "Being the approved, verified, sympathetic and natural Egyptian Secrets or . . . " ' He peered at the ceiling to summon the lettering. ' "White and Black Art for Man and Beast, Revealing the Forbidden Knowledge and Mysteries of Ancient Philosophers"!'

'Clara Goodwater's you say?'

'Walking along, I had a good chance to peek at the front pages, no harm in that. "Hidden Secrets of Life Unveiled by that celebrated Student, Philosopher, Chemist, Naturalist, Psychomist, Astrologer, Alchemist, Metallurgist, Sorcerer, Explanator of the Mysteries of Wizards and Witchcraft, together with recondite views of numerous Arts and Sciences – Obscure, Plain, Practical, etcetera." There! By God, I got a head like a box Brownie. Got the words, even if I haven't got the sense.'

Elmira stood looking at her iodined finger as if it were pointed at her by a stranger.

'Clara Goodwater,' she murmured.

'Looked me right in the eye as I handed it over, said, "Going to be a witch, first-class, no doubt. Get my diploma in no time. Set up business. Hex crowds and individuals, old and young, big and small." Then she kinda laughed, put her nose in that book, and went in.'

Elmira stared at a bruise on her arm, carefully tongued a loose tooth in her jaw.

A door slammed. Tom Spaulding, kneeling on Elmira Brown's front lawn, looked up. He had been wandering about the neighbourhood, seeing how the ants were doing here or there, and had found a particularly good hill with a big hole in which all kinds of fiery bright pismires were tumbling about scissoring the air and wildly carrying little packets of dead grasshopper and infinitesimal bird down into the earth. Now here was something else: Mrs Brown, swaying on the edge of her porch as if she'd just found out the world was falling through space at sixty trillion miles a second. Behind her was Mr Brown, who didn't know the miles per second and probably wouldn't care if he did know.

'You, Tom!' said Mrs Brown. 'I need moral support and the equivalent of the blood of the Lamb with me. Come along!'

And off she rushed, squashing ants and kicking tops off dandelions and trotting big spiky holes in flower beds as she cut across yards.

Tom knelt a moment longer studying Mrs Brown's shoulder blades and spine as she toppled down the street. He read the bones and they were eloquent of melodrama and adventure, a thing he did not ordinarily connect with ladies, even though Mrs Brown had the remnants of a pirate's moustache. A moment later he was in tandem with her.

'Mrs Brown, you sure look mad!'

'You don't know what mad *is*, boy!'

'Watch out!' cried Tom.

Mrs Elmira Brown fell right over an iron dog lying asleep there on the green grass.

'Mrs Brown!'

'You see?' Mrs Brown sat there. 'Clara Goodwater did this to me! Magic!'

'Magic?'

'Never mind, boy. Here's the steps. You go first and kick any invisible strings out of the way. Ring the doorbell, but pull your finger off quick, the juice'll burn you to a cinder!'

Tom did not touch the bell.

'Clara Goodwater!' Mrs Brown flicked the bell button with her iodined finger.

Far away in the cool dim empty rooms of the big old house, a silver bell tinkled and faded.

Tom listened. Still farther away there was a stir of mouse-like running. A shadow, perhaps a blowing curtain, moved in a distant parlour.

'Hello,' said a quiet voice.

And quite suddenly Mrs Goodwater was there, fresh as a stick of peppermint, behind the screen.

'Why, hello there, Tom, Elmira. What – '

'Don't rush me! We came over about your practising to be a full-fledged witch!'

Mrs Goodwater smiled. 'Your husband's not only a mailman, but a guardian of the law. Got a nose out to *here!*'

'He didn't look at no mail.'

'He's ten minutes between houses laughing at post cards and trying on mail-order shoes.'

'It ain't what he seen; it's what you yourself told him about the books you got.'

'Just a joke. "Going to be a witch!" I said, and bang! Off gallops Sam, like I'd flung lightning at him. I declare there can't be one wrinkle in that man's brain.'

'You talked about your magic other places yesterday – '

'You must mean the Sandwich Club . . . '

'To which I pointedly was *not* invited.'

'Why, lady, we thought that was your regular day with your grandma.'

'I can always have another Grandma day, if people'd only ask me places.'

'All there was to it at the Sandwich Club was me sitting there with a ham and pickle sandwich, and I said right out loud, "At last I'm going to get my witch's diploma. Been studying for years!" '

'That's what come back to me over the phone!'

'Ain't modern inventions wonderful!' said Mrs Goodwater.

'Considering you been president of the Honeysuckle Ladies Lodge since the Civil War, it seems, I'll put it to you bang on the nose. Have you used witchcraft all these years to spell the ladies and win the ayes-have-it?'

'Do you doubt it for a moment, lady?' said Mrs Goodwater.

'Election's tomorrow again, and all I want to know is, you running for another term – and ain't you ashamed?'

'Yes to the first question and no to the second. Lady, look here, I bought those books for my boy cousin, Raoul. He's just ten and goes around looking in hats for rabbits. I told him there's about as much chance finding rabbits in hats as brains in heads of certain people I could name, but look he does and so I got these gifts for him.'

'Wouldn't believe you on a stack of Bibles.'

'God's truth, anyway. I love to fun about the witch thing. The ladies all yodelled when I explained about my dark powers. Wish you'd been there.'

'I'll be there tomorrow to fight you with a cross of gold and all the powers of good I can organize behind me,' said Elmira. 'Right now, tell me how much other magic junk you got in your house.'

Mrs Goodwater pointed to a sidetable inside the door.

'I been buying all kinds of magic herbs. Smell funny and make Raoul happy. That little sack of stuff, that's called thisis rue, and this is sabisse root and that there's ebon herbs; here's black sulphur, and this they claim is bone dust.'

'Bone dust!' Elmira skipped back and kicked Tom's ankle. Tom yelped.

'And here's wormwood and fern leaves so you can freeze shotguns and fly like a bat in your dreams, it says in Chapter X of the little book here. I think it's fine for growing boys' heads to think about things like this. Now, from the look on your face you don't believe Raoul exists. Well, I'll give you his Springfield address.'

'Yes,' said Elmira, 'and the day I write him you'll take the Springfield bus and go to General Delivery and get my letter and write back to me in a boy's hand. I know you!'

'Mrs Brown, speak up — you want to be president of the Honeysuckle Ladies Lodge, right? You run every year now for ten years. You nominate yourself. And always wind up getting *one* vote. Yours. Elmira, if the ladies wanted you they'd landslide you in. But from where I stand looking up the mountain, ain't so much as one pebble come rattling down save yours. Tell you what, I'll nominate and vote for you myself come noon tomorrow, how's that?'

'Damned for sure, then,' said Elmira. 'Last year I got a deathly cold right at election time; couldn't get out and campaign back-fence-to-back-fence. Year before that, broke my leg. Mighty strange.' She squinted darkly at the lady behind the screen. 'That's not all. Last month I cut my fingers six times, bruised my knee ten times, fell of my back porch twice, you hear – twice! I broke a window, dropped four dishes, one vase worth a dollar forty-nine at Bixby's, and I'm billing you for every dropped dish from now on in my house and environs!'

'I'll be poor by Christmas,' said Mrs Goodwater. She opened the screen door and came out suddenly and let the door slam. 'Elmira Brown, how old are you?'

'You probably got it written in one of your black books. Thirty-five!'

'Well, when I think of thirty-five years of your life . . . ' Mr Goodwater pursed her lips and blinked her eyes, counting. 'That's about twelve thousand seven hundred and seventy-five days, or counting three of them per day, twelve thousand-odd commotions, twelve thousand much-ados, and twelve thousand calamities. It's a full rich life you lead, Elmira Brown. Shake hands!'

'Get away!' Elmira fended her off.

'Why, lady, you're only the second most clumsy woman in Green Town, Illinois. You can't sit down without playing the chair like an accordion. You can't stand up but what you kick the cat. You can't trot across an open meadow without falling into a well. Your life has been one long decline, Elmira Alice Brown, so why not admit it?'

'It wasn't clumsiness that caused my calamities, but you being within a mile of me at those times when I dropped a pot of beans or juiced my finger in the electric socket at home.'

'Lady, in a town this size, *everybody's* within a mile of someone at one time or other in the day.'

'You admit being around then?'

'I admit being born here, yes, but I'd give anything right now to have been born in Kenosha or Zion. Elmira, go to your dentist and see what he can do about that serpent's tongue in there.'

'Oh!' said Elmira. 'Oh, oh, oh!'

'You've pushed me too far. I wasn't interested in witch-craft, but I think I'll just look into this business. Listen here! You're invisible right now. While you stood there I put a spell on you. You're clean out of sight.'

'You didn't!'

'Course,' admitted the witch, 'I never *could* see you, lady.'

Elmira pulled out her pocket mirror. 'There I am!' She peered closer and gasped. She reached up like someone tuning a harp and plucked a single thread. She held it up, Exhibit A. 'I never had a grey hair in my life till this second!'

The witch smiled charmingly. 'Put it in a jar of still water, be an angleworm come morning. Oh, Elmira, look at your-self at last, won't you? All these years, blaming others for your own mallet feet and floaty ways! You ever read Shake-speare? There's little stage directions in there: *Alarums and Excursions*. That's you, Elmira. Alarums and Excursions! Now get home before I feel the bumps on your head and predict gas at night for you! Shoo!'

She waved her hands in the air as if Elmira were a cloud of things. 'My, the flies are thick this summer!' she said.

She went inside and hooked the door.

'The line is drawn, Mrs Goodwater,' Elmira said, folding her arms. 'I'll give you one last chance. Withdraw from the candidacy of the Honeysuckle Lodge or face me face-to-face tomorrow when I run for office and wrest it from you in a fair fight. I'll bring Tom here with me. An innocent good boy. And innocence and good will win the day.'

'I wouldn't count on me being innocent, Mrs Brown,' said the boy. 'My mother says — '

'Shut up, Tom, good's good! You'll be there on my right hand, boy.'

'Yes'm,' said Tom.

'If, that is,' said Elmira, 'I can live through the night with this lady making wax dummies of me – shoving rusty needles through the very heart and soul of them. If you find a great big fig in my bed all shrivelled up come sunrise, Tom, you'll know who picked the fruit in the vineyard. And look to see Mrs Goodwater president till she's a hundred and ninety-five years old.'

'Why, lady,' said Mrs Goodwater, 'I'm three hundred and five *now*. Used to call me SHE in the old days.' She poked her fingers at the street. 'Abracadabra-zimmity-ZAM! How's *that*?'

Elmira ran down off the porch.

'Tomorrow!' she cried.

'Till then, lady!' said Mrs Goodwater.

Tom followed Elmira, shrugging and kicking ants off the sidewalk as he went.

Running across a driveway, Elmira screamed.

'Mrs Brown!' cried Tom.

A car backing out of a garage ran right over Elmira's right big toe.

Mrs Elmira Brown's foot hurt her in the middle of the night, so she got up and went down to the kitchen and ate some cold chicken and made a neat, painfully accurate list of things. First, illnesses in the past year. Three colds, four mild attacks of indigestion, one seizure of bloat, arthritis, lumbago, what she imagined to be gout, a severe bronchial cough, incipient asthma, and spots on her arms, plus an abscessed semicircular canal which made her reel like a drunken moth some days, backache, head pains, and nausea. Cost of medicine: *ninety-eight dollars and seventy-eight cents*.

Secondly, things broken in the house during the twelve months just past: two lamps, six vases, ten dishes, one soup tureen, two windows, one chair, one sofa cushion, six glasses, and one crystal chandelier prism. Total cost: *twelve dollars and ten cents*.

Thirdly, her pains this very night. Her toe hurt from being run over. Her stomach was upset. Her back was stiff, her legs were pulsing with agony. Her eyeballs felt like wads of blazing cotton. Her tongue tasted like a dust mop. Her ears were belling and ringing away. Cost? She debated, going back to bed.

Ten thousand dollars in personal suffering.

'Try to settle this out of court!' she said half aloud.

'Eh?' said her husband, awake.

She lay down in bed. 'I simply refuse to die.'

'Beg pardon?' he said.

'I won't die!' she said, staring at the ceiling.

'That's what I always claimed,' said her husband, and turned over to snore.

In the morning, Mrs Elmira Brown was up early and down to the library and then to the drugstore and back to the house where she was busy mixing all kinds of chemicals when her husband, Sam, came home with an empty mail pouch at noon.

'Lunch's in the icebox,' Elmira stirred a green-looking porridge in a large glass.

'Good Lord, what's that?' asked her husband. 'Looks like a milk shake been left out in the sun for forty years. Got kind of a fungus on it.'

'Fight magic with magic.'

'You goin' to *drink that*?'

'Just before I go up into the Honeysuckle Ladies Lodge for the big doings.'

Samuel Brown sniffed the concoction. 'Take my advice.

Get up those steps first, *then* drink it. What's in it?'

'Snow from angels' wings, well, really menthol, to cool hell's fires that burn you, it says in this book I got at the library. The juice of a fresh grape off the vine, for thinking clear sweet thoughts in the face of dark visions, it says. Also red rhubarb, cream of tartar, white sugar, white of eggs, spring water and clover buds with the strength of the good earth in them. Oh, I could go on all day. It's here in the list, good against bad, white against black. I can't lose!'

'Oh, you'll win, all right,' said her husband. 'But will you *know* it?'

'Think good thoughts. I'm on my way to get Tom for my charm.'

'Poor boy,' said her husband. 'Innocent, like you say, and about to be torn limb from limb, bargain-basement day at the Honeysuckle Lodge.'

'Tom'll survive,' said Elmira, and, taking the bubbling concoction with her, hid inside a Quaker Oats box with the lid on, went out the door without catching her dress or snagging her new ninety-eight-cent stockings. Realizing this, she was smug all the way to Tom's house where he waited for her in his white summer suit as she had instructed.

'Phew!' said Tom. 'What you got in that box?'

'Destiny,' said Elmira.

'I sure hope so,' said Tom, walking about two paces ahead of her.

The Honeysuckle Ladies Lodge was full of ladies looking in each other's mirrors and tugging at their skirts and asking to be sure their slips weren't showing.

At one o'clock Mrs Elmira Brown came up the steps with a boy in white clothes. He was holding his nose and screwing up one eye so he could only half see where he was going. Mrs Brown looked at the crowd and then at the Quaker Oats box and opened the top and looked in and gasped, and put the top back on without drinking any of that stuff in there. She moved inside the hall and with her moved a rustling as of taffeta, all the ladies whispering in a tide after her.

She sat down in back with Tom, and Tom looked more miserable than ever. The one eye he had open looked at the crowd of ladies and shut up for good. Sitting there, Elmira got the potion out and drank it slowly down.

At one-thirty, the president, Mrs Goodwater, banged the gavel and all but two dozen of the ladies quit talking.

'Ladies,' she called out over the summer sea of silks and laces, capped here and there with white or grey, 'it's election time. But before we start, I believe Mrs Elmira Brown, wife of our eminent graphologist — '

A titter ran through the room.

'What's graphologist?' Elmira elbowed Tom twice.

'I don't know,' whispered Tom fiercely, eyes shut, feeling that elbow come out of darkness at him.

' — wife, as I say, of our eminent handwriting expert, Samuel Brown . . . (more laughter) . . . of the U.S. Postal Service,' continued Mrs Goodwater. 'Mrs Brown wants to give us some opinions. Mrs Brown?'

Elmira stood up. Her chair fell over backward and snapped shut like a bear trap on itself. She jumped an inch off the floor and teetered on her heels, which gave off cracking sounds like they would fall to dust any moment. 'I got plenty to say,' she said, holding the empty Quaker Oats box in one hand with a Bible. She grabbed Tom with the other and ploughed forward, hitting several people's elbows and muttering to them, 'Watch what you're doing! Careful, you!' to reach the platform, turn, and knock a glass of water dripping over the table. She gave Mrs Goodwater another bristly scowl when this happened and let her mop it up with a tiny handkerchief. Then with a secret look of triumph, Elmira drew forth the empty philtre glass and held it up, displaying it for Mrs Goodwater and whispering, 'You know what was in this? It's inside me, now, lady. The charmed circle surrounds me. No knife can cleave, no hatchet break through.'

The ladies, all talking, did not hear.

Mrs Goodwater nodded, held up her hands, and there was silence.

Elmira held tight to Tom's hand. Tom kept his eyes shut, wincing.

'Ladies,' Elmira said, 'I sympathize with you. I know what you've been through these last ten years. I know why you voted for Mrs Goodwater here. You've got boys, girls, and men to feed. You've got budgets to follow. You couldn't afford to have your milk sour, your bread fall, or your cakes as flat as wheels. You didn't want mumps, chicken pox, and whooping cough in your house all in three weeks. You didn't want your husband crashing his car or electrocuting himself on the high-tension wires outside town. But now all of that's over. You can come out in the open now. No more heartburns or backaches, because I've brought the good word and we're going to exorcise this witch we've got here!'

Everybody looked around but didn't see any witch.

'I mean your *president*!' cried Elmira.

'*Me!*' Mrs Goodwater waved at everyone.

'Today,' breathed Elmira, holding on to the desk for support, 'I went to the library. I looked up counteractions. How to get rid of people who take advantage of others, how to make witches leave off and go. And I found a way to fight for all our rights. I can feel the power growing. I got the magic of all kinds of good roots and chemicals in me. I got . . . ' She paused and swayed. She blinked once. 'I got cream of tartar and . . . I got . . . white hawkweed and milk soured in the light of the moon and . . . ' She stopped and thought for a moment. She shut her mouth and a tiny sound came from deep inside her and worked up through to come out the corner of her lips. She closed her eyes for a moment to see where the strength was.

'Mrs Brown, you feelin' all right?' asked Mrs Goodwater.

'Feelin' fine!' said Mrs Brown slowly. 'I put in some pulverized carrots and parsley root, cut fine; juniper berry . . . '

Again she paused as if a voice had said STOP to her and she looked out across all those faces.

The room, she noticed, was beginning to turn slowly, first from left to right, then right to left.

'Rosemary roots and crowfoot flower . . . ' she said rather dimly. She let go of Tom's hand. Tom opened one eye and looked at her.

'Bay leaves, nasturtium petals . . . ' she said.

'Maybe you better sit down,' said Mrs Goodwater.

One lady at the side went and opened a window.

'Dry betel nuts, lavender and crab-apple seed,' said Mrs Brown and stopped. 'Quick now, let's have the election. Got to have the votes. I'll tabulate.'

'No hurry, Elmira,' said Mrs Goodwater.

'Yes, there is.' Elmira took a deep trembling breath. 'Remember, ladies, no more fear. Do like you always wanted to do. Vote for me, and . . . ' The room was moving again, up and down. 'Honesty is government. All those in favour of Mrs Goodwater for president say "Aye".'

'Aye,' said the whole room.

'All those in favour of Mrs Elmira Brown?' said Elmira in a faint voice.

She swallowed.

After a moment she spoke, alone.

'Aye,' she said.

She stood stunned on the rostrum.

A silence filled the room from wall to wall. In that silence Mrs Elmira Brown made a croaking sound. She put her hand on her throat. She turned and looked dimly at Mrs Good-water, who now very casually drew forth from her purse a small wax doll in which were a number of rusted thumbtacks.

'Tom,' said Elmira, 'show me the way to the ladies' room.'

'Yes'm.'

They began to walk and then hurry and then run. Elmira ran on ahead, through the crowd, down the aisle . . . She reached the door and started left.

'No, Elmira, right, right!' cried Mrs Goodwater.

Elmira turned left and vanished.

There was a noise like coal down a chute.

'Elmira!'

The ladies ran around like a girls' basketball team, colliding with each other.

Only Mrs Goodwater made a straight line.

She found Tom looking down the stairwell, his hands clenched to the banister.

'Forty steps!' he moaned. 'Forty steps to the ground!'

Later on and for months and years after it was told how like an inebriate Elmira Brown negotiated those steps touching every one on her long way down. It was claimed that when she began the fall she was sick to unconsciousness and that this made her skeleton rubber, so she kind of rolled rather than ricocheted. She landed at the bottom, blinking and feeling better, having left whatever it was that had made her uneasy all along the way. True, she was so badly bruised she looked like a tattooed lady. But, no, not a wrist was sprained or an ankle twisted. She held her head funny for three days, kind of peering out of the sides of her eyeballs instead of turning to look. But the important thing was Mrs Goodwater at the bottom of the steps, pillowing Elmira's head on her lap and dropping tears on her as the ladies gathered hysterically.

'Elmira, I promise, Elmira, I swear, if you just live, if you don't die, you hear me Elmira, listen! I'll use my magic for nothing but good from now on. No more black, nothing but white magic. The rest of your life, if I have my way, no more falling over iron dogs, tripping on sills, cutting fingers, or dropping downstairs for you! Elysium, Elmira, Elysium, I promise! If you just live! Look, I'm pulling the tacks out of the doll! Elmira, speak to me! Speak now and sit up! And come upstairs for another vote. President, I promise, president of the Honeysuckle Ladies Lodge, by acclamation, won't we, ladies?'

At this all the ladies cried so hard they had to lean on each other.

Tom, upstairs, thought this meant death down there.

He was halfway down when he met the ladies coming back up, looking like they had just wandered out of a dynamite explosion.

'Get out of the way, boy!'

First came Mrs Goodwater, laughing and crying.

Next came Mrs Elmira Brown, doing the same.

And after the two of them came all the one hundred twenty-three members of the lodge, not knowing if they'd just returned from a funeral or were on their way to a ball.

He watched them pass and shook his head.

'Don't need me no more,' he said. 'No more at all.'

So he tiptoed down the stairs before they missed him, holding tight to the rail all the way.

The Happiness Machine

On Sunday morning Leo Auffmann moved slowly through his garage, expecting some wood, a curl of wire, a hammer or wrench to leap up crying, 'Start here!' But nothing leaped, nothing cried for a beginning.

Should a Happiness Machine, he wondered, be something you can carry in your pocket?

Or, he went on, should it be something that carries you in *its* pocket?

'One thing I absolutely *know*,' he said aloud. 'It should be *bright*!'

He set a can of orange paint in the centre of the workbench, picked up a dictionary, and wandered into the house.

'Lena?' He glanced at the dictionary. 'Are you "pleased, contented, joyful, delighted"? Do you feel "lucky, fortunate"? Are things "clever and fitting", "successful and suitable" for you?'

Lena stopped slicing vegetables and closed her eyes. 'Read me the list again, please,' she said.

He shut the book.

'What have I done, you got to stop and think an hour before you can tell me? All I ask is a simple yes or no! You're *not* contented, delighted, joyful?'

'Cows are "contented", babies and old people in second childhood are "delighted", God help them,' she said. 'As for "joyful", Leo? Look how I laugh scrubbing out the sink . . .'

He peered closely at her and his face relaxed. 'Lena, it's true. A man doesn't appreciate. Next month, maybe, we'll get away.'

'*I'm* not complaining!' she cried. '*I'm* not the one comes in with a list saying, "Stick out your tongue." Leo, do you ask what makes your heart beat all night? No! Next will you ask, "What's marriage?" Who knows, Leo? Don't ask. A man who thinks like that, how it runs, how things work, falls off the trapeze in the circus, chokes wondering how the muscles work in the throat. Eat, sleep, breathe, Leo, and stop staring at me like I'm something new in the house!'

Lena Auffmann froze. She sniffed the air.

'Oh, my God, look what you done!'

She yanked the oven door open. A great cloud of smoke poured through the kitchen.

'Happiness!' she wailed. 'And for the first time in six months we have a fight! Happiness, and for the first time in twenty years it's not bread, it's charcoal for supper!'

When the smoke cleared, Leo Auffmann was gone.

The fearful clangour, the collision of man and inspiration, the flinging about of metal, lumber, hammer, nails, T square, screwdriver, continued for many days. On occasion, defeated, Leo Auffmann loitered out through the streets, nervous, apprehensive, jerking his head at the slightest sound of distant laughter, listened to children's jokes, watching what made them smile. At night he sat on neighbours' crowded porches, listening to the old folks weigh and balance life, and at each explosion of merriment Leo Auffmann quickened like a general who has seen the forces of darkness routed and whose strategy has been reaffirmed. On his way home he felt triumphant until he was in his garage with the dead tools and the inanimate lumber. Then his bright face fell away in a pale funk, and to cover his sense of failure he banged and crashed the parts of his machine about as if they really did make sense. At last it began to shape itself and at the end of ten days and nights, trembling with fatigue, self-dedicated, half starved, fumbling and looking as if he had been riven by lightning, Leo Auffmann wandered into his house.

The children, who had been screaming horribly at each other, fell silent, as if the Red Death had entered at the chiming of the clock.

'The Happiness Machine,' husked Leo Auffmann, 'is ready.'

'Leo Auffmann,' said his wife, 'has lost fifteen pounds. He hasn't talked to his children in two weeks, they are nervous, they fight, listen! His wife is nervous, she's gained ten pounds, she'll need new clothes, look! Sure – the machine is ready. But happy? Who can say? Leo, leave off with the clock you're building. You'll never find a cuckoo big enough to go in it! Man was not made to tamper with such things. It's not against God, no, but it sure looks like it's against Leo Auffmann. Another week of this and we'll bury him in his machine!'

But Leo Auffman was too busy noticing that the room was falling swiftly up.

How interesting, he thought, lying on the floor.

Darkness closed in a great wink on him as someone screamed something about that Happiness Machine, three times.

The first thing he noticed the next morning was dozens of birds fluttering around in the air stirring up ripples like coloured stones thrown into an incredibly clear stream, gonging the tin roof of the garage softly.

A pack of multibred dogs pawfooted one by one into the yard to peer and whine gently through the garage door; four boys, two girls, and some men hesitated in the driveway and then edged along under the cherry trees.

Leo Auffmann, listening, knew what it was that had reached out and called them all into the yard.

The sound of the Happiness Machine.

It was the sort of sound that might be heard coming from a giant's kitchen on a summer day. There were all kinds of hummings, low and high, steady and then changing. Incredible foods were being baked there by a host of whirring golden bees as big as teacups. The giantess herself, humming contentedly under her breath, might glide to the door, as vast as all summer, her face a huge peach-coloured moon gazing calmly out upon smiling dogs, corn-haired boys and flour-haired old men.

'Wait,' said Leo Auffmann out loud. 'I didn't turn the machine on this morning! Saul!'

Saul, standing in the yard below, looked up.

'Saul, did you turn it on?'

'You told me to warm it up half an hour ago!'

'All right, Saul, I forgot. I'm not awake.' He fell back in bed.

His wife, bringing his breakfast up, paused by the window, looking down at the garage.

'Tell me,' she said quietly. 'If that machine is like you say, has it got an answer to making babies in it somewhere? Can that machine make seventy-year-old people twenty? Also, how does death look when you hide in there with all that happiness?'

'Hide!'

'If you died from overwork, what should I do today, climb in that big box down there and be happy? Also tell me, Leo, how is our life? You know how our house is. Seven in the morning, breakfast, the kids; all of you gone by eight-thirty and it's just me and washing and me and cooking and socks to be darned, weeds to be dug, or I run to the store or polish silver. Who's complaining? I'm just reminding you how the house is put together, Leo, what's in it! So now answer: How do you get all those things I said in one machine?'

'That's not how it's built!'

'I'm sorry. I got no time to look, then.'

And she kissed his cheek and went from the room and he lay smelling the wind that blew from the hidden machine below, rich with the odour of those roasted chestnuts that are sold in the autumn streets of a Paris he had never known . . .

A cat moved unseen among the hypnotized dogs and boys to purr against the garage door, in the sound of snow-waves crumbling down a faraway and rhythmically breathing shore.

Tomorrow, thought Leo Auffmann, we'll try the machine, all of us, together.

Late that night he awoke and knew something had wakened him. Far away in another room he heard someone crying.

'Saul?' he whispered, getting out of bed.

In his room Saul wept, his head buried in his pillow. 'No . . . no . . . ' he sobbed. 'Over . . . over . . . '

'Saul, you had a nightmare? Tell me about it, son.'

But the boy only wept.

And sitting there on the boy's bed, Leo Auffmann suddenly thought to look out the window. Below, the garage doors stood open.

He felt the hairs rise along the back of his neck.

When Saul slept again, uneasily, whimpering, his father went downstairs and out to the garage where, not breathing, he put his hand out.

In the cool night the Happiness Machine's metal was too hot to touch.

So, he thought, Saul was here tonight.

Why? Was Saul unhappy, in need of the machine? No, happy, but wanting to hold on to happiness always. Could you blame a boy wise enough to know his position who tried to keep it that way? No! And yet . . .

Above, quite suddenly, something white was exhaled from Saul's window. Leo Auffmann's heart thundered. Then he realized the window curtain had blown out into the open night. But it had seemed as intimate and shimmering a thing as a boy's soul escaping his room. And Leo Auffmann had flung up his hands as if to thwart it, push it back into the sleeping house.

Cold, shivering, he moved back into the house and up to Saul's room where he seized the blowing curtain in and locked the window tight so the pale thing could not escape again. Then he sat on the bed and put his hand on Saul's back.

'*A Tale of Two Cities*? Mine. *The Old Curiosity Shop*? Ha, that's Leo Auffmann's all right! *Great Expectations*? That *used* to be mine. But let *Great Expectations* be his, now!'

'What's this?' asked Leo Auffmann, entering.

'This,' said his wife, 'is sorting out the community property! When a father scares his son at night it's time to chop everything in half! Out of the way, Mr Bleak House, Old Curiosity Shop. In all these books, no mad scientist lives like Leo Auffmann, none!'

'You're leaving, and you havn't even tried the machine!' he protested. 'Try it once, you'll unpack, you'll stay!'

'*Tom Swift and His Electric Annihilator* – whose is that?' she asked. 'Must I *guess*?'

Snorting, she gave *Tom Swift* to Leo Auffmann.

Very late in the day all the books, dishes, clothes, linens had been stacked one here, one there, four here, four there, ten here, ten there. Lena Auffmann, dizzy with counting, had to sit down. 'All right,' she gasped. 'Before I go, Leo, prove you don't give nightmares to innocent sons!'

Silently Leo Auffmann led his wife into the twilight. She stood before the eight-foot-tall, orange-coloured box.

'That's *happiness*?' she said. 'Which button do I press to be overjoyed, grateful, contented, and much-obliged?'

The children had gathered now.

'Mama,' said Saul, 'don't!'

'I got to know what I'm yelling about, Saul.' She got in the machine, sat down, and looked out at her husband, shaking her head. 'It's not me needs this, it's you, a nervous wreck, shouting.'

'Please,' he said, 'you'll see!'

He shut the door.

'Press the button!' he shouted in at his unseen wife.

There was a click. The machine shivered quietly, like a huge dog dreaming in its sleep.

'Papa!' said Saul, worried.

'Listen!' said Leo Auffmann.

At first there was nothing but the tremor of the machine's own secretly moving cogs and wheels.

'Is Mama all right?' asked Naomi.

'All right? She's fine! There, now . . . there!'

And inside the machine Lena Auffmann could be heard saying, 'Oh!' and then again, 'Ah!' in a startled voice. 'Look at that!' said his hidden wife. 'Paris!' and later, 'London! There goes Rome! The Pyramids! The Sphinx!'

'The Sphinx, you hear, children?' Leo Auffmann whispered and laughed.

'Perfume!' cried Lena Auffmann, surprised.

Somewhere a phonograph played 'The Blue Danube' faintly.

'Music! I'm dancing!'

'Only *thinks* she's dancing,' the father confided to the world.

'Amazing!' said the unseen woman.

Leo Auffmann blushed. 'What an understanding wife.'

And then inside the Happiness Machine, Lena Auffmann began to weep.

The inventor's smile faded.

'She's crying,' said Naomi.

'She can't be!'

'She is,' said Saul.

'She simply can't be crying!' Leo Auffmann, blinking, pressed his ear to the machine. 'But . . . yes . . . like a baby . . . '

He could only open the door.

'Wait.' There his wife sat, tears rolling down her cheeks. 'Let me finish.' She cried some more.

Leo Auffmann turned off the machine, stunned.

'Oh, it's the saddest thing in the world!' she wailed. 'I feel awful, terrible.' She climbed out through the door. 'First, there was Paris . . . '

'What's wrong with Paris?'

'I never even *thought* of being in Paris in my life. But now you got me thinking: Paris! So suddenly I want to be in Paris and I know I'm not!'

'It's almost as good, this machine.'

'No. Sitting in there, I knew. I thought, It's not real!'

'Stop crying, Mama.'

She looked at him with great dark wet eyes. 'You had me dancing. We haven't danced in twenty years.'

'I'll take you dancing tomorrow night!'

'No, no! It's not important, it *shouldn't* be important. But your machine says it's important! So I believe! It'll be all right, Leo, after I cry some more.'

'What else?'

'What else? The machine says, "You're young." I'm not. It lies, that Sadness Machine!'

'Sad in what way?'

His wife was quieter now. 'Leo, the mistake you made is you forgot some hour, some day, we all got to climb out of that thing and go back to dirty dishes and the beds not made. While you're in that thing, sure, a sunset lasts forever almost, the air smells good, the temperature is fine. All the things you want to last, last. But outside, the children wait on lunch, the clothes need buttons. And then let's be frank, Leo, how long can you *look* at a sunset? Who *wants* a sunset to last? Who wants perfect temperature? Who wants air smelling good always? So after a while, who would notice? Better, for a minute or two, a sunset. After that, let's have something else. People are like that, Leo. How could you forget?'

'Did I?'

'Sunsets we always liked because they only happen once and go away.'

'But Lena, that's sad.'

'No, if the sunset stayed and we got bored, that would be a real sadness. So two things you did you should never have. You made quick things go slow and stay around. You brought things faraway to our back yard where they don't belong, where they just tell you, "No, you'll never travel, Lena Auffmann, Paris you'll never see! Rome you'll *never* visit." But I *always* knew that, so why tell me? Better to forget and make do, Leo, make do, eh?'

Leo Auffmann leaned against the machine for support. He snatched his burned hand away, surprised.

'So now what, Lena?' he said.

'It's not for me to say. I know only so long as this thing is here I'll want to come out, or Saul will want to come out like he did last night, and against our judgment sit in it and look at all those places so faraway and every time we will cry and be no fit family for you.'

'I don't understand,' he said, 'how I could be so wrong. Just let me check to see what you say is true.' He sat down inside the machine. 'You won't go away?'

His wife nodded. 'We'll wait, Leo.'

He shut the door. In the warm darkness he hesitated, pressed the button, and was just relaxing back in colour and music, when he heard someone screaming.

'Fire, Papa! The machine's on fire!'

Someone hammered the door. He leaped up, bumped his

head, and fell as the door gave way and the boys dragged him out. Behind him he heard a muffled explosion. The entire family was running now. Leo Auffmann turned and gasped, 'Saul, call the fire department!'

Lena Auffmann caught Saul as he ran. 'Saul,' she said. 'Wait.'

There was a gush of flame, another muffled explosion. When the machine was burning very well indeed, Lena Auffmann nodded.

'All right, Saul,' she said. 'Run call the fire department.'

Everybody who was anybody came to the fire. There was Grandpa Spaulding and Douglas and Tom and most of the boarders and some of the old men from across the ravine and all the children from six blocks around. And Leo Auffmann's children stood out front, proud of how fine the flames looked jumping from the garage roof.

Grandfather Spaulding studied the smoke ball in the sky and said, quietly, 'Leo, was that it? Your Happiness Machine?'

'Some year,' said Leo Auffmann, 'I'll figure it and tell you.'

Lena Auffmann, standing in the dark now, watched as the firemen ran in and out of the yard; the garage, roaring, settled upon itself.

'Leo,' she said, 'it won't take a year to figure. Look around. Think. Keep quiet a little bit. Then come tell me. I'll be in the house, putting books back on shelves, and clothes back in closets, fixing supper, supper's late, look how dark. Come, children, help Mama.'

When the firemen and the neighbours were gone, Leo Auffmann was left with Grandfather Spaulding and Douglas and Tom, brooding over the smouldering ruin. He stirred his foot in the wet ashes and slowly said what he had to say.

'The first thing you learn in life is you're a fool. The last thing you learn in life is you're the same fool. In one hour, I've done a lot of thinking. I thought, Leo Auffmann is blind! . . . You want to see the *real* Happiness Machine? The one they patented a couple thousand years ago, it still runs, not good all the time, no! but it runs. It's been here all along.'

'But the fire – ' said Douglas.

'Sure, the fire, the garage! But like Lena said, it don't take a year to figure; what burned in the garage don't count!'

They followed him up the front-porch steps.

'Here,' whispered Leo Auffmann, 'the front window. Quiet, and you'll see it.'

Hesitantly, Grandfather, Douglas, and Tom peered through the large windowpane.

And there, in small warm pools of lamplight, you could see what Leo Auffmann wanted you to see. There sat Saul and Marshall, playing chess at the coffee table. In the dining room Rebecca was laying out the silver. Naomi was cutting paper-doll dresses. Ruth was painting water colours. Joseph was running his electric train. Through the kitchen door, Lena Auffmann was sliding a pot roast from the steaming oven. Every hand, every head, every mouth made a big or little motion. You could hear their faraway voices under glass. You could hear someone singing in a high sweet voice. You could smell bread baking, too, and you knew it was real bread that would soon be covered with real butter. Everything was there and it was working.

Grandfather, Douglas, and Tom turned to look at Leo Auffmann, who gazed serenely through the window, the pink light on his cheeks.

'Sure,' he murmured. 'There it is.' And he watched with now-gentle sorrow and now-quick delight, and at last quiet acceptance, as all the bits and pieces of this house mixed, stirred, settled, poised, and ran steadily again. 'The Happiness Machine,' he said. 'The Happiness Machine.'

A moment later he was gone.

Inside, Grandfather, Douglas, and Tom saw him tinkering, make a minor adjustment here, eliminate friction there, busy among all those warm, wonderful, infinitely delicate, forever mysterious, and ever-moving parts.

Then smiling, they went down the steps into the fresh summer night.

Calling Mexico

And then there is that day when all around, all around you hear the dropping of the apples, one by one, from the trees. At first it is one here and one there, and then it is three and then it is four and then nine and twenty, until the apples plummet like rain, fall like horse hoofs in the soft, darkening grass, and you are the last apple on the tree; and you wait for the wind to work you slowly free from your hold upon the sky, and drop you down and down. Long before you hit the grass you will have forgotten there ever was a tree, or other apples, or a summer, or green grass below. You will fall in darkness . . .

'No!'

Colonel Freeleigh opened his eyes quickly, sat erect in his wheel chair. He jerked his cold hand out to find the telephone. It was still there! He crushed it against his chest for a moment, blinking.

'I don't like that dream,' he said to his empty room.

At last, his fingers trembling, he lifted the receiver and called the long-distance operator and gave her a number and waited, watching the bedroom door as if at any moment a plague of sons, daughters, grandsons, nurses, doctors, might swarm in to seize away this last vital luxury he permitted his failing senses. Many days, or was it years, ago, when his heart had thrust like a dagger through his ribs and flesh, he had heard the boys below . . . their names, what were they? Charles, Charlie, Chuck, yes! And Douglas! And Tom! He remembered! Calling his name far down the hall, but the door being locked in their faces, the boys turned away. You can't be excited, the doctor said. No visitors, no visitors, no visitors. And he heard the boys moving across the street, he saw them, he waved. And they waved back. 'Colonel . . . Colonel . . . ' And now he sat alone with the little grey toad of a heart flopping weakly here or there in his chest from time to time.

'Colonel Freeleigh,' said the operator. 'Here's your call. Mexico City. Erickson 3899.'

And now the faraway but infinitely clear voice:

'*Bueno.*'

'Jorge!' cried the old man.

'*Señor* Freeleigh! Again? This costs money.'

'Let it cost! You know what to do.'

'*Sí.* The window?'

'The window, Jorge, if you please.'

'A moment,' said the voice.

And, thousands of miles away, in a southern land, in an office in a building in that land, there was the sound of footsteps retreating from the phone. The old man leaned forward, gripping the receiver tight to his wrinkled ear that ached with waiting for the next sound.

The raising of a window.

'Ah,' sighed the old man.

The sounds of Mexico City on a hot yellow noon rose through the open window into the waiting phone. He could see Jorge standing there holding the mouthpiece out, out into the bright day.

'*Señor . . .* '

'No, no, please. Let me *listen.*'

He listened to the hooting of many metal horns, the squealing of brakes, the calls of vendors selling red-purple bananas and jungle oranges in their stalls. Colonel Freeleigh's feet began to move, hanging from the edge of his wheel chair, making the motions of a man walking. His eyes squeezed tight. He gave a series of immense sniffs, as if to gain the odours of meats hung on iron hooks in sunshine, cloaked with flies like a mantle of raisins; the smell of stone alleys wet with morning rain. He could feel the sun burn his spiny-bearded cheek, and he was twenty-five years old again, walking, walking, looking, smiling, happy to be alive, very much alert, drinking in colours and smells.

A rap on the door. Quickly he hid the phone under his lap robe.

The nurse entered. 'Hello,' she said. 'Have you been good?'

'Yes.' The old man's voice was mechanical. He could hardly see. The shock of a simple rap on the door was such that part of him was still in another city, far removed. He waited for his mind to rush home — it must be here to answer questions, act sane, be polite.

'I've come to check your pulse.'

'Not now!' said the old man.

'You're not going anywhere, are you?' She smiled.

He looked at the nurse steadily. He hadn't been anywhere in ten years.

'Give me your wrist.'

Her fingers, hard and precise, searched for the sickness in his pulse like a pair of callipers.

'What've you been doing to *excite* yourself?' she demanded.

'Nothing.'

Her gaze shifted and stopped on the empty phone table. At that instant a horn sounded faintly, two thousand miles away.

She took the receiver from under the lap robe and held it before his face. 'Why do you do this to yourself? You promised you wouldn't. That's how you hurt yourself in the first place, isn't it? Getting excited, talking too much. Those boys up here jumping around — '

'They sat quietly and listened,' said the colonel. 'And I told them things they'd never heard. The buffalo, I told them, the bison. It was worth it. I don't care. I was in a pure fever and I was alive. It doesn't matter if being so alive kills a man; it's better to have the quick fever every time. Now give me that phone. If you won't let the boys come up and sit politely I can at least talk to someone outside the room.'

'I'm sorry, Colonel. Your grandson will have to know about this. I prevented his having the phone taken out last week. Now it looks like I'll let him go ahead.'

'This is *my* house, my phone. I pay your salary!' he said.

'To make you well, not get you excited.' She wheeled his chair across the room. 'To bed with you now, young man!'

From bed he looked back at the phone and kept looking at it.

'I'm going to the store for a few minutes,' the nurse said. 'Just to be sure you don't use the phone again, I'm hiding your wheel chair in the hall.'

She wheeled the empty chair out the door. In the down-stairs entry, he heard her pause and dial the extension phone.

Was she phoning Mexico City? he wondered. She wouldn't dare!

The front door shut.

He thought of the last week here, alone, in his room, and the secret, narcotic calls across continents, an isthmus, whole jungle countries of rain forest, blue-orchid plateaus, lakes and hills . . . talking . . . talking . . . to Buenos Aires . . . and . . . Lima . . . Rio de Janeiro . . .

He lifted himself in the cool bed. Tomorrow the telephone gone! What a greedy fool he had been! He slipped his brittle ivory legs down from the bed, marvelling at their desiccation. They seemed to be things which had been fastened to his body while he slept one night, while his younger legs were taken off and burned in the cellar furnace. Over the years, they had destroyed all of him, removing hands, arms, and legs and leaving him with substitutes as delicate and useless as chess pieces. And now they were tampering with something more intangible — the memory; they were trying to cut wires which led back into another year.

He was across the room in a stumbling run. Grasping the phone, he took it with him as he slid down the wall to sit upon the floor. He got the long-distance operator, his heart exploding within him, faster and faster, a blackness in his eyes. 'Hurry, hurry!'

He waited.

'*Bueno?*'

'Jorge, we were cut off.'

'You must not phone again, *señor,*' said the faraway voice. 'Your nurse called me. She says you are very ill. I must hang up.'

'No, Jorge! Please!' the old man pleaded. 'One last time, listen to me. They're taking the phone out tomorrow. I can never call you again.'

Jorge said nothing.

The old man went on. 'For the love of God, Jorge! For friendship, then, for the old days! You don't know what it means. You're my age, but you can *move*! I haven't moved anywhere in ten years.'

He dropped the phone and had trouble picking it up, his chest was so thick with pain. 'Jorge! You *are* still there, aren't you?'

'This will be the last time?' said Jorge.

'I promise!'

The phone was laid on a desk thousands of miles away. Once more, with that clear familiarity, the footsteps, the pause, and, at last, the raising of the window.

'*Listen,*' whispered the old man to himself.

And he heard a thousand people in another sunlight, and the faint, tinkling music of an organ grinder playing 'La Marimba' — oh, a lovely, dancing tune.

With eyes tight, the old man put up his hand as if to click pictures of an old cathedral, and his body was heavier with flesh, younger, and he felt the hot pavement underfoot.

He wanted to say, 'You're still there, aren't you? All of you people in that city in the time of the early siesta, the shops closing, the little boys crying *loteria nacional para hoy!* to sell lottery tickets. You are all there, the poeple in the city. I can't believe I was ever among you. When you are away from a city it becomes a fantasy. Any town, New York, Chicago, with its people, becomes improbable with distance. Just as I am improbable here, in Illinois, in a small town by a quiet lake. All of us improbable to one another because we are not present to one another. And so it is good to hear the sounds, and know that Mexico City is still there and the people moving and living . . . '

He sat with the receiver tightly pressed to his ear.

And at last, the clearest, most improbable sound of all — the sound of a green trolley car going around a corner — a trolley burdened with brown and alien and beautiful people, and the sound of other people running and calling out with triumph as they leaped up and swung aboard and vanished around a corner on the shrieking rails and were borne away in the sun-blazed distance to leave only the sound of tortillas frying on the market stoves, or was it merely the ever rising and falling hum and burn of static quivering along two thousand miles of copper wire . . . ?

The old man sat on the floor.

Time passed.

A downstairs door opened slowly. Light footsteps came in, hesitated, then ventured up the stairs. Voices murmured.

'We shouldn't be here!'

'He phoned me, I tell you. He needs visitors bad. We can't let him down.'

'He's sick!'

'Sure! But he said to come when the nurse's out. We'll only stay a second, say hello, and . . . '

The door to the bedroom moved wide. The three boys

stood looking in at the old man seated there on the floor.

'Colonel Freeleigh?' said Douglas softly.

There was something in his silence that made them all shut up their mouths.

They approached, almost on tiptoe.

Douglas, bent down, disengaged the phone from the old man's now quite cold fingers. Douglas lifted the receiver to his own ear, listened. Above the static he heard a strange, a far, a final sound.

Two thousand miles away, the closing of a window.

THE WORLD'S GREATEST SCIENCE FICTION AUTHORS
NOW AVAILABLE IN PANTHER SCIENCE FICTION

Frederick Pohl

The Man Who Ate the World	£1.25	☐
Survival Kit	£1.25	☐
Drunkard's Walk	£1.25	☐
Man Plus	£1.25	☐
The Age of the Pussyfoot	£1.25	☐
Jem	£1.50	☐
The Gold at the Starbow's End	40p	☐

Harlan Ellison

The Time of the Eye	£1.25	☐
All the Sounds of Fear	£1.25	☐

Jack Vance

Trullion: Alastor 2262	85p	☐
Fantasms and Magics	75p	☐
Servants of the Wankh	40p	☐
The Houses of Iszm	65p	☐
The Languages of Pao	65p	☐
Son of the Tree	65p	☐
The Five Gold Bands	95p	☐
The Blue World	60p	☐
The Pnume	50p	☐

Chelsea Quinn Yarbro

False Dawn	£1.50	☐

THE WORLD'S GREATEST SCIENCE FICTION AUTHORS NOW AVAILABLE IN PANTHER SCIENCE FICTION

Robert Silverberg

Earth's Other Shadow	75p	☐
The World Inside	75p	☐
Tower of Glass	60p	☐
Recalled to Life	95p	☐
Invaders from Earth	80p	☐
Master of Life and Death	75p	☐

J G Ballard

The Crystal World	75p	☐
The Drought	80p	☐
The Disaster Area	95p	☐
Crash	95p	☐
Low-Flying Aircraft	75p	☐
The Atrocity Exhibition	85p	☐
The Venus Hunters	95p	☐
The Unlimited Dream Company	£1.25	☐
Concrete Island	60p	☐

SF581

THE WORLD'S GREATEST SCIENCE FICTION AUTHORS
NOW AVAILABLE IN PANTHER SCIENCE FICTION

Ray Bradbury

Fahrenheit 451	£1.25 ☐
The Small Assassin	£1.50 ☐
The October Country	£1.25 ☐
The Illustrated Man	£1.25 ☐
The Martian Chronicles	£1.25 ☐
Dandelion Wine	£1.50 ☐
The Golden Apples of the Sun	£1.25 ☐
Something Wicked This Way Comes	75p ☐
The Machineries of Joy	95p ☐
Long After Midnight	95p ☐

Philip K Dick

Flow my Tears, The Policeman Said	80p ☐
Blade Runner (Do Androids Dream of Electric Sheep?)	£1.50 ☐
Now Wait for Last Year	85p ☐
Zap Gun	75p ☐
The Three Stigmata of Palmer Eldritch	85p ☐
The Penultimate Truth	95p ☐
A Scanner Darkly	95p ☐
Ubik	75p ☐
A Handful of Darkness	95p ☐
Our Friends from Frolix 8	60p ☐
Clans of the Alphane Moon	50p ☐

All these books are available at your local bookshop or newsagent, and can be ordered direct from the publisher or from Dial-A-Book Service.

To order direct from the publisher just tick the titles you want and fill in the form below:

Name _____

Address _____

_____

Send to:
Granada Cash Sales
PO Box 11, Falmouth, Cornwall TR10 9EN

Please enclose remittance to the value of the cover price plus:

UK 45p for the first book, 20p for the second book plus 14p per copy for each additional book ordered to a maximum charge of £1.63.

BFPO and Eire 45p for the first book, 20p for the second book plus 14p per copy for the next 7 books, thereafter 8p per book.

Overseas 75p for the first book and 21p for each additional book.

To order from Dial-A-Book Service, 24 hours a day, 7 days a week:

Telephone 01 836 2641 – give name, address, credit card number and title required. The books will be sent to you by post.

DIAL-A-BOOK